Also by Sherwood Smith:

The History of Sartorias-deles
INDA
THE FOX
KING'S SHIELD
TREASON'S SHORE

BANNER OF THE DAMNED

The Dobrenica Series
CORONETS & STEEL
BLOOD SPIRITS
REVENANT EVE*

*Coming in Fall 2012 from DAW Books

SHERWOOD SMITH

'BANNER OF THE DAMNED

DAW BOOKS, INC.

DONALD A. WOLLHEIM, FOUNDER

375 Hudson Street, New York, NY 10014

ELIZABETH R. WOLLHEIM
SHEILA E. GILBERT
PUBLISHERS

www.dawbooks.com

First Printing, April 2012
1 2 3 4 5 6 7 8 9

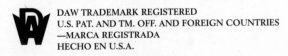

for Hallie O'Donovan

ACKNOWLEDGMENTS

Thanks to:

Francesca Forrest, Pilgrimsoul, Beth Bernobich, Amanda Weinstein,

and especially to:

Kate Elliott, Hallie O'Donovan, and Rachel Manija Brown
for duty above and beyond.

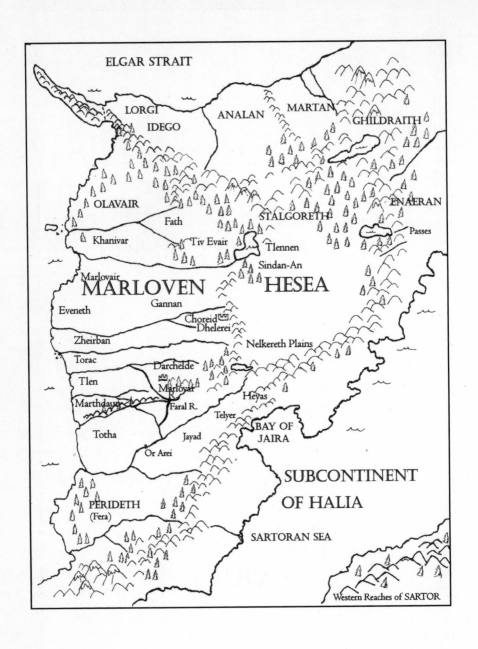

PART ONE
COURT

ONE

OF THE SCRIBES' FIRST RULE

The scribes have three rules.
First Rule: Do not interfere.
Second Rule: Keep The Peace.
Third Rule: Tell the truth as we see it.

I can see your ironic faces, those of my judges who know that I began life as a scribe. This, my defense testimony, shall show how I tried not to interfere, that I meant to keep The Peace; and I will reveal the means that enables me to tell the absolute truth.

I will begin with the first important day of my life, just before the Hour of Daybreak, the spring I turned fourteen.

While Princess Lasthavais Lirendi—known to everyone in Colend from queen to shepherd as Princess Lasva— danced happily off to bed after her triumphant introduction to court in the grand ballroom, I awoke in a different part of the royal palace: the attic chamber for kitchen servants.

It was still dark when the hand touched my arm. I lunged up, shocked awake, then remembered that I was not on bread duty. So who was this silhouette barely outlined against the high window?

"Emras. If you wish to be examined for your Fundamentals, present yourself at the Hour of the Sun at Golden Gate." She was a scribe teacher!

Fundamentals! The test we scribe students called The Fifteen, as that was the customary age a student took it. But then I was the youngest in our class. Or had been before my exile to the kitchens half a year before.

I *must* not say the wrong thing. "Am I permitted a question?"

"Yes."

"Do I wear my kitchen garb?"

"Do you test as a scribe or as a baker?"

The silhouette did not wait for my answer, but moved away in a rustle of fabric. One girl at the end of the row of beds mumbled in her sleep, turned over, and her breath slowed once again into slumber. The other girls slept on.

My hands trembled as I crouched at the foot of my bed and lifted the lid to my trunk. Quietly I set aside my books and writing implements, then lifted out the plain undyed linen robe we scribe students wear, which I had nearly burned half a year ago.

If I'd burned it, I would have had to wear my kitchen smock, and that would have been the first mark against me. The thought made me sick with anxiety as I raced down to the bath. There was so much they did not tell you, that you were supposed to know by reason or calculation or observation.

I splashed in and out of the bath and, still damp, flung the robe over my head, breathing deeply of linen and of the cedar wood trunk where my robe had lain for half a year. It no longer brushed the tops of my feet. I tugged, but it hadn't caught anywhere on my scrawny body. I stared down in dismay at my bare ankles and my exposed feet like a pair of fans at partial unfurl. Not only was my robe too short, but the hem—the entire robe—was puckered in wrinkles. No help for it.

I dunked my servant's tunic in the barrel. Magic flashed over it, making it clean. I wrung it hard once or twice, then put it in the air-chamber next to our bath for it to dry, my longing never to touch it again so strong that I shivered. I had done good work in the kitchens—I'd even made friends—but oh, to feel paper and pen in my hands again instead of dough, to read instead of knead, to listen and talk about history and the world today instead of enduring long anecdotes about past banquets!

So hurry, I scolded myself.

My old slippers no longer fit. I put my feet in my kitchen shoes. I'd cut off my hair on a hot autumn day. It was still too short to braid, so I tied it back with my crumpled old scribe ribbon, and paused. For the first time in six months, I was a scribe again. That meant I could carry a scribe's tools. I had not been instructed to, but the prospect of slipping my travel pen, screwed into its inkwell, and a small roll of paper into my tool pockets was too overwhelming a joy to resist. No one had to know they were there.

Then I ran.

Twice in the year, spring and autumn, the Hour of the Sun actually coincides with the sun's appearance. The spring morning was already warm, the sky blue in the east as I gave wide berth to the royal residence portion of the palace and cut through the annexes and across the public gardens between wings. Why must we meet at Golden Gate? It had to be the farthest of the palace gates. Only the city gates were farther, I thought irritably as I pounded past the herb garden the courtiers were currently calling Isqua's Assent for some typically obscure reason. I breathed in the fragrances as I leaped the low, vine-covered wall without bruising a single blossom. That would have angered the gardeners, who were beginning to appear in order to whisk away any withered flowers before the courtiers woke.

Down I ran the entire length of the Rose Walk, alongside the princess's wing of the royal residence. I slowed when I spied the polished copper of the former palace's twin bud domes glinting with ochre shading on the eastern curves, above the wild tangle of the old park.

There was the point of the inflexed arch of Golden Gate. I'd been given plenty of time, but I wanted to arrive early, to see who might be there and to discover what would happen when they saw me for the first time in half a year.

The others pressed in a cluster directly under the Golden Gate. Its wall was long gone, but no one wanted to be marked for error. The only thing scribe students knew about the Fifteen Test was that each year it was different.

Someone must have spoken for they turned as a group, their faces lit by the sun just rising behind me. Waves of shyness made my skin prickle and my mouth dry. My parents had taught my brother and me that scribes were unobtrusive. From the time I was four I'd earned a treat if I entered and left a room without sound, and a bigger treat if I managed to enter a room without being noticed.

Being stared at made me feel I had erred. But I had been ordered to be here, so I stared right back.

There was the oldest boy, tall Nashande, and a girl who must have been

promoted to the royal scribe school while I'd been exiled to the kitchen.
Already testing? She had to be smart. The urge to compete, to find a place
above her, made me anxious again as they glanced at me with indifference.
Scrawny Thumb, who for once was not blotched with drawing ink, didn't
even look. He was studying the mossy lily carvings on the gate.

Not indifferent was my cousin Tiflis, until six months ago my best
friend and study partner. Secret sisters, we'd called one another. She,
Sheris, and Faura stared at me with interest but no welcome.

I shifted my gaze before my burning eyes could disgrace me with
tears, and movement distracted me. There was the boy we called Birdy,
juggling again. I glanced at him in scorn and annoyance as he lurched
and bobbled those ever-present little silken bags of sand, dropping one
every couple of throws. In four years he'd not gotten much better. Birdy's
crescent eyes were set close on either side of his beaky nose. But the
nickname came when he was ten from the way his rust brown curls
stuck up in shocks and his ears stuck out like little wings, making him
look like a startled bird. His hair was longer now, pulled back into a neat
braid that swung as he twitched and sidled in a desperate attempt to
keep the sandbags in the air. He looked more awkward then ever, bony
and clumsy—he had to be every day of sixteen, I thought in disgust.
Why did he still make such a fool of himself?

Birdy had been my toughest competitor in classes, calling me The
Baby and smirking when I was wrong. I'd smirked right back at him,
gloating when he was given deportment marks for that ridiculous juggling. Scribes were supposed to be quiet and unobtrusive. He then made
remarks to his silken bags about nose-lifted 'shadow-kissers'—our slang
for fawning and flattery.

Old habit made me turn to my cousin for safety.

Tiflis met my eyes, looked away, cut a glance back, and our eyes met
again. "You're here, Em."

For six months I hadn't seen her. When my Name Day came and went
unobserved by anyone except messages from my parents in Ranflar and
from my older brother on another continent, I'd cried so hard that the
senior cook took me aside and asked why I grieved.

So I told her. Her answer was, "Would you not have done the same, if
your positions had been reversed?"

It took me a week to admit that Yes, I would have done the same, for
fear that Tiflis's disgrace would somehow pull me into disgrace.

I said to Tiflis, "I'm here."

Then I took my place on the other side of Nashande, because I knew that even had I avoided Tiflis if she'd been sent away, when I saw her coming to rejoin the scribe world I would have run to meet her.

But she only said, *You're here.*

The whispers ceased, and Birdy straightened up, his silk bags vanishing into his robe pocket. Just as the city bells pealed out the sweet cascade of chords signifying Sun Hour, toward us strode . . . none other than Scribe Halimas, the *senior* scribe, his pace vigorous enough to make his thin gray queue swing against his bony back, his bony knees poke the white linen robe, his cloud blue overrobe billow. He taught the elite, those who would become royal scribes, or maybe even herald scribes— the ones who decide what writings are kept in the archives.

We all straightened up, wondering why he was bothering with *us.*

"Let us not waste time." He marched around the gate without slowing. "Now. Who will give me a concise history of the old palace? Three to five hundred words."

I find I can still recite every question he asked, so full of portent and importance they seemed to me. Mostly about Sartoran history. Oh, the joy of questions whose answers you know!

But that, we discovered, was just the preliminary. Then came the questions no one could have studied for.

The first was when Scribe Halimas led us to the massive carved doors to the shell of the old palace and asked, "What do you see?" indicating the intricate carvings.

Four voices said, "The Treaty of Sovereignty." Sheris, who shadow-kissed the adults (Tif and I had called her the Empress), declared with that self-important lilt that had always made my insides tighten, "They finished carving them in 3615."

Faura, who shadow-kissed Sheris, put in, "Almost eight hundred years ago." Then she flushed, when everyone but Sheris looked at her. What? Faura was always at Sheris's side.

The class looked away as quickly. We were on our best behavior, the Second Rule of the Scribe Guild having been repeated by tutors, and by us, since we were very small: *Scribes keep The Peace.*

Scribe Halimas was famed for sarcasm, but he only flicked a glance at Faura, eyebrows slanting steep enough to furrow his forehead. Safely behind him, the young girl I didn't know rounded her eyes in the Too Obvious to Be Interesting expression.

"Anyone?" the senior scribe had paused.

That meant he was waiting for something else. I studied the door, which was enormous—you could drive a coach and six through it. The wood shone with rich golden highlights in the clear light of morning. It had been carved from a great goldenwood tree, brought all the way from the middle of the continent, the entire tree used in cleverly fitted pieces.

That much I knew, and I had seen the deep relief carving once before, when we first arrived at the palace school and were given our tour. I stepped around tall Nashande, who frowned at the figures in their old-fashioned clothes, elaborate cloak-jackets over tight vests and trousers, pointed shoes, their hair braided over and under the broad diadems with the dangling decorations either side of their faces.

Central was King Martande I, our favorite because he was that rarity, a scribe-herald become king.

I stared at his handsome figure, trying to come up with an observation that wouldn't get me the Too Obvious eye-roll. "Everyone is bowing except the king," I said under my breath, because if anything seemed Too Obvious, it was that.

But Faura didn't think so, for she took my comment as her own, saying loudly, "It depicts the very first sovereign bow."

The senior scribe raised both brows. "I have ears."

Faura shook her golden curls back with a pretence of nonchalance, as others stifled laughs.

Scribe Halimas did not address me—since I had addressed the ground. He put his hands to the lily-stalk door handle. It took only medium effort to open those beautifully hung and balanced doors. We entered the cavernous hall, a slice of morning sun shooting inside past our elongated silhouettes on the mosaic floor of patterned lilies and lighting up the three-story mural on the opposite wall. Now that we were inside, everyone shifted or even hopped so that no one committed the rudeness of stepping on anyone else's shadow. Then we turned our gazes to the lit square on the opposite wall.

Diadems and elaborate arm bracelets and golden belts gleamed. Then gloom shrouded the figures to vague shapes as the doors swung shut again, closing with a boom more felt than heard.

Ah-yedi! I thought, but managed not to exclaim what had begun as a Sartoran epithet, *Rue the day*. All three syllables were considered inelegant, and the tutors did their best to smooth that high "di!" from our diction; the soft, sighed "ah-ye" was permissible.

Ah-yedi, I think now, as I pen this defense, for the next question is one of those coincidences that aren't, when you reflect.

I do not claim that the following conversation caused my subsequent actions, but did it shape them? I've had occasion to think back over every one of the following words.

"Before I bespell the light," the senior scribe said, "I require each of you to tell me what greatness is."

Sheris quoted confidently, "'Greatness is service to the kingdom.'"

Scribe Halimas did not respond.

Birdy gave another quote that we'd often written when practicing our handwriting, "'Greatness is the term we give to those whose virtue earns them a position of outstanding eminence.'"

"Verbose," Scribe Halimas observed. "But good practice for your hands when you are ten. Come, come, I said everyone, and we have much more to do."

He turned to Tiflis, who said, "It's the quality of . . . of influence." We could not use any form of a word in a definition, so she'd avoided saying 'great influence' but at the cost of making sense.

"Nashande?"

"I'm not entirely certain," the oldest boy said in his ponderous manner. "When we were young, it seemed clear. Greatness is implied in the doing of a mighty deed that, as one might say, alters events. For the better, as it were. But . . ."

Scribe Halimas prompted, "But?"

He wasn't sarcastic, yet Nashande hurried his words together into almost normal speech. "I . . . wonder sometimes, is it great from everyone's view?"

"I am quite certain that the Chwahir whose remains so sanguinely decorate the mural we are about to scrutinize would not—had they lived—have considered Martande Lirendi great. But they do not have my sympathy, as they ought not to have invaded our land in the first place. Emras."

Nashande's words hadn't made me think of the Chwahir, but of the senior cook. Startled by hearing my name, I said, "Could it be that greatness is a lot of little deeds? That add up, I mean."

No one scoffed in words, but I heard it in the tiny scrape of a foot on the cold inlaid marble floor and in a soft breath, not quite a snort, from someone directly behind me.

Scribe Halimas said mildly, "It's a fine idea, but the truth is rather more pragmatic. Most of us will live exemplary lives, doing good work every day, and no one will call us great. Few will even know our names. Yet our civilization will, perhaps, be called great. Faura. Since you appear to find little wit in Emras's answer, you may now stun us with your great wit."

Faura wriggled her shoulders. Her chin lifted as she enunciated, "Greatness can be a state, a quality, a condition, or a virtue. Of eminence."

"A virtue of eminence. I am almost afraid to ask what that means."

Faura made a little business of flinging her hair back, obviously struggling for a response. But the senior scribe gestured to the rest, who'd by now had time to think. They offered familiar quotations in well modulated voices.

He listened, gazing on the mural, until they were done. "Next question. It's probably unfair to ask, and no doubt the lower school tutors will tell me so. I usually put this question to the journey-scribes, and so it would have been for you. But Queen Hatahra has recently decreed that this building be pulled down, once the mural here behind the dais is recorded by the herald-mages for the archive. As you all know very well, archive portraits and paintings are intended to fit against the archive display wall." He flung out his arms, fingers perpendicular. "Reducing a work so mighty and awe-inspiring to a wall five paces in length is . . . a necessary disservice. Never again will people experience this hall as King Martande intended. You should regard yourselves as privileged. So tell me what you see."

He whispered the light spell. The glow globes set in entwined lily sconces lit, and there was the mural of King Martande and his allies fighting against the Chwahir. At least a hundred paces long, it towered above our heads, so that the central figure of the king must have been the size of a ten-year-old oak. Age-spotted mirrors on the other side threw back the color, intensifying the fiery reds in flaring cloaks, the rich glint of gilt, the twilight blues and summer greens and daffodil yellows and stately violets of the outlandish clothing worn so proudly aback those dashing chargers. Even the horses looked proud, eyes fiery, manes tossing in winds that seem to come from all directions at once, the better to stream tails and capes like gonfalons.

"It's very barbaric," Sheris the Empress pronounced.

I sneaked a look Tiflis's way. We used to share private grins if we didn't dare signal our disgust at the way Sheris *always* pushed to be first.

But Tif just looked up solemnly as Sheris elaborated into the silence: "What makes it barbaric are those swords and blood. And those dead people lying on the ground."

"'War is the failure of civilized negotiation,'" quoted Birdy. His beaky nose pointed up at the mural. "According to Queen Alian II."

"Look at them wearing metal all over themselves, along with swords, like outland brigands," said the new girl.

"The patterns on the metal are old knots, from the Venn," began the quiet boy we called Thumb, on account of his inky fingers. "Those patterns came out of the west, from—"

"The figures are way too large," Tiflis interrupted Thumb while looking Sheris's way. For approval? From Sheris the Empress? "The king must be twenty paces high. That style is very outmoded." Tif was repeating what Sheris had said—she *did* want her approval!

"So say our artists, and the queen concurs. What is the effect of the painting?" Scribe Halimas asked. "Nashande?"

Nashande blushed, his slow voice rumbling as he measured out his words. "Its being larger than life gives emphasis to, I will say, a sense of power. The swords add to the impression."

The tutorial gaze flicked my way. "Emras? Do you see power?"

"Yes, Senior Scribe Halimas," I said, hoping that I showed no sign of the wild mix of disgust, anger, and perplexity that assailed me. Tif and Sheris? Friends?

"How is it powerful? Besides the presence of steel weapons."

The back of my neck tingled as I struggled for sense. I would *not* sound like the Empress, no matter who admired her. "Like Nashande said, it's larger than real life. And, ah-ye! It's the way they wave those swords, and the bright contrasts of colors, and everything flying in the air. Their clothes and hair. Not the horses. They are galloping. Though actually horses stretch their necks out when they gallop. They don't arch like that. And . . ." I was acutely aware of babbling.

"Go on."

Everyone stared at me, Sheris with a curled lip. Faura flicked looks between Sheris and Tiflis and me, then curled her lip. Tif had turned Sheris's way. Oh yes. Things had changed not only between Tiflis and me, but between all the girls in our class.

Birdy bobbed his head in tiny motions, as if urging me on, but I did not know if he was teasing or encouraging me. The tingles of warning worsened.

"And the jewelry. I didn't think they wore all that golden jewelry in battle. I thought they had armor," I finished uncertainly.

Senior Scribe Halimas addressed the group. "They did embellish their armor with the intention of impressing the enemy. Warriors traditionally will bedeck themselves to appear larger or fiercer or more imposing. I believe what we are seeing here, and perhaps it is too soon for you to understand it, is a calculated augmentation of personal beauty. Martande Lirendi, as you all know, was not just presented as handsome by heralds bent on enhancing his prestige, he really was. He used that as well as prowess to knit the kingdom into a single state, and then to beguile the Sartorans into accepting us as a separate entity."

The senior scribe stepped back and swept his gaze over the enormous figures with their flowing braids and the golden diadems with winking gems framing their faces, the tight clothing emphasized by flaring jackets, the men turned so that their broad shoulders were their widest point.

"Now." Scribe Halimas smiled at us. "You are to take yourselves into the antechamber, and you have a quarter glass to write out your impression of this mural, in Old Sartoran. You may use what I told you, providing your own examples of how the mural illustrates—or disproves—my conjecture."

For a heartbeat we stared as the senior scribe perched on the edge of the empty dais where queens and kings had once presided, turned his glass over, then clasped his hands around his bony knee as he surveyed the riotous colors of the mural.

Then we filed out at our hastiest walk, taking care not to make noise.

A quarter glass later Scribe Halimas took us outside to the garden, where he indicated the silver blue junipers so large their pointed tops were level with the palace roof. They soughed deeply, stirring in the breeze.

"We used to study here," the senior scribe said in a reflective tone that I would not understand for a long time.

He turned our way and raised his brows. "Sit. Wait. Nashande, you are a year overdue and then some, so let us begin with you."

They settled under a king willow so old that its foliage hung down in a solid curtain. The rest of us sat where he had left us.

Though the willow curtain warded sun and sight, it did not ward sound, but the senior scribe pitched his voice so that we could not hear the words. None of us had that control of modulation. We certainly heard Nashande's slow recitation of the different forms of written diplomatic discourse, ending with his answer to the easy question, *When are scribes permitted to use blue ink?* Nashande was not even roundabout and ponderous when he said, *Only when directed by the royal family*.

The new girl was called next. It was unsettling for me to see someone younger, and I didn't understand until that moment how proud I'd been of that distinction.

"There goes the brat," Sheris whispered. "Always pushing herself first."

"She only has to see a page, and she can remember it in its entirety," Birdy whispered to me.

Birdy, not Tiflis.

The girl's voice was so light that we heard nothing of her interview.

The senior scribe called me next and took my rolled paper. "Emras, I will ask a question, then you may ask me a question," he said when I sat on the waiting mat.

The willow formed a green curtain all around, but I was aware of the others all listening a few paces away. I braced for close examination in dates or the minutiae of court protocol—anything but, "Why were you sent to the kitchens half a year ago?"

I clipped my lips tight on the response, *But you sent me there!*

He waited, his face blank.

The emotions stirred by that memory were so immediate that I forgot about modulating my voice. "Kaleri the day servant asked me to get the tray of dishes after Tiflis's Name Day fête. Kaleri was in a hurry. I told her to do it herself, because I am a scribe. We don't—didn't—don't do kitchen work." My face burned. "And so you sent me to the kitchen to work. You said, being a scribe is not a rank but a vocation. If I was—am—was truly a scribe, I would find a way to stay with my studies on my own time. I would find the time to visit Scribe Aulumbe for instruction and assignments, and bring work back to her when finished."

I could not look up but waited miserably for a repeat of the lecture on arrogance, and how I obviously did not understand the Second Rule, every word of which I could have repeated.

"Your turn for a question," the senior scribe prompted.

I still could not look up. "Does my question have to be about that?"

"You may ask me anything. My second question. What did you learn during your sojourn in the kitchen?"

Instinct prompted me to say, *Never be arrogant to servants*, or I could say *Never break the Second Rule*, but that sounded Too Obvious—and I heard it inside my head in Sheris's voice. Smug.

I could repeat the angry conclusion I'd reached during my first few

weeks in the kitchen, which was, "Never be *overheard* breaking a Rule."
Except that as my anger faded I'd come to wonder if that wasn't break-
ing the Rule after all. You're not keeping The Peace if you only heed
Rules when others are watching.

So what did I learn in the kitchens?

"Since I was too ignorant to help with pastry or cooking, I learned all
the different kinds of bread. I learned that bread can be an art, and that
messages are conveyed in bread, from the measure to the knead to the
shape. I learned who loves making bread and wants to spend a life making bread, and who . . . who . . . who . . . wants to be famed for their
bread. That's what I meant by lots of little deeds. Ah-ye, some think
pastry the true art, and . . . " I'd talked myself into a tangle.

But when I halted abruptly, he did not comment on my lack of reasoned, elegant diction. "We spend all these years instilling the first two
Rules into you students," he said. "The First Rule—*do not interfere*—is seldom an issue when you are young. The hardest to live by is the Second."

His fingers lifted, inviting my question, so I asked it, though my stomach knotted with dread. "Am I to return to the kitchen?" I could bear
it—the work was important and some loved it above everything—but I
had never lost my desire to be a scribe. Even after half a year's exile.

"You will recommence classes today. Who among your class was the
most helpful, while you were striving to keep up?"

Now I was truly caught. Tattling was scorned, diplomacy was prized—
those came under the Second Rule. And yet, there was the painful
awareness of six months of avoidance. Of being forgotten on my Name
Day, except by my family. "I worked alone," I said, trying hard to sound
neutral. But my voice shook.

"Your last question?" he asked.

My mind careened wildly, trying to think up some historically significant question—something to show off the studies that had kept me up
until midnight so frequently, even when I had to rise before dawn for
duty—but need was too strong. "When will we know how we did on this
test?"

He smiled. "You will all find out when you are assigned your new
classes, at the Hour of the Quill." He made The Peace, palms together,
the signal that my interview was over.

TWO

OF THE SECOND RULE

I made it to an archway before the tears came.

I knew my face was blotchy and my eyes red when I appeared in the kitchen dorm. At least the only ones there were the early morning bread-makers, all asleep. I scrubbed my face and hands. Then I put my trunk on a roller and made my way back to the scribe students' quarters above the heralds' hall. My sense of triumph was dashed by grief when I discovered that someone had taken my old bed next to Tiflis's, where I'd slept for almost five years. We entered the school aware that we did not own anything but our tools and clothes, yet I'd thought of that bed as mine. And I knew that if Tif had been sent away, I would have done everything I could to keep it empty against her return.

I ran down to the dining hall, wanting to be the first so either Tiflis would sit next to me like the old days, or she wouldn't. She must choose. I could bear her walking away slightly better than being south-gated, that is, turned away.

I heard their voices. My stomach roiled as Tiflis sat across from me. Not next to me, but at least she didn't sit at the end of the table. The girl who sat next to her with a chin-lifted, proprietary air was Sheris.

"After your interview. We all got protocol marks for not helping you." Tiflis wrinkled her nose at me.

"You didn't help me," I said, hands flat in Observation Without Judgment mode.

"And the tutors know it." Birdy took the place next to me. "Nash said we would have gotten them anyway, and Emras would have gained one for lying if she had said we helped her." He addressed Tif, who gave a tiny jerking shrug, like shaking loose a leaf that has fallen on her shoulder. Or the touch of a hand.

Faura sat on Sheris's other side, running her fingers through those golden curls of which she was so proud, as none of us were old enough to earn a wage to pay a hair dresser for a better color. She always had some excuse for not tying her hair back—but the tutors didn't always believe her, and so she'd often gotten deportment marks.

Deportment marks—like having a disordered robe or forgotten tools—meant tending ink pots and cutting paper for the tutors for a week. A protocol mark meant recreation time would be spent in service for as long as the tutor giving the mark deemed appropriate.

Faura fingered her hair and glanced Sheris's way, but Sheris ignored her. "Protocol marks, and we didn't even know. I so wish they wouldn't *do* that to us."

"Life in the palace is always a test," Birdy said.

"Ah-yedi!" Tiflis exclaimed, eyes rolling in Too Obvious. "Remind us your sister is on the queen's staff, Birdy. We might have forgotten." She wrinkled her snub nose again. Though she's a year older, we look enough alike that people think we are twins, as our mothers are twins. We are both small and wiry, with round faces. Only Tiflis got our grandfather's dark waving hair, and my hair is plank-straight and light brown.

Tif nudged Sheris the way she used to nudge me. "So who do you think is out?"

Their speculation was boring, mostly justifying the brilliance of their own answers. I was glad when Sheris signaled she was done, and Tif and Faura followed her out, leaving Birdy and me alone.

"Want to know what I don't think you heard?" he said.

"Yes."

"There is likely to be a single opening in the royal staff, for the princess."

Princess Lasva was still "the princess," for her sister was still trying every Midsummer to get an heir via the Birth Spell. If Lasva were to be proclaimed the royal princess, or heir, she would be given a staff of scribes and tutored in statecraft.

"That's why the senior scribe tested us," Birdy finished.

I touched a dab of wine jam to a finger biscuit and set my knife down. "Why us? Won't the princess pick from among the journey scribes?"

"None of the three is eligible."

"No one eligible? What is amiss?"

"The fellows are elas. If one was elan or elor. . ." He shrugged.

I stared.

I had dropped through an unseen hole in the familiar world when I was summarily sent to the kitchens. Now I was back in the scribe world again, but it seemed as soon as I had stepped on the familiar ground it had opened once again, dropping me to a new and terrible world in which Tiflis turned away.

Birdy's words caused yet another drop. "Why should anyone care if they like women, or men, or no one at all? Rule One is no interference or influence—"

Birdy flicked another look down the table, then said in a low voice, "My sister says that elas or elendre fellows all seem to go zalend over Princess Lasva."

I will not assume you understand our idiom. There are many words with elen, to love, as base. The feminine suffix "as" joined with third person singular "el" meant a preference for women, as "an" was the suffix for a preference for males, elendre meant a preference for both, and elor, for the person who prefers to remain asexual. And, combining zad, or storm, to the adjective form of love, elend, indicated a wild passion. We all used the term—but about food or fashions or the momentary ecstasies of youth. None of us knew what the adults meant, though we all thought we did.

"They'll want to pick a female for her, unless the princess asks for a male. For sure it must be someone excellent not only in writing but parroting."

Being trained to hear and repeat conversations was common among scribe families. The toughest tests were in languages one did not actually speak. My parents had made it a game, becoming more serious when I turned six and showed my readiness for the family trade. "Parroting" sounds more difficult than it is. There is a trick to recognizing the patterns of speech, anchored to root words, and remembering the whole.

But not everyone could do it. The first elimination of potential royal scribes happened around age ten, and the inability to master parroting was most often the cause for students to be sent to less arduous, less prestigious training.

So I was still eligible to train as a royal scribe—and the others had known it. That explained my lack of welcome. "So the class wanted me out." Yet another hole to drop through.

Splat! One of the bags landed on the table, knocking into my cup. "You're too loyal to that cousin of yours," Birdy muttered.

I righted the cup, which at least had been empty. "I thought we are supposed to be loyal to each other. Isn't that part of the Second Rule!"

"So did I." Birdy started the bags circling again, a little faster, as he lurched from side to side on his cushion. "So did I until I woke up that day and they were south-gating you for being sent to the kitchen, even though we were all there in the room when Kaleri asked for help, and we all ignored her."

"You didn't say anything to her. I did."

"Don't you see? We really were all to blame, because we were complicit." He said the word with a slight emphasis, the pleasure of knowing just the right word. "After you were sent off, the others were glad. And, yes, I was glad, too. Not that you got into trouble, but that you were gone. Out of the competition."

One of the bags flew beyond his fingers, and crashed into his cup. He flattened his hand on the top of the cup. "But then we heard you at The Fifteen, and I think we were supposed to. I think the test wasn't about what we know. They know what we know. I think the test was about how we act, how we treat others."

∙ I said, "You always used to talk about shadow kissers in my direction."

"Yes." Crash! A bag clattered into the serving bowl, causing the students at the other end of the table to look our way.

Birdy made The Peace in apology. "You were always so good, though you're the youngest. Never a deportment mark. I thought there was no difference between you and Sheris, who also never got deportment marks. As soon as you were gone Sheris started praising Tif. Soon as Tif started following her, she shoved Faura away. That's not the Second Rule, it's a pretence at it. Do you see?"

"Maybe Tif was lonely," I said, feeling my way. Yes, that explained Tiflis's turning from me. I could understand it. Maybe I could forgive it, if she came back.

"See? See?" He tossed the bags in the air. "They pretend to live by the Second Rule, because today, when Scribe Halimas gave us the protocol mark, as soon as he was gone, they blamed you, and not themselves. But when you gave your answers there under the tree, and we all heard you, I thought, you are trying to live by the Second Rule. You didn't blame anyone but yourself."

He thrust the juggling silks into his pocket, put his dishes on his tray, and left.

THREE

Of the Hierarchy of Style

As soon as we're born, we become a part of patterns, the intimate ones we create with those we live among, and the patterns so large that it takes a lifetime to perceive a fragment of the possibilities.

Our first lesson was to differentiate between what we observed, what we had learned, and what we conjectured, or assumed, because sometimes cause and effect are not so simple to identify.

I know it will seem fantastical (if not prevarication) to add to my defense testimony parts of other people's lives—incidents that you would think I could not have seen, and words I did not hear spoken at the time. Thoughts that the thinkers locked inside their heads.

I promise these are not surmises.

———

At the far northeastern end of the kingdom, Lady Carola Definian sat down to breakfast with her father, the formidable Duke of Alarcansa, as the palace bell rang the three-note chord of the Hour of the Leaf. This was the time the duke had been raised to consider the most civilized and decorous for an aristocrat to begin the day.

The duke had not criticized her for well over a year. "You've turned out prettier even than your mother," he'd said last winter on her six-teenth Name Day, after eyeing her meticulously: dainty and small, but perfect proportions, straight back, rounded at bosom and hip, hair that never required a curling iron. She had the best of the Ranalassi looks (for which her father had married her mother), and the Definian brains. "If you demonstrate *melende* commensurate with your breeding, I will take you to court."

I must pause here and remind those not familiar with Colend that *melende* does indeed come from the Sartoran *malend*, or the *love of-grace-in-movement*. In Sartor, "malend" came to be used for the dance. In our Kifelian, as always, the singing three syllables of *melende*—emphasis in the middle—connotes what has often been translated in other tongues as "honor" or as "the court mask."

The definition of honor differs from land to land, culture to culture. I will have more to say about that eventually. But *melende* is the life of art, it means control and grace even when you are alone in your chamber, even if a lightning storm burns down your house.

Carola shared her father's conviction that a Definian must always excel in everything—that the Definian *melende* must transcend style, rather than merely harmonizing with it.

In anticipation of her presentation at court, she'd paid a poor courtier connected to her mother's family to sketch the latest fads and fashions each month. She spend a small fortune luring a well-regarded court dancing master to Alarcansa, and she practiced at baronial balls and fêtes. If she could not excel (and no amount of practice made her riding or singing any better) she dropped an activity. Meanwhile she ordered an extensive wardrobe that could be adapted at the last moment, so when her father determined by his internal standard that she was ready, she would be able to give her servants a single command, and they could depart the next day. That was style, the outward-most form of *melende*.

So when her father bade her good morning, examined her from pink hair ribbons to satin-covered toes, and said, "Tomorrow we shall depart for Alsais," she was able to reply with complete composure, "Very well, Father."

She reveled in the minute relaxing of his narrow lips that indicated approval, and said the thing she knew would please him most. "I will make my farewell visits to our dependents."

Visiting the dependents was the tedious but necessary dictation of personal messages to be dispatched to baronies of Alarcansa, then the equally tedious carriage ride to call on the principal guild masters and mistresses in Alarcansa's capital, and last of all, on the palace people.

She fully intended to carry out this duty. But first, the delicious triumph of giving the news in person to her two female cousins, who awaited her in the dining room as Cousin Falisse tried to coax Carola's silver-tailed parrots to quote poetry.

Tatia Definian, whose mother was younger sister to Carola's father, would accompany Carola. Her joy was expressed in gales of high, tiny giggles and breathless, fawning praise. Carola smiled, turning as she always did to the mirrored insets along the wooden inlay in the wall in order to assure herself that her smile accorded with *melende*.

Falisse Ranalassi, cousin through Carola's world-traveling mother, was not to go to court. The Ranalassis were well connected, but Carola had so many excuses—the expense, the smallness of the palace suite allotted to dukes, the problem of servants—everything but the truth, which was that Falisse was as pretty as Carola, could dance as well, and she had a beautiful singing voice. Tatia was scrawny and plain, her chief skills shadow-kissing and scudding around noiselessly in her tiny court steps, spying on conversations, so that she could report them to Carola.

Tatia was indispensable, Falisse unthinkable.

A sly, triumphant glance from Tatia, that superior little smile when Carola's light gaze met her own eyes in the mirrored inset, and Falisse could not resist observing, "I hear Princess Lasthavais is the most beautiful girl in court."

Tatia tittered as she swiveled to Carola, who broke her gaze from the mirror. "That's what everyone says about princesses," Carola retorted, watching the shape of her mouth as she spoke. *Melende* required that she never speak a word that made her lips ugly. "It's a convention. Father told me they said it about the queen when she first appeared, though she looked like a toad standing on its hind legs."

Falisse flirted her fan in amusement mode. "From what I've heard, Princess Lasthavais is the image of the greatmother for whom she is named."

I assume everyone knows the history of Lasthavais Dei the Wanderer, who at the age of thirty-nine came to the court of Alsais, dusty and travel-worn, and the king, notorious for his casual affairs, never looked at another woman for the rest of his life. He not only married her, but rebuilt most of Alsais to please her and then began expanding Colend, some say to remake the world around her.

This praise of the princess was not new to Carola. Far more irritating was Falisse's glee. Falisse was a pensioner, her family too poor to keep their own house. Falisse was a dependent, but she never acknowledged it properly. And now? Now she was *gloating*.

Carola whirled and with palm cupped, wrist straight, and arm propelled from the shoulder blade, struck Falisse across the face.

Falisse gasped in shock, a hand rising to cover her throbbing cheek. Though Carola was in the habit of slapping her personal attendants (and Tatia, the rare times Tatia annoyed her) until now she'd respected Falisse's mother, her quick-tongued aunt, enough to never strike her child.

Years of pent-up anger at Carola's slights and sweet-voiced cruelties boiled up inside Falisse. What was the use of *melende* when she was never to go to court, just because she happened to be as pretty as Carola? She launched herself at Carola to claw that complacency right off her face.

Carola instinctively threw up an arm to ward, and with the other hand, caught hold of Falisse's hair, yanking viciously to throw Falisse off balance.

Falisse screeched in pain and anger.

Carola shrieked, "How dare you! How dare you!"

The mingled screams echoed down the marble hall, reaching the duke in his scriptorium as he was giving his scribe last instructions.

The duke, accustomed to decorum in his household, entered the formal dining room to discover one of his four hundred-year-old lyre-backed chairs turned over, the table linens all askew, dishes lying in pieces on the floor, with food scattered about the crane-patterned Bermundi rug. Expensive parrots flitted from drapes to furniture, squawking, as his daughter and niece-by-marriage rolled about, kicking and scratching.

"What." His voice was like a whiplash. "Is this?"

The girls fell apart, Falisse weeping with rage and pain as she fingered her tender scalp where Carola had pulled out a huge chunk of her hair.

"It is entirely Falisse's fault, your grace," came Tatia's obsequious mouse squeak.

The duke ignored Tatia as his gaze traveled from the lock of hair on the floor to Carola's angry face and disordered appearance.

"Carola. When you have restored yourself to order, you will attend me in my interview chamber."

The door snicked shut. Carola whirled to her feet, her voice shaking with rage as she turned on Falisse. There was no thought of how her lips shaped each word now. "I will deal with *you* later."

She had her explanation all worked out by the time she had changed her ripped gown and had her maid brush out and bind up her hair again in a fresh pink ribbon.

The only person in the world she feared was her father, though he had never raised his voice or his hand. But he made his disapproval plain in ways that hurt much, much worse. Her palms were damp by the time the footman let her into the formal room where the duke dealt out judgment to those whose rank preserved them from the more public office on the ground floor.

"Father," Carola began, "permit me to explain—"

"The spectacle I was forced to witness is not just risible but offensive."

She gulped, rigid with the effort it took not to exclaim at the unfairness. It was all Falisse's fault!

"It appears I erred in believing that you understood the rudiments of civilized behavior."

"But Father—"

He pointed his fingers at the floor in the sharp gesture that once preceded the deliberate stepping on another's shadow, but now meant *Shut your mouth*. It was as shocking as a slap. "A Definian never forsakes *melende*. Even in death."

Carola trembled, struggling to control her breathing.

"A Definian exerts authority through choice of word and precision of tone."

Then the real blow came; the duke was irked, and wanted to teach his heir a lesson, but he also welcomed the prospect of postponing the tedium of introducing her to court, a place that had ceased to interest him almost twenty years ago. "We will defer this journey to Alsais until I am assured that you are able to conduct yourself in civilized company."

Carola could only curtsey and retire. Her first impulse was to return to Falisse and claw her face to ribbons, but Falisse would only shriek again.

So. Whether her father postponed the journey a day or a year, Carola would still triumph, because she would devote every day she was stuck at home to demonstrating the perquisites of authority to Falisse, without raising her voice or touching her. With style, the outward form of *melende*.

She smiled.

FOUR

Of White Linen and Ignorance

When the collective age of any class reached sixteen, we all knew the Interview could come at any time. It was individual, and it determined the rest of your life. We all had hopes of being chosen as royal scribes, serving the most important people in the kingdom.

After a year of very hard study, Scribe Halimas entered our history class one afternoon as usual. Instead of offering a topic to research and discuss, he said, "At the midday meal today, you were joined by a journey herald who insisted that Adamas Dei left Sartor for the west in 3391 when he discovered that he would not inherit the throne."

He paused long enough for us to comprehend that what we thought was a conversation-turned-debate had actually been a test.

"It's the same question we discussed in class the night before. During our discussion, you all employed admirable skills in politely confining yourselves to facts, without attempting influence, according to the First and Second Rules. But today, one of you used elementary diplomacy techniques to persuade: apparent agreement, then question, or apparent agreement then correction."

Birdy flushed to his ears.

"Two of you did stay with the facts, but in attempting to avoid any imputation of influence, got bound up in a tangle of justifications and qualifiers until no one could make sense of your point. It seems, including you."

It was my turn to look down at my pen case, and I heard Nashande shuffling his feet.

"One of you escalated in emphatic statements, rude in tone, and finally in word. Yet in class, these statements, when repeated, were couched in language that can only be termed an attempt at flattery. As if a buttery tone and a smile excuses emphatic repetition."

Shadow-kissing, in other words. Sheris looked away—and Tiflis looked startled, then uneasy. Faura just looked lost.

"And one of you thought it best to parrot the flatterer."

Tiflis blushed.

Over the past year, Tiflis had responded to my attempts to get back to our old rhythms by being friendly in public, but any time I tried to talk to her alone I was cut short by the ever watchful Sheris. That had hurt so much I'd tried to bury myself in work, studying even during recreational times—especially when they all turned sixteen and went off to the pleasure house, where I couldn't go yet, unless I stayed in the children's rooms downstairs. So I didn't go at all.

Now Senior Scribe Halimas surprised us further by saying, "You also did not know that this past ten days were your year tests. We have saved you a week's effort in trying to gain knowledge that you should have spent the year accruing, and we have also saved ourselves a week of listening to what you think we want to hear."

The others' shock, commensurate with my own, revealed itself in tiny shiftings, the sighs of indignation.

The corners of the senior scribe's mouth curled. "I am going to dismiss you to your Interviews, and thence to your new studies. Tiflis, you will attend me. Sheris, you will wait outside the door. When they are done, I will send someone to fetch the rest of you."

Tiflis cast a triumphant smile at the rest of us, though her shoulders were stiff. I suspected she wasn't quite certain she was being singled out first for a good reason.

The Interviews did not take long. Birdy and I were last.

He had been kindly, if distant, this past year. I fancied that he looked down on me from his great height, from the vast worldly knowledge of a sixteen year old who regularly went off to the pleasure house, while babyish me stayed alone at our dorms and studied.

Birdy addressed me abruptly. "My sister told me if you get called out first, it's because you're being sent from the royal scribe pool." He'd transgressed unspoken etiquette by referring to family, but it was acceptable if the family member in question was employed at the palace—a fellow scribe. Everyone knew that one of his twin sisters, who were older even than my brother Olnar, was a royal scribe, employed by no less than the queen. "I think Sheris is being sent away."

"Sheris?" I repeated. I was used to thinking of her at the top, because she acted as if she were at the top. The rest of us had accepted her at her own valuation.

"Did you notice her nails?" Birdy asked.

"No."

I looked back in memory, and yes, Sheris's hands were always hidden, except when we wrote, and then everyone's attention was on work. "She bites them?" I asked.

Birdy tossed one of his sandbags in answer. "Wager she gets sent to Archive. Not for herald training—she could never decide what is worthy of keeping—but as a scribe."

"She'd be perfect there." Neat, orderly details, ranks and rows of indexed books and scrolls. Facts. "Perfect."

But it was no place for Tif. She'd hate that. Facts had always been her weakness. Her interest was in people.

We were called soon after, to discover that we were joining the very small pool of royal scribes in training. As I made my way to Housekeeping to order my new plain bleached-white linen robe of the journey-scribe, I began to suspect that the Interviews had been nothing more than a compassionate gesture keeping us out of the way so that those not chosen for royal scribe training could gather their belongings and go.

Sheris went to Archive, which meant she lived across the courtyard from us, and Faura to the public scribes. Her new dorm was on the other side of the palace, overlooking the city.

Tiflis was sent to prentice with one of the most prominent book dealers in the city, which meant she had to leave the palace altogether. I hid in the stairwell, ready to pop out to hug her, to commiserate, to say anything, if she even glanced toward me as she trundled her trunk along.

But she marched down to the canal, face red, mouth angry, without a look my way. Once again I crept to my room and wept, in spite of my promotion. When I got up, I resolved to bury feelings altogether. I was going to be the best royal scribe ever, even if I was the youngest in training.

Here is another of those coincidences that shape us, though we have no idea at the time.

Among our many new duties was the beginning of our training in sitting still for long periods. Scribes were expected to remain in the background, observing, ready at an instant to serve but otherwise separate from events.

Because of those long periods of sitting, the senior scribes now required us to choose a method of exercise. I loved dancing, but that class was already full. So I scurried to the class meeting down by the canal to learn graceful boating. When I recognized the back of Sheris's head among those waiting to join the class, I backed away in haste, to discover Birdy waiting for me.

"Come do fan form," he urged.

"What is that?"

"You will see."

Since I had to choose something, I went along with him.

We were required to move slowly, in exactly prescribed patterns, back and forth across the floor, a fan in each hand, our steps in time to softly played music.

Afterward, Birdy left with me, already juggling. "Like it?"

"Boring. So slow!" I hopped out of the way when Birdy dropped one of his bags and dove down stork-like to retrieve it. I was startled to discover how long his arms were—how tall he'd grown. "I can't believe that the fan form was truly for training warriors. Not that I know anything about war. But one would think that by the time you finished that first sweep, wouldn't the warriors on horseback have trampled you and gone on to another city?"

Birdy shot a bag into the air and nodded assent. "You didn't hear her say that they used speed for attack?"

"Even so. Whether fast or slow, waving a fan in a circle does not seem martial."

Birdy grinned. "I know. Well, it's to strengthen our wrists and hands, and to keep them supple—that I learned when I talked to the instructor yesterday. I can use that. Since I won't be going to any wars, I don't care if waving a fan is lethal or not." He let the bags plop to the marble floor and clapped his hands in The Peace. "Shall you say it, or shall I? It is down to you and me. For a single position."

I made The Peace in return. "For the garland," I said, as the courtiers did before a race.

He laughed. "For the garland!"

Classes were now individual, or at most in twos and threes.

I had Sartoran translation with Birdy, and we all came together again for Discourse. We had to delve for corroborative evidence, then we had to present our thoughts succinctly and politely. We would never be permitted to argue with those who employed us, so from now on, we were to regard our classmates as employers. Credits were earned (or marks garnered) on our manners and abilities to correct factual error yet avoid the attempt to persuade unless our opinions were sought. We had to discern the difference, because our employers would not always be clear which they wanted.

I caught sight of Sheris from time to time. Faura sometimes appeared in the staff dining room—she had made new friends and, judging by the decrease in hair fingering, she had gained by the transfer.

I never saw Tif, who lived in the city.

"Should I send her a message?" I asked our counselor, old Scribe Aulumbe, when I was summoned for progress interview.

"Why have you not?" she asked.

"Because it might be felt that I am gloating."

"Are you gloating?"

"No . . . yes . . . it is difficult to define. It's just that we both wanted to be where I am, and the entire family wished to see us there. And I miss her."

"Do you miss her, or do you miss your childhood relationship?"

"Are they not the same?" I asked.

"You must decide that. For now, do you have family gatherings at which you can be friendly outside of the environment of our labors?"

"No. We're all scribes. I go at New Year's Week to my parents in Ranflar, and she goes to her mother in Sartor, or our grandmother up in Altan."

The scribe touched her fingertips together and said, "You might send her a friendly note and see if she returns the wish for contact."

That friendly note, so simple to suggest, turned out to be more difficult to write than I thought. No, it turned out to be impossible, for it seemed that my entire life might be seen as a reproach, or a gloat. And so the days slipped by as I thought about it and even wasted some paper in attempts, but I could always hear Tif's scorn. And Tif never wrote to me.

The rest of the royal scribes were friendly enough, and I kept my friendship with some of the kitchen folk, but it was casual friendship—

talk at mealtimes. They continued to go off without me for recreation, even after I turned sixteen. It wasn't exclusion; I could see it was habit. To them I was still "the youngest." So I studied harder than ever, which made the loneliness recede.

Over winter the stonemasons began dismantling the old palace—work that ceased as soon as court returned, so that the nobles would not have to hear the noise and breathe the dust. Because it would, therefore, be a very slow process, they'd let the back garden grow wild to hide the unsightliness.

I was listening to the thumps and clatter of great stones being dislodged as I stood by the open window of the scriptorium, waiting for Scribe Halimas, who had summoned me.

He came striding out, robe panels flapping. "Good. You are here. Come inside." With a sweep of his long sleeves toward the window he said, "The queen is there herself, pacing out where the new wing will be built." His brows slanted steeply. "The dukes have already argued over how much space each should get."

Many courtiers bought or hired enormous, handsome houses along the Sentis Canal. But the dukes had been granted the right to housing in the royal palace by decree, when King Martande bound his nobles to him for the spring and summer season—what used to be considered the season of warfare. Rooms in the royal palace, cramped though they might seem to nobles accustomed to their own palaces, were a fiercely guarded privilege.

Scribe Halimas eyed me from under his bushy brows, then flashed a quick grin. I'd never seen him grin before. "You have a comment, Journey scribe Emras?"

The veins in my arms ran cold. I made the Peace. "You did not ask my opinion."

"Then give me an opinion of this. The Princess has asked for her own scribe. We have decided to assign you as first candidate—if, that is, you haven't discovered you're elas."

"I don't have any preference yet," I said, feeling childish and awkward.

He shrugged. "It may happen later. Or you may be elor, like your aunt, which is a very good thing for a royal scribe, as you know. That is one of the reasons why she serves in Sartor as Colend's scribe guild representative."

"Because royal scribes can never marry," I said—trying not to sound impatient, since I'd grown up hearing that.

He looked closely at me. "Some ducal families also require that of their personal scribes, because no one in a position of power wants . . . divided loyalties, let us say. I suspect a more detailed discussion of this matter lies a year or two off, though you've passed sixteen."

I made the Peace, internally shrugging.

He frowned at me. "And yes, we know you should have another year or two of training. Eighteen is the customary age for royal scribes to take up their duties. But the princess wants a scribe, and you are the best candidate we have. We still have your public training to complete, and a few lessons about court, courtiers, and protocol, then you will be sent to her to see if you suit."

I trembled all over, wondering why they had not selected Birdy. Oh, of course. If he had inclinations, and they tended toward females, then he was out of consideration. What an odd thought, Birdy and attraction! A butterfly of hilarity swooped behind my ribs as I gave the formal answer that is appropriate to just about every situation, "I wish to serve."

Another impatient swoop of the sleeves, and the Senior Scribe was back to business. "At first the queen's staff will continue to handle all state correspondence—such that the princess has—but you will take over her private communications, now that she is officially public enough to have a private life."

I smiled at the mild joke, though I still trembled.

"From all evidence she has inherited her famous great-mother's style and taste. Your pen work, your selection in paper and scents and seals is excellent. She has agreed to wait for your last lessons—she did ask for someone young, and understands that your training was not quite finished. Though you'll continue to work with Scribe Selvad in getting your note taking to speed, you will also get used to public appearance."

He sent me to the Grand Seneschal.

As soon as I reached the cool marble hall, Birdy appeared around one of the columns. He flung out a scrawny arm to steady himself, his beaky face joyous. "I was summoned just now by Senior Scribe Noliske. They want me to shift to the heralds. For training in diplomacy. And I'm to be part of the staff for no less than the King of Chwahirsland, who is coming to Alsais!"

"The king? A Chwahir?"

Birdy clapped lightly in happy affirmation.

"You've always been the best of us at suitable persuasion."

Birdy shrugged, his smile odd. Then he leaned close and whispered, "If I do well over the next few weeks, and the Chwahir don't take against me, I'm to go back to their capital with him. An embassy! I'm to wear a magic transfer token to bring me home in case of danger, and I must learn the diplomatic code, and everything!"

I waited impatiently for him to finish, so eager was I to impart my own news. As soon as he paused, his expression one of inquiry, I said, "I'm in the last training before they send me to interview with the princess."

He grinned. "I hoped they'd pick you. I'd begun to hope so since winter. You'll like a lifetime of cutting, writing, and folding pretty finger-scrolls about dances and picnics and all that. I confess I like the idea of danger. Not a lot, but some."

Once again, that sense of question, more felt than seen.

I turned my palms out in Do Not Cross My Shadow. "Not me. I hate the idea of danger."

Birdy spun around in an awkward circle, then out came the juggling bags, arcing high in the air. As usual, he dropped one almost at once; while bent down, he turned his face up toward me and laughed. "Ah-yedi! I am so happy! Though she warned me that this first assignment, where we're to go now, is the definition of tedium."

"You've been sent for? You go to the Grand Seneschal?"

"Yes."

We walked together. The herald scribe who awaited us said, "Since the court is just beginning to arrive for the season, we give this first month to you youngsters for your first public appearance. You'll be monitoring the coming and going of courtiers in specific chambers from the Hours of Leaf to Stone, which is when they gather in the conservatory for the Queen's Rising."

He paused, but we were too schooled to react beyond making the Peace with our fingertips, showing that we understood.

He smiled. "This is not make-work, tedious as it sounds. The Grand Seneschal reports to the queen on how the rooms are used, which dictates next year's changes."

When he saw our comprehension, he went on, "At first, you count the courtiers as they come and go. As you learn names, note them down. If you discern patterns in their movements, good. If any of them sends you on an errand, you see to it, but return as quick as you can. If you see a page and can hand off the errand, do it. They're used to it."

The salon I was given to monitor had been built around a central fountain carved of ice-white marble in the shape of twined lilies, the sprays arching up to plash in a pool with lily pads. Most of the room was white marble, except for insets of polished black stone that outlined the triple ogee arches, and the ceiling vaults. Argan trees grew in marble pots with gilt rims in stylized leaf patterns. The trees' silvery leaves turned toward the light in the triple-set trefoil windows far above.

Surrounding the fountain, the semi circles of marble benches bore black satin cushions, their tassels hanging to the floor. Everything clean, the air moving in slow breezes with the faintest scent of spice.

My first glimpse of courtiers in their complicated layers of robes made me nervous and self-conscious. Like the layers of their clothes, their modes and manners were far more complex than ours: they grew up knowing how something as simple as the turning of the wrist, and where that hand is poised in relation to one's head, can change the meaning of everything said, heard, and displayed. And that was before they learned the silent communication of their fans.

I soon observed the truth of what we'd been told, that courtiers had little interest in anyone but one another. To intrude on their notice if they did not require you was to find yourself summarily removed from public service.

To strive for invisibility was to remain safe.

FIVE

The Dangers
of an Unguarded Smile

While serving as monitor in the fountain chamber, I first observed four of the six important people whose lives crossed mine and brought me here to my prison cell.

Contrasts were the fashion then, and cool-toned, frosty shades of white hair against the warm browns of skin were prized as well as contrasts in clothing and in the lacquer on one's nails.

The first thing I noticed about Princess Lasva was her laugh. Laughter was a matter of a smile, sometimes half-hidden by a fan, and any utterance no more than a soft fall of notes. It could sound as artificial and artful as a cascade of silken flowers, but when there was genuine humor in it, like Princess Lasva's, laughter was charming.

She entered, trailing young courtiers like a comet's tail. For a heartbeat I saw her profile: she had the round cheeks and clear brow of seventeen. Her complexion was the prized shade we called russet—honey-brown with rose underneath it. Her blue eyes were framed by dark lashes and crowned by elaborately dressed silver hair.

She moved like a cloud, her little court steps soundless, her gait so smooth that her ribbons streamed in a long arc, never bouncing or jiggling.

The second person to draw my eye was Lady Carola Definian, just arrived at court for her first presentation.

Three mornings I observed Lady Carola as she crossed in a deliberate pattern, arm in arm with her cousin Lady Tatia, who was yew-branch thin, her best feature thick curling hair colored blue-white.

I was training to be observant, so it frustrated me that I could not identify why the subtleties of the princess's manner called to my mind the drift of a cloud in a summer sky, but Lady Carola—so petite, so beautiful she seemed more doll than human—her manner reminded me of softly falling snow.

The third person excited the most whispers of all. He became my first lesson in the tension between rank and social hierarchies.

I heard about Lord Vasalya-Kaidas Lassiter long before I saw him. In rank he was merely the heir to a ruined barony. The Lassiters were notorious for their gambling, sports-madness, and not so long ago for their duels, before a succession of three strong queens convinced their courtiers that wit was preferable to the messiness caused by steel. Any who reverted to the bloody customs of their ancestors could go home and live on their ancestral estates for the remainder of their lives. Consequently courtiers wore embroidered slippers, not boots, and no man or woman marred the elegance of their robes with steel implements. Their former sanguinary nature was confined to their nail colors, varying shades of crimson. The lords moved sinuously, rather like cats, except for the Lassiter heir with his impatient, quick stride and the negligent way he kicked up the hems of his robes.

In a court where control was prized in all things, to be known as carefree was risky: so "carefree" became "uncouth" or even vulgar.

Lord Kaidas Lassiter was tall, well made in the way those who are active can be, with a face all planes and a broad smile that creased his lean cheeks down to his well defined jaw. His hair was long—longer than most—indicating carelessness rather than affectation because he rarely changed the shade from a serviceable silver and never had it dressed, just tied back with a long ribbon that matched his clothes. The courtiers called his style The Fresh Arising, a jest that I didn't understand for a couple of years. Few dared to emulate it, except in private.

I soon perceived that the courtiers crossed and recrossed in patterns that appeared to be random but were not. Some lingered, sitting on the edge of the fountain, talking and trailing their fingers in the scented water as they covertly observed the hallways leading off.

Lady Carola appeared with other young ladies that third morning at the Hour of the River, then stilled, her light gaze reaching beyond her companions.

And there was Lord Kaidas Lassiter in company with two other young lords, one of whom twirled his fan in laughing challenge at the ladies as they passed by. The ladies and lords acknowledged each other with graceful dips of heads, except for Lady Carola, whose profile tracked Lord Kaidas's journey in the revealing long gaze of The Garden Arch, named for the arc a flower makes in following the sun. She watched him all the way across the chamber, until he vanished down a hall.

The last day of my service at that post, my fourth important person appeared: tall, pale-faced, awkward King Jurac of Chwahirsland, his black hair undyed, invariably wearing, in dark green velvet, a semblance of their military uniform. He was newly arrived on his diplomatic tour of Colend, walking on the arm of Princess Lasva, whose lovely laugh trailed behind.

The courtiers watched him, gazes cold as glass, fans at Life's Ironies as they bowed, but he only had eyes for Princess Lasva.

My next assignment was to learn the bewildering series of chambers, alcoves, halls, and intersections in use by the courtiers, then practice moving through them without attracting notice.

The palace was built in squares, the serving corridors winding laboriously around, through, and sometimes under the chambers used by the nobles. Servants popped in and out of discreet doors. We scribes (and the heralds) were often on call, which meant using the same halls as the courtiers. We must know how to move without catching eye or ear.

The first official event of the royal day has been called the Rising for centuries. It was an ancient Sartoran practice, the heralds say, a custom that sounds awkward and disagreeable now, specifically the king or queen's rising from bed. Sartoran history says that the day began in the royal bedroom, crowded with the chief courtiers, each with a grand-sounding title centered around the ritual of dressing the monarch. Awkward indeed, but a fine way to leash aristocrats who might otherwise be out stirring up rebellion, as this was the only time for private converse with the monarch. The rest of the day was conducted in public.

The Rising was now held in the Conservatory, the coolest place in the palace, and as the queen walked along the carefully tended stream, the courtiers could advance and request private converse. In Sartor, we're told the Rising means the Rising of the Sun. In Colend, during the courtly season, the Rising did not occur until the Hour of Stone, the hour before Midday—before the heat of summer set in, but accommodating to late-sleeping courtiers.

Since I knew court would all be gathered in the Conservatory, I used that time to practice moving through their territory.

On my second foray, I was startled by the sound of voices as I approached the enormous gold and marble royal gallery. I paused, peered around a leaf-carved marble column, and was so surprised to discover Princess Lasva and King Jurac there that I froze in place.

"Ah-ye, like this and this. Keep your weight on this foot. It's only a brush with the other." Princess Lasva swept up her filmy robes to reveal her ribbon-tied slippers as she demonstrated the basic step of the complicated line dances.

The king of the Chwahir was absorbed in trying to get his feet to move in a way they obviously never had. When he hopped and caught the marble balustrade to keep from falling, he blushed.

Her laugh was soft, his a painful bray. "It's tricky, but do try to just brush the free foot as you turn on the other. Do not step. See? See? Now pivot on that same foot, and you're ready to start off in any direction. The free foot crosses behind. That frees your left. See? Then cross behind. If you can get that much, you can do a turn, or a dip, or cross over and behind, but it is always the same basic step."

"I think I see it," he said. "Like this?"

"Yes! Yes, that is it. Now, we're going to try the waltz. You steady yourself here at my waist, I steady myself at your shoulder, we take hands here—and we're off! Step two three, step two three, ah-ye-di, ah-ye-di, always turning—"

I knew I should not have been there, but I was so astounded to find a princess secretly teaching a king to dance, I watched them waltz along the gallery as her ancestors gazed down—among them her ancestor who had fought his on this very site. When they reached the end and turned back I recollected myself and fled.

The next day I dined in the staff hall with friends from a mix of services. Kaleri, who had been promoted from kitchen page to guest wing page, came in very late, her face flushed. I had long since made friends with her, after begging her forgiveness for my affront at Tif's Name Day gathering. Kaleri was round, fair, and loved to be happy. She could never be angry long.

She plunked herself down next to Delis, another kitchen friend, a pastry-maker.

At the other end of the table, Birdy's sister leaned forward. ". . . and the Gaszins are taking wagers that Jurac of Chwahirsland will not know how to dance. They all intend to ask him at the Dance of the Spring Leaves." She was tall, long-nosed, her eyes so close together they seemed crossed, her smile as merry as her brother's.

"Which the Duke of Gaszin is hosting." Garsun raised his forefinger, signifying a shadow kiss—everyone knew the Gaszins were trying to win concessions from Queen Hatahra.

Tall, craggy-faced Garsun had indeed been hired as a scribe by the Duke of Altan—but like several of the ducal families, the Altans left their staff to eat at crown expense when the family was in Alsais attending on the queen.

Kaleri said on an outward sigh, "Well the Ice Duke and his daughter won't be there to see it."

"The Alarcansas are leaving?" Garsun asked. "Before the court season has officially begun?"

Kaleri laid down her fork. "It's Willow Gate for her," she said, laughing. "You did not know? That's why I'm so late—several of us got summoned to help their people pack them up."

"Why?" Birdy asked. He turned sideways on his cushion. Out came the bags—

"Birdy, might I request you perform your . . . your practice after our meal?" said his sister.

Birdy looked startled. "Oh." He looked around at all of us, then put away the silk bags, grimacing a little.

His sister patted his hand. "It's just that we like our dishes to remain where we set them when we eat. You will forgive me, will you not?" And to the others, "The Duke of Alarcansa sent a page to request an interview of the queen before I went off duty. I assumed it was more demands or more complaints about protocol slights."

"Protocol slights?" Birdy leaned toward me. "Do you share the sense that we are coming at the news backward?"

Garsun said, "This is what I know. The Gaszins were laughing about how furious old Alarcansa had been when the queen accepted the Duke of Gaszin's offer to host the Dance of the Spring Leaves. But I didn't think he'd depart over it—not scarcely three weeks after their arrival."

"They're going to say that the Duchess is ill." The drop in tone on the nickname "Duchess" (for Lady Carola had not been granted any such rights, she was heir only) made it clear that she had not endeared herself to the servants. "But the hall page overheard Tatia Tittermouse warning the second chambermaid not to gossip about. . ."

At this juncture I will shift the narrative to Carola's memory (again, I promise I will record how and why I was able) which turned up in her nightmares over the next several years. She stood before her father, her muscles locked tightly lest she tremble, or weep, or reveal any emotion.

"It is not just the betrayal of our name," he said, "by lowering yourself to the sort of subterfuge that entertains the vulgar." He used a silver letter opener to lift Carola's scroll from the letter salver. It was written on the most expensive rice paper and tied with heart's red. He refused to touch the invitation with his own fingers, but flicked it into the fire from the letter opener, which he then wiped on a cotton silk handkerchief. "It is the vulgarity of your taste, chasing the tail of someone so indiscriminate that if he, and his father, hadn't chanced to be born to titles, they would no doubt be employed on their backs in a common doss house."

His voice on the word "common" was like the snap of a whip, and Carola recoiled as if she'd been struck.

"Honor lies in our reputation. I will not have Definian besmirched by the noisome mirth that you would have stirred up had this thing been delivered. It is clear that you cannot be trusted in court. You will write an appropriate letter to the queen, regretting a summer illness. You will smile and exchange bows as we depart in the morning."

Carola made it outside the room, though she had to stiffen her knees. When the door was closed, she leaned against the wall as black spots floated across her vision.

"Oh, was it bad, darling?" Tatia cooed. "Here, I will help you to your room. We can tell everyone you were taken by headache."

"Illness," Carola murmured. "Summer illness."

"What?" Tatia asked, guiding Carola slowly to their end of the suite.

"Why should an invitation to a private picnic be vulgar?"

Tatia said, "My mother once told me that your father hates the Baron Lassiter more than anyone alive. Something about your mother. Maybe he's visited that hatred onto his son. I'm so sorry, dearest darling coz, sweeter than a sister."

Once she'd reached the safety of her room, Carola turned around. "I shall take a stick to Denra," she snapped. "How *could* she be so clumsy as to let my father see her taking the letter? Or maybe she even gave it to him—in expectation of extra pay—oh, I will beat her senseless, and then turn her away."

"And have everyone whispering?" Tatia raised her hands in Don't Cross My Shadow. "You know that such an action would cause the exact sort of interest that you would despise. How people would laugh!"

Carola paused and turned to study herself in the mirror to see if she revealed any traces of her disgrace. "But she betrayed me. How else would he have gotten that letter?"

"It could be that Uncle's own man was lying in wait," Tatia said. "At any rate, you know you cannot trust her. Go on exactly as usual. You will just never again give her anything to whisper about. But really, darling, in the future, you must entrust such things to me. Who is better to guard Definian secrets than a Definian?"

"Oh, Tatia, you are so good."

"Now, you just lie down. I will fix your favorite tisane with my own hands and see to your arrangements. You only have to rise, dress, and hold your head high on the morrow."

Carola retired to her bed.

What follows is not Carola's memory. Carola had no idea that after Tatia shut the door softly she gave orders to the waiting servants before she flitted down the hall to the formal chambers. There she made herself busy until at last the duke crossed from one room to another. He caught sight of her and beckoned. When she neared, he said, "You have done well, niece."

"It was my duty, Uncle," she said humbly, with a low curtsey. "Though it hurt me, oh-so much, for Carola is dearer than a sister. But I am a Definian, and our name is even dearer."

The duke smiled tight-lipped and walked on.

Back to our servants' table, and the gossip that the duke deplored.

"*Zalend*," one of the servants commented.

Garsun said, chuckling, "And doomed to exit through Willow Gate because her veins don't run with ice like her father's."

Not that the ducal party would depart through the Gate of Silver Willows. The duke would see to it that they departed through the Gate of the Lily Path, as was proper, even though it was located on the west side of the city nearest the palace, and Alarcansa lay directly east. The Gate of Silver Willows was used for mourning corteges, or for those signifying a wrong done them. When mentioned in conversation, the Willow Gate inevitably meant grief, sorrow, or tears, most often for badly ended love affairs.

This matter taught me three things.

First, that you might "whisper," that is, entrust a privacy to a confidante about a third person, but your listener might not feel the need to keep the secret if they feel no loyalty to that third person. In fact, it might be regarded as a weapon.

Secondly, that I now understood the look I'd seen on Lady Carola's face the day she watched Lord Kaidas Lassiter: it was *zalend*. The storm-love.

Third. It was identical to the look I'd seen on King Jurac's long face as Princess Lasva demonstrated the brush-and-step in the gallery of her ancestors.

———

I was to discover that shadow trespass is specifically a Colendi convention. Even as children at play we are taught not to step upon someone else's shadow when we are indoors, for if the space was not well lit, to blend your shadow with another's was to request or declare intimacy, or to challenge another for place. The only time one is safe from shadow etiquette is when one wears a shrouding domino veil, which means one is regarded as invisible.

All Colendi, even the most poor, try to light their rooms in all four corners.

Lighting from a single source can be startling, dramatic, full of expectation. A popular game among youth newly come to the years of interest is to walk amidst a circle of your friends gathered in a dark room where a lamp swings freely. Whomsoever your shadow touches, you must kiss.

The gesture for shadow kiss—sycophancy—was a forefinger held up, as I have said. In court, the fan closed and held upright.

But the courtiers also had the moth kiss, (forefinger touching the lips) was regarded as the highest style in insult—far above the clumsiness of what the rest of us called south-gating. The moth kiss appeared to be flattery, but its purpose was to humiliate the victim, exposing him or her to the amusement of the group.

Lady Ananda Gaszin and her brother, Young Gaszin (as the heir was known—nearer thirty than twenty, he favored the nod to his fleeting youth), aspired to begin the season at their father's Dance of the Spring Leaves, which was held on Flower Day, the day the sun rose at Daybreak and set at the Hour of the Cup. The game was that everyone would be seen assiduously obeying the queen's injunction to be friendly to the Chwahir king, to mask a courtly moth kiss.

Lady Ananda was so confident of triumph that her outer robe was made of sheerest moon-glow silk, woven in curled-leaf patterns, with the tiniest gems caught in the gossamer fabric, like drops of rain, her sleeves draped in the then-popular fan shape. Her first underrobe was pale green, her innermost underrobe a darker green, its sleeves, neck, and hem visible a ribbon-width at the edges of the pale green; her nails were tipped with tiny emeralds.

That hint of dark green was considered presumption by many, as it was the custom at this dance for the royal family to wear the color of spring and the court to wear shades of white and silver, symbolizing the crown's liberating the season of warmth from winter's isolation. Although Lady Ananda's intent was to highlight her incipient triumph by mocking the Chwahir forest green—which Jurac invariably wore—most saw her gesture as arrogance, presuming on the royal prerogative.

All this Kaidas Lassiter saw at a glance when he arrived at a ball he'd very nearly skipped. He was only there because Young Gaszin insisted that he join the game by making a very expensive wager on Jurac of Chwahirsland's ignorance of Colendi dance. Wagers were always fun, and it was even funnier that every dancing master in Alsais had been hired away by the Gaszins.

Purely on whim, Kaidas wagered . . . against Young Gaszin.

He arrived late to find everyone in motion. There was Ananda sporting dark green, there was Young Gaszin, uncharacteristically paying assiduous court to the queen.

And there was Princess Lasva waltzing down the middle of the room with King Jurac.

"When's he going to fall down?" he asked Lord Rontande behind his fan.

Lord Rontande laughed silently; he followed Young Gaszin because the latter was powerful. Rontande enjoyed Ananda's flushed face, her modulated laugh that rang the false note to sensitive ears, causing her urbane father to send a long look her way. And he especially enjoyed Young Gaszin's failure to distract the queen, who had proved time and again to be distressingly observant.

"He isn't," Rontande said, the diamonds braided into his silver hair shivering as he suppressed laughs. "Someone taught him to dance."

By then, while Lord Rontande gloated at the fall of his clique's leader, Lord Kaidas had taken in the entire room. His circling gaze returned briefly to the besotted Chwahir king, who appeared to be utterly unaware of his near brush with ignominy, then stayed with the princess, whose smile, whose laughter, rang the true note of merriment and fun.

SIX

OF HONEYFLOWER WINE
AND LILY-BREAD

S everal mornings later, Birdy came straight from the baths, his hair still wet and pressed flat against his skull. He seemed more restless than ever. Out came the silken bags. He'd sent the salt bowl tumbling and nearly overturned the entire table in a lunging dive to keep a bag from falling into the butter rolls when I said, "Birdy, I apologize for sounding ill-natured, but must you do that now?"

Birdy turned scarlet, nipped up the bags with far more dexterity than he displayed when juggling them, and said contritely, "I didn't think you minded."

I took refuge in quotation, as people will when they want to say something but find it necessary to mask personal intent with someone else's words. "I am weak, and my serenity is easily disturbed when I can't anticipate the next assault upon the dishes."

"Assault! Oh. Queen Alian the Second." His smile was pained, but present. "And why she did not like picnics."

"The diving of bold birds is an apt comparison to the swooping of your silken bags," I said. "But if I have to point out the analogy, then it is clumsy."

"I'm the clumsy one. It's just that . . . we leave tomorrow for Chwahirsland," he said, as abrupt as any of his bags' attacks upon plates, glasses, and bowls.

"I thought you wished to go."

"I do. But—" He pressed the silken bags in his fingers, so that the sand bulged against the fabric as he gave me a comical look of regret. "but . . . Chwahirsland."

I opened my hands in Heartfelt Assent, not wanting to say that I would loathe going there or to anyplace like it. "I hope it will prove to be fascinating, and that you are so valuable that promotion comes swiftly. Will you write to us?"

"Us?" he repeated.

He made The Peace and bow over his hands, but he remained silent as more of our friends arrived. He left without speaking—without eating, even—and I did not see him for the rest of the day.

Next morning I discovered through casual talk by his sister that Birdy had departed with the ambassadorial staff who accompanied King Jurac. I found myself looking for him at fan practice, at meals, at the archive late at night where we went for extra study. Then I would remember that he was gone. He had not said farewell, nor had he said anything other than that "Us?" It made me think that maybe heralds were not permitted to correspond with scribes because of the secret nature of diplomacy.

The only thing I was sure of during the next extremely tedious month, as I reviewed every detail of royal etiquette and protocol, was that there was a Birdy-shaped hole in my life. I would even have welcomed the juggling.

In the wake of the Chwahirs' departure, the whispers eddied out, the most common topic being how Jurac of the Chwahir had offered anything short of his kingdom to arrange a marriage treaty with the princess, to be turned down by the queen. But Queen Hatahra worked out a trade agreement for wood and sailcloth and, in turn, Jurac agreed to accept the ambassadorial mission in place of the old trade agents.

The month after Birdy's departure, it was time for my formal evaluation.

At the Hour of the Quill, I presented myself.

The scriptorium's formal chamber, used only for important matters (it was there that Scribe Halimas had exiled my shivering thirteen-year-old self to the kitchens), was formed of cool, slightly glistening moonstone. The senior scribes gathered on a wide bench carved of old rosewood. The only decoration was a tapestry that dated back to

Colend's early days, depicting King Martande (then a herald scribe) with his pen. No swords or horses or bodies of dead Chwahir. This room was a testament to the power of the word.

"Scribe Emras," old Senior Scribe Selvad said, her voice wavering. "You are come before us for your final evaluation."

I stood facing them, my hands together in the formal gesture of peace, and bowed my head so that my chin touched my fingertips. "I am."

Senior Scribe Halimas tapped his finger on his bony knee, ignoring a sidelong look of mild affront from short, newly appointed Senior Scribe Aulumbe. "And so?" he prompted.

It was then that I realized that they were not to provide the evaluation. It was my responsibility.

I had to breathe to control my nerves, for hard as it had been to brace for the prospect of hearing all my faults and shortcomings enumerated by my seniors, self-evaluation would be much harder.

I said, "My best skills are art script and history. My parroting is best in our languages, but I usually test with high reliability at five thousand words in unknown tongues."

"Good enough for your present post," Senior Scribe Louvian observed, his red brows lifting. "But Princess Lasthavais may well be proclaimed heir, or she might marry a king. If you wish to remain in her service, I counsel you to continue in expanding your limit. The heralds are not released into regular service until they have highest reliability at twenty thousand words. You should make that your goal."

"With respect, my dear colleague," Senior Scribe Noliske said, her thin old fingers gesturing with grace. She was at least as old as Selvad, but her voice was firm, if husky. "With respect. If the princess marries abroad, the custom in Sartor is now for the home scribes to be left behind and fresh scribes appointed in the new kingdom. In fact, it is sometimes a note in treaties."

"Quite right, quite right," several murmured.

Senior Scribe Louvian lifted a hand in acknowledgement.

Senior Scribe Selvad turned her black eyes on me. "I counsel you to exert yourself to build rapidity in script. You are not quite fast enough for thorough accuracy at the pace of conversation, and such a skill might be required as the princess gains experience. She will not have the leisure to keep up with correspondence. You must learn to be fast and accurate under all conditions—perched at the edge of her bath, in the dark if she wishes to dictate letters before falling asleep, on a shred of paper if you are summoned at a meal and have only a pocket scroll."

"Agreed, agreed," echoed the others.

Then Senior Scribe Halimas said, "Now for your evaluation of us as instructors."

There's no use in reproducing my speech. It was as earnest and as pompous as we can be at seventeen, when we're so sure we have the world figured out much better than our elders. My inner self brimmed with gratitude as I informed them that they had done well in training me, and they accepted that with the grace of long experience. I did see subtle signs (no more than a lifted shoulder, a slightly canted head) that they waited to hear what I would say about my six months of exile to the kitchen.

It would be a number of years before I understood the risk they had taken in so drastic a correction, not just in sending me away but in requiring me to study on my own for half a year. When I told them that I had returned from the kitchens to the scribe world to see it anew and to appreciate what I had chosen rather than accepting my training as my due—this shoulder dropped, that canted head tipped back, and the rustle that soughed through them reflected back to me as relief.

My heart expanded with thankfulness that their training had brought me to what I wanted most, and they were thankful that their experiment had produced such a well-trained, observant young scribe.

On the tri-toned notes of the Hour of the Seal, which is the time when the most formal contracts are traditionally made, Senior Scribes Halimas and Noliske each took hold of the shoulder of a new cloud blue overrobe and brought it to me. I slid my hands into the tulip sleeves with their cunning inner pockets, the open front placket falling over my white linen robe.

I was a scribe.

We celebrated by sharing the gold-edged cups of the complex golden wine called honeyflower. A perfect blossom floated in each cup—the highest accolade. The very best dainties, such as paper-thin carrot slices folded into the center of breads formed in the shape of a lily, were so light and delicate they melted in your mouth.

Then we rose, and for the first time I exchanged The Peace greeting as equals with my new colleagues.

Then, with the complex flavor of honeyflower still on my tongue, and my blood feeling as if it had been replaced by water (especially in my knees) I made my first scribe journey to the princess's suite. I knew I must arrive at the Hour of Spice, but I was so familiar with the palace and how long it took to get anywhere, I was not particularly anxious.

The royal wing lay behind the main building, separated by Alian's Garden. The lower floor comprised the chambers used by the royal family for personal entertainments. The main building was not only for state events; the outer rooms could be utilized by courtiers who wished to host a public entertainment—the definition of "public" varying, because all of these were by invitation.

The simplest way to explain is that there were generally understood degrees of privacy and exclusivity. Where you chose to hold an event was a communication equally important as its guest list.

The royal wing, the most exclusive part of the palace, was to be my home. The royal family lived on the second story, and Princess Lasthavais had the entire western suite of rooms as her own, overlooking the Rose Walk, down which I had run to my Fifteen test. Beyond that path flowed the Canal of Silver Reeds, a tributary of the River Ym. The princess's quarters were the most private, their serene view unimpeded by stables, servants, or petitioners.

The back and east side belonged to the queen and her unofficial consort, Lord Davaud, cousin to the Baron of Estan. The queen was an early riser, and she liked looking out over the outlying portions of the palace complex before she went to work in the mornings.

I crossed Alian's Garden for the first time and entered the rose marble foyer of the royal wing, slowing so that I might reach the stairs when the bells began to ring the Hour of Spice. As the first note rang, thrilling me, echoing rapidly from wall to vault, I raced up the stairs then turned to the left as the last echoes died away.

A twelve-year-old page popped up from her bench, laid aside her stitch-work, glanced at my new cloud blue overrobe, and clapped her hands together in salute. "Scribe Emras?"

Scribe Emras! Oh the glory of an earned title!

I signed assent.

"I am to bring you to Seneschal Marnda. Please come this way," she said, her enunciation formal, her gesture correct but too new to be natural.

I had memorized the names and positions of the princess's staff, of course. Seneschal Marnda had once been first handmaid to the old queen.

The little page carefully opened the door carved with trumped vines and butterflies, and we entered a cool hallway with open arches leading to a circle of rooms. The air smelled deliciously of fresh caffeo, which I was to discover was the princess's favorite drink. The biggest room lay directly across from the carved door; blond wood and pale gold silk hangings made the most of the indirect light.

Though the tall, slender seneschal was the same age as the queen, her hair was still dark, her large, sunken eyes *sunrise*, that is, paler than her skin—like the princess's. Only where the princess had inherited her great-grandmother's remarkable blue eyes, Marnda's were a subtle hazel.

Second most important on her staff was Head Dresser Dessaf, compact and gray-haired, with a quick, ever-alert gaze and a small, prim mouth.

They were both waiting for me but afterward, I almost never saw them together, they were always so busy.

There were sixteen more women and girls crowded into the room, the pages and housemaids against the wall, and those with skills—seamstresses, dressers—stood forward. All wore variations in the soft blue-shaded gray robes, some with peach-colored aprons.

"Welcome, Scribe Emras," Seneschal Marnda said.

The page had vanished into a small chamber. She reappeared, her posture self-important as she carefully bore a beautiful silver tray with a service of pale blue porcelain cups with silver reeds painted in the harmonious pattern of *spring breeze*. The air filled with the perfume of wine as Seneschal Marnda poured, observing the solemn and graceful ritual.

"Let us celebrate your joining us."

I thanked her with the customary words, then took the proper three of the bite-sized ceremonial breads, each perfectly shaped, as Seneschal Marnda named the princess's staff. I was glad I already knew their names. Now I could put faces to those names.

"Scribe Emras, you may summon any duty page on the princess's behalf. If you summon anyone else, it is a courtesy among us to include, at least briefly, the reason. That can save time, if an item is to be brought, for example."

In other words, I could summon no pages on my own behalf, but this I already knew. Some scribes had their own staff. I did not. The possibility for such lay not only in my future but also in the princess's. In the meantime, I must be my own page until ordered differently.

The seneschal said to the others, "In turn, you may not summon the scribe. If she is seated doing nothing, you may not assign her tasks. Her duty time will be different from yours. If there is a question of procedure, you bring it to me."

Then back to me: "Within the princess's inner chambers, we remove our house slippers and wear chamber slippers. We all keep pairs by our doors."

I made The Peace. I already knew about courtiers and their costly carpets.

"In recreation time, the two back rooms are open to you, as to us all, and of course, there are the servants' halls. We always have fresh caffeo and steep available. There is a strict rule, from the queen herself, against fermented or distilled drinks on duty."

"What is your custom for meals?" I asked.

She made the two-finger gesture of appreciation for my discreet wording. "We do not know yet how your meals will fit into our practice. You might have noticed that my staff does not dine with the rest of the palace staff."

I signed assent.

She continued, "We always have hot breakfast cakes, morning steep, and fresh caffeo in the sun room at dawn. For supper, you may join the queen's personal staff who, you probably know, are served separately."

A privilege indeed. Impressed as well as intimidated, I placed my hands together, and Seneschal Marnda mirrored The Peace, then dismissed the staff. She then showed me to my room, on the same hall as the princess's outer salon. It overlooked the Rose Walk. The summer bed lay under the window, the desk and trunk against the inside wall on the low platform—the sleeping platform in winter, when the vents under it would be opened to the warm air of the furnace. This platform, and the narrow door at the other side of the room, were signs of prestige indeed: I would not have to retreat to a dormitory in winter, and further, I had my own entrance to the bath.

"You may call upon the services of Anhar once a week," she said, and I remembered the personal dresser whose pale, moon-round face made me wonder if she were half Chwahir. Her hair was a dull shade of light brown not unlike mine. "I understand scribes like to keep their nails pared, so you may make private arrangements with her when she is not on call. Here you will see that we have put in one of the new cleaning frames."

Marnda indicated the door to the bath. "If you haven't time to bathe. You've only to pick up the wand there and then step through. The wand passing through the bespelled doorway enables the magic to function. You and your clothing will be clean, but the magic does not remove water, or wrinkles." Then she added, "For intimate recreation, our rule is to take it to the pleasure house. No staff relationships. We have an account at—" She bent and peered at me, her brow perplexed. "Are you old enough for this conversation?"

"I am nearly seventeen," I said, with the dignity of the young. (At least she did not laugh.) I neglected to add, however, that although I'd had to say the Waste Spell to bring on monthly flow for half a year now, I as yet had nothing more than a vague, academic interest in sex.

"If you have questions, please come to me," she said, and the subject rested there as she indicated my trunk, which had already been sent over.

On it sat a row of little notes, almost all folded in the congratulatory shape called *crowned lilies*.

Seneschal Marnda smiled as I bent over them, touching the largest of the crowned lily shapes, which was tied with a heavy white silk ribbon. I suspected this one was from my parents. Three of the others were tied by silk threads, most likely from fellow journey scribes, and one with a gold ribbon—it had to be an extravagance from my brother Olnar.

I smiled, moving to the blossom made of shell pink paper—Tiflis's favorite—with a full ribbon. I stared at it, overcome with surprise and joy.

"I'll leave you to—" began the seneschal, then halted at the sound of Princess Lasthavais's voice from beyond the open door.

"Where is my new scribe?"

Marnda's gaze flicked to my feet, but I'd already slid out of my house slippers when I'd entered. I shoved my feet into the waiting pair of silk chamber slippers as the princess scudded swiftly into the main room so her robes fluttered, and her hair ribbons—they wore them very long that year—streamed in an arc behind her.

Her tiny steps slowed. I stepped out of my door. She clapped her hands lightly then flung them wide, almost as if to hug me, but her fingers spread apart in the Bird on the Wing, a gesture seen rarely in Alsais's court. It was graceful, enthusiastic—so charming I was late in remembering to place my hands together and bow deeply.

"Come! You've made your duty bow. But please, The Peace will do from now on, except when my sister is here. She likes the niceties. Truly. Ask dear Marnda," the princess said in a quick rush of words.

Her voice was what we call fluting: somewhere between husky and breathless, yet musical. "Do you like cats?" she added, as two glossy felines paced out from behind her.

"I do, very much," I said, bending just enough to hold down a hand.

The nearest cat gave me a delicate sniff then put up its tail, so I ventured a pat. The animal sinuously rolled its back under my touch then passed on to scour its head against the princess's leg, tail high.

"I am so glad you like cats. But the bows must go when we are private." The princess chuckled, a small and pleasing sound. "I came late to a presentation one day, when I was small. There I was, running from the south door, and oh, there was the entire court in full sovereign bow—with heads lowered—but you have no notion how that appears from behind." She laughed again, as I struggled to control my own flutter of hilarity at the sheer unexpectedness of words and image. "And as I passed, I caught such looks! Ah-ye, I know manner is important, but meaning is, too. I never see a room full of deep bows without thinking of those silken backsides."

She did not wait for my answer. "Now, come with me. Tell me all about yourself," she continued, whirling so fast that her blue silk hair ribbon caught against my side. Then it slithered and fell as she sped across the little tiled hall and into a wide chamber as large as all the service alcoves together.

I gained a swift impression of raw silk cushions in a subdued blue the color of winter ice over water, a fine tile floor patterned in Venn knots made in shades of sand and beige and cream interleaved with blue. Potted argan trees arched overhead and, arranged abundantly below, were a variety of fragrant ferns.

From there I followed her into yet another room, a bower of living things—potted lindens and stalked starliss under broad western windows, set on low platforms framing a sunken circle in the floor, fitted with couches around a mosaic patterned table. The floor had the largest rosebud carpet I had ever seen, made of thousands and thousands of hand-rolled silken buds of palest first-dawn rose.

The princess dropped onto a darker rose brocade cushion, noticing my fascinated glance, for I had learned that rosebud carpets were favored for the intimacy of lovers. And here was one in a semi-public space!

She chuckled again. "I have been given three rosebud carpets," she said confidingly. "This one is here so I can run my toes over it. The maids put it through the cleaning frame every night, so if you ever feel headachy, feel free to run your feet over it. I assure you, it kills the pangs in moments!" She gestured, the turn of her hand both graceful and inviting. I never once had thought I would actually sit in her presence unless recording, so moved uncertainly until she patted a cushion. "Sit! My neck hurts, craning up to see you! I asked for someone my age," she said, her gaze direct as she studied me. "Are you younger?"

"Nearly seventeen, your highness."

"No titles when we are alone. I am telling you now so that you will not form the habit. Try it."

She waited, so I said, "Nearly . . ."

"Lasva."

I could not get that past my lips. Yet I knew it was hypocritical, because among my closest friends we dropped the titles as often as not, though I had taken great care to be formal if I might be overheard by anyone in authority. And I had always referred to her as *the princess*.

Lasva's eyes narrowed in speculation. She said slowly, "I think you have the habit already, do you not? There is that in your face—here." She touched her cheeks, and her chin. "You say 'Lasva' among your friends, do you not? Or is it Lasthavais? Or something worse?"

"Never," I exclaimed.

"Then you've heard it from others." Again the chuckle. "So. I'll be nineteen soon. You know, my Name Day is not Midsummer, unlike my sister, my mother, my grandmother, and in short, all orderly Lirendis for whom the Birth Spell worked." She chuckled deep in her chest. "I persist in thinking that the reason my mother tried the Birth Spell at the age of seventy-nine, on a winter's day, was whim. Or even a dash of wickedness. Or at least humor, though everyone insists she was always very good. And I should think, very dull and dutiful. There, are you scandalized? I never knew her, you see. I may say what I like: she brought me into the world and then, in effect, abandoned me, as she died not long after."

She smiled, her cheeks dimpling. Then she said, "Tell me about your education. I am guessing it matched a great deal of mine."

My mind flashed to the kitchen—and she said, with that narrow glance, "You are laughing inside. I can see it! Why?" Then she waved her hands. "Ah-ye, I can see it is a secret—my sister warned me not to pester you. I know you must obey, I know that trust comes when it will, and not by order. Someday, someday. Now, let us talk about your duties. Oh! They will have told you that staff is *strictly*—" She gestured toward Thorn Gate with an ironic flourish. "—forbidden to have passions with one another. However, I know that you scribes are trained to be discreet. So twistle with anyone you like, but . . ." She laid her finger to her lips and smiled. "You understand, I am sure! You scribes are trained to observe. So are we, and yet, so much of what we are taught is the art of *melende*, which conceals instead of reveals."

She paused, so I put my hands together in peaceful assent, feeling very grown up.

"My sister often asks her scribes, after an interview, what did you see?" She touched the sides of her eyes. "And they will tell her, 'I saw anger in the tilt of her head.' Or, 'I saw the wariness of a liar in the angle of his shoulders.' I am beginning to have more social correspondence than I can deal with, but here is where we begin our trust."

I bowed. She clasped her hands again. "What I really, really want is for you to observe like my sister's scribes but for me. Because you must know by now, everything I hear is flattery. Everything. I want to descry the truth if I can."

This surprised me so much I hesitated, and again she laughed.

"Shall we begin while traveling to Sartor for the music festival? I always leave the morning after Midsummer's Day. You can carry the scrollcase I promised my sister would always be near me. I hate that thing, it ruins the hang of my gowns. I'll continue to carry the emergency transfer token—they made it a finger ring." She touched her smallest finger.

"I am ready to travel if that is your wish, your h—"

She raised a hand, chuckling. "I think I will have to play the game with you. Poppy! Ah-ye," Lasva cried when the little page appeared. "We will save the cakes yet. I want you to run in and out, so that I may get Emras accustomed to addressing me. Now, if she's gone, you must say 'Lasva.' And when she appears, then it's back to all the titles. You know that so-called privilege is a matter of social agreement, do you not? That in the baths, we are all skin over bones?"

Poppy dashed in, her laughter light and free.

"Your highness," I said, when Lasva rose and nodded to me, her face full of fun.

Poppy ran out, and at the royal gesture I said obediently, "Lasva."

Three or four more times we played this game. Then the princess had to ready herself for her part in a musical quartette for, at that time, courtiers created what were called air poems—extemporaneous verse while playing insuments. Though often enough the most witty (or that deemed the most witty if someone was courting someone else's favor or favors) would appear in illustrated form the next morning, delivered by silent night pages, to be enjoyed over morning drink and discussed during the fountain chamber stroll before the Rising.

Lasva whirled away, saying over her shoulder that I was free to settle in—I had liberty that night but would begin my duties in the morning.

So I retired to read my congratulatory notes. My mother had folded a queensblossom in hers, a sign that she was pleased—and a warning to live up to my new status. My father sent a gold coin under his seal.

I saved Tif's for last, and with trembling fingers opened it.

The note had only two lines, the first the customary words of congratulation, and then, "Come visit me when you can. On Restday eve you can find us at the House of the Thistle, our favorite pleasure house, or at whichever play is newest."

SEVEN

OF THE PRICE OF STYLE

O f course I must go see Tiflis!

I'd only ventured into the city twice, both times in company with other students. I put on my new pair of outside shoes for my first venture into public as an adult scribe.

Tiflis lived over Pine House on Alassa Canal. Competition for living space is vigorous in the city. My father had joked that it was probably a Water Guild conspiracy that made addresses on the canals so much more prestigious. The canals were lined with brick walkways, so that people could stroll along them as well as boat on the water.

I proudly offered my gold coin to a young water girl on the Crown Skya Canal. This was personal business, so I would not use the palace pass.

She broke my gold piece into satisfyingly heavy six-sided silvers and a handful of small square coppers, and then she and her partner rowed me into the city as the sun began its slide toward the west, lighting up the whitewashed buildings with warm, peachy rose, and intensifying to jewel tones the painted shutters and flower boxes and vine-trailing iron work.

That bend in Alassa Canal was largely made up of book sellers. The front windows of their shops displayed books and scrolls, old and new.

Pine House's specialty seemed to be illustrated travel records, memoirs, and biographies.

The Hour of the Lily was when many shops closed and others, mostly places of entertainment, opened for the evening. Booksellers catering to the court and to richer folk usually stayed open late. Tif's shop was open, its door carved to resemble the outer edges of an open book.

Inside, the fine display shelves and little reading tables were presided over by a woman wearing a rich overrobe in the deep V-fronted style called "swan wings." It was embroidered in yellow knotwork over brown linen silk. Merchants dressed to signify success, as everyone believed that success bred more success. "May I be of service, Scribe?"

"I am here to see my cousin Tiflis, if she is off-duty."

The woman's inviting smile lessened at this evidence of mere personal business, but few dared to be rude to a royal scribe. "Second floor."

I found Tiflis in a parlor filled with fine papers, desks, and inks. Wide windows in all four walls let in the florid sunset colors; still-dark glow globes in sconces waited for someone to bespell them to light.

At my entrance Tif laid aside her book, her manner casual, as if it had been an hour, a day, and not a year since we'd last seen one another.

She introduced me around with obvious pride, ending with a thin girl our age dressed in a robe with great curling leaves of dull gold over pale eggshell blue silk. This girl, named Nali, eyed me speculatively from under a curled fringe of red hair as she made her Peace.

Then Tif led me up to the third floor dormitory.

The view from the journey scribes' curtained cubicles (each had a window) was over the complexity of pattern-tiled roofs and balconies on the alley behind the shop.

"It's pretty," I said.

"You know it's against the law to let any part of a property lapse into unsightliness?" she said.

"I mean your space. The way you have fixed it up, with this book shelf over your sleeping platform."

"It's small. I'm sure yours is ten times as grand."

My pay would be small, but I would always live in a palace. Tif knew that, but because she was Tif, she had to offer a challenge.

"I hope you will invite me to see the festival of lights," I said. "Which I will never see from my room."

"Oh, I will. But only if you bring some of those good cakes from your friends in the kitchens." After this reminder of my service in the kitchens, she sat on the bed, waving me to the desk chair. "So you got free time already? I hadn't expected you to come for a week or more."

I couldn't resist—and the moment the words left my lips, I saw my mistake—"The princess gave me leave." I tried to mitigate the error by adding, "Tell me about your life here."

To her peers Tif had shown me off, but now that we were alone, the competition narrowed to us. I saw it in how her spine lengthened, her chin came up, and her voice sharpened as she launched into an affected speech about how hard *they* worked, how difficult it was to copy books while keeping an eye to beauty on every page—a hint at how much easier it was to make full scribe in the palace than here in the world of commerce, where life was fast and challenging, and how much harder it was to design beautiful books instead of being a mere copyist. "Towers scribes are responsible for making every page look exactly like the original. Any ten-year-old can do that, once you've got the knack of measuring off your page. But to design each page so that it is a work of art . . ."

She described how they were always on the watch for a book that might become popular—but they had to determine whether it would appeal to people who collected fine books or just to those who liked reading parties. Most people, she explained, liked hearing a book, especially when read by a Reader, but rarely wanted to own it or even hear it a second time.

Gradually her voice and mood lightened, leaving me wondering why it is that so many of us humans may love a thing, but we still test its value against others' opinions: She was happy here, but she still wanted me to envy her, because she envied me being employed by a princess, even if she had scant interest in the actual work.

". . . and so I'm hoping to find an illustrator to pair with me. Nali says you get promoted faster if you can create a style together. Nali also told me, in the first week, that everyone wants illustrated books, at least the capital letters, these days."

That was the fourth "Nali says." I wondered if Nali had replaced Sheris in the way that Sheris had replaced me.

"How about Thumb? " I asked. "He was one of us—he was easy to get on with—and I never saw anyone draw as well as he did. Remember that sketch he made of Scribe Aulumbe when she stuck the quill behind her ear when it was still full of ink? Three lines, it seemed, and he had her very expression."

"Thumb's already been promoted to inker, and they say next year he'll be an illuminator, youngest in thirty years. Way beyond me from the start. He's at Laurel House, doing erotica, so I couldn't get him as my illustrator even if he wasn't so far ahead of us all."

"Erotica," I exclaimed, trying to imagine absent-minded Thumb illustrating people cavorting in sensory abandon.

Tif grinned, clasping her hands around her knees—the princess now forgotten, I hoped. "Did you know that most men arouse seeing drawings, the more detailed the better, but most women prefer poetry and text? But it all changes when they give one another pillow gifts." She shook her head. "I don't quite get it yet, though Nali insisted I go to the pleasure house with her a year ago winter, for my first time. And it was fun, but . . ." Tif wrinkled her upper lip. "Here I am, already eighteen, but it still takes forever to warm up. I like practicing on myself, and at the House of the Thistle, I play cards. I am deemed quite good, especially at Riddle." She turned her head cantwise as she regarded me. "Have you and Birdy twistled yet?"

"Birdy!" I exclaimed. "We never—"

"Em, you're not a baby anymore." She threw up her hands in *don't cross my shadow*. "The way he used to stick to you, we thought he was sweet on you."

"Only as a study partner. And he recently left for Chwahirsland."

"Poor thing! What an ending for the fellow who thought himself the smartest of us. So you two never trysted?"

"Never even thought about it." I was about to say I hadn't had time, but I was afraid she'd think me bragging about how important my time was. "As for pleasure houses, Mama offered to take me for my first time, last home visit. When I didn't particularly want to, she told me she didn't warm until she was twenty."

Tif snickered. "Maybe you'll warm if you hear her highness groaning away—she's sure to be better at it than everyone, like we hear about everything else she does. How close are her rooms to where you sleep? Does she really have rosebud carpets on her bed as well as all her floors?"

The princess hadn't been forgotten. Tif's voice was casual, but the way she leaned forward, her breath caught as she waited for my answer—this is why I was invited. *It wasn't family, it wasn't our old friendship. It's ambition.*

Betrayed, even affronted as I was, enough of the old bond remained for me to say evenly, "I have not seen her sleep chamber, but I'd be surprised if anyone hears anything."

"Then again there might be nothing to hear. In the new play at the Slipper, there was a new Handsome wearing a blue bow all the way through, and the Veil couldn't see it, though everyone else did." "The Veil" was always a royal figure, usually the princess, and the blue ribbon in Handsome's hair meant that the court's most popular man had his eye on someone royal. Except that no one gossiped about the queen's private life, so it had to mean Lasva.

Tif peered intently into my face. "You are now the closest to her. If you tell me—I am determined to find out any way I can, because it's the only way to get ahead—then I'll know what to do. And you needn't think I will tell anyone who my source is. I don't want you stolen, so any secret you tell me is perfectly safe."

What a blow to my heart—and, it must be confessed, to my pride. Here was the real reason Tiflis had written to me at last. She was using our family connection to delve for whispers!

I knew I should get up and march away. But what would happen? Tif would do what she said she would do, find another way to worm into Lasva's private life.

So . . . what if I tell her what Lasva doesn't mind the world knowing?

"They have to be making up something that isn't there," I said, and because Tiflis gave me a skeptical smirk, "I see Princess Lasthavais every day in court. There is no veil hiding her expression, so I can attest to the fact that she's never taken the least interest in Lord Vasalya-Kaidas Lassiter, if he's the new Handsome. Nor, from everything I've seen, does he in her. He's too busy with his many flirts."

My tone, my hand in Lily-Gate mode—openness—caused Tif to sit back. "Ah-yedi! If you haven't heard anything, then it's only smoke, to sell seats. I thought so. I shall take great pleasure in telling Sheris she's made a hum of herself yet again."

You have to remember that everything that had to do with the Chwahir culture was despised by us. For generations Colendi were scolded out of the otherwise innocent human penchant for humming because of the famous Chwahir humming choruses. To be a hum was to be risible.

"Sheris thinks the new playwright at the Slipper is a courtier in mask. She only comes over here to brag about how the archive is the center of any news. Hum! Now, my friend Nali says . . ."

I left soon after, my emotions in the greatest turmoil I'd felt since the day of the Fifteen.

My cousin pretended an interest, but what she really wanted was news. However, that didn't disturb me nearly as much as her words about Birdy.

EIGHT

OF A DISINTERESTED IMPULSE

For days Tif's remark continued to disturb me. I could not define why. Not loss. Not regret. I was unsettled. *Birdy?* Interested in *me?* Birdy with the jug ears and the juggling, always ready with a joke? I never would have thought of Birdy that way. He was just a friend. Yet the more I thought about it, the more I became convinced that the look in his eyes when he had said "us" had been hurt.

I am going to sidestep into another's thoughts again.

Lord Kaidas (called "Handsome" after the male figure in court plays, representing the latest male who'd caught a royal eye) was impatient with formality.

It had only been impulse to wager against the Gaszins. He couldn't have said why. He hated trouble. But the Gaszin brother and sister had been a shade too smug, and so, for the sake of a moment's laugh, he promised more money than he had to wager against them.

The result? He was the slightly embarrassed recipient of a small fortune. Though he was continually stressed for funds to support his racing stock, those things were separate in his mind: his racing wins went to racing needs. A windfall must be spent on whim. So when court left after Midsummer (and still no heir) he travelled south for the first time, to attend the Music Festival in Sartor.

His friends practiced their well-honed wit on him at this sudden curiosity for old culture. At that time, few knew about his talent with painting.

After two days of slow travel, he hated the journey.

No, he did not *hate* it.

Nothing bothered him enough for hatred. It was even a matter of pride. As his father frequently said, you regarded the vagaries of life with a sense of humor, and if you didn't like something, you did something else. Hatred was too fatiguing an exertion and never flattering to one's style.

His father had also said when Kaidas first went to court, "If you don't want to end up exiled like Thias Altan for five years, then stay away from Hatahra. And her pretty little sister, when she comes to court."

Kaidas, young and already popular, had said lazily, "Right now I have trouble finding time to be alone."

"That can change with a snap of the royal fan," said the baron, his expression sardonic. "Ask Thias someday how many friends he had left after a half a year exiled to his estate. He laid out more money than we'll ever have in either of our lives in his attempt to set up a second court. But they all go back to Alsais sooner or later."

The baron rarely spoke seriously. His son listened when he did, and avoided the crowd around Princess Lasva. Not that that was any hardship. Court was full of attractive people.

Then came the Dance of the Spring Leaves, and that smile she gave Jurac of Chwahirsland. He was intrigued enough to stay assiduously away from the princess. Too assiduous; when he realized that his determined distance was causing idle speculation, he left court entirely, claiming he had to get ready to go south for the music festival.

He was going to find out what sort of nature lay behind that smile, but he was going to manage it without causing gossip. That made it a game.

He lived for games.

———

Above all, humans crave happiness, we are told.

Sublime is the sense that *now I am happy*. The curious thing, at least in my experience, is that one can look back and think, *I was so happy then,* even if at the time one thought the day filled with an unending stream of small vexations.

Lasva's elaborate entourage set out for Sartor.

I reveled in belonging to the royal carriage, which would never have to halt for other traffic. My place was with my back to the horses, and I could not command a stop when I was tired, or demand food and drink when hungry and thirsty, but I had earned my place.

The happiness was unalloyed only in retrospect. At the time, I was also anxiously determined to observe something of use for Lasva. I longed to make so penetrating an observation that she would clap her hands and throw them out in Bird on the Wing, overjoyed with my perspicacity. And if I didn't, would she want another scribe?

After a day or two at Skya Lake's peaceful shore, in order to recover from the exertion of the gentle ride down the river road, the courtiers set out again. They paired off as we rolled west through aged forest shaded by what some said were a hundred types of oak and hickory, stippled by red maple and white ash. We're told that many of these trees were brought in hoarded bags of acorns through the World Gate eons ago. If so, here was evidence of the trees' children, grandchildren, and blended descendants, all in the green glory of summer.

I watched courtiers flirt—not that I witnessed anything worth relating. We scribes are supposed to remain invisible, which means we must never be caught staring. The eye is quicker than the mind at catching other eyes. Though I also tried listening, the courtiers' soft voices in the musical cadences of our language revealed even less than visual clues. I began to fear that the princess would be disappointed in me and send me back.

At an elegant riverside village we stepped into waiting barges for the ride up the Eth, and then another road journey along the north-flowing river on whose barges we would return to Colend.

Now I must return to Kaidas, who had taken a different barge from ours. Lasva did not know he was attached to our company, he was so careful to remain on the periphery. Ananda Gaszin, Rontande, the beautiful Isari, tall, thin Sharith, and other young courtiers circled around him, ready to smile, to flirt, to get up an impromptu dance or ensemble, for in those days courtiers still made music with instruments that looked well being played, such as strings and crystal-bells.

Though he was circumspect, his presence prompted enough glances, smiles, and witty rejoinders to send him on a stroll with Lady Darva of Oleff one Restday evening. "Aunt Darva" was the only one of his father's many lovers who had been kind to him when he was a youth, giving him gentle advice when needed. On this day they strolled an embankment where the princess's barge was docked. They were well along a meandering path that dipped down to the rush and chuckle of the river before he asked, "Aunt Darva. Am I the subject of a wager?"

Lady Darva had bent to examine the puffs of foam flower among the cattails. As she straightened up, the snow cloud of blossoms poofed into the air, and several ruby-glowing dragon-wings whirled skyward, humming. The last of the setting sun glowed in fiery tones through the insects' long tails then vanished against the emerging stars.

"I think so." She gave him a pensive smile. "I don't understand the impetus, but Lissais says that some have noticed you've never danced with the princess. They're wagering on when and how you will change that."

"They're wagering on how well I will dance?"

"On how you, oh, get her attention. Have you taken an interest in that direction? You have joined her party, if in the public sense." Her tone was peaceable, but he was annoyed anyway.

"Very public. It is the largest party going south." He knew it was hypocritical to be annoyed. He'd wagered carelessly on others' caprice.

Darva turned her back on the trees with nut-sized glowglobes winding up the trunks into the branches. The mellow sandstone village transformed to silhouettes among a forestland of lights. "Are you disturbed?"

"Isn't everyone, when precious self is the target of wit's arrow?"

Her shoulders lifted slightly, but she did not remonstrate with him for using such ugly images. Arrows! For centuries Colend had been part of the Accord banning the use of arrows. Better to leave such images to the barbarians of the western subcontinent.

He said, "Do you have a book of boring poems?"

She laughed. "Why would I bring such on so long a journey, when packing is already a puzzle?"

They were in sight of a mossy old arched bridge, along which travelers and villagers crossed to and fro, many with swinging lanterns carried by servants, their laughter wafting on the fragrant summer air.

"I want boring poems . . . for diversion."

"Ah. I believe I have what might be almost as good. The Altans always bring a scribe who is my age—a connection of some cousins. He's also a

Reader. Used to be able to quote pages and pages of bad poems, recited in comical accents, or voices of a cat or a mouse. A horse. So amusing when we were young and the winters were long."

"Is he discreet?"

"You know how scribes are." Her fan flickered in Surprise.

"As I recall, not all are discreet."

Her smile vanished. "Ah-ye! I'd forgotten that dreadful—but surely that would be the exception, and explains why we remember."

"Since my father's private life furnished his fund of particulars, I've inherited Father's distrust for the ubiquitous blue-clad scufflers. But I'm willing to be proved wrong."

"Let us turn back. I will introduce you, and you may judge for yourself."

She was considerably surprised—so was everyone—when at the gathering that evening, Kaidas asked the duke's permission to address his scribe in public, and then, as several listened, the two began a long discourse on Sartoran poetry during the Symbolist Period—sometimes considered the most obscure poetry ever written. Few would have claimed that Kaidas knew anything about poetry, and Rontande drawled that he hadn't known any Lassiter could read.

For several days afterward Kaidas amused himself with quoting poetry to anyone who came near—especially certain among his old friends and lovers. The effect was to encourage them to find other pursuits with as much haste as would not be unseemly.

While he was intent on rerouting curious courtiers, the entire court left the river Eth and began the journey along the Margren River, toward the transfer point. The inn at Arvin is an enormous structure but not a palace—that is, not a great building whose grand design uses space, fine materials, and artistry to impress as well as to please the eye. This inn had been added to over many centuries. Children saw the place as a labyrinth or challenge and ran from garden to garden or above our heads across bridge-ways that linked the many wings. They pounded along halls, shrieking and chasing in an uninhibited way that I never had.

Here, at the second-to-the-last stop before transfer, Colend's court found themselves among people from all over the eastern part of the continent; as I followed a servant along a wickerwork bridge built over a stream that tumbled between two buildings, I counted five languages.

Sauntering in the crowd behind us was Kaidas Lassiter, who couldn't afford a carriage. Not that he told anyone that. Famed for his riding, it was a tribute to his style that he was admired for the freedom with which he could trot from carriage to carriage at whim. If anyone got too speculative about why he made this journey, he pulled scrolls of obscure Sartoran poetry from his sleeve pockets and favored them with choice pieces. None of the courtiers knew he thus observed Lasva from afar.

Lasva travelled with half her household. When he comprehended the extent of the inn, with its private wings and tree-shadowed balconies, Kaidas Lassiter followed us.

We found the rooms of our suite warm and stuffy. Most courtiers retreated to the parlors at the front, which were cooled by magic, but Lasva surprised us by remaining as the servants labored to make things comfortable.

As Marnda and Dessaf supervised the duty housemaids, Lasva and I moved at her desire to the narrow wickerwork balcony, which was shaded by the balcony of the rooms above. The waterfall splashed into a pool below. Layers of leafy trees rustled in the air, moving slowly above the falls, giving us a semblance of coolness.

"What did you see today?" Lasva asked me, as had become habit.

I strove always to have something to say, and so I offered my observation about the running children and their freedom from constraint.

She perched on the edge of a table carved in the shape of a tree that framed the glass top. "Time," she said. "Here it seems suspended. And my childhood the blink of an eye." She rubbed at her forehead.

As if reading her thoughts, Marnda appeared behind us. "Your highness. Shall I send a page for refreshment?"

"Thank you, just send the hair dresser, please."

I caught Marnda's look of surprise as she turned away. Though she was in a sense Lasva's *hlaras*—heart's mother—she could not question orders.

"Go on, Emras."

"I don't know if my thought is worth the effort of speech in this hot air. Merely, I wonder if I should be sad or glad that childhood slipped away without my notice. We remember dramatic things—contrasts in emotion, as all the poets say."

"And dramatic contrasts in scenery," Lasva added as she untied the ribbon of her hat. She tipped her head. "You've heard Isari. What do you think lies behind all these hints about how tiresome it is to attend to the color of our hair while we travel?"

"Is it troublesome?" I asked. "Sitting quietly every few days, so that no vestige of root growth mars the sheen of silver or moon-blue or lemon-froth? The hair dresser is the one who makes the effort to create the magical spell that transfers the colors to your hair."

Lasva's dimples flashed. "So exhausting, to sit for a hair dresser, when otherwise we sit in a carriage. I cannot decide if she wants me to begin fashions—or to make myself a hum."

"I don't think there is any danger of that," I said.

"Neither did I," she said, "but whenever I think I am safe from ridicule because of my rank, I only have to remember that poor fellow from Chwahirsland. He was a king, but they would have stepped on his shadow if they were not so afraid of my sister, who'd invited him for treaty purposes. So they hummed behind his back. What do they chirp behind my back?"

The hair dresser arrived, showing no reaction when the princess gave the order for her hair to be restored to its natural color. The hair dresser had set out her pots but put them away again. Then she performed a different set of spells, that sent the false color into the ground in the manner of the Waste Spell we all learn soon after we begin to walk.

Kaidas had slipped up the stairs, found the suite empty (Lasva always hired the floors above to prevent footsteps from disturbing us) and made his way to the balcony, from which he heard our voices.

When the hair dresser left, Lasva peered in the mirror at her newly dark hair. "It makes me look . . . pale." She tapped her fingers to her lips in distaste, but said nothing more.

I never heard her say a cruel thing, though all around one heard casual slanging of the moon-pale or slug-faced Chwahir. The word "pale" alone carried enough derogatory associations. "I will need fabrics that bring my skin tones out again." She shrugged, then whirled away, arms raised. "I'm still stiff. What was that I saw you doing on the private terrace at dawn yesterday? Is that what they call the Altan fan form?"

"Yes."

"Why do you do that? I never heard they taught it to scribes."

"It keeps the wrists strong, as well as the body."

Lasva clasped her hands. "There is something compelling about it, suggestive of strength. Almost the opposite of dance, which exhorts us to be light and fluid as water. Teach it to me." And when I began a protest, she waved a hand, "Ah-ye, I know. You are not a proper teacher. I will hire an expert if I take to it. Now, all I want is to experiment."

I fetched my long fans from my trunk. Lasva took one to spread and inspect. Neither of us was aware of Kaidas standing on the wickerwork balcony above us, caught by the sound of Lasva's voice.

"I read that people actually fought with these fans," Lasva said. "Did they really, or is it metaphor? I have yet to read of anyone truly treading on someone's shadow, yet our language is rife with references."

"The instructor told us that the first Duke of Altan won his land after a duel with fans. See the points on the blades? These are rounded, and made of the light wood, but I did some research and learned that centuries ago they were thin steel, as sharp as carving tools."

"That must have been quite heavy. Even these have heft." She turned the fan over. "Black on one side, white on the other. Why is this? Caprice?"

"It's so the master can see your moves. For certain forms, correct style requires only one side visible at a time."

"Low shoulder," she said, touching the blades below the plain white-sided mount. "Ours have high shoulders."

"Gives the fan more strength," I said. "Court fans merely have to set a breeze going."

"I still do not see how one could engage in battle with this." She poked it into the air. "With a sword, I know you press the point into the opponent. That frightful mural in the old palace made that evident."

"I will demonstrate, with your permission. If you will hold the paper thus."

I gave her one of my practice scrolls, which I could easily mend.

She smiled in anticipation as she held the scroll stretched between her hands.

"Hold it taut," I said, and she snapped it taut.

The fan form is done slowly—that is what keeps our muscles supple. The word "form" is meant to imply dance. Some centuries ago any reference to actual warfare was smoothed away, and the *arts of war* became *arts*. "No one actually practices at speed, or against others, at least, not in Alsais," I said as I set my slippers and my cloud blue robe aside and began the first moves. "We are told that the Altans have guards who still practice at speed. It's because of their proximity to the pass and to the Chwahir. Our teacher is from Altan."

As I said the above I moved with gathering speed, the fans closing and opening in my hands, until at last I stepped, whirled, and with a swift cut of the open fan, dashed it across the scroll, which ripped across.

"Yedi!" Lasva exclaimed, leaping back and dropping the ends of the scroll. "I did not expect that!"

I finished the form, picked up the scroll ends, and examined the tears. "Oh, I would get a bad mark for the jagged rip. A good strike cuts the paper cleanly straight across."

She picked up the fans, then canted her head. "Is this why the challenge fan has points painted on it?"

"The challenge fan is a descendant of these, we're told," I said.

No one in court carried the intimidating fans with thorns or clawed figures painted on them anymore. Now anger was signified with the snap or angle of an ordinary fan, or an oblique reference to Thorn Gate, which had been the old place of punishment during our very early days. Thorn Gate no longer existed—had not for centuries—but in referring to dire judgments everyone pointed north as if its shadow still lay over that end of the old castle.

Lasva whisked herself into her room and returned with her two largest fans. These were half the size of my Altans and had lace or painted mounts on only one side of the blades, but they would suffice.

We pushed the furniture to the edges of the room, then she removed three of her filmy outer robes, until she stood in her cotton-silk body robe of pale peach. I carefully set the queen's scrollcase on top of my robe for instant retrieval, though Lasva had told me her sister was no letter writer. That would make a communication all the more imperative.

I showed Lasva the first steps, which I warned her would have to be practiced over and over.

Without our knowing, Kaidas moved along the balcony until he could see through the wickerwork, down to the top of Lasva's now dark head.

That dark hair startled him. He bent down cautiously so that he could see better. He watched Lasva mirror me through the fan form across the balcony, and when we turned, he glanced at me, only to dismiss my scrawny, chipmunk-faced self. (Seeing oneself in others' eyes can be disconcerting at best. But I will have more to say on that later.)

The important thing at that moment was this: Lasva caught and held his attention, the living breathing image of her great-mother, the famous Lasthavais Sky Child, who had wandered into Colend and ended up married to a king.

He bent even lower, looking for flaws, for differences from the centuries-old magical image caught from a few moments of Lasthavais Sky Child's real life. His father had shown him the gallery his first week at court. *This*, his father had said, *is beauty. Not just her face, or her figure. Listen to her laugh and watch her movements. Such a woman would never cease to set you aflame.*

On our second journey across the balcony, Lasva had learned the basic pattern enough to resume converse. "Can you tell we are nearing Sartor?"

"Turn your wrist up. That's right. Yes, I thought the air smelled differ-ent. And it seems . . . bluer, somehow."

"I felt the same when we reached this point my first year. It was thun-dering, then." She dashed her sleeve over her face.

From above, Kaidas observed how her hair coiled in ropes of dark silk about her head, glinting with golden highlights, the hairpins in her fa-vorite rose color matched the topmost outer robe spilled like a puddle of gleaming silk on the far table. A fresh glow enhanced her russet com-plexion. Her voice was low, and husky, as though she was on the verge of a laugh.

She gripped her fans in the right pose, and we began another set. "You'll see when we get there," she said, "the forests are older. Denser. That haze against the mountains is denser, too. Like silvery smoke."

I said, "Bent knee. Stay on one level. Like your court walk but lower, for when you strike you will lunge out on one leg."

"What a strange posture!"

"I'm told it is much the same when manipulating a sword." I paused, straightened her wrists and arms, then took up my fans again, falling into the stance. "I remember when I was eight, we learned that one could find in Sartor evidence of every type of green thing that grew on the world."

Lasva laughed, then lifted her lip in a slight grimace. "This uses my arm muscles in a different way. I suspect it will ache."

"Would you like to stop?"

"Not at all. That ache builds to strength, I learned that when I first commenced dance lessons. Let us keep going until I master this first form. So. I used to count types of flowers and trees and birds. I wonder if children always do that, as a way of learning the world?"

"We did. How high will the mountains get?"

"I'm told they touch the sky, with peaks always white, but we will not see them. Pirun, our next stop, is where we use magic transfer—or it would take months to reach Sartor."

"Magic transfer," I repeated and hid my aversion.

She touched her fingers to her lips, smiling in agreement. Though I appreciated the speed with which I could get home for my New Year's Week visits, the reality of transfer was wrenching, leaving me with nau-sea and a headache that took a while to fade.

Kaidas watched and listened, his heartbeat accelerating as Lasva started back again, one arm rising over her head, the other extended, hands turning the fans over, her body graceful in the clinging body robe.

". . . Like the idea of ancient geliaths honeycombing those mountains,

older than Colend—far older—some say back to The Fall." I snapped a
fan open. "And the idea that the Morvende might not be human any
more—slow. Stay low. Do not bounce up when you step."

Laughter, soft and calculated, drifted along the aromatic air from behind Kaidas. He recognized one of those voices and forced himself away.
His heartbeat thundered in his ears as he ran through the archway to the
inside landing and forced himself to a semblance of calm. Several courtiers wandered in.

The Gaszins formed the group's center. Kaidas did not wait for
questions—for Ananda's restless, avid glance to take in Kaidas's sur-
roundings, and her ready ears to hear the princess's voice below.

He marched forward, slid his arms in each of theirs, and quoted a passage he'd memorized for such an occasion.

They were too well-trained to interrupt, and so he bore them through
the opposite arch and along an adjacent balcony, boring them in a different manner the entire way.

"Ah-ye," he exclaimed at the end of the verse. "Do I have to lay a wager? Who can furnish the next line?"

"If you want to play games of wit, then give us a poet we've heard of,"
the Sentis heir complained.

"Why should I make it easy? If I go to the trouble of enriching my
mental archive—and listen to this passage . . ."

On they walked, as he uttered more lines in a sonorous moo.

At the end, Ananda flirted her fan. "I make it a rule never to duel in
poetry. Musical roundelays, yes, but the other arts? Ah-ye, not fair to
either. And distresses my sensitivities." Then she turned to her brother,
"You know how very sensitive I am to poetry—"

"—both air and written," Kaidas inserted smoothly, when she paused
for her admirers to add to her self-praise. "Reminding me of the immortal lines . . ."

Off he went again, drawing them down yet another hall, until at last
Young Gaszin pulled away, laughing. "You're a wit-wanderer, that's what
it is."

"It's true. I admit it."

Rontande drawled, "We'll have enough poetry, won't we, when we
get to Sartor?"

"There's never enough poetry," Kaidas declared, and because the princess's voice still whispered in memory, and the image of her charming
arms arching with those fans insisted on repeating against his inner eye,

he added, "And so I fear I must leave you all. I am too impatient to serve as audience. I'm off to write immortal verse."

They were startled into real laughter.

". . . and visit my cousins on the border. They do persist in begging me to help them chase brigands. Maybe the queen will smile on my poetic afflatus if I prove diligent, eh?" He bowed, and they bowed, and he ran down the stairs, laughing when Ananda called to halt him.

Soon he was galloping toward the east, his hair freshly restored to its natural black, his court clothes sent by wagon to his ramshackle ancestral home.

How long before the beautiful Lasthavais Sky Child got bored with the great King Mathias? His father had observed as they stood side by side, admiring the centuries-old portrait. *We never hear about that. I wonder just how soon she crooked a finger at all those kneeling hummers of such high degree, who waited like beggars for her smiles.*

Admire, son. Always appreciate art of whatever kind. But don't touch it. Keep your melende and move on.

NINE

OF CATS AND GOLDEN CAGES

My life was not entirely consumed by the pleasure of being the princess's scribe. When I passed my seventeenth Name Day, I left the calm of childhood behind.

How quick is the eye of youth! Once one begins to look, one might see desire or speculation in a stare that is actually someone's absent gaze, or mistake interest when there is only politeness. But the time came at last when the lingering eye, and the inviting smile, meant what I thought they did whenever I encountered a certain footman with dark curls. How alluring is the tingle and glow when that eye lingers! How subtle is that invisible boundary between the waking of physical desire and the emotional appeal of thinking oneself in love. His interest both intrigued and scared me.

By the time we are ten years old, we scribes learn how trite some expressions are—for example, the moth to the flame. Even so, that is exactly how I felt.

I was intrigued by my footman's interest in me to the point that I thought about him thinking about me, and I found myself seeking excuses to traverse the hall where he would be on duty. I adjusted my schedule so that I would attend staff meals when he did. I felt grown-up and interesting when he singled me out for walks along the canal, or to sit beside at entertainments. Yet when he wanted to be alone with me, I was uneasy. I was only aware that he was too close, that I did not like the clamminess of his palms, or his hot breath on my cheek. When he touched me, I always had some reason to rise, to stretch, to claim hunger, thirst, or a need to return to duty.

It was curious, what a relief I felt, yet how hurt I was when he no longer sought the place beside me. Then the day came when I saw him go off alone with Delis, my friend from the kitchen. It was awkward for me when we met in the halls or the staff rooms, though he was never unfriendly. I was glad to go home for New Year's Week.

Because I was now a scribe, my parents hired one of the finest rooms in Ranflar's best pleasure house, where we had a succession of delicacies served while nearby six musicians on winds and strings played for us.

During this meal my parents praised me for my diligence and dedication, but gradually I became aware of my mother's preoccupied expression, even though I was describing my recent duties.

". . . and so the princess hired an instructor for the fan form on our return. She often goes out in domino veil to visit the Rose Walk, and because she's in domino veil, no one bows or speaks to her, so she can walk and walk. But she said she missed running, which she was scolded out of at an even younger age than we scribe students were!"

My father smiled.

"She's begun to lead fashion," I went on. "You know it was she who got rid of the silver hair, while we were in Sartor. The young courtiers now all wear their own hair color. Lady Isari first, because hers is the true red."

"Either that or they are paying for flattering natural colors," Mother observed.

"True. Though the older generation still silver their hair. Lasva said that the queen told her that her face would never be more pale than her hair."

"An insult aimed at the Chwahir," my father said. "She's had that predisposition all my life." He spread his hands, and we understood the gesture as *What can you do?* I felt very grown up—he was including me in a mutual recognition of the fact that our all-powerful queen had a shortcoming, but we were left with the comfortable sense that at least it did not concern us.

"The next fashion the princess introduced, or reintroduced, is the Reading in the Reeds."

My mother's brows went up. In my wish to show off my grown-up knowledge, I interpreted her reaction as question.

"Stationing readers among the reeds and flowers along a canal," I explained. "When the boats near, the reader offers a poem. So the guests in the boat slide along from poem to poem. The custom dates at least to the days of Lasthavais the Wanderer."

My mother said, "We know what Readers in the Reeds are."

My father's straight brows furrowed. "Who has your loyalty, Em?"

"Colend, of course. Need you to ask?"

Mother touched her porcelain cup. "Who has your loyalty, the queen who houses and pays you, or the princess who employs you?"

The sense of ease had vanished. I looked from one earnest, worried face to the other. "I believe that my housing and essentials, as they call it, come out of the princess's budget."

"Who, in turn, gets her budget from . . ." Mother prompted.

"The queen." I set aside all eating things. "Please honor me with the reason my loyalty is in question?"

Mother bent her head, thumb and index finger working slowly over her closed eyelids, back and forth. The skin was so fragile, marked by lines I'd never seen before. Sorrow swooped through me. *I do not want my mother to age.*

Mother said, "You understand the . . . the hidden responsibilities, the cost of being a royal scribe."

I made The Peace. "I know I can't marry, but I don't have any interest in such things. I also know what being a personal scribe means, as opposed to a public royal scribe. They have been very careful to teach us to understand the responsibilities. Again, why is my loyalty in question?"

Father's gaze flicked her way, then back to me. "Emras, we want you to see what we see. We are proud of your promotion, as we've always been proud of you and your skills."

"When you learned to read so young, we hoped you would reach the higher levels," Mother said.

"But . . . well, if you will pardon advice—"

I made the gesture of acceptance, keeping my head at the angle of gratitude. Annoyed as I found myself to be told what I knew—to be treated not as an adult, but as a student again—I could also see that something worried my parents.

"Keep the distinctions in mind." Father's voice dropped, and he leaned forward, his body tense. "Only permit yourself to hear that which you can in good conscience keep in confidence."

Mother signed agreement.

Disquiet stifled my irritation. "You mean, the queen might . . . might summon me to reveal Las—the princess's secrets?"

Mother said, "It's one of the reasons why we hired this room in a discreet house. Ranflar's palace is notorious." She made the old-fashioned signal for spywells, left over from the days when mages could put spells over rooms so that conversations could be spied upon. But those spells had long since been warded against. Now the gesture just meant that there was a danger of being overheard.

"People spy on you in Ranflar?" I asked in disbelief.

"Ah-ye! Just that the air conduits often carry voices as well, whether by accident or design," Father said. "Here, we can talk freely."

Mother touched my hand. "You have risen high at a very young age."

"But Lasva is not the heir—there is nothing political in her life," I protested. "You said as much, and I have seen nothing political. All I do is write what she dictates. For important notes she chooses the paper, the scent, the ribbon, the flower, and I even fold them as she directs. Her choices are for style and beauty. She has never mentioned politics. As for the Readings in the Reeds, she has asked me to hunt out the poems."

"So the Readings began," Mother said. "Poems were chosen for their beauty, but even beauty can embroider themes. And later, you know, people brought their own poems, to surprise. Or to convey delicate meanings."

"Yes, we talked about that. They were arranged by those who wished to make an oblique comment upon state affairs—or personal things. Princess Lasva tells everyone that I pick the poems, to make certain no one will think there is any hidden meaning. The Readings have been very popular. Her themes are things like autumn, water, friendship."

"There is still no heir," Father said, his fingers absently stacking the cups in a neat tower. "Everything her highness does has political prospect."

"And if you get summoned to the queen in what is decreed a matter of state, the line between private and public blurs—from a queen's point of view."

"The princess would never order me to find poems that—oh, but you are talking generally. She would never confide in me something that would be . . ." I could not even force such words as *treachery* or *treason* past my lips.

Mother shook her head. "Emras, nothing is safe when you find yourself involved in state matters. And the affairs of a princess one step from a throne can be personal and state at once."

"But we trust in your good sense. Our conversation is a reminder, as I'm certain your scribe guide will also remind you when you go for your first review. Just remember the Rules," Father said.

"Especially the First Rule: Do not interfere," Mother added. "*Especially the first.*"

I worried about that First Rule as I traveled back to Alsais and discovered that Lasva was involved in such a round of flirtations and dalliances that I scarcely saw her, except at noon, when she met me to go over the day's correspondence.

Since court was not yet in season (though some courtiers lived in the city year round, especially second sons and daughters and cousins who had no duties of heirship at home), there were few public events for me to witness. Therefore I plunged back into my studies and practice. I had gone to Ranflar feeling adult, but had returned feeling like a student again.

As for romance, I decided in my teenage wisdom that it didn't exist—that it was just poetic words for desire. When I wanted to be social, I joined the kitchen folk or the friendlier dressers on excursions to the pleasure house, but when the others went upstairs, I stayed below where the company was merry and there was singing and poetry, and people got up impromptu play readings. I was popular, trained as I was to read well, so I had a good time in the public areas. As for romance, and desire, I kept thinking, *Maybe next year I will want to go upstairs.*

When spring warmed the air, I was summoned by Noliske to my first year's review, two hours past midday at the Hour of the Quill. I knew that I was not in trouble; an admonitory interview would have taken place at the Hour of Stone, before midday.

When I arrived, I found two senior scribes, Halimas and Noliske, there to interview me, instead of the traditional one.

I told them everything, including my conversation in Ranflar.

At the end, Noliske said, "You have been diligent and hard-working, Emras. We hear nothing but praise from everyone you work with, including Seneschal Marnda."

Halimas said, "She reports that you are discreet and polite. No higher praise can come from Marnda. You know that when we were young she was first handmaid to Queen Alian."

As I put my hands together in agreement, Halimas ran his quill through his fingers. "We deem it time to let you know that you are an anomaly. You are what the princess asked for, but you are not the older, experienced scribe that Queen Hatahra would have preferred to give her sister."

"That is why there are two of us," Noliske said. "You must understand that the anomaly is not just you. In truth, the princess herself is also an anomaly—her birth took everyone by surprise—though everything has been done as if her birth had been planned for."

Here was a new trapdoor to fall through. *Is this what adult life is, then?* I thought. *Surprises at every turn?*

"Is this why I have not been interviewed by the queen?" I asked. "I thought at first she was too busy, then I wondered if my work was amiss."

"She is never too busy for any royal matter," Noliske said. "Especially those relating to the princess."

Halimas said, "But when the princess turned sixteen the queen gave her control of her own staff. And in turn, the princess kept her old staff, though they had been appointed by the queen. Consequently the queen has been careful not to interview you, to avoid the appearance of interference."

"So . . . the queen would not have hired me because there is something amiss with me as a person?" I asked.

Noliske laid her hands together in The Peace. "It is my pleasure to negate so reasonable but painful a question. The subject is before us so you will truly comprehend that everything the princess does raises questions. She was born when the queen was an adult, so in a sense she was never like a true sibling. And there is no heir."

"Yet," Noliske said quickly.

"Yet. This is why we waited a year for this conversation, rather than telling you when you first commenced your position," Halimas said. "We did not want to burden you before you had learned what you have in this past year."

Scribe Noliske stretched a finger toward the lily petal floating in the cloud blue porcelain wine cup. "You have done well. Continue to do well. Just . . ."

"Just be aware of what you say. And to whom," Halimas finished.

"Especially when off duty." Noliske made the spywell gesture, to emphasize discretion. "Now. Let us celebrate your excellence by partaking of this fine honeyflower wine. The almond-cakes were sent by your friend Delis, who was recently promoted to pastry."

As I said, in Kifelian there are so very many verbs and nouns for *love*. Not to say that other languages do not furnish many variations in meaning, it's that (I've found, so far) they tend to rely on metaphor or variation in the descriptors: a new love, an old love, an ardent love, a tranquil love. In Colend, we seem to delight in words for the sake of words, and so I find that I must choose from many in order to convey what I mean in languages that have no equivalent.

Therefore. If I say "flirtation," it means the easiest of relationships; what some say is light in heart and some say involves no heart. People come together for enjoyment, sometimes to share passion, and then go away again with no emotional ribbons binding one to the other. I counted seventeen nouns used by courtiers for this type of relationship, but I will not list them or how each differs from the next. Flirtations vary from public to private in duration and degree.

"Dalliances" are usually more ardent and are conducted privately. They end, usually with a fading of interest into friendly indifference or sometimes in equally passionate anger, hurt, or hatred.

At the time I write about, the various noun-ramifications of "flirtation," and "dalliance" were modified by names of scents, from mild to strong, representing degrees of intensity. The courtiers talked about them endlessly, entertaining themselves with extended metaphor, the more oblique the better, as they strummed or sang or composed elegant poetry.

A week after my interview with the senior scribes, I entered Lasva's outer chamber with new poems for another Reading in the Reeds.

I found Lasva looking out her window. I said, "I seem to have misplaced my lap table—"

That was when I discovered that Lasva was not alone. Lord Rontande sat on the couch in the sunken circle. He'd been partially obscured by one of the potted flowering plants. I made my formal bow, which hid my blush at having been caught in error.

"Sorry, scribe," Rontande said with a soft, pleasant courtier's laugh. "Need you your table now?"

He sat at his ease, long legs crossed one over the other, their shape outlined by the silken night robe that he wore. His dark hair lay loose on his shoulders.

My inks lay open on the lap table, and with quick strokes Rontande was painting. His question, so simple if you are not Colendi, did not allow for negation. Courtiers avoided negations to one another, and for one such as I to deny a lord or lady would be unthinkable.

"Your pardon." I bowed. "It is an honor to relinquish it to your use, my lord."

Lasva turned away from the window. She, too, wore only a silken robe that matched his in shade. His was embroidered with geese in flight, chained round it and flying upward; hers with entwined lilies. Pillow robes.

"I told him you wouldn't mind if he was careful," Lasva said to me. "Are those the poems?"

"Nature poems, your highness," I said, striving for normalcy. "The chrysalis, the surprise. Kileili of Jhamond, two centuries ago."

The young man's hand rang my brush against the inside of the water glass, then he scrubbed it to loosen the color faster. I hid my irritation—not that he bothered to look my way.

"We were thinking," Lasva gave a breathless laugh, "of cats."

"Cats, your highness?"

She gestured toward Rontande's painting, and I took that as permission to satisfy my curiosity.

Sketched so swiftly—no more than a suggestion of figures—was a row of cats seated on the window sill, staring out. Rontande's skill was quite good.

"Six of them." Lasva's hand opened toward the opposite window. "Watching so intently."

"May I ask what, your highness?"

Lasva put a hand to her cheek. "That's the mystery—I don't know. Could be some birds teased them."

"You shamed them with your beauty." Rontande smiled up at her, brush in the air.

"Cats are cats," she retorted, leaning down to caress his cheek. "I don't think they see beauty. Or do they?"

She turned to me, question in the faint contraction of her brow. Question outside of her words. Had she seen my reaction?

"I thought they see ghosts, your highness." I strove to smooth voice and manner into neutrality, next to invisibility.

"If they do, they don't seem to care," Rontande drawled, giving me to understand that my opinion was unessential to his experience of art and beauty.

"Well, if ghosts are part of their daily life, why should they care?" Lasva asked.

"You are always full of these questions." Rontande's low tone was intimate. "Do not make me laugh, I beg. If one is to offer oneself as a skilled painter, one cannot stutter one's efforts through laughter that later cannot be explained away with grace."

"I will be as quiet as a cat," Lasva retorted, slipping down beside him. She put her hand on his free arm, her chin on her hand. "And watch."

I performed my bow to their averted heads and left to return the book to the archive, where I exchanged it for one containing poems about cats.

A few days later she came to my chamber and said, "Rontande wanted me to change the reading to cats."

I brandished the book. "I thought you might."

But she did not take it. She stepped close, regarding me wide-eyed. "You did mind. Didn't you?" She sighed. "You did."

"I shouldn't," I said. "You—and her majesty—own these things, so I—"

"*You* own them. They are your tools. The moment you set your hand to them, they became yours." Lasva prowled around my small chamber, then bent and extended a finger toward one of my quills. But she did not permit her finger to brush the feathering. "I am willing to share my things, and so I thought you would not mind. But you did." She straightened and pressed her hands together. "I'm trying to understand where the difference is. Is it that he did not ask you? Though I was sure you would have assented."

I said slowly, "I would have assented."

Her eyelids flashed up. "You had to assent, is that it? Ah-ye, I who thought I saw so clearly! But no one ever denies a princess, and so I never see denial, though I know it exists. So he asks knowing you cannot deny . . . and of course, you would never ask if you could share his."

Relief sighed through me. "That's it."

She looked through her window, her voice meditative. "Just as no one would presume to ask for the smallest of my infinity of possessions, thus limiting the scope of my generosity. A humbling lesson! It is a week for lessons, it seems."

My window looked west, but even so there was enough light to reveal pink eyelids and a faint puffiness below her eyes.

She turned my way. "I believe myself observant, yet my attraction for Rontande clouded my perceptions. I thought his heart was involved, as mine was beginning to be."

"It was not his heart, but his ambition?" I ventured.

"Did you see it, then?"

I said, "The way he kept bringing the subject back to himself. Or to flattery of you."

She sighed, flinging her hands out wide in the mode called Bird on the Wing. "That is the fourth one. And I was so careful, this time! Is it always this way? No wonder my sister refuses to marry, though I always thought Davaud the kindest of men. My sister has always been formal and distant. I thought it her nature, until I began to understand some whispers about the past. Or is it always this way for everyone? Ambition first, no true interest in the other person, as a person? Is that arrogance, that I want to be desired as Lasva and not as a princess?"

When I saw that she wanted an answer, I said, "Yet he painted for you."

She breathed a soft laugh. "You did not know that painting is the new fashion? Come."

We moved through her suite to her private chamber, the one with access to her sleeping room. This room was enormous, but that was the end of my met expectations: in the place of fantastic art and textiles there was a complicated climbing structure covered in old carpet-work, much shredded, and around the room hosts of pillows, and even miniature houses in and out of which cats paced; the faint flash of magic from inside the houses indicated that the Waste Spell had been laid on them, instead of on wands, as is usual wherever people have pets. Extremely expensive to lay those spells time after time on the houses, but it meant that there would never be any smell, and the sand within the houses would always stay clean. And no servant had to come in to wave the wand over the boxes, as is common elsewhere.

On the wall above the bed someone had affixed the painting of the cats, framed within two dyed-silk mats in contrasting shades of dull gold and rust.

"They're all busy with their brushes now," she said as she took the painting from the wall and carried it to the outer chamber where she held her parties. "Those who can. It's more popular than extemporaneous music. Did you hear what happened in the east?"

"My parents mentioned a new treaty on the border. That is all I know."

"It was made by Kaidas Lassiter, whose father Hatahra loathes. Maybe the son isn't so . . . so frivolous. I do not know. I only met him to exchange bows. There was some sort of skirmish with brigands on the border with Khanerenth, when Kaidas was visiting his cousins. Some countess or duchess on the other side of the border was involved. Kaidas and this countess or duchess vanished into her castle, and for a time no one knew if he was a hostage, a prisoner, or what. After a week—this was New Year's Week—they emerged, he with a new treaty and she bearing a lover's cup, painted in her own colors and decorated with her favorite motifs. Though it was a pillow gift, she put it on her mantel. Peace, and so romantic! Now the style is painting."

"Ah-ye," I exclaimed. "And so Lord Rontande made the cat painting for you."

"But do you not see? I didn't, at first, but I think you did, didn't you? That was not for me, he wants me to display it for others to see on my wall."

Pillow gifts are always private, intimate. Kept in one's inner chamber and never shared. I hadn't seen his intent, but I had seen his motivation.

Though I wasn't sure what to say, she was studying me carefully.

She clasped her hands. "I love dogs as well as cats. However dogs can hurt you with their eyes, they are so devoted, and all they ask is love. And sometimes you are too busy to give it. What is the—the responsibility of love, and how many can one love? With cats, it doesn't matter so much. Rontande reminds me of a cat. He is so . . . so smooth. But he's not as interesting as a cat, who never bores one with its ambition."

She turned away to wipe her tears. I reorganized my pens, reversing their order, that I might keep my hands and eyes busy.

"Remember when you first came, Emras? I asked you to see for me. Just like my sister's scribes do for her. At my next party—nothing large—an informal reading, an evening of music, either our own or a concert—you must be my eyes, and if there is something I don't see, you must tell me. Will you do that?"

I bowed.

She fluttered her fingers in the Butterfly-in-the-Wind mode, the delicate lace at her wrists floating. "As for Rontande. When he comes to my party, he will find his painting in my outermost chamber where the servants most frequently walk. Ostensibly a place of honor, in the public eye. But I think he will take my meaning about his ambition."

I bowed again, thinking to myself that if the queen asks me what we talked about, I will say it was only cats, as I walked to my room.

There I found an invitation from Tiflis: another summons to mine for gossip. *She's heard about Rontande.*

TEN

OF SARTOR AND GARGOYLES

I loved going to Sartor with Lasva. On each of the twelve days, I willingly followed her to the different stations around Ilderven, listening intently to the remains of Old Sartoran ritual and to scraps of poetry celebrating what our ancestors thought were important events in the history of human life. And when given free time, I enjoyed going off with my fellow scribes to the Scribe Guild to debate long lost meanings, as we have for centuries.

When we returned the following year, I used my own money to take one of the horse drawn cabs, feeling very grand and grown up.

By then I had met my chief accuser, and as Greveas will no doubt have told you, we became friends. She and her peers said that they found charm in my Colendi-accented Sartoran, and I found their quickly spoken, idiomatic Sartoran good practice.

The year after, Greveas and her friends took me to a concert where I sat high in the gallery with others in service, listening to the beautiful Falisse Ranalassi who, after the brawl in the Alarcansa dining chamber, endured two weeks of refined cruelty from her cousin Carola Definian—cruelty so deliberate and so well hidden from the adults that Falisse ran away and worked her passage down the river to Sartor by singing ballads with a group.

She auditioned at the music guild and commenced several years of intense training. Nicknamed Larksong, she would win the Silver Feather, and go on to world fame. And ever after she would say that it was her cousin who inspired her.

Later that visit, I was taken to the Guild archive, where Greveas and her friends traded off giving me a history of the New Year's festivals throughout the world—certain guilds responsible for certain plays, costumes always a certain way, centuries of symbolism. "This is how we have always taught each new generation morals, ethics, and history," Greveas said, her slanted eyes wide on the last word. "Our ancestors knew that we learn the most through play."

"Colendi plays are a social dialogue," I said with what I now recognize as rather pompous earnestness. To their smiles, I responded: "A duel of wit, Scribe Aulumbe used to say, between the rituals and conventions of government and the wishes of people who need, desire, or flirt with change."

My Sartoran friends laughed at me. "For all you Colendi claim to be so civilized, only in Colend have playwrights, actors, and sometimes audiences been imprisoned. And twice in your history riots broke out after a performance," Greveas said.

"Our *early* history," I said, and they only laughed the harder.

One of her friends leaned forward. "Early? Early? You are still early. It is only, what? four generations? Five? since your emperor decided that Independence Day sounded too much like a rebellious child and changed the name of the festival to Martande Day."

They laughed the more heartily, Greveas saying, "Wait until your second millennium before you begin to talk about 'early.'"

Oh, that comfortable superiority! Yet this was the beginning of my discovery of the Sartoran paradigm, how very differently you Sartorans see the world!

At the time, I could scarcely conceive of the fact that the Scribe Guild building is four thousand years old. One of the scribes insisted it was older, though admitting that it's been torn down and rebuilt twice with the same stone. The last modernization was just after Queen Alian Dei married King Connar Landis in 3355, well over a thousand years ago.

You see, I remember these things. They are important to me. Historical paradigm and how it shapes perspective! My mind fills with the vivid image of that shared fifth-story salon that looked south over Ilderven, Greveas and the other young Sartoran scribes sitting about on the low curule couches, talking over centuries-old gossip as if it were current. All the figures of history were living and breathing people to them. One of their favorite pursuits was finding contradictory accounts, to figure out who was lying and why.

The fourth year, I had my usual review after my return home—which was always in time for the Martande Day that you Sartorans so tolerantly scorned, when all Colend dresses in white and blue, our royal colors, to celebrate the accession of our first king. I brought up what Greveas and her friends had said about the Colendi view of history, and Halimas flashed me that unexpected grin. "We were going to wait another couple of years before getting into royal truth, archival truth, and personal truth."

"Don't forget social truth," Noliske said. She was always serious, though sometimes she displayed an irony that matched the queen's.

"There isn't any social truth," Halimas retorted. "Which," he turned to me, "is why I am not scribe to the queen but stayed, instead, with education. Sartor's view of history is so long that we call it archival truth—they will talk about patterns that take centuries to change."

"The problem with that, as we see it, is that such a very long view can lose sight of personal motivations," Noliske put in.

"So. Continue to tell the truth as you see it, but question every account, now that you have enough experience to perceive what might be the motivation behind its slant—whether royal, historical, or purely personal."

Now you are thinking that I am going to begin excusing my actions on the basis of scorn for Sartor, its guilds and its archival truth

Rather than offer protestations that will seem self-serving, let me share a memory.

In that salon at the Sartoran Guild in Ilderven, symbolic home to the scribes of the world, a fire stick burned in a cheery low fire on the grate, for those stone buildings can be chilly. Greveas's bright red hair was outlined against an age-darkened tapestry depicting scribes a thousand years before. She and her friends sat about in their dark blue robes, toasting corn cobs in wire mesh so that the kernels popped into crunchy florets.

Despite the scrupulously scrubbed floorboards (new floors get laid down every century or two) and the cleanliness of the plain furnishings, those buildings whiffed of mildew, a scent that forever after reminded me of Sartor. At each visit I sat in the window embrasure, my favorite place, as I rubbed my thumb over a smiling gargoyle—a toad with a cat face and artichoke leaves for a ruff, paws out as if it would spring onto the street below.

Magic protected it from the wear of wind, rain, and time, so my fingers buzzed slightly as they gritted over the stone. The cat-toad creature had been carved directly below the window in a long line of rioting fish and frogs and other animals of water, land, and air, fanciful and not. From below, one could not see any of those details.

The first time I saw the stonework I wondered who it was for—who was intended to see all that detail—until I glanced across the street into the tall windows of Twelve Towers Guild. The elongated carvings of ancient figures, each holding a scroll or book, gazed with monumental patience back at me. They, too, would be difficult to make out from five stories beneath. But from the high windows the scribes and the archivists could see one another's buildings, and enjoy the sight.

There might even have been silent messages in those stone shapes, now forgotten, so that only the art remains. It is a memory that has offered me consolation.

ELEVEN

Of Love and Power

"What did you see, Emras?"

After our return, and the Martande Day cakes had been consumed, and the blue clothes put away for another year, the round of late summer activities commenced.

"I saw your guests enjoying themselves. I saw everyone join the *Roundelay of the Summer Lark*. They played a second round, through all the minor keys, after Lord Jantian added the counterpoint with his finger-cymbals."

"That is what they wanted us to see. What did you see when my back was turned?"

"That Lady Ananda—"

"Lay aside the honorifics, Emras. We are alone."

"I saw Ananda's smile fade as soon as you turned away. She put her twelve-stringed tiranthe down and picked up her fan, then turned it over in contrary mode when she met the eyes of Isari. I saw Suzha make the spywell sign twice to gain their attention."

Lasva's voice dropped a note. "We make music, which we are taught adds harmony to the world, but are we ever truly harmonious? We gather friends around us, but I see the little evidences that each thinks only of herself. Or himself. Or what is secretly entertaining, rather than the entertainment by the artists. Did anyone listen to our music?"

"Farava. Her eyes were closed the entire time you played."

"Farava of Sentis lives in a world of music. Some say of spirits, and unseen things." Lasva sighed. "I did think I'd find a friend. Lissais was a friend, but she was sent from court. Farava does not seem to trust words. I get nothing but politeness from her."

Heedful of my parents' cautions, I reminded myself that I was a scribe, asked to observe. I was not a *spy*, who tries to winnow out secrets to carry to those who will pay to possess those secrets. I would observe if asked, but secrets must stay secret, whoever they belonged to.

Therefore I did not tell Lasva that Tiflis, who interrogated me on all the court chirps she overheard from the hopping birds in Alsais, had said that Lissais was sent away because she had fallen in love with the princess. Her family did not want the trouble of an unrequited grand passion: she was the fourth so sent, three lords having departed summarily for Sartor, or Sarendan, one family having sent their heir all the way north to Lascandiar, on the north continent.

Lasva faced the window, hands stroking the butter-colored cat, who purred and stretched. "In my dream last night, I floated down a canal. The voices in the reeds whispering poetry were those of Lissais, and Calres, and Demiran." She named three of those sent away. "I float out of reach of their voices, though I try to linger, to catch their tone and their words."

She turned from the window, and reached down to stroke the butter cat and the smaller black who twined about her feet, tail high. "But I cannot seem to catch a friend. I think I am done with Readings in the Reeds. They only give me bad dreams."

The glance of interest, the speculative smile: it happened again. Warily, I returned the smile and moved on to the storage rooms of the Wardrobe, where former Lirendis had stored their favorite clothes. Lasva was attending a century party, and all must be as it was one hundred years before.

"Will you hold this length against yourself, scribe? As you seem to have nothing else to do."

That was Torsu, the newest clothes dresser. I'd already noticed her sense of style—not that Lasva's gowns were ever less than perfect. But Torsu had a way of standing back, sturdy arms folded, her eyes narrowed. Then with a twitch the fabric would drape perfectly. The newer styles had opened the overrobe all the way up the sides, and the underrobe was more of a gown now. It did not wrap but followed the line of the body. The two long lines of the overrobe complemented the shape beneath. Some wore lengths of gauzy silks in loops and swoops over all.

I took the length of heavy silk, loving the luxurious hiss, the cool sheen. The rules were that I was not to be ordered to do others' work, but I was mindful of my arrogance to Kaleri so long ago, and so I stood there as Torsu walked around me and the green silk. The staff bound their hair up simply, usually wrapped with thin ribbon, but Torsu's straight dark hair was artfully bound in blossom knots at each side of her head, to make her face into the heart shape. So complicated a style meant that she either had friends or influence with the hair dressers in the staff.

"Who comes and goes from her rooms now?" Torsu asked.

"What?" I replied witlessly. "The cleaners, or—"

"Who is she sleeping with now?"

"I don't know."

"Oh, come, you are not sightless. I only want to find out what his tastes are—or hers. Does she like the women?"

"I don't know." The question—Torsu's tone of intimacy, of knowing—made my nerves tingle.

"A lover's tastes can be charmingly added to a gown. Just a hint."

"I don't know," I said.

A rustle from behind was all the warning we had.

Torsu looked up, quick as a bird, and Marnda was there, her lined cheeks mottled. "Thank you, Scribe Emras, for your forbearance." She cast me a glance of rebuke before turning on the dresser: I should not have taken the silk.

"If you wish to stay in the princess's service, you will spend the next year as a mender, Torsu," Marnda whispered, her voice tremulous with anger.

Marnda held out her arms, and I surrendered the shimmering lengths of spring-colored silk to her. Beyond her shoulder Torsu glared at me in reproach—my profession of ignorance had protracted the conversation long enough to catch Marnda's ear. I may as well record here that she never spoke to me again, and the intimations that I conspired with her are not only false but absurd.

The interested eye was so dark it was black, the better to reflect light. Framed by curling lashes. The smile curved lips already enticingly curved. Black tight curls, the faintest scent of cinnamon. Silver blue nail lacquer enhanced her beautiful hands as she noted the return of the ivy gown.

"Thank you, Scribe Emras." She knew my name.

Lady Carola Definian stood at the sidelines at a horse race. "Look at him ride." Carola sighed.

Her cousin Tatia sent a quick look her way. "And so?"

Carola breathed in, exerting all her control to hide that burst of laughter that burned behind her ribs every time she thought of her father found sprawled on the floor between his bed and the door. Sprawled like a drunken peddler, only dead instead of drunk. She'd had to go inside her clothing storage and bury her face in her old gowns so she could let out the shrieks of laughter at his utter lack of *melende* in death.

Alarcansa was hers. And oh, the joy of giving orders instead of getting them!

Tatia mistrusted that smile. "So Handsome Lassiter rides well. What of it? You can hire better riders. You can bed them afterward. Then dismiss them."

Carola snapped her gaze at her cousin. "You do not want to see me married?"

Tatia raised her hands to ward shadow trespass. "Ah-ye, darling cousin, I live only to see you happy. I just thought. . . ."

Carola scorned to ask what she thought. Hirelings—even well-trained hirelings—were nothing to the sight of these high-born courtiers, rich and wanton, matched with horses equally high-bred and striking. And at their head, his long body tight, hands loose, smile free, his hair windstreamed like the mane and tail of his horse, rode Kaidas Lassiter.

It was whispered that he was as good a lover as he was a rider. It was whispered that when he found a lover who could match him ride for ride, before he galloped on he painted them a lover's cup—a fragile round cup with no handle, that it might be shared between two.

Carola remembered her father's excoriating diatribe about the vulgarity of her infatuation with an indigent baron's son who could bring nothing of worth to Alarcansa.

She turned her angry gaze on her cousin and whispered in her father's deadly tone, "I want *him*."

———

It was easy enough to find her name: she was Shuras, First Scribe to the Wardrobe, under the Grand Seneschal.

I made an excuse to return—I had "forgotten" the jeweled shoes that went with the ivy gown. Shuras gave me a spray of starliss and one of those smiles.

———

I had come to understand that Tiflis's craving for "chirps" was bound to her work—her livelihood depended upon knowing the very latest chirpings of the little birds busy pecking and fluttering around the edges of court, for the booksellers were always trying to figure out what might become popular.

Chirps were gossip, what courtiers called *whispers*, a term descended from the days of the spywells. The bird metaphor used in Alsais came from the Heralds' tradition of crying the news in the city squares at the Hour of the Bird just after Daybreak in the morning. The most entertaining chirps usually found their way to the plays.

Tiflis's journey scribe's project, a book depicting famous loving cups with each illustration's story told in poetry from the time the cup was made, had earned her a position as clerk. I'd hired Delis to make her a splendid set of lily-frosted queen-cakes to celebrate her promotion, knowing that Tif would glory in the display before her new peers.

"They say that not two weeks after the death of the Duke of Alarcansa, Lady Carola Definian, the new duchess, rode all the way to Estan for the point-to-point." Tiflis's eyes widened with enjoyment. "Ah-yedi! She laid out fantastic amounts in entertainment, and wagers on Handsome Lassiter's garlanding the bucks, and on his animals when he did not race. All to catch his eye—before she even came before the queen to swear fealty!" She waved in the direction of the palace, where the Duchesses of Gaszin, Altan, and Sentis had united to give a flower-filled, expensive party in welcome of the new duchess.

"Did she get a lover's cup?" I asked.

"Not that I heard. Handsome Lassiter hasn't deigned to paint one for anyone in this kingdom since Lady Talian of Deshlen got one, and he found out that she straightaway put on her outer salon mantle, where all can see it—like a trophy garland after winning a race."

By now I had refined my comportment in these meetings with Tif. I reacted enough that I could see my cousin react to my reactions—like mirrors distort the infinitude of reflections between them.

If a chirp might be harmful to Lasva, I'd sit unmoved, for I'd discovered that Tif would then denounce it as mere rumor. If the chirp did not relate to Lasva, or couldn't harm her, I'd press my lips against a smile—or smooth my robe over my wrist—if I had heard it was true. And off it would go, chirping its way into Alsais and beyond.

Was I breaking the First Rule? Was that influence? I wondered as I walked back to the royal wing one warm, rainy evening, as Lasva danced at a ball given on the marble terrace of the new ducal wing—watched by Kaidas Lassiter, as Carola in turn watched him.

No, I decided, for I never whispered, and this was only my cousin, not some powerful court figure. And I was not a spy, for *I* did not chirp, nor was there any material gain.

———

Shuras's rooms overlooked the Grand Skya, off which breezes flowed. She had aromatic flowers to sweeten those breezes and wine mulled with her own hands over a tiny brazier. Her touch was like silk, but when it became ardent, again, my interest froze, and I found her too close.

She smiled the more, read me passionate poetry, offered to brush my hair, and when I was relaxed, she murmured, "Do you share any tastes with the princess?"

"I do not know," I said, and said so again and again when the drifting talk circled lazily back to Lasva.

I got up, thanked her for the lovely evening, but as soon as I reached the hall I wept, for *I* had not been courted. It was Lasva's scribe who had been courted by one of Tif's chirping birds.

———

"What did you see at my party, Emras?"

"I saw The Garden Arch," I said, referring to the gaze named for the arc a flower makes in following the sun.

Lasva sighed. "I felt it, though when I spoke each smiled and deferred, and I believe those new cakes with the tiny sugared bluebells were lauded by all. They certainly ate them. But yes, I was aware of all eyes following not me. They followed . . ."

"Lord Vasalya-Kaidas Lassiter," I said.

"Yet he did nothing to draw their attention," she responded. "Not that I could detect. He's not even all that handsome. Rontande is far prettier, especially with his hair dyed that shade of lemon, though I prefer his hair black. Young Gaszin catches the eye as well, if you like them chiseled. There are a dozen men who have better clothes, or finer features, or more grace in their movements. Martande of Ranflar makes us all laugh, and he know the latest music from Sartor. Yet when this Kaidas gets up to fetch the fan that he so carelessly dropped on the window sill, they all watch him, man and woman. What does he do to draw the eye?"

I had not said—yet—that her own gaze had become The Garden Arch. Maybe I would not say it. "He moved," I said instead, groping my way, as if in an unlit room. "But the way he moves causes the eye to linger."

She clasped her hands. "Yes. The way he moves. He laughs inside his own body, as it was said about my famous forebear. Any man may pick up a fan, but the way he does it makes my skin curious for the warmth of his touch." She tipped her head. "Here is what I ponder: whether he does it consciously. Is he collecting lovers like others collect garland trophies or gems? Ananda talks on about those lovers' cups he paints."

Tiflis had reported:

There was a court play at The Slipper called 'The Hart's Hearts,' about racing deer and wagering on them. The yellow-haired doe, who everyone said depicts Lady Ananda Gaszin, was desperate to get a garland of heart-blossoms from the buck dressed as Handsome. The garlands were shaped like lovers' cups.

Lasva said, "Is there a competition to gain them? Who is collecting whom?"

They sold out all the seats, and Nali says that the word about Handsome Lassiter and his lovers' cups is, the only one he's given out since Lady Talian of Deshlen got hers was to Lord Adamas Dei in Sartor. Or Sarendan, or somewhere.

"You would think," Lasva said, her brows lifted, "a parting gift from a lover would be kept secret, like a pillow gift. Unless you parted with him. In which situation, why would anything he gave you keep value? Or why would you part?"

In the play, the deer with the coronets were wagering up to two thousand apples, the highest contenders being the yellow one and the crimson one, crimson being the chief color of Alarcansa.

"Here's what I do know: I will stay far away from him," Lasva vowed. "Even if my sister didn't despise his father, I don't intend to become his latest trophy."

I was glad I'd said nothing more specific about The Garden Arch.

———

"What did you see, Emras? Was there something amiss in my manner? In my words? The play was one Carola said she liked. The musicians promised they knew all the songs popular in Alarcansa."

Queen Hatahra preferred what we call the formal plays—all old, usually set during important times, most often in verse. The words are poetry, the movements stylized—everything expressing *melende . . .* and often quite dull.

I have since realized that many were not dull when first written, but in fact were much like today's city plays, which comment obliquely on current events that are eventually forgotten, leaving only the pretty words and the high-minded version of incidents the writer wishes remembered.

Most courtiers had to memorize pages of the old plays during their early training, so they all knew them. Courtiers might arrange extemporaneous versions of famous scenes, in honor of one another.

Lasva had gone to great trouble to hire the best players and pay for new costumes, and she had made a request for regional music from Alarcansa. All this as an offering of friendship to Carola, who returned Lasva's friendly overtures with diamond-precise politeness—and as much warmth.

I had watched Carola instead of the play. When Lasva asked what I'd seen, I replied: "I saw politeness."

Lasva sat down on a hassock, the strong morning light catching in the blue of her eyes—a pretty contrast to the shades of pale apricot in her overrobe, slit up the sides to the waist sash in the new mode, the underrobe of deep forest green. Forest green ribbons tied the filmy moth-gauze above her elbows and at her wrists, making graceful drapes of the sleeves. "Is that all?"

"I saw . . ."

I remembered Carola's straight back, her small hands so perfectly placed and as empty of expression as her face below its high-piled corn silk hair threaded through with rubies and diamonds. Her gown was moon-gauze and silver over so deep a crimson it was almost black. She wore many diamonds all about her person, so she glittered even when she breathed.

"I saw . . ."

When Kaidas rose, beckoned by Young Gaszin, Carola turned her head. And when he strolled back, he'd passed by Lasva's chair, smiling at her, though she was talking to someone else. Light flashed along the diamonds on Carola's gown as her muscles tightened.

My instinct insisted that she was angry, but after the play she used none of the hasty movements, the brittle words of anger. Reason said courtiers did not get angry—*melende* did not permit the distortion and discourtesy of anger. Anger was destructive, and angry nobles before the days of civilization had caused wars.

"I saw how she watched, when Kaidas greeted you."

"All he did was walk by."

Lasva let out a long breath, then got to her feet and moved to the window to look out over the Rose Walk. There was no use in saying what we both knew, that she had been aware that he was there.

That next morning, at the Hour of Reeds, several men crossed through the fountain room bearing fans with poppies sketched on them in compliment to the crimson of the lovely new Duchess Carola of Alarcansa. Young Gaszin's fan was scarlet.

Kaidas Lassiter's alone was neutrally plain.

Lasva and Kaidas turned and turned again, sun and moon in opposition, just as the court, like the brilliant stars in the summer sky, turned about them both. The sun is oblivious to the flowers that arch their faces in its path: the Garden Arch no longer captured the mode any more than the word "flirtation" expresses the breathless intensity of those brief interchanges—never more than a single question, a word or two in response in the time it took to walk past one another.

Theirs were the fast, slanting glances across the entire width of a ballroom.

Neither ever danced with the other at court parties or balls.

The Colendi have the word *rafalle*—as always, our three syllables come from a pairing of Sartoran words, "re" for "sun," "va" for "water" with the added pun of "al" meaning "bright." Light and water are always beautiful together, but sometimes, if the sun and the water and the viewer are all in the right place at the right time, the water coruscates into "white fire." The term was understood by us Colendi to mean that nearly palpable attraction between lovers whose passion so matches the other's that they always know—whether their gazes meet or not—when the other is nigh. And when their gazes meet: *rafalle*. They feel it. Others see it.

So it was with those two, all the remainder of the year.

And every time their gazes met, even briefly, Carola was watching.

The New Year's ball was usually a small gathering, given for the queen's particular friends and others she wished to honor, without distinction of rank. I was invited, at Lasva's wish, so I postponed by one day my yearly visit to my parents.

The elderly Grand Seneschal was there, as was the Chief of the Kitchen, and a couple of musicians with whom the queen was pleased, as well as a number of us scribes. Since I was not there on duty, I exchanged my beloved scribe's cloud blue and white for a gown of heavy brocade in layers of green, yellow, and amber.

It didn't matter who I danced with. Male or female, they all asked questions about the princess. I returned the most boring and conventional politeness instead of answers.

The queen had still never spoken to me. From a distance I saw her summon Lasva, and from Lasva's stillness understood that a conversation of import was taking place.

The queen, I had learned, liked everything orderly and important information imparted on important days. So I was braced when Lasva told me as soon as we'd reached her suite: "Hatahra wishes me to organize the Dance of the Spring Leaves for her this coming season."

"Organize it?" I asked.

Lasva's smile reminded me unexpectedly of the queen, who otherwise did not resemble her beautiful younger sister at all. "Yes. She is annoyed with the dukes and duchesses."

I put my hands together in The Peace, surprised to hear this small bit of politics. Queen Hatahra seldom referred to state affairs—even those touching on court—at these events.

I forgot that, when Lasva bent toward me and whispered the following. "She said that this year Midsummer, she will try again for an heir. As always. But here is where things change: she will try again every day thereafter, for one year. With Davaud and without. She will even take the hand of certain others whose families might contribute to a good heir, for you know the magic of the Birth Spell somehow partakes of both families."

"Yes."

Any talk about magic stirred my mind, but it would settle again like a pond left to itself. Scribes had nothing to do with magic. Instead, I considered this sudden second-hand confidence from the queen.

"And so, if by next Midsummer there is still no baby, then she will proclaim me heir. And begin my training in state craft."

I had no words, so I only bowed.

"She asked if I should keep you, and I said yes. If you agree, and I am named heir, you will have to hire a staff, and begin your own kind of training, for we shall be plunging into diplomacy and matters of state."

Her pupils dilated, so black I could see my reflection in them, as she asked, "Does this news please you?"

My nerves chilled.

"She said that whomever I choose to dally with, I must keep that part of my life and statecraft separate." Lasva turned around, facing the beautifully gilt and painted walls sightlessly. "She also said that Carola Definian has spoken to her about the possibility of a marriage alliance with the Lassiters. The baron is enthusiastic on his son's behalf."

Of course. The baron's debts were legendary. A third surprise. Was this a royal warning?

Lasva turned my way, her forehead troubled. "My sister said she favors the idea of Definian order taming Lassiter recklessness."

Oh yes, it was a warning.

TWELVE

OF THE *RAFALLE*

E very so often the moon and the sun meet in the sky, creating a coro-
nal ring of fire. So was my perception of their emotions when Kaidas
arrived unexpectedly, the week before most of the courtiers began their
return to court, and met Lasva for the first time with no courtly witnesses.

It was distant music that drew them, that Restday afternoon. Lasva
and I sat in her outer chamber, cats rubbing against us and walking across
our laps as she talked over her ideas for the Dance of the Spring Leaves,
and I stored them all in memory, to later be written out neatly. It was
excellent practice.

She'd opened her windows, though the air was chilly. The vents blew
warm air all around us.

Through the windows drifted a series of braided flourishes, cadenzas
spiraling upward, played by at least two flutes, sometimes three or more.

Then more instruments joined in so compelling and joyous a song
Lasva faltered in the middle of a question, head raised. "Open air music,
while there is still snow in the shadows? Let's take a walk," she said. "We
can still consider ideas. You always remember everything anyway."

We set out in the direction of the music—which ended before we
reached the Rose Walk. But we had a destination: the winter garden ter-

race at the extreme western end of the palace, hard against the Gate of the Lily Path, where Alsais's gardens meet the palace gardens and many weddings are held.

Kaidas had heard it, too.

The iron-hard ground had loosened, breathing the clean scent of moist soil ready for the gardeners to bring out the bulbs and shoots. Grace-thin trees, silver-barked and bare, framed the south end of the Rose Walk.

We mounted the shallow marble steps before the Gate, the stone frigid under our walking slippers. Later I'd find out that the music was to accompany a wedding of two musicians. As soon as the ceremony was done, off they went to warmer air to celebrate.

By the time we arrived, the only sounds were the whisper of wind amid the budding twigs, the rustle of wintry-pale silk—and then breathing.

There were the subtle signs: the speculative glance, the quickened breath, the arch of neck and stillness of hand, the snap of interest between these two when we found Kaidas standing below the carved gate, thumb to cheek, chin resting on curled fingers, elbow on his other palm.

"I wondered," he said, as if he'd expected us—maybe he had— "if the sounds I heard were summer's music unborn. And if the metaphor of scent as modifier for the subject of love might be better replaced by sound."

Lasva said in her court voice, "And so your wish is father to court's deed?"

He evaded the question with his hands opened wide. "I hoped that it would be your wish." The slight tilt to his head gave his quick grin the air of a challenge. "And your deed."

"What about your wish?" Lasva had stilled. "Is my deed to form a garland blue-inked on your mantle?"

I cast a fast glance at Lasva. To bring up that countess or duchess in Locan Jora who'd displayed his pillow gift on her mantel was rude, and I had never before heard her be rude.

He bowed, amusement not only in his face but in the line of his shoulders, the turn of his wrist. "I stopped giving those damned cups away as soon as I found out about the display on the mantel."

His tone was so genuine, his amusement so open, that Lasva relented enough for me to discern a change in her breathing.

"And the rumors about your skills as a lover? I take it you are fashioned like other men?"

Now I did not hide my surprise.

Nor did he. "I believe so." He patted his chest. "The skills? Ah, that secret is no secret at all, not if you are fond of any kinds of animals."

Lasva's head lifted. "Animals?"

"Dogs. Cats. Horses. Run your nails along their skin, press your thumb over this muscle and that, and watch a dog's bones melt. Cats, too. And humans. It's the art of giving, not of taking, or of tending *melende* so closely that the simple pleasures diminish before the demands of grace." He chuckled. "You know that twistling isn't graceful if you're really having fun."

That surprised a laugh from Lasva. She turned. And turned back. "My feet are cold. I must go."

He bowed, gave me a slight smile and a salute—quite proper for a scribe to whom he had not been introduced. He could have ignored me—etiquette declared I was invisible unless presented—but the friendliness of his easy gesture warmed me.

"Is that his secret?" she asked, when we were halfway along the Rose Walk. "He's blunt?"

"You were blunt first," I ventured.

"I was, wasn't I? I don't want to find him attractive, but I do. I have. Here's what I just discovered: I suspect he doesn't want to find me attractive, either." She tipped her head. "Maybe that's why it works, this manner of his. Of course this seeming spontaneity could be scheming."

"It could," I agreed. "But he seemed to be as interested in what you would say as you were in his words."

"I know not to believe the flattery of those city plays—as empty as the flattery of court. But my dresser Anhar told me something that was said in *The Rose Veil*, which she thought I'd like. And that is, 'The secret of her charm is to make everyone feel as special as one actually is.' Here's my point: I wonder if that is his charm. That he makes me feel . . . singled out."

"You've been singled out all your life," I said. "Did that make you *rafalle?*"

"*Rafalle!*" She repeated, and I don't think she was pleased. "Is that my manner, then?"

I amended the truth. "It was today."

"*Rafalle.*" She breathed the sounds. Then smiled. "It takes two to make the *rafalle*, sun and water. You are accusing me of *zalend.*"

I bowed, hands in full Peace mode, and we finished the walk in silence. Before we reached the entrance to the royal wing, she said, "I think I will meet him again. Just once. But Emras, I don't want anyone to know. So I will ask if you are willing to wear one of my rose gowns, one well known, and walk about in a domino veil, as if you were me. If everyone assumes you are me, no one would dare to approach you. I do not ask you to misdirect by words, only by appearance. But if it seems wrong—"

"I will do it."

She lifted her face upward. "I shall find out the name of that song. Whatever it is, I shall think of it as *rafalle*."

Three times over the next few days I walked around the garden, dressed in layers of mothwing silk, a veil floating behind me. I enjoyed myself, pretending to be a princess. I enjoyed the deference, though I knew it was not for me. I contemplated the absurdity of human social hierarchies—some are deemed better than others by accident of birth.

Two weeks later, the Duchess of Alarcansa arrived to settled into the newly decorated ducal wing.

Carola walked the perimeter of her party. It was daring, to use winter as her theme but she had counted on the spring warmth for contrast with the expectation of the Dance of the Spring Leaves in a matter of days, to be hosted by the queen herself.

Carola's magic-flashed ice sculptures glittered with blue highlights, like mighty diamonds. How she loved diamonds! So brilliant, so commanding of the eye. Their complicated facets so precise. Her gown of ice blue glimmered with diamonds, as did her fair hair. She could see herself from every angle in the glass and mirror insets she'd added to the walls, which in turn threw back the light.

Everyone in court was here—everyone, even the queen, sitting there next to her hum of a sister. Carola was thoroughly sick of hearing about Lasva's beauty, Lasva's taste, Lasva's kindness, but she could ignore it all as long as *he* could.

Carola smiled and slipped her fan into half-furl. Its intricately carved blades, set with a complicated line of silver, glinted on the back of the silk mount: Hatahra might not bring *melende* to the discourse but she embodied *melende*. Carola was courted by dukes in a silent power struggle with the same queen they chatted with so suavely. Carola wanted to laugh. How they must despise one another! Yet here they were at her party, by her will and desire.

All of court was here. She'd forbidden herself to look *his* way; already Tatia had spied out whispers. Yes, there was that red-haired Isari on the watch. Near her that snake Ananda. Carola laughed inwardly at the whispers about Ananda's failure to attach *him*, though she'd contrived earlier in winter to get herself snowed in at the estate where he visited. If she had managed to bed him, she had not gained a lover's cup for her efforts. Carola wanted to laugh every time she saw Ananda watching him.

On the other side of the room that bone-thin Sharith talked with two others, her restless gaze moving about. A Definian must never be the object of the gossips' mockery. Carola gripped herself, consciously laying aside rage. Kaidas Lassiter was here. That was enough. Last year she had, perhaps, been too precipitous, and he was known for his vagaries—an unpolished gem. She would cut order into his life and polish it with passion, and he would glitter the brighter for reflecting her love.

Just one look. In a mirror, so nothing was direct.

She knew where he was—always—even without the sound of his voice amid a group of men. She turned her shoulder. The pearls looped through her high-piled hair trembled against her temples. She loosed a glance.

There he was, lounging against the back of a white-on-white brocade chair, his ring hand near that bore Rontande, who'd turned his head up to listen to whatever Sentis and Kaidas were saying.

But then Kaidas lifted his chin, ever so slightly. His breath stilled— Carola could see the pulse in his throat between the lappings of his velvet overrobe—she cut her gaze fast to see what drew those dark eyes—and there was the princess equally still.

Then the princess turned toward the queen, but Vasalya-Kaidas pushed away from the group and walked across the room as if drawn by an invisible thread.

Carola's heartbeat drummed in her ears as he passed within touching range of the princess. They did not touch, they did not speak.

That private smile, quicker than the flit of a butterfly's wing, was enough: *rafalle*.

For the rest of that interminable night Carola moved about and smiled, talked, bowed, and used her fan, her control steel-hard. She was especially gracious to Isari, inviting her to an intimate gathering to interview a new musical consortium. She complimented Sharith on her slipshod hair arrangement, calling it charming and daring. She moved around every one of Lasthavais's "roses," as the older generation had begun calling the young women around the princess. So disgusting. Carola was glad she'd never pandered to the princess by wearing her favorite rose.

At the very end, after she'd complimented each one of the roses, promising an intimate gathering later, Carola leaned down and murmured to Tatia's avid face, "The princess was as ravishing as ever. I wonder if anyone wagers on how many men she collects to garland her mantel?"

PART TWO
LOVE

ONE

OF RUMBLES IN THE DISTANCE

I have presented four of the important people whose lives intersected mine: Princess Lasva, Kaidas Lassiter, Carola Definian of Alarcansa, and King Jurac of Chwahirsland.

I have summed up my early life and four years of serving as Lasva's scribe in Colend's capital.

Now it is time to introduce the fifth person, whose appearance changed all our lives.

The sixth—some might say the first, for that one is the most important of all—comes later.

"Road's too quiet," was Prince Ivandred Montredaun-An's first comment that morning, as he, his second-cousin, his sister, and their company rode at a leisurely pace alongside the Fal River toward Remalna, where his sister Tharais would marry a king on New Year's Day.

Prince Macael Elsarion, second-cousin to Ivandred and Tharais, shook his head. "Well, it's hot enough today. Travelers're probably all tucked up in inns, drinking cold beer and waiting for a breeze."

Tharais looked at the broad, slow-moving river flowing peacefully along, then at the land on both sides. The countryside here was open, reminding her of the plains of home. A lot of the same plants grew at the other end of the continent: leddas along the riverbank, from which shoes and belts and suchlike were made; away from the mud grew tangles of hemlock, white ash, and fragrant spicebush, the myriad wildflowers dotted with golden queensblossom and crimson tulips and pale blue starliss.

Ivandred ignored the plants. He sniffed the air for lingering traces of fire, of horse, any sign of trouble.

They'd been warned before they came down through the Adrani Mountains that the entire river valley, already known for constant upheaval, had been left unguarded due to a badly thought-out treaty. Three kingdoms all wanted the territory.

The terrible roads testified to neglect.

"Faleth is a byword for brigandage," said the Queen of Enaeran, Tharais and Ivandred's great-aunt, and Macael's mother. "That's if you get past the Adranis. Every second person in Old Faleth is a thief, and the first is a jumped-up noble whose father was a thief. I suggest you hire a ship."

But once they were alone with Macael, Ivandred said, to Tharais's relief, "No ships. The Adranis hate you Enaeraneth, not us. As for the sea, I get too sick."

Tharais agreed fervently. "Can't see standing up at all those parties waiting on us in Remalna when I've been heaving my guts out for weeks. Longer, if we get becalmed. At least on a horse, you can move, regardless of what the wind does."

Macael had shrugged. He, like Ivandred, was in his mid-twenties, and though he, too, was a prince, he was a mere second son and so had few claims on his time. "My Elsarion cousins insist the Fals are mostly a lot of talk and sword-waving."

Everyone laughed—except Ivandred, whose expression had not changed. Tharais's worry escalated. She'd worked hard to get her brother away from Marloven Hesea and all the dangers there.

Hitherto the trip had been uneventful. The farther they got from home, the more Tharais relaxed and enjoyed herself. Now her brother wore that blank expression again, reminding her of home.

She looked around in the clear summer air, and found reassurance in the sight of her own entourage. Most were young women wearing the dark gray of skirmishers, bows slung at their saddles, who had been sent by their father as protection as well as for Tharais's prestige. But there were also young men—a group of chattering young Enaeraneth nobles who'd obviously been bored at home and wanted any excuse to be out looking for adventure. Even as tame an adventure as escort duty to Prince Macael. Her uncle had sent them ostensibly to enhance his second son's prestige, but Tharais's great-aunt had told her bluntly that the king was getting rid of them to give the Enaeraneth court a breather.

Riding behind the Enaeraneth lords, in strict paired columns, was Ivandred's handpicked honor guard, academy trained and eager to be selected for the Marloven First Lancers. The young warriors looked superficially alike in their severely cut long skirted, old-fashioned gray coats, their hair braided back. They were silent, alert, riding aloof from all the rest on their beautiful Nelkereth horses, teardrop-shaped shields at one side of the saddle and, hanging at the other side, their steel helm. To the tops of these helms was affixed what looked like long hanks of horse hair. The Enaeraneth lords thought them absurd.

Tharais was thinking about that and smiling somewhat grimly at their happy ignorance—she hoped they would not find out the truth about those hanks of hair—when Cousin Macael gave a long, low whistle. "Anyone doesn't know us would take us for a party of tutors with a lot of youngsters playing at riding shield."

"Eh?" Ivandred said, slewing around.

"You Marlovens are too short to look intimidating," Macael observed, from his scarcely two finger-breadth's greater height.

Ivandred snorted. "I think we look like a party of toffs. It's all that lace, Cousin. And that baggage of yours, Thar."

Tharais sighed, thinking of the six great wagons trundling behind her brother's remounts. Three of those wagons were full of her possessions, one belonged to the cooks Macael's mother had sent along and the other two carried the personal effects of Macael's friends, who, though they sought adventure, preferred to do it in comfort. Behind those wagons rode their palace-trained servants.

Tharais opened her hands. "What could I do? Father insisted I bring all my furnishings—as if no one else in the world knows how to make a proper sitting mat or table." She also had a castle's worth of sheets, quilts—heirlooms all—golden candlesticks, plate, clothing, and what she actually valued (knowing that all the foregoing would probably be jumbled up into an attic on her arrival): her horse gear. "Well, if some needy thieves happen along," she said, "they can have most of it."

Macael laughed. "And upset my boys, who will need their pretty clothes if they're to properly impress your future subjects? Not likely!"

Scouts appeared, riding back at a canter. They halted before Ivandred, and one said, "Town ahead."

"Maybe we can find out what local rumor says about these empty roads," Macael suggested.

Ivandred opened a hand in affirmation. "And I could use a cold drink." He gestured to his scouts to reconnoiter. The cavalcade passed slowly through their hanging dust, everyone longing for shade and something good to drink, preferably from a barrel kept in a nice cool cellar.

Round a couple of river bends they went, then over a little bridge that spanned a feeder stream, and they reached the town at last, finding mostly empty streets and shuttered low houses made of whitewashed stone and brick. From behind shutters faces peeped. The market square was entirely deserted, heat waves rising from slate tiles.

On the other side of the square was a rambling two-story inn. Ivandred tipped his head toward it, and they drew up before the barred doors.

Macael uttered a low whistle, shaking his head.

Ivandred nodded to his personal runner, who leaped from his horse and strode up to the iron-reinforced doors. He pulled a knife from his sleeve and used the hilt to rap loudly.

Nothing.

He rapped again.

A window opened above, and a heavy woman with untidy gray hair peered out. "We're closed," she said, in the flat-sounding Sartoran dialect common in these parts.

"Why?" Tharais called.

A man spoke in the background. The woman glanced back, then said swiftly, "Find shelter, girl, if you can. We've heard from three separate sources that Dandy Glamac has taken to the high road."

"Dandy Glamac?" Tharais replied.

From behind the woman came a roar: "Shut the window, damn you. Who says they aren't with the Dandy?"

Slam!

"Whoever he is, it would seem he's not much liked, despite the merry nickname," Macael observed. "What now?" he asked Ivandred. "I don't think we're going to get our beer, cold or hot."

"Ride."

Tharais watched her brother's eyes widen, pale blue as the morning sky, as he gazed around the deserted square. She watched the way he smiled, motionless except for quick, minute movements, as if he sensed something out of sight or hearing. She'd seen that before, almost always before something violent happened.

"Camp somewhere," Ivandred said. "We have enough to eat."

She bent down to thumb her horse's sweaty neck, to hide her uneasiness. "I suggest we water the animals first."

Her brother flicked an approving look her way. "My thought as well."

They rode on through the town to the feeder stream, fording it at a shallow place. The animals drank and splashed. The humans did not mind the splashing at all. It felt good.

After they crossed the stream, Ivandred called a halt as his Academy riders withdrew. When they started up again, he had changed their riding formation around Macael's noble friends and their attendants. Tharais's women still rode in pairs at points along the cavalcade, but their bows were now strung, their arrows within reach. The honor guard still rode in column, but their helms were on their heads, the hanks of various shades of hair swinging against their sturdy winter fighting blacks. They had thus made the mental transformation from Academy trainees to warriors.

Some of the Enaeraneth seemed amused to find these light-built mostly yellow-haired boys riding guard. Were they all boys? A couple of them had girlish faces. The more jovial made remarks, to be steadfastly ignored. They'd discovered that this honor guard interacted little with anyone else.

Tharais sighed to herself. So it had been during the entire trip, though she and Macael had both worked hard to blend the Marlovens and Enaeraneth. She was popular now, and the fellows seemed to genuinely like her, but she would never forget how horrible it was when she first came over the Pass from Marloven Hesea to stay with Macael Elsarion and his older brother, the heir to Enaeran. She was twelve at that time. Her antiquated Sartoran accent had filled them with as much mirth as the carefully made gowns that she discovered were two hundred years out of fashion. It had taken a couple of summer visits to Enaeran before her cousins and their friends stopped teasing her.

As the light slowly slanted west, shafts glowing golden between the trees in full summer leaf, only Tharais appreciated the sight and that only intermittently. She sensed that her brother was uneasy by the way he kept suggesting camping spots, each of which Macael and the other Enaeraneth turned down because it was too hot, not enough shade, too rocky.

Ivandred said, after the fourth such rejection, "Dandy Glamac and his band are sure to attack at full dark. I'd like to be camped with a perimeter in place."

Macael waved that off. He was tall, well made, trained in the noble rules of dueling; his broad mouth was attractive as were his wide light eyes.

He sat back on his mount with the comfortable conviction that a brigand attack meant a lot of yelling, maybe showing off some horseriding skills before the brigands realized they were dealing with not one but two princes and scampered off with their tails tucked under. It had certainly been that way in Enaeran.

Before Ivandred could form an answer, his scouts galloped up, and reported a great many hoof prints "along the river," and "beyond the ridge" that ran parallel to the water.

Macael only heard "river." "Let's make for the bank," he suggested. "Won't that feel good, the cold water, after this hot ride? Damn that innkeeper anyway for a coward and a fool."

Ivandred stilled, frowning down at his hands. "We should camp here," he said. He hated an unclear chain of command—but he had grown up with anomalies. His life had depended on not listening to what was said so much as what was unsaid.

What he heard now was, *It is my party*, from his cousin. The young nobles around Macael followed their prince's lead.

Ivandred did not understand the ways of diplomacy outside of Marloven Hesea, but he had listened when Thar tried to explain them. So he said, trying to find a compromise, "If we ride fast, we might reach the river before sunset."

The Enaeraneth brightened at the thought of a gallop—even a necessarily short one, given the tiredness of the horses. At least the heat was fast diminishing.

The attack came as the sun sank beyond the mountains, melding the shadows. The tired, thirsty party was riding down through thick trees toward the river's edge when they heard sounds: first the rumbling of hooves, then the whining buzz of arrows.

Arrows! Despite the Compact agreed to by the civilized world, *No weapons that cannot be wielded in hand*, these brigands shot *arrows!* Macael and his friends exclaimed at the discourtesy—the criminal action. They wondered what authority might be sought, then sustained the sick realization that their law, and those who protected their law, resided far beyond the mountains.

Oh, but the Marlovens had arrows—everyone knew they were barbarians. It was certainly good to have barbarians on your side now! They turned to Macael, who mirrored Ivandred's motion to gather behind a thick copse of trees a few paces away.

An Enaeraneth servant gave a choked cry and fell, an arrow in his chest. The second arrow struck Macael in the shoulder.

The cavalcade reined in behind the trees, terrified Enaeraneth horses nearly out of control, the Enaeraneth and their servants yelling commands and questions that no one listened to as the Marloven women spread out, bows at the ready, their animals alert, even if their hindquarters quivered.

The enemy ranged in a line behind a hedgerow in the gathering shadows. A brigand called something, the words in a slow drawl, the consonants affectedly prissy.

Ivandred turned to his cousin. "What's he saying?"

"That's Lamancan," Macael whispered, his breath hissing. "I know that much . . . but I only have a few words."

Tharais said quickly, "It's enough like Remalnan for me to understand—if he keeps talking slow like that. They said we can all go if we throw down our arms and turn loose the horses. We can keep our food, but the rest is theirs."

And another shout, which she translated: "We have to decide now."

An arrow whistled right overhead, glancing off a shield snapped up by one of the women. Tharais ducked, but Ivandred did not move. A last glint of the fading day reflected briefly in his pale eyes as he tracked the shot—and the defense—then he raised his voice just enough to be heard by his academy riders: "Spoke form."

The honor guard vanished somewhere behind the wagons, blending with the gathering shadows as the unseen brigand shouted and his line galloped to the attack.

On the command of their captain, the women encircled Tharais and her fallen cousin, their bows humming as they shot arrows with astonishing rapidity. The bewildered Enaeraneth rejoiced when nearly every arrow hit a target.

Here was another shock, women (some middle-aged) defending young lords trained in the art of the duel. A tall, hardy young lord rallied the Enaeraneth with angry shouts, and they galloped to meet the enemy, roaring with fury.

Tharais mustered the terrified servants to help get their prince off his horse before he fell. Someone spread a cloak on the grass and laid him on it.

Macael, struggling with every breath to hold onto consciousness, perceived milling horses, bodies, heard the whang and clash of swords, shouts of his own friends, and yells in foreign languages.

The Enaeraneth reached the brigands to find themselves surrounded. The brigands, in turn, became aware of the drumming of hooves from behind, and then "Yip! Yip! Yip!"—an inhuman cry that would echo through Enaeraneth nightmares for years—Ivandred's honor guard hit the brigands from both flanks. Only twelve of them on either side, but the fury of their attack felt like hundreds.

The brigands' order was utterly destroyed, and within a very short time, so were they.

"Drink." Tharais pressed something pungent to Macael's numb lips.

He gasped as fiery liquid burned his mouth and down into his chest, a fire almost as strong as the shredding pain in his shoulder.

"Another. Big one."

He drank again, realizing what had to come next. The thought of the arrowhead having to be pulled out made him swallow so much his nose burned, but by then a dose of strongly steeped listerblossom and willow bark assuaged the worst of his anguish, and he lay back, panting.

"Bite onto this." A bitter-tasting wedge of treated willow bark was pushed insistently into his mouth. He wanted to gag, to spit it out—but then white lightning ripped into his shoulder, and his teeth clenched.

One of Thar's women was winding a bandage round his shoulder and chest when he became aware of Ivandred kneeling at his side. "Was it bad?"

Macael tried to talk, but he couldn't get his lips to move.

"Nasty enough," Tharais said, from somewhere behind. "But he'll live. We'll have to ride easy for a time."

To which her brother replied, "No difficulty. They're all dead. I've got Dandy's locks right here." And something long and waving dangled from his hand, catching the campfire light; it was bound at one end by something ragged and pinkish-brown. "Where's my helm? Weather's too hot to wear it."

Macael's gut churned. Those helms were decorated with hair from human scalps.

"A hundred and forty, or close to it," Ivandred went on. "Nearly three to one. I've given my riders permission to do a victory dance."

He laughed then, a young laugh, that Macael—who knew him from only two visits—had never heard before. Tharais, of course, had, and her usually cheerful face sobered into a hardness that emphasized her resemblance to Ivandred.

But in her usual pleasant voice she said, "Go ahead, Van. Dance with them. They'll want you. I'll stay with Cousin Macael."

Macael wanted to ask questions, oh so many, but he lay, watching her firelit profile for a time, the square jaw and subtle line of ridged cheekbone that characterized all of them, framed by long butter-colored braids.

From a distance came the sound of drums, and then singing, in cadenced minor key melodies that sounded warlike to Macael's ears. And then came the rhythmic crashing of steel, more drumming, and he fell asleep at last, dreaming of horses riding over the plains and hooves striking the ground in galloping rhythm.

TWO

OF SILVER CORONETS

All that spring Lasva lived in two worlds. There was the world of court, which saw the exact same smiling, graceful, witty princess as always. She made extra efforts to appear so, for she had taken my obser-vation about *rafalle* to heart.

So too did Kaidas Lassiter, who for the first time was not careless of manner, or word—though he worked hard to sustain the impression. They wore no ribbons. They did not dance together in public, and spoke together rarely. They controlled the impulse to watch the other in a room. There would be no whispers of the garden arch.

They met in secret, all in all to one another. That was the second world.

He could not afford a staff. He had a man who oversaw his horses and lent a hand with his things when necessary. This gave Kaidas freedom of movement. I took many domino veil walks, and with my permission, they used the bath stair through my room to avoid the notice of the rest of the staff.

But no one can live successfully in two worlds. We are finite.

"What did your princess do, Em?" Tiflis asked when I took cakes and wine over for her Name Day. "In the last court play at The Slipper, the *Rose Veil* was collecting silhouettes of coronets decorated with hearts."

"Coronets decorated with hearts," I repeated. "Since I've never seen her flirting with anyone at court this year, I wonder whose hearts she's supposed to be collecting."

Then a month later: "What's going on in court, Em? They got out that old play about the mermaid who lures sailors to dive into the sea, so she can drown them, and they dressed her in rose."

To which I replied, "Princess Lasva hasn't done anything cruel. She doesn't flirt."

"Not even with Handsome Lassiter?" Tif leaned toward me, her brows furrowed. "Here's what I find confusing. The city chirps about how half of court is wagering on whether or not she's twoing with Handsome Lassiter. Does anyone know? Even court doesn't seem to, or they wouldn't be wagering."

I said, "You know no one chirps to me. Or even whispers."

"Well, I'm chirping like a tree full of birds," Tiflis said plainly. "I would love to know if there is a book in it. What has she to be secret about? She's the *princess!* No one can do anything to her! Anyway, how can she be collecting all these other hearts if she's with him?"

"I don't know anything about it," I said.

"Of course you do," she retorted, but not angrily. "Well, I don't tell you my secrets, either."

I walked back, greatly troubled, for in spite of my words to my cousin, I'd begun to catch some of the whispers, the canted looks, the flit and snap of fans when Lasva danced or even moved about in a gathering.

I could not figure out *why.*

The high, sweet bell rang the five notes of the Hour of Repose—the last hour before the dawn of Midsummer's Day, and the Queen's Birthday.

Lasva walked out of her bedroom onto the balcony that overlooked the Rose Walk, singing under her breath the melody she called *rafalle.* The name of the song was actually "Laughing Fountain," and she'd introduced it to court at the Dance of the Spring Leaves. Now it even had its own dance. By making it so public, she could hear it all around her and revel in its secret meaning. The canal beyond was barely visible, the color of slate. She did not want the happiest night of her life to end, but since it must, she would watch through the old meditation hour as dawn banished the shadows.

She and Kaidas had pledged their lives to one another. Who had spoken first? Now she could no longer remember, but did it matter?

The intensity of her exhilaration almost frightened her. It was time to let the world discover their love: tomorrow, she and Kaidas would travel down to Sartor together.

A gift? All I ask for in life is for you to bind my hair with your white ribbon, he had said as he reluctantly robed to leave, for the entire court must be in formal dress for the Midsummer Rising.

And you will bind mine, she had said.

He kissed her, then brought from his pocket a gift wrapped in a square of silk. *It's Midsummer's Day, and I know your sister will expect you to attend her before the day's festivities, so I'd better leave. But first I wanted to give you this.*

Her fingers cradled the lover's cup, made from porcelain so fine that light shone through it, gathering with a golden glow. She lifted it to gaze on the delicate roses painted in the wind dance pattern around the rim in shades of red, pink, peach, apricot, and mauve, leaved with gold.

The pure light of daybreak had painted the roses at her feet with their natural color when the joyous peal of Midsummer Daybreak rang out.

Lasva listened with her eyes closed, hands cradling the cup, mind lingering in sweet memory of their last moments together, feeding one another slices of crisp apple. The long reverie was broken by voices from her private bath chamber, which, at this time of year, was always open to the air.

"Oh Dessaf," Seneschal Marnda's voice was so high Lasva almost failed to recognize it. "Oh, it has happened."

"Boy or girl?" That was Dessaf, the princess's chief wardrobe mistress.

Lasva stared down at the Rose Walk, so rich with blooms the perfume rose on the soft summer breeze. She shivered, her heart cloud-light with elation, and wonder. "Boy or girl" could only mean one thing: there was now an heir.

"Oh, a girl, a girl," Marnda said. "The queen is so happy. I saw her myself just now, when the nursemaid took her out to put her Name Day clothes on! A princess! Her eyes will be dark like the dear old queen's, mark my words."

"How lovely," was Dessaf's whispered response. "How perfect! For of course she'll carry the dear queen's name."

Lasva and I had talked about magic on the last journey to Sartor. As far as I could discover, not even the mages knew why the Birth Spell worked for some and not for others, why sometimes a person alone, man or woman, could produce a child, who was nearly always a throwback to a distant ancestor. It came when it willed—when someone willed it?—to the poorest street-wander or to kings. Colend's rulers had been relying on it for centuries, and because it had nothing to do with nature's child-bearing cycle, their custom was to wait as long as they dared. Though heirs were necessary to those in power, no one liked them appearing too soon. Historically, heirs were impatient to inherit.

Heirs.

I am no longer potential heir, Lasva thought.

She only realized she'd stirred when she heard a soft intake of breath from the other room, and there was tall Marnda, who ducked out and then returned with a silver tray on which rested Lasva's morning caffeo. Her thin face was flushed with elation.

Lasva slipped the sleeve of her robe over the lover's cup.

"Oh, my princess," Marnda said, her low voice tremulous with emotion. "Your royal sister begs you attend her before the Rising."

Lasva forced a smile at the perfect blend of fresh-scalded coffee and fresh-ground chocolate, all frothed up in steamed milk, but her stomach was closed. "Thank you," she said.

Marnda made a sign to the page waiting beyond the archway, out of Lasva's view, who would speed down the hall to apprise the queen that the princess was awake.

She was still The Princess, but now there was a Royal Princess, heir to the throne. Lasva began to wonder what that would mean.

"Tell me what happened," Lasva asked, as Marnda lingered in the doorway in a manner completely unlike her usual brisk busy-ness.

Marnda's smile and indrawn breath were full of wonder. "It was just as the Daybreak carillon rang out. Just an hour ago and how the world has changed! The queen took Lord Davaud's hand . . . and the magic came to them." Marnda clasped her hands again, almost a clap, in an effort to contain so much joy. "They said the spell together, though no one could quite catch the words. The maids said it was very like Old Sartoran, and very like a song. And then she said it was as if a star blinked into the room, and the babe was suddenly there, on the waiting cloth they held between them, the child kicking and looking around." Marnda opened her hands, turning them upward. "She said the queen's face—her face—" Her voice suspended.

Lasva scarcely heard the last part. *The babe was suddenly there!* Awe sent a chilly tingle through Lasva's nerves. Somewhere outside of time in the world that babe had spent its eight months growing, between the moment the spell was spoken and the appearance of a new, live, human being. The thought of something so impossible becoming real gripped

Lasva by the vitals. One knew such things all one's life and yet did not truly *know* until they became manifest. "I must go at once."

Lasva ran to her inner chamber, bare feet skimming the silken bud carpet, where she had so recently lain with her beloved.

Alone there, she gently closed the lover's cup inside a carved and gilt treasure box that fit inside another box. The inner one had a lock, which she turned, then secreted the key in the cleverly made pocket, among the branches of the hanging cedar that sheltered her bed.

Lasva walked to her bath and sank below the surface of the water, her long dark hair floating among the freshly picked herbs. Magic snapped and rippled over her scalp, her flesh, her teeth.

Dessaf stepped into the wardrobe beyond the bath and issued her orders in a rapid voice. Her staff, excited by the news—by change—rushed about to fetch gowns, ribbons, lace, a choice of fans. Slippers.

And so, when Lasva rose from the bath, hanging beside her dressing table were two moth-light layered morning gowns, both formal, appropriate for both Midsummer Day and a royal audience. One was many shades of yellow and forest green, touched with silver embroidery. The other's main color was peach, with an array of contrasting or complementary emerald green and silver ribbons for the sleeves and waist.

No blue, though it matched her eyes. Today was a day of change. The babe would be robed in royal blue.

Lasva chose the yellow gown, the color of sun, of new beginnings. Dessaf gestured, and the dressers came forward to towel the princess. Lasva shut her eyes, her skin still sensitive to touch. Their hands were gentle but impersonal as they helped her into the most intimate clothing, then flicked her underdress over her head and twitched it to lie smoothly over her body, precisely fitting her shape. A pair of dressers brought the paneled overgowns and floated the layers of silk (called "cloud-gossamer") one after another, to fall in ordered folds of pale yellow, shimmering gold, and then the last filmy layer embroidered in lily-patterns with forest green silk thread.

Lasva sat down, shutting her eyes as her hair dresser used a carved ensorcelled comb to stroke the wet from her hair and then brought the ruddy-gold-threaded dark locks up into the complicated knot of loops popular for morning in the summer.

Should she wear a white ribbon today, signifying before all the court that she was heart-given? She knew it would delight Kaidas. But the real delight would be to wear it for the first time when they rose together, before they left for Sartor, tied by his fingers.

The very idea made her shiver, causing Dessaf to scold the dressers for being slow. Lasva opened her eyes and said, "I am merely tired."

Dessaf bowed. "Your crown."

Oh, yes. Today she must wear a crown, for the Rising would also be Name Day for the new royal princess. Formality required the silver band of the royal family. The beautiful band of the heir's gold—brought out in case only the day before—would be quietly retired to the treasure room.

Dessaf herself offered the silver band worked into the shape of ivy vines. It had belonged to some long-dead aunt, for it was a royal sibling's crown, worn before going into the world to make a dynastic marriage, as custom decreed.

Lasva took up a fan of painted with orchids, then she left.

I had been waiting in case I might be summoned, so I was there when Torsu whispered to the new mender, "Turfed out of a crown. Did she throw things when they told her?"

"I don't know. I think Marnda herself went in," whispered the new girl, so new she still wore the yellow and gray of the palace servants. "Maybe to see if she had somebody handsome in the bed—"

Dessaf stalked across the room and slapped the new maid and Torsu across their faces, hard enough to sting. "You are inappropriate, Torsu. This is your last warning. Nereith, you are new, so this is your first. We never gossip. *Ever*. There are far too many who want to know what is said and done in these rooms, and always for the wrong reasons. Always." Her voice lowered to a hissing whisper. "So if you still wish to remain in the royal service, then you will both remain silent until Martande Day. You will *not* go to Sartor. You will be given work here, which you will perform in silence. *No* word to family, to friend."

She gave them the command direct, strengthened by the word "no." Both dressers curtseyed in apology, Nereith with tears dripping down her cheeks. Torsu looked submissive, but her lips were white with fury.

THREE

OF THE GREAT MAP

Lasva entered the queen's rooms to find her sister alone, except for the cotton-wrapped babe on her lap. Lasva curtseyed deeply.

Queen Hatahra's mouth trembled, and the soft flesh under her chin quivered. "I did not think," she began. "That joy could be so painful."

Lasva sank down onto the hassock beside her sister's chair. "Pain?" she asked.

"The realization that all my work will pass to these little hands. Who is she? Yesterday, I merely longed for her existence." Hatahra bowed her head, and tears spattered on the soft robe, but the sleeping babe did not stir.

Lasva was amazed. She thought she knew all her sister's moods—brisk, businesslike, sarcastic, blunt.

Not since the very first birth attempt, fourteen years ago, had her sister spoken on this subject. At that time it had all been plans for the future, and Lasva had been a child. Her sister's consort then had not been Lord Davaud but the sophisticated, powerful Lord Mathias Altan, heir to a dukedom—already married with two children, although the marriage, once it produced an heir, had settled into a distant partnership.

He'd laughed after the queen tried the spell and nothing happened. Not out of cruelty, only mere carelessness, unexcited at the prospect of another squalling babe (though he did like the idea that this son or daughter would inherit a kingdom) but all the while thinking his position secure. A mistake. Favorite though he was, by that night she'd unribboned him, and he was riding back to his estates, his belongings in wagons behind him. It was five years before she relented and permitted him to return to court, but by then he had been replaced by Davaud.

That was Lasva's first lesson in the complexities of love when you wear a crown.

"Pain also because my courses ended two years ago. I wish I could nurse."

"But surely the Healer knows a way . . ." Lasva tried to hide her surprise, but Hatahra, always observant, smiled wryly. "Perhaps. But the fact remains that I am too old for it to be natural. And I do not have the time. I assure you, the desire did not come to me until the babe was born. It will probably pass as quickly, especially if she wakens in the night, as several have said will occur. As it is, poor Pollar must have spent weeks selecting this year's wet nurse." Her chin lifted, and she said in a lighter voice, "Would you like to hold your niece?"

Lasva held out her arms, thinking, *Surely this will make it easier for me to ribbon Kaidas without the necessity for treaties, now that I'm not the heir?* But it was not the moment to ask. In the time it took for Hatahra to settle the tiny bundle in Lasva's hands, Lasva consciously set aside her own joy, to more fully partake in her sister's.

Lasva had never held a baby before. The royal princess was unexpectedly light. She smelled sweet, though it was a sweetness not identifiable with the scents of mere flowers. Her features were small, the head large, her body felt boneless. Her mouth made faint nursing motions, and Lasva smiled, finding the sight unexpectedly endearing.

But as Lasva watched, the little mouth puckered and then frowned. Then eyes the indefinite hue of a shallow stream opened, and they too puckered.

"Ah!" came a thin little voice.

"Pollar!" the queen cried.

Pollar, who was Marnda's sister, bustled in with quick steps, and behind her was a cheerful looking young woman unlacing her bodice.

The babe was surrendered to the wet nurse. The servants departed, and Queen Hatahra got up from her chair—a small, square woman, her wavy, honey-colored hair still untouched by gray. (She'd finally given in and abandoned the silver hair as old-fashioned.) Hatahra's maternal effusion seemed to depart with her baby. She moved briskly past Lasva, her light gaze acerb, a slight frown furrowing her straight brows.

Lasva followed Hatahra to the great table in the queen's private withdrawing room, with its twelve bowed windows looking southward over the rose garden, and beyond, the royal canal. On the table lay an enormous fine-drawn map, detailed to the exact shape of each noble's home, in tiny but proportionate rendition. Something only a king or queen could afford.

"And so," Hatahra said, "today's Midsummer Rising will be her Name Day, as is traditional." She smiled wryly, waiting for Lasva to pick up her cue.

But Lasva stared down at the map as though her future lay there. Of course it did, Hatahra thought. Best to get it over with.

Lasva was observing the fact that her sister had told her nothing she did not know. Sometimes Hatahra introduced difficult topics by prefacing them with statements on which they already agreed.

Hatahra continued in the same wry tone. "All court will look their best. Right now they must be working out the most flattering congratulations in hopes I will be granting requests or handing out posts with the same freedom with which I toss flowers at the Martande Day regatta when you all return from Sartor."

Lasva curtseyed, her fan spread gracefully in Expectation of Pleasure, which made her sister bark a short laugh, snapping her fan open and sweeping it over the great continent that stretched nearly two thirds across the southern hemisphere. "I do appreciate, even in my happiness, the irony that she comes in the very last year I was to try."

Lasva said, "I did not want to say this at New Year's, but our mother had me when she was seventy-nine. The Birth Spell came to her then. Surely . . ."

"And how long did she live past your birth? Not a year. Maybe I should tell you the truth about that day. For now, know this: I had decided I would not have a child past my next Name Day. To go beyond that, well, who can know how long one will live? I would not condemn you to the unwanted task of a regency, raising the one who would always have precedence of you. Oh, I know you would have done your duty, and with grace, but a regency is seldom a stable government, especially when you have ambitious nobles stepping on your hem. And you deserved a better life."

Hatahra leaned on the map table, her gaze serious. "Lasva, you are now free to choose among the world's kings and princes, either to court, or to be courted, as you wish. That much I can grant you."

Lasva's heart constricted. But she only curtseyed.

"We will very soon be receiving royal suitors, and I need the sort of treaty only a king, or future king, can bring. Altan and Gaszin are getting stronger. And while the Sentises stay aloof from the machinations, it is only because they are fishing in royal Sartoran waters—specifically, young Sentis wants to marry Adamas Dei, giving him equal rights of government. It is said they will even combine the names."

"Ah-ye, it is such a romance," Lasva exclaimed, hands open in Shared Joy.

"A romance, yes," her sister returned dryly. "But Sentis ought to know better: marriage has nothing to do with romance when one's person represents government."

Lasva bowed. "I had forgotten."

Hatahra smiled. "But the world hasn't. Which is why every prince in the east—royal or not—will be haunting Alsais soon, but you won't be courted by any royal princesses."

Lasva had never before considered the meaning of what she'd grown up knowing: that dukes and royal persons did not have the freedom of those who were not regarded as living symbols of law. There could be a single queen, as had been for three generations. There could be single kings, as was Jurac Sonscarna. But no land had two kings on a single throne, or two queens, just as there was no kingdom populated exclusively by men, or by women.

Marriage between government figures seldom had much to do with love, or with lovers. They might never sleep together; they might not even make an heir together. If marriage there must be, it comprised a treaty between a man and a woman, as representatives of those who identified themselves as male and those who identified themselves as female. Government, according to Old Sartor, from whom most traditions descended, was more stable if represented with gender parity.

Hatahra was watching her sister closely. "There is enough unbalance in the world between the sexes. Some say that the Chwahir keep the sword in the hands of men. Where does that leave women? It sounds to me like they are overdue for a run of queens to inherit and balance things out. Or there will be trouble."

Lasva bowed, chilled to the heart. The message was clear: *a princess cannot marry for love.*

Hatahra snapped her fan open. "From the hypothetical to the specific. My dukes and duchesses want all the privileges of power, but one by one wish to discard the inconvenient responsibilities. Ah-ye! I can use that to break their alliance. Carola Definian has made overtures to me; she wants, who knows why, the Lassiter heir, and I favor that because I'd rather avoid a marriage alliance between Alarcansa and either the Altans or the Gaszins. They're courting her. I know it. Either of them joined with Alarcansa's wealth and land would effectively control a third of Colend, which would press me hard to resist their demands."

Lasva said, "You have never discussed these things with me before."

"I dealt with the politics so that you could preside with grace and the ease of detachment from political machinations. You would have begun learning had you been declared heir. But now Alian is here to take that responsibility, so your responsibility is to bring me a strong alliance with another kingdom—one that permits me to get a harness on Gaszin and Altan at last." Hatahra lifted her gaze to her sister's stricken eyes. "Lasva, I speak only of treaties. I'm a tough negotiator. As I said, you shall have the choosing of your royal prince or king, I promise you that."

Hatahra's eyelids narrowed as she studied her beautiful sister in exasperation and tenderness. "You are not pleased?"

Lasva's fan swept in the pretty arc of Harmonious Assent. "It is so soon to think of having to leave Alsais." She despised the lie—she despised herself for lying—but she could not bring herself to believe that all her careful plans, talked through so lovingly the night before, might be smashed.

Hatahra touched her sister's wrist. "I know you love life in Alsais. Of course you do. Our city is the fairest in the world. The pleasures of our court the finest, even surpassing Sartor, I do believe, though the Sartorans might say differently."

Lasva said, with a little of her sister's irony, "But?"

"But think. If you were to stay—if we did not need a good, strong treaty—the years would pass in an eyeblink, until one day you would come downstairs at the beginning of the season to find a sixteen-year-old Royal Princess there to take precedence of you, and thereafter you'd dwindle into an aunt, sought more and more by those who wish you to serve as conduit to either me or my daughter. I would give you a better life than that."

Hatahra stopped there. She had her own secret thought. She had looked down into the little face born that day, and in spite of a mother's enchantment with her infant, she had seen vestiges of her own plain features with perhaps her consort's big ears and hawk nose.

Lasva had been beautiful from the moment of birth and would remain so until she died, and what kind of problems might arise from the future heir being overshadowed by her aunt? Humans, Hatahra thought, of whatever degree, however refined their education, have a tendency to behave like humans. And jealousy is a distinctly human trait. Time to give Lasva—whose looks were the fault of their shared ancestors—some alternatives."

Lasva seemed startled at the idea, her sky-colored eyes round. Then she made a wry face, dimples winking in her cheeks. "The only two un-wed kings I know of I would not court."

"I know. We will certainly leave out the cursed Chwahir, though I think they would do better for a queen. Even if that braying Jurac comes riding through Lily Gate to offer you a crown, I will not have you any Lammog."

Lasva winced, remembering the story of the Chwahir Queen Lammog who had been murdered by her brother the century before, some said for being too popular.

"Ah-ye," Lasva whispered, thinking of awkward Jurac, who'd been so grateful to be taught to dance. She'd felt sorry for him, but pity was no reason to marry.

The carillon rang in the distance, signaling Hour of the Leaf.

"I had better dress," Hatahra said.

Lasva began her curtsey, then paused. "My birth." Her fan opened at a pretty angle, indicating Discreet Inquiry, but the unhappiness of her lifted gaze was revealing. "I always thought it was caprice that caused our mother to try the Spell. Marnda has said more than once it was her age, and a wish to see the sweetness of youth before she died."

Hatahra's brow was severe. "That's because Marnda doesn't know the truth. None of them do. Our mother was even more private than I am, and our battle of wills, harsh as it was, stayed between us. Very well, then, here is the truth, but do not imagine the telling any kind of allu-sion: I preface it by pointing out that all our lives I have avoided forcing you into choices."

Lasva curtseyed. Her sister's low tone warranted no less.

"I wanted to marry," Hatahra said, speaking with care. "It doesn't mat-ter who. The fellow came from a family known for being dashing and attractive, both men and women. In short, I was in love with him, and I can see now—as our mother did then—that he was in love with the idea of acting the part of a king. A dashing king, of course." She grinned. "I will say he had little desire for power, only for the fun of presiding artistically—making 'dashing' the royal mode, you might say."

Lasva closed her fan, hiding her hands in the soft folds of her skirt.

"But being dashing is not the purpose of a king—not of a kingdom the size of Colend, with its unending demands. Besotted, I did not see this, or pretended I didn't see it. I insisted on marriage, not mere ribbons, or the private agreement of a consort: a ring-marriage with promises of fidelity, which I claimed were for love but, actually, I thought to bind him. Hum-bumbler that I was! You do not bind others, they bind themselves. My mother said that if I married him, I would not inherit the crown. Instead, she would try the Birth Spell. I did not believe she would—that she could have any success—but that very night she spoke the words, and there you were. I had to make my choice at that moment, or she would have declared you the heir the next day."

Lasva's chill spread to her limbs. "How—did your favorite—?"

"Oh, he didn't dust off the moment he realized he would never rule Colend. He had far too much style for that. But each day I could feel his attention wandering farther afield, and by summer I knew that he was courting someone else. He professed eternal love for me, but by then I had faced the truth: he was in love with what I could give. He did not ever know me. Within five more years, my own eternal love had dwindled to indifference, and I thought I was in love forever with Mathias Altan. Which in turn didn't last."

She touched Lasva's wrist again. "It's the way of human nature, despite all the songs."

FOUR

OF ROSES IN BLOOM

"So our Rose has been supplanted?" asked Isari of Ananda.
Ananda Gaszin glanced at the fine pearls Isari had threaded through
her bright red hair and looked away again. Pearls! In the morning! The
Icicle Duchess's fashion. Court had become both expensive and . . .
strange, since Carola Definian began hosting such expensive parties that
few dared compete.

Ananda flicked her fan up in a graceful whirl, languidly fanning her
face without disturbing a single corn-silk curl. Pearls . . . but Isari did not
have a lover's ribbon in her morning hair dress any more than the Icicle
Duchess Carola did.

They were joined by tall, thin Sharith, recently betrothed. Sharith's
mouth twitched. "Let us enjoy the fragrances, shall we?" And her fan
opened slowly

Time to talk over the astonishing news: the queen had an heir at last.
What did it mean—besides Princess Lasva being changed from conjec-
tural heir to marriageable princess? They stepped along the mosaic pathway leading to the conservatory, their draperies fluttering in the slow,
aromatic breezes that flowed off the canals and over the palace gardens.

Low couches shrouded by planters made inviting circles throughout
the space. There was no obvious center and certainly no dais or throne.

The focus of the room was inevitably toward the fern-shaded, grassy area near the waterfall, where the queen sat. Those who wanted her attention made it their business to place themselves as close to that miniature dell as their rank permitted—or as need required.

The three ladies were joined, at languid pace, by a fourth: Fiolas, whose lateness and tired eyes were noted by the others. Her abundant brown hair was done up in a charming disarray, scarcely curled, as though she had risen in haste—The Fresh Arising. Behind her back, Carola's eyes semaphored to anyone watching about the vulgarity of a style at least three years out of fashion. Not that Carola cared anymore, with her heart's desire so close to her grasp, but she did not have him yet, and it would not do to reveal anything until she did.

So she commented on life's ironies in the language of the fan, as though nothing else were on her mind, as Sharith flicked her skirts with one hand, her ribbon-tied wrist arched. Ananda held out her arm and Fiolas took it, her touch lighter than a butterfly's wing. Isari smiled. The four young ladies known as Lasva's Roses, once secure in their ascendance, would stand together.

"It is time." Isari turned a shoulder in the direction of the conservatory.

Queen Hatahra, like her foremothers, did not care for trumpets. A single, pure *ting!* from a silver bell brought all to their feet. The Roses joined others already at their station near the pale yellow orchids as, through the main doors, the queen and Princess Lasthavais arrived together, followed by Davaud, the royal favorite who, by sharing parenthood, now would be confirmed as Duke of Alsais, which in the eyes of court established him as the Royal Consort.

The traditional responsibility of the Duke or Duchess of Alsais was defense of the royal city, though none had ever had to perform that duty. But the monarchs held the honorific in reserve for consort-parents whom they did not marry. As Duke of Alsais, Lord Davaud would now take precedence of the other dukes in his own right, instead of being conducted there on the queen's arm.

Soft, modulated voices had scarcely carried over the sound of plashing water. At the sight of the bundle in the queen's arms, the court bowed low, hands together in full Peace mode, acknowledging the queen and the new queen-to-be as the royal party made their stately way.

"So small," Fiolas breathed through slightly parted lips. "And so unwitting of how much change she has made in so short a time alive."

"Ah-ye," Isari sighed behind her fan. The others knew she'd staked a fantastic sum on Princess Lasthavais succeeding where no one had for four years: ribboning Kaidas Lassiter. "The Icicle Duchess will ringshackle Handsome now."

"Why should she want him as anything but a pillow boy?" Ananda's fan twirled.

Isari drawled, "They say the Lassiters are near to broken, their debts are so large."

Sharith said, "It's the baron's debts. Not his."

Fiolas said in the soft courtly whisper, lips nearly unmoving, "And the queen hates the baron."

They glanced across the artfully scattered groupings of courtiers (all actually in strict order of status), easily picking out the petite, fair-haired Carola, Duchess of Alarcansa, and near her, Young Gaszin, wearing her colors in his nail lacquer and talking idly with a couple from Ranflar.

Carola, who paid no heed to Young Gaszin, shifted her gaze to the queen's small bundle in its silken wrappings. A tiny fist was visible. Triumph made the edges of her vision glitter, but she banished it. She would not permit it until she had her heart's desire.

Isari said, "The chase is no longer worth the garland."

Sharith said, "You appear to think that she wants Kaidas solely because Lasva has him. Had him."

"Lasva probably sent him a parting gift before breakfast," Ananda said. "As for Carola, she'll have my brother." Ananda flicked her fan toward Young Gaszin. "The rest is persiflage."

"Camouflage," Isari said, fan hiding one eye.

Fiolas said to Sharith, "She chased Kaidas Lassiter simply because he didn't chase her."

Sharith expressed her disbelief with an artful twirl of her fan.

Fiolas flushed slightly, and slid her arm in Ananda's. Neither of them had succeeded in catching Kaidas's eye, and both had tried. As the two former rivals walked on, Sharith said, "Fiolas does not seek the simple motivation for simplistic comfort."

"Nonsense. They all do," Isari murmured. "All of them. Kaidas Lassiter is popular because he's wayward. Ananda and Fiolas wanted him because they couldn't have him. Carola wants him because Lasva has him."

"I still cannot believe Kaidas and the princess are together. I have seen no sign of it."

"That is why they are together. Or were." Isari glanced at the queen. "To continue: Young Gaszin thinks he's in love with Carola because she won't have him."

Sharith finished, "The princess collects hearts because she can—"

"*That* rumor is fog."

Sharith sighed. "You see her the center of every group, courted by many, accepting none."

"That much is true," Isari said. "But she's not heartless."

"Then how did she get the reputation, in a court where hearts are hidden?" Isari marked.

Who hurt you? Isari thought, but she said, "I wondered about that, after the whispers began before spring. Aunt Darva says that Tatia Tittermouse spread it about, and I believe her."

"What do the old know? All I know is what seems most obvious: that everyone wants what they can't have. It's that simple. How absurd life is! I believe there is a poem in it."

Already written a hundred times, if not more, Isari thought as Sharith flicked her fan mockingly. "Everyone can see how *zalend* Ananda's brother is for the Icicle. She and Young Gaszin will lead this court by next season." She plucked a bud from deep down so the plant was not marred, and tucked it behind her ear.

Ananda and Fiolas had rejoined them. Ananda said, "I confess, court would be more fun if Young Gaszin reigned. His parties—always amusing. Remember when he invited those city guild hummers and convinced them the cook was his father? The way they bowed and scraped . . ."

Fiolas sighed. Few subjects were duller than past parties. "Wager." She watched Ananda's fan flick in Delicate Indifference, though Isari could see in the tightened grip that Ananda was not indifferent at all. *And isn't that what makes court entertaining?*

Ananda said, "I'll wager The Icicle makes a move before we leave for Sartor tomorrow."

"Young Gaszin," Fiolas whispered.

"Altan," Sharith drawled, just to annoy Ananda, who had been courting the heir to the Altan duchy. She did not want to see Ananda made a duchess.

"Never." Isari surprised them all by saying, "Kaidas Lassiter." Then, after another look at Carola, she surprised and intrigued them all by adding, "by tonight."

"Stake?"

A hesitation. All were aware of how much Ananda had lost by wagering she could win a lovers' cup from Lassiter.

Isari said, "A gown's length of rose lace. Gold-edged."

Rose. Gold-edged, as for a formal court appearance—or for a princess.

Ananda laughed, thinking that Isari might be kind, but at least she covered her kindness with wit. "Done."

Carola, Duchess of Alarcansa, permitted herself a quick, reassuring glance at the stream channel pooled at her feet and the scene mirrored there: ferns and flowers framing her own dainty figure, setting off the fresh spring green of her gown; her hair, its curl more regular than Lasthavais's clumsy curls which were surely hot-ironed; the curve between waist and hip a far purer arc than the princess's; her bosom higher and rounder, her under-lip fuller. The princess's earlobes curved outward in a most vulgar manner, unlike Carola's own, which lay elegantly flat to her head. And her own over-lip was much more shapely, especially when she pronounced the difficult consonants. Lasthavais was often quite careless in her speech, but no one professed to notice—but then courtiers were sheep. Carola had proved that! As for that face, Carola's own face was shaped in a perfect heart, it needed no arrangement of hair to suggest it. So *why . . . ?*

It didn't matter why. She had only to get Kaidas away from that royal grasp—more likely now that there was no chance of a future crown. If the queen assented to the match—and Carola was certain that Hatahra was in the mood to assent to almost anything—he would gain a coronet, and from someone who could make him into the greatest duke in Colend's history.

Carola said behind her fan to her cousin Tatia, "I believe I will gain my wish." She sent a fast glance at Kaidas, lounging by the fountain with most of the other young lords, the provocative bones of his profile drawn against the granite as if by an artist's hand, his dark hair tied back, with no flourishes or even gems to adorn it. But he did not need adorning—except for his hair to be bound by the white ribbon of fidelity to Carola Definian.

As the queen beckoned to Carola with a welcoming smile, the Duchess of Alarcansa stepped toward her triumph, blind to the bitterness in her cousin's face.

FIVE

OF ROSES UNDONE

Just after the bells of Midday, Kaidas slipped free at last. As soon as he reached the terrace behind the conservatory, he ducked through servants' unadorned halls to evade courtiers who strolled outward in order to gossip. His mind burned with questions, his eyes burned with exhaustion. His heart panged with the knife-sharp irony of memory, how he and Lasva had longed for Midsummer's Day to be over, so they could set out for the journey south.

Well, Midsummer Day had brought its own surprise.

Lasva had looked so solemn at the Rising, so . . . lost. He'd watched her obliquely while pretending to listen to chatter about the trip to Sartor. He'd ignored everyone but Lasva, who had given him no signals, but he was used to that. Surely their situation was better, now that Hatahra had her heir. Surely the queen would release Lasva to do what she wished?

After all, Kaidas never expected a title—didn't want one. Though she said she would marry him, he didn't care. He'd be Lasva's footman, or stable master, or whatever she wanted.

Yes. But in spite of all these arguments, he'd seen that look in her eyes. *Something* had happened, and it wasn't her being displaced by that infant, because one thing he did know: Lasva cared nothing about being queen. She never talked politics, she had no ambition. The birth of that little scrap of humanity would be seen as her freedom.

Wouldn't it?

Impatience impelled him toward the safety of his rooms. He had to contain it. They were still at court, and courtly etiquette ruled the outward forms of their lives. He had to wait for her invitation to talk, for she was still a princess, and he the heir to a debt-ridden barony. Another thing he knew for certain: he was ready to run if she wanted it.

He made it to his rooms, dismissed his servant, removed his plum-colored brocade overvest, and his violet damask undervest as well. Who knew when he'd ever have the wherewithal for another new suit? Life was like a mad dash down a river—exciting, but there were submerged boulders or logs to shoot your boat up into the air and toss you into the rapids.

He rolled back the sleeves of his fine cambric shirt, glanced down at his trousers, then shrugged. If he got paint on them, he got paint on them. Instinct set his heart racing. Something was going to change, he felt the same poised tension of an impending race. No, it was more severe than that, more like the moments before the single battle he'd ever been in.

Meanwhile, there was duty. Reckless as always, he took out a porcelain cup. He'd bought half a dozen in case he ruined the painting of Lasva's—a ridiculous expense—but then when your debts were already mountainous, what was a few hundred twelve-siders more?

Now he was glad to have the extras, for he knew what he must do.

He had taken up his paints when the first visitor arrived. There was no scratch at the open door, only a flicker of color, then his father sauntered in.

Kaidas dipped his tiniest brush in liquid gold.

The baron lounged against the table, as was his habit, but he knew enough of painting to stay out of the light. He scrutinized the fine porcelain cup in his son's hands. "Nice," he said, his eyebrows aslant. "But you're a strumming hummer to be painting that thing with the door wide open."

"The intended recipient is unlikely to complain, as she was born this very day," Kaidas retorted.

"Ah!" His father gave a crack of laughter. "For the royal brat. Of course."

Kaidas shrugged. "The announcement of a Name Day party is sure to be circling soon. One must have a gift."

"I hope," his father drawled as he kicked the door shut, "you realize what it means now that your princess lost her crown."

Kaidas did not pause. "Come to impart wisdom on the subject of princesses?"

"I am not such a hypocrite," the baron retorted. He leaned back against the door, his gaze sardonic. "The poets say history sings a repeated chorus if we have the wit to hear the tune. Something I always doubted."

Kaidas did not pause in the delicate task of painting budding queensblossom round the rim of the cup, though warning gripped the back of his neck. "My intentions remain unchanged, Father. A crown was never part of them." He paused to count the tiny dots that formed each petal. "So you are here to suggest a different melody?"

His father was tall, rakish, careless in how he wore his clothes, though he wore only the best. He stood beside the curtain, his profile toward the window, through which he saw what he'd expected to see: a diminutive, shapely blonde heading this way with the straight-backed assurance characteristic of the Definians.

He snapped his fan outward, brushing the panes. "Comes your little duchess, as I expected." He faced his son and spoke bluntly. "The queen was just smiling on the Definian girl. It's time to give her an answer."

"I gave you my answer. It's you who has been courting her on my behalf, so you may tell her no."

No, the flat denial that courtiers avoided. Not *ah-ye,* not words rearranged into compromise and ambiguity.

"Kaidas—"

"No."

His father sighed. "Kaidas. We're talking about a treaty marriage. You don't have to live with the damn girl, you don't even have to bed her, as long as she agrees at the outset. All you have to do is marry her, and when she chooses, partner her in making an heir. I don't know why she wants you, but she does, and we need that treaty."

"You mean you need money."

"*We* need money. And what of it?"

Kaidas paused, sending his father a frowning glance before he resumed painting. "How well do you know Carola Definian?"

"Enough. She's well born, though we're an older family. She's rich. She's polite, she's got style, she's beautiful, and the queen just now gave her Hither." He held his fan in a mockery of the royal beckon. "Gaszin and the Altans are after her."

"She scares me."

His father burst out laughing.

Kaidas painted on.

The baron wiped his eyes. "Hatahra scares *me*. She just publicly favored the suit, my boy. Didn't you see it?"

No point in saying that he'd only had eyes for Lasva. Kaidas's hand poised above the gold paint. "Father, I don't want to marry. Not for twenty years. Thirty."

The baron drawled, "Of course not. You're a Lassiter, and we never think of the future if we can help it."

"Do you want to hear the truth?" Kaidas asked, turning around to face his father.

The baron stared down into those wide black eyes, unblinking, intense, and this time opened his fan full out, angled north toward Thorn Gate in anticipation of dire outcomes. "Not," he said, "if it will bring ruin to the family."

The pleasure of speaking aloud the words—*I love Lasthavais Lirendi and will love her until I die*—vanished like smoke. Kaidas made an airy gesture with the paint brush.

His father said grimly, "The only truth that matters is that your princess is no longer heir. She's a king's bride, soon's Hatahra finds her a king. And she intends to, she made that plain to Mathias and the dukes. My guess is that Hatahra won't have to lift a finger, because the suitors'll come at the gallop the moment the news gets out. But Hatahra knows that the best treaties aren't made with princes who have to take their future queen with a worthless baronial heir attached as her lover."

"Most of those princes probably have their own lovers," Kaidas pointed out wryly.

"Probably." His father tapped the table next to the paints. "More important—much more important—the other news going out right this moment is that you won't be consort to a future crown with unlimited funds. And so our creditors are going to close in."

Kaidas painted on, his fingers steady, four, five tiny royal lilies, each perfectly formed.

The baron expertly assessed his son's tight mouth and the tense jut of his jaw. Promise or stubbornness? The boy had inherited the Lassiter will, which goaded them all to ride free—too often straight to disaster.

"You might be thinking of a run for freedom. For love. But what will you do when you climb out of bed?" The baron twirled his fan. "Pretty as you paint, you could never earn enough to even feed that race horse of yours, much less pay servants. Your princess, if she's hummer enough to flout the queen, won't be welcomed in any court on the continent. What can she do besides collect cats? Nothing. And she owns nothing. Every stick in her rooms, every stitch on her body, belongs to Hatahra."

Kaidas did not look up.

His father said, "You are free to revile me for being lazy and worthless. I am. But listen to this last thing, then I'll bow out. If you marry yon duchess, you not only save our family, you save Princess Lasthavais from a life of drudgery and indifference. Because this you can believe: so-called true love does not last. If you two run off to Sartor, one will tire of the other—it happens, it's nature—and what's left? An old age amid broken furniture, under a leaky roof. Do you really want her to wake up one day in ten years, or five, or next season, and hate you for what she lost? How much better is a quick break, if you can't manage it with grace?"

He thrust open the door. With a quick swing of gray-streaked black hair, he was gone, leaving the barren truth: the cost of saving the Lassiter family was Kaidas's life. He had nothing else to offer Lasva. Not even a lifetime of love, if his father spoke the truth. He could bear anything but Lasva waking one morning and looking at him with hatred.

Kaidas dropped the brush and gripped the table. The pain nearly took his breath away. He could not imagine not loving Lasva. It had come by degrees, like the sun returning after winter. He'd fought it, but had no more success than a man fighting against the sun's warmth and light. First attraction, then the giddy pleasure of her voice, her wit, the un-thinking, generous kindness with which she regarded a silly world. And finally the passion as eager as his, as ardent, as inventive. As tender.

Would she really come to hate him? She was young—younger than he by several years of variegated experience. He couldn't see her hating anyone, but this he could believe: she was so loving that she would easily find someone else to love. Someone who would give her the life she deserved.

Leaving him only honor.

Kaidas went to the door and opened it.

Then he returned to his task.

He was counting queensblossom petals in a soft voice when Carola found him. She paused in the doorway, noting that it was open, noting her intended in shirtsleeves and busy with a paintbrush. He wore a fine court shirt, lace at wrists and throat, not a painting shirt, and she inter-preted it thus: he wanted to be alone but did not expect to be.

It was possible he was expecting *Her*. Fury seethed inside Carola, until her gaze was caught, as always, not by the old-fashioned artistry of the apartment's decoration, but by a sliver of her own reflection in the gloss over a miniature painting of the Lassiter mansion.

Carola studied the smooth heart shape of her face, steadied by the reassurance that her countenance gave no clue to her thoughts. So absorbed was she, that for that moment she was unaware of her beloved's attention.

He studied the startling mirror images, profile to profile, one highlighted with the bright rays streaming in the window, the other reflected darkly against the rich wood of his door. He remembered the last time he'd attended one of Carola's parties; the heat, the stifling mental atmosphere. Everyone invited sat in a circle around her as she talked in her sweet, light, precise voice about the latest play. Later she'd paused, encouraging others to speak as she watched her own reflection in the rain-streaming windows.

He returned to his painting.

No betraying emotion showed. Restored to the slow, steady breath of composure, Carola looked into the bright room at Kaidas, who painted on, apparently unaware that he was more compelling than any mere daubs, his paint-stippled hands moving with delicate care. She scratched at the open door.

He set aside his brush and got to his feet to bow. She intuited from his lack of surprise that he had known she was there. The lure of the hunt quickened in her. She would woo him, and she would win him all to herself. But first she must bind him with all the honor she possessed.

She curtseyed back. All quite proper. She would rather he have waived the bow, or better if he'd walked over and shut his door—the sign he wished to be intimate—but his behavior was perfectly correct.

Heat flamed again under her ribs. What was that he was painting? One of those damned cups! The heat of rage overwhelmed desire, burning all the way up to her throat. She'd been able to discover where he went and how long he stayed, at great expense, but so far, she had not been able to determine if he'd given Lasva one. *How* she longed to find and destroy them all.

At least this one, painted so in public, would have to have an appropriate purpose—yes, there was royal blue queensblossom intertwined by graceful golden vines with royal lilies of white. Relief made her breathe easier. "That is a thoughtful gift for the Royal Princess," Carola said, coming forward and examining the cup. "Ah, how delightfully you paint! I wish I had such an eye. I could look at it forever, I confess."

"May I finish it?" he asked. "If I wait too long, I lose the rhythm of the pattern."

"It would be my pleasure to watch." She smiled.

The cup was striking. The queensblossom petals were so tiny, each blossom perfectly made. He touched his brush to the liquid gold and with deft strokes finished the last curling stem.

Then he laid down the brush, picked up another, and dipped it into the cobalt. He began painting stylized ivy vines around the base. When she was certain his attention was absorbed in his task, she shifted her gaze to him, craving the exclusive right to kiss the long lashes shuttering those black eyes under the wicked lines of his brows. She yearned to caress him, to revel in the certitude that no other hand would be permitted to touch the hard jut of his cheekbones; to have at her command the choice, whenever she desired, of playing with the single lock of hair that fell neglected over his broad brow—*his* curls, not hair dresser's art. Her hireling had insisted he had no hair dresser nor even a body servant. Just a man who tended his horses and came inside to tend his clothes. He did not even paint his nails, though few of the most dedicated riders did.

Strictest etiquette required the person of superior rank to make the proposal, but, before that, go-betweens would normally have made certain what each party expected.

She would—she *could*—no longer wait. "Will you marry me?" she asked, and when he looked up, his expression impossible to interpret, she said what she had not intended to say, "The queen favors my suit."

She should not have to say it—by all reason he should be the supplicant here. But he wasn't. She was.

He said, "I know." Then he bowed, the low, correct bow of assent, and relief eased the tightness in her chest. "I accept. When should this event take place?"

"We have nothing to wait on," she said, triumph restoring her poise. "And sufficient reason to make it soon." A delicate hint about the debts.

"True."

Was that mockery? He bowed again, quite correct, except for the paintbrush still gripped in his fingers. He seemed to see it, and with another slight bow, "You will permit?" He tipped his head at the paints.

She gestured. She would be generous toward his little idiosyncrasies. They were so much a part of his style. He must, however, understand what becoming the Duke of Alarcansa meant. This was the difficult part—the part that ought to have been arranged between them by a mutually accepted party. She could not wait, but she could not risk bluntness, for if he refused—if he repeated the conversation—how court would smile behind her back!

How *She* would smirk in triumph.

"I will return home to Alarcansa when the court leaves for Sartor to-morrow," she said.

One, two leaves, and then he paused to dip the brush. Kaidas under-stood the statement. As delicate as a diplomat, the duchess had given a command to escort her home.

His eyes, so dark you could not distinguish the pupils, were impossi-ble for Carola to read.

"You are tired of Sartoran music, then?" he asked finally.

He did not know, or pretended not to know, that she had never visited Sartor. A surge of terror made her grip the back of a nearby chair. No, wait, *did* he know? "I love good music and find it both civilized and inspiring," she said. Her words were measured, rational. Elegant. "But I have musi-cians at home. And Sartor hasn't produced anything new for years."

There. That was oblique enough, surely?

It wasn't. Where she heard elegance, he (not looking at that practiced, smooth countenance) heard the quick breath, the slightly hissed sibi-lants of demand and anger: marriage with Carola did not come with freedom. She wanted him in Alarcansa, under her eye.

He showed no reaction as he painted with quick, sure touches. Kaidas knew his duty. His father—devoted only to his own pleasure—had even bestirred himself to make certain he knew his duty. But he waited—a heartbeat, a breath—gripped by an image of Carola's pretty little fingers inexorably binding white ribbons not around his hair but around his neck.

There was no escape.

Duty required him to speak.

His own honor required the words to be given with *melende*. "Permit me to offer my escort."

Carola dipped into a low, gracious curtsey. These words came as sweet relief, followed by sweeter triumph. Far sweeter.

He asked, in a polite voice, "When would you depart?"

"Once we have paid our respects to the queen." When he heeded her wishes, she would always be generous. "There will be pleasant events enough in Alarcansa this summer, which ought not to be neglected while our wedding is being arranged. And not just in Alarcansa. I would not want to miss your father's hunt. He said he's bringing out the new doe, is that true?"

"True indeed," he replied, his fingers steady, steady. "She's reputed to be as fast as Kansl."

Kansl was the Lassiters' most famous buck, running hunts for almost ten years and the garland only thrown around his neck by three extremely good riders. Comparing the Lassiters with their wild, beautiful deer had become trite, but that was the way Carola thought of her beloved. He was a wild buck, to be garlanded with Alarcansa crimson.

"Ah-ye! I shall enjoy making a wager or two in support of the doe," she said, conscious of graciously offering him a long rein. "What is her name?"

"Vriss." Another leaf painted. The ribbons were wound round his neck. *Melende* demanded that he run with grace. "If you wish to stay with us, our house is what the others have forgivingly termed 'rustic.' But it has its comforts," he said, painting a curling vine.

It was acceptance, but not surrender.

Carola unclasped from around her neck a huge, faceted blue stone in the shape of a great tear. She swung it before the window and said, "I had thought to give the newborn royal princess my grandmother's sapphire, which was given her by a queen, because it matched the color of her eyes. The blue, framed by your blue-and-gold cup, would make it the more beautiful. Is that not a charming idea, to join the stone with this cup as joint gifts?"

His hands stayed steadily on his task. In a court filled with people who either had unlimited wealth or affected to, gifts were meaningless unless they were either made by the giver or carried historical significance.

The Lassiters had no principle jewels, no medals awarded by kings or queens, nothing famed for cost or art or acquisition. Whatever they once had, his father had sold over the years, to satisfy debtors. Kaidas had discovered his talent for painting at a young age, grasping that art was not valued unless it was rare.

"Kaidas. You who love beautiful things, do you not admire?" The high, precise voice insisted.

He paused in his painting.

Carola held the gem to the window. Blue shards caught the summer sunlight and danced around the room, startlingly brilliant. "Blue and gold are lovely indeed." She smiled. "The Lirendis knew that when they chose them for royal colors. Yet I find I much prefer the crimson of good wine, drunk from the cup made by a master hand."

Alarcansa crimson. Not a ribbon, then, he thought, glancing at that swinging prism as she dropped her hint about her expectation of a lover's cup, but a chain around his neck.

Exigencies put the chain there; style determined how he wore it. "Shall I send the gem with my finished gift, then?"

"The two will complement one another beautifully," she replied in that determinedly gracious tone and stepped toward him.

He could not forbear a bid for a small measure of freedom. "Will you be good enough to place it there, within reach?" he asked, not pausing in his strokes.

She understood enough about painting to know that there was a rhythm to the execution of patterns, and so she said, "I will wait until you finish the ivy vine."

He looked up then, and she smiled her most understanding smile. "This gem, gift of a queen, gift to a future queen, must not be risked in the hands of careless servants or awkward visitors." She watched his hands at their steady task, then studied his expression. He seemed to be absorbed in painting, and so she added, as lightly as possible, "The Dukes of Alarcansa, ever since the Definian family inherited the title, have always safeguarded our treasures. I will show you that record before we wed." His mouth tightened, and though it could have been on account of his exacting task, instinct warned her that her message had been clear enough. So she chattered on, as pleasantly as possible, "You will have to read the record of my great-great-grandfather, when the Chwahir last tried to conquer us. You might not know that they came over the pass above us, trampling our vineyards. It's terribly exciting."

He laid down his brush then, and she closed the distance between them at last, clasping the gem about his neck, then, with a quick twitch, making certain it lay outside his shirt, where it looked quite handsome, she thought. He was now hers.

He picked up his brush again. "I must finish."

Of course, he must be left to paint.

"Someone is surely organizing something. Wear the gem to the party, at which time we will present our gifts to the royal princess together."

He bowed his assent.

Tatia waited in the garden, her eyes anxious.

"He will escort me home," Carola breathed, and Tatia tapped her fingers lightly on her fan in applause. "And he wears my gem for the Name Day gift—we will give our gifts together before the entire court."

"Oh, Carola, I would not have dared. But I am so happy for you!"

"And I am so happy."

"The princess shall soon be mourning at Willow Gate," Tatia cooed as they entered the Rose Walk.

"I'm sure of it." Carola spied a new-bloomed rose at the very top of a bush. With a quick snap of her fan she struck it from the stem. "It is a good lesson even for princesses to learn that to wish is not always to have." She laughed and struck another rose, sending petals spinning and fluttering in the breeze. "As for him, I will give him anything he wants. I will adore him and make every day over to pleasing him. But first he must understand that I will never sleep in an empty bed." She struck another rose so sharp a blow the petals scattered all across the path as the bees buzzed angrily, and birds scolded overhead.

SIX

OF PORCELAIN SHARDS

The bells had rung the Hour of the Wheel, and only the magic-enhanced breezes that ruffled upward from the indoor pools and fountains kept the palace from becoming stifling by the time Lasva escaped the last courtier. The one pair of eyes she'd sought had not been there amongst the curious, the triumphant, or the sympathizers.

She made her way to her rooms, and found me awaiting her.

"Any private messages?" she asked, her forehead tense.

My throat hurt. I knew what she wanted to hear, but I could not give it to her. "Just public ones. All lily-shapes. Congratulations."

"Emras, two things." She pressed her fingertips to her eyelids, then dropped her hands. "First, will you organize the Name Day party, and send out verbal messages? Everyone is waiting in expectation. I know I can trust you to arrange it with appropriate style. Second, may I borrow your robe?" She ripped her sleeve ribbons free and dropped them, a careless gesture I had never before seen.

Then she stripped off her overrobes, which settled in a sun-yellow puddle at her feet, leaving the cream-colored body gown.

I handed her my cloud blue linen, and she fled. I stepped into the hallway, feeling undressed in my white linen. I glimpsed her flitting to the maids' entrance as she flung a neutral domino veil around over her head, transforming herself into a scribe sent on a private errand.

Then she vanished.

This was the customary resting time to recruit one's energies for the night's festivities. The hallways of the palace guest wing were mostly empty, doors closed, as Lasva traveled a circuitous route to the far end and then up the back stairs.

She crossed the landing in the upper level and saw the afternoon light glowing in a lengthening rectangle on the wall opposite his open door. Was he painting, then?

Lasva smiled. She did not begrudge anyone their lover's cups. Her own was a precious secret, a gift of love—perhaps she was part of a secret bond of beloveds, a notion that partook of grace.

She stepped to his doorway, flinging the domino veil back so she could see, and he could see her. There he was, framed by the window. Painting, as she had surmised. She scratched at the door post, and he looked up swiftly, and there she was, robed simply in blue, the exact color of her eyes.

When he smiled, it was sudden, his own dear smile, but the warmth tightened to politesse, and that's when Lasva saw the great blue gem gleaming on his breast: the famous Definian sapphire.

Her breath expelled. It was all the reaction she made, but color rose under the brown skin of his cheeks.

He set aside his paintbrush and bowed.

"Ah-ye, not that." She flung up her palms.

He sat down again, more quickly than he'd meant to, his face blanching.

And for a painful stretch of time they stared at one another.

What could she say? She knew immediately what had happened: Hatahra had won. She had ridded herself of the Lassiters and broken the ducal alliance all in one blow. However it had come about, Kaidas had chosen duty over love.

She must leave but could not. Was there nothing left for her? She pointed at the cup, painted queensblossom in the royal blue and gold. "For the babe?"

He flicked his brush in Assent.

"A beautiful gift. My sister will be pleased."

"I am nearly finished." He saw her anguish, he heard it in her thready voice, and the pain made his chest hurt. He kept his hands steady by act of will, by not looking at her, though he could smell the clean wild-herb scent she favored, and his heart labored, his knees trembled, and his hands faltered with the ache of wanting to hold her.

She stood there looking at that cup, and his hands painting the cup, because she couldn't bear to turn away. The gem there on his breast forbade the direct speech that had been so brief and so precious a night ago. Honor required that much. It was for him to say what this token stood for. Some treaty marriages were in name only. But if he'd made such an agreement with Carola Definian, surely he would not be wearing her gemstone.

As the silence stretched she felt oddly dizzy. "Your plans," she began, a catch in her voice.

"The Duchess of Alarcansa honored me with a request for my company," he said. "We leave tomorrow, by her desire."

Honor. She could see the cost of those words. She heard that he took no pleasure in the words.

But he had spoken them.

So she forced a court smile. "I came to tell you. The Name Day celebration? At the sunrise room in the royal suite. Hatahra would be pleased to receive your gift from your hands."

She was gone on the last word.

Behind her, Kaidas painstakingly set aside the cup and his brushes and paints. With equal care he set the remaining cups on the floor, each perfectly made, holding light within its circle.

Then he smashed them all to dust.

I whirled into action, dispatching the entire staff to put together a party suitable for a queen and a future queen; the kitchens had already begun the baking of the specialties appropriate to the day. The Grand Seneschal gave me the royal sunrise chamber, and loaned me a staff to set things up as Princess Lasva wanted them. I issued my orders as if they were hers, then dispatched an army of pages to inform the waiting court of time and place.

No sooner was the page gone than Carola sent her own page to Kaidas, to settle their arrival together. She could not wait for the pleasure of viewing Lasva's face when they appeared, her future duke wearing her jewel.

And so the day closed with Lasva presiding with smiling grace over a charming Name Day party, the babe the center of talk, and Lasva serving

out the spun sugar queensblossom lily cakes and star-shaped berry tarts
with her own hands.

Those on the watch for such things observed Carola and Kaidas arriving together. Attention arrowed straight to the gem he wore, and from
thence to the princess, as he bowed before her.

She did not hold out her hand to be kissed.

The queen, observing over the babe's lacy headdress, watched with
approval as he laid the Alarcansa gem and Carola set the newly painted
cup on the tray for gifts, then sat together on the opposite side of the
room from Lasva.

Fiolas whispered to Ananda and Isari, "I shall expect my lengths of
lace to match a traveling gown."

SEVEN

OF SPICED WINE

Torsu slid into her chair in the servants' quarters of the royal palace in Alsais, as she had for the last eighteen days. Eighteen days! It seemed forever—over two weeks—and it would be two forevers until the princess returned around Martande Day.

She stared in resentment across the table at that hummer Nereith, without whose big mouth they never would have been living out this humiliation.

Nereith ate steadily, her lowered gaze never rising from her plate. The dinner was superb. The cooks were experimenting again, something light and delightful, tasting of wine and herbs and cheese, to serve Them if it was a success. But Torsu was too angry to enjoy it.

She was a dresser and good, too. She could unerringly cut a length of fabric by measuring with her eye. So why was she being treated like the stupidest shit-wander on the street, just for a comment about Princess Lasthavais that no one would have repeated anyway?

Here was the irony—the princess was far kinder than her noisome servants.

Several women laughed at the other end of the table, and Torsu grimaced, pushed aside her plate, and reached for the ice-drink. Even the taste of lime and berry and a hint of apple, usually so refreshing, did nothing to cool the heat of her anger.

The Princess had gone to Sartor without any lovers. Her rooms had been thoroughly cleaned, all her remaining clothes taken out, mended, reordered against autumn. Dessaf should have said, "You've kept silence well, Torsu. You may speak again."

Torsu turned toward the stable hands' table and happened to catch the eye of the new bridle-man. He smiled and saluted her with a little lift of his cup.

Torsu didn't smile back, of course. Just watch some poke-nose at her table see that and go chirping to that old toad Dessaf!

"And maybe a little more butter," someone was saying.

Still talking about that humming cheese-pastry!

Torsu turned a little on her chair, so she could peek over at the stable hands' table without being obvious. The bridle-man—what was his name? Kivic. He mostly sat alone, though sometimes the old coachman talked to him. Some said that he looked too much like a Chwahir, with his round, flat-cheeked face, but he wasn't any Chwahir. Everyone knew they had black hair and pale skin, and he was normal brown with some darker freckles, his hair a rusty color.

"Nobody likes new people," she thought, remembering how long it had taken to get anyone to speak to her after she'd been hired. Thinking back to her high hopes when she'd left her boring little town and her triumph at being hired at the palace after only four years' drudgery in Alsais, made her lips curl sourly. She hid her face, pretending to drink. Dessaf had sharp eyes, the fat old claypot.

So why sit here? It wasn't like she could speak. She left her dishes there for the kitchen maids. Let them do their jobs. She'd help them out if anyone ever showed the least sign of helping her out.

The air out in the vegetable garden was only marginally cooler, and the atmosphere felt thundery. Rain would be a relief. She breathed deeply, wishing she could shout to hear her own voice.

Only that would get her into trouble. She glared at the carrot tops. What made her furious, more than anything? That no one seemed to care that she couldn't talk. After all those weeks of flattering the upper maids and pretending an interest in the other dressers, how far had she gotten? They knew her name, but none had spoken to her since Dessaf landed on her so unfairly.

"Hot night, eh?"

She whirled around, stared up into a round face. Kivic!

She nodded.

Kivic looked down into that mutinous face, the full lower lip, and laughed softly. He checked in both directions. "I know you cannot speak, though I don't know why. But you can drink, yes? I have an ice-jug my cousin gave me, and it contains sweet wine. Surely you can spare enough time for a sweet cup of wine."

She wavered. Dressers were forbidden to dally with other palace servants; that was the very first rule she had agreed to. For sex, they were to go, always incognito, to the pleasure houses where the crown-steward held an account.

But he wasn't offering sex, only a cup of wine. And she was already laboring under the effects of one soul-sucking rule.

He leaned close. His breath stirred her hair. "I like silence. When it's companionable."

Her nerves tingled.

"Meet me on the north side of the winter-carriage barn. No one ever goes there in summer. I live right above." His breath stirred her hair.

She whirled around and made her way through the extensive vegetable garden. When she glanced back, he was nowhere in sight.

She took her time, making certain every few steps that no one followed. When she reached the huge barn, the moon was now fully covered by clouds, and the heat was stifling. Thunder muttered in the distance.

"This way." Kivic led her inside a narrow side door and up rickety steps. His room was at the top, tucked into a corner. Private, though it must be a longer walk to the stables.

The room was plain, clean, smelling faintly of oats and hay. He snapped his fingers and a small glowglobe lit. "Take my good seat," he offered, shutting the door and pointing to a low chair near the narrow bed. "Few like being housed here, but I find it's out of the way. The others are all gone into town to The Slipper," he added. "So no one will see you leave."

He didn't say when that might be. Torsu watched him open a trunk and lift out a fine stone jug. It had moisture beads on the side, a sure sign of its being magic-made.

He pulled out a pair of plain cups, poured, and handed her one. "I salute us, the invisible newcomers," he said, raising his cup.

She raised hers and drank. The wine was delicious. "How—" She remembered and stopped, blushing.

He shrugged. "Go ahead and speak. Who would I tell? I'm new," he said ruefully. "No one ever talks to me."

Who indeed? She sighed. "In truth, it feels good to speak," she admitted. "How can you afford such a wine? It's good."

"Isn't it? My cousin works at a vineyard to the north. He sends it to me."

That was hardly sinister. Feeling relieved—she hadn't even known she was uneasy—she sat back, sipping more.

"I probably shouldn't say this," Kivic admitted, laughing over the rim of his cup. "But you know what the stable hands call Dessaf?"

"I know the kitchen helpers call her Princess Pickle." Oh, it did feel good to talk!

Kivic's eyes quirked appreciatively. He had quite nice brown eyes. "That's good. Her nose does have that shape, doesn't it? Though I think the boys have it closer when they call her Gruska." Gruska—the gray mushrooms found under trees after long rains.

Torsu groped for meaning, then the image came, superimposed over Dessaf's sniffy face. "Ugly, and not even good to eat." She burst out laughing, and Kivic leaned forward to refill her cup. "Oh, this is good," she said, coughing, then wiping her eyes. Outside thunder rumbled closer, and fat droplets of rain tapped, pocketa-pock, on the roof directly overhead. "Just this, then I'd better go. I don't want to get drenched. It would cause all kinds of questions."

"That's right, you girls are forbidden to consort with the likes of us, eh?" And on her nod, he sighed with disgust. "Is that because that old broomstick Marnda's too dried up to ever look for a lover, and no lover with sight would look at Dessaf?"

Torsu snorted. "Ah-ye. They think that if we take lovers on staff we won't be able to keep our mouths shut. As if we're too witless to know not to blab—as if they wouldn't find out! We can only go to the pleasure houses. You can't even marry or have a child for ten years." *Not that I want either*, she thought. *I have better plans than that*.

Kivic whistled. "Now, that's a swindle. Is the pay bad? It is for gear men, though I've ambitions. I'm learning from the farrier."

The storm broke right then, lightning reflecting so brightly through the tiny window it was almost blinding. Before the thunder died away the rain began, a steady roar on the roof.

Torsu looked up apprehensively, and Kivic said, "You watch. It'll be over before your third cup is drunk."

The wine, its sweetness and warmth, the coolness rain brought after the relentless heat, all conspired to make Torsu very well satisfied with her place now, in contrast to her lonely bed up in the dressers' dormitory, surrounded by chattering hummers to whom she could not speak.

Kivic poured out more wine and made a motion as if refilling his own cup, though he hadn't yet finished his first.

"They pay us well enough," Torsu admitted, shrugging sharply. "But it's not what a person could make who has ambitions."

"I take it that means you're saving your wages?"

She grinned, bumping her cup against her teeth. "Someday, when I have all the secrets of the royal wardrobe, I'll move to a wealthy town where the women have pretensions, and I'll be rich in a year. But I'll need stock." Torsu had never told anyone that.

"A fine ambition," Kivic said.

The rain ended as abruptly as it had begun, except for steady drips from the cornice outside Kivic's room. She'd drunk too much. She'd better go.

"Now, I bet you have to pay extra for a simple massage," Kivic said. "I know we do. And what a shame. Because, if you were a horse, I'd say you had tension here and here."

He set aside his cup and stepped behind her. Finger pressed on her shoulders either side of her neck—the very muscles that got so tired sewing the fine stitches that had earned her her position. "Oh that's right on the spot," she breathed.

He chuckled. "You know, this is good practice. I could pretend you were a horse, and you don't even have to pay, like you would at the pleasure house. How's that?" As he spoke he pressed his fingers into her muscles. He wasn't as adept as the pleasure house men, but she was a little drunk, and she liked the slow circles that sent sparks of pleasure down her back, to pool, like warm wine, in her belly.

"It's good," she muttered hoarsely.

The fingers moved outward along her shoulders, to the muscles inside of her shoulder blades, and she breathed in, leaning into his fingers.

"So many knots. A race horse doesn't get so many. They must work you girls a whole lot harder than anyone knows."

The fingers shifted down to her collarbones. She winced when he dug in too hard. He shifted to light caresses outward, and the tingles spread before them. She knew by now that he was seducing her—the massage was clumsy, but the slow approach to the places that tingled was so . . . so different from the pleasure house men who gave expert massages before sex, always so matter-of-factly, always with an eye to the sand glass. Kivic seemed to be in no hurry, and her muscles melted into warm wax. She closed her eyes, scarcely aware when a hand lifted, nipped the cup from her lax fingers, and set it aside, while the other smoothed and smoothed at the base of her neck.

Scarcely aware when a piece of cloth was cast over the glowglobe, so the light on her eyelids cozily dimmed, and when, at last, slow fingers moved to her bodice strings and untied them, one by one, she welcomed the shivery feeling of air on her flesh as she stretched out on the bed that she discovered was conveniently nearby.

The storm boiled furiously overhead then diminished into the east, taking the thunder with it. The single toll of the third-hour bell echoed through the rain-washed night air as Torsu hurried back to the dormitory, smiling with pleasure at the dripping trees, flowers, plants.

Kivic had asked nothing about the princess, nothing at all. Dessaf was an old Gruska, and meanwhile, a girl had a right to pleasure, hadn't she?

Kivic stood at the top of the barn and watched as she skimmed along the pathway, holding her skirts up. He stretched, laughing to himself, then returned to his room, and hastily straightened up. Not long after, he heard voices as the rest of the hall's inhabitants returned in a group, now that the rain was gone. He snuffed the light, lay down, and pretended to sleep.

Sure enough, a rough hand banged his door open, a drunken voice muttered, "Oh, he's dead to the world."

"We better be, too. Dawn bells next, high-steppers!"

Raucous laughter echoed down the flimsy wooden hallway as doors slammed.

Kivic rose, touched the door, muttered a sealing spell. Tested it. When it held, he snapped on his light and then pulled out paper and pen, pausing to smile. Almost four months, he'd watched the royal cooks, runners, dressers, cleaners, all. Patience, he thought. Thinking back over the sweetness of the night was its own reward.

He wrote, chuckling, *My liege, I am in.*

Wasn't that the truth! And he'd be in again before week's end, if he wasn't mistaken. By the time the princess returned, if he continued to be patient, he would be "in" the princess's chambers at last, through a very sharp pair of ears.

He put the paper in a transfer case, tapped it as he said the spellword, and on the other side of the mountains, far to the north, King Jurac Sonscarna of the Chwahir felt the mental alarm that signaled a communication from his most trusted spy.

Jurac rose, snapped on a light, retrieved his transfer case, read the note, and threw it into the fireplace, where it flared briefly and burned out. Though it was summer, Chwahirsland was seldom warm enough for the fires to be doused.

He got up, though he'd had scant sleep. Events had transpired so rapidly—in a matter of days, and all his way. After years of effort and waiting. He'd always known that old woman would have an heir, but until he'd found Kivic, he'd never been able to get anyone past the layers of invisible barriers in that palace.

Now, in the same year, he had both the perfect spy, and his princess forced out of inheritance.

His princess. He laughed, walking about the room and rubbing his hands as he remembered her beautiful face, her smiles, all the more brilliant while she was surrounded with those smirking, drawling courtiers. Of course she would want to be a queen, but that had been taken away from her in Colend, as he'd always known it would be.

Now she could again be a queen, and he was going to make her one. Sleep was impossible. Joy and anticipation made his heart race too fast for that. It was time to issue orders and make ready to ride south. Time to claim Lasthavais for his bride.

EIGHT

OF ROYAL WAGERS

"So what do you think?"

Tharais studied her beloved, whose gaze mirrored her anxiety, despite his darling smile. She couldn't see it, but she sensed a question underlying the spoken question.

"I love your home, of course," Tharais exclaimed. One arm was looped most satisfactorily through his, so she waved her free hand to sweep around his world. "I love your arches and your tiles and all those pretty paintings that run along the tops of rooms."

"Athanarel is not as large as what you're used to," Geral observed.

"I'm not marrying a huge castle, or even a huge palace. I'm marrying you," she replied and kissed him.

He kissed her back, thoroughly, until they both ran out of breath and broke apart, laughing.

"I dug up an old map soon as I got home," Geral admitted. "I suspect it's long out of date, but from what I saw, your father rules a kingdom so large all of Remalna might fit right into your royal city."

"I'm not marrying a kingdom, either," she retorted.

Geral's brow puckered. "Yes, you are."

Tharais sighed as she guided him out of the upper hallway in the royal residence wing, which he'd been showing her so they could decide what to get rid of, what to keep, and what to change—always with a mind to the budget.

Tharais had never had to deal with the concept of budget before, but she'd mastered it quickly enough. The royal coffers here were not unlimited. She could see that Geral lived comfortably but not with the extravagance of the Enaeraneth court, or with the unstinting eye for military advantage that she saw at home in Marloven Hesea. None of which mattered a jot to her.

"I love the palace and the kingdom," she said, before her mind slid back to those cold winters at home and the constant fear she lived with in the royal city, with the ever-impending violence when her father grew angry, or Ivandred grew angry, especially at one another. Yes, the castle in the Marloven royal city was huge, but not huge enough. People had sometimes died as a result of Van's standing up to the king, but mostly Van suffered savage punishments that he would then pretend had never happened, except he'd go very quiet.

A chill tightened Tharais's shoulder blades, and she kissed the watching Geral again. She didn't know that he'd seen that bleak expression again. He'd learned that it meant she was thinking of Marloven Hesea. Macael had once admitted seeing it, too.

I've never gone over the mountains to visit my Marloven cousins, though Thar's invited me, Macael had told Geral. *But anything that could make her return to us so stiff and jumpy on her first days back in Enaeran is nothing I ever want to see. Especially as she never tells us why.*

Tharais broke into his thoughts. "I know I'll marry a kingdom, Geral. And I know its size, and the principal families, and what you trade where. The tutor you sent taught me all that, too, while we practiced your tongue. And I speak it well, do I not?"

"With the most charming accent." Geral's grin was merry, the first thing she had noticed about this otherwise unprepossessing fellow. Geral was her height, stocky, his thinning hair mouse brown. He'd been easily overlooked at the Enaeraneth court, except that Macael had liked him so much, joking with him until Geral's quick wit drew her attention and slowly but surely, her admiration.

His wit was not only quick but also kind. He liked everyone, he found everyone interesting, no matter what degree, and it was that aspect of him that had sharpened her admiration into attraction. That and the fact that his military knowledge was negligible—just enough to know who, in his kingdom, to talk to when it came to keeping peace.

"Accent? Me?" she said, tweaking his ear. "I do not have an accent. It

is all of you who do. Ther-r-ray-ezzz. I hear that, and think they are talking about someone else. And Van says it took him the better part of two
days to figure out who 'Yah-vandrath' was."

At the mention of her brother's name Geral pressed his lips together,
then he looked away and said, "Why don't we take a ride while the
weather's nice? You can show off your splendid horse, and I'll show you
the garden. I put in a plantation of fruit trees—"

"Geral." She stopped him with a hand flat against his chest. "My
brother hasn't . . . said anything or done anything to you, has he?"

"Oh, no, of course not," Geral said quickly. "He's been most polite. To
me, to everyone. He never makes demands, unlike some of those pup-
pies Macael insisted on bringing. Life! My steward tells me she had to
hire a dozen extra day-servants, just because of those fellows' constant
demands. You'd think they were the heirs to gigantic kingdoms and
not—"

"Geral." She pulled him outside into the lovely sea breeze. She sniffed
the enticing salt air. As long as she didn't have to be *on* the water, she
could get used to this proximity to the Sartoran Sea.

They walked down the broad, shallow stairs, past the new wing that
Geral's father had begun and then abandoned, and that Geral was hoping to begin again. When they were on the pathway between the flow-
erbeds, where she could see if anyone approached, she said, "Something's
wrong, and it has to do with my brother. It would be better if I knew."

"But he hasn't done anything wrong—at least, not to any of us. Not
that I have a right to comment on."

"Oh." She winced. "Don't tell me someone's been spying on their
drill."

Geral's cheery face suffused with color. "Yes. That would be me," he
admitted.

"What happened?"

The young king sighed. "You have to realize that news of what you
did up on the Fal River reached us long before you rode in. I mean, for
well over a year there's been rumors about that rascal Denlieff, who calls
himself the new King of Lamanca, and how conveniently certain lawless
types vanish into his kingdom. I'd heard of Dandy Glamac—bad, horribly bad. No one even *tried* to stop him. But you and your brother, with
a handful of boys and girls, put them out like a doused fire." He paused,
looking unhappy.

"Go on."

"So when you arrived, of course, people toasted you and all that, and when your brother asked for a garrison court, a private one, so he could exercise his fellows, I had to agree. And I made sure that no one has any business along that wall, though there aren't any windows. There are peepholes, though." Now he looked guilty.

Tharais snorted a laugh. "Our castle is riddled with 'em. Go on."

"My great-aunt showed me that peephole when I was little. Never mind why—the reason no longer exists. Main thing is, I had heard all that, and I couldn't help going to watch them drilling to see if rumor had made a tree out of a twig, as it usually does."

"Not always," she said in a grim voice.

He searched her face, saw that she was not angry with him, and said, "Well, and so I watched. And they *are* good. So good that I couldn't even tell you what it is they do, except swing lances until they hum, and throw one another using what seems to be a thumb and a knee, and ride like they were stuck to the horse's back. I couldn't see the least error, but they sure could, because at the end, your brother called two of them out, and whipped them himself. He didn't use a stick, the way the tutors did in my grandfather's day. He used a short leddas whip, and the boys stood still for it, then went to the ensorcelled bucket to wipe the blood off. Then they put their shirts back on and went right back to work, though I saw one of them faint not long after. I hope he didn't get beaten for that."

"No, he wouldn't," Tharais said. "There is a limit even to their—oh, call it methods. Or so I understand. No one is permitted to see what happens at the Academy. No one. But I know this: to stay in the Academy—to work for the chance to be chosen for the First Lancers— they will do anything. And so the last finished in any drill gets beaten, and he who makes an error also. Even my brother. Especially my brother, until he learned to never be last. And to never make mistakes."

"But someone has to be last, right? Stands to reason!"

"The ideal is they all finish together. Without error."

Geral leaned toward her and whispered, "But I think some of them are women."

Tharais couldn't help a laugh, but she turned it into a hiccough. "Three."

"Women," he repeated. "And they get the . . . beatings?"

"If they aren't fast enough," she said. She added, as he turned his head aside, "They don't take off their shirts, but everything else is the same. Geral, they choose to train. The competition is terribly strict, but it's an honor. They have to be as strong as the fellows. Which is probably why you couldn't tell the difference at casual glance." And when he continued to look troubled she added, "This is why I don't talk much about my home. It's different, there. You don't know what life there is like. Please don't judge."

Geral pleated his fingers, looking very like a guilty young boy. "I won't. But I wish I hadn't seen your brother do that."

"Since you have," Tharais said, "it makes it a whole lot easier to ask a question that my aunt and I have been mulling over for a year now. And you were the one I hoped to put it to, if I could find a way."

Geral looked hopeful.

"You have to understand that I love my brother," Tharais said, as they skirted a pond in which silvery fish leapt and splashed. Frogs sang a pleasantly lugubrious note. Oh, she would adore living here! But. "He's always been good to me. No matter what his summers were like, he always was the first to greet me when I came home for my winter visits, and always had a surprise for me. And rough as his friends were, he never let them tease or bully me. With me he was . . ." She looked away, "He was. . . at his best with me, you see, which is what leads me to my question. Is there a smart, strong princess you know of looking out for marriage? You've traveled all over this end of the continent, you must know someone who isn't already taken."

"It has to be a princess?" Geral raised his brows.

She sighed. "Van has to have the best, because he's had to be the best at home. Think of what you saw, then imagine it far worse. Many times worse. He has to have an equal, and the one woman who would have done—" She paused, thinking of tall, strong, hard-riding Tdiran Marlovair, but shied from that last terrible memory. "Well, it didn't work out."

"I don't think any princess would work out, not if he has to have a tall, strong, hard-riding one with anything like those skills," Geral said, guessing at least at some of what his beloved did not tell him. "*No* one I know rides like you people—boys or girls, royal or warrior. And I am willing to wager anything you care to name that no princess I've ever met has broken the Compact and drawn a bow. Though there are a couple of east coast girls who are rather good with the rapier," he amended. "But then, life is different there, you might say, because of the unending problems with pirates. However, one of them is married, and the other—" He grinned. "—won't have anything to do with boys."

Tharais sighed, and because she looked so unhappy, he said impulsively, "I have an idea. Let's ride."

A stable girl came running out, but Geral sent her away, and the two of them saddled their own mounts, Tharais quicker than any ostler.

While she performed a chore she'd been doing since she was six years old, she thought happily about her own life stretching ahead. The pretty Nelkereths she'd brought could be bred to the king's stud, and she would introduce riding games to a young court that seemed to be looking for entertainment. As soon as she could, she'd get rid of those ridiculous bell-shaped gowns (who could possibly ride in those?) and introduce riding fashions, only in fine fabrics so the daughters of counts and barons would think themselves smart.

So she was still smiling, though pensive, as they trotted out on the bridle path. At last he said, "Maybe what he needs is a different kind of princess altogether."

"What kind?"

"Well, I heard not a day before you arrived that the Queen of Colend has an heir at last. And that puts Princess Lasthavais out of inheritance. Which means Colend'll be looking about for some dynastic marriage, though no kingdom on this continent is as strong or rich as Colend—unless it be Sartor, and there are debates on that."

"Tell me about this princess. There were rumors in Shiovhan that she is beautiful, but that's what everyone says about princesses, unless they are awful, or interesting."

"You have a branch of the Dei family living at your end of the world, don't you?" Geral asked.

"Not any more. They left the south when the civil war broke out and my great grandfather took the throne. But there's a portrait in my aunt's rooms of Joret Dei, who married into the Elsarions, and I've seen sketches of Lasthavais Dei the Wanderer, or Sky Child as some call her. Oh. Has she got *those* looks?"

"Yes."

Tharais grimaced. "But if she's stupid or a stinkweed it wouldn't work. Beautiful girls are usually stinkweeds," she added, thinking of the two reigning court beauties in Enaeran.

"Recent whispers give her a reputation for being frivolous and heartless, but when I was at the Colendi court, I never found her so," Geral said. "Though she's several years younger, she was as kind to me as if I'd been the King of Sartor, instead of a visiting prince from a tiny, outlying land no one could be the least interested in. And though you could forgive a girl of sixteen for being rude to a fellow who is ugly as mud, and has a personality to match, she was even kind to that glowering Chwahir prince—who was about as ill-favored a fellow as you'd never want to see."

Tharais gave a sudden yip that caused Geral's horse to sidle, tossing its head. "Sounds better and better! We need someone at home who's strong and smart. And if she were beautiful, too, why so much the better."

"Well, the rep for heartlessness is very recent, so maybe she's changed. One thing for certain, half that court is reputed to be in love with her. Won't your brother's—" He hesitated, but briefly. "Won't it make things worse if he went courting her and, well, it didn't take?"

Tharais looked thoughtful. "Who says he has to *court* her?"

———

"There they go!"

A morning storm had been too brief to muddy up the fields to the east of Geral's palace, Athanarel; it had been enough to cool the air. Some even felt the promise of autumn in the cool breeze.

Horses thundered down the track, and again Tharais was first, the ribbon streaming behind her until she slowed, laughing as she gathered it up. Young Remalnan nobles cheered, many of them with an eye to their king. Geral grinned with pride.

Tharais shook her head when the call went out for the next horse race. She'd let two of Geral's friends ride a pair of her horses, as everyone agreed the pretty horses from Marloven Hesea were, despite their dainty heads, much faster than any others. But it was clear that you needed to know how to ride a fast horse. She'd won two races (the second so the first wouldn't seem a fluke) and then refused to run any more, though she gave those who wished it permission to ride her mounts, as long as they exhibited light hands.

Geral deeply appreciated his queen-to-be exchanging cheerful comments with the people gathered along the grassy ridge on their blankets and quilts. Two races was exactly right. Had she kept racing and winning, it was only human nature that admiration might turn to resentment.

"That was fun!" She sat down beside Geral, but as was her habit, sought her brother to assess his mood. Of course he wouldn't race against the Remalnans, but he seemed to like watching her ride—the pride of the teacher.

Ivandred turned up his palm. "Mare looks good."

There followed a detailed exchange about the demands of training versus breeding, while the last couple of races were run.

Those who had made wagers completed their exchanges, most of them being for tokens: a scarf, a pin, a ring. Then the spectators dispersed, town folk to the streets, palace folk inside to change for dinner.

Much later Macael joined them and the four gathered in Geral's personal rooms. Talk ran generally on races, roads, and traveling, and at last Tharais signaled Macael with her eyes, and he said, stretching, "I smelled autumn on the air today. Maybe it's time to ride on."

Ivandred looked over, brows lifted in question. "On?"

Macael said, "Well, what's waiting at home? A soggy month of rain shut up with the same people."

"Passes west close up with snow by Tenthmonth," Ivandred reminded him.

Macael spread his hands. "And so? What's to do at home in winter that you can't put off for a year?"

Ivandred looked down at his hands, considering the academy, his father, his magic lessons. What his father's mage, Sigradir Andaun, had said. *Get some experience of the world outside our borders, Ivandred. Getting away will do well for you and your father.* And the Herskalt who taught him magic had smiled, saying, *There is always magic transfer,* reminding him that he could not only get home fast from anywhere in the world, but he could also be found.

A summer away meant he would miss Tdiran Marlovair's wedding. He looked up.

Macael leaned forward. "Wouldn't it be more fun to go take a look at the most beautiful woman in the world?"

Ivandred looked surprised. "Who's that?"

"According to rumor, Lasthavais of Colend." Macael kissed his fingertips and flicked them out in salute. "Newly supplanted. Her old toad of a sister finally had an heir. Colend always marries off the royal siblings. That's how they gained control of half the east, you know."

Ivandred snorted. "Colend. Beauty. She'll have every prince on the continent at her feet."

Macael shrugged. "Of course. And her sister'll see she picks the richest or most powerful, but we're not looking to marry her, are we? Women are going to flock to Colend to try their hand at prince-nabbing. I say we join the merry throng, test the truth of rumor, and have ourselves a dalliance or two. Maybe add a wager to the fun."

"Wager?"

"If one of us can get this princess to kiss him."

Ivandred laughed. "You know how to talk to women of that sort. I don't."

"But you ride well. Females like that." On Ivandred's snort of disbelief, he leaned forward again. "Admit it. You'd love to give these sniff-nosed Sartor-trained snobs the back of your hand. Just think how they'd chew their pretty silks if you won a kiss."

"What language do they speak?" Ivandred asked.

"Kifelian. Colend was once a collection of Sartoran provinces. Their language is similar to Sartoran, but with a whole lot more words adopted from other languages. The best poems, supposedly, are in Kifelian, if you like that sort of thing. We can practice it on the ride north. We can even join with their court if we ride out soon—they're taking barges back from the Sartoran music festival. We'll learn their fashions and the language of ribbons."

"Language of ribbons?" Tharais asked.

"Colendi men don't wear ribbons on clothing any more, just in their hair," Geral told her. "What color you wear, and how you wear it, signifies your status in rank and romance."

Macael dropped his head into his hands. "All my pretty ribbons," he moaned. "Though if I get to keep ribbons for romance, I think I can live with that. What color ribbon signifies 'will dally with any beautiful woman'?"

"If you are free," Geral said, "you tie back this part of your hair." He grabbed the back of his own. "And let everything forward of your ears free in what they call lovelocks."

"Lovelocks," Macael repeated. "They weren't wearing those when I was there. Everyone's hair was dyed silver, and they wore it loose. No, the women had just begun to wear long ribbons in it, hanging down to their heels."

"You're obviously not up to date," Tharais said, dismissing Macael with a playful wave of her hand. "Go on." She grinned at Geral, who grinned back and continued: "Colend's court changes their clothes as often as their bells ring the hours. Anyway, if you pair off with someone exclusively, then you choose a color and both wear it in your hair, and fellows bind back their lovelocks. If a pair is exclusive, they both wear white."

"Well, that's all easy enough," Tharais said.

"Yes, but if it was that easy, then people wouldn't make mistakes that cause scandals," Geral said. "For example, the newly betrothed or married can't ribbon with another for a year. It's considered indelicate. But if it's a marriage purely for treaty, they might be ribboned with a lover or ribboned meaning they're *looking* for one. Sometimes it depends on what time of day they wear ribbons. Or not."

Macael laughed. "Symbolic ribbons! That sounds *just* like Colend."

Geral laughed. Tharais laughed. Ivandred shook his head, still grinning.

Everyone noticed he didn't say no.

After supper, when Tharais caught Macael alone, she said, "Thank you. If you can keep him away from home for the rest of the summer, well . . . you know."

Macael placed his hand over his heart, his generous mouth curving in a grin. "Yes, O Queen. Any further commands?"

She gave him a mock stern look. "Indeed. Since my brother refuses to use his unless the world is ending, you are to use that golden scrollcase of yours, and if anything at all happens with this princess, you are to write to me every single night."

Macael laughed. "I promise. But you know, I did wonder about his never using his scrollcase. He's learned some spells—he could even *make* one—so it can't be a matter of not trusting magic."

Macael's laughter vanished at Tharais's grim expression. So grim, her resemblance to Ivandred was unsettling.

She said softly, "He has it in case the world ends. The world, to him, being home."

NINE

OF WATER AND MAGIC

The summer that everything changed, we traveled to Sartor in the company of the compassionate Lady Darva, her younger sister Lissais, and several others.

We Colendi have a word for the grief of a broken romance, which is a play on "river" and "tears." Until that year I thought the "river" meant only the quantity of tears (which would be true) but I came to understand that it also meant the ceaseless flow of grief-stricken words. In private, Lasva talked about Kaidas, endlessly, examining every turn of his head, the exact meaning of every smile, his tone as well as his speech.

In public, Lasva spoke social nothings from Alsais all the way south to the aromatic pine forest of Barhoth, always endeavoring to smooth the ribbons of conversation that Ananda tangled. Ananda was still angry that Kaidas had actually married Carola. Young Gaszin was too experienced to exhibit any sign of emotion for the entertainment of court, but those who knew him best remarked on the sharpness of his sarcasm.

Then things changed, and the blame is mine.

One rainy day, as Lasva repeated every motion and word of a conversation that I had already discussed exhaustively with her, I thought, *So much for the reality of human passion,* as I clenched my teeth hard on a yawn, my eyes watering. I would swear that I showed no sign of how stifled I felt that humid day, but Lasva must have seen, or sensed it. She tipped her head in that considering way, murmured that she was tired and, thereafter, all we got from her was the same superficial politeness she gave the world.

For one day, it was a relief, but then Marnda and I hovered in worry, striving to find little ways to please Lasva, to win a genuine smile, to ease the unexpressed suffering from her gaze. Guilt kept me awake nights.

When we reached the lakeside town Pirun, she began practicing the Altan fan form alone in her room, sometimes to music played by hired musicians, other times accompanied only by the sound of rain, or the river beneath the windows.

The day after our arrival was Restday, so everyone was free. I set out for a long walk, grieved that I had failed Lasva when she needed me most. I stepped down from an arched bridge, examining a window that overlooked that bridge. It was so beautiful a scene but the shutters were closed, carved with ancient acanthus-leaf patterns blurred by wind, weather, and time. Why would the inhabitants not look out?

It's like Lasva, I thought, and made a vow to bring her outside the prison of her grief.

I returned, and it became my turn to talk endlessly—about the gardens growing aromatic blossoms both familiar and strange, about what kind of life people might have when most of the town was comprised of inns that catered to the yearly pilgrimage to the Sartor festival.

Lasva listened but gone was the delight of past years, the questions and debate. When I offered information she thanked me, but the subject died after her gratitude. I had become another social obligation. I don't think she was punishing me. I don't think she was aware. She had fallen into so deep a reverie, emerging occasionally to read and reread a book of poems that she had copied out herself; they belonged to the old seasonal mode, but they were really poems about sorrow.

From Pirun we transferred by magic to Lirendi House in Ilderven, which was owned by Colend's royal family. As soon as I recovered from the wrench of magic transfer, I ran to fetch and sort through all the waiting correspondence. In the front vestibule—a plain room tiled in blue and white that served as a weather buffer—was a large shallow bowl carved from pink marble into which city runners and personal pages put letters. In Sartor they do not fold notes into shapes. They merely crease them into thirds and close them with a blob of wax, stamped with a signet or carved seal.

Among the many notes to Lasva there was one for me, from Greveas, who had been watching for sign of our arrival.

Emras: there's a new fad this year. They're carrying decorated albums around, filled with sketching papers, on which they are to draw one another while listening to the music. You'll want to have one ready—come as soon as you can.

Early the next morning, I hunched into my cloak as I hurried through the nearly empty streets.

Ilderven's buildings are commonly five and even six stories, unlike Alsais's, which are never more than three. Ilderven is mostly bare stone—shades of gray, warm sand, honey-brown, even a reddish rock that contrasts beautifully against the dark green pine forest on the mountain slope north of the city. The closer you get to the palace, the more marble you find.

I'd turned two corners and was heading toward the double spire above Twelve Towers, when I heard my name above the splash of my feet.

"Emras!"

I stopped at the running approach of a tall fellow wearing outlandish clothes. His round cheeks glowed with effort. Round little nose. Button chin—

"Olnar?" I gazed up in disbelief at my brother, who'd left the scribes for the magic school when I was six. I'd seen him only intermittently since, and he'd grown at least a hand since I saw him last.

"You shrank, Em," Olnar said, grinning.

"What are you doing here?" I exclaimed.

"I've leave. Mother thought you might be here. I was heading for Lirendi House when I saw you bolt out like a horse from a barn, and I've been running after." Olnar looked strange to me with that short tunic of shale blue coming to mid-thigh, worn over loose dun trousers tucked into low blue-weave boots. "It's winter up north. Haven't had a chance to change."

Up north—he meant on the other side of the world.

"Where are you running off to?" he asked.

"Guild. There's a new fashion—"

"What?" he exclaimed. "Sartor doesn't *have* fashions. They repair and redo and replant, but it looks like it did a thousand years ago."

The surprise encounter had shocked my wits into a tangle. I glanced around wildly, for I could not speak of my foremost problem—the desire to distract Lasva from her private grief—and my gaze caught the stylized knotwork in the corbel above us, a motif echoed in the collar around a gargoyle across the street. "Isn't this city amazing? I wonder how old yon bird-creature is. And if it represents something real."

"You'd be surprised what lives in the north, especially the wilds of Helandrias," Olnar said grimly, eyeing me. "So what's this fashion that seems to have you running from shadows?"

"Sketching albums. They're sketching one another this year, while they listen to the music."

"Why don't you just send a page to the bookmakers for a bound book, and come to breakfast with me?"

I frowned at him. "Is this a hint that you find my work frivolous?"

"Ah-yedi, sister! Enlighten me." He tapped his fingers together in peace mode.

"Olnar, she's a princess. What album she'll carry reflects on me. I need to see the paper, the covers, and the ribbon marker, and I'll want to make certain the binding is good." It was reasonable, it was true, and it also concealed my worry about Lasva.

Olnar rocked back on his heels, squinting up at the crouching owl creatures staring down with hooded stone eyes. Mist beaded on his eyelashes. "Ah-ye," he said. "So it has to be the best. And even if everyone else throws theirs away as soon as they get home, she's a princess—maybe even heir—so hers becomes an artifact."

"She's not the heir anymore."

"I'm behind in southern news. Ah-yedi! I will come along with you, and we can catch up."

He fell in step beside me as I told him briefly about Princess Alian's birth.

At the end, he peered down into my face, furrowing his nondescript eyebrows so like mine. "You're hiding something. If you talk about something else, your tone is normal. As soon as our conversation touches the princess, you go flat. Em, I hope your heart is not given."

"Heart-given!" I hiccoughed on a surprised laugh. "My heart is ungiven, and so is hers," I said. "It's just that . . . things are difficult right now."

"With her losing a crown? I can imagine."

My tongue shaped the words to deny that, then I hesitated again. Why not let him believe it? The world probably did.

So I sought another subject and found one. "Now the problem becomes all the suitors everyone expects. But I can leave that to the queen.

And the Grand Seneschal, who will have to find room for them. Olnar, why magic? When I asked you before, all you'd tell me was that I'd find out later. Cousin Tiflis and I both found that very condescending."

Olnar grinned. "It's an odd thing. I know your age, but in my mind you are still six."

We dodged around a party of workers carrying bits of scenery—looked like a false castle—across the square. Then I said, "Can you tell me now?"

"It was a girl," Olnar admitted. "I'd passed my Fifteen late, so I was near sixteen by the time the practice rotations put me at the palace relay desk."

"Oh, that was so tedious," I said, remembering that month of monitoring the ensorcelled tile to which magically transferred messages were relayed. We had to note in a log book when messages were received, and who they were for, then file them in the slotted shelves against the wall.

"There was a mage student on pickup rotation. Never mind her name. Our passion faded within a month, which is to be expected at sixteen. But in that month I found every excuse I could to delay her, and so I asked questions about magic. The more I heard, the more I got interested in it. We stayed friends, and so, when I was hauled in for my career discussion that next winter, and I asked about transferring to scribe mage, she was the one who showed me around. I'm a full mage now," he said, taking me by surprise. "Happened just this spring. I've a head for spells, it turns out. But we don't write about what we do in letters. So I tell Mother and Father what I can, and you know how discreet they are."

We'd reached the boulevard lined with venerable linden trees, one over from Quill Street. "So tell me how magic works. I know that spells do different things—you have to gabble Old Sartoran codes and make comic gestures."

Olnar frowned. "Emras! You know mages don't talk about it. They must have told you that a hundred times in scribe school."

I sighed. "I do not want the secrets of spells, I only want to know how it works. But if you cannot tell me even that . . ." I made the formal Peace.

And my brother blushed. "Well, there's no harm in generalities," he said, and I tried not to see condescension in that. "Shall I come with you, since I've the time? I miss fine paper and inks, I have to admit."

"I would be delighted in your company. Please, go on, if you will."

"So. Generalities only! Think of magic potential as a giant lake. Got that image?"

"Yes."

"And magic is the water."

That seems obvious, I thought, but I only repeated, "Yes."

"You're standing at the edge of the lake. You're thirsty, but you haven't a cup, or a thimble, or even hands. You have no lips. How do you drink?"

"I guess I don't."

"Our ancestors—so we are told—used to be able to think magic into action. But we need the lips to sip, and the cup, and the hands to hold the cup. That's what spells are: the lips, hands, and cup. The water is still water—its nature doesn't change—but we need all these things to get and use it."

We'd reached the corner of Quill Street, with Twelve Towers Archive on one side, the Scribe Guild on the other, and the royally appointed paper and book makers on either side.

"We used to hear warnings about Norsunder, the land of death beyond time, and their use of dark magic. 'Dark' meaning that its uses are evil, sending magic out of the world. But it made little sense. How can you send anything out of the world?"

"Think of steam—ah-ye, that's not right, for steam beads up into water again. Think of the water boiling dry, and forget the steam. Think of the danger of the fire that is doing the boiling."

"So boiling a pan dry is evil?"

Olnar rubbed his hands together as he squinted up at the statues of ancient writers. "It's not evil itself, but most of those who use that kind of magic—no safeguards and spending it profligately—use it for evil purposes. And use it faster than nature can replenish it."

"So light magic doesn't spend it faster than it can be replaced?"

"Correct—which is where the word 'light' comes in, from the sun that returns each day. Light magic is used in small amounts. Bound to the thing being made or protected. Slowly it leaches back into the lake over time. It isn't burned up, as in a house consumed by conflagration. That's why all our things need to be respelled over and over."

"So you go around renewing bridge spells, and road protections, and binding spells on walls and roofs?"

"I have done so," he said slowly. "All this last year. But I'm training for wards."

"I hear about wards. At borders. But not what they do."

"They are invisible walls to keep out specific types of spells." He made the flat hand gesture once used to negate spywell enchantments. "They can be as wide as a kingdom or as small as a single person.

Kingdom-wide wards are built by a team of mages, working together. Those are the most powerful ones. Except the wards that put things beyond space, which is what banks use."

I had never thought about banks, for I would never have a fortune to be kept for me. Banks in Alsais are run by a branch of the heralds, their storage all being shifted to magical space.

"And so Norsunder is not just a story to frighten children. It really exists—beyond time and place," I said, hunching my shoulders when I saw how his mouth tightened.

"Oh, it exists," he said in a low voice. "And the lords of it really are thousands of years old. And they really do smite you with a thought. But they seldom come into the world we know. We're taught that the resumption of the pull of time and the weight of existence in the material world exact a cost even on them."

We'd stopped in the street outside of the Guild. "Oh, I want to hear more. But I do not wish to miss Greveas."

"Greveas," he repeated.

"She gets up early—ah-ye! You know her?"

He shrugged. "We met. Look, your selection will require thought and attention. How about we try to meet again when you really are free, before I leave? We can catch up on family news without having to worry about duty."

Of course I agreed. I gazed after him, wondering if Greveas had been a girl in his life. That was the only explanation I could think of for his sudden change of mind.

TEN

OF FIRE AND WATER

I n her private diary, Countess Darva of Oleff wrote later that summer:

You must remember, my darling grandchildren, or grandchildren of my grandchildren—whoever reads this—I cannot know what fashion will decree in heralding the movements of courtiers by the time you are born, but in my day we all had handsome panels that attached to the sides of our coaches, and when we wanted our movements publicly known, the panel was taken off and hung on a hook outside the castle, or palace, or suitable posting inn, proclaiming our presence. On our river and canal barges, the panels hung from the taffrail: the most important in the middle, and the others moving outward by rank and degree.

So you see the picture, my dears? We are at a posting house along the Margren River at Arva, at the very southwest corner of Colend. This is a large affair built of pale, patterned brick and decorative stone, located above Great River Fork, and there along the low roof are all our panels, including that of Princess Lasthavais, and behind the inn are gathered the prettiest coaches we can afford, for it's here that we will leave the river and start eastward toward home.

Then rides up, in the sort of military formation you only heard about in very old songs, a group of young men, most with braided hair the color of sunflowers, wearing these plain coats of servant gray that were not cut like anything our servants wear: made tight to their arms and chests, high at the neck, but the skirts long and full, down to the tops of their high blackweave boots. And, oh my dear you would never believe the horses! Riding at the front, all dressed in black except for the golden buckle on his belt, is their leader, who stops his horse and raises his hand.

The foremost rider throws a javelin to strike down into the ground before the inn door. Attached to that javelin is a peculiar banner—a length of cloth, all black with a fox face on it—a strange sort of fox that almost looks like a hunting bird, a ruff fanned around its head in pet- als shaped like flames.

And I knew at the very moment that javelin struck the ground that everything in our lives was going to change.

Hindsight, of course, is always accurate in prediction.

The Countess did not lie. She was there and saw Ivandred's personal runner throw down the javelin bearing the Montredaun-An fox banner— which had, historically, been the heir's and was again, now that they were back on the throne of Marloven Hesea.

The Countess, her younger sister Lissais, and Ananda Gaszin had been walking about on a shaded knoll under carefully tended fruit trees, glad to stretch their legs after the long barge journey. Each carried her travel album. On seeing the newcomers they all stopped, the albums' tassels dancing in the wind as the ladies took in the blue-eyed leader.

The other fellow was not as exotic, though perhaps more dashing; taller, handsome, with a generous smiling mouth, his blond hair worn loose. And he was dressed in the latest fashion: dupion silk woven in green and blue, edged with silver braid.

A short time later Ivandred stood in the center of a spacious chamber, the walls hung in pale green watered silk, the quilt matching, a copper bath in a small room adjacent, with tiled knobs that released magical spells summoning (and later transferring underground) heated water. Ivandred, scrutinizing that bath, was impressed. At home, posting houses and castles had general baths in great pools siphoned off from under- ground streams, with the water-heating and cleaning spells on them.

"Will it suffice?" asked his cousin, Prince Macael.

Ivandred glanced aside, a hand still on the copper rim. "Fine. I don't know about that bed, though. Looks like a whole lot of pillows. Stifling."

"Then sleep on the carpet." Macael cast himself gratefully into a chair. "No one will know, unless you invite someone in. But you'd better get rid of the day's sweat and dress for dining, unless you want to lose our wager by offending the princess's pretty nose."

Dress for dining. Ivandred reflected on that as his cousin shut himself into the bath. At home they dressed for dining once a year, on New Year Week's Firstday, after he stood behind his father's throne and listened to the jarls renew their vows. He wore the same battle tunic every year, handed down from his grandfather.

Ivandred approached the empty fire place and raised both hands, concentrating as he intoned a spell. Heat built behind his eyes, his teeth vibrated, the sense of danger increased rapidly but he pictured the spell held between his outstretched hands, finished the words of power, and—

There! Flames shot up the flue. He clapped his hands lightly and spoke the word of quittance. The flames went out, leaving the acrid tinge of hot stone.

Too slow, he thought as he opened the window, and fresh air off the river scoured out the smoke. If only he had time to practice!

———

When we first arrived at the inn, Darva had watched Lasthavais's blue gaze read the salon as if a written record, for she was always kind to those excluded, or troubled in countenance. It was this quality, remarkable in one so young, and not her beauty, that made Darva love the princess.

Lasva was emerging from her bath when Darva called.

When I told Lasva who had requested to see her, she assented, but with that blank smiling countenance that had become painfully familiar. We entered the small outer chamber together.

Darva observed, "The day has been long."

"The summer has been long. I am grateful for any signs of autumn's approach," Lasva was tired enough to admit.

Darva curtseyed. "I told the innkeeper to send for musicians. Until they come, we have been reminiscing over the drawings."

In other words, Darva promised her a peaceful evening, if she could contrive it.

I was glad. Too many evenings we'd spent shut in, Lasva lost in reverie as I contrived to keep myself busy until it was time to retire.

As for her reverie, here is what she was thinking when she withdrew to dress for the evening and stood looking down at her fans. *How strange.* For a moment she saw the familiar fans as bizarre objects. *I think about which I shall choose and what message that sends, and I use it to say things I cannot voice.* Some things you couldn't say even with a fan, such as how much she hated Ananda's angry obsession with the news from Alarcansa. *I'd thought that was idle attraction. Was it more, did Ananda love Kaidas, too?* Lasva thought, her fingers tracing up and down each fan, then back again. *Do we share a grief?*

Ananda wrote every day to her cousin in Alarcansa, who was connected to a baron there. It was as if she could not forbear plucking at a healing wound. She insisted on uttering daily bulletins in a wicked voice, mocking Carola and her newly wedded duke with his hair tied back in a white ribbon.

Lasva never answered the slanders or joined the mirth at Carola's and Kaidas's expense.

She tried to wish he'd found love, but it was her mind exhorting her heart without effect. She dreaded seeing him again and picked up a fan at random, moving away as if she could leave the familiar pain behind. "Emras, do you have my album? Thank you."

We walked out, silence between us.

"The dining rooms are that way," Macael said to Ivandred as they walked downstairs. He pointed with his thumb in one direction, along a carpeted hallway with inlay paneling. "The private ones have closed doors, my man told me. The one at the end, double doors open, is for anyone who didn't request private dining."

"Private dining," Ivandred repeated, entertained by the notion. "If the princess is dining in private then we won't see her. Why don't we sup with my riders?"

Macael shook his head. "We should join Nanvo and the boys in the public dining room, and practice our Kifelian. We all need it," he added.

Ivandred could not argue with that. He'd discovered on the month-long ride north and east that Geral had been right. The language itself was deceptively easy to learn, for it was related to Sartoran. But the way people spoke it was quick, curiously drifting, with convoluted tenses whose meaning was difficult to grasp without reflection, and word clusters separated by pauses that appeared to convey yet another layer of meaning. In addition to that, these courtiers seemed to sing, almost, the way their voices rose, fell, paused, with drawn-out vowels that sometimes changed notes.

At times, the language seemed less like expression and more like code.

I stepped back to permit Lasva an unimpeded view of the inn's main salon, which had been hired by the Duchess of Gaszin. Lasva returned bows and curtseys, her fan held open at the neutral Anticipation of Artistic Pleasure, giving a smile and polite word here and there, as she made her way across to the room to the table by the fire.

The focus of this side of the room was Lord Rontande, whom I had quite unreasonably hated ever since he used my desk without asking and hurt Lasva by his ambition. I knew he was no worse than any others, and some said he was better than most. But experience shapes emotion.

His hair was dark again, contrasting with his robes of a subtle straw hue. He was holding forth to Darva's smiling sister Lissais, another popular lord, and a very bored Ananda, leaving a young lady new to court sitting all alone.

"May I see your album?" Lasva asked Farava as she took her place on a satin couch next to her.

Farava blushed and handed it over. The Duchess of Sentis cast Lasva a grateful look for this attention to her niece, but Lasva did not see it as she bent over the silk-bound album.

Lasva leafed through the heavy, crackling pages of finest rice paper, looking at the sketches of Farava, ranging widely in skill (and in the case of the written ones in wit), halting at one marked with a golden ribbon. There was a fast but well-executed sketch not only of tall, thin Farava, her merry brown eyes caught by a masterly hand, but in the background, Lasva discovered a sketch of herself, standing pensively framed in a window. No, a mirror, and she wore a lace mask. But her gown was unmistakable.

"That was at the Twelfth Night Masque. Isn't that a wonderful drawing?" Farava whispered, leaning forward. And, in an under-voice, "He said I am as beautiful as a princess, which is why he sketched you and me together like that."

Sketches of masks and mirrors conveyed their own hidden meaning.

The drawing was not signed, except by a quick semblance of a coronet: the younger Landis prince.

Marry me, he'd said to Lasva, bending over her chair and laughing as if I was not seated within arm's length. But then scribes are supposed to be invisible. *We are so alike*, he'd whispered.

Perhaps they were, in mirrored rooms and decorated with court masks, but not in the realm of the spirit, or he would have seen that her acknowledging the truth of his remark did not admit of it being a compliment.

"If I have to marry, it will not be to a mask," she had said to me as soon as he moved away. That was the first observation she'd offered in days.

Lasva paused, bending a little closer to Farava's album as she stared down at an arrestingly beautiful likeness of Farava, each eyelash, the glimmer of light on her ear-gems, all lovingly and faithfully rendered. "Oh. How brilliant."

"I love it the best," Farava whispered.

Lasva's brows rose in surprise at the initials below: R.A. for Rontande Altan. She had not known that moody, wayward Rontande had found someone to train him to far better skills than the days of his cat sketches. What surprised her more was that his ignoring of Farava was not cruel intent but protection against idle gossip.

"You know he's painting a great mural for his cousins at Altan Castle?" Farava asked.

"My dear, recall that the princess has spent her life surrounded by work from the best artists in the world," the Duchess of Sentis put in, drawing attention to royalty seated with her niece, as Rontande bowed ironically in the background.

"Such as that of Mazin Phee," came Ananda's voice, brittle as glass.

Lissais sat down beside Farava, her light gray eyes wide with interest. "I heard before I left that the queen hired Phee to paint the royal princess on her first Name Day!"

"By then he ought to be finished with his present . . . challenge," Ananda said, deep quirks on either side of her pouting mouth.

Lasva had turned her head, and I knew she wished she was elsewhere.

Rontande flipped his fan up before one eye for just a heartbeat, and Farava was too young to resist displaying her curiosity. "What? What is it that makes you smile?"

Ananda's fan dipped into Art is Eternal but mocked the pose with a questioning flick. "My cousin Suzha had the news two days ago from Tatia Tittermouse. It seems that the Icicle Duchess hired Phee to paint the newly wedded pair—in the fashions of Lasva Sky-Child and King Mathias the Builder." Her fan arced at a plangent angle, a mockery of Becoming Modesty.

"Oh!" Lissais and Farava said together, stunned into silence.

Lissais whispered behind her fan, "She's not *that* beautiful."

A baroness whispered back, "But some think *he* is." Her fan twirled slowly in Ananda's direction. "I don't see how. Those Lassiters are as raw-boned as the horses they prize so much."

Ananda stilled then caught a slack-lidded, warning glance from her mother, the Duchess of Gaszin.

"I understand we're to have music," Lady Nollafen spoke up from her chair near the duchess, her fan fluttering in the Heedless Youth mode. "Where can the musicians be?"

The Duchess of Sentis rose, smoothing the silken layers of her robes. "I believe I will seek the music of the river. A walk would be refreshing."

Though her tone was kind, the rebuke was felt by the Duchess of Gaszin, who sent her daughter Ananda a long glance.

Ananda gazed over her fan—trailing ribbons of the pale gold called Summer Thunder.

Lasva smiled at Farava. "Let's see who else admires you," she said into the silence, turning over the next leaf of the album with enough deliberation to shift attention, although she longed to be back on the river, watching the moon trail liquid light over the dark waters, far from Ananda's scalding whisper, *Alarcansa . . . Alarcansa . . . Alarcansa.*

Lasva forced herself to listen as Farava told every detail of the parties she'd attended with her elusive, complicated cousin, now betrothed to the equally romantic Lord Adamas, second son of the problematic Dei family.

". . . and I hear they will combine their names. Dei-Sentis. It sounds . . . historic," Ananda said.

"Well, you know that the Deis have married into royal families," Farava was saying. "In fact, someone in Sartor said that they have more royal blood than any other family."

"*King-makers but never kings,*" Rontande drawled. "But the Deis seem to be the more romantic for all that."

Lasva turned the subject yet again, and Darva sat back, staring at Ananda's fan and its ribbons swaying to and fro, as she contemplated the lingering poison of Carola Definian. She did not understand: why pursue and then bind a man who shows no interest? Was it *because* he showed no interest?

It sounded too simple, as it sounded too simple to attribute Carola's obsessive and barely hidden hatred of the princess to mere jealousy. Carola had more power than the princess did and her own wealth, yet all spring Darva was convinced that Carola had whispered evil of the princess through that tittering, tittupping cousin of hers: imputations, questions, hints that together besmirched Lasva's reputation, painting a distorted image of her as a heartless flirt. Carola had taken up the pale gold as tribute to her own coloring, determined to make *summer thunder* her personal sigil; Ananda was just as determined to keep *summer thunder* as the fashion of Lasva's Roses.

Lasva did not see the sketches though her head was bent and her hand leafed the pages. After a proper time she returned Farava's album and glanced wearily past the row of soberly dressed people carrying their musical instruments. She *must* hope Kaidas was happy. She did not want him hollowed out by the memory of passion the way her body, mind, and spirit seemed hollowed out.

How she missed his touch, the sound of his voice, the sweet fire of *rafalle!* Her gaze drifted to a stir inside the doorway, and her weariness gave way to mild interest. People parted, their attention on the musicians, and a few on the newcomers, in particular a pale-haired young man dressed all in black.

Lasva gazed as he sauntered to the doorway with a heart-catching swinging stride, and lightning struck.

But it was not lightning, for there was no thunder, or rain, or burn. The shock was entirely inside her skull, leaving her staring witlessly at a pair of eyes that were not black, but pale blue, the exact shade of Skya Lake's deep-winter ice.

ELEVEN

OF SUMMER THUNDER

I vandred and Macael followed six musicians into the music room as the crowd stirred to make way for the entertainers. Ivandred scanned the room, looking for the remarkable Dei features that occasionally appeared every couple of generations, and there she was.

Ivandred stopped dead, staring.

The first impression was of blue and silver complementing warm shades of brown skin in a perfect oval face framed by curling dark hair threaded with glints of gold. Extravagant winged brows arched over brilliant eyes the dense blue of a summer sky over the plains. Dark lashes lifted, and their gazes met.

Sound and sense vanished, leaving only the drum of his heart against his ribs.

"Come along," Macael urged. "We're direct in the doorway."

Ivandred was nearly dizzy, so sudden was the shift from deafness to being acutely aware of people to either side of him, waiting for him to cease blocking the doorway.

He shifted as the musicians bustled about, four bearing wind instruments of various sizes, one with a twelve-stringed tiranthe, and another brandishing a percussive tambour with bells around it, which he rang to gain attention.

The musicians took up a station opposite the fireplace, and struck up a lively melody. More people entered, drawn by the music, until the room became quite crowded.

Ivandred elbowed Macael and jerked his head toward the door.

Outside the air was much cooler, the sound only some night birds, and the rush of the river downslope from the back of the inn. He could breathe again.

"Don't you want to stay and talk to her?" Macael asked. In the reflected light from the long row of windows Macael looked interested, even amused, but not the least stricken by desire.

"Hear her talk first," Ivandred said. His skin hurt, and his heartbeat thundered in his ears. "Later."

"For once rumor was, if anything, stingy," Macael offered. How strange these things were! Here he was, a practiced flirt, but he had not managed to garner more than a distracted glance from the princess, whose face and form transcended rumor. But his appreciation was aesthetic.

Ivandred, who had obviously shared that thunderbolt of instant attraction—so very, very rarely did it go equally both ways—did not answer.

Lasva said, "Emras, will you find out who they are?"

Alone of the Colendi, who had been busy finding seats for the music, I'd seen the *zalend* in his face. And when I turned to Lasva, I found it mirrored in hers. Not *rafalle*, this was something different. Purely physical, for they had not exchanged a word.

I hoped that the two young men had scribes with them, for that would make my task easier. As it turned out, I did not need that middle step, for the same moment I left the salon, Macael re-entered the inn.

He cast his gaze over the knots of people in the hall, and when he saw me, his eyebrows lifted. "Ah," he said. "Scribe, right?" He spoke Sartoran with an accent.

"I am." I recognized the signs of superior rank, and wondered how to politely demand his name. "Scribe Emras, in service to Princess Lasthavais of Colend."

He smacked his hands together and rubbed them, grinning. "Am I the best, or am I not?"

"The best what?" I said, hiding laughter and surprise.

"At finding the right person at the right time. So." He looked down at me, his lazy lids narrowing as if he, too, was hiding laughter. "You wouldn't happen to have been sent to find out who we are? Who *he* is." He jerked his thumb over his shoulder toward the double doors, opened to let in the cool summer air. "I saw that look of hers. Didn't even know that my handsome self was in the room. Or alive. Whew! We call that 'the clap of thunder' at home."

There was no protocol for this moment, so I fell back on decorum. "Her highness gave me a task."

Macael chuckled. "Scribal discretion! I recognize it from home. Come on outside. It's cooler. He's gone. You talk to me, I'll talk to you. How's that?"

He took my arm, the way he'd take that of a friend. I pulled away, saying, "I was sent on a simple task."

Macael flashed a knowing grin. "I'm not going to pry anything out of you that you don't want to give. I know how tight-lipped you scribes are, though I also know you and the heralds have got everyone's secrets scribbled down somewhere. Never mind, I won't figure in any histories. Too fatiguing. But people are starting to take an interest in you and me standing here like this."

It was true. A few speculative glances were cast our way from servants passing to and fro and even from courtiers. There was Rontande, lips pursed, strolling arm in arm with another courtier. So I walked outside with a prince, uneasy and curious all at once.

He gestured toward the grassy knoll nearby, where earlier the Countess Darva and others had observed the arrivals.

"I am Macael Elsarion, second son to the Queen of Enaeran," he said. "And in a complicated web of intermarriages that would bore anyone but the heralds, a cousin to Ivandred Montredaun-An, heir to the throne of Marloven Hesea." He tipped his head toward the door.

"Marloven Hesea," I repeated. He did not say "Hes-ay-ah" in our manner, but "HESS-yah."

"Yes, and what you're not saying is, 'Those barbarians?' Or maybe, 'Oh no, I'd better run before those nasty Compact-ignoring Marlovens shoot me.'" He grinned, his teeth showing briefly in the light pouring from the row of open windows. "Am I right?"

"I know very little about that side of the continent," I said diplomatically and bowed. "Thank you for the information, your highness."

Macael was rubbing his shoulder, evolving an idea. "And what you've heard is probably pretty bad. Look. You've heard of Elgar the Fox, right?"

I stopped, surprised by this unrelated question. "Of course I have."

"Bet you didn't know he was not only real, he was a Marloven."

"He wasn't real," I said with conviction. "No more real than Peddler Antivad, he of the folk tales. We studied Elgar the Fox as a lesson in how kingdoms borrow myths to bolster their own history. You will find that he's claimed by every kingdom from Khanerenth to Bermund and Bren."

"He was," Macael stated, "a distant relation of mine. No, I can see you don't believe that. Then how about this. You've heard of a book written by another of my ancestors, *Take Heed, My Heirs*, right?"

"It is a memoir by the Adrani king several centuries ago, the same king who married an ancestral connection of my princess. Her name was Joret Dei."

He applauded lightly. "*Take Heed, My Heirs* is required reading for all princes except your Colendi royals, no doubt."

"I think they read it, too," I said.

"Interesting. My point is, you know it was written by a specific king—in fact, another ancestor of mine. Far more direct, I can show you the records, if you like. That is, if I could go to Nente and not be arrested on sight, because of the split between us and the Adranis. But I know the record is there, and so is the fact that King Valdon Shagal wrote it for Elgar the Fox's wife. She ended her life in Nente, though she was a Marloven."

I said, "That is very interesting, thank you."

He went on as if I hadn't spoken, "And she talked about having read another record of Elgar's life, written by one of Ivandred's ancestors. His name wasn't actually Elgar, by the way. It makes interesting reading, if you like adventure. I even happen to have a copy, right here, with me— because Van's sister translated it as a gift for her new husband. She gave me her work draft, before she copied it out fair."

I hesitated, trying to find a diplomatic way of saying *So what does this information have to do with me?*

Macael gave me a wry grin. "I'm telling you this because Van's my cousin, and the farther east I get, the more I hear about barbarians. If your princess wants to meet him, well, it occurred to me, here's something about his people that she might find interesting. Maybe even help his cause a little—boost his prestige. I know you Colendi are proud of your famous ancestors. Well, everyone is. If they have 'em."

He made a quick gesture, expressive of regret, even embarrassment.

I'd been thinking rapidly. Lasva had shown interest in something—in someone—for the first time in weeks. I had no idea if her interest would last long enough for her to wish to speak to this Prince Ivandred, but I was so glad to see an expression besides her shuttered misery that I would do anything to encourage her. And this Prince Macael cared enough about his cousin to want me to think well of him.

I said, "I would very much like to borrow it, if I may."

"Excellent. Come along. I'll give it to you right now."

He led me back to the rooms they'd taken, where servants were busy setting things to rights. The Marloven prince was not there. Macael dashed into one of the bed chambers, leaving me alone with the busy servants, who ignored me. Moments later he returned and placed a heavy scroll in my hands.

"We're riding along with the rest of you into Colend," he said. "So you can give it back any time you like. Go ahead and make a copy for yourself—my cousin is about to marry a king, so she won't care. In fact, I think she'd like this plan of mine. Share it with anyone you think might be interested. The more the better, if it helps Van's cause."

I departed and returned to Lasva, who glanced at the scroll in my hands. "This is one of their histories," I said, offering it. "It's supposed to be about Elgar the Fox, who Prince Macael insists was a real person. This was written at the same time as *King Valdon's Advice to His Son*."

"Hatahra had me read that when I was ten." She looked away from the scroll. "It was funny, but what a horrible time in history. Wars, pirates, a dreadful time—and my own ancestor, as you know, was King Lael the Recumbent." She touched her lips in the moth kiss, the sign of courtly humiliation through flattery, and I thought of the king who was known only for the excesses of his flirtations—and how he used to test for too-ambitious ladies by farting to see whose expression stayed sweet.

Lasva said, "Would you mind reading it first? You know the kind of things I like."

A week went by.

I read *An Examination of Greatness*, which was the title of the Elgar the Fox story translated by Princess Tharais. At first I'd found it difficult. Not the language, which was serviceable if old-fashioned Sartoran, but the many words not translated that hinted at a way of life that seemed impossibly foreign. And disagreeable.

Still, the "Elgar" who emerged—and the unfamiliar world underlying our familiar world—was real enough to convince me that Indevan Algara-Vayir had actually lived, and so, following impulse, I began to copy his history out in fine script. After a page or two of that stilted Sartoran, I decided to translate it into Kifelian.

We saw Prince Ivandred twice more, as he and his silent riders paced us from a distance. Lasva was always surrounded by Darva and Ananda and the others. Their second encounter was too brief to record—except for the way their gazes met then quickly shifted away—but Ivandred and Lasva's third encounter occurred at the end of that week, when a thunderstorm boiling up made everyone on the road within a half-bell's ride take shelter in a guard post above the river.

The river being the border, the guard post was not a Colendi building—we did not have such things as guard posts, except along the mountains shared with the Chwahir. It not being Colendi meant it had no comforts. So there were all these courtiers caught in a barren building with only plank tables and benches to sit at, as the storm poured all around. I stood near Lasva. Abruptly she turned around.

Later, I realized there must have been sounds—the slow tread of the Marloven heeled boots—maybe even scents, like the combination of horse and wildgrass, that signified the new arrivals. But at the time, I was surprised when she stilled, her body tense, poised in the same manner as when we met Kaidas on the Lily Gate wedding terrace early in spring. Her chin jerked up, just the breadth of a finger, and again she locked gazes with Ivandred of Marloven Hesea.

Lasva forgot the world. It was I who looked around anxiously, relieved that everyone was too busy with their own concerns, as Lasva thought about how Kaidas had brought her gradually to feel that way. This Prince Ivandred set fire to her bones by looking at her across a room.

She knew it was mere attraction, as ephemeral—and as trustworthy—as a butterfly in a wind. It had happened twice, but in crowded rooms, because when was she ever free? If she ordered them all away, the consequence would be unending inquiry, gossip, innuendo. If they were to meet and talk, it must be in private.

Dear Tiflis:

You have often asked me to be on the lookout for a likely book, or subject, that might appeal to court. I think I have such a subject. We met some foreign princes on the road. They are coming to Alsais. It could be that people will find them interesting, as one of them has as an ancestor none other than Elgar the Fox. And since the writer is dead, you wouldn't have to pay the Writer's Fee. The translation into modern Sartoran was done by Princess Tharais, soon to be queen of Remalna, who donated her draft. It was translated into Kifelian by me.

I knew Tiflis's scribe sigil. I had never trespassed by using crown funds for expensive magical transfer, but I did so now.

I wrapped up the copy I'd made, which was considerably less weighty than Macael's scroll, and sent it to Tiflis.

TWELVE

Of Horses in Flight

"Talk to her," Macael said to Ivandred a few days later.

"No. Not with these ribbon-prancers all jostling for her attention."

Macael smothered the urge to laugh. Ivandred was easily the most formidable human being Macael had ever met, heir to a kingdom at least the size of Colend, yet he was chary of speaking to the most polite princess on the continent. "What do you think she will do, bite you?"

"I'd like her to bite me," Ivandred said, flashing his rare smile. "But supposing I elbow my way into the crowd always around her, we'd have to fumble through a conversation about music, or plays, or some other thing I have no experience of, without any talk to the point."

"The point being . . .?"

Ivandred turned his hand over as he squinted up to assess the weather. The morning breeze was cool, bearing a hint of winter each time the sun passed behind fluffy clouds. "I want to talk to her alone," he said finally. "She doesn't walk out alone."

Macael could have left it at that. He was sorely tempted. But he'd promised Tharais. "Did you do treasure hunts for your Name Day celebrations?"

"No." Ivandred did not explain that his Name Day had never been celebrated, probably (so his aunt had told him, because there was no written record) because on the day his father came of age he had killed Ivandred's grandfather.

"A treasure hunt is when you search around, find clues of various sorts, which lead to other clues, and then at the end you get your surprise."

A small forest creature darted across the road. Ivandred's mount was far too well-behaved to do more than snort and toss his head. Macael's own horse pranced, eyes rolling.

"Give me a scout report, not a guessing game."

"Well, this scout report is going to be another type of comparison. You know those drawing books all the younger courtiers are carrying around?"

Ivandred flicked his fingers in question.

"It's a fad. You purchase this bound book of drawing papers, as expensive as you can afford. When you are invited somewhere to hear music or poetry, your hosts, or guests, or companions, male or female, draw in this album while you sit and listen. The object is to do a portrait of you. It could be a written portrait, if they don't have the knack with a drawing-chalk." He paused. "You know. Poems, or the like."

Ivandred lifted his eyes, tracking a dart of birds skyward, over a field of ripening wheat. His gaze arrowed back to the cause: it was only a trio of bounding young dogs. "Go on."

"So then, it's a matter of who drew in your album, and who asked to see it after. It's a kind of social competition. Except for the princess. Everyone wanted to draw in her book. She didn't have to ask, she left it with her scribe to fetch back and forth because anywhere she went there was always a long line. See?"

Ivandred stroked his chin with his gloved thumb. "I see. Her rank puts her above everyone."

"Well, it's going to take some maneuvering to talk to her alone. The road is filling up, d'you see? And she's at the center, whether she wants to be or not, and they're all competing for her notice. Think of it as duels with words."

"One set of weapons I don't have." Ivandred opened his hand, smiling a little. "I don't even know the rules."

Macael snapped his fingers. "Don't camp with your boys tonight. There's supposed to be a play in the next town. They're all talking about it The playhouse arranged the performance in expectation of this cavalcade. You come with me. Maybe you'll see the rules better."

Ivandred agreed, and so, later that evening, after he'd seen his people camped, he rode into the town and found the central inn, located on one side of a square paved with patterned stone. Opposite the local guild hall was a huge playhouse.

He found Macael sitting on one of the many benches set under flowering trees. The air was cooling now that the sun had gone down, carrying unfamiliar scents.

"You've seen plays, right?" Macael asked as they crossed the square through crowds enjoying the rapidly fading light.

"Of course I have," Ivandred said, surprised. "We do have plays in Dhelerei. You should come over the mountains and see one some winter. Always plenty of action. Good singing of the old ballads, as well." Sometimes the ballads were so popular the entire audience would join in and maybe even insist on singing it through twice, drumming on the benches or anything to hand, before the stage battle recommenced.

Glowglobes on elegant poles lit all at once. The playhouse was much bigger than the chamber used for plays in the royal castle at home. There had once been a city playhouse, down on Harness Makers' Row. But it had been destroyed during the Olavairs' civil war and was now an armory and waystation for the city guard.

In this one, people sat on benches in the back, or in the rows and rows of plush chairs, or in boxes built into terraced balconies along the sides, affording a modicum of privacy. Macael paid for one of the last available boxes. The playhouse swiftly filled, the air permeating with the subtle blossom scents that Colendi seemed to like to wear.

The cousins pushed the empty chairs back, paid for wine, then watched as a hanging curtain was drawn aside, revealing an illusory chamber fitted up in Colendi styles.

The light was brilliant. Macael, in a whisper, pointed out what Ivandred had instinctively noticed: that Colendi public spaces eradicated shadows. But not, apparently, for reasons of security.

Before a word was spoken, already this play was utterly unlike anything at home where the opening scene would either be outside, before some castle or river location of the first battle, or else in a throne room or jarl's hall where the command to battle would be given.

Ivandred sent a considering look at his cousin. "Why did you bring me here?"

"I've been to two of these things, now, while you've been sitting around your campfire sharpening arrows or swords, or whatever it is you do. I believe this will demonstrate better than I can how they think," Macael replied, sitting back with his arms folded.

Ivandred turned his attention to the neighboring boxes and met a speculative glance from a pretty woman with a dimpled chin and brown ringlets, who promptly transferred her gaze to Macael. She whirled her fan in one of those butterfly patterns, and Macael smiled back, touching his folded fan to his eyebrow in salute.

Then the glowglobes in the audience portion dimmed, and everyone faced the stage with an air of expectation. The characters came out, one in a stiff brocade overvest, rapier at his side. He minced, nose in the air. From the other side strolled people in plainer clothing.

"I have decided to court a princess from a great land," the man in brocade declared.

"Why so far away, your lordship?" asked one of the bowing men in plain clothes. Ah—of course, a servant. Imagine putting servants on stage! In home plays, runners only appeared to deliver messages. Servants, never.

The audience laughed. No great lands near home, was that the joke?

"Hum-mumbler! Because it is the fashion," replied his lordship. "Fashion defines the man of royal rank."

The servants looked at one another and gave exaggerated shrugs. Then the second one said, "But does not the man of royal rank refine the fashion?"

The audience laughed again. What was the joke this time?

Ivandred looked around, wondering if he'd missed some action in another part of the stage. No, they were all looking at the servants. Macael watched the stage, a slight smile on his lips, the light reflecting in his eyes.

"How is that funny?" Ivandred whispered.

"Secondary meaning to 'refine' has to do with taking lovers. It's directed at some northern prince, who apparently has a rep as uncouth."

"Like me."

Macael grinned. "You don't have any rep yet. Here. Just listen."

Ivandred did. The play unfolded, not at all like the plays he knew. It wasn't even like the play he'd seen in his aunt's court before they left on their journey. That play had been about a historical event, but talky, with little sword fighting compared to the fun brawls he was used to at home.

He followed the spoken words here easily enough, but what happened on the stage was bewildering. The servants kept asking questions that the unnamed lord answered in a pompous, foolish manner, and people laughed more.

Then the scene shifted to a palace setting, and there was a woman in a spectacular rose-colored gown, also unnamed, her face hidden behind a veil. Macael whispered that any royals depicted on stage always wore veils, as well as went unnamed. But everyone knew who they were.

That had to mean they also knew who the various foolish nobles were who drawled obscure things that sent the audience into breathless mirth.

Satire. Ivandred had forgotten the concept, though he'd once known it. The idea of lampooning contemporary people, events, and ideas by putting words into the mouths of historical characters had caused riots in his own country's past and had gotten some play-makers flogged to death for treason.

Ivandred could not tell what it was in those knots of silk braid or bunches of colored ribbon that so clearly identified otherwise unnamed characters for the audience, but he could see they not only knew who was being lampooned, but somehow their manners said things about the characters. On entrance there were sometimes laughs and once a gasp, though Ivandred could not figure out why.

It ended with the buffoonish lords and servants looking foolish, the favored lords and ladies and servants pairing off, and the veiled princess in rose reigning benignly over all, without choosing a suitor—though she had not escaped satiric arrows shot her way for her wish to display suitors as art on her mantle.

And afterward? Nothing happened. No royal decrees, no duels, nothing but laughing people and whispered comments behind fans. Names flitted by, too quick for Ivandred to catch.

Macael said in his home language, "Some of the gallants represented on the stage were in the audience."

Ivandred did not ask who, or why they'd been lampooned. None of it mattered. He understood that he was not going to master the ins and outs of fashionable attire, much less the manners of fashionable people, before he met Princess Lasthavais.

He and Macael walked back across the square in silence. Then Macael said, "Well?"

Ivandred shook his head. "I need to think." He left abruptly, as he usually did.

The next morning, as always, he found Macael's group in the long cavalcade. The column trotted at a distance parallel to the roadside, like a vanguard.

Ivandred had been thinking, but he'd come to no conclusions except that he still wanted to talk to this princess, but on his own terms. Or somewhere between his terms and what he perceived as Colendi terms. This land was so strange, and as yet the real princess was veiled, like in the play, between memory and mere conjecture. In this place, with these people, he had no power but that of his hands and his brains.

Ivandred didn't see the road curving eastward with its steady procession of beautiful coaches followed by a train of baggage carts and servants in gigs, or the slow stream crossing under a bridge, the cows in the field to the left, a town far to the south. He saw Lasthavais's dense blue gaze, and even in memory its impact had not lost strength.

Macael waited, and finally Ivandred spoke.

"I will ride to Colend, but not jostling with all them." Ivandred jerked his thumb over his shoulder at two men riding side by side in an open carriage, drawn by four horses in harness, several other men following in another carriage.

Macael snorted at the sight of the high-stepping animals. "Square shoes on those poor beasts."

Ivandred huffed a laugh. Macael had been learning from the farrier, had he? Then Ivandred shrugged. Carriages that wasted four good animals—even if they'd been more wisely shod—to carry one or two, even three people made as little sense as the idea of wearing a rapier in places like inns and withdrawing rooms. Didn't matter that he'd been told it was ancient custom for escorts to go armed.

That wasn't his idea of armed. And no one fights in drawing rooms. But these courtiers dressed differently, thought differently, spoke in a different language that had very little to do with translating words.

"So what's your plan?" Macael asked.

"Ride another route. Horses need a decent run anyway, they've been walking and breathing dust off these roads long enough. I'll go to their Herskalt—"

"The royal seneschal. No. In Colend, I think they call him the Grand Seneschal."

"—whoever keeps the gate. Prove who I am. Ask for an interview, which sounds like it's as close to their rules as I know how to get. When she gets home, either she'll want to meet or she won't. If she doesn't, we'll go home." Ivandred looked around, then back. "Want to come, or stay on this road?"

Macael's own countrymen were riding at a little distance behind, talking and laughing. Ever since they discovered the truth about the hair on the helms, they had become wary around Ivandred.

Macael said, "I'll stay with my boys. That's preferable to hard riding. If the princess doesn't take notice of me, I'll find another flirt and cheer you on. One of us should win our wager."

"Anon." Ivandred lifted his gloved hand in the longed-for gesture.

His outrider blew a wild call on a horn, as Ivandred kneed his horse and thundered across the field to rejoin his column.

"Yip yip yip!" the Marlovens cried, and their horses leaped to the gallop.

Seen from the open chariot behind them, one moment the mysterious Marlovens were riding sedately in that compellingly strict formation, the next they crossed country with the speed of raptors, the horses seeming not to run through the fallow field but to soar.

Three of the Roses, riding together in a splendid coach farther back, pressed against the windows. They were like girls again.

The Sentis heir, driving himself in a single two-horse gig beside Young Gaszin's chariot, said admiringly, "Look at 'em ride!"

Young Gaszin raised his hand against the morning sun. He tracked that straight black figure with the pale hair, riding the lead horse, and thought, *Maybe this fellow will stand up to that old toad Hatahra*, for he was still certain that the queen had banished Carola of Alarcansa to her duchy the day after Midsummer, just to keep her from uniting with either him or Altan and fostering a ducal alliance.

His friends in the carriages fore and after turned his way, expecting him to make some observation, but he only shook the reins to pick up the pace. He hadn't made it to age thirty in the court most known for words being used as weapons without learning that opinions were best locked behind your teeth.

———

Later that evening, Lasva sat in an inn withdrawing room indistinguishable from all the other withdrawing rooms she'd seen on this long journey. Music, albums, who in Sartor had drawn in whose, and how much. The chatter made her head ache. She sat next to the fire, staring down into blue and red and gold snapping flames.

Here came Ananda's voice, tremulous with false laughter.

". . . and Tatia tells my cousin that Icicle Duchess has decided they will spend their autumn devoting themselves selflessly to their eternal gift to the world of art, and after that, together give a dance for the wine harvesters."

"Poor Kaidas will need some drink, eh?" Rontande observed.

"We'll have to ride up. Take some brandy to him, you think?" Jenstiar of Isqua said, laughing.

Lasva longed for solitude. Why was she so giddy? Her emotions tumbled through her mind like, well, like summer thunder: first the sharp disappointment when the word came that the Marlovens had left the road, then Ananda's refined torture as she tried to make others as angry as she was herself.

What could she do to occupy the endless stretch of time? She remembered the scroll. She was looking around for me at the very moment I experienced an internal *ping!* The tiny, silvery note was startling—I'd forgotten the queen's scrollcase, though I'd now carried it to Sartor and back several times. The queen had never used it.

Until now.

I signaled to Lasva, who retreated to her private sitting room as rain fell musically in a shallow pool outside. I opened the scrollcase and took out the note.

Lasva:

I want you home at once, but it must be in secret. Marnda and your scribe must travel as you, and arrive before Martande Day as customary. Chwahir have been seen massing in the mountain passes to the east. Use your transfer token as soon as you have seen to your entourage.

———

". . . and I'm afraid all our quiet is going to end soon," Torsu finished at last, as Kivic poured out more hot mulled wine.

By now they had a comfortable little fiction going, all of her own making. He had reassured her during the delicate days of pique, smile, provocative comment, that this was no *dalliance*. Nor did he ask questions—such as, "The princess? Returning?"

No, to answer such direct questions would be *telling*.

He said, "I suppose we'll all find ourselves hip deep in extra work soon, right when the weather is starting to nip at the fingers and toes."

Extra work. Torsu's lip curled. *She was so easy to suggest ideas to. You picked the ones both selfish and lonely and gave them what they wanted. Torsu wanted sex outside of the rules governing everyone else, and a sympathetic ear while she complained.*

"I haven't heard anything but rumors," he went on, sipping his wine and sighing. "I don't suppose you have a hint of when we start bracing up against all that extra demand."

Second rule: create a sense of "us" against "them." "Us" being Kivic and the one he wanted information from, and "them" being those he wanted information about. We are the heroes, they are the enemies.

"Oh, put it this way. By Martande Day, I'll be stuck upstairs standing around in case Someone decides on impulse that this ribbon or that silk rose or the other embroidered lace is too ugly and has to be fixed on the instant," she said sourly, looking out the window. *She always did that when she revealed something she shouldn't, as if by not looking at him she could pretend he didn't hear it.*

He knew better than to repeat it. "Well, here's to the last days of freedom, or what passes for it here." He raised his cup.

She raised hers, they drank, and she frowned. "It's already cooling off."

"That's because my room is cold," he agreed. "Better a cold room alone than a warm one working like a drudge, that's what I always say. I sit here and work on my harnesses, and no one orders me about."

"Orders! You don't know what orders are until you've been under the tongue of the likes of Dessaf," Torsu started, and went on to give a bitter description of her labors.

There wasn't much about the princess's rooms he didn't know now: who worked when, who slept where, what everyone's schedule was like, and where they would all be at any given time. Weaknesses, strengths, all of it winnowed out with flattery, sympathy, and pleasure.

When Torsu finished her wine, she sighed and rose. "I had better go," she said. "Can you believe bed checks at midnight? It's Dessaf being vindictive."

"Of course, of course," he soothed, giving her a lingering caress. "But you don't want to be on the receiving end of another of her artistic chastisements."

"Ah-ye, to be avoided." With that, Torsu gathered her shawl close about her, and he walked her to the narrow stairway then leaned against

the door as she ran lightly down and sped over the path behind the vegetable garden.

Same way she had taken last visit—and the one before. He turned
away, tsking to himself.

Habit was lethal in the spy business.

Marnda had been granted the evening off. I found her at the other end
of the inn, dancing with some locals and staff who had free time. As soon
as she saw me she made her way toward me, followed by her dancing
partner. "What is it?"

I said, "The princess has a headache. She wants a scented bath and soft
music, so that she can sleep."

Marnda wiped her damp brow on her sleeve, her expression unchang-
ing at our private code "headache" and "music"—which meant urgency
and privacy. "I have to go," she said to her partner.

Second valet to a baron from the north, he rolled his eyes. "I wouldn't
work for a princess for a gold piece a day and my own coach."

Marnda followed me out the door, where the noise and music diminished. All I had to do was show her the golden case, and her brow lifted.
Together we hurried to Lasva's suite, where she told us the plan, finishing, "Marnda, you'll carry on as if Emras is me, and give everyone to
know I took cold in the rain today, and so I must regretfully decline any
entertainments and dine in my chamber."

We curtseyed.

Lasva twisted the ring she wore on her smallest finger, whispered her
transfer code, and was wrenched out of the world then shoved back in
again, stumbling on a Destination carpet in Hatahra's inner chamber.

Lasva groped, found a chair, and sat down abruptly, to wait for the
hideous reaction to magic transfer to pass. The ache in her bones passed
swiftly, the dizziness dissipated, and she was left staring not at her sister,
as expected, but at Lord Davaud, the consort. She stared at his jowly
face, his intelligent gray eyes, as if she'd never seen them before. Slowly
her wits returned.

He was dressed formally, his overvest velvet, not silk, his undervest
gemmed brocade, meaning there had been a grand ball. "Would you like
a glass of wine?" he offered.

"Thank you. I'm all right now."

"Queen Hatahra is attending a play in her honor, but she should be here soon."

"The babe is safe?"

"Everyone is safe," he said. "Except, quite possibly, you."

"Me?" Lasva looked surprised, and for a fleeting moment thought of the Marloven prince. But that made no sense, and she dismissed it impatiently. "The Chwahir, seen in the passes? So said her note. I'm having trouble understanding the connection."

"We don't know that there is one," came Hatahra's voice from the doorway, and both turned. "But I mislike the timing, so soon after Alian's birth. When I put that together with Jurac Sonscarna's attempt to bully me into a marriage treaty between you and him, and the fact that our ambassador fields far too many questions about you, I think—until we find out why Chwahir are swarming at the passes—the entire royal family will stay here in the palace, warded, and you shall stay hidden in your rooms. Let the world think you are traveling home for the Martande Day regatta."

Lasva rose and curtseyed.

Hatahra sat down tiredly. "Have the heralds been sent?"

Her consort pointed at the big map on the table. "To each House within two weeks' ride of the western and eastern passes, which is where the border magic has been crossed."

"What about the middle pass?" Lasva brushed the mountains north of Alsais.

"Even the Chwahir are not mad enough to try that one." Hatahra gave an ironic sniff. "To get an army through past the magic wards, they would have to slip them across one by one through what I am told is a very narrow passage. I assure you, the massing of hundreds of platter-faces would give cause for complaint by the people in Ymadan." She snapped her fan open.

Davaud said to her, "To all the other northern Houses I sent a herald ordering them to be on the watch. And in your name, a suitable host to be raised against need."

"Most of them will probably require the added time," Hatahra said wryly. "The dukes will hate it and will inevitably cause a lot of unnecessary bustle."

Davaud wondered where the bustle would begin. It was his place to command the defense of the city, something that until recently had meant overseeing orderly traffic, maintenance of roads, and peace in city and on canals. Now, suddenly, his royal consort expected him to command the forces being raised and sent to the outer passes.

Hatahra broke into his thoughts. "Come, Lasva, and see your niece, who smiles all the time now, the innocent smiles of one who demands only love. She is a refreshment to the spirit."

Lasva followed her sister to the baby's adjoining suite, in the old nursery where once she had lived. There before the doors stood heralds wearing rapiers, something not seen at the palace in generations.

PART THREE
COLEND GOES TO WAR

ONE

OF WHITE RIBBONS

For the next five days, each morning before dawn, the Grand Herald, Lord Davaud, and the Grand Seneschal met in the latter's rooms.

Their aggregate age was almost two hundred ten years, not a day of which had been spent in any military exercise. The Grand Herald had been digging through all the House Archives to read up on what was actually entailed in the "oaths of support" that each noble swore on accession.

The Grand Seneschal, who had been chosen by the old queen for his ability to smoothly organize and manage a royal palace, had no idea what the etiquette of defense could possibly be, with the result that he, too, had assigned a squadron of young scribes to go spelunking in dusty old archives, commiserating with them when they emerged day after day empty-handed.

"What can I tell her majesty today?" Davaud asked, as he always did.

The Grand Seneschal rubbed his age-spotted hands through his sparse hair. "No personal records, so far. Only scribal versions of old family stories. We've found two references to eyewitnesses at the Battle of Skya Lake. We will keep searching."

"Thank you," Davaud said. "If you require the aid of her scribes, her majesty bids me offer you their services." In other words, keep digging.

The Grand Herald knew the ducal houses were already in a struggle with the queen over whose responsibility it was to maintain royal roads, the ducal houses united in asserting that royal roads should be the royal prerogative to maintain as well as to order built. He wondered how much trouble the ducal houses were going to make now or were already making. It cost good money to feed warriors and horses, furbish up old armor, and maybe scout out new swords—money that many thought wasted on such impedimenta. Life at court was expensive enough.

Davaud turned to the Grand Seneschal. "We'll need more armed heralds, too, to keep order in the palace."

The Grand Seneschal gazed back, appalled. "Has there been rumor of possible disorder?"

Davaud opened his hands. "Is disorder not part of an attack?" It was clear that no one had an answer, so Davaud went on. "The queen desires armed heralds in the private wings. And everyone accounted for, at all times."

The two gray heads opposite bowed. "It shall be done," they said, almost in unison, though they wondered how to arrange such a thing. Very few heralds trained at arms—when they had time. And where were they to get the weapons? The Grand Seneschal knew the barge men had some extra rapiers, the old-fashioned heavy ones, for there was sometimes trouble on the waters, but he also knew they wouldn't relinquish them without fierce negotiation.

The Grand Herald, presuming on a lifetime of amity, said, "Ducal houses are balking, perhaps?"

They all thought back fourteen years, to when Thias Altan—then the ducal heir—had been abruptly, and without explanation, sent packing by the queen at the very height of the season. Now Altan was the leader of the dukes.

"All." Davaud sat back, arms folded. "Except one—the newest duke: Kaidas of Alarcansa."

———

"You are not happy," Tatia Definian observed, linking arms with her cousin Carola, Duchess of Alarcansa, as they descended the staircase toward the dining room.

"*Melende*," said the silver-tailed parrot riding on Carola's shoulder.

Carola gently stroked the parrot's head, a pucker between her brows. "Would you be happy after hearing that the wicked Chwahir might be coming to conquer us?"

"They won't succeed." Tatia giggled as she sent a complacent glance down the marble sweep of the staircase. Her ancestors had built this staircase two centuries before—and that had been to replace an older, narrower one. "They never have succeeded. They are stupid and uncouth. The queen will easily stop them, as her ancestor did."

The parrot shook itself, lifted its tail, and made a dropping. Tatia watched the ensorcelled silk cloak over her cousin's shoulders sparkle blue, and the dropping vanished. "*Melende* crowns Definian," said the parrot.

"Master Nolan reported disturbing news yesterday." Carola chirped, and the parrot obediently hopped down to her wrist, where she could more easily stroke it.

"Master Nolan?" Tatia watched the bird lean into the patient forefinger as she considered the astonishing turn of events. What had mages to do with prospective war? "There's to be a . . . a magic battle of some kind? Oh, I trust not here, near *our* lands!"

"He received word from one of his people that the watch-wards on the pass were dissolved. That's why it took so long to notice the massing of the Chwahir." Carola glanced in the direction of the mountains, which were high and rocky, and the only three passes—one east, one west, one central—were narrow. Colend had kept it that way deliberately.

A good portion of Alarcansa lay on the southern slopes below the eastern pass, where the vineyards that formed their greatest trade asset basked in the late-summer sun.

Tatia fought against impatience. The Chwahir did sound like a problem, but Queen Hatahra had more than enough mages and counselors to address the matter of wards, whatever those were.

No, there was something else disturbing her cousin. When Carola acted like this, her fan or forefinger snapping and tapping like the twitch of a cat's tail, Tatia knew it had to do with *Her*, Princess Lasthavais, the person Carola hated worse than damnation. Or else it had to do with her new duke, the person Tatia hated worse than damnation.

How to get closer to the real subject? Tatia reached to stroke the bird—knowing what would happen—as she said soothingly, "The mages know what to do. Also, you have a duke now to obey the Oath Summons. You do not have to lower yourself to such tedious duty." And she saw by the slight jut of Carola's perfect chin and the tightening of her smooth cheeks, that she'd hit close.

Time to humble herself, lest Carola's temper snap. Tatia reached again to stroke the parrot, which squawked, raised its wings in alarm, and snapped its beak at her finger. Tatia squeaked and jumped back. Carola laughed.

But the reassurance that the parrot loved her, and only her, did not smooth her mood as it usually did. "Come," Carola said. "Let us see if there is something to trouble me." And she scudded up the other side of the staircase, Tatia following with a growing sense of dread.

Carola ignored her cousin and the bird riding obediently on her wrist as she sorted through memories of what she'd believed until recently had been a superlatively happy month—ever since her wedding day. She now had everything just as she had always planned, or almost everything. There remained one tiny thing, a tiny round porcelain thing, or rather, not the thing itself—she could buy better ones with a single command—but what it symbolized. So maybe two small things, both of which shared the same meaning.

She let her breath out slowly, counting the triumphs. She and her beautiful Kaidas spent each morning completely alone in her handsome suite, redecorated with his colors as a surprise for him before the wedding. They breakfasted together on the terrace above the herb garden, and then he attended her while she did business, with the idea that he would one day take his share, especially of the vineyards. Not yet, of course. He had to learn how she wanted things, as she had spent years learning from her father.

They rode around together, so that he would know Alarcansa, and Alarcansa could know their new duke.

And in the evenings, there was always entertainment— either musicians, or parties. Twice she'd given expensive masquerade balls for the baronial families who owed her fealty, because she'd overheard Kaidas, during her first spring at court, say that he loved masked balls. And after that, to bed, together, where she gave him all her attention. He, in turn, was skillful and attentive, just as she required.

And every morning, before that intimate breakfast, she dismissed her maid and his new valet, and with her own hands she tied back his beautiful hair with a fresh white ribbon.

Tatia had sentimentally informed her that the household considered that romantic. Carola calmly acknowledged the tribute, not telling anyone that the act gave her as exquisite a flame of pleasure in her vitals as did the touch of his hands where she wanted them, each night.

More, truth to tell.

More, because the pleasure of sex with the one she desired most was heightened by the triumphant reminder that he was hers, and by the mental image of Lasva waking in her empty bed. How she lingered in the aftermath of bliss, imagining Lasva distraught with the same pain that Carola had once felt when the eyes of the man Carola had chosen— the most desired man in Colend's court—had dared to drift indifferently past her to that damned princess, and then smile.

Kaidas was hers, all hers. She was munificent with love-gifts; each day for the two weeks after they were married, and now every time he did something she asked. He would learn that she was generous when he bent his mind to pleasing her: clothes, rings, a racing carriage, two fine new race horses that she'd ordered all the way from Sarendan.

She turned her head as she passed a window, dissatisfied with her elaborate coif, the white ribbon bound artfully into her pearl-braided coronet. She would wear her hair as simply as a peasant girl if the ribbon were tied by his hands. Surely even a man would one day waken with the idea of making his own romantic gesture and bind up her hair. However, he was too careless about such things; she suspected that if she did not perform that sweet office, he would never remember to tie up his own hair. He certainly never looked in the mirror after she'd tied it for him.

So, though the white ribbons gave her pleasure, she was not certain that their symbolism was *true*. The real proof that she at last possessed his heart was the single thing she could not ask for. The idea must be his alone: to paint for her a lover's cup. One? She wanted the palace full of them, one to each room. But the first one was yet to come. She'd ordered a room fitted up for painters, complete to an astonishing array of expensive colors ordered from all around the world. She'd instructed her servants to discover who the best porcelain-makers were, especially of cups, and she'd paid a crushing sum to have an entire case of them delivered.

But as yet he had not set foot in that room, past the day she'd taken him there as a surprise.

Well, it was early days yet. There had been so many other things to do. Like that damned herald from the queen four days previous.

She considered that moment yet again.

They'd begun hearing petitioners when her steward cleared the crowd, saying, over and over, "Message from the queen. Make way for the messenger from the queen."

The herald said, "Her majesty, having received word of the border being breeched by the Chwahir, requires your oath-stipulated defense force to be raised at once and sent north to the pass, there to await command from the consort Lord Davaud."

Carola remembered her own disgust. It meant a great to-do, assembling people who were far better employed at the grape harvest. In specific, it meant horses, strong and sturdy young men and women, swords, mud, sweat. Surely she would not be required to preside over something so dreary. But now she had an active man at her side who had spent time riding the eastern border with his Thora-Dei cousins, patrolling against incursions from Khanerenth troublemakers. What could be more perfect?

So she'd turned to her duke, saying, "I believe this charge of the queen's must fall to you."

And his face had changed. For a heartbeat only. She might have missed it had she not watched him constantly in her hunger to know his secret mind. She thought she knew all the range of his expressions, but she had never seen that lifting of the eyelids, the sudden, unguarded deep breath of . . . of joy?

She reached the round windows above the east court, where the stables circled what long ago had been a garrison. Now those buildings were storage: old furniture, the best of the silk, the best wine.

It was in some wise a garrison again, some of the rooms having been hastily cleared out against the fifty expected young people, mostly men, as she had guessed. Lower servants and commoners stood down there with him now, in their shirt sleeves despite the cool air, swinging their swords round and back and up in a kind of rhythm that Kaidas must have learned with his Thora-Dei cousins.

"Again!" she heard him shout. "I want tighter circles and convincing blocks. Then we'll get out the wooden swords for some bouts."

"Hurrah!" some of the younger ones shouted, dancing about with glee.

"Now! One! Two! Three!" Kaidas barked in a voice she'd never heard from him, and his little army hastily took up their positions again, swinging their weapons.

Trailing her cousin, Tatia looked down. Sword-swinging meant nothing to her. As for the duke, the fool was clearly having fun, but he was a man, and they were notorious for liking to get sweaty and bruised up with such hummery.

What was Carola sulking about now?

Stroke, stroke went the forefinger along the parrot's head.

Tatia said, "What is amiss? Are you thinking of the labor gone to waste when those lackeys ride off to the mountains?"

"I only have to provide fifty of my own people, and I have distributed the remainder of the numbers through all my Definian holdings, so we'll have enough laborers to pick grapes when they are ready. The Oath only stipulates two hundred for this kind of summons. I don't intend to go over that number by one single lout. Unless, of course, this turns out to be a real alarm."

"Is that why you frown?"

"I frown," Carola said, abruptly turning away, "because I don't like the timing." Though that was not her real reason. She would not speak of her duke's sudden smile.

Tatia looked surprised. "Chwahir invasions can't possibly have anything to do with *Her*. Why, she's not even in Colend for the next couple of weeks."

Anger burned through Carola, but she mastered it.

Kaidas had *not* gone to Sartor with *Her*, and everything was as it ought to be. Carola had seen every letter sent to Kaidas since the wedding, and Tatia, under the pretext of showing his manservant where to put his personal things, had searched every single item of his, leaving out not the smallest paint brush or inkpot. Carola herself had gotten up their very first night and searched all through his clothes, right to the seams, finding no sign of any of those horrid magical scrollcases or any mementos that could be attributed to *Her*.

Everything indeed was as it should be.

But. There was that smile. . . .

"What should I do?" she addressed the bird.

Tatia suppressed a flash of irritation at Carola's asking the bird for advice. But then, she reflected, Carola wanted to be told what she wanted to hear.

"Definian in *melende*," said the parrot, giving the sounds that got the most treats.

"Smart darling," Carola cooed. "Yes. I must think of duty above comfort. I believe I shall ride with him. I believe we will raise more volunteers if I am seen."

Tatia's head turned, and she pursed her lips. "You will go outside the palace, in a possible war situation?"

"It is only to circle Alarcansa. Why shouldn't I go?" Carola paused when she caught sight of her reflection in the window, with that thin white line braided into her hair by her maid. "Perhaps it is not a good idea to leave my steward in charge as I do when I go to court, for she's old and doesn't like change, but why don't I leave you? Until I have a child you're my heir—they all know you. And you know how I like things done."

Tatia turned to hide her hot rush of triumph from her cousin's quick eyes—triumph followed by fear and dismay. *Until I have a child.* "Of course," she said, in her meekest voice. "If it is your desire." She cooed at the parrot, "Smart birdie," and once again reached and once again avoided the snap of its beak.

She jumped back. Her incessant giggle sounded, Carola thought irritably, exactly like the dying bleat of a mouse impaled on the claws of a cat.

But Tatia was so devoted, so obedient, just like her darling birds.

"I know exactly how you like things done," Tatia said, putting her hands behind her back. The instinct to slap the bird into the wall was so strong, so strong. But she'd learned as a child that any pet who showed an inclination for anyone but Carola didn't last long. "Every command will be as you would wish." *Every command.* What sweet words!

TWO

OF VEILED PLAYS

I vandred looked down at the innkeeper. "Do I speak wrong? How can there be no garrison in so large a town?"

The innkeeper gazed uneasily up at the fair-haired young man in black. There had been no harsh words, no threats uttered. But that black coat, so unlike anything anyone wore, the knife hilts in plain evidence, the slightly curved sword in the saddle-sheath instead of the usual rapier decently shrouded in a baldric and half-covered by robes, even the fellow's accent—all added up to potential trouble.

The innkeeper tried not to look at the two lines of armed young men behind him, the horses so still, the fellows sitting straight and alert. Though they were dressed in unadorned servant gray, the cut of those coats was somehow intimidating, and the warriors sported more weapons than you'd find in the entire town of Binnam.

The innkeeper said, "Well, if you want to find—" He groped in the air, as if swinging a sword. "The duke's peace patrol, you'd go to see the duke. But if rumor is right, they might be in Alsais. Everyone's talking about how there might be some kind of trouble. Hmhmhmh." The man hummed tunelessly, then made a rude gesture toward the northern mountains.

Ivandred had heard several versions of this hum coupled with vague references to rumors of trouble from the north.

"I don't want the duke or a peace patrol," he said, trying to be exact in this exasperating language so rich with inexactitude. "All I want is a map of the roads of Colend, so I can make my way to your royal city."

The innkeeper's forehead cleared. "Oh, is that all! You don't need a map. Stay on the royal roads. The ones marked with a crown all lead to Alsais. You must have seen the sign stones."

Ivandred had seen the waist-high plinths indeed, some of them marked with a crown at the top and an arrow. Below the crowns were local town names, and more arrows, pointing off toward various roads. "So that was a king's road, then?" Ivandred asked.

The innkeeper spread his hands, and all the people by now gathered around with their baskets and bright clothing, nodded at one another. A young boy said, "We have *good* roads here in Colend. All paved. Didn't you see?"

Ivandred gave the boy a grave salute, then tossed a gold coin to the innkeeper, whose expert fingers nipped it out of the air and made it vanish beneath his apron.

"You don't wish to stop here first?" Strange-looking this foreigner might be, but he also had a free hand with the largesse.

"We'll be on our way."

Ivandred lifted a hand, and it seemed to the watchers that a heartbeat later his entire force was in flight toward the bridge out of town.

Once the animals had had a good run, the columns slowed to a walk. Ivandred motioned Haldren Marlovair to him. Their horses gave one another a sniff and a flick of ears.

"Did you hear yon innkeep?" Ivandred asked, chin motioning over his shoulder.

"Royal roads." Haldren's countenance expressed his question.

They studied the road, which was broad and so well paved no grass grew between the joins of the sandstone. Yet it curved about lazily, with no attention to the straight line, the fastest route.

"These can't be military roads," Ivandred said. "They either keep those to themselves, or—"

It was inconceivable that there weren't any military roads. But this kingdom was already so unlike Marloven Hesea. Observe these Colendi houses. Rich or poor, they had big windows, even door-windows that opened right onto gardens, for summer living. How can you defend any house with all those windows and no perimeter walls, only gardens? You couldn't.

Hard to believe they shared the same world, Haldren thought, looking from a pretty farmhouse to the royal road sweeping around a lake, swooping south into a shallow valley, then northward to skirt the forested side of a hill.

"Maybe they don't have any military roads," Haldren observed.

Ivandred gestured, palm to the sky. "We'll find a likely campsite, and I'll hail my cousin tonight."

Haldren dropped back to the rear of the column, and they rode on until they made camp beside a stream.

The sun had set when Ivandred exchanged his dusty coat for a clean one, resettled his belt and his weapons, then walked a little ways away from his warriors, shut his eyes, and muttered the transfer spell. Heat built rapidly. The inward wrench was thoroughly nasty, but when the sensation passed there was Macael, sitting at a private table, watching him with a bemused expression.

Macael had felt a brief sense of impending lightning, then there was his cousin. Curtains fluttered and candle flames glowed bright in the burnt-smelling air he stirred up.

Ivandred sank into a convenient chair, wiping the sweat from his brow. Transferring like that left him dangerously weak for too long, but he didn't have transfer tokens and did not know how to make them.

"I take it there's some reason you couldn't write me a note," Macael said, pulling his notebox from his inner pocket.

Ivandred made a repudiating gesture. The Herskalt had taught him how easy it was to suborn those message boxes. He knew how many had died because messages had been waylaid by magic, without writer or recipient knowing. *All for the good of the kingdom, that's what my ancestors say.*

"Very well." Macael sighed. Then gave his cousin a speculative glance. "You transferred here without a token," he observed.

Ivandred turned his palm up in assent, then frowned down at the tiny lapidary wine cups, which held little more than a sip. How strange it was that these Colendi seemed to prefer dishes that would better befit a doll.

He helped himself to wine right out of the bottle, as Macael went on: "Pardon me if I'm wrong. I know almost nothing about magic, short of what the traveling mages tell us when they come through once a year and renew all our spells. But isn't a transfer without token dark magic?"

Ivandred hid his impatience. "This 'light' and 'dark' distinction is nothing but moral posturing," he said. "Why not blue and orange?" The Herskalt had explained all that to him when he first began tutoring.

Macael toyed with his wine cup. "I thought dark magic was dangerous. Mages avoid it, except . . . eh."

Ivandred made a flat-handed gesture. "If I have to use any magic outside of the transfers necessary for this journey, it will be an emergency. I have to be fast. I assumed it would be all right to fix on you as a transfer destination."

"You're welcome to fix on me. It's well, though, that you didn't two nights ago at this time." He grinned ruefully, as Ivandred looked surprised, then snorted a laugh. "I didn't consider that. And should have. Sorry."

Macael waved. "So. Something has happened, I take it? Where are you, anyway? Er, where did you come from?"

"Near the Alessandra River. East of a town called, ah, Benind? Binnam. They don't have maps or garrisons. Only this royal road that seems to wander up and down the countryside." Ivandred gestured with his palm down, as though pushing aside the royal roads. "Everywhere we go, we hear about rumors of trouble. They hum, they point toward the distant mountains. Does this mean imminent war with the Chwahir?"

"Nobody has the faintest idea," Macael said. "The word from Alsais is just as vague. 'Trouble' about sums it up. Then they conjecture, based on stories of wars that are centuries old." He grinned.

Ivandred gave a short nod. "Talk of war, this I understand. I will send Haldren ahead at the gallop."

He muttered and vanished by magic, leaving the candle flames flickering and streaming wildly.

Emras:

I thought you might like a report on what has happened since you sent me the scroll. I think I told you, if you want everyone eager to read something, you must catch the toffs first. They won't read anything the tradesmen discovered, no matter how popular. So I waited until I had the right person, the Duchess of Altan, who stayed in Alsais this summer—the chirp-birds insist that she and the Duke are leading the rest of the coronets in some campaign to force the queen to rescind some tax. The duchess wanted something unrelated to music. Then came these rumors about the Chwahir, and possible war, and that was my chance!

You will love the design. I found an old-fashioned style of paper, ink, and for illustrations, I looked up all the old family sigils of those early days. And as the battles were mostly about the Venn, what could be better than Venn styles?

I skimmed through Tiflis's description of the book—"book," not "scroll," as books were enjoying popularity over scrolls, though they were harder to make. After the Duchess sat for two hours in one of the reading chairs, then insisted on buying that very copy, Tif detailed triumphantly how her employer not only took the risk of putting all the copyists in the house to the job, she also paid for a night crew. They sold every copy within two days, and she had just seen the list of all those waiting for new copies.

. . . everyone at the palace says that the stay-at-home toffs are smirking about the toffs still on the road, who don't know of this latest sensation. And it is a sensation! Is it true that one of these Marlovens is coming east with an army of hundreds?

In the Grand Seneschal's formal audience chamber, the Grand Herald and two ducal heralds were locked in a bitter war of wills between the queen and her two strongest dukes: while everyone agreed that the Oath stipulated that each ducal territory send two hundred warriors, the ducal alliance was determined to make the queen pay their expenses, and Davaud and the Grand Herald were determined that the dukes were to cover supplies as well as furnishing bodies.

The Oath was so old that its exact meaning had become obscured enough for a variety of interpretations.

This war was conducted by the Grand Herald (with Lord Davaud present), his attackers the ducal heralds, their weapons a formidable mass of historic detail, delivered in the blandest of voices accompanied by formal manners.

". . . and my lord duke requests that I furnish this copy from the Altan archives," the first herald was saying to the Grand Herald, his face smooth and innocent as he bowed, then proffered a paper written in the court hand of two hundred years ago. "In it, his grace begs you to honor with your attention, you will find the marriage treaty between Prince Gaelan Lirendi and Lady Phosar Altan on Firstday Sixmonth, 4191. Under the third head, please note that the Lirendi Family would henceforth provide all sums required in an Oath Summons for Defense, the Altans being held to the number of riders. It was agreed that sums included the purchasing of equipment. His grace begs you will honor him with perusal of this statement here."

The Grand Herald pretended to look at the paper, but he already knew what it said. Two days ago he'd read the identical copy (duly noted and sealed by magic-seal) in the royal archive. It was now time to unleash his own weapon, discovered by one of his army of scribes, who had been searching both the royal archive and the general, night and day.

"You must convey," he said smoothly, his formality a degree more elaborate than the herald's, "to his grace my infinite respect and duty, along with the following, which no doubt escaped his attention: 'equipment' was defined, by law under Emperor Mathias the Magnificent in 4258, as covering 'war horse, saddle, sword, shield, armor and any appurtenances required thereto.' The crown, therefore, sees its responsibility limited to fodder for mounts, and food for the warriors. Tents and clothing being considered 'appurtenances.'"

"If you will forgive a moment's interpolation," the herald from Endralath interposed with the bland smile of anticipatory triumph, "we might be able to clear up this matter with reference to the exact definition of 'equipment,' for in our own treaty with House Lirendi, in 4317—which you will all agree postdates the reign of the glorious Emperor Mathias—"

The sound of horns startled them into silence—silver horns, blown with sweet and heart-racing precision in triple falls of notes. The unprecedented fanfare issued forth from directly outside the Grand Seneschal's formal audience chamber.

A young herald-apprentice ran in, wringing his hands as if shedding decorum. A door herald clattered behind him, tugging at ill-fitting armor painted in the garish styles popular two centuries previous. "Forgive me, sir," this latter said, his eyes round with apprehension. "The Prince of Marloven Hesea rode right past the outer reception areas. They are *here!* They rode *horses* straight to the *throne room doors!*"

"Who?"

"Where?"

"Marloven what?"

Davaud slipped away and vaulted up the stairs. The Grand Seneschal, seeing him gone, motioned to a footman.

In strode Haldren Marlovair and his second cousin Tdan Marthdaun.

They were, on their prince's orders, not dressed formally in their own House tunics but in their fighting blacks, with gold buckles to their belts, which transformed the whole into Montredaun-An black and gold. Their heads were bare, their pale hair neatly braided. In their left arms they carried their helms with the long hairs swinging down. In their right hands each bore a banner on a spear, Tdan the screaming eagle of Marloven Hesea, and Haldren the fox head, Ivandred's personal banner.

The heralds and the old Grand Seneschal stared at these newcomers in their martial coats, knives at their sides, in their high boot tops, and visible at their wrists. No one knew what to say.

Haldren and Tdan found all those open mouths funny, but they were under orders to bear themselves as they would before the king, Ivandred's father.

"We bring greetings from Prince Ivandred of Marloven Hesea," Tdan said, his back sword-straight.

"—who requests an audience with the Princess Lasthavais Lirendi," Haldren finished.

"Most irregular," a woman whispered from the row of heralds in the back, busily writing down the proceedings for the archive.

Above, unknown to anyone but the Grand Herald and Grand Seneschal, the queen sat by a listening-post, its opening lost in the splendid carvings all around the ceiling of the interview chamber, as Davaud joined her, puffing for breath.

The queen sent a page for Lasva as below, the Grand Herald sent a royal footman out to Ivandred, then hedged for time by asking once again for the young men's names, that they might be correctly entered in the records.

"So the suitors are showing up," Hatahra said, as Lasva joined her and Davaud. "Kholaver of Bren has been prowling around impatiently, as I told you. Now I hear that Hathian of Sarendan is on his way. And here is the mysterious Marloven."

No reaction from her sister. Lasva seemed lost in reverie.

Hatahra tried again. "Somehow I did not expect a royal suitor all the way from the barbarian west. And a descendant of Elgar the Fox, no less."

"Elgar the Fox," Lasva repeated. The name made no sense at first, then she said doubtfully, "The pirate in history?"

Hatahra leaned forward, her brows beetling. "So says the legend. But we will deal in facts. The single thing I know about the Marlovens is that one of their kings, perhaps an ancestor of this very prince, is the one whose threat to join the Enaeraneth caused our own ancestor, Mathias the Magnificent, to think better of bringing his empire of peace to that part of the world."

"You judge the Marlovens ill because of that?" Lasva asked, surprised.

"I do not," her sister rejoined crisply. "I would be a fool to hold against anyone a defense of their homeland. My point is this. This king—perhaps his ancestor—returned Mathias's peace offering with a warning that Marlovens do not negotiate, though the Enaeraneth might. We have *that* exchange reported by a herald scribe, kept in the royal archive. I've seen it. However, it was centuries ago. Maybe they are more reasonable now."

When Lasva bowed, vouchsafing no answer, Hatahra said in a different voice, more speculative, "Did you meet this Marloven prince in Sartor?"

And Hatahra saw it again: the catch of breath, the widening of pupils. Lasva, for once, was not aware of her outer response, which amazed Hatahra and Davaud.

Lasva was only aware of the quickening of her heartbeat. "We did not meet to speak. I only glimpsed him once or twice on the river road," she said.

"Yet the city is suddenly talking about ancient pirates as if they'd sailed their ships up the Ym into town. It's the illustrious history of this man's country that is now the most popular thing. I understand The Slipper has abandoned their current slam at us to mount a new rendition of *Jaja the Pirate Slayer*. And I hear some of the younger girls are wearing a new fashion, shades of amber and maple in layered mantles on their gowns, called a fox ruff. Is this coincidence?"

Lasva was genuinely puzzled. "I don't know. That is, my scribe did mention something about a scroll, and Elgar the Fox. But that was before you summoned me home by magic transfer." She did not have to add that that was nearly three weeks ago, and she'd been sequestered in her suite ever since.

"This new fashion has sprung up in the city over the past five or six days. What was that about your scribe?" Hatahra asked, and at Lasva's bewildered reaction, used her fan to dismiss the matter. "I have an idea."

She reached for the bell-pull that would summon a page, then paused. "Before I investigate further, let me ask you if yon Marloven prince is someone you wish to acknowledge formally as a suitor? If no one has met him, then we don't know, after all, if he's even less appealing than that young hum from Bren, whom we must tolerate if we're to honor our treaties with his father. We have no treaties, no embassies, nothing, with these Marlovens. That gives us the freedom of response."

Lasva drew in a deep breath, and once again she was back at the riverside inn, weary, dreading another long night of joyless music—and looked straight into those startling winter-blue eyes. "What have you in mind?"

Hatahra said, "To snap my fingers under Thias Altan's nose. He's the leader of the ducal faction, not Gaszin. They're trying to get back at me for smashing the Gaszin marriage alliance with Alarcansa. Except for Thias, who's pushing me because he can," she added with a thin smile.

Lasva flicked her fan over the lower part of her face in Surprise then flipped it, indicating the opposite.

Hatahra flashed a grin. "If we were, as publicly as possible, to offer this martial Marloven a royal alliance and request him to aid us against the Chwahir, it might undercut Thias and his allies at a stroke. If the Marloven does, indeed, know something about military matters, Davaud could all but promise him the supreme command, and watch our dukes fume. Nothing they can do, if half the servants they're stuffing into old armor to fulfill their ancient obligations are still straggling this way with lagging steps, while the dukes try to force me to pay to equip an entire army."

Lasva smiled. Her thoughts veered from memory of that hapless King Jurac to Kaidas, then recoiled from Kaidas to Ivandred's pale eyes. Attraction and mystery.

If he agreed, they would meet. Speak. Would either mystery or attraction survive their first conversation?

Her heart sped. "Do it, then."

THREE

OF SILVER TRUMPETS

When the bells rang the chords precisely one hour past noon—the Hour of the Wheel—the throne room doors opened, and Prince Ivandred Montredaun-An of Marloven Hesea walked alone down the center aisle.

Over the last two days, whispers had spread through the palace faster than a fire. All of court and everyone else who could find an excuse to be there ranged on either side.

Hatahra watched that straight, slender figure with the fearless pale gaze, the callused hands, the hard-heeled stride so unlike the sinuous cat-grace of her courtiers, and gloated inwardly at this challenge to her court.

The young man came directly to the foot of her throne. He did not bow but stood with his booted feet slightly apart and struck his right fist against his heart.

"Welcome to Colend, Prince Ivandred of Marloven Hesea," she stated in the clear, steady cadence that made it easiest for the heralds up in the left-hand gallery to take down every word spoken. "You are welcome as friend and as an ally to be trusted in time of need."

Again he struck his fist against his heart, a gesture she found strange and intimidating, then he cooperatively spoke the single line she, Davaud, and the Chief Herald had wrangled over all night:

"You have only to state your need, and I will prove that trust."

He said it clearly in that clipped accent. What did the words mean to him?

She lifted her voice once more. "When can you be ready to ride to the aid of Colend against the threat of Chwahir invasion?"

"Now." He smiled briefly.

As whispers susurrated outward, Hatahra almost laughed. Oh, this little drama would be talked of for days. Maybe years.

She turned to her consort, who stood behind the throne in a splendid battle tunic modeled on a gold-leaved illustration the heralds had found in the Archive. She thought he looked quite distinguished, so tall and sturdy with the long blue tunic worked with golden stars down its front, the gleam of chain mail at the gapped sides, his rich sword belt and gem-studded rapier. These were artifacts from the Lirendi treasury, along with the splendid shield, half as tall as he was, with the Lirendi lily in the old-fashioned crowned dagger shape that furniture artisans had spent all night silvering afresh, then adding ten layers of cobalt to deepen the blue. It still smelled faintly of lacquer.

He looked noble and imposing, but not as . . . martial as this young fellow in his plain black, relieved only by the golden belt buckle at his narrow waist and the long knife he wore at his side. If he wore chain mail, it was hidden beneath that tight-chested, long-skirted coat.

"Are you ready to ride, Lord Davaud?"

"I am, your majesty," Davaud replied, the sonorous drawl pitched to be heard in the gallery where the scratching of quills could be made out over the profound silence below.

"Then I bid you go. Protect our kingdom," she commanded.

Lord Davaud stepped down from the daïs to Ivandred's side. The Marloven turned, coat skirts flaring, and matched pace with the consort. Together they walked out of the throne room to the great courtyard, where the courtly carriages had all been sent away, and the only people permitted were those ready to ride with the consort—including twenty-four Marlovens, still and straight on their exquisite horses.

As many courtiers as could crowded out behind the grim-faced Duke Mathias Altan of Altan.

The court peered past the milling herald-guards in their old-fashioned armor and hastily sewn (or age-green, attic-resurrected) battle tunics, waiting in disorder next to the still double column of horsemen all dressed in black, as Prince Ivandred mounted, then raised a gloved hand. One of his boys (*were* they all boys? That one next to the redhead had a womanish turn to her throat) blew a stirring air on a trumpet, a sound unheard for centuries. Twenty-four lances with black and gold fox face pennants rose at exactly the same angle. Then the prince's horse leaped into a gallop, tail high, and his twenty-four followers wheeled and raced after, the columns strictly side by side, horses nose to tail, the riders so easy on their backs the racing enthusiasts among the court felt their hearts seize.

Behind them galloped Lord Davaud's riders in a mass, borrowed weapons and armor clattering and jingling.

The court turned away, everyone talking. The queen stood alone on the top step between the massive doors.

The Duke of Altan rubbed his heavy jowl, then indicated by sign that he wished to speak. Hatahra gestured permission, and he stepped up beside her. "All right, Tahra, you win."

"Try to catch them, Thias." She breathed a laugh.

———

Servants found their own vantages from which to observe history being made. The favored view was from the roof of the carriage storage building, where Kivic sat, exchanging joking comments with co-workers. One raised a tankard. "Ah-yedi! Look at those foreigners ride! Wouldn't you love to get your hands on their horses?"

"You won't get within sniffing distance of them," scoffed a stableman from Kivic's other side. "Those Marlovens pull a sword if you so much as touch one of their hoof-picks."

"Ye*di!* They do all their own grooming? Imagine one of our fine lords knowing what a hoof-pick is, never mind what to do with it," offered a third, to knowing chuckles.

The dust had begun to settle behind the riders when Kivic stretched and yawned. "Duke Pinch-Copper Altan looks like he's going to snap his fingers for his saddle at last."

Genial curses met this announcement. They slid off the roof onto the bales of fresh-harvested hay and dispersed.

Kivic eased away. In his locked room, he wrote: *My liege, the crown is sending a force east. Among them, twenty-four Marloven boys and girls as honor guard. There may be a more substantial number out of sight. Rumors are wild about a Marloven army, though no specifics.*

Jurac Sonscarna waited a day's ride north of Alsais, well outside the range of Hatahra's magic wards. He frowned at Kivic's message. He and his force had crossed the border one by one, dressed as day laborers. There was no disguising their pale Chwahir faces, but this close to the mountains, Kivic had assured his king that Chwahir were often hired on the cheap for harvesting. They had to make certain no one saw them en masse—something that would have to be addressed later. For now, Jurac waited for news of his princess. Kivic had only to find out where she was, then he could act.

But Marlovens? Even if each of the twenty-four fought with the prowess of an Elgar of the legends, they could not defeat a thousand marchers massed up in the eastern pass, waiting on his word to engage the queen's fan-waving fops, and make them all look like the fools they were.

But if there was a Marloven army on the move somewhere, masked by the mass of courtiers flowing toward Alsais. . . . Kivic must find out.

Jurac threw the paper into the fire. Kivic now had five spies out on the western road below Alsais, along which the courtiers were straggling. How long could they hide a traveling princess—or an army?

Davaud soon regretted having chosen to ride.

At least they did not gallop long. Marlovens knew how to make an impression, but they were equally careful of their mounts. Ivandred gave the signal for them to holster their lances and slow the animals.

Davaud welcomed the signal with intense relief. His hips hurt almost as much as the inner parts of his legs, and the back of his neck was awash in sweat from the sun beating down on the four layers he wore: silken brocade over thick quilting, over a heavy linen shirt, and over that the chain mail. The damned shield dug unmercifully into his thigh, but no matter how he tried to shift it, it either disturbed the horse or thrust against his boot, or something. It seemed to have twenty corners instead of five.

Davaud glanced at his companion, whose shield, an odd tear shape, hooked over the horse's gear at a slant so that it stayed out of the way. The Marloven prince wore black, which soaked up sunlight, but he did not look red or sweaty. Summer was nearly over, and that coat had to be hot. On closer look Davaud suspected the weave had more linen than wool. But did he wear chain mail underneath?

Ivandred had been scanning the countryside. He turned Davaud's way and said in heavily accented Sartoran, "What can we expect?"

"Expect?" Davaud was grateful for the Sartoran, because the meaning was confusing enough even though he could define each word. "You mean, how many are there?"

Ivandred turned his palm up.

Taking that for assent, Davaud answered, "The wards in the passes signal alarms if more than fifty gather in a given space. We do have some limited trade with the Chwahir, and there is even some visiting back and forth and seasonal workers hired, but no one travels in large groups. Forbidden either side," he explained. "Since the first alarm, our people have been trying to count them. Several hundred at the least, probably with more coming up their side of the pass."

Another open-handed gesture. "Any warning sent? Demands? Threats?"

"Nothing. Only the wards broken."

Ivandred's voice showed no emotion. "What kind of tactics can we expect?"

Tactics? Davaud had felt like a fraud ever since the queen had informed him he would be in command of this defense. But he wasn't one. He'd spent long, wearying nights reading every first-hand record of a battle that the heralds could find in the archives. Most of them were not only ancient, they took place in other lands. Colend had had skirmishes aplenty, but was short on wars.

He'd begun with the Battle of Skya Lake four centuries previous, when the Sentis family had faced off the Lirendis and lost. Then there were several abortive Khanerenth incursions, a brawl at Pansan Bridge in Gaszin, and a ducal scuffle over inheritance that the former queen Hatahra had to settle. He'd finished by plowing grimly through the long-winded chronicles of the last Chwahir invasion, the enemy having been repelled by Martande Lirendi, who subsequently made himself king. The archaic language turned out to describe, in detail, the heroism and glory of the aftermath, and furnished not a scrap of instruction on exactly what you were supposed to do to get there.

"Tell you what," he said to the waiting prince. "You take a look at these records yourself and tell me what you think."

He gestured to the servant riding discreetly behind with the baggage. The man trotted up, and Davaud handed off the shield, then retrieved the neat copies made by Hatahra's scribes from the side-pouch on his carry-all.

These he handed to Ivandred. Then he turned his neck from side to side to ease the stiffness that had somehow resulted from that wild gallop. When had he last galloped like that? Probably the time he fought his only duel—when he was twenty, and he and that hothead Basya Isqua hadn't known how to back down from a witless quarrel forced on them by a flirt. That duels were forbidden had only added to the . . . intensity. He recalled the anguish of those days with an inward flutter of laughter. Now the flirt was a staid matron, married to a southern baron. But in those days, she wanted to heighten her prestige by getting someone to fight over her, so she could court the brother of the King of Sartor, visiting at the time. They'd all lost, in the sense that the old queen had demanded they make restitution for flouting laws.

The purpose of a court, he thought, trying to ease his right hip by listing to the left, *is to avoid this war savagery*. He had lived too long to expect everyone of high degree to have brains, moral principles, and good will, but the layers of language, behavior, even dance and fashion, all diffused the clashings of intent. People might, and did, get wounded, but not by steel. And so they lived to learn their lessons, as he and Basya and Firandel had, or they did not learn. But no one lost their lives in the process.

The Chwahir, he knew, did not have that luxury. Neither did these Marlovens, it seemed.

"Parade," Ivandred said.

"What?"

Ivandred handed the papers back. "These are not battles. They are parades, at least this Skih-huh Lake one, and this other that took place near this bridge."

"Do you mean the Battle of Skya Lake?" Davaud corrected with an apologetic gesture. "Parade? If you will honor me with a clarification, I would be most grateful."

Ivandred pointed at the papers. "These rules binding who marches first, how close they come, maneuvering around one another, the heralds all at the side conferring and sending messengers running back and forth, with scribes to write it all down. At the end, all that about hostages and ransom, and what is required of each rank, and the court lined up watching their favorites. That's a parade, a mock battle. It is not quite a war game."

Davaud looked surprised. "But there have to be rules, or who's to stop a wholesale slaughter?"

Ivandred's pale eyes narrowed, revealing the amusement he was trying to hide. Davaud's nerves chilled.

Ivandred said, "These Chwahir, they are mainly foot warriors and rely on numbers, or did in this report. How old is it?"

Davaud told him.

Ivandred turned up his palm. "Seven centuries ago! Much could have changed since then." Again, he was trying to hide his amusement. "So we shall assume a similar tactic, at least until we see them. If you have a map, I can show you how to plan for that and break them up quickly."

The clatter of galloping hooves interrupted. An excited page rode up, his voice cracking as he announced that Duke Thias was behind them.

Davaud knew his duty. "We are about to be joined by more of the queen's force. Perhaps we can all plan over the map together," he suggested.

To the east the Duke and Duchess of Alarcansa completed their third day on the road, stopping by the duchess's command at the western limit of her lands, where Baroness Mayra Valsin had a comfortable palace.

"We will stay with Mayra, in a civilized manner," she said, after summoning her duke to her carriage. "There is time enough to ride north tomorrow, for the next leg of our circle."

Kaidas bowed.

Carola realized her voice had been short, and fought against irritation. She prided herself on her excellent manners, on no one ever knowing what she was thinking. She especially hated being short with her beloved, but it was difficult to maintain serenity after a second long, hot, boring day alone in this carriage, jolted horribly because of the speed that war seemed to require. Kaidas had politely refused to ride in the carriage, saying that he must remain with his force, to be seen by them, to be accessible to them each time they stopped, so he could answer questions and talk to the new recruits at each point.

Was that a necessity of the warrior habit of mind? She had no experience of it, so no argument could be made. She used her rank to commandeer an inn for the first night, but it had been extremely late when he came to bed where she lay waiting; and worse, far worse, he had risen before she awoke, ruining her cherished morning ritual for the first time. She'd had to scold herself into reason: if he'd made this stupid trip alone, she still would not have had her morning with him.

After dressing far more swiftly than she liked, she emerged from the bedchamber to discover that the putative warriors were all gathered in the courtyard, ready to ride. Her carriage waited and a meal, thoughtfully arranged for her to enjoy in the comfort of the coach.

To eat alone, while her duke rode with the louts.

It happened again the second morning. She was forced to hasten in a manner she did not consider commensurate with *melende*, but that night, when she requested her duke to wake her when he woke, he replied, "I shall if you desire, but first I must ask. Do you wish to go out to the stable in the dark and examine the animals' shoes, and see to their feed? Because that is my task as soon as I rise."

She did not wish. But she woke when he did and insisted on tying his hair before he went.

A rider was sent ahead to inform the baroness that she would be honored with a visit from her duchess and duke.

Mayra came to her gate herself to welcome the ducal cavalcade, assigning her own rooms to the duchess and her duke. As the baroness labored through dinner to entertain the two tired and tense people who had displaced her in her own home, the duchess responded with rigid politesse, and the duke, aching after a long day in the saddle, longed for rest. Everyone was relieved when at last they retired.

The duchess was determined to retire early so that she would waken before dawn and not be denied her morning time with Kaidas. Mayra's bedroom was comfortable enough, but it was not Carola's own. While Kaidas stood at the window, she wandered about the room, looking at things and fighting to resume her serenity. Her dressers, unfamiliar with the palace, were late to attend her. Finally she sent a waiting maid in search of them, and stood in the middle of the room, furiously tapping her fan on her palm.

Flick, flick, flick.

The sound was not loud, but it was distinct. Yet she seemed to be the only one to hear it. And what was her husband doing? She turned her head, and there was no attentive duke, making her distress his own, but an absent one staring out through the window, as if whatever existed there held more importance than his duchess. The realization was one more affront to the refined mind. Enraged past endurance, she said venomously, "Chwahir. The first time in hundreds of years. It would be like Lasthavais to be at the root of it."

Kaidas spun around.

Carola had never seen that narrow look, the white mouth. Anger flamed, blood-hot, but she kept her teeth gritted, wishing she had not lowered herself even that much. Until now she had never permitted any mention of the selfish, grasping Princess Lasthavais to cross her lips. Carola would not permit *Her* to destroy Definian *melende*.

But Carola's disgust with her lapse was subsumed under the rage caused by that reaction of his.

His answer was utterly unexpected. "What makes you think there is a connection between the Chwahir in the pass and the princess?"

He didn't say her name, or attempt to defend her, Carola thought with a spurt of triumph. *His anger is justly with the Chwahir.* That observation was so comforting she regained her customary well-modulated tones. "The birth of the heir, the rumors of suitors, and the arrival of these Chwahir, all three at once, raise my suspicions. But if the queen apprehends no connection, no doubt it is mere coincidence. I don't pretend to comprehend the warrior mind."

He didn't hear this gentle reminder of her forbearance. His eyes were turned toward his wife, but his mind reviewed the map of Colend. The pass. Alsais. Heir, suitors . . . and, back in memory, Prince Jurac Sonscarna, refusing to dance with anyone but the princess, scandalizing the entire court.

The possibilities assembled into conviction as he followed his wife's lead in her evening routine. By now he had learned to shut his mind away, leaving his body to follow orders. A month's habit set his thoughts free to consider what was likely, and what must be done, while the rest of him performed his part in Carola's long sexual rituals.

He had learned after a single day in company with his wife-to-be that she was consumed with an angry jealousy, and so he had made a private vow never to mention his beloved before Carola. He would not have his memories sullied by her acrimony.

Jealousy, he had learned, distorted everything it touched. Carola's notion that Lasva could have somehow caused the Chwahir to threaten was preposterous. Yet might there be a spark of truth in it? Why else would Jurac Sonscarna suddenly send warriors over the mountain the same year—the same season—that an heir was born?

Containing his impatience, Kaidas waited until, at long last, his wife's demands had all been met and she sank into deep sleep. Then he picked up his clothing, splashed through the bath long enough to rid himself of her scent, dressed, and penned a note to his wife before his valet had managed to rouse the stable hands and get eleven animals saddled.

Kaidas hesitated, studying the note.

Carola:

I realize you were right, and the Chwahir must be making a feint toward Alarcansa while riding on the capital. As we have no magical communication cases, I ride to warn the queen.

No mention of Lasva. He knew he ought to add some diplomatic sentiment, but he resisted. If he was wrong, it would never be enough. If he was right, the accolades of the court would diffuse his true motivation. Carola's pride in the accrued glory to Alarcansa might even overcome her jealousy.

But more important, he could not bring himself to gainsay what mattered most: the love that must stay locked inside his heart, and the guardianship of what remained of his honor. He would never paint another lover's cup, and he would write nothing that was not true.

He signed his name and left the note on her bedside table. Soon he was riding west, breathing clean air through a misting rain.

He and his small band traded off, the two riders in front lighting the way with bespelled torches that burned somehow in spite of the rain. When it was Kaidas's turn to ride at the front, his partner was his favorite man, a burly smith named Neas.

They rode side by side, the smell of singed honey from the torches, the hiss of rain hitting fire not unpleasant, though Kaidas discovered that holding something aloft was irksome. There were enough glowglobes in the houses they passed to shed faint light on the road that wound down to run alongside the river. The darkness was not absolute but made up of shades of blue, broken by distant pinpoints of golden window lights.

Kaidas did not realize he was smiling until Neas, who'd been giving him increasingly puzzled glances, said doubtfully, "Pardon me, your grace, but have you ever seen war?"

Kaidas's smile faded. "Yes," he said, as his horse snorted and shook water from its mane. "That is, I was present at a skirmish."

"What happened, if I may ask?"

"Ask away. Though there is little to tell. A few years ago I rode with some of my border cousins. Nothing much happened—mostly the

Khanerenth border riders and us playing hide'n'find. But once, some brigands tried raiding across the border. We found 'em, defeated 'em. I say we, but I mostly followed, sweating so much my sword was slipping out of my fingers."

Twin gleams from the torchlight reflected in Neas's eyes. "Go on, if you've a mind."

Kaidas's expression resumed the grimness Neas had thought habitual until this sodden ride. "What can I say? The actual fighting was appalling to witness. I wasn't the only one on our side constantly muttering the Waste Spell lest I lose everything I'd eaten for a week as people hacked one another to bloody splatters."

Neas said, "Ah-yedi! So it is."

"Why do you ask?"

The big man bunched his shoulders in an embarrassed shrug. "Nothing. Only wondered."

You wondered because I must look as happy as I am, Kaidas thought. He was not angry with Neas. How could he be? But it forced him to acknowledge that though he was riding steadily toward the prospect of having to hack up unknown Chwahir, or be hacked up, he *was* happy.

He was, for the first time in weeks, free.

Riding west away from Alarcansa was like leaving prison. There was no wifely gaze watching him every moment, no sweet, precise courtly voice catching him up by asking what he was thinking. He had not, until this moment, permitted himself to consider how she watched his every breath, every move, every bite and sup; how her neat, small hands rifled through every belonging of his, no matter how inconsequential; how she calmly made herself mistress of the contents of every one of the few letters he'd had occasion to pen, as if she had the right; and how—he discovered through the single personal servant he'd brought with him (all the rest were hired by her)—every letter sent him was seen first by her.

She would watch his thoughts if she could.

He had chosen this life and must abide by his decision. He could preserve a semblance of honor only by never speaking these thoughts aloud.

The truth was this: freedom was sweet, and even sweeter was the possibility that he would see Lasva, that he might even, somehow, get her alone long enough to say the things he had locked inside himself since the morning of the heir's birth and his father's visit. Just once. To speak the truth. Once. And the memory would have to last a lifetime. He would never come to court again.

FOUR

Of Empty Hands

"Books?"

It was midnight, and Torsu, having been sent to the queen's rooms to bolster the sewing teams assembled to stitch together all those battle tunics, was about to leave when she encountered that silly rabbit Nereith coming from the princess's rooms, her arms laden with books.

"Books?" she said again, for they'd finally been permitted to speak. Not that she was grateful—it was long overdue, and Nereith should have been silenced longer, as it was all her fault. Torsu couldn't resist: "I didn't know you could read."

Rain tapped against the windows, and lightning briefly flared. Nereith jumped. "It's that new book, the one about Elgar the Fox—not for me."

Torsu did not care about books, old or new. "You mean she's back?"

Nereith's mouth rounded. She was not supposed to tell anybody, but surely that didn't mean other dressers, did it? Just people outside the princess's staff, didn't it?

She leaned toward Torsu and whispered, "She got here by magic. The queen's making her stay hidden. I'm not sure why."

Torsu gave the younger girl a derisive smirk. "It probably has to do with this war talk flying every which way."

"War. But what would that have to do with—" Nereith's eyes looked wild. "I'd better go."

Don't you listen to anything? Torsu thought, and as the girl flitted away, Torsu walked on, laughing to herself.

———

Ivandred was amazed at how long it took to convene Colendi nobles for a simple strategy session.

First a city of great silken tents had to be erected, each in some predetermined reference to the others that necessitated many takings-down and pacings-off. After that, an elaborate supper was served by the light of a hundred paper lanterns, followed by a long, polite debate about precedence at the war negotiation in the morning—who would stand where, and who would have to wait outside the tent.

Then they retired to recoup themselves for morning. Ivandred took his people off for practice, returning early, battle-ready, when the servants slowly began to stir.

As the dukes and barons and their followers slowly rose and clamored about calling for rapiers and shields and some for armor, their servants crowded around with folding chairs, towels for muddy boots, and refreshments, despite the plan for an elaborate breakfast as soon as the strategy session was deemed finished. While the sun hid behind building clouds, more servants ran back and forth with messages for Davaud and Duke Thias, sent from the city half a day's ride away, until at last the Colendi were gathered.

Davaud and the duke had agreed that Ivandred, as the one with highest rank as well as being the new ally, had the position directly before the royal map. This map was duly unrolled by the herald who had carried it like a couched lance, bound by ribbons in the royal colors, golden seals dangling and swinging at every step.

Ivandred assessed the enormous map as the dozen men and women of various ages around him covertly scanned their own territories, evaluating how the royal heralds had drawn them. Ivandred took in the elaborate drawings of what appeared to be ducal and lordly emblems, tiny etchings of palaces and old castles—almost down to the level of gardens—but not one hint of where forges lay, or ore mines, or military establishments. There appeared to be no military roads at all.

Ivandred laid a finger on the easternmost of the three golden-labeled passes. "You say it is here, they come?"

"Yes," Davaud said. "This pass, above Alarcansa. We should be meeting the new duke on the road within a day or two, if we ride faster, and take carriages at night—"

"What is here of strategic importance?"

Strategic importance?

Ivandred saw the uncertainty in the well-mannered faces around him, and said, "Your royal castles—holdings? Mines and forges? What would the queen lose that the Chwahir king could take here?"

"Nothing but vineyards, really." Davaud made a vague, apologetic gesture, to beg pardon for the trespass against good taste in implying a duchy had nothing of importance. "The pass is closest to Alarcansa land, but it's very rocky up there. The principal ducal castles are all south."

"There was no threat? No demand?"

"Such communications have been absent."

"If he wants the kingdom, your royal city lies here directly below the middle pass."

"But that pass has the most wards protecting it. Only one Chwahir is permitted through at a time," Davaud said. "And never warriors. As for our royal city, it has transfer wards all over it, extending out a full day's ride in all directions. No one can transfer except to the proper Destinations warded by our mages. Anyone who tries a transfer anywhere else will be re-transferred directly to the mages."

Ivandred waved that information away. "How long have the Chwahir been seen in these mountains?"

"About three weeks since the first notice was taken."

"Doing nothing? Then they wish to be seen, to draw your forces."

"Of course."

Everyone made signs or cultured murmurs of assent. It made perfect sense. If you were to have a battle, a place was appointed, the forces lined up, everything according to expected rules.

"No," Ivandred said.

They reacted to the baldly spoken word, some frowning, others stepping back.

"You do not comprehend," he continued. "This is not an attack. That makes no sense. It is a—a—" Ivandred lifted his hand, miming a feint before a strike.

"A trick?" Davaud asked, feeling impending disaster. He tried to recollect all that military reading. "A ruse? A diversion?"

"Diversion, yes," Ivandred said. "But to draw our attention from what?"

"A ruse." "A ruse?" The word whispered back through the crowd.

Ivandred looked around. These people were not stupid, they were inexperienced. How to educate them quickly?

"Suppose it was possible to slip warriors, the number doesn't matter now, through one of these other passes. Over a period of time previous. What would they want to take first? Assuming they are not mad enough to try to take the royal city without a full army."

Duke Thias immediately thought of his own home and the mines in his hills, but Davaud cast back several years to Jurac Sonscarna's visit. His second cousin was the ambassador, so he knew that Jurac was still angry that Hatahra had not stopped her courtiers from high-handed treatment of a hated Chwahir, nor had she entertained his proposal for marriage between him and Lasva. Ever since then, the Chwahir ambassadorial staff had endured various diplomatic insults. The only Colendi who had treated Jurac with respect, even kindness, was . . .

"Lasva," he whispered. Then he shook his head. "Ah-ye, even a Chwahir wouldn't do that," he said aloud, thinking of Lasva safe in her rooms, no one knowing she was there.

"Take the princess?" Thias said, cutting one of his own barons off mid-word. "Jurac would. Remember how he followed her around like a hound after a tidbit? And didn't the young ones laugh!"

"But she's somewhere on the road," the Countess of Isqua pointed out. "How could all these fellows in the mountains get past us to the royal road? They cannot! I believe we must spread out, guarding the road."

"By magic, of course."

"Who can do that kind of magic transfer?"

"Dark magic!"

"Norsunder!"

Few listened as they waited for the speaker of higher rank to pause so they could slide their own observation in.

"Obviously," a countess stated, "the Chwahir have allied with Norsunder."

"Norsunder certainly would covet the Chwahirs' ready-made army, and our land."

Low-voiced, Davaud said, "We've had Lasva safe in the palace for days. Or what we thought was safe."

Ivandred's eyes narrowed. Matthias Altan voicelessly repeated the words, *We thought.* If Jurac had people swarming around at either end of the kingdom, drawing the Colendi galloping madly eastward and westward away from Alsais, there wouldn't have to be any mysterious magic.

Jurac was perfidious enough alone; if, say, he slipped men over the middle pass one by one, while waiting for the princess to arrive home—

It was Thias, and not Davaud, who lifted his head and without so much as a gesture of pardon, roared, "Ride back! At once! We have to search the city!"

Ivandred said, "Wait—" But his voice was lost.

He didn't bother with a second attempt. Instead, he remained at the map, measuring with his eye. Assume the Chwahir king had indeed come over with abduction in mind. He couldn't have arrived in the city with a force without being unnoticed. That meant he had to be hiding within a short ride to the north, waiting on a signal.

Ivandred looked around. The nobles were running about the camp, leaving their servants holding fine silver trays filled with uneaten dainties, and two herald-scribes busily scribbling down everything they'd heard.

Ivandred ran out, whistling to his trumpeter. He was in the midst of issuing his orders when Davaud arrived, panting.

Ivandred said briefly, "Ride north. Intercept."

Davaud fought for breath. Elsewhere in the camp, Thias was ordering everyone about. The servants obeyed, then paused as their own counts, countesses, barons and baronesses called out conflicting orders according to their own ideas, for they did not like their own servants given commands by Thias Altan. It would set a dangerous precedent at court.

Servants stood in disorder, faces turning from side to side as the courtiers assumed manners of elaborate politeness and vied for primacy, some still convinced that they should proceed to Alarcansa, and others that they should guard the road.

In contrast, Ivandred said three or four things in his home language, and the Marloven tents snapped to, the horses' shoes were checked, weapons stashed, bows slung.

"I'm riding with you," Davaud said.

"We will ride fast," Ivandred warned. "And we have only our own remounts."

"I can borrow a mount from someone who has fast horses," Davaud said, thinking regretfully of his hips. But he could see Hatahra's face. Whatever the cost, he had to be there. And so he would be.

He left behind his servants, baggage, and that stupid shield he wouldn't have known how to use. They rode out, unnoticed by Thias—who was arguing with the Duke of Gaszin, the Countess of Isqua, and several barons about which way was most efficient to surround the royal palace—and unnoticed by the servants, cooks, and stable hands buzzing about like bees over their half-cooked breakfast in the shambles of their camp.

———

By morning, Torsu had worked herself into resentful anger. Why was a rabbity hum like Nereith trusted in the princess's secret presence, and not someone who actually had brains—and art?

They don't need my art if Princess Lasthavais is hiding, of course, Torsu reasoned. But she knew when she'd been south-gated, and it rankled.

When she happened to see Kivic at breakfast, and he happened to look her way, it was instinct to whisper, "She's back—and I didn't even know it. What's more, that bird-wit Nereith did. Can you imagine?"

Kivic grimaced sympathetically, his eyes wide and smiling with promise. "Come along, tell me all about it."

"I can't. I have to get to the queen's rooms. It's lace day."

"Too bad. You'd get a laugh out of the chirps I'm hearing from the stable hands. Here, I'll come with you. Wait till you hear about the near fight between Altan and Sentis's hummers."

"Fight? What about?" she asked as Kivic fell in step beside her.

"Oh, they're all in an uproar. Seems half the court is stringing out along the roads, all hoping to watch the play—er, I mean the war." He grinned. "Here, let's take the longer route, through the old gardens. Then you can cut back and not be seen."

Torsu agreed. She certainly did not want to be seen, and so she paced beside him as he retailed gossip in a joking voice. He led the way behind the new ducal wing to the old juniper garden, as yet untouched, as it hid all the unsightly construction that was only carried on when court was absent.

When he was done, he asked casually, "Where would Nereith be now?"

"Asleep, of course, since she had night duty."

"Perfect." He halted under the shadows of a great, spreading juniper. His hands slid up Torsu's shoulders to her neck, and he smiled down into her face. "And here's a lovely thought to hold to: she'll never bother you again."

Torsu looked up in surprise as his hands stroked her throat, his thumbs brushing over the pulse above her collarbones. She opened her mouth to ask why, but no sound came out. With faint regret, and a real sense of gratitude for the pleasure she'd given him, he made her death both clean and quick, then laid her gently down, rolling her body under the deep green branches far enough that the scent of broken needles and resin made him sneeze.

Then he loped back to his room to report. Jurac would have to move *now*.

Getting the princess out could not be done by magic, as the entire palace was warded against transfer.

Kivic had already ascertained that Lasthavais drank caffeo, and he knew whom, from the kitchens, to relay false messages to and whom to commandeer. Things were agreeably chaotic already as servants ran to and fro packing traveling baskets for courtiers who had taken a sudden notion to ride east.

Kivic slid in, got his caffeo, and it was easy enough to find an isolated corner so he could slip powdered sleepweed into the porcelain pot. He hailed a passing page. The armed heralds weren't even there any more—the queen herself had sent them the day before to guard her consort on his ride east.

"Here, Nereith said that this is to go to the princess's suite," he said.

The girl rolled her eyes. "But she isn't here."

Kivic smiled his charming smile and shrugged. "Orders."

The girl sighed, giving an irritated shake of her shoulders, but she took the tray. Everything had gone crazy, it seemed, but she was obedient, and so she carried the tray upstairs, and scratched at the princess's outer door. And to her surprise the door opened and Poppy, the princess's page, appeared. She looked down at the tray, hesitating.

"Nereith sent it," said the palace page.

With a shrug Poppy bore the tray inside, then closed and locked the door. She brought it to Lasthavais's inner parlor, where the princess was immersed in the book about Ivandred's ancestor.

"Caffeo, from Nereith," Poppy said, when she looked up.

"I didn't order it, but now that I smell it, it seems a good idea," Lasva said, smiling. "Thank you."

She took a sip. Was the chocolate not quite sweetened? It had a bitter edge. She poured the cup back and swirled the pot around, poured more, and drank that. A little better, though some of that taste remained. Enough so that the desire for it went away after one cup.

But one cup was enough. The handsomely written words on the page flickered and swam, and a huge yawn forced her jaw open.

She rose. The sound of her moving brought Poppy running. "I think I will retire," Lasva said. "You needn't wait. Is that the bell for the Hour of Spice? Go, have your meal, and on your way back, please ask my sister's people if there is any news."

Poppy curtseyed, delighted to be ordered to listen to whispers. She locked the door and sped downstairs, not realizing until much later that her mistress's thoughtfulness had saved her life.

Kivic used a heavy dose of sleepweed on the four remaining of the upstairs dressers, via cups of caffeo with distilled liquor to mask the taste. Three of them were glad enough to break duty rules and take a refresher. One, though, lectured Kivic on daring to approach her during duty, and with liquor in the caffeo—she could smell it! Still smiling his cheery smile he cut her remonstrance short, strangling her with a lot less finesse than he'd used on Torsu. He did not enjoy being lectured by these Colendi fools he would never see again.

As he'd done with the previous three, he dragged her body to one of the brocade-covered tables that lined the halls, and left it underneath. The others would waken to considerable surprise and aching heads. This one would have to be found.

Kivic climbed over one of the balconies in the empty consort suite and made his way to Lasthavais's chambers. The windows were un-locked, open to the air. He found no more servants. As well. There would be no chance of getting them to drink sleep potions, and he hadn't looked forward to killing little Poppy or some other young page, all of whom were both friendly and harmless.

The princess lay on her bed alone, deeply asleep.

He looked down at her face. He had never been this close to her. Even in sleep the curve of her lips was entrancing, her coloring warm, her brow intelligent. What would be her reaction if she opened her eyes?

It was strange. He was alone with the princess half the continent seemed to want—more, if the news about the Marloven fellow was true. He ran his hands lightly over her peachy-rose gown, exquisitely stitched in a floating, gleaming fabric unheard of in Chwahirsland, where the women dressed sturdily against the ever-present cold. Her curves, after all, were just female curves. The pleasure in touching her was too mild to be termed pleasure; for that to ignite, there must be the pleasure of her response. Interesting.

But not interesting enough to linger. So he searched her with quick efficiency for hidden pockets and transfer tokens, or magical scrollcases. Nothing. She had expected to be alone.

Beautiful she was, supposedly with will to match wit to wit. What would her life be like with Jurac Sonscarna and his somber moods?

Kivic laughed soundlessly, located the wardrobe, and pulled out a summer cloak with which he wrapped her up.

Then he trod to the doors to unlatch the locks, and there were two of Jurac's men, wearing lamentably ill-fitting House servant garb that Kivic had smuggled out the previous week.

They took up station, watching in all directions, and there was Jurac himself. He alone did not wear servant garb, but there was no one to see him as he looked around appreciatively, and then at Kivic's open-handed gesture went to claim his bride.

She never even stirred as Jurac picked her up. In silence he stood holding her against him, at last, at last, the subtle scent in her hair making him almost dizzy.

"Let's go." he said to the waiting men.

FIVE

OF A BLACK COAT

D istant bells rang the midday hour as Kaidas and his little troop
stopped for something to eat. The stable hand went to scout fresh
mounts. Stupid with too many nights of shorted sleep and then one
night with no sleep at all, Kaidas sat over his wine-fish and lemon-
touched butter beans as he tried to force his tired mind to examine the
reasons for his increasing uneasiness, that sense he was too late.

Why did his mind keep circling round that conversation with Carola
in the baroness's bedroom? If he could recapture the chain of logic—
Jurac—courtship—the possibility that Chwahir had slipped over the
passes one by one while everyone was paying attention to the outer two
passes. . . .

What if Jurac was already *in* Colend? If half the court was busy galloping east toward Alarcansa, and the rest were turning their faces westward in expectation of an attack from two fronts . . .

"Here's your caffeo, my lord," said his valet.

Kaidas drank it off, his eyes stinging against the scald on his tongue.
Good. He gasped, fighting the pain. At least it cleared his head.

Assuming Jurac wanted Lasva, and not the city, then he wouldn't
need an army. All he needed were a few people, who would wait—

"North."

Two of the men said, "What?"

Neas came stomping in, a wide grin slashed across his sun-browned face. "Horses ready, your grace. Royal city isn't far now."

Kaidas realized he'd given voice to his thought. He shook his head. "We either waste time talking, or we go north and sit on the quickest road to the middle pass, and intercept him going either to the city, or from it, if he's already been there." *And just waiting for Lasva to arrive home from Sartor.*

Neas crashed his mighty fist onto the massive oaken table, making all the dishes jump. "Let's go!" the man roared.

They ran out. The rain was steadily increasing. *Good,* Kaidas thought, veering between weariness and exhilaration as he mounted up. *If it slows us up, it will slow the Chwahir, will it not?*

Jurac had never actually carried anyone before. It seemed to take forever to get out of the palace, not because they'd be seen. Royal privacy was absolute, which was why I'd only seen the back garden behind the royal suite—the very route Jurac was taking—after the senior scribe had gained permission for our Fifteen test.

So the problem for the Chwahir was not being seen, but the slowness of Jurac's progress, as he had to stop frequently and rest.

In spite of the many pauses to rest, by the time they were proceeding through the tangled growth hiding the rubble marking the old palace, his shoulders and wrists ached, and his breath came short and fast. He regretted having given over the old courtyard drills he'd had to do as a boy. Kingship meant inspections of parades, not parading. It also meant hours of magic study on top of other demands, leaving little time for sweating at target practice.

But he was not going to let anyone else touch her.

So he hitched her up once again, shifting the burden, grateful that Kivic had thought of the sleepweed. Carrying an awake woman who might be struggling—

He veered away from that thought, and resisted the impulse to grip her tighter. Let him get her to Narad, and make her a queen, and give her anything she asked for. Then she would change her mind. Yes, that was the way to think.

He forced himself to walk faster. Though they were well beyond the palace, they were in no wise safe. What if some fool ran up to that room

to see if she wanted her ribbons changed? He wasn't afraid of a fight—
would welcome it, preferably with some of those strutting, drawling
windbags whose sneering insults behind fluttering fans he'd been forced
to ignore years ago—but he knew that slaughter of her countrymen
wouldn't help his cause with Lasthavais.

At a nod his men spread out as they slogged through the overgrown
gardens, churning up the rich red soil that was so very scarce north of
the mountains, until at last they spied the woodland whose cover he'd
counted on to hide his small force. He breathed in the sharp smell of the
evergreens that reminded him so relentlessly of home. It was the leafy
trees, with their startling orange and gold and red leaves, that were so
strange. Not enough sun penetrated Chwahirsland for any but the hardi-
est to grow. Evergreens he had in plenty.

Mixed with the scent of crushed needle-mat was the smell of his own
sweat (pouring down his back, despite the rain) and crushed flowers.
The world seemed unreal and made him want to laugh.

"Fence ahead," a man cried.

Excellent. That wall marked the last of the palace grounds, beyond
which was scrub forest. And relative safety.

Jurac had a new thought, and turned to find Kivic's snub, cheery face
not far behind. Kivic had shed his Colendi servant tunic and wore plain,
dark clothing. "I take it you cannot return?"

Kivic smiled mischievously. "Afraid not. You wanted speed. Once they
figure out she's gone, it won't take them long to think of me."

Ivandred kept an eye on Lord Davaud, who rode at their speed without
complaint. When his riding companion's face had grayed to nearly the
color of his hair, Ivandred whistled for the duty runner. "Give the Colendi
a willow stick."

Davaud was concentrating so hard on staying in his saddle he was
startled when a horse drew near, and a young Marloven appeared.
Davaud looked in surprise at a rain-washed face with feminine lines to
the neck. Was that a young woman? The warrior held out what looked
like a twig or a strip of something.

Ivandred said, "It's treated. Medicinal. Chew it."

Davaud bit down. The bitterness caused his tongue to pucker and his
nose to burn, but he kept grimly at it, and the reward was a gradual but
steady easing of the pain radiating out from his hips and thighs—causing

him to reflect on what kind of life was led by these boys . . . these. . . . He couldn't accustom himself to the thought of women warriors, though he knew history was full of them, including in Colend.

What kind of lives did warriors—of either gender—lead, to have need of medicine that you could chew on the road?

A familiar jut of hilly land brought him back to the present. "We're close. The palace is a short ride that way." He pointed to the southwest.

Ivandred raised his hand, and the cavalcade halted. "Lead," he suggested, indicating Davaud take the forward position.

"I've never actually approached the palace from the back. Let me have a look from that hillock right there, to orient myself." Davaud pointed to his right, where a cluster of wild hickory and young oak grew in profusion above a little waterfall.

He urged his horse up a path adjacent to the fall, while Ivandred had his riders gear up and change horses.

"Do we fight to kill?" Haldren asked, in Marloven.

Ivandred considered, while watching the old Colendi lord up on the hillock. Lord Davaud was smart enough to keep himself screened behind shrubbery as he peered around.

"Not our quarrel," he said. "No honor, either, if there are fewer of them than us, which is probably the case if they're doing a covert grab-and-run."

Haldren flicked out a hand in assent. Abductions of women were known in Marloven history, though not recently. They'd happened back in the days when the kingdom was splintering under the terrible Olavair kings. Right around then the old baby-betrothal custom was also breaking down. Sometimes the brides planned the abductions themselves— those were the only successful ones. The other kind tended to end in disaster, sometimes with the bride killing the groom, other times torching off a war between entire clans.

"Fight to disable, unless they threaten her," Ivandred said finally. "If there's any danger to the princess, they're yours."

Tdan asked, "If we're outnumbered?"

"Anything more than double, go for the kill, and you can take trophies."

Fierce joy rippled through the two columns, but no sound was made, not on a reconnaissance pause.

Davaud made his way back down and said, "I spotted the palace roofs that way. So we must cross this stream, and go over yon hill. I believe we will catch up with the old road that runs to the wall at the edge of the palace ground."

Ivandred motioned to his two scouts. "Ride ahead, and watch for a sign," he said.

They took off, Davaud and Ivandred following more slowly.

———

Lasva was dreaming of swimming in Lake Skya. Marnda kept calling for her to come out, that winter was coming, and Lasva obediently tried to swim her way, but the lake shore kept receding, the waters gradually getting deeper and darker, and she was cold, and tired, and—

And heard rasping breathing above her, not her own. And voices, talking softly, but not in Kifelian. Her neck hurt, and her legs from the knees down tingled as if she'd been kneeling too long. She was being carried, and the voices were speaking Chwahir.

Instinct to panic, to fight for freedom, flared through her, but she controlled it. Better to stay as she was, listen, and learn. She was in enemy hands, that was obvious, though how or why was unclear. But she was quite sure if they knew she was awake, she would lose the only advantage she had: surprise. She lifted one eyelid—to discover that her face was covered by cloth. Very well, then. Steady, steady, listen.

Jurac felt Lasthavais stir and her muscles tighten. He looked down, but her face was hidden. She relaxed again, and relief pooled inside him.

———

Queen Hatahra scowled. The Hour of the Lily had long passed—five hours past midday! Her sister was late and had not even sent a page. Hatahra had not thought Lasva capable of such discourtesy.

Hatahra had whiled away the hour by watching her daughter, who waved her arms and made noises that were endlessly fascinating. But now she was hungry.

Hatahra looked over the baby's head to the duty page. "Will you find out if my sister has been detained?"

When the girl was gone, Hatahra picked up the latest message from the heralds who were on watch below the eastern pass.

The Duchess of Alarcansa is traveling north, having so far raised a force of—

"Noooooo!" The scream ripped through the halls, echoing everywhere.

Hatahra whirled, grabbing her baby up tightly against her. The two remaining armed heralds opened the door and looked out, then at each other, then back at the queen for orders, their hands gripping the hilts of their rapiers.

The royal page stumbled in, her face greenish white. "Sindra is *dead*!" She wrung her hands.

"What?"

Everyone exclaimed in questions. Hatahra rapped out: "Silence!"

The page forced words past her chattering teeth. "The hall. Empty. Her tray-table, the cover crooked. I, I straightened it, and my foot felt something 'neath. I looked, and it was her. H-her face, all purple—" She broke down again, weeping into her hands.

Hatahra turned to the herald guards. "Guard the babe." She motioned to Pollar, the head nursery maid, to take Alian, and waited until they had gone through the nursery door. Then she shut it, locked it, and yanked the bell-pull.

Servants came running, some to the summons, others to report finding another dresser shoved under a table, snoring deeply.

Hatahra herself led the investigation, terrified of finding her sister's dead body. Yet too stunned, she had to observe, to comprehend, before she could conjecture why and what it meant.

It did not take long. Lasthavais's locked door was swiftly opened, to disclose an empty room. The queen turned to her servants. "You will say nothing. To anyone. But guard every door. I will send the entire staff of heralds on a search."

The Marloven scouts sped over a rise thick with silver-leafed aspen, their forms dark shadows flickering between pale trunks.

Davaud and Ivandred halted.

"Horsemen waiting over that rise to the north. Ranged for someone coming up the cart path from the south. About to join them, looks like. Not sure of the numbers. We heard voices beyond the wall, in a wood. The two groups'll meet fairly quick."

"Terrain wood?"

"Yes. Rough, rocky—ancient ruins, looks like."

Ivandred motioned, dividing his small force. "No lances or bows. Swords only."

One group to attack from the south, making all the noise possible, the others to close in from the north. A scout went with each party as guide, and they rode out.

Chwahir do not fight on horseback for a number of reasons, including the fact that their kingdom is mostly too rocky. They heard the thunder of horse hooves just before they saw a tight wedge of yellow-haired warriors on horseback soar over a jumble of rock and a fallen tree trunk, and then everyone was fighting.

Lasva chose that moment to jam her elbows out, in the exact movement the fan instructor had taught her. Taken by surprise, Jurac dropped her with a squelch into the mud.

The second Marloven party closed in from the north.

Ivandred saw within two heartbeats that he was going to win, for the Chwahir had no time to assemble into any kind of defense, and further, they did not know how to fight upward toward mounted warriors.

With the habit of years of war games, he scanned for their leader, spotting the tall figure the Chwahir all watched for orders just as Lasva tumbled out of his arms and fell with a splat into the mud. She flung the cloak back from her face and rolled over, coming to her knees as the tall man bent over her, hands out.

Instinct was faster than reason. Ivandred pulled a knife from his sleeve and spun it to Lasva, recalling as it left his hand that she was no Marloven woman to nip it out of the air. It might even hit her, or she'd squeal and jump out of the way, thus providing her assailant with a weapon. Maybe to use on her.

But as he leaped from his horse to her aid, she put up her hands.

She misjudged, for never in her life had she even seen a knife thrown. Her wrist turned in the fan sweep as if to knock it aside, but there was no fan in her fingers. The honed steel blade scored across her hand and wrist. Unaware of the sting of pain, she ducked down to snatch the dagger up from the mud.

Jurac stepped toward her, then rocked back when she dragged herself to her feet, her gown ripping, mud sliming her from hairline to heels. She held the knife with both hands.

"Touch me, and I'll use it," she said in a low, angry voice.

Her desperate gallantry caused Ivandred's heart to constrict.

Jurac stared at her in anguish as she glared back, her mind veering between unconnected thoughts like a toy boat tumbling down a waterfall: her ruined gown—Prince Ivandred, how could he possibly be here?—Jurac all grown up and strange, so strange, right there in the middle of his bony face, those gooseberry eyes were *Landis* eyes. Sartor's royal family stared back at her from those eyes.

"I offer you a kingdom," he said numbly.

Lasva stared back, too stunned to speak.

Ivandred joined them in three steps, Davaud limping behind.

"That's King Jurac, all right," Davaud said, wheezing from renewed pain. "What do you suggest we do?" he asked Ivandred.

Ivandred flicked a look from the tall, dark-haired Chwahir with the aggrieved face to the grim, mud-covered princess. The Chwahir stood there empty handed, while all around, the fighting swiftly ended, both sides looking to their leaders, awaiting command.

Ivandred shifted his gaze away from Jurac's anguish. He knew that face. Had felt it when he watched Tdiran Marlovair go.

He had no desire to kill this Chwahir king, but then he wasn't the one who'd been wronged. He turned to Lasthavais to ask her judgment. Saw in her averted face, her shivering body, that she just wanted Jurac gone, which surprised him; at that point he was unaware of how little she knew of statecraft. Well, it was not his affair.

"Take off," he said to Jurac. And to Lasthavais, "We'll return to your sister."

Lasthavais made a mute gesture of agreement. Now that the excitement was wearing off she was only aware of cold, the grit of mud, a searing sting across her hand and wrist, and a crashing headache from whatever it was she'd drunk. It took all of her dwindling strength to stand up straight, to avoid entertaining that staring Chwahir with a wild bout of weeping.

Davaud *did* know about statecraft. He watched, wondering if he ought to demand that they seize the Chwahir, but he was not sure the Marlovens would obey him. And anyway, he had no idea what they might do with a captured king, what Hatahra might do with him. Brandish him to the Chwahir? The idea of an entire kingdom mobilized to the kind of violence he'd just witnessed chilled him.

No, things were better this way. Hatahra could rant about missed opportunities if she wanted. At least her sister was safe.

Jurac looked around—his men disarmed, some disabled—his plans a ruin. He took one step, then another, each more painful.

Kivic had slipped behind a friendly oak at the first sign of trouble, watching in helpless dismay as his schemes for future influence crashed down with every exchange of steel. He slunk out, rapidly evolving plans to regain his position with his king—while Jurac, catching sight of him, thought angrily, *This is all your fault.* Retribution would start with Kivic, who'd promised it would be so easy.

"Let's go," Jurac commanded, and his men picked up their weapons and their wounded.

Jurac did not look back.

Ivandred held out a hand and helped the princess to her feet. Her touch, muddy and clammy as it was, sent fire along his nerves. He heard her breath draw in, and she lifted those wide blue eyes, and once again her gaze flashed heat through his entire body.

As the steady rain washed the last of the mud from her face she looked down at her bleeding wrist, the mud-sodden cloak hanging uselessly from her shoulders. Ivandred flicked it off, and she stood trembling in her wet cloud-gossamer gown that outlined every curve of her body, the knife held slack in her fingers.

With a quick, decisive movement he unfastened his knife belt and slung it to Haldren to hold, then he shrugged off his coat and set it around her. Last he wiped his knife on his clothing, resheathed it in his sleeve, and put his belt back on. A runner brought up a clean bandage, which he himself wrapped around her wrist. The only sounds were the thrummings of rain, and the thunk and squelch of the departing Chwahir.

Ivandred snapped his fingers and his horse danced up, head tossing. He lifted Lasva up to the saddle then mounted behind her, riding in his shirt sleeves. Davaud saw that he didn't even wear mail.

The Marlovens all removed their helmets and slung them at their horses' sides, then mounted up and resumed their formation. Their discipline was extraordinary.

Davaud winced and heaved himself back into the saddle, and they began riding south, back down the cart path leading past the dismantled palace.

Lasva's awareness of Ivandred's proximity blinded her to anything else. The musky smell of male sweat and his scent rising off the stiff, heavy coat sent the flame of desire through her to form a pool of hot fire low in her belly.

Jurac was already forgotten.

"Thank you," she said, when she was certain she could control her voice. "I am sorry about the knife."

She gave a breathless little chuckle. "I'm sorry I didn't catch it. Could I learn?"

His arm tightened around her. "You could."

Then they heard the sound of horse hooves as the outriders ripped their swords from the saddle sheaths.

SIX

OF A LOCK OF HAIR

K aidas knew before they sighted the towers of the palace through the rain that this rescue was going to be a disaster. He'd counted on finding fresh horses halfway, but there had been none anywhere. They'd all been claimed by those still streaming to the east expecting to witness the panoply of a heroic smiting of the despicable Chwahir.

Kaidas and his troop plugged grimly on, their animals drooping, the warriors sodden and shivering from cold and exhaustion and hunger.

So when they sighted mounted figures riding out from between the aspen trees, Kaidas did not hand out any orders. He let his poor horse come to a stop while he squinted into the rain.

Two riders resolved out of the gloom first, wearing black coats of a military cut. These had to be the Marlovens he'd heard about. How had they got here? Of course they'd be the first to figure out the feint.

The fact that he'd been right gave him about a heartbeat of relief. Then came the worst blow. Behind the outriders was Davaud, barely recognizable hatless, his fine battle tunic sodden with rain, his gray hair writhing down onto his shoulders like worms. Finally, across the withers of the horse next to him, shrouded in a severe military coat, sat Lasva, her rain-washed face splendid with heightened color. What had to be the Marloven prince rode behind her on the same horse. He was dressed only in shirt, trousers, and boots.

"My lord duke," Davaud called, smiling wearily. "You figured out the Chwahir ruse, I take it."

"And I take it I am too late," Kaidas returned.

Davaud bowed from the saddle. "The thought is taken as the deed. As you see, we are safe." His glance fell on young Haldren's helm and on the long curling hank of auburn hair that never was grown by creature of hoof, and he wondered what quality of "safe" he could promise the queen.

Kaidas paid the accompanying Marlovens no attention. He forced himself to face Lasva.

Equally determined, she braced herself to meet Kaidas's steady dark gaze. His upper lip was long, his mouth tight.

How could she speak, when he rode there with that rain-sodden white ribbon hanging down from his hair?

"Return to the palace with us?" Davaud asked, gesturing.

Kaidas compelled himself to observe the two on a horse, for he knew that memory must be exact, or the questions would torment him the worse. So he noted the arc of the Marloven's strong arm holding Lasva. It was an intimate grip, and she permitted it. She seemed to be leaning into his grasp.

Kaidas briefly met the cool light gaze of the Marloven prince, then he gave in to the overwhelming need to look away toward the marble towers of Alsais's royal palace.

He recalled the question, and understood that they all waited on his answer. "Ride on, my lord," he said to Davaud, grateful for the years of court training that gave him *melende* awake, asleep, and in defeat. "You seem to have everything well in hand. I must return to my wife."

Wife. The word acted on Lasva like the sting of a lash, and she closed her eyes. Ivandred's arm tightened round her, sending new fire along her lacerated nerves.

Oh, Lasva! Kaidas could not forbear one last glimpse, knowing it would be his last.

Just in time to see her turn her face into the Marloven's chest.

It took the remainder of his strength but he rode eastward from the palace, and the canals, and the royal city, his tired, dejected troop with him. Presently he had to occupy himself with the little details of life: where they might stay, how he could get mounts, his lack of funds, how to arrange for more. Oh, but he was wealthy now. He had only to give his name, his new name, the Duke of Alarcansa, and he had instant credit, smilingly offered.

Rain fell steadily, and his mind ran on and on, making logistical decisions.

Only once did he give in to impulse when, following scouts' reports, they arrived at the inn the Duchess of Alarcansa had ordered readied for her arrival. Kaidas's valet was among the laboring servants and set about ordering a warm, clean room, and fresh clothes.

While his man was doing these things, Kaidas took out the knife that he'd never used and hacked off his hair, throwing it and the ribbon into the fire.

When his man returned, his eyes widened in surprise, but he said nothing.

No one said anything, except Carola, when she arrived later. Her mood was vile. She hated rain, and coaches, and isolation, all made worse by the royal road being clogged with nobles as well as commoners. Rumors were even more wild, the latest being that the Chwahir had abruptly vanished from the eastern pass.

She received with well-bred politeness the news that her duke had arrived before her. She readied soft words—not rebuke, never that, but a gentle question. Why did he not rejoin her yesterday? Might he have spared a thought for his wife, compelled to sit in that stuffy carriage as it jolted along behind the crowds?

The words vanished when she confronted the astonishing spectacle of short curls falling unkempt on his forehead and over the tops of his ears, his neck bare. Hair far too short to be tied back. It changed his face. Made it harder. Or was that her imagination?

She said in her sweetest tone, "My dear Kaidas, I am almost afraid to ask what happened to your lovely hair."

"An act of war," he said.

SEVEN

OF ROYAL VEILS

I was still rolling along the road in Lasva's carriage, wearing Lasva's clothes, eating meals cooked and served for a princess, and sleeping in luxurious rooms.

During those days in early spring when I'd taken those solitary walks in Lasva's two outer robes and the domino veil, I always wore my own gown underneath. On this masquerade, Marnda insisted I put on the princess's clothes lest some sharp-eyed courtier spot the plain linen. (For we did not then know about Kivic's even sharper-eyed spies, constrained to watch our progress from a distance.)

When the first body gown fell to the tops of my feet without touching my spare form anywhere, it seemed as if I had become neutral, unwomaned. Though I view the world through a woman's eye, and a woman's hands worked below the level of my gaze, I wondered for the first time what others see when they see me. Not a man, certainly, but something between the two—a genderless scribe. And that led me to consider how much we define gender by our relations with others.

Marnda brought the dresser Anhar into the secret so that she might wear my clothes and pretend to be me. She was half a head taller than me. Surely her round face, which looked so Chwahir to me, could not possibly be thought to resemble my own at a distance? It had to be her light brown hair, similar to my own shade.

Anhar, so quiet and subdued in the princess's chambers, turned out to have a sense of humor, and she loved plays. We had a good time talking in the coach, and she even admitted that, though she'd been trained as a personal dresser, she'd wanted to be a player. She went to The Slipper often. "Every time they get something wrong about court, my sister and I treat ourselves to a dinner at the Geese in Flight, and every time they get something wrong about the princess, we give ourselves a music dinner on a barge. We had four barge trips just this spring alone," she said.

We speculated on what "Chwahir massing at the passes" might mean, but with the comfort of knowing that it was a matter for the queen and court.

So we were not prepared to roll into the inner stable reserved for the royal family's use, to find a very senior, white-haired herald waiting among the expected stable hands and pages.

Waiting for *me*.

"I must change." I indicated Lasva's clothing on me.

She lifted her brows slightly. "And keep the queen waiting?" At my shock she relented. "She knows about the masquerade, Scribe Emras. There is nothing amiss."

How unreal it felt to walk through the queen's side of the royal wing while wearing Lasva's lavender and silver! My gaze touched the golden inlay of lilies worked into the carved rosewood doors. I breathed in the scent of cinnamon and bee-balm wafting off the tended shrubs in pots below the high windows; I listened to the rapid tattoo of my heartbeat, in counterpoint to the hiss of our slippers on the marble floor. I did these things to restore a sense of reality, but I felt the more removed from normal life.

One, two, three, four doors (all opened by heralds, not pages) and for the very first time, I was alone with the queen.

Lasva's gown rustled in folds about my feet as I pulled off the veiled hat and then bowed deeply.

"Come here, Scribe," the queen said. Where Lasva's voice had a slightly husky, breathy sound, her sister sounded gruff. "Ah-ye. Quite odd, to see your round apple of a face atop one of my sister's gowns. Now, tell me about this."

The queen threw onto a fine carved table a slim book bound with silk-covered stiffened paper. I glanced in puzzlement at the elegant, elongated Venn knotwork, then made out the stylized lettering: *An Examination of Greatness.*

Then I looked up at the queen.

People use the words "beauty" and "plain" and "ugly" but what do they really mean? Beauty is often likened to perfection, with discussions of symmetry, harmony of features, and dramatic coloring. "Ugly" is spoken of as distortion. "Plain" is me, harder to define—cheeks too round for my small chin, nose a mere blob. My lips are thin, my eyes just eyes below brows so unremarkable they are nearly invisible.

The queen's cheeks are like mine, but squared, somehow, in a broad face. Her nose is also broad, her eyes small and widely spaced, but their expression is called penetrating because she can stare you right in the eyes without fear of offending. Most of us just touch the gazes of others, then let our eyes slide to other features, or away, unless we are in love or in anger.

The queen leaned toward me, attention unwavering. I did not find her ugly, or even plain, but so intimidating my armpits tingled with perspiration, and my heartbeat sped as if I had committed a breach of protocol.

With a rapid flow that would have pleased Halimas, I gave a summary in under five hundred words: Lasva's request that I find out more about the newcomers, speaking with Prince Macael Elsarion, Tiflis, her letter.

What did I leave out? Lasva's and Ivandred's exchange of glances, and my real motivation for sending the book, which was to make Ivandred's suit easier, because I was so glad to see Lasva's wall of grief broken.

When I finished, the queen thumped her hands on the arms of her satin-cushioned chair. "Laudable! And I hope your share brings you a stiff sum."

My share of what? I dared not speak.

"I am very pleased when something turns out to benefit us all. You've done well, Scribe Emras." She looked aside, then back. "Very well. If . . . ah, events transpire as I wish, you will be part of the plans. So. Go talk to Halimas. He will tell you what happened before your arrival, while I deal with the aftermath. I expect you will be in here again."

She gave me a short nod of approval. I bowed myself out and followed the waiting herald, who refused to take me upstairs so that I might change. Wretched with embarrassment, I followed him to the scriptorium, where I found many of the senior staff waiting for me. As I made my bow, I spoke an apology for my appearance. As much as I had felt a private pleasure at being taken for the princess by those who did not know the secret, I was made equally ill-at-ease by being seen as myself in her clothes.

No one said anything about my appearance. The senior scribes and heralds wanted a full report on what had happened. Again I left out Lasva's private grief, but told them everything else.

When I was finished, Halimas brought me up to date on what I had missed, finishing with these words, "The queen is very pleased with you for having foreseen the need to create prestige for the Marlovens before they even appeared, by arranging for *An Examination of Greatness* to be published."

"'Foreseen,'" I repeated, squashing the impulse to say that my motive had been personal, not political.

He smiled at me with obvious pride. "You've seen how we are always refining our educational methods. The court several generations ago made a game of seducing the handsomest scribes. As a result our beautiful young students were encouraged toward vocations outside of court. Around the time you were born, a young, ambitious scribe used his position to sell to a bookmaker intimate stories from an infamous baron's bedroom, so we did not teach your generation of students how to earn extra money on the side. Instead, we stressed secrecy, the First Rule, and so on, assuming that you would learn on your own. And indeed, you figured it out and discreetly made your arrangement with your cousin. I hope you got a full finger of the finder's fee."

"Finger," I repeated. "Not quite." Now I understood the purport of Tiflis's letter—it was the beginning of a negotiation.

Halimas laughed. "You can wrangle with her later. The point is, you gained permission to use an ancient text, which avoids not only the international squabbles over Writers' Fees, but also political implications. You appointed your cousin to act for you, thus avoiding any question of trespass against the First Rule. And you saw the opportunity first, whereas most were apparently laughing at how strange these foreigners are."

He smiled at me, and I tried to return the smile, feeling far more false than I had walking through the palace in Lasva's clothes. I hadn't foreseen any of these things—except the chance of making the Marlovens popular for Lasva's sake. And since I was not going to explain that, I must accept praise I didn't deserve.

Halimas closed with a compliment on how I'd turned that long, exhausting journey to good use. "One trip to Sartor was enough for me," he admitted as he accompanied me to the far door. "They can keep their thousand-year-old hassocks and their rooms that stink of mildew. I'd rather read about Old Sartor in the comforts of civilization." He opened his hands to take in the palace.

The first change I saw in the royal wing was the pair of heralds guarding Lasva's suite. One was quite young—my age—the other, about the age of Senior Scribe Halimas. The older one recognized me from shared service.

"That's the princess's scribe," he muttered to the other.

They'd tightened their hands on swords, but eased their grips, their expressions relieved. I passed inside, but no one greeted me—not even Poppy, the day page.

I headed toward my room to bathe and change into my own clothing, but no sooner had I entered the hall than Lasva ran out, one hand bandaged, the other holding a book that I now recognized. "Oh, Emras, it is such a relief to have you back at last."

Despite the marks of sorrow in her face I was giddy with joy. *Relief to have you back*—I cherished those words as she drew me inside her chamber.

Her words tumbled out in a breathless rush as she told me of the kidnapping from her perspective. When she got to the rescue and its aftermath, she described with precise detail how Kaidas looked—how he did not speak—how he sat there in the rain, astride his horse, with Carola's white ribbon binding his hair.

"That means he has sworn fidelity, whether his heart belongs to her or not." Her voice faltered. "I should hope he loves her, should I not? Only why does it hurt so much?" She wiped her eyes, and out came a quick rush of words, so fast I could scarcely comprehend them. "I am attracted to Ivandred. I embrace it. I never thought I'd feel anything again, except the pain of parting with Kaidas. Is that how one finds love again, to follow the body's inclination, despite what we are taught about reason staying in control?"

I had no answer, and was spared having to invent one when Marnda appeared, her eyes raw with weeping, for she was great-aunt to the maidservant, Sindra, who had been strangled. And Torsu had been her responsibility.

"Permit me to explain the changes in rules the queen has desired we adopt," Marnda said to me, as Dessaf wiped her eyes in the background.

EIGHT

OF THE RISKS OF SHARED MIRTH

Hatahra strode back and forth in her private chamber, her heels coming down so hard her arms and chin jiggled.

"We were definitely caught with our butts to the fire," she stated.

Davaud had sunk into a chair by the hearth, steeped listerblossom leaf in his hands to ease his aching joints. He gazed at his consort in surprise. Only once before had he seen her this angry, and that time she had gone silent. He had never before known her to utter vulgarities—he would have sworn she did not know any.

She spun, her skirts brushing his knees. "What about the foreigners? Did they really ride around all night?"

"That they did," Davaud said tiredly. His orders had been to stay with Ivandred until the investigations were complete, and stay he had. Most of the night and all day. "Perimeter search, they called it."

"I take it you were unsuccessful in convincing them that we have plenty of guest chambers here in the palace?" the queen asked with irony.

"They prefer the back barns. It was the only place I could think of where they could be close to their horses, which they won't permit anyone else to touch, and also perform their military exercises."

"Military exercises?"

"Ivandred said something about daily drill. I think that's what they were doing this morning, out in the fields."

"That's what we need," Hatahra said, snapping her fan northward toward Thorn Gate. "Or at least, some training scheme that doesn't leave my armed heralds standing around looking like they've lost their wits."

A servant scratched at the door. Hatahra whirled. "Enter!"

"The Grand Herald and the Grand Seneschal are here at your majesty's request," said a young page, frightened and excited.

"Come in," Hatahra said. As soon as they had filed in, she shut the door in her curious servants' faces. "Speak!"

The Grand Seneschal said, "We have searched the entire palace, and interviewed every single person, as your majesty ordered."

He did not mention that it had taken all night and a good part of the day and while they were still carrying on their regular duties. They knew the queen hadn't slept either, any more than the consort had. "Nothing's changed since yesterday," he continued. "Only those three of the princess's dressers were found sleeping under tables. All had taken sleep-weed served in caffeo laced with distilled liquor, offered by Kivic, a bridle-man."

"Did you find out what a bridle-man was doing in the royal residence?" Hatahra demanded.

The Grand Seneschal looked down. "There was no one to stop him, it seems, your majesty."

"It was your majesty herself who ordered the armed heralds to attend me," Davaud said.

"Lay aside the protocol for now." Hatahra cut a glance at the Grand Herald. "Though you'll put it right back in when you write up this conversation. Everything with due decorum."

The Grand Herald bowed.

Hatahra snapped her fan out and glared at them. "We're all going to sit down at dawn tomorrow and address the fact that even in civilized Colend the unthinkable can happen. We've been complacent for years. For generations. No more." She scowled at the fan. "But. Those three servants must have smelled the liquor in the caffeo, and I know that Marnda forbids duty staff to drink anything but what she keeps for their refreshment. That does not include wine. Therefore they broke two rules."

"Yes." The Grand Seneschal made an apologetic bow. "And we assume that Sindra Kereis did not, which is why she is dead."

"Augh," the angry queen exclaimed, and now she really did stomp to the fire and back. "How can I in justice dismiss those three, when they can point to Sindra's example and declare that the reward for fidelity is death?"

No one answered.

"I trust no more dead people turned up?"

"Correct, your majesty," the Grand Seneschal said. "I believe Torsu Emberit, the dresser found out in the garden, will be the last. The search has also included the old palace foundation. We found footprints and what we think might be splashes of gore—that would be the fighting his grace Davaud reported—but no remains."

"Do you know yet by whose hand Torsu Emberit died?"

"We must assume that same Kivic." He looked down, the thin hair over his scalp spangled with sweat. "He was newly employed in spring."

"A spy!" Hatahra kicked a tasseled hassock. "I don't want Thias using this as an excuse to declare war on Lasva's behalf." She swung around. "Let's give the court something new to whisper about. Since the Chwahir have also gone from the passes, let us give out that they were driven off because they greatly feared our new alliance. Let's get everyone talking about the Marlovens."

"We're going to put it about that the entire Chwahir army was driven off by the threat of twenty-four riders?" Davaud asked.

In answer, Hatahra crossed the room, picked up Tiflis's book and cast it down before our eyes. "While you were all busy, I had a most informative interview with our Twelve Towers Archivist, and with Prince Macael Elsarion, who is cousin to Prince Ivandred. He arrived last night."

"*An Examination of Greatness*?" The Seneschal read the title, then looked up, puzzled. "Is this about Prince Ivandred?"

"It's about one of his ancestors—none other than Elgar the Fox. And it has turned into the latest fad." At the surprise in their faces, the queen snapped her fan open. "I don't care if it's all wine fumes. By nightfall tomorrow, when I give my victory celebration, everyone will believe that Prince Ivandred's ghostly ancestors chased off the Chwahir."

Davaud laughed. The Grand Seneschal shook his head, and the Grand Herald permitted himself a small smile. "The Chwahir will hear that rumor, too. I predict they will not like the inevitable imputation."

Hatahra grinned at her consort. "If Jurac does not like people calling him a coward, then he never should have come sneaking over here in the first place. As it is, he will shortly receive notice that all trade is ceased until he extradites that Kivic to make life-restitution to two families." She slashed her fan down in shadow-challenge.

The Grand Seneschal mentally re-sorted his staff and their schedules, and the Grand Herald mentally organized the report that his heralds would be reading in all town squares, not at the Hour of the Bird, but the more official Hour of the Stone.

"I will set my seal on the archives of the true events and on this conversation," Hatahra said, rounding on the Grand Herald.

He bowed, unperturbed.

"Two changes will take place as of now," the queen said, snapping her fan open and shut, open and shut. "The easiest first: We will, for my lifetime at least, hire no more staff who are not in some wise related to those already here, and thus spoken for."

The Grand Seneschal bowed. That would actually make his life somewhat easier.

"Second, and more difficult: we need better wards."

The Grand Seneschal asked, "Shall I send to the Mage Council for a ward-mage, then?"

Hatahra knew of and shared his misgivings. History was far too full of stories of powerful mages who couldn't resist meddling in government affairs. Mages who made wards were trained in Sartor; they were disciplined and smart, and they often had Sartoran views.

"Only until we get one trained here whom we can trust. I know how difficult this magic is. But I tell you this." The fan snapped open again. "I am already changing my mind about my daughter's education. She shall learn to read a year earlier than I'd designed. She will be smart because Davaud and I are smart. She is going to learn ward-magic, as many of my royal ancestors did."

Davaud whistled soundlessly, pitying that poor child lying on silken sheets in the far chamber. Magic lessons and all the other educational requirements of a future queen meant that Alian would have little time to herself for many, many years. *I hope she's more like her mother than like me*, he thought.

The queen faced the Grand Herald. "One more order for you. I want your most diligent minds to dig up as much information about our new allies as possible, in case we do put together a marriage treaty. I do not like being ignorant, and my sister might be going to live among them. Speaking of ignorance, why were we not warned of Jurac's trickery by our embassy in Chwahirsland?"

"Because they were told that King Jurac was inspecting ports along his coast. There was no evidence to the contrary, and our people can't follow the Chwahir king around."

Hatahra sighed. "Our training is in the subtleties of courts. It is not sufficient to anticipate blunt actions, and so we were very nearly given a royal moth kiss on our doorstep, and by a hum-bumbling Chwahir." She gestured dismissal with her fan.

The Grand Herald and the Grand Seneschal bowed and withdrew.

The moment the door shut on them, the queen turned to her consort. "What is he like, Davaud? Do these Marlovens experience the unthinkable as thinkable every day, is that what makes them so . . ." She waved her hand in a circle. "So different? I remember what you told me this morning. Now tell me again, more slowly."

Davaud complied. The queen did not interrupt until he reached Ivandred and Lasva sitting together on the horse, and then she asked him to describe exactly what he had observed in Ivandred, Lasva, and the Duke of Alarcansa.

"You've a good eye for detail," Hatahra said grimly. "All right. Here is my next change. You said that Vasalya-Kaidas Lassiter was the only one outside of the Marloven who saw through Jurac's plan."

"Correct."

"I've been thinking about this all day. We will call him back to court. It's time to relearn defense. I already know how everyone, of whatever degree, would resist with all their might. But. Putting a smart duke in charge will make it a fashion. Reminding them of ancient oaths would cause resistance, but fashion," she showed her teeth, "will get 'em all scrambling to be first."

Davaud laughed, then winced and put a hand to his hip. "Oh. Oh! It's brilliant, Tahra."

"No," she said—flat denial, all humor fading from her face. "It's dangerous."

"Dangerous," he repeated, and because he had laid aside his fan, flicked his fingers in query.

She snapped her fan open in Direct Address. "It took several generations to get swords out of the hands of nobles, and now I must put them back. But only outside the palace. I also need real guards, but they must be trained in manners. They must also look good, and that means weapons decently hidden, so we'll redesign their livery with that in mind. I believe this puts them under the seneschal. The heralds have enough to do and enough power."

Davaud made The Peace in assent.

She kicked the hassock again. "Not that there isn't danger even when court's hands hold pens, fans, ribbons. There is another attack that disturbs me nearly as much."

"Another *attack?*" Davaud asked.

"Yes! I feel like I woke up in a world of venomous snakes! You know I've never interfered with those hummers at The Slipper and the Skya Playhouse. They can put a crowned veil over a horse, hinting it represents me, and I just shrug. I know what I look like. I also know my motives and those of my chief antagonists—Thias, for all his bluster, does care for the good of Colend."

When she paused, Davaud signed assent.

"But I take exception when they start putting a rose veil on a grasping, venomous serpent, as they did this past spring. Whence came this poison? I asked myself—for I *know* it's not true. But those plays echo the chirping birds on the streets, which it's important to know when all I'm surrounded with is the warble of practiced flattery."

Davaud did not lift his head, and the queen gave a short bark of laughter. "Oh, I acquit my closest trusted people of lying, or we would not have this conversation. And truth to tell, I never took the rumors seriously. I know my sister isn't heartless, so what matter? If she were to inherit, it would be better for a queen to have a reputation for hardness. But when has Lasva ever been spiteful, or toyed with someone out of idleness?"

"Not once in my experience," Davaud said.

"Exactly. None of us were aware that the whispers about Lasva collecting hearts began directly after Carola Definian returned to court after her father's death."

Davaud did not hide his surprise. "Definian?" He thought of the sweet-voiced young duchess and shook his head. "All I've ever seen is quiet manners and fine taste in dress and display. And you favored her suit with the Lassiters. You told me, in this very room, that you thought her good sense would settle young Kaidas down—or at least his progeny."

"My grandmother would have commended Carola's superlative sense of moral geography," the queen stated, her brows sardonic.

"Moral geography?"

"Look in my grandmother's private writings. They're on the shelves opposite the bed." They had separate bedrooms, the queen seldom being able to sleep through the night. What reading she did was always in those night hours, while the kingdom either slumbered or entertained itself. "Carola is a Definian, and they have always been raised to believe that ducal privilege extends to every aspect of life. To want is to have. And everyone else exists to serve that want."

Davaud said, "When I first came to court, the former duke was called 'his imperial highness.' But the girl seemed so . . . so perfect an expression of courtly style."

"You are caught in a maze," Hatahra stated, "but Carola is caught in the act. It was that lackwit Ananda Gaszin, just arrived today, who inadvertently exposed her. In the general scramble yesterday, she left a letter in Darva's coach. I acquit Darva of nosiness. It's not like her. Says she opened it, thinking it hers, and saw Lasva referred to in an unmistakable manner. And seeing it, she decided it was better to send the letter to me."

She pulled from her pocket a little scroll and cast it onto Davaud's lap. Davaud held the letter up to the lamp-light.

My dear Ananda, Tatia reports that Carola wishes to know if foreign attack as courtship is to be the latest royal fad? If so, I pity our dressers! Tatia says the duchess made the baronesses helpless with mirth, asking if we all have to employ Chwahir in order to capture lovers. I laughed so hard! Is it true? Let me know at once what they say at court. Luzha.

Davaud set the letter down and wiped his fingers on his handkerchief.

"You know," Hatahra began, "they call Tatia Definian 'Tittermouse,' and it's not just because of that giggle of hers. Whatever they say about that Kivic, he's no worse than Tatia Tittermouse, who's worse than the spywells of old tales." She wiggled her palm back and forth. "Tatia Definian was directed, same as Kivic was by his king. 'Carola says.' More like Carola commands!"

"Impossible, impossible."

"But don't you see how cunning it is? Carola, I will stake my life, has never lowered herself to making a direct accusation. Instead she asks these venomous little questions, sometimes in a droll tone, always soft and sweet, and Tatia is relied on to spread 'em."

Davaud sighed. "This makes me feel unclean. Like turning over a leaf on a thriving garden shrub and seeing a worm gnawing away its vitals."

The queen whirled around. "Here's what I learned when I first took the throne. Either one is first because everyone agrees on the fiction of rank, or one is first because one has the power to make everyone else bow down or die." She kicked that hassock. "Then there's human nature, which puts the beautiful and charming person first. Lasva is beautiful, and charming because she genuinely takes an interest in others, a quality she will have even when she's old. Because young Lassiter hurt Lasva so badly, I would very much like to see her get out of court. Out of Alsais. Out of Colend. The sooner the better."

"You don't want Lasva and the duke to meet again."

"Exactly. I didn't take their passion seriously—that is, I doubt he's capable of it. He's a Lassiter. But Lasva? I did not know until you described their faces during yesterday's little affair how wrong I was. I don't want Lasva hurt, and if the new Duke of Alarcansa actually has a heart, I don't want it bruised, not if he's going to be serving the crown. So let's do everything we can to foster this romance so suddenly sprung up under our noses. As for Carola, I will begin the next season by honoring my duchies with a royal tour." Hatahra's fine, even teeth showed. "I will begin my tour with Alarcansa and stay, enjoying her tasteful, spectacular and so *very* expensive entertainment, until she has to wear dish cloths for clothes."

NINE

OF IMAGES AND EXPECTATION

The next morning, as the queen shared breakfast with her sister, she talked about palace changes. In the middle of her list she mentioned that she was going to summon the Duke of Alarcansa to commence the new training for such eventualities. Then she outlined the celebrations she had taken great pleasure in planning during a sleepless night; she intended to honor their new allies, the Marlovens.

When Lasva returned to her suite, I was horrified by that expression of mute misery I had hoped never to see again. "I have to get away," she whispered to me. "I have to get away before he comes." And she told me what the queen had said about summoning Kaidas to his new post.

It was time to get ready for the Rising, at which the first celebration would take place. It was to be an "impromptu" award ceremony.

The Grand Seneschal saw to it that the Marloven prince knew where and at what time to appear. The Grand Herald dug up from the treasury underneath the Archive an old beaten-gold shoulder chain that had an impeccable history, dating from the days before Colend's borders had consolidated; days when enterprising would-be heroes went out looking for trouble to settle (or cause).

The queen watched the courtiers watch Ivandred. The Grand

Seneschal and Grand Herald watched the queen smile. Lasva and the mysterious Prince Ivandred watched one another.

He looked so striking, so . . . *aware*, but our word was not quite right for that alert stillness as he stood there in his black and gold, the chain arcing with metallic grace over his straight shoulders and across his chest. He just moved, and people deferred, yet he was not arrogant.

At the sumptuous banquet in his honor, he sat between the queen and the princess. He ate very little, which stirred well-bred wonder. A gobbling barbarian was expected, if not hoped for.

No one heard Ivandred mutter to Lasva, "You have no spoons."

Lasva hid a flutter of laughter and slid her fingers over her shaped gold eating implements. Colendi implements are not ubiquitous, so I shall describe what Ivandred saw: a fork with tines close together—long-handled so that one's arm did not lift clumsily high, dragging one's sleeves into the food—and the elegant but dull-edged knife against which we balanced a bite, or gently pressed a bite smaller, so that the face never distorts after the food passes behind the lips, and one never makes a noise.

"Is aught amiss?" Lasva whispered.

"They eat like butterflies," he answered after a long pause.

She realized he did not understand the question, but discussing eating was unforgivably vulgar, so she let it pass. How much they had to learn about one another!

At the queen's signal, the company moved into the ballroom, where musicians struck up soft music as a preliminary to the dancing.

Ananda contrived to drift by Ivandred several times as he sat beside Lasva, watching the dances. She leaned down to ask occasional questions—did you go to the music festival? *No.* Have you ever traveled to this end of the continent before? *No.* And, toward the end of the evening, Is it true that Elgar the Fox was one of your ancestors? *Yes.* The pleasurable shock of such simple denial—she found it immensely daring and attractive.

Not just Ananda but several court ladies glided near him to hear anything Ivandred might say. They glanced over their fans, close enough to trail their subtle scents; they even smiled their enigmatic smiles at him but gained no smile in return.

———

The poets, Lasva reflected as she led her silent guest up the broad sweep of the pink-marble stairway, often likened the faces of a crowd to a great sea. Perhaps the image worked for those who had glimpsed a sea. Lasva never had, and while she acknowledged the beauty of lakes—Lake Skya being the principal lake in her life—she could not reconcile the image of that quiet, sky-reflecting infinitude with a gathering of courtiers.

In her early childhood, the faces of court were like a vast garden of flowers, all nodding heads, light-reflecting eyes and gemmed and ribboned hair graced with different colors and shapes. And so there were times when she strolled the Rose Walk she fancied the blossoms were a crowd, breeze-tossed petals nodding, their faces turned toward her.

When she was a girl, courtly gazes had been warmed by smiles of admiration, of friendship. Or so it had seemed until the sexual neutrality of flowers vanished, and she arrived at the age when faces divided into men and women, the scents and *melende* masking individual emotion and motivation.

So here she was with their honored guest, in the gallery where once she'd taught that Jurac to waltz. It was one of the few places in the palace she knew they could be private, yet it was neutral space.

She cleared her throat. "Here is the first king of Colend, Martande Lirendi, though he was actually a herald-scribe in Kei Fael, before the unification." She listened to the sound of her own voice, dryly recounting history as they stood side by side staring up at the life-sized, gold-framed painting of a handsome man with a smooth beard, gem-studded braids, and a strange outfit made up partly of gold-worked armor and partly of what appeared to be hangings of the long-famous silk that had made Kei Fael the wealthiest province on the whole eastern continent—second only to Sartor.

Her voice echoed slightly as she talked about the secrets of silk, guarded on pain of death. Her voice sounded high. Alone.

He said nothing.

She continued on, dropping her voice to damp the echoes as she moved down to the second portrait. ". . . grandson of Martande the Great. He finished the castle whose outer foundations you saw north of the juniper garden. They are to be plowed under next year."

Ivandred's profile revealed naught. She could hear his breathing. Awareness of the sound flooded her with warmth. Memory of the strength of his arm around her, the strangely enticing smell of horse and man and some unnamed herb, clean-scented and strange, seized her. But hard on that was the equally strong memory of Kaidas's last glance, his tight line of a mouth. *I must return to my wife.*

Kaidas, soon to return to Alsais, was bound by that white ribbon.

Lasva *had* to get away. Was the other side of the continent far enough to diminish the pain?

Ivandred made a gesture. "Do you not want to show me these things?" he asked.

Lasva's lips parted. She'd let the pause stretch to silence, and so his response was natural, but so direct a question seemed curiously difficult to answer. Courtiers were not usually direct, but Kaidas had been. Once, had been.

She fluttered her fan in Query mode, though by now she knew he did not notice the fans except as distraction. "Do you wish to see my ancestors?" she asked.

Ivandred glanced across the landing to one of the other great portraits. "I have read a little about your emperor," he said. "To hear you tell about them, that is interesting."

Was that flirtation? Habit caused her fan to sweep into the pretty arc of Possibility as she said, "Were I to visit your capital, would you take me on a similar tour?"

His eyes narrowed briefly in amusement. "We have not so many portraits," he said. "It would be a short tour."

"Portraiture is not a custom in your kingdom?"

"It was not for my ancestors. When the throne was seized, the new king usually burned everything belonging to the old family." His amusement increased for a moment. "Summary endings are our custom, some say." He stopped, one hand groping, a curious gesture, almost of appeal. He squared himself to her. "I will confess, I know not what to say to you. Not about ancestors. Not in your manner." His open hand now indicated the portraits around him, of sophisticated kings and queens, intelligent, many of them handsome, surrounded by the symbols they chose to represent their interests, talents, and power.

He added with a rueful quirk to his mouth, "It appears to be custom, from what I hear, to liken you to the roses." He indicated the windows. "I haven't the skill with words to say one thing and mean another."

She sifted his words for hidden meaning. There were no gestures, no lifts to brow or alterations of stance, the subtleties that courtiers employed with such grace and style to convey what could not be said— what must not be said.

"The language of diplomacy," she said slowly, "is different where you live?"

"Diplomacy," he repeated. "Diplomacy." He gazed at the marble floor, question furrowing his brow. "The word might mean different things to us. I understand 'diplomacy' as negotiation of treaties between states."

Is that not the very definition of royal courtship? she thought, remembering her sister's exhortation.

Heat flushed through her, followed by a sickening chill when she remembered waking to discover herself in the arms of Jurac Sonscarna. Ivandred's quiet, direct speech freed her from the arts of deflection, and she spoke in a quick, low voice: "So what do you see when you see me?"

Her intensity sparked fire in him, too long banked. He stared down into her summer-sky eyes, aware of the splendid glow of color in her beautiful face, the quick rise and fall of her bosom under the layers of floating gauze, and he said, his hands out, his tongue dry, "Beauty."

She made a gesture of repudiation, turned away, and then turned back. "Let me tell you about my beauty." Her eyes widened. Her voice was quiet. "I've never told anyone this, outside of—" *Kaidas.* "When I was, oh, about ten, I was full of self-importance as a child is who has discovered what rank means, but who has not yet seen the true motivations behind those smiling words of admiration. I used to come here to touch the magic spell over the portrait that captured moments of my ancestor, Lasva Sky Child. I'd been encouraged to learn to walk like her, you see, and I used to practice over and over."

Lasva's fan swirled upwards to the left, flattening at the angle of False Triumph. He did not know the mode but he suspected the self-mockery from the angle of her face and arm. He glanced from living woman to painted image, and there Ivandred saw Lasva's face on the most fabulously framed portrait of them all, a secretive smile on the lips, the gown a fantastic working of gold and gems over pure white silk, a golden crown on the curling dark hair—painted in later, because she had refused to be any more than royal consort, though history called her Queen.

Lasva approached the portrait. She touched the lily-shaped gem worked into the frame, and the magic spell released the captured moments of the living woman.

They had chosen a bright day, so her face was lit from the high windows, her blue eyes gleaming as she laughed over her shoulder. According to the records she was forty-two at the time. There were the tiny lines about her mouth and eyes that revealed her age, but her expression was so full of inner light, of fun and joy, her beauty transcended mere physical features. The king had gone to the extreme expense of causing the mages to bespell sound as well as light, so she said in Kifelian with a strong Sartoran accent, her voice higher than Lasva's, and more sibilant, "What shall I say? This feels odd. I know! I'll do a little dance, from the village of my birth."

She hiked up the costly brocade of her skirt and lightly twirled and stepped, her long curls bouncing as she hummed a tune, for in Sartor, there was no discrimination against wordless voices in music. Then she looked up again at someone she loved because there was so much tenderness in her face, so much shared laughter. Then the image winked out.

"That smile was for the king," Lasva said. "It's attested to by the mage, the artist, and a scribe."

Ivandred had heard about this portrait magic, but his forebears either did not know it or the portraits, and the spells, had been destroyed. *Most foreign kings and queens make speeches*, the Herskalt had told him. *They want to be remembered, and no one will tell them, or can tell them, how very boring they sound. The portrait magic seeps away over the years, unused, and unrenewed by indifferent progeny.*

But this famous woman, whose family had intermingled with his own, mother of the most powerful emperor in several generations, had chosen to be remembered dancing about like a village woman.

"I can still do every step, every move, of that dance." Lasva's mouth quirked sardonically, mirroring the enigmatic smile above. "And I practiced what I thought was that smile, secure in my own perfections, for did not everyone tell me constantly how much like her I was?"

Ivandred made that gesture again, an open hand, as if handing her something. Maybe it was appeal. "So on one particular day, two court women stood talking, right here where we are now. I heard my name, so I hid behind that column over there. I thought I was going to hear praise of myself—I don't know why I hid, since I'd never been the sort to do that. But I was soon disabused of my vain desire to hear praise."

He stepped nearer, listening to the breathless flow of words.

"With the detachment of people discussing the design of a table, or a wall-hanging, they compared every feature in my face to those in the portrait—which is reputed to be exact—something my ancestor insisted on. She is said to have inspected each day's painting and withheld money for anything she deemed flattery."

Ivandred looked up at that intelligent, slightly mocking blue gaze, faithfully captured on canvas.

Lasva uttered a soft, sad breath of a laugh. "So I listened to this catalogue of my flaws: eyebrows too faint, nose too pointed, upper lip this, lower lip that, ears not quite another thing, until they had thoroughly assessed every single feature, then they moved on, leaving me feeling like . . . like a commodity handled in the market place and dropped back into the basket to be fingered over by the next idle passer-by."

She dared a look at him to find his attention wholly on her, so close, so fixed, that again she felt that heat and ice running through her veins and nerves. Her heart hammered against her ribs, and her fingertips tingled.

"It was not the criticism that upset me. After that long catalogue, even praise would have caused me to feel shop-soiled, though it would have wounded me far less. I was never a person to them, you see, but an object. *Do* you see it?" She kept her hands at her sides, no art in voice or gesture. "So when I ask, what do you see when you see me, you understand I don't want flattery?"

He thought of her smeared with mud, her gown ruined, her hand bleeding as she faced the Chwahir king. "Gallantry," he said.

"Oh." Her eyes stung. "Oh." A word so long outmoded it gained all the charm of the unexpected.

He did not understand, though he listened with all his attention. When she held out her hands he sensed appeal, and so he extended his own and closed her thin, cool fingers in his callused grip, once again sustaining the pleasurable shock of her touch.

He said, and it was many years before she understood the courage it took, "What do you see when you see me?"

"Safety," she said.

A word so alien it carried all the power of redemption. Disarmed and defenseless, he stared down into her eyes, unable to speak. Lasva did not know that he was breathing a scent that reminded him so curiously of home. "Rose" they might call this princess, but she did not drench herself in attar of roses, as did many of her ladies. The scent was clean wild-growing sage with a hint of anise, reminding him of galloping over the rain-swept plains of Hesea, and she looked to him with trust.

Her voice was almost a whisper. "Why are you here?"

He put his cold, tense hands behind his back. "It was at first a wager. Who would gain a kiss from you."

She lifted her chin in acknowledgement of his honesty. "Is it still?"

"No."

She wished he would put that arm around her again that she might push against it and feel its strength.

He hesitated then went on. "It changed when I—I don't have the right words, for so much of importance, in your language."

Lightning flared, thunder crashed outside. Memory: lying with Kaidas, warm and sleepy as they watched a lightning storm and discoursed on words for *zalend* in three languages. She shook her head, a quick snap, then said, quickly, huskily, "If you want to marry me, will you do it at once, and take me away?"

TEN

OF THE WORLD OF BOOKS

L asva knew she should tell her sister before she did anything else.
She offered her hand. He brought his out in that open gesture,
hesitant, curiously appealing. His palm was rough-skinned, closing
around hers with latent strength, and again she shivered, thinking, *I shall
marry him.*

"Come," she said. "We must tell my sister."

He accompanied her down the marble halls, past paintings and cartouches glowing with warm color. The queen had gone to bed, which
was not surprising, but they found Davaud playing harp with two friends,
who accompanied him with tiranthe and chimes. Ivandred followed
Lasva. She sat on a cushion against the far wall, so he sat beside her,
mentally reorganizing the next day as the music tweedled on.

Since he had taken her on his horse and she had tucked herself against
him, he had not permitted himself to look past the next moment. He
was going to have to, now: the idea of taking this impossibly beautiful
creature back to Marloven Hesea was strange.

The song ended. The man and woman rose, bowed, and took their
instruments with them as the queen's consort cast a cover over his harp.

Lasva told Davaud the news in a few whispered words, unexpectedly
lacking in the long, ornamental phrases Ivandred thought unavoidable.

Davaud bowed to Ivandred, who dipped his head, finding the movement awkward and odd. In Enaeran, he'd refused to bow, but here, he
wanted to do everything right.

Davaud said, "I will tell the queen as soon as she wakens. You should
know that she will be well pleased."

Lasva made The Peace as she wished Davaud a good night and led the
way out. She felt uncertain, for Ivandred did not acknowledge her cues.
Here they were, beginning a relationship. They knew nothing about one
another, and she did not know where to begin without inadvertent trespass against *melende*. Did he wish to join her in her suite, or not?

He hesitated, and because she said nothing about his staying, he laid
his hand over his heart. "I will return in the morning. If there is a need
before then, you've only to send a runner to my camp."

He walked out, leaving her thinking, *runner?*

The following morning, after a series of intense, disturbing dreams whose
terrifying logic fell apart with the rise of the sun and the prospect of a
new day, Lasva rose, looking around her bedroom, thinking, *I am going to
leave this place forever.*

She walked out quickly, trying to leave the dream behind as she approached the staff's private chamber, where we were marveling over the
recent excitement. When Lasva appeared—something she had never
done before—we fell silent and bowed.

"I am going to marry Prince Ivandred of Marloven Hesea," Lasva said,
aware of the possible transforming into what would be as the words
reached the servants' ears.

At the looks of shock and dismay, she stared back, also shocked and
dismayed. Of course they would go with her . . . wouldn't they?

"No one shall be forced to go west with me—"

Poppy gave a deep sob, tears rolling down her cheeks.

That set Nereith off crying desolately. She sank down onto her knees,
hiding her face in her hands. "I don't want to leave Colend," she sobbed
over and over, too distraught to heed Marnda's hiss of affront at this
breach of the rules. "Spare us the barbarians, oh please, your highness,
spare us from having to live in barns and carry swords."

I stood in the back, numb with shock. *What have I done?* That was my
first conscious thought. I had only dared hope that they would find one
another for a time of passion, long enough for Lasva to forget Kaidas.

Then he would conveniently fade away, like mist before the sun, and we would carry on with our lives, restored to the tranquility of the days before Kaidas came to hear the *rafalle* song and met Lasva.

I watched the three servants who had been drugged exchange low-lashed glances as Lasva stooped over poor Nereith, stroking her disarranged curls and whispering, "It's all right. It's all right. You do not have to go."

Marnda finally drew Nereith up. "Stop weeping. I am certain that Pollar will admit you to the Royal Princess's staff, as her royal highness will need dressers before long."

Marnda confined herself to stern looks at those who wished to remain, then stated, "*I* will go with you, my princess. Even if I have to walk all the way." Her tone said, *I know what loyalty is, even if no one else does.*

Anhar also agreed to go, so calmly that I was surprised. I did not know then that she was very ready to leave a kingdom where she had only a sister to be social with, because everyone else looked at her and whispered, "Chwahir." In Marloven Hesea no one would even know who the Chwahir were.

Lasva turned to me last. "You will not fail me, will you, Emras?"

"Never," I said, though my throat nearly closed.

The Hour of the Leaf—the queen's breakfast hour—was nigh, so Lasva let us go as she withdrew to dress in her finest morning gown. She expected a royal summons, as this was also the queen's favorite time for personal interviews.

Her being readied left me with nothing to do, so I walked to my room without being aware of going there. As always, a page had brought a flat-basket of messages, most for the princess, but one for me.

I dealt with the princess's messages first, then read mine. It was from Tiflis, a lily made up of gold-dusted parchment, tied up with green and gold ribbon. This could only be an invitation to her formal acceptance into her guild.

I left the invitation sitting on my little desk. I knew that Lasva would give me leave to attend. The emotion that overwhelmed me as I stood there staring at the pretty shapes of the princess's messages was one of loss, of fear. Of guilt. Had I not interfered, in direct breach of the First Rule?

It was only just that I pay the cost, leaving this dear little room, the comfort and beauty of the palace, for life on the other side of the world.

The Hour of the Deer chimed. I thought Lasva would have been sitting with the queen for the past hour, but when I went to lay the letters in her chamber, I discovered her moving through a set of Altan fan dances to the soothing melodic strains of reed-pipe and harp in the Swan Variations, as cats came and went, tails switching in annoyance at not having the room to themselves. I quietly withdrew.

Near to the Hour of the River, Lasva changed to a day dress, and she herself came to my door, her manner one of question when she said, "My sister the queen desires you to attend her as well."

Lasva led the way, moving quick and nervy as a dragon-wing. Queen Hatahra met us in her personal interview chamber, all rose marble with an exquisite carved ceiling with oval insets, painted pale blue, centered around her favorite birds in flight. An array of refreshments had been brought in, from honeyflower wine to Sartoran steep, and fresh-baked lily cakes.

The air was filled with enticing aromas, but no one touched the food. The queen looked tired. "Lasva, I am very pleased with your alliance, and I beg your forgiveness for the long wait." She smiled grimly. "Others are not so pleased, which, in part, I count as a success. The dukes are upset. They seem to have convinced themselves that if they do not back down at last on the road question that Thias has been vexing me with for a year and more, Prince Ivandred is going to raise hundreds of his lance riders out of the ground to fight for me. I'm not denying a thing."

She paused, clearly expecting the princess to laugh. Lasva's hands fluttered in I-share-your-mirth mode.

"So I am well pleased. But where is your swain? Lasva, I beg your indulgence for treating you like a page, but we do not want to risk insulting him—making him think he is summoned—might you find him yourself, that we three might negotiate our treaty? I think the sooner we hold your wedding the better, so that court need not go home just to return. Why not on Martande Day? I am thinking of a magnificent masquerade, a thousand candles set in the air like stars, and everyone in their blue below, like a great sky. Our great-mother Lasva Sky Child had just such decoration after her wedding. It would be a fine touch, do you not think?"

Lasva bowed assent, and then left.

The queen lifted her chin. "Davaud? Where is that boy?"

Boy? I could not believe that even the queen would call the Prince of Marloven Hesea a boy, but then Davaud moved to the far door and opened it.

In walked a tall, imposing young man in a herald's robe. Familiar? The beaky nose—the ears almost tamed by thick dark hair with a trace of rust at the temples, pulled back. He flicked me a look, his mouth curling in a half-suppressed laugh—

Birdy?

A sun burst behind my ribs, so sharp and sweet it was painful, followed by a faint echo of that embarrassment when I remembered the last time we had seen one another, and how I had hurt him all unaware. The queen cut a glance at me, and I ceased to breathe until I saw that it was an abstracted glance. I had betrayed nothing. She shifted her attention back to this tall, unfamiliar Birdy. "Sit."

We knelt, hands on our thighs. I was distracted by the sound of his breathing. Birdy!

The queen glared at the window. "I am going to talk fast, so listen fast, the both of you. You may have noticed that I am not like my sister. She is sensitive. So the facts I am about to tell you are not to burden her. Are we agreed?"

We bowed, and I forced my attention away from Birdy.

"Scribe Emras. I asked the Grand Herald to find out more about Marloven Hesea. He had the effrontery to contact the Heraldry in Sartor, and they had the effrontery to send none other than Herald Tzan of the Mage Council to me."

She paused, snapped her fan, then grudgingly said, "Oh, I suppose the Sartorans see their action as compliance with duty. I see it, however, as a mighty stretch of their so-called First Rule, but the thing is, the Sartoran Mage Council is all a-chirp about the Marloven king's mage, and whether he might be using dark magic. They think that the Marloven king's chief mage, a Sigradir Andaun, has been treating with Norsunder in some wise."

In some lands, careless tongues speak such curses as *May Norsunder take you*, or *Ugly as Norsunder*. Now, with a few words, the queen had made the vulgarity of invective into terrifying reality. *Treating with Norsunder*—meaning actual contact, as in someone from there coming into the world . . . or someone in the world going there.

"The Mage Council claims that the Marloven king won't permit their mages to cross their borders. There is even a proscription against Sartoran heralds and scribes, whom this king calls spies. I find myself unsympathetic. What business is it of the Sartoran herald and magic guilds, if their First Rule is not to interfere? That sounds like interference to me, over nothing more than rumor! That young man courting Lasva is no more Norsundrian than I am, I would swear."

We made The Peace in assent.

"Interference in royal affairs . . . it's an old problem. Tzan said their Mage Council would be pleased if 'someone' were to find out about Norsundrian dealings. This someone could get word to the Mage Council. Hummers! They wish to put spies among my sister's entourage, and endanger them for their own purposes? I think not. But."

The queen snapped her fan shut and pointed it at Birdy. "You were the only one, I am told, who had the wit to be suspicious about Jurac Sonscarna."

Birdy flushed to his ears. "I did not guess at his plans, your majesty. I only guessed that something was amiss, because of the way they curtailed our access to news, these past few months. Before, there was access to street chirps."

"Yes, and you had the wit to listen to street chirps, while my older, experienced appointees scorned such. Ah-ye! I learned young that birdies chirp more, and at times more truly, when the hawks are not right overhead. Thorn! Lasva will return soon, and I want this finished and you two gone, because she has enough to contend with right now, getting to know this man she is to marry. The sooner she can get her heart turned westward, the better for her—for us all."

We made The Peace in assent once more.

"This is what I would like from you two. I'm not letting those Sartoran hummers put spies among you. Let them see to their own politics. But you will be watchful for my sister. You, Herald Martande, I know you have experience in stables. I would like you to take charge of Lasva's horses, and go with her coachman. But. There is something else."

Herald Martande. How strange! I had forgotten that Birdy was named for the first king.

"Lord Davaud has discovered from his military reading something called a stalking-horse. You will be this. It's inevitable that the Marloven king will be investigating us just as everyone else is investigating them. He will probably discover that you are really a herald, but with that discovery will be the fact that you are appointed by me, as a conduit of news about my sister. Let him surround you with spies, because you will be a good stable hand, and you will send me letters about Lasva that can be seen by many eyes. Steward Marnda will cooperate with you in this. My sigil on correspondence should protect you, as I'm certain they won't want trouble with me any more than I want trouble with them. But mostly I want you writing letters meant for them to see. You and I will discuss code words anon."

Birdy swallowed. I saw his neck knuckle go up and down.

"Now to you, Scribe Emras. Who bothers with a scribe, if she is not writing? Especially a little apple-faced thing like you? You will *not* report to me, in fact, you will get rid of your personal scrollcase, if you have one, so that no one thinks of you as a scribe. Let them think you a servant. You will be the closest to Lasva, so she is going to need your watchful eyes. I want you to learn everything about magic that you can. Discover if there is anything in these rumors, once you reach Marloven Hesea. Specifically, if there is a Norsunder threat to Lasva." She frowned. "Question?"

"Do you wish me to listen to this Sigradir Andaun?"

"I want you to stay away from him! If he's truly treating with Norsunder, then he is dangerous, perhaps the most dangerous man in their kingdom. But this I believe about great evil, which is our definition of Norsunder: it can't be subtle. If you find evidence of Norsunder's magic, then you tell Lasva, or Marnda, if Lasva is surrounded by spies. Marnda will know how to reach me, and if I have to, I can end the marriage treaty, though I hope and trust that none of it is true." She paused to take a breath. "Right now, I do not plan to burden her with any of these vexing rumors and accusations, and anyway, you can be certain that when she arrives in her new kingdom, she will be surrounded by court flatterers who will hum whatever they think she wants to hear. But you scribes are trained to hear past the flattery." She finished with her fan aslant in Life's Ironies.

I made The Peace a third time.

Davaud moved to the door, then turned his gaze to the queen, who said, "Ah-ye! They come. We will meet later. You two may leave through that door there."

We withdrew in proper order. I even waited until we got safely beyond the second door, to the public corridor beyond, before I exclaimed, "Birdy!"

"Yes. I'm back." His ears stuck out as always, his hair was barely contained, and he was *tall*.

"What happened?"

"We're to say that our embassy is completed, but King Jurac couldn't have pushed us through the door more thoroughly than if he'd done it with his own hands. We had to leave everything and use our transfer tokens! Ah-yedi." He rubbed his forehead.

"You are all back?"

"All but the ambassador, who is still in Narad, with our trade agreement in the balance. I don't envy him." He fell in step beside me, even though his legs were so long and mine so short. "What happened here?"

I gave Birdy a quick summary, but my mind was on the past. Twice we had to defer, our backs to the marble walls as courtiers drifted across our path, but as we approached the eight-sided fountain chamber, I put out a hand.

He stopped. I stopped.

Then I gazed up at him, my being so filled with emotions I could not define that words failed me. He clenched his jaw against a yawn, but his eyes watered, betraying him, then he grinned ruefully. "Em?"

"I—I missed you," I managed to say.

He chuckled. "I missed you, too. All of you."

All of us.

I knew I should let him go, but the urge to explain was too overwhelming to suppress. "Before you left," I began. "When I said—'Will you write to us?' and you said 'Us?' and you sounded so sad . . . I didn't know what you meant."

His grin widened. "Emras. There were two of us not knowing what the other meant, that day. It's past, and here we are again. Shall we begin where we left off, and pretend that particular conversation never happened?" Another yawn caught him. He hid it behind his hand, but his eyes watered again.

"Agreed. Have you slept at all?" I asked.

"There was no time for that." He dashed his sleeve across his eyes, then said, "One thing I'm curious about is this book you apparently found in time to smooth the way for that Marloven prince. The Grand Herald gave me the briefest summary, and it seems they all think you have an eye to making money through Tiflis and the book sellers, but unless you've changed more than I expected, it doesn't seem like you."

"You're the only one to say that. Even Halimas thought I wanted to make some money of my own. The queen called it laudable."

"She called it laudable because of the laudable outcome," Birdy said. "Ah, I am so tired. But we are here." Birdy looked around the familiar anteroom to the staff dining area, plain cream-wash on the walls, arched accesses. He breathed in and smiled at me. "You have no idea how good it is to be home—"

He fell silent as a very new, young page scudded up to us with a breathless summons for me from Seneschal Marnda. I took my leave of Birdy, rejoicing in the knowledge that he was back, and not angry with me for my sixteen-year-old obliviousness, as I followed the little page back to the west wing.

From that my mind leapt to the astonishing nature of the queen's orders. I had agreed because what else does one do? But doubt and then dismay assailed me. How was I to learn what I must know?

"Did the queen speak with you, Scribe Emras?" I was startled by Seneschal Marnda's voice.

I made a swift Peace, then said, "I am ordered by the queen to learn about magic. If Norsunder is truly allied in some way with the Marlovens, then I am to tell the princess or you. I remember one of the senior scribes saying that when the queen was young, she attempted the study of magic. Has she some books that I might borrow?"

Marnda rubbed the bridge of her nose. "The queen was only instructed in theory, I remember, for it was part of my duty to fetch and return the books the mage sent. She always commented about them before she sent them back."

"How much magic did she learn?"

"None. They would not send a teacher unless she would give over more time than she was willing."

"Why?"

Marnda opened her hands. "They said only that one must train the mind to the consequences of power as much as one is trained to use power. Even when a girl, the queen knew she was already learning those lessons. But the Mage Council was adamant: one must learn slowly and must be tested often by their methods, or not at all."

I left, resolved to comb through the archive though without much hope. My studies had made them familiar to me, and I knew what they held.

So I turned to the one person I knew could help me, my brother. Even so, I had doubts, for I remembered what he had said about magic studies—corroborated by Marnda.

I hesitated over the wording, partly for this very reason. The queen did not entirely trust mages. My brother, once a scribe, was now a mage, and he'd made his loyalty clear. So I worded it generally, asking for referral to any text from which a scribe could learn about the presence of dark magic—and I said it was a research question asked on behalf of the princess.

To my surprise, I received an answer from Olnar as I was readying myself for Tiflis's ceremony.

It was written in evident haste:

Em,

Would you ask a glass-blower for a text on how to parrot a thousand line poem in Old Sartoran? Especially if it was full of political significance whose false interpretation might break treaties? Your prin-

cess knows better, if you will forgive my bluntness—plain speaking being the prerogative of family. If she has any kind of question about dark magic, then she should send an inquiry to the Sartoran Mage Council, who are certain to send a properly trained mage to consult with, or to investigate, if the matter is serious.

I could hear his voice, the fond exasperation, for he did not mean to patronize. But I had to find a way to follow my orders, or the queen might replace me. My position was already anomalous, with the princess leaving the kingdom.

I was in a sober mood as I picked up the net of golden lily blossoms I'd ordered and took a boat to the Crown Gate—or, rather, as close as I could get. All the book sellers seemed to be there. As the city carillons sounded the chords of Hour of the Harp, I tried to squeeze close to the rail to see Tiflis's lily-decorated barge sail through—but so did everyone else. I only succeeded in glimpsing heads and shoulders. I flung my blossoms when everyone else did, and the shower of gold petals was lovely in the light of the glow globes, first glittering and tumbling in the air, then alighting on heads and shoulders and hands.

As the crowd broke up, most walking toward Alassa Canal, small children threaded among us and gathered lapfuls of petals to cherish or to shower over one another.

On Alassa Canal, every window in Pine House glowed with golden light. The double doors stood wide. I reflected everyone's Peace as I entered, returning smile for smile until I found my cousin in the central place in the room at the owner's right hand, resplendent in plum brocade over carnation and sea green panels.

Tiflis greeted me ecstatically, then presented me to the room. "Here is my cousin, Royal Scribe Emras, who was the finder for my mastery work."

The entire circle finger-tapped their palms in approbation. Caught completely without a clue to the proper response, I made The Peace generally.

"What happened with the warriors?" the book seller asked.

"Was there really a pitched battle with the Chwahir?" someone else asked.

"Did they truly attack the palace itself?"

I began assembling words, but Tiflis forestalled me. "She will only say what the heralds cried in the streets at the Hour of the Bird. Even in the family, you may as well be talking to a wall as to a Royal Scribe for real news."

They laughed and returned to their small groups as Tiflis drew me toward the banquet table to press into my hands a gold-rimmed cup full of the best honeyflower wine. A pure white petal floated on the surface.

"I'm moving tomorrow," she said, raising her own cup to me. "It's not on Skya Canal, but—"

A tall young woman with hair dyed shades of flame slid her arm around Tif's shoulders and bent to kiss the tip of her ear. Her robe featured a capelet of pointed layers in ruddy shades. Here was the fashion the queen had mentioned: *The fox's ruff.*

"—but it's a splendid little place," this newcomer said, turning a smile to me. "And we have a fine view of Alassa Canal from the parlor."

Tif caught up her lover's hand and kissed it. "This is Kaura," Tiflis said to me. "My artist partner, and my partner in art." Her hands shaped the heart symbol on the word "art," her manner and their immediate laughter making it plain that this was a standing joke between them.

Kaura's brown eyes rounded. "I was the first to read the book. I could hardly believe they were real people! But Inda was a prince—they don't lie, do they?"

"How can they," Tif answered, "when all it takes is a herald to poke his beak into their portrait gallery, if not their archive?" She turned to me. "Kaura thought of that design," she said proudly. "The Venn knots make the book!"

Kaura blushed. "If the chirps are true, and the princess is going to marry the Prince of Marloven Hesea, how will she manage in such a kingdom?"

Surprised, I said, "I do not know."

Tiflis put her head back and sighed. "Em. *Everybody* is talking about the match. It's hardly a secret!"

My cheeks burned. "I meant, I don't know anything about his kingdom, except that that book is about a time four hundred years past. They must be more civilized now."

Kaura said with a friendly smile, "I'm certain everything will settle out sooner or later. Right now, I want to thank you for thinking of Tif."

"Yes," my cousin said, setting down her cup. "We need to settle on our own part. You got my note, of course."

Once again I found myself without a clue to expected behavior. From the way others gathered around, I surmised that this was the negotiation

Halimas had talked about—begun in Tif's letter to me on the road—and further, that it was important to her. If I left the amount to Tif, would it be perceived as an insult, as if I was too superior to care? I said slowly, "Yes, I got it. I did not answer as my hand was still resting from all that copying I had done."

Everyone exchanged a look, and I heard an "Ahhh," behind me.

"All of which had to be corrected by us," Tif said. "But I honor you for the excellence of your work."

So like a court negotiation for place—establishing who must defer to whom. Now I knew how to respond. "And you were my first thought, as soon as I began reading the scroll that Prince Macael Elsarion loaned me," I replied.

Tiflis flushed with pleasure. "To be the first choice of a Royal Scribe honors not just me but our House."

After a few more complimentary exchanges like that, Tiflis referred to Kaura's talent in designing the book to catch the eye, to which I answered that I'd had to translate the scroll from Sartoran to Kifelian. I expected that to be dismissed—translation in and out of Sartoran had been part of childhood training—but those gathered around acknowledged it with little signs, and soon Tiflis offered me a full finger—ten percent—of her earnings.

Once we sealed the agreement by finishing the honeyflower wine, her fellow book makers gradually closed into their own groups. Tif saluted me. "I'd hoped to negotiate you to a flit." She lifted her little finger. "But when you mentioned that Prince Macael, I had to come up." She lifted her longest finger. "He's already got a reputation. *Everybody* on the canal will be chirping by morning. And long may the birdies sing."

My heart thumped as I leaned toward her and murmured, "Instead of paying me, perhaps you could locate and buy something for me?"

Tif's eyes rounded, and so did her mouth. *Is that apple-faced?* I wondered, distracted.

"I need a book on magic. As good as you can get."

"Magic?" Kaura repeated. "Why?"

"It's an assignment. For understanding."

Tif pursed her lips, hands at the angle of Surprise. "Magic! Why you, a scribe? Can't your princess summon a herald or two?"

"Not on the road. I need to understand the process of magic . . . if I travel."

Kaura's feathered fan touched her eyebrow in Discretion, and Tif took her bottom lip in her teeth.

"I have a cousin whose lover teaches something or other about elementary magic to the heralds," Kaura said doubtfully.

"Elementary is perfect, actually," I said gratefully. I was thinking that the description of magical history for the heralds would be less about politics and theory and more about how it was used, when and why, which seemed closer to what the queen wanted.

Kaura's lips parted, then Tiflis said swiftly, "If you, on your . . . travels . . . find any good books, you'll remember me, won't you? Of course you will. You already did." Then, in a low voice: "You're a good cousin, Em—like a sister. When I think back to what a brat I was, how jealous I was that you were so much quicker at learning, well, you're better than I deserve." She gave me a strong hug. "You'll get your book."

I hugged her back, wishing her success and happiness. Lightning flickered in the distance; I made my excuses and departed.

ELEVEN

Of Secrets and Empty Rooms

From then until the wedding the memories come in splinters. The clearest is fan practice in the early mornings, now that Birdy was back. I'd retreated to the staff area as Lasva was either with her sister or her betrothed, or involved in the many tasks of readying for the move.

Birdy and I spoke little, as others were always present. It felt good just to have him next to me, to be falling into our old rhythms, even though he'd grown two hands taller in the time he was gone. From time to time I remembered Tiflis's promise, and tried not to fret, for none of my other avenues of research turned up anything useful.

For a few days fan practice was the only time Birdy and I saw one another, but gradually, during brief free moments, I'd find him at a meal, and it seemed natural to sit by him and continue catching up on each other's our lives.

"No juggling?" I asked one day, after he dug his fingers into his pocket, and I expected to see the old silken bags. But instead, out came a note. He frowned at it, replaced it in his pocket, then looked up, his mouth awry. "Is that relief on your face? Ah-ye, do not answer. Everyone else was relieved. No more juggling, not after the ambassador forbade it that first winter, when we were all shut up together."

Though I had maintained a scribe's reserve—perhaps because I did—

he made a comical grimace. "You too? Nobody liked my juggling." His tone shifted. "That's because I never got any better at it."

"Would it offend to request enlightenment on why you did it?"

"I don't require formality, Emras. Before I came to scribe school, my Uncle Issas, who is a player, told me that juggling makes the hands sensitive and clever. Something a scribe needs. But I never got better at it. Partly because . . ." He looked away, then back. "Because I wanted to keep my hands busy, especially when my mind wandered where it shouldn't. So I thought no one would mind music. I bought a tiranthe. But I haven't any better musical sense than I do juggling sense. So then I tried carving. That one lasted two weeks, until I tired of the sting of ink in the cuts on my fingers."

I accepted that with The Peace, wondering what he'd been about to say. But it felt intrusive to ask.

"Trousers," he said a few days later at a staff meal. He turned on his cushion and wiggled his legs. "They look so simple, but if you don't manage them right, I hate to tell you what they do to your parts. If you have 'em." He grinned at my kitchen friend, Delis.

A young journey-scribe sitting across from us said, "I always wondered about that. Can't you just wear a robe?"

"You don't want to know what happens to the hem of a robe in the stable." Birdy touched his nose. "There's a reason stable hands wear trousers, and it has nothing to do with guild commonality."

After the laughter died, Delis said, "Is it a demotion, going from herald to stable?"

"I like to think of it this way." Birdy's fingertips sketched Shared Empathy. "There are no openings for heralds or scribes just now, but among the horses, there are. I like their company just fine! They don't waste ink, and they never dictate boring letters or require me to make diplomatic speeches."

There was another laugh, and as he went on talking about the horses' personalities, people returned to their own conversations.

So it seemed natural to wander in the direction of the stable if I had free moments, and—if I found Birdy—to share a meal, or talk, or do fan practice. I did not think we met often or for long; every meeting was interrupted by either a page, a bell, or both, and our conversations, though friendly, could easily have been carried on in public. The queen, however, had something to say when she finally called us back. She dictated a few orders concerning the journey, then finished with this: "Apparently you two are friends." Her fingers flickered in the old-fashioned Silken Screen mode, left from the days when people ate behind portable folding walls. "But I do not want my plans ruined. Curtail your public socializing, at least until we know that Lasva is safe, and that the rumors are mere rumors. There is no use in a stalking-horse if he's being ridden by the very scribe who is supposed to be inconspicuous."

She dismissed us. Birdy was silent as we walked out.

I had reached the second landing before the implication hit me. "Ridden?" I protested.

Birdy turned deep red. "You know how people are. If they're twistling, they see pairs everywhere."

"Ah-ye," I breathed. "If that's what people are thinking, then I guess the queen is right." I said wistfully, "I'd looked forward to sitting next to you in the carriage."

"I'd looked forward to that, too. We could practice our Marloven," Birdy said.

"That's right!" I said. "We've another language to learn! But how? From what I see, the Marlovens hold to themselves."

"It will be a very long journey." Birdy signed Rue with his fingers.

————

Two days before we left, a hired courier was waved upstairs, where she picked her way past all the boxes and piles and bags, moving from person to person until she found me kneeling before my trunk, trying to reduce its few components and wondering in despair why our archive was so scanty on the important subject of magic, for I'd spent most of my time sifting the relevant shelves only to come away empty-handed.

In surprise I took the package, and handed the courier the last of my spare coins. When I had my room to myself, I opened the neatly wrapped package and discovered a book, newly bound, the ink so fresh I could smell it.

On a strip of pink paper was Tif's scrawl in out-of-practice Old Sartoran: *Here is the best we could do in so little time. Remember us!* I paged carefully through the book and gazed in gathering puzzlement.

Question, discovery of magic; wait for "Women/indigenous beings" questions. What spells do you think asked for first, why?

Second lesson: Question, what are angels? Indigenous beings—forms of living being—forms taken to communicate with humans—magic and power.

What questions?

This was *less* than we were taught! Where were the explanations?

When I encountered the words *First lesson in basics,* with a list of abbreviated cautions and warnings, I paged impatiently farther along to find no historical details, no maps or explanations, just columns of code, sometimes with odd drawings next to clusters of words. These drawings were brief, cryptic, with arrows, not unlike notes on fan forms.

I turned over a handful of pages, by training too careful to fling them over, though I wanted to. It made no sense! For a time I tried decoding the marks in some of the old archival scripts that we'd had to learn, and then the truth became a possibility: this was not a record.

It was not a history of magic as taught to heralds.

I had in my hands *a book of magic.*

It had to be an instructor's book, perhaps the very instructor that Kaura had mentioned knowing at Tif's celebration. I'd assumed that my cousin would approach this person for recommendations. Instead, she had—somehow—got hold of this.

I laid it on my knee as if it were more fragile than porcelain.

I am not supposed to have this book.

My first instinct was to wrap the book again and send it back to Tiflis with a carefully worded note explaining her error. But as I considered what I would have to say to her, I hesitated for three reasons. First, I did not want to offend my cousin, who had done her best to fulfill my request, probably at great cost. Second, I wondered if lessons for a beginning mage might furnish me more of the sort of knowledge I needed to know than a history of magic, suitably distanced as such things inevitably were. Third, and probably most important—though I thought it least important at the time: I was curious.

I wrapped the book up again, and laid it at the bottom of my trunk. I would not make a hasty decision.

The following days passed rapidly as I helped Lasva sort through her belongings, and I continued my research. She had burned all her rosebud carpets the night before we left for Sartor, which had shocked Marnda, but no one had dared say anything.

Most of the rest of her things were given away. Courtiers adopted the cats—as much as cats are ever owned by humans. Let us say, the cleanboxes and the food were shifted to new locations and cat-windows refitted. Mostly, the cats vanished, though a few wandered through until the very last day.

Heirlooms went back into storage. About other things Lasva said only, "Take it away." Like Rontande's painting of cats. I don't know what the servants did with these, but I suspect they were sold as once having belonged to the princess.

The only new things were those items she had ordered to take west as gifts. As her household shrank to packed trunks in bare, sunny rooms, she seemed to withdraw into herself.

I did not discuss my secret book with anyone. My orders from the queen had been clear about not burdening Lasva, and I understood that the less Birdy knew about what I would be doing, the less the Marloven king would be able to winnow out if Birdy (in his place as stalking horse) might come to be questioned. Besides (I am trying to be honest in this record) I knew he would tell me to send it back as quickly as possible so that I might get a suitable history. Not that I'd been able to find any such suitable history.

As for reconsidering my decision to keep it, I was too busy. Or so I reasoned. When it did intrude on my mind, I found myself arguing, not reasoning: I would learn just enough to understand, to see magic from the inside . . . what harm could it do? I would never use it. Knowledgeable, I could protect Lasva so much better, could I not?

Lasva was also isolated. Here are some of the memories she later cherished:

"This is the waltz," she said. She'd brought Ivandred to her own suite for the lesson. Though it was smaller than the gallery, she did not want any reminders of waltzing with Jurac of Chwahirsland.

Instead, the reminders of Kaidas were like the thorns hidden behind the rose blossoms. Here they had stood . . . no. And, there they had—no.

She forced her attention to the dance steps, which he caught in a surprisingly short time. But the way he watched, with his eyes narrowed, his body so still before he moved, and then, when he did move, it was neatly, lightly, with controlled guestures mirroring hers all the way to the fingertips. It was strange to find her own style so adroitly copied.

When she said, "Let us try it together," her heartbeat quickened.

She took his hand, surprised at the roughness on his palms. She placed the one at her waist, which he barely touched, and the other clasped her fingers, cool and light. The first step was awkward; she bumped into him, and her hand on his shoulder slid down his back to steady him, but he did not stumble or sway.

He stilled.

Then moved, slowly, matching her step, her dip, her turn. His clasp was cool but the internal heat flared again, and she welcomed it desperately, hungrily, craving to annihilate the memory of Kaidas's body, taller, bigger in the bones. Smoother under the skin. Ivandred was built like a cat, but so muscular, his contours were ridged and molded, and she wondered what it would be like when they . . .

But he did not seem to understand the signals inviting him into intimate space. Colendi enjoyed the subtleties of advance and retreat, the lingering eye, the inviting curl of private smile. Seduction was best done subliminally, never any word that later would be regretted, or worse, reported.

She sensed a corresponding fire in Ivandred, but he did not see the signals, nor did he speak any lover's words. In fact, he didn't speak at all.

So she made the mental retreat from intimacy. They had plenty of time. And anticipation was so much better than grief.

Faces flashed by as she waltzed with Ivandred at the queen's ball. Curious eyes, envious, laughing, puzzled, haughty, familiar faces all. Ananda, trying to catch Ivandred's eye, then giving up and seducing the quite willing Prince Macael. Aunt Darva's worried gaze. Little Farava, clasped in the arms of Rontande Altan, for once not sulky or pouty, but intent; so intent he looked like a man at last, rather than an aging youth.

The first storm that carried a hint of autumn sent the brightly colored leaves swirling into the canals, which in Colend is called The Scattering of the Jewels. But she would not be there to hear the autumn songs about the first fire, the first hint of winter wind, the lowering arc of the sun, and always about drawing into the warm circle of loved ones.

So she turned from that thought to the good memories again: the last hunt of the season, Ivandred's pale hair windblown as he rode his silky-maned horse straight as an arrow shot from a bow, the glimpse of him riding easily next to the young buck as he leaned out and wound the garland around the nearest antler. He didn't toss it, like the Colendi did. Riding back, he looked as if nothing happened. Admiring whispers rustled through the courtiers like wind through autumn trees.

She felt nothing as her suite vanished around her. She felt nothing when

Hatahra laughed and then gave a sudden sob. Just one, as Pollar showed everyone the royal babe's first tooth. There was Alian—hard to think of her as a niece—waving her arms and trying to wriggle out of her nurse's grasp, her embroidered and lace-edged gown entangled over sturdy, chubby, short limbs; strings of drool hanging down off her bran-colored nubbin of a chin as Pollar moved from person to person showing the tiny bud of a tooth. *I should feel something,* Lasva thought, touching the baby's fat cheek.

She felt nothing when her rooms were empty at last, and she took her last bath before the wedding.

The wedding.

It was no longer spoken of in future. It was now.

There was the throne room, her sister, the consort, and her betrothed, distant as statues as she listened to their voices reciting the very old words. First his voice, husky, low, the strange accent, then her sister's, firm, but with a tremble just once. And her own voice, high, clear, and remote as the stars.

She walked out, his arm under hers. *I am married.*

As she danced through the night, surrounded by people wearing every shade of blue, except for that central figure in black and gold, the few who knew her well realized just how much grace would leave the court when Lasva was gone. Two people, Darva and the queen, watched Lasva from opposite sides of the brilliantly lit ballroom built of translucent blue-veined marble. The blue cast, usually so cool and beautiful, seemed to shroud Lasva in sorrow as they recognized in her distant gaze, her absent smile, and in the hint of winter's bite carried on the rising wind, that Princess Lasthavais the Rose was already gone.

Ivandred, too, moved in a haze, mostly of exhaustion, for he was not used to late nights of dancing or card parties or performances. Marlovens do not sleep from dawn until almost noon, and then rest again in the afternoon. He forced himself to stay awake and aware.

As they completed the ritual that seemed so foreign to him, and he took hands with his new wife, Ivandred tried again to envision her gentle manners and ribbons and web-soft, drifting clothes in his home of stone and steel.

"Safety," she had said.

Marlovens prefer to depart on long journeys at dawn. The queen and consort walked out with us into the bleak bluish light, where the

Marlovens, Prince Macael and his diminished entourage, and Birdy (or Stable Hand Birdy, as he was now known) waited with the princess's carriage, which was the first of the three carriages containing servants and belongings.

Bare-headed, Ivandred sat astride his horse as Hatahra and Lasva embraced one last, lingering time that made it clear neither expected to see the other again anytime soon—if ever. I climbed into the carriage in the backward seat, my travel bag gripped in my arms. The hours had rung, the days had passed, and the courier remained un-summoned, the note to Tiflis unwritten, the dangerous gift unreturned. Instead, it lay at the bottom of my carry-bag, wrapped in my second-best underrobe.

I'd decided that my very reluctance to return the gift was my strongest reason to keep it. By accepting the gift, I kept faith with my cousin and also with the queen. Yes, I was breaking the mages' rules, but I trusted myself not to use for influence whatever knowledge I gained, much less for ill. I only wanted knowledge for the sake of knowledge, a laudable goal at any time but especially upon venturing into a new land and a new life.

I watched the wind lift Ivandred's pale hair as he looked down his assembled rows, baggage and remounts at the back, black and gold banners flagging on their lances.

Hatahra raised a hand in farewell.

The prince of Marloven Hesea struck his hand to his heart in salute to her, then turned Lasva's way. She sat there, still and composed.

Ivandred lifted his fist in the air.

The Marlovens did not leave at the gallop, but at a quiet walk, falling in two by two behind our Colendi carriages until there was nothing left in the courtyard but a low cloud of dust settling swiftly in the cold wind that already smelled of winter, and three cats watching, twitch-tailed, from the roof.

PART FOUR
Magic

ONE

Of Foresight and the
Serving of Food

We were shocked when we discovered that our princess was not going to travel the way princesses always traveled—in a sedate cortege, with outriders going ahead to requisition the finest inns and see that all was ready.

The Marlovens did their best to accommodate us. They put together two of their tents just for Lasva, as befitted their idea of a princess, and they'd gathered fine embroidered cushions and hangings for it.

That first night, as Lasva and we, her staff, crowded into the already-stuffy, cramped and unfamiliar space of the tent, wondering where to put our things as well as ourselves, it was clear from the sharp angles of elbows, the pitch of voices, how tired and irritated everyone was. We stood uneasily around the edge of the light cast by the lamp, no one daring to move lest she inadvertently cast a shadow over someone else. The violence inherent in that light disturbed some of us and excited others—you could see it in their shadow-emphasized features. Single source light is crude in its harsh and sudden revelations, emphasized by the *rudeness* of shadow.

Lasva had her palms together in The Peace. "I want us to travel in harmony. If the Marlovens can endure this kind of travel, so can we." There was nothing more to be said until we were in private.

She retired behind one of the hangings that screened off the back of the tent, then reappeared and handed me her gold scrollcase. "Will you take charge of this, Emras? Tell me at once if my sister writes, as always."

I bowed my assent. She let the cloth fall and vanished from sight but not from hearing. Seneschal Marnda motioned the staff and me outside.

I hesitated, not certain if I should follow, for my orders came directly from Lasva. Until now, the chain of responsibility had been clear. I was still Lasva's scribe, even if in secret. I was not a serving maid under the seneschal, except in seeming.

Marnda beckoned again, a firm gesture that left me a choice between obeying (thereby setting a precedent I might come to regret), or causing resentment in her.

I picked up my cloak and followed.

In darkness we trampled over the rough ground as occasional drops of rain splattered us. I gritted my teeth when my slippers stuck in muck. Soft exclamations escaped the dressers, barely seen in the uncertain, flickering light of the cooks' fire and the bobbing torches carried by what we would soon learn were inside perimeter guards. These guards protected us from attack, but it seemed to us that their true purpose was to shoo wandering Colendi back inside the circle, much like a shepherd chasing errant sheep.

When we'd gone a distance from tents or fire, Marnda stopped, and we gathered around her in the deepening nightfall. Marnda issued orders to the dressers for who would sleep where, when, what their duties that night would be, and then sent them off one by one.

Then we were alone. "That gold case should be mine, Scribe." Her voice quivered with emotion. "The queen was specific. Her highness must become accustomed to the new life as soon as possible. That means, no letters from home should disturb the princess's repose, unless she expresses the desire to see them. We already know that the queen will not write, unless there is some great cause."

"Seneschal Marnda, you know my orders from the queen." I made The Peace, though she probably could see as little of me as I saw of her. "And you just heard the orders from the princess. 'Always' means I summarize any letters not from the queen, and the princess dictates an answer if she does not wish to answer herself."

After a painfully long silence, Marnda said, "Then you must read whatever comes, but do not summarize unless she asks. If a week goes by and she does not ask, then answer them in her name, on the queen's orders to *me*."

"But I did not hear those orders. And my doing that seems a breach of the scribes' First Rule."

"But you can break that Rule when ordered. Scribe Emras, the queen said—these are her words—that the sooner our princess turns her heart west, the sooner she will again be happy."

"Yes. The queen said that to me as well."

"So this is how I interpret Queen Hatahra's orders: do not let her highness see any letters from home that will cause her pain. She *must not* experience reminders that might keep her heart back in Alsais, so if you find that you are unable to answer those letters, I am putting myself forward to carry out that duty."

"I am her scribe. I will do it."

I trudged back to the tent, sick at heart. The tent was not empty— from the sound of low voices I could tell that Lasva and Ivandred sat behind the hanging. He asked a series of questions about her comfort, what could he do, what could they do, and she returned polite answers. Without the distraction of seeing them, I could hear from their tones how they spoke past one another in their effort to be accommodating. He in that outdated, stiff Sartoran became more specific and she more vague, garlanded with more words of gratitude, but I sensed her tension mounting from the very gentleness of her tone.

He left, bidding her a good night.

That set the rhythm of our days. And I do mean days. The Marlovens did not stop even for Restday. Anyone who has traveled rapidly (the Marlovens wanted to get home by winter) without being able to stay in hostelries (the Marlovens did not like foreign inns) would understand at once how rare and precious are a few moments alone.

As fine as a tent is, in theory, what you have in reality is a canvas enclosure of stale air that does not shut out cold, damp, or noise. The only bearable place was near the brazier, then your front cooked as your back chilled. Colendi are accustomed to closing off the intimate details of life behind doors. Privacy was the privilege of birth: the higher your birth, the more doors between you and the world. The powerful chose when they would be seen, but even we who served had recourse to a semblance of privacy, and we each had our own sleeping space, tiny as it might be.

Living almost on top of one another in tents, then bumped up against each other in carriages, we were forced into continual intimate proximity. It did not help that there was no staff to attend to our needs. We either had to do for ourselves, or rely on each other. Anhar offered to attend to our nails as best she could, and Pelis to repair our clothes. However, Belimas, the hair dresser, refused to touch anyone else's head but Lasva's because (she said) our hair was disgusting as we could not bathe every day. I was glad that I'd cut my hair short again, but the others were miserable until they learned to finger their hair into simple braids, at least.

Belimas, in her hatred of the journey, was not content to stop there. She and Anhar quarreled interminably in short, hissing whispers. At first I did not hear any particulars, but one night, I was there when Belimas scolded Anhar, calling her a moon-faced hummer and an oaf for deliberate shadow-trespasses.

Anhar? My incredulity caused me to look her way, and I saw in her tight lips, her downward gaze, that this accusation was not new. But there were none of the angry little signs of someone who has been caught doing wrong. Just the opposite.

I said, "I believe the campfire is at fault." When Belimas turned my way, looking as surprised as if a tree had spoken, I addressed her. "As you can see, the shadows are uneven. Anyone might find a shadow forming *after* she placed her foot." I made The Peace.

Belimas flushed, but she returned The Peace in a stiff manner.

After that I was listening, and as the miserable journey wheeled its way west, I became aware that Anhar tried to keep a distance from Belimas, but there was no distance to be kept. And Belimas was always on the watch — the way Anhar folded her bedding, or offered to trudge through the mud to take meals to the stable hands who could not leave the horses for long, or even the way she climbed into the carriage — as though by catching Anhar in error she could justify her own wretchedness.

These accusations seemed to drive invisible wedges between everyone, and they angered me sufficiently that if I overheard one, I began to offer excuses that were less justifiable, until the day I offered one that was outright preposterous—"I believe a bird flew over the sun"—causing the second dresser, Pelis, to snort with laughter.

Thereafter Belimas would not speak when I was around. I expected that. I was glad not to be the recipient of her complaints. The thing I did not expect was how Pelis began sitting next to me in the coach, and sometimes she turned my way when offering observations, even joking.

Marnda's instructions became more frequent and longer as she endeavored by force of will and attention to the tiniest detail, to impose order on the messiness of nature. She followed Lasva about, straightening things with angry little twitches and shakes almost as soon as the princess set them down.

Lasva reacted by closing herself inside her skull, leaving us with a polite, pleasant, utterly blank simulacrum.

———

Life did not halt behind us.

King Jurac wished it would. For a time, he wished the entire world blasted to splinters by Norsunder. Nothing could be worse than the humiliation of defeat. If only he hadn't gone himself! But he'd had to. Nothing else showed her sufficient honor.

And that Marloven prince had come himself. The problem was, he'd succeeded. Why was that? Because he had better information, from no less than the queen's consort.

Jurac transferred to his capital, leaving his defeated men to travel the mountains home. The first thing he did was rid himself of the Colendi, except for the ambassador, who was the necessary link to that vital trade.

Kivic had figured out within heartbeats after the disaster that the blame was going to fall squarely on him, probably sooner than later. On the long, wearying journey, he put in useful time forming friendships with the guards, expertly teasing out those most responsive to "us" against "them" thinking.

When they arrived back at Narad, the king ordered the guards to fling Kivic into prison, citing Colendi demands. Everyone knew it was for form's sake. The spy protested his innocence all the way, but that, too, was just for form's sake. A few weeks later he was summoned before an unsmiling, remote king, to be told, "In accordance with my agreement with Queen Hatahra of Colend, you will be remanded to their custody to make restitution according to their laws, since you committed murder of their people on their ground."

The ambassador bowed and withdrew. Before Kivic was led away, Jurac said, "It was a *stupid* idea, Kivic. That should have been me, on the horse, coming to the rescue."

Kivic didn't bother to say that the wretched woman had done her best to rescue herself—that if there'd been no Marlovens, and Jurac *had* gotten her back to Narad, his life would have been reduced to a misery.

You don't tell a king that the princess in question didn't want him as a man or as a king; that she'd wanted the other fellow. So he kept silence as he paced past all the guards, until he came abreast of his man. "Fun ahead." He breathed out a laugh.

———

"That's it," the Duke of Alarcansa said, and the tailor stepped back, his mouth an unhappy line.   ¹

Kaidas made an experimental turn. Once again the damned sword thumped his side. And the folds of his robe covered the hilt again; he glanced in the mirror. Yes, the line was ruined. Now he understood why those Marlovens wore their coats so tight to the waist—though they hadn't worn their swords. Maybe they did at home. In the salon? In the dining room? In the bedroom?

"It will have to do," he said, glancing at the sandglass. He must not be late for his interview with the queen. Who wanted him wearing a sword.

It thumped and rattled against his side as he crossed the palace from the wing hastily given over to the new military arm. It tried to tangle in his legs when he mounted the curving stairway, and when he kicked it impatiently, it did its best to spin, nearly tripping him. He caught himself on the balustrade, glanced around to see who had witnessed his near fall, and caught the gaze of an armed herald at the top of the stair—*her* sword decently hidden behind a panel of her new livery. The corners of her mouth tightened. Yes, she was laughing, but he sensed from the angle of her brows the sympathy of one who had been in the same ridiculous position.

He banished his anger and smiled, fingers flicking in Irony before he put his hand on the hilt and pressed down so that the tip of the sword angled safely behind him, which permitted him to lengthen his strides. Much better. He'd just have to march around with his hand on the hilt, feeling like a strutting rooster in a barnyard.

On the first reverberating strike of the Hour of Stone the heralds opened the door to the white-marble and slate interview room that was reserved for military matters, and as such, had not been used for years. Kaidas walked in, imagining the scurry of servants scrubbing the marble and polishing the ebony-lacquered furnishings.

The queen was there, dressed in judgment robes of dark blue and white.

"The murderer Kivic will be presented at the border arch in the middle pass in three days," the queen said. "You will oversee his delivery into the hands of the Judicial Masks to commence restitution for his crimes. You will take as many of your defenders as you think necessary, at crown expense." Her fan snapped. "You will see to it that nothing interferes with justice, for I do not trust that hummer Jurac past my next breath."

Since his marriage, Kaidas had become an expert at shuttering his emotions. He employed that skill now to hide his abhorrence. Guard duty, that was what "defenders" really meant.

He bowed, withdrew, and returned to the Alarcansa suite, where he found his wife walking back and forth in the vestibule so that no wrinkles would crush her silken panels of sheerest silver, embroidered with moon-pale pond lilies and redbirds with tiny rubies at their wingtips.

She lifted her fan upward, as if toward the bell towers, for it was not commensurate with the *melende* of a Definian to remonstrate.

He bowed, hand out in polite apology. "We will not be late to the Rising, for I was summoned to a private interview with the queen in my new capacity," he said as he removed the exasperating baldric. The Grand Seneschal had been exact about the etiquette: when summoned to the queen on Defender affairs, he was to wear the sword. The rest of the time, the weapons ban was to be observed.

He resisted the impulse to fling baldric and sword and handed them to the waiting man in the hallway. "Tell the tailor we need more of an angle," he said, and the man bowed and vanished.

He handed the new service robe, edged in royal blue, to another waiting servant, shrugged into a brocaded robe with rubies studding the swinging tassels at the shoulders—all without breaking a step—and offered his arm to his wife in the correct manner.

She slid her fingers over the smooth linen silk of his sleeve and smiled as he matched his pace to hers. On the surface, everything was as it should be. The new duke of Alarcansa had alone (the departed barbarians, whom she had never seen, were effectively forgotten) figured out the Chwahir king's evil plot, and had been recognized for his foresight by the queen with his new position as Defender of the Crown. Carola herself, on arriving in Alsais, had been personally welcomed by the queen, and before all the court had been appointed Chief Lady in Waiting to the Princess Royal. And *She* was gone with the barbarians. Gone and it was to be hoped, soon forgotten.

All as it should be. But every time Carola glimpsed her duke after even a brief separation, there was the shock of that short hair. *An act of war*, was all he had said in explanation, and the strict demands of *me-*

lende prohibited her from pressing further. Until he chose to explain, she would wait.

This lapse might have been forgotten with time had not every hothead who wanted to swing a sword cut off their hair, male and female. Carola was convinced that Lady Isari, striding off to the military practice barn each morning, had more swords than her own on her mind. But who would want her, with that ridiculous short hair flying untidily about her face?

She could not speak any of that, but *melende* permitted questions about duty. "More military matters?"

"I am sent to fetch the Chwahir murderer. Apparently the heralds' judiciaries can't be trusted, though they have handled restitution for generations."

"The murderer is a Chwahir," Carola stated, flourishing her fan in No Matter. "Of course the queen would send you." He showed no sign of regret for his imminent departure, and once again, she could not prevent the pent-up words, "You are pleased to be going?"

Kaidas gave her a glance of surprise. "Pleased to be riding out in bad weather, with a damned sword rattling my thigh at every jog? No doubt to be kept waiting by the Chwahir, who won't be in any hurry to spare us wind or weather. I would rather be running the Ym Hunt. I would rather be tending the two-year-olds. But we have both been honored with calls to service."

This reminder of her own honor should have been a triumph, but it wasn't. Within a week of her new duties, Carola's vision of elegant and select little parties—at the queen's expense on behalf of her daughter—as courtiers came to pay calls upon the infant, had vanished when no one seemed inclined to call upon a babe-in-arms. Carola still had evenings free, but with her freedom curtailed by her not-very-onerous duties, she felt her influence over the ever-changing eddies of court slipping.

"You will be pleased to return, then." She recovered modulation as they approached the double doors leading to the conservatory, where everyone was gathered for the Rising—and Carola would have to follow the royal family back to the royal suite to begin her day as Chief Lady in Waiting. "I will offer you consolation with a masquerade and invite your particular friends, if you will honor me with a list before you leave."

There was nothing like an exclusive party to tighten one's grip on the court's inner circle.

TWO

OF PATTERNS VISIBLE AND INVISIBLE

"Hai ho, it's another letter from Macael," Tharais exclaimed, opening her scrollcase.

I still have yet to hold a conversation with Lasthavais (wrote Macael), *whose manners are so good that I cannot tell if hers is the silence of nothing to say or nothing to think.*

"Ouch." Geral picked up his goblet of spiced wine, more to warm his fingers than to drink, and sat back on the cushion they shared, ready to be entertained. "Where are they now?"

Tharais bit her lower lip, scanning rapidly. "He says, 'another miserable, wet, befogged road just like the past four days.'"

A fresh fire burned on the grate, but it had not yet taken the chill off the room. "Go ahead," he told her. "Read it, if you've a mind to."

"There isn't much." Tharais fingered the tiny curl of paper.

"Uh oh. Trouble, I gather?"

"I don't know." Tharais offered the letter. "Here. Tell me what you think."

Geral took it from her callused fingers. *"Your brother still goes off in the mornings, but he's always back by dawn. Lasva the Rose doesn't emerge from her tent.* Her tent?" Geral looked askance.

Tharais lifted a shoulder as she sank back on the silken cushion, her blond curls spreading around her. How she adored varieties in custom! In Marloven Hesea, you used cushions when you traveled but tables and chairs in your home. Here, cushions at home, tables and chairs if you traveled outside the borders of this small kingdom with its famous goldenwood trees, guarded, it was said, by tree-spirits.

"It's not necessarily a problem," she said slowly. "One thing I learned between Marloven Hesea and Enaeran, there are different notions of privacy. Tents are only private up here." She touched her forehead. "They might sleep separate for her sake."

"All right," Geral said, and looked askance. "Are you sure you want to know what I think, when I don't even seem to know how to read this thing? Your customs are as much a mystery to me as is your brother. Or for that matter, as is Princess Lasthavais the Rose. Frankly, I am astonished that she married him, given the number of princes who must have been crowding in to court her."

"Fair enough." Tharais's capable fingers rolled the paper into a little ball as she stared out the window at the sleet plunking momentary craters in the light brown, soupy soil. The winter breakfast room faced north, where the faraway sun arced lower each day against the bleak gray sky. "Geral, I hope this makes sense, but until she married Van she wasn't real to me. Now she is. I . . . I have to talk to her."

"Because?"

Tharais turned her face toward the fire, knowing that it was impossible to hide her reaction to the memory of Van's parting with Tdiran Marlovair. "Can we invite them here?" she asked.

He sank down beside her. "Is that wise?"

In spite of the color flooding her cheeks she looked unexpectedly like her brother as she said, "I think I need to tell her certain things that she had better know."

When the carriages got stuck in the mud left from an earlier storm, Ivandred called an early stop. It was Restday—but there was no rest. We were not in sight of any civilization. The Marlovens pitched the tents with their usual speed, then vanished beyond a distant line of tall ash that must once have marked a border. Marnda marched all the dressers to the river to wash everything we had, to make full use of precious daylight. Birdy was busy with the animals and the carriages.

Macael invited Lasva to join him and his noble friends, as the remaining pair of Marlovens established the perimeter circle around us.

So I had the tent to myself. Oh, a precious moment alone!

I hung up my water-warded cloak to drip at the far end of the tent, plunged my hands to the bottom of my modest trunk, and yanked out my book of magic. I was deep into puzzling out patterns in the nonsensical phrases when quick footsteps outside the tent made me wrap the book and plunge it back into my trunk. The tent flap opened, sending in a draft of cold, clean air, droplets catching the lamplight like fireflies.

"Supper," said the Prince of Marloven Hesea.

He left, moving between the light and me. So it always was, the Marlovens and Enaeraneth flashing shadows over us without the slightest gesture of politeness. *They don't know anything*, so we kept saying, but the implied rudeness—they *should* know—was a continual source of irritation, like ill-fitting shoes that rubbed blisters on your feet. But hard on that was the unsettling surprise of a prince coming to fetch me. He could have been passing by, but in Colend, no royal would take a single step out of the way for that. That's what pages were for.

But Marlovens didn't seem to have pages. They had runners, whose purpose we couldn't define.

I pulled my water-bespelled cloak around me and followed Ivandred to the other side of the camp, where the Enaeraneth had set up their row of tents. We found Lasva sitting neatly on her cushion, the way Colendi ate in formal company. My job was to serve her the way we Colendi liked to be served.

The rest lounged about on their cushions, careless of light and space, talking while Lasva sat and smiled.

"You're late," Macael observed, smiling lazily up at his cousin.

"Change of my outriders." Ivandred sat down next to Lasva. "Short drill, as we'll ride early tomorrow to make up the time. If you concur?" He turned to Lasva, who (as always) gestured Harmonious Agreement and smiled. Smiled. Smiled.

The Enaeraneth waited politely for me to fix Lasva's plate, which she accepted with her smile already going absent. She formed a portion of the corn-meal and fish into a tiny ball in her fingers and passed it behind her lips, her movement small and neat and noiseless. She knew, as I knew, that it was not for the Enaeraneth or the Marlovens to adjust, but for us. Every day, every cold breath, was a reminder that we moved farther from Colend.

Ivandred leaned forward to tap a scroll lying on the table near the food. "This latest map must be a generation out of date. The road goes nowhere. I sent a pair to scout," he said. "I'd rather we don't encounter any more Dandy Glamacs lying in ambush."

"To which I agree." Macael spread his hands, rings glittering. He was friendly and was certainly pleasant to look at when he sat back on his cushion, his hair like corn silk, hanging long and loose over his open jacket, revealing a brocaded waistcoat and cambric shirt. His hands, negligently holding a half-eaten cabbage roll, were well-made. "Do you think we were sold an old map as a setup for ambush?"

"Possible," Ivandred conceded. "If so, they will learn their mistake." His teeth showed. "Though I'd rather not lose the time."

"Speaking of travel. Your sister wrote to me moments ago. She wants us to come to Remalna. She promises a proper bride party for Lasthavais." Macael made a graceful bow in her direction. "You can take ship from there. I smell winter on the wind."

"Lasva?" Ivandred turned her way.

Lasva said, "I will leave that to you. I know so little of the terrain past our border."

The lords and Macael heroically kept up a three-way conversation about hunting customs across the continent: in the east they chased and garlanded deer, but deer were rare in the western plains, where they hunted the trained fox, and hunted to kill the marauding wolf. In the case of the trained creatures, animals that often won were prized so that stud fees might cost as much as a castle, and they compared the prices of fast horses against what they'd heard about fast deer in our part of the world.

The meal ended at last, and we picked our way over the muddy turf back to our tent, where I discovered the scrollcase full of notes. Of course it was—today was Restday, the courtiers' favorite day for writing letters to those far away, and for some of the letters in the scrollcase, a week had passed.

Mindful of my promise to Marnda, I did not tell Lasva, nor did Lasva ask.

From Isari:

> *. . . and Kaidas summoned us after the Rising with tidings that we ride tomorrow to the middle pass to fetch the Murderer. He thinks the enemy capable of anything, while here we are, attempting to learn.*

Kaidas has sent to his Thora-Dei cousins for a sword master, but this person will not be here before harvest. . . .

From Ananda:

> *. . . but why do you not answer my questions, Lasva dear? Do we cease to amuse you at a distance? You would laugh if you saw all the fellows in that horrid short hair. And Isari! I could have gone my entire life without having to contemplate just how absurd necks look from the back, and as for that grunting and stamping as they wave those rapiers about, believe me, my dear, the tang alone is enough to keep one away.*

From Darva, the Countess of Oleff, and from the look of it, more worries about Ladies Lissais and Farava, and Lord Rontande of Altan:

> *L. now goes down with F. to watch R. at the Duke's swordplay. I think she may join them. The defenders look quite odd with their hair shorn; they seem to find it martial, though I think it makes them look absurdly young. Alarcansa, when pressed, said it's more practical, if you're to wear a helm and . . .*

I scanned to the next page.

> *L. seems to share everything with F., including falling in love with R. Or perhaps she is in love with F. and so tries to adore R. because F. does. The Duke of A. shows all the signs of favoring him as an aide . . .*

As always, I avoided the use of the word "I" and answered on precious strips of lily-paper. For Darva I described the slate shade of a slow moving river framed by red mud, a gnarled, ancient hawthorn from which a flight of brilliant crimson tzilis burst, plumage streaming as they flew skyward. For Isari I described how handsome the Marlovens looked, riding in their orderly columns, banners at the front, snapping in the wind. For Ananda, I described Haldren Marlovair's striking profile, and how the Marlovens' braids stayed neat over days, so they did not have to tidy their hair twice a day like we did. I never responded to any mention of the Duke of Alarcansa.

Lasva retired behind her screen, and the other dressers returned with clothes to hang over every available surface in hopes they would dry sufficiently overnight, aided by the heat from the brazier, to be packed at dawn.

I was on the last letter when Ivandred himself arrived, just as I was describing those droplets gleaming on his pale braids. He acknowledged me by a lifted index finger then said, "Lasva?"

Marlovens, I had discovered, were strict about the hangings, as if they were real walls. To Lasva it was just more damp cloth. She flung it aside so we could see her and said as sweetly as always, "Please join me."

"I wrote to my sister." Ivandred ducked inside and sat next to her, but he did not touch the hanging. It was for her to decide the degree of privacy.

To her, there was no privacy.

He said, "We will take a ship from Mardgar. That will quicken the journey."

Lasva tried to use his open-handed gesture as one of gratitude and politeness, but he saw it as a beckon, a come-hither.

Color ridged his cheekbones, then he took her by the shoulders and pulled her close. When she raised her hands to his face he bent his head and kissed her. I watched the shock of the kiss go through Lasva's body, as though the tension—the difficult emotions one sensed leashed within him—struck through her.

She groped toward the hanging. I brought it down, then took up my cloak and stumbled over the uneven ground into the darkness outside the tent. I knew that nothing would happen in there. Lasva could not bear the idea of intimacy heard by all—her own private space in Colend had been beyond three sets of doors. So he would leave soon, but before then I had a little time to myself, which I always needed to shed the residue of guilt from my trespass against the First Rule.

Ten steps outside the tent, I tripped over an unseen root and landed full length on the rough turf. I'd paid no heed to where I was going. Then I was startled when hands reached under my armpits and hauled me to my feet.

"You are a little thing," the dresser Pelis exclaimed as she brushed mud off me. She glanced around, laughed softly, then said, "I love the way you've south-gated Belimas, but I hope you know that with Anhar you are stroking the wrong plumage."

"I am doing what?" I responded, completely surprised.

Then I became aware of the way she was holding my hand as her fingers caressed the dirt from mine. It was gentle but insistent in a way that caused me to stiffen.

She freed my fingers, chuckling. "And so am I, it seems!" She fluttered her fingers mockingly and walked off.

Thoroughly unsettled, I walked randomly in the other direction. There beyond a tangle of trees was the campfire of the Marlovens. They sounded like ordinary folk from a distance, talking, even laughing. Then I recognized a familiar voice among those laughing: Birdy!

The voices were clear on the night air. He was trying to speak their language, and they seemed to find his attempts funny. I turned away, groping so I wouldn't smash into a tree, for their firelight had dazzled my vision. I couldn't bear the idea of them making game of Birdy, and I stumbled away.

I hadn't gone far when Birdy himself appeared out of the darkness, arms moving, elbows poking . . .

He was juggling again. "Emras?" he whispered. "That *was* you! Did you get lost?"

"Merely walking about." When he dropped one of those silk bags, I said, "I thought you gave that up."

"The ambassador took me aside in Chwahirsland to advise me that I looked stupid when I practiced my juggling. His actual words were 'hum-bumbler' which, when you consider that we were in the Chwahir capital at the time, had added spice. I thought, if the queen wants me to look harmless, what could be more harmless than a hum-bumbler? So I'm at it again. There's a stream over yonder."

We started down an incline, barely visible in the weak starlight peering through the parting clouds. He added with a laugh no louder than a breath, "Between the inner perimeter sentry points. I've learnt that much."

"What does that mean?"

"It means that though the fellows posted to guard the camp can still see us, because these Marlovens are far too efficient to permit a blind spot, we're at enough distance that they will just see a couple of inept Colendi fumbling around. And the outer patrol, on horseback, won't see us because they are looking outward, so the firelight won't cloud their vision."

"You've learned a lot," I observed.

"I've learned a little," he countered, pocketing the silks as he turned his head. "Very little, as I discover anew each day." The glance to the side was quick.

I turned, but it was only Anhar, and not a Marloven or our own fretful seneschal.

Birdy continued, "But as the queen ordered, I am making myself as useful as I can." He pointed toward a huge boulder, barely discernible in the weak blue light. "We can sit on that for a short time, I think. We're too boring for any of them to wonder what we might be doing, but a long absence will cause notice."

The water-repelling spell on my cloak kept me from getting wet, but nothing warded the cold or the hardness. As I fell in step between the other two, I shivered, and he said, "Ah, getting to chat in our language feels so good. But Emras, you don't look happy."

As always, the temptation to tell Birdy about the book was intense, but he could not know any more than Anhar could. "You do not mind being damp and dirty all the time?"

Anhar's hands came up in the shadow-ward, and Birdy chuckled. The firelight exaggerated his bony eye sockets, the edge of his jaw, and his ears. "I'm glad I was with the Chwahir so long. I learned all about sleeping in terrible places and bathing infrequently. Not that I mean to slander the Chwahir, for if our kingdom was half as cold as theirs, we wouldn't bathe often, either. How are you two doing learning the language?"

I said, "They don't talk to us but rarely and then in Sartoran."

"I do not know a word." Anhar gazed downward, revealing two fingers breadth of dark hair on either side of the part. "Are they giving you the south-gate?" she asked, looking up earnestly into Birdy's face.

"Ah-ye, it's more that they're a closed circle. Like what people say about courtiers: you can walk with them, but not among them. How long did it take before I realized that three of Ivandred's lancers are women?"

"Women?" I repeated, as Anhar threw up her hands again. "I did not know that."

"They do look all the same, don't they? Anyway, they're not south-gating me. I know the difference—the Chwahir south-gated us as much as they dared. *How* they hated us Colendi! I only learned these things after I bought a Bermundi coat and hat, then walked about the streets of Narad unintentionally incognito."

"So are you learning anything now?" Anhar asked.

"Yes." The ruddy firelight was just bright enough to outline the sharp angle of his nose and catch in curly wires of light his unruly hair. "We'll have to sell these carriage horses when we reach the river, and since my orders are to go all the way to Marloven Hesea, my partner really wants to return home."

"But why sell the horses? The queen's horses aren't good enough?"

"They aren't trained for riding," Birdy corrected. "And most important, they aren't trained for fighting." He yawned. "The Marlovens can't afford to transport the carriages and the carriage horses. I don't know what they do for money in their own kingdom, but Prince Ivandred's purse is thin, so when we get to the other end of the Sartoran sea, we'll all be riding. That means throwing away any 'extra' baggage. Except for the princess's. You know whose will go first. Be aware of that when you repack." He yawned again. "The perimeter guard will be around soon to shoo us back to camp. Sleep well! I fear we'll be riding by torchlight well before dawn to make up for lost time."

His footsteps chuffed through the mud, and the two of us returned to our tent, each silent. I could not prevent Seneschal Marnda from going through my things as well as the belongings of the other staff, if she was ordered to.

I would have to parrot the entire book, though I still did not comprehend it. When we reached the river, I would get rid of it. That would meet everyone's demands.

"You should have seen them! Or maybe not, for I tell you, we were in danger of falling off the roof, we were laughing so hard," Kivic said, as they toiled up into the mountains, coats pulled up against occasional spits of sleet. "There was no hope any of them would catch up with the Marloven boys, no matter what their titles."

"Tell 'em about the duke who put the shield over his butt," one of the men said.

"It wasn't a shield, it was a breastplate," another corrected. "Tell him, Kivic!"

The tale had grown in the telling. What harm did it do to embellish a little? Kivic laughed with them, though the spark of his amusement was at the predictability of human behavior. He'd picked his man—the one who couldn't resist finding duty near Kivic's cell to hear more, and out had come the little anecdotes, one by one. This man carried the stories to his cronies among the guards, exactly as Kivic predicted.

Their favorite story was how the arrogant Colendi, trailing ribbons and lace, scrambled all over one another to mount their horses and chase after the Marlovens. It was amusing and also reassuring, not only reinforcing how incompetent the Colendi were, but reminding them that the hated Marlovens were long gone, probably halfway across the continent by now, where they could cause no one any grief.

". . . and the Duke of Altan bawling at his servants to find the tents as he danced around, wrestling with the baldric. Which ripped right across."

Guffaws, as someone repeated, *Ripped! Ripped!*

"I promise you, it ripped. They wear silk even to battle, those fools. And this baldric, judging from the faded color, had to be at least five hundred years old. I'm surprised the moths hadn't gotten to it generations ago."

"It's certainly moth food now," someone said as they pulled up behind the captain.

"Ho, here we are," said the captain, as they rounded the last towering cliff, runnels of slushy rain slanting across the road.

The animals halted, heads drooping. The Chwahir dismounted, leaving the horses to the equerries.

"Let's just take a look," the captain said, eyeing the massive stone arch with its narrow passage that the Colendi had built generations ago to mark the border. Kivic had always wondered if any of them knew about the epithets painted and even carved on the Chwahir side. There was no such mar on the Colendi side, but the carvings were insult enough, intertwined thorny vines representing their Thorn Gate. "Stupid as they might be, there's no use in our riding down blind," the captain said, sending a speculative glance Kivic's way then shifting his attention to a scout. "Thassler. Take a look through the glass."

This was the first sign of suspicion, making Kivic wonder what the king might have said to the captain, as the scout slogged through the mud to a standing stone, pulling his field glass from his belt.

No matter. Kivic maintained his most innocent demeanor, and as the captain raised a hand to peer down the Colendi side of the road into the mist, Kivic shot a grin at his guard, who had ranged himself with his chosen fellows in a line. All he needed were a few moments of mad scramble to make his getaway. He'd marked his escape route on the retreat with Jurac, while everyone else was grumbling and cursing. Among the scattering of animals trails there was an overgrown path, probably the one used before the road was laid.

"Two ribbon-pricks with the pair of buckets," the scout reported, the epithet "bucket" pertaining to the judiciaries' hoods. "Waiting about thirty paces down the road."

The captain turned Kivic's way. But before he could speak, Kivic said with all the disgust he could muster, "Look at 'em. Summoning us like we're servants."

If he'd done his work right, that "us" could goad the captain, along with the memory of that humiliating defeat. If the captain said "you," then it was on to plan two, far less easy.

But the captain reacted with a grim face, his horse shifting beside him. "If they want him, let 'em come and get him," he said, and Kivic's pet guards reinforced that with *Yes, let 'em fetch*, mutterings.

After that, everything proceeded as Kivic had hoped. The masked judiciaries didn't speak, of course, for justice is supposed to be neutral, but the sodden defenders in blue nudged their horses forward, one calling in Colend's language, "Send the accused forth."

The captain, bolstered by his men, called, "What?"

The Chwahir grinned.

The fool in blue repeated his request in passable Chwahir, but the captain, enjoying the grins of his men, said again, "What?" causing a general chuckle.

Kivic was thrilled—people were so predictable!

The pair of Colendi rode a few steps closer over the flagged road. "Send forth the accused," the one repeated in Sartoran, gloved hands cupped around his mouth.

"Come and get him," the captain roared back.

The pair trotted closer to the stone arch, and the judiciaries also rode forward, as if pulled by strings.

When they were nearly in reach, Kivic's guard spoke right on cue, "Let's teach these scum a lesson."

"Let's see how stupid those buckets look with their bare faces hanging out," Kivic said to the men nearest him then stepped sideways until he was outside of the captain's peripheral vision. From there he shied a small stone at the nearest Colendi. Up came the sword—out came all the swords—the Chwahir roared through the archway, nearly stepping on each other's heels in their hurry to get through the narrow gap, and the fun was on!

For about two heartbeats. Then the hillside erupted with Colendi, who had been crouched like brigands behind rocks and trees. Who would have thought they'd have the wit to plan for an ambush? Ah, well. All Kivic needed was for the brawl to spread fifteen paces down the trail.

He slipped past a knot of struggling men, slid in the mud, righted himself, ducked through the arch, got his feet on the flagged stones and shifted past another knot, ignoring the surprised hail from his guard, "Hey, Kivic, give us a hand here. . . ."

Kivic dashed past, found the old path—and came up short when a man stepped out from behind a juniper, sword in hand. "Where are you going?" the man asked pleasantly.

Kivic stared. Tall Colendi in a theater version of a battle tunic, edged with heavy blue silk, black hair under the towering, silver-chased helm that didn't keep the rain from pouring down his neck, black eyes. Wasn't this the destitute baron who'd married his way into a rich dukedom?

Kivic drew in a breath of pleasure. His kind of man! He leaned forward and said conspiratorially, "I can make you a king."

The black eyes widened, then the fellow threw his head back and laughed.

Shock flashed through Kivic, followed by anger and intent.

For Kaidas, it was the first time he'd laughed since he and Lasva were together. But the reminder of Lasva doused the hilarity and just in time, given that the Chwahir whipped a knife out from his clothing and darted at Kaidas, quick as a snake.

Kaidas belatedly swung the rapier, but not before the point of the knife struck him a palm's width above the navel. The point turned on the fine mail the queen had ordered him to wear, but the force of the blow nearly doubled him.

He gasped, choked for breath, alarm bringing his arm around to protect his front, the sword swinging with it. The Chwahir darted out of the way of the blade, then lunged again, this time for the throat. Kaidas stumbled back, the sword swinging but too slow, damn the soulripping thing. Fury burned through Kaidas, white fury, his breath rasping, as he put his entire body into a two-handed swing, the correct forms of dueling forgotten.

The blade caught the Chwahir on the side of the head, sending him staggering. Kaidas brought the sword around in a whistling arc. Kivic raised an arm to block the blow, fell to a knee as the steel cut to the bone. Kivic recoiled in shock and disbelief, and the blade struck him again, this time across the face, breaking his nose. He fell back, legs churning up the mud as he tried to get away. Kaidas struck again and again, until the man lay hacked and bloody, obviously dead.

As suddenly as it had come, the hot fury vanished, leaving Kaidas trembling, his body awash in sweat inside his clothes, his breath wheezing in a raw throat. He looked from the blood splatters down his fine battle tunic to the blood fast congealing down his sword in streaks and clots, to the revolting mess he'd made of a once-living man, and nausea clawed at the back of his throat.

He shut his eyes and fought for control as sound rushed around him. An eternity later the weird rushing noise ebbed. Other noises resolved into voices, and then words. "Here he is! Oh, is that the *prisoner?*"

". . . and so we witnessed, before the duke ordered the body restored to the Chwahir side of the border, along with the other dead man and the two wounded," came the cadenced voice of the judiciary.

Kaidas could not prevent the unwanted image of mud-smeared gray hair, a middle-aged woman's mottled face, cheek opened by a knife, lifted by her fellow judiciary from the muddy ground, hood then quickly restored. It felt like personal trespass, so ingrained was the rule that you did not speak to or approach judiciaries acting as Judicial Masks. He did not know if she was among the judiciaries present. Or what happened to them if unmasked.

". . . we both saw that the accused had attacked the duke with a weapon. The evidence was the knife in his hand and the condition of the duke's overrobe, with a great rend at the front," the judiciary went on. "As a result, we are satisfied that both the deaths of the prisoner and of the Chwahir warrior were the result of self-defense in battle, your majesty."

The queen thanked the judiciaries and indicated that they could withdraw. She then sent the scribe out, so that she, Kaidas, and Davaud were alone.

"Now I want your version, Commander," Hatahra said.

Kaidas did not mistake the privacy of this interview as complimentary, not under that unwavering gaze. He answered bluntly, without any courtly arts: "The one thing I learned from my cousins was how to plan an ambush. I thought I'd better do that in case the Chwahir tried anything. So each day—it took three—I placed my people in position on either side of the road, sent two defenders to accompany the judiciaries, and we waited. When the Chwahir arrived on the third day, they ordered the defenders forward to collect the accused, which seemed to me that they were drawing our people in for an attack. So I signaled to ready swords."

The queen gave a short nod, the fan flicking to avert shadow trespass. "They attacked. We defended. We outnumbered the Chwahir by three, which they soon saw. Most of them ran the moment they could disengage, except the ones who attacked the judiciaries. The accused tried to run. As it happens, the path he chose was where I'd stationed myself to watch. He attacked me. I killed him."

The queen's eyes narrowed. "No heroic claims?"

I could make you a king.

"It was not heroic," Kaidas said, after a short pause. "He had a knife. I had a sword. I was also wearing mail, as ordered."

The queen's fan snapped shut. "The kingdom is going to hear about a heroic defense," she said. "And as no Colendi lives were lost, we will call it a triumph." She smiled thinly. "I will reward you at your wife's masquerade. I want everyone to know that service is always rewarded. I will also announce my kingdom tour and that the honor of the first stop will be bestowed on Alarcansa."

The queen smiled broadly.

.

THREE

OF AN ACT OF WAR

W e reached the Mardgar River, Birdy and the other stable hand
sold our carriages and horses. Birdy was kept on, as foreseen, and
the coachman paid off and sent back to Colend. The Marlovens (and
Seneschal Marnda) oversaw the repacking of our belongings, but the
book was in the waistband of my knickers. As soon as night fell, I moved
to the back of the barge and quietly slipped the book over the edge,
where it fell away into the black waters, every incomprehensible word
now in my head.

———

"Truly," Queen Hatahra said with lifted voice, Carola standing in proud
triumph at her left, and her duke at the queen's right. "Truly, this masquerade surpasses anything I have ever seen. Nothing," she declared,
"will ever match it."

Carola lowered herself in a deep court curtsey, wishing that thorn
Ananda present only to witness her triumph. But no, it was far better
to break the circle of the so-called Roses (thorns, every one of them)
by not inviting them. Carola would shut them out of her select inner

circle and thus rid court of the last of *Her* influence. Court would be the better for it.

As she rose from her curtsey, she permitted herself one triumphant glance upward at the floating lamps, each in an expensive crystal tulip that reflected its light in spangled beauty. They shamed the floating lamps at *Her* wedding—and had probably cost twice as much—but all the rest of this season, court would talk only of this masquerade, and those who had not been invited would . . .

". . . so glorious," the queen was saying, "that I find I cannot wait to discover what delights lie in store. And so I have decided that my progress will not begin at New Year's as is customary, but at Harvest Festival." She smiled at Carola. "I am humane. You are released from duty so that you may make Alarcansa as beautiful as rumor praises it. Nor would I dream of separating the newlyweds. If the kingdom requires defense, my lord duke, you will have a transfer token for instant return."

Carola dropped into another formal curtsey, her duke bowed, the entire company bowed, and the queen held out her hand to her consort, which was the signal for the music to begin again.

Carola straightened up, having exerted every nerve to maintain her composure, though her throat tightened with the desire to weep for triumph. Newlyweds, honor, she had reached the pinnacle of courtly influence far sooner than she had anticipated. With *one* masquerade!

Melende required a modest demeanor and an elegant finish to whatever one did, whether dressing or regaining influence over court, and so she walked among her guests, giving graceful replies and gestures in return for complimentary words and deferences. She looked for signs of envy and jealousy. There were long glances and oblique angles to the fans of some of the older women, like the Duchess of Gaszin. Jealousy? When Carola attempted to drift by them in order to hear their conversation, they always seemed to be on the other side of the ballroom.

No matter. People really were a collection of petty desires and spites, as her father had said. She gave up, determined to enjoy her triumph until the last guest departed.

When the high windows showed blue of impending Daybreak, she left on her duke's arm, her purpose to retire to a well-earned rest before making a leisurely departure for Alarcansa. So busy was her review of her triumph that she did not prompt him for his thoughts, as she might have. *We shall have time to converse as civilized beings, riding together in the coach,* she thought. And there was that little flutter of victory when she remembered the word the queen had spoken before all court: *newlyweds.*

So rare a word, so very romantic, she was thinking as she walked into her wardrobe, where the ever-vigilant maids waited to help her out of gown and jewels. Newlyweds! How much gossip had reached the queen of those white ribbons? Even the queen took the Duke and Duchess of Alarcansa for a devoted pair, and that was a triumph, too, in its way. But it was an outer triumph, almost . . . hollow, for it reminded her of her lack of personal victory.

Perhaps, when they were alone, just the two of them, and no horrid wars or royal demands to distract them, she could delicately remind him of that one last sign. He seemed to have given up painting, but she didn't care for lover's cups so long as no one else had one. The real sign was so very simple a thing! Kaidas had only to wave aside her maid of a morning and offer to tie up her hair. So small a gesture, yet so very, very important, akin to the garlanding of a stag at the end of a long hunt. . . . Was there perchance a painting in that?

She designed the painting while she soaked in her perfumed bath. It would be full of secret symbols, to remind her of her triumphs each time she glanced at it.

She emerged smiling from the bath, dressed in her wrapper and ready for bed, but instead of finding him awaiting her in their bedchamber, he was still in his ball dress, staring out the window at the rooftops in the weak light of dawn. Only his mask was gone.

She let him hear the whisper of her slippers on the mosaic tiles. He did not turn, but said as he gazed out at the pale sky, "I think I'd better go."

"Kaidas," she said his name tenderly, to soften the tone of remonstrance. "Surely you remember that the queen released us both from our duties? We may leave at our leisure," she finished, conscious of her admirable restraint.

He made a quick sign with his fingers, too quick to catch, but she perceived his impatience. "Yes, I comprehended; I intend to depart for Alarcansa at this moment. And travel fast. I've been standing here contemplating that challenge, and the work that shall be required to meet it."

"Challenge?" she repeated, too surprised to hide her astonishment.

He turned, and there was *that* expression, the one she'd seen when he said, *An act of war.*

Here was his explanation at last; she was aware of her ambivalence about hearing it, and for the first time questioned her desire to hear his every thought.

He said, "Surely, you did not mistake her remark about newlyweds as anything but irony?"

Carola was so shocked that she shivered and closed her hands around her arms, hugging them against her as the ice was followed by the scorch of rage. The words were out before her tired mind could control them: "You will ride home too fast for me? Would you have been so considerate of Lasthavais's comfort?"

If she could have snatched the words out of the air, like those Elgars of legend snatched arrows when shot by enemies, she would have. But rage had forced them, and they were spoken. She watched their impact in the tightening of his mouth, the quick dilation of his pupils.

He said evenly, "Please honor me by appreciating the fact that I have never introduced her name into any conversation between us. I beg the honor of a similar forbearance."

She curtseyed, and though she trembled with fury, the years of control her father had inculcated permitted her to imbue every line of her body with the irony he seemed to think her unable to perceive.

His brows lifted. "Since you *have* introduced her name, twice, and since I would not have any lack of answer subsequently used to fuel your slanders, I will take leave to state that if I had—"

Slanders? "I have heard enough," she said, in her father's tone.

"If I had ridden with Lasva at the speed I will shortly travel, she would have laughed and made a joke of it, she would have spared a thought for the comfort of the servants, of innkeepers and stable hands, and of the horses and myself. Everyone, in short, but herself."

"I have never slandered anyone," she began, hating the necessity to defend herself.

He turned away. "I will end my part of this distasteful conversation by observing that the first time I heard your voice, you were making a remark about the King of the Chwahir that your cousin faithfully carried through court, embellishing its venom at each repetition but always prefaced by *my cousin says.* Do you really believe the queen was not aware whose wit inspired Tatia's tattle about her sister?"

The shock knocked her back a step. "The queen has *never* said . . ." Carola paused, the hot rage subsumed by horror. The queen's penchant for irony was well known. Carola had enjoyed the occasional moth kiss aimed at Altan, at Gaszin, at that hummer from. . .

Oh, but surely, never toward Alarcansa. But the idea, like her first words to Kaidas, could not be caught and smothered. That very evening, a courtly moth kiss in the word *newlyweds.*

Carola's gaze shifted to his face.

He saw the pain under the shock and anger and found a breath of humor at his own heated righteousness. With considerably less temper he said, "My part of the queen's ire was earned by my father when I was still in the nursery, when he apparently dallied with her. Do you see it? The queen is going to arrive in state, expect entertainment on an imperial level, and beggar Alarcansa before she moves on to either Altan or Thora-Dei, whoever she wants to intimidate the most."

Beggar Alarcansa.

Carola's chin came up, and intent stiffened her spine and shoulders. Behind her breastbone was that strange numbness that one gets just after touching hot metal, before the pain. The pain of burn was going to come, oh yes. A very angry queen, who had been far, far more observant than Carola had ever conceived. *Do not ever underestimate an enemy, once you identify him,* her father had said when Carola was scarcely ten years old. *Or her,* Carola had thought, remembering her cousin Falisse, and her intolerable smugness over everyone calling her Songbird. How Carola had done everything she could to take away that pride, that preeminence, but she could not take away that voice.

She said, "I will ride with you."

"I am going to travel fast. That means no languor of a morning," he said. It was that same tone again: *an act of war.*

"I shall be ready before the glass changes," was her response, and she whisked herself back into her bedchamber, surprising her yawning maids in the act of stowing her cleaned jewels and rolling her ribbons.

She issued orders in a determinedly low, pleasant voice that sent them scurrying, and then, when they were safely out of the room, she moved to her ribbon drawer, and pulled out the waiting white ribbons. She was about to pitch them in the fire, then hesitated. No. That would only cause comment.

Just how much subsequent slander had been aimed *her* way, that she didn't know about? Before this she had never considered the possibility that a Definian could be mocked. But that was before the queen had given Alarcansa a moth kiss before nearly all the court, at an Alarcansa masquerade.

No, that was a *royal* moth kiss. Carola carefully replaced the ribbons that she would never touch again and walked to the wardrobe to dress for riding.

In spite of the rude, even vulgar incivility of this mode of travel, her *melende* required that she match Kaidas pace for pace; she would show concern for others, including animals; she would never bring up the forbidden name unless he introduced it first. She would demonstrate through her actions that anything that fool Lasthavais Lirendi could do (or Kaidas believed she could do—because Carola knew that the princess had never so much as sat bestride a horse) a Definian could do with more style and grace.

And so, because they traveled largely in silence, she had time to think.

Carola had to appreciate the queen's mastery. In spite of all her flourishing words about loyalty and romance, heroism and defense. *My part of her ire was earned* . . . Carola had known about the queen's antipathy for the Baron Lassiter. It had never occurred to her that the queen had accepted Carola's suit not just as an effective break of the prospective ducal alliance, but as a personal strike at the Lassiters, father and son.

And now the queen was going to strike again.

Carola regretted those damned floating lamps.

When she rose on the third morning of their journey, and the early light outlined the familiar ridge that marked the distance to her home, her mood was more uneasy than relieved. Too much had changed. From a lifetime of habit she yearned to share her thoughts with Tatia, and yet there was that *my cousin says*. Those particular words had *never* been on Carola's orders. She had always been quite clear that if Tatia shared her views, she was free to speak of them, but to tell her to say something? What could Tatia have been thinking? Carola was tired of conversations in her mind, both with her silent duke and with Tatia.

This was her firm conviction: she could duel with the queen, style for style. Since it was going to cost, she might as well create an entertainment that would be talked of as the epitome of fashion, if not by an antagonistic queen, then by her entourage. Even in beggary a Definian would display more style—more *melende*—than a Lirendi.

They rode into her courtyard just after the sun had cleared the mountaintops. She dismounted and said, "Shall we breakfast at the Hour of the Deer and form our plans?"

Kaidas bowed and strode off. She had matched him pace for pace, as she had promised. He did not acknowledge it, but neither did she see any of that withering sarcasm.

Taking in a small breath of relief, she walked inside her palace. It was quiet. She encountered one of the maid-servants carrying a silver chocolate service. The girl looked so startled the dishes rattled as she curt-seyed. "Oh, your grace," she said. "We did not know you were to come!"

"Who is that for?" Carola asked, annoyed that her personal dishes—the ducal dishes—were being used. *Surely* the servants did not dare—

"Lady Tatia," the girl said quickly.

"Return it to the kitchen to be kept warm. We will breakfast at the Hour of the Deer," Carola said, smothering the impulse to add *as always*.

She trod at a deliberate pace up the stairs to Tatia's rooms, which were empty, the bed stripped, the finer furnishings shrouded. Carola looked around, puzzled. Where was Tatia—visiting a vineyard? No, that maid had been taking chocolate to her.

Carola started out, and it was then that she noticed things out of place: a mirror gone from the wall there, where Carola customarily took one last look at her dress and coif before descending the stairs to public view. The side mirror gone from outside her own suite, where she liked seeing herself as she entered and left her private rooms. The parrots' cage was missing from the small anteroom.

She spied a footman carrying a dusting cloth to the formal rooms and asked, "Where are the silvertails?"

The man bowed, not hiding his surprise. "We were told it was your orders to put them in the cellar until your return."

"It was not my orders. Lack of sunlight makes them ill. Restore their cage at once."

Carola whirled and marched to the ducal suite, flung open the doors, and there was the private parlor with the furniture every which way and no sign of any of the lovely things she had ordered for Kaidas. Carola surprised two servants in the wardrobe, amid shimmering piles of Tatia's favorite pinks and mauves and lavenders.

Fury ignited in Carola as she strode into her own bedchamber—her own room, where she and Kaidas slept—and there was Tatia in the great bed, like a skinny worm in the heart of a—

"What are you doing in here?" Carola demanded.

Tatia sat up, flushed, then put her hands on her hips. "I did not know you were coming home, cousin," she retorted, flinging her hair out of her eyes. She seemed to see Carola's anger, for she mooed in her usual ca-ressing tones, "If you had sent a messenger, everything would have been just as you like it."

"Why was it not left the way I like it?"

Tatia said, "But surely . . . as I serve as your voice, and after all, I *am* your heir. . . ."

The quiet clink of something set down reminded Carola of the servants in the wardrobe behind. She smiled, preserving her *melende* as she said in her sweetest voice, "Yes, quite true. You are my heir. I have ordered breakfast for the Hour of the Deer. The queen is honoring Alarcansa by beginning her progress here, and there is much to be done."

Carola walked out, hearing the satisfying sounds of hasty dismantling behind her. She did not have to lower herself to giving orders for all to be restored. She walked back down the stairs, and out through the vestibule and then the side garden to the court, where she discovered her duke surrounded by the garden and stable staff.

At her appearance they all bowed. "Please finish," she said, and waited.

Kaidas said, "That's enough for a beginning, don't you think?"

Everyone bowed again and hastened away.

Carola walked with him to the foot of the lily pond, which still had few plants and fish. She was too weary and too heart-sore to feel the fierce enjoyment she'd gotten from seeing the rose garden ripped out and this canal dug. She forced her attention to Kaidas, to be surprised by a smile. A *grin*. "I have an idea," he said. "I am quite certain that Hatahra is using this progress to beggar this province. Do you agree?"

"I have come to the conclusion that you are right," Carola said, wondering at his startling change in mood.

He said, "The queen duels with wit, so let's choose the same weapon. We'll start a new fashion by bringing back an old. We will have everything redone, but from the period of artistic austerity. She's expecting to be showered with gifts, and so shall she be—but music. Poetry. Plays. She won't be able to walk ten steps without having verses quoted at her. When she ventures into the garden, every bush will hide a flute player, and every tree a harpist. Meals will be in high art mode—"

"From the period of austerity, when plates were largely empty, save lightly dressed garden produce, all arranged to appeal to the eye." Carola was surprised by her own laughter. It banished enough of her anger to enable her to broach her own new idea: "I have a notion of my own. I believe we should consider an heir."

FOUR

OF THE MERCILESS MELODY

Remalna is one of many small kingdoms bounded by intersecting rivers along the northeast coast of the Sartoran Sea, above the enormous delta where the Mardgar River empties into the very east-most point of the sea.

We transferred from barge to a wide-bottomed ship. The journey to Remalna only took a day through quiet waters, but even so, Ivandred spent all of it at the rail, along with several others. It was astounding to me to witness those black-coated Marlovens exhibiting human weak-ness, as more than one of them leaned foreheads against horses' necks, hands gripped in manes in their struggle against seasickness.

The ship wallowed into a small natural harbor. At the end of the pier we were met by the king and his soon-to-be queen, along with a host of servants liveried in pale violet and white. The king, princes, princesses, and lords sped up a paved road in fast carriages. The rest of us waited for the horses to be coaxed down the ramp to the pier—a job Birdy helped with, exchanging brief and easy remarks with the Marloven servants. After that we had to fetch all the baggage.

Athanarel was a long crenellated castle made over into a palace by the addition of marble inside, sunstone outside, and widened windows. It was fashioned in squares around carefully pruned formal gardens, readied for winter.

The Remalnan version of Sartoran sounded strange to us but comprehensible. As soon as we were shown to our quarters, I left Marnda and Pelis not quite arguing over the low platform all the way around the chamber. They spoke in the enforced polite tone of ill-hidden irritation as they attempted to determine whether people sat on the cushions on the platform, or was it storage, and they sat in the middle of the room, like normal people? Marnda had plenty of servants at hand, and I had the queen's orders to think about, so I slipped away in search of a bath.

A hot bath! Clean skin! Dry clothing! Oh, the sweetness of rediscovering things I had always taken for granted.

After my bath, I approached a passing attendant and was directed to the central portion of the palace, upstairs.

The archive was a large, airy room with windows on one wall overlooking an enormous open garden, unlike our discreetly walled Colendi gardens. The shelves were knee to eye height, very comfortable for walking along, containing the expected mixture of scrolls and books. Most of the section on Sartoran history was not only familiar, the books and scrolls were from the Sartoran Twelve Towers, which gave me hopes of finding something about magic.

My search along the shelves brought me three quarters of the way around the room to an archway covered by a tapestry instead of a door—as were most entrances in that palace. The tapestry was pulled halfway up and pinned by a hook, so that I could look in. And I found myself face to face with Greveas, my fellow scribe student from Sartor.

"Emras," she exclaimed.

"Greveas?"

"I'm here to replace a scribe who strained her arm," she said, answering a question that I had not asked. She indicated the desks. "We were hired by the new king to translate the—"

Her greeting, the quick gestures, and the sense that she was offering an excuse, rather than information, formed into a new idea. I said, "You expected me."

She flushed to her hairline, the two different shades of red startling. "I am a messenger. " She took a step closer to me, moving from polite to private space.

"Messenger to whom?"

"To you. I work as a scribe, yes, but my true vocation is field mediator for the Mage Council."

"The . . . the *Sartoran* Mage Council?" Then a new surprise bloomed, and I said, "My brother Olnar. He knew your name. Is that why he wouldn't visit the guild? Because you were there?"

"It's not what you think." She grinned. "We studied together in Bereth Ferian, in the far north, and it's hard to pretend you don't know some-one when you've shared the same table for three years. Listen, Emras. This is my first assignment on my own, and it's very important. See, I was to talk you into being a messenger, too, since we've already met. They said I could explain as much or as little as I thought best, and I'd so rather tell you everything."

"Please."

"We *must* find out if the Marlovens are dealing with Norsunder. There have been disturbing . . . no, I won't tell you that. You might go looking for what might not be there. You know how human nature is."

I touched my fingertips in assent.

"All we ask is this. I am to offer you a ring. If you find sign of Norsunder, you use the ring in a simple spell. It will let us know. You need do noth-ing else."

"A ring," I repeated.

"Not to be worn on your hand," she said quickly. "I know that you Colendi see symbols in everything you wear, and someone might ask why if they saw a ring on your hand. But if you were to wear it on your toe, well, the only person who might see it is a lover, and I understand that you Colendi have different customs for intimate things."

So many questions crowded my mind I couldn't lay tongue to one.

A sweet sound caught my ear, silvery, bright. At first I could not de-termine what made it, then I recognized it as a silverflute, a musical in-strument I'd only heard in Sartor. It was not popular at court in Colend, as blowing a wind instrument distorts the face. Another flute with a deeper range joined it, and a third much higher, then more as three separate melodies wound in a roundelay.

"Practicing for tonight's banquet," Greveas said, gesturing.

"It's so beautiful!"

"Emras, listen to me, not to the octet."

I flushed, bowing with my hands open in Pardon.

Greveas leaned toward me. "I don't know if we can speak again like this. It is generally believed that the most dangerous man in Marloven

Hesea is their king. And he is dangerous, everyone says. You had better walk soft and look around every corner twice, as we Sartorans say. But your real danger has to be Sigradir Andaun, the king's mage. We think he's the one treating with Norsunder."

"But that sounds like spying," I protested. "You are asking me to spy on behalf of the Sartoran Mage Council?"

I could just hear Queen Hatahra's response to that.

Greveas looked affronted, and I said quickly, "We had a spy in the palace. A Chwahir spy. He killed two of the princess's staff."

"You would not be a spy in that sense—an agent of some monarch, intending harm to another. You certainly aren't going to harm anyone. All you do is live your life." Greveas brought her hands together in a clasp. "You are not pretending to be anything other than Princess Lasthavais's scribe, and you will see and hear many things because you know how invisible we scribes are."

"First Rule."

"Exactly. And you won't break the First Rule, because all you will do is listen. And if you find out that Norsunder is invoked, or involved, or gives Sigradir Andaun power or even just spells, you take off the ring, say the spell, and it vanishes. Then you are done."

Here is one of those crossroads we reach in life.

I had come to the archive seeking information about magic, so that I could understand Tiflis's book, now lodged in my head and repeated every morning to keep the memorization fresh. I considered confessing to Greveas.

But I heard again her own words, *You are not pretending to be anything,* and I heard the queen's words about Sartorans and their interference, and all during my student days I'd heard about how jealous mages were of their training and skills. If she told her superiors about the book in my head, would the mages demand that I be removed from my position? What would be the repercussions?

Traveling in isolation had made such questions seem distant. Now the questions were as close as Greveas's watchful eyes.

And I still had my orders. "I will do it on one condition."

Greveas gripped her fingers tightly. "Which is?"

"If I am to recognize magic, any kind of magic, I need to hear it done."

"Is that all?" Her eyes closed and her jaw softened in relief. Then she smiled at me. "Of course. Nothing easier. Here. See the flames?"

She pointed to the fire stick burning on the grate. "I will borrow a bit of the fire to light a candle. We seldom do such a spell. It takes as much effort to get a paper-twist and light it in the fireplace, then touch the flame to the candle, as it does to expend magic. Summoning fire from far away is exponentially harder, as you may surmise."

She uttered some of the gibble-gabble. My heart thudded when I recognized the syllables, but she said them fast, and her fingers flickered as if winding yarn and pulling, then she leaned over the candle sitting on a sideboard, opened her hand, and a flame sparked into being on the wick. And burned steadily.

"Magic will sound like that. If it's a complicated layer of spells, what we call an enchantment, there will be a lot of it. Norsunder's magic is destructive. You won't be able to miss it, as there is a terrible feel, as if the world has been scorched. And it will do something terrible . . . I don't know how they use it, though most certainly to conduct wars. The Marlovens always seem to be involved in wars."

I thanked her, accepted the ring, and departed, nearly running into a familiar round face framed by blue-black hair.

"Anhar?" I rocked back on my heels.

She flushed. "The staff has a hair dresser here, who restored my natural color."

The glossy hair framed her round face, highlighting how light her skin was by nature, for there had been no time in recent months to sit outside in the sun in order to gain color. The black hair emphasized how large were her black eyes, yet it wasn't just the hair. Her gaze was more direct, her chin up as I took in the truth: Anhar was definitely Chwahir.

Out loud I said, "It is flattering." Which it was. I am aware of how abominable it will make me, and by extension, the rest of us Colendi sound, but I had never before considered that there could be any beauty to the Chwahir in person or culture. Anhar, in her quiet way, was beautiful.

———

The carefully planned dinner began as an anxious ordeal for Tharais and as a bore for Macael.

Tharais found Lasthavais Lirendi to be as stunning as reputed. She looked and moved like a portrait, with her smooth gold-threaded dark hair, her wide blue eyes framed by the longest lashes Tharais had ever seen. Her stillness, her slightly breathy voice, her fascinating singsong Colendi accent. Lasva mirrored everything Tharais did, to eating the same food and drinking the same amount of liquid. She praised everything she'd seen. Her manners were so exquisite they were exhausting, like the first time Tharais saw Macael's palace, so full of colored marble and carvings and art that she could not determine where the doors were.

Tharais avoided Macael's ironic gaze after a relentlessly polite conversation about travel, and made the private sign for the musicians earlier than she'd planned. And Macael avoided Tharais's, so he was watching Lasva when Tharais signaled the first of the carefully chosen Colendi airs her octet had rehearsed in honor of their illustrious guest.

Flute, horn, and there was that lilting melody called "Laughing Fountain," brought straight from Alsais's court, everyone said.

Lasva stilled, every muscle taut. Her eyelids flashed up then shuttered, her face blanched with pain, as if she'd been struck. Macael was so surprised he leaned forward. Her face smoothed out a heartbeat later, no sign of any emotion, like a lake closing over a rock that briefly broke its surface.

He was alone in seeing it. Ivandred was reassuring Tharais that the Colendi all seemed fond of music. Tharais divided her attention between her brother and Geral, whose attention was solely on her.

For the remainder of the concert, Macael watched Lasva, his boredom gone. There was no return of that expression—what was it? Sorrow? *Grief.* Not what you'd expect from a witless princess. He was aware of the intensity of his interest, and laughed inwardly at himself. Why was human nature so absurd, that this beautiful woman would bore him mercilessly, but the first sign of inner pain made her interesting?

By the end of the evening when he saw in his cousin's taut focus on Lasva, and in her heightened color, that the long-postponed wedding night was about to be shared, he discovered not only regret but the sting of jealousy. If he stayed, he would get himself into trouble.

And so he informed one of his dallying lords that he had an urgent message from home, and they would depart at first light.

Tharais suggested an early retirement, and no one demurred. She watched anxiously as Van took Lasva's hand, and the Colendi princess showed all the passion of marble as the pair vanished into the guest suite.

At first, all Lasva could think about was the relief at being clean again, chafed skin soothed with herbal balm, hands and feet properly attended to, the knots of travel smoothed from grateful muscles.

It was so very good to be in civilization again, and Ivandred's sister so friendly, that Lasva was the more unguarded, which made the pain of that song all the worse. It took all her strength to hide her reaction. Her head was throbbing when at last it was time to retire. She could feel anticipation in Ivandred's touch and hear it in his breathing. And so when they reach their suite, she whispered, "I will return after I bathe."

He uttered a surprised laugh. "Did you not bathe before this meal?"

"Will you indulge my Colendi habits?"

He saw only her beauty and her poise, but he was sensitive to pain in others. Puzzled, wary, he stepped away, and she vanished with those gliding steps that made it seem like she floated.

Lasva summoned Anhar to knead the strain out of her neck and shoulders, then soaked in aromatic water. The ache lessened, as it does. Life would go on with all its vagaries and little mysteries. Like, why did Anhar appear with this black hair? It was surprisingly flattering, but it made her look . . . was it possible that Anhar had Chwahir somewhere in her family? Lasva frowned at the bathwater. Had she ever employed the term "hum" around Anhar? Probably. Everyone used it—meant nothing by it—*I must never say it again.*

Lasva rose from the bath, found Anhar and complimented her on her hair color, then went in to dress. It was good to wear silk next to her skin again.

But when she reached the bedroom and found Ivandred waiting, she made a discovery: that Marlovens did not wear wrappers, at least while traveling. He, too, had bathed, his light hair lying loose, and she knew that he had done so for her. He wore a fresh shirt and trousers, and there was no sign of weapons anywhere.

The sight of him standing there so still, his empty hands turned a little outward as though in appeal, the drape of his shirt sleeves over the contours of arms and shoulders, caused her heart to beat a little quicker.

One hand came up, the palm open. "I told you I am not good with words," he said, his tone tentative. Like a preamble.

With Kaidas there would have been words, oh so many, enchantingly oblique, quick as a duel only with poetry and wit, scored by laughter and kisses. With a flicker of anger she untied her wrapper and let it drop to the floor. No arts, no allurement, blunt and direct. She held out her hands. "We will do away with words."

When Lasva reached the age of desire she'd delighted in all the arts of pleasure, at first for pleasure's sake. Then came the birth of tenderness, followed by the blossoming of love. And then love's flower had been cut, leaving a void in body, mind, and soul. But here was the man she had married, who woke her body's hunger. She was determined, even desperate, to employ all her arts in easing the mind and soul.

He was not at first certain how to begin; his habit was rough and ready but he would not handle this beautiful, fragile creature with that roughness. Sex for him had been confined to the Academy, brief and violent, sometimes mixed with laughter, often with anger. And few words. She trailed her newly painted nails from his brow to his collar bones and then down and down, urging him flat on the bed, and he obeyed. So began a long, slow, striving that was not combat yet engaged all the senses—from the enticing fingernails along the contours of muscle as she undressed him to the soft touch of lips on his eyelids, in the hollow of his throat, and on all the places where the skin is most sensitive—until he was nearly out of his mind with desire. But he did not act because she had not given him leave to act, and the waiting, the anticipation, was far more intense than any intimate act he'd ever known.

The smell of her hair fresh with herbs he could not name, the taste of her, the whispering sigh of silken sheets over his skin, her secretive smile and clever hands that touched him in ways he had never experienced—all these reasons gave him at last, at last, the to mount and ride, to gallop to the rim of the world: "Obliterate me," she breathed.

It is one thing to imagine giving hints on marriage to a famous princess, Tharais reflected as she prowled around the room just below her freshly swept dining platform, and another thing when that princess appears and looks at you from unreadable eyes, her manners so good and so polite and so . . . so like a swan, or a lily, or anything that isn't human.

Tharais had ordered Colendi delicacies. The table was Geral's finest; carved bluewood, the edges a braiding of ivy leaves, a symbol from her own home, the cushions brocade in the cable pattern in deep violet silk. The dishes were fine porcelain of the type she'd heard they used in Colend, the food thin wheat cakes in rolls no bigger than a child's little finger, daubed with a fluffy thing made of butter with thrice-boiled molasses whipped into it, making a light, frothy pale gold sweet. Tharais had never heard of such a food, but when she stuck a finger in it, she discovered it was delicious.

There were tiny cuts of tangerine, and another new item, caffeo, which turned out to be coffee, chocolate, honey, and fresh milk with the cream still on it, all whipped together into a light froth. Assembling the ingredients for this drink cost nearly as much as the dishes.

Time in Remalna was measured by marked and colored candles. Mid-morning's Hour of the River was called Third Gold, which was when Lasva had been invited to join Tharais for breakfast.

She appeared, her arms full of rich silk worked in patterns of narrow leaves. As Tharais gazed in wonder, Lasva laid the bundle down on a side table, opened it, and disclosed what first appeared to be hundreds and hundreds of rosebuds, mostly crimson in graded shades.

"Ivandred told me you like crimson," she said. "This is my gift to you for your wedding."

The rosebuds were tiny rolls of silk connected by exquisitely embroidered silken leaves. It was a carpet! Gorgeous, probably too fragile to actually step on, it seemed to symbolize Colend. "It's beautiful," Tharais said. "I . . . have never seen such a thing." She dared not ask, *What is it for?*

But Lasva heard it, or saw it, and smiled. "They are found in our private chambers. Many enjoy lying on them when engaging in dalliance. Some keep them for their use after a bath, as the sensation on the bottoms of the feet, when tender from the water, is so pleasant. They can be washed, but far better is to have your chamber servant put them through a cleaning frame after each use."

"Of course," Tharais repeated, not saying that cleaning frames—though admittedly useful—were crushingly expensive, and that she did not have a maid whose single job was to tend her bedchamber. She expressed her gratitude as they took their places at the table. Though she intended to store so precious and frivolous a thing, as the breakfast went on, her fingers kept straying to it so she could rub her palm over the silken buds.

Geral had warned Thar that Colendi did not talk with food in their mouths, so she was careful to ask easy questions between bites. She'd never been aware of how like a dance eating can be. But Lasva's manners were so dance-like.

"Would you like music?" Tharais asked, ready to signal those waiting in the antechamber. "My wind octet awaits our word."

Lasva's quick intake of breath, the way her fingers stiffened slightly, gave indefinable emphasis to her polite, "Thank you, I hoped you would choose to honor me with just your company."

So they ate in silence, Tharais trying not to make noise or drop her silver, or clatter the utensils on the plate. She ate as little as she dared, mostly confining herself to tiny sips of the Colendi caffeo, which was delicious.

Lasva also ate little. Tharais watched anxiously, and as soon as it seemed there was no danger of either of them being caught with food in their mouths, she said, "I've found you a fine ship. That is my wedding gift to Van." Tharais laid her right hand over her heart. "For you, I have picked out four of my own women to accompany you, because you'll need them, oh, in so many ways. I don't mean as a bodyguard, for Van will see to that. But I shall make certain that you have the eyes you need, the ears you need, the wit to answer your questions when you get home." She waited, and when Lasva bowed her thanks, she said tentatively, "As you will be the first queen in generations."

Lasva's brows lifted in surprise. "No queens? Has this to do with the . . . the martial elements of your culture?"

"It has to do with the fact that our kings don't usually marry."

Lasva took in Thar's wide, pale-eyed gaze so like Ivandred's yet so un- like, then shifted her own gaze to the window, beyond which bare, silver- barked trees rustled in the rising wind. "It has been the same in Colend for several generations. No kings, only consorts."

Tharais breathed out. "I can see Van is . . . happier." She hesitated.

"But?" Lasva prompted, her fluttering fingers poised at an inviting angle.

Tharais had all Lasva's attention, which made her nervous. "The last time I saw Tdiran and Van together . . . well, it was the morning before she left. She was bruised here and here." Tharais touched her face, her jaw, and her wrist. "That was her visible flesh. And two weeks later came the news that she was going to marry Danrid Yvanavar."

Lasva crossed her forearms over her chest, closing her eyes on the vivid rush of images and sensations, memories all the more intense for the sensitivity of her flesh. *So much can be concealed through intimacy, and so much revealed. And not always through intent.* When she opened her eyes, she found a sober question in Ivandred's sister. *This is now my life,* she thought. *These are the people I have chosen to live among.*

Aloud she said, "I thank you for the . . . is this a warning? Did you see him?"

Tharais looked startled. "What?"

Lasva said, "Did you see your brother?"

Tharais's eyes widened, then narrowed, and she blushed crimson. "No. I did not."

Tharais's lips parted, making her look younger than her nineteen years. Then her gaze dropped, her shoulders tight with guilt. "My father is so violent, and I was afraid that Van might . . . especially since he spent all those years there, but then Tdiran is also one of *them*. I should have remembered that."

"Them?" Lasva prompted, leaning forward to lay two fingers briefly on the top of Tharais's hand.

Tharais did not understand this gesture inviting her to a private circle, but she found it soothing. "The Academy. Tdiran and Van had been together since the Academy," Tharais said quickly, squaring up with assurance. "Van won't talk about this, either, because he doesn't see it as a danger, but it is . . . because you share his heart with it—with the Academy. You cannot come between him and the Academy, or expect him to choose between you."

Lasva made a graceful gesture. "I know what that is. It is your training school, for your leaders. I read about it in your record about Indevan the Fox."

Thar shook her head. "You read about the way it was four hundred years ago. It's different now." She drew in a deep breath, eyes closed. "Very different."

FIVE

Of Rocks in the Sea

The first sign that we had finally become one party was when the Marlovens let us hear their music. At the same time, we began to perceive them as individuals with names. Although it would be overstating to say that leaving the Enaeraneth was the reason, it contributed. But so did living cramped together on a ship for what seemed to be endless days (about two weeks) during which it would be difficult to say who suffered more, Colendi, Marloven, or horses.

But one by one we recovered enough to gather on deck, or in Birdy's case, to climb to the upper masts with some of the younger Marlovens, where I would hear them talking away in a language that I was still struggling with.

My magic experiments were total failures. Yet it had looked so simple when Greveas did it.

"It is interesting, the things people think important," said Tesar Jevair, two days after we landed on the coast of the Bay of Jaira, as she stood with another lancer, looking down at the open trunks containing Lasva's things.

Tesar was the lancer I'd been assigned to ride with. I should note here that among themselves, on duty, they only used their family names, something never done in Colend, where family names are used only in formal (or ceremonial) situations. It was especially confusing because so many of the Marlovens were related—there were two Jevairs—and almost half of the males had been named for the king. But they also had private names, which we adopted and which will serve for this defense.

To resume. Tesar observed, "What do you think this is?" as she held out a rosebud carpet to Lnand Dunrend, the lancer Anhar had been assigned to ride with.

Lnand bent over it with her hands on her knees, her pale braid slipping over her shoulder as she examined the carpet without touching it. "It looks very, very costly."

"Ah-ye! This must be held with care," Marnda exclaimed, hands high. "Emras! Have you nothing whatever to do but stand about at your ease gawking? Please show them how the rose rug is to be held."

Lasva turned their way and smiled, her voice a contrast to Marnda's sharpness. "It is a gift for Prince Ivandred's aunt. It will be safest sent in the trunk. Might Emras demonstrate how we wrap it in the brocade covering?"

"Is that a command?" Lnand whispered.

"Best to assume so," Tesar whispered back and handed the rug to me—who hadn't been standing about at my ease. I was stationed at the cedar chest, packing each item the princess decided must be sent by magic transfer, a very slow process with Marnda questioning every choice in that humble-but-hear-me voice.

The tension centered around a fine box of polished darkwood with flying herons in cedar inlay. Marnda tried every way she dared to discover what was locked in it and the princess deftly, politely, but firmly evaded.

"The box stays with me," Lasva said for the third time.

Marnda gasped and rushed away to the tent, where Anhar was shaking out some things. Her scolding voice drifted back; the word "hum" shrill, like an accusation.

Birdy was waiting to carry the chest I was packing. He lifted his head, watching them with a slight frown. "You like Tesar? She asked to be assigned to you."

Tesar was a full hand taller than me—nearly Ivandred's height and as tall as many of the men. She was built on spare lines, enormously strong. Her smooth braids were about the same color as my own lank locks— plank brown, and her eyes were an unremarkable gray.

"She keeps calling me Er-mas," I said. "But then correcting herself. She speaks slowly, which I appreciate. Why did she pick me?"

"Because you're the smallest, next to the seamstress, who is rounder," Birdy admitted, chuckling as he indicated Nifta. "And Tesar's the biggest of the women. Easier on her mount."

"'We all want to be interesting to someone.'" I signed Rue as I quoted the old proverb from childhood.

Birdy tipped his head, one hand mirroring Rue, the other making juggling motions. I remembered our orders—and I could see him remembering—because we consciously moved away from one another. Birdy walked off to check on the progress of the staff, who were busy adapting our sturdiest robes for riding, using the pattern that he'd already developed when making his own clothes. Marnda followed him, her voice rising as she unnecessarily pointed out the precautions everyone should take with Lasva's clothes.

I did not intend to overhear Lasva and Ivandred. The problem here was how we all understood the space of privacy.

". . . I begin to realize," she was saying, "how much our civilization is centered around *things*. What I have thought necessary for daily life is not necessary at all, from what I am seeing in the faces of your company."

Ivandred said, "Have any of my people offered you a, how did you say it, a discourtesy?"

"Never," she responded. "Never. It's merely the incomprehension I perceive in their countenances, when they look upon my necessities. And yet I am thinking, if I throw this or that away, am I throwing away my semblance of civilization?"

His voice lowered, but passion heightened his articulation: "You could walk naked and make it look civilized."

Shock! Just like that, I was trespassing. I hastened away, glad of my quiet step as he grabbed and kissed her.

I circled all the way around the edge of the camp as the sun vanished and the shadows closed in. As Lnand and Tesar carried a last trunk, Lnand muffled a soft laugh. Tesar whispered, "'Hes-*ay*-ah.' It is so comical, how she says that." They set down the trunk in a line of trunks and other baggage and retreated. Ivandred moved along the line, stretched out a hand and slowly said a string of magical words. Each trunk vanished, sending out a puff of wind that smelled faintly of singed wood.

I stilled. He was not using transfer tokens, he was doing the magic himself. But then, some rulers did.

I recognized some of the pattern of words, and the hairs on my arms rose. I know now what it felt like: one of those rare, hot dry winds that sometimes blow from over the northern mountains dividing Colend from Chwahirsland, usually before a tremendous storm.

I could feel how Ivandred drew magic to him *through* the words and gestures.

In memory, my brother spoke again as we stood on the Sartoran street, talking about magic. *What was it Olnar said, that magic is "the cup and the lip"?*

While everyone got ready for the next day's ride, I paced a little way from the campfire in the gathering darkness, positioning myself between two sentries. Then I crouched down with my two candles, misshapen from my desperate grip as I attempted magic.

Ivandred had used familiar patterns but shorter than those spoken by Greveas. I wondered if that was because Greveas was a new agent of the Mage Council, which would mean her magical skills were those of a beginner.

So I recollected the shorter phrases that he'd used and tried to draw magic in. Twice I had to stop when I was startled by that sense of dry heat, but when I used concentration breathing—the way we'd been taught while doing the Altan fan form—and spoke the words all the way through, a brief, intense internal heat flared behind my forehead . . . and flame leapt from the lit candle to the unlit one.

By my magic spell.

The sense of victory was as powerful as the day I was made a scribe.

SIX

OF THE PATIENT WILLOW

The sun was just lifting the darkness over the ocean behind us when Ivandred swiped his hand in a circle—the "mount up" signal. Birdy drifted into step alongside me. "Do your fan stretches as you walk right now," he whispered. "And no matter how badly you feel later, do them again tonight. And in the morning. You won't get as sore."

He passed by the other Colendi staff, murmuring. I heard Anhar's higher voice, and Birdy's soft chuckle, then he was gone.

Tesar lifted me to the back of her horse. I felt as if I sat on a roof, an unsteady one as she mounted behind me. She tucked an efficient arm around my middle, and the rocking shifted to jolting.

Two, three steps, and I was very glad for that arm.

Most of the next week may be summed up in a word: ache.

The weather at least was benign as we followed a river up toward its source in exceedingly dramatic, slate-dark and tumbled mountains. When we began the descent into the long, gently inclined valley called Telyer Heyas, tension increased.

The Marlovens' tension was due to military alertness. Within our little circle, it was due to Marnda, who fought the impossible battle—to impose cleanliness, beauty, and order over a muddy, tumbled camp. She hovered over Lasva, counting every bite until the princess gripped her eating utensils with white knuckles, her eyelids shuttered. Marnda's anxious, low pleading often sounded like a woman addressing an infant.

Marnda had only to see the rest of us to unloose a pent-up string of orders. As I had foreseen, my acquiescence had set a precedent. I was helping with plain sewing and laundry, so that the dressers could use their more skilled fingers for fine work.

The first nights, we hurt so much we did our work and went straight to sleep. Gradually that changed. When Lasva sat with us, she liked hearing poetry. At first, I was called upon to recite and then to read from one of the few books that Lasva had chosen to bring along.

But one night, when I had made an excuse to distance myself from the camp in order to practice my magic, I returned to discover Anhar reading. I had been trained to read well and to mimic the style of the speaker if I had to deliver a spoken message, but she was able to vary the voices of the poems' different narrators.

When Lasva was alone with Ivandred in her tent, Tesar, Lnand, and Fnor Eveneth sat around the campfire. The female lancers traded off teaching Marloven lettering to Anhar, tall, thoughtful Pelis, and me. Occasionally Birdy joined us, sitting between Anhar and me and glancing from side to side as she wrote with her left hand, and I with my right.

I forced myself to practice magic each night before I laid my aching body at last in the bedroll. I thought about magic during the ride— better than thinking about how much I hurt—and each night I tried something a little different. I lit one candle, then two. One night I pulled a lick of flame from the campfire instead of another candle. The point of heat behind my brow intensified for a heartbeat, as it did when I lit two. But now I expected it, and instinctively enclosed it as soon as it appeared, like closing walnut shells around a spark. The faster I did that, the stronger the flame. Speed and control, then. Pull, speed, control.

Now that I understood the process, I began reviewing the patterns of syllables I'd memorized. As if someone had clapped on a glowglobe in a dark room, everything began to make sense. So I started from the beginning, and worked out how the patterns fit together.

The easiest was illusion, as it was ephemeral, a trick of light. It still did not mean I knew how to weave more complicated spells, but I could see that magic built on syllables that were fragments of Old Sartoran.

The pain from riding was incrementally less agonizing. I had learned to be grateful for those moments of rest, for the bitter willow-bark steep that Tesar made for me, and even for the crude pan rye bread with cheese and boiled greens that formed our usual night meal. Ivandred had offered to find cooks familiar with Colendi food, but Lasva—of course—had said, "We shall begin as we shall live and eat the foods that you do."

Belimas wept silently the rest of that night.

One night I squatted before the campfire, briefly alone. I used my time to make tiny illusory blossoms grow on my palm. They lasted no longer than a bubble, but I was charmed with my success. I made illusory blossoms until others of the staff joined me, talking as they often did about how much we might be paid once we reached Lasva's new home. Nobody thought of it as *our* future home.

Then the Marlovens joined us. Tesar and Lnand brought out the slate on which Ivandred sketched the day's map and how they would divide up their patrols. Lnand used her long pale braid to clean the chalk off, and they sat before the fire near two of the dressers. The Marloven women's movements were easy and strong.

"Let's see what you remember of the alphabet," Tesar said, her gray eyes black in the ruddy firelight.

Chalk was difficult to write with, but I gripped it tightly and scrawled the letters.

"Good."

Lnand smiled at Pelis, who blushed a little as she handed the slate back. "Good! You learn fast." She smudged with her finger, then gave a soft chuckle, her breath clouding. Firelight gleamed in her eyelashes and warmed the brown of her eyes as she said, "When we were girls. We used to draw the vowel-sounds as close to circles as we could. When my grandmother was young they made them slanting down, see? Between the letters, like tufts of grass—"

She stilled, head lifting in a tiny jerk.

All I heard was galloping. Tesar exchanged a glance with Lnand while tipping her head, a hand briefly turned palm down. This was like fan language, but no signal I understood.

Tesar rose and loped away into the darkness, where I heard low, urgent voices. Then Lnand handed the slate and chalk to Anhar. "Before we rode into your country, people sometimes said to us, *Do not take 'no' as 'no' and 'yes' as 'yes' from a Colendi*. We spoke so little to your people when we were there. So I ask you, does 'no' mean 'yes' and 'yes' mean 'no'?"

Pelis blushed. Anhar smiled. "Sometimes."

"It is our custom to avoid a flat denial," I said, "In particular in public, except with children or for purposes of instruction." *And to assert rank.* "So we have words of compromise and degree, and gestures that modify."

Tesar reappeared within the golden circle of firelight and dropped cross-legged to the ground in a single easy move.

I said, "May I ask if something might be amiss?"

Lnand's lips moved as she repeated my words. Then she said, "By treaty, we must let the Telyers know if we cross the border."

It was now us Colendi who turned from one to the other, each seeking enlightenment but only finding our own puzzlement mirrored. What could be worrying in so sensible and civilized a rule being properly observed?

Anhar said, "And so?"

"And so we have," Lnand said.

She and Tesar waited, as if that explained everything. Lnand's brows puckered. She could not have been over eighteen. Tesar was, at most, around twenty, like me. From a distance they had seemed older, harder, made of stone and steel.

"Shall we resume?" Lnand held up the slate in her scarred, callused hands.

———

Later, I walked out into the cold air, to check on our laundry scrupulously segregated from the plain Marloven cotton-linen. Segregated, but taking up exactly half of the available drying line. I looked at those drying clothes, aware that we Colendi numbered far fewer than the Marlovens, and remembered something disturbing that Nifta had said about bloodstains on some of their shirts.

I felt that sense of being observed. When I turned, there was Birdy with a cluster of Marlovens. The urge for civilized conversation—for his particular perspective—was irresistible, and so I said, "I would offer my aid with the animals if it might help." I found it difficult to speak a conditional sentence in Marloven. Their verbs seemed variations of what must be, rather than what might, could, should, or would be.

Birdy said politely, "I don't believe you have been trained."

"I would like to learn," I said, equally politely.

Birdy said in a dismissive voice very unlike his own, "You can scrub saddles. But don't touch anything until I show you how." I knew Birdy, so I could hear the laughter down deep, forming just the faintest tremor on the word "anything."

That is how we ended up alone at a stream far from anyone else (except for the eternal roving guard) as I forced my protesting muscles to learn yet another new thing in soft-brushing quilted pads and saddle gear, so that Birdy could carry it back to air out near the picket line, as it was a clear night.

"Just copy what I do," Birdy said in Old Sartoran. "They will assume that I am instructing you exhaustively the way they did me. As if I was four years old. Though I must say, their ways really are quite effective."

There was a quick step. We both turned, and there was Anhar, carrying in each hand one of the Marlovens' plain round travel cups. She held them out to us, saying, "Pelis made a tisane to warm us up and take away the aches."

I took mine and gratefully sipped the listerblossom mixed with Sartoran leaf. Birdy sipped, closed his eyes, then held his cup out to Anhar and said, "Shall we share?"

"I thank you for the kind thought, but I already had mine," Anhar said. "Birdy, are we in danger?"

"I was going to ask that very thing," I exclaimed. "Nifta said she thinks that someone among them had been beaten. Why? They never do anything wrong."

"A scout chose the wrong road. We're having to correct that as best we can."

"That's reason to thrash someone?" I asked.

Anhar threw up her hands in the shadow-warding. "Is that going to happen to us?"

"They've never touched me," Birdy said. "And I've made plenty of mistakes. They seem to have a different standard for themselves. It's like court has its rules that are more elaborate than the rules for the rest of us Colendi." He handed his empty cup to Anhar and the brush back to me, hefted a load of gear, and carried it swiftly away.

She looked after him, then sighed. Marnda was watching. Anhar took my empty cup and started back to our tents.

I remained where I was, working with the brush by the light of lanterns. Birdy's voice drifted back, quick and assured in Marloven, and then came the swift chuff-chuff-chuff of his returning footsteps.

I tried to lift the saddle gear, and my lower back muscles protested.

"Don't," he cautioned, and then laughed, a puff of breath. "I couldn't either, at first. You'll want to bend at the knees, like the low sweep with the fan, and lift with your legs, not your back." He stretched out his fingers to brush them against my back.

It was not a possessive caress, but—like Pelis's touch on my hand—the signal was there: interest, question.

I backed away instinctively, saying, "That is most awkward." I sensed in the way his hand dropped to his side, the subtle stiffening of his shoulders that I'd hurt him, so I pretended that the moment had not happened as I reached behind me to press my knuckles alongside my spine. "Can you tell me this, at least? *Is* there danger?"

"I don't know. Prince Ivandred sent the outriders two days ahead instead of a day. That's why you won't see but two of Fnor's women—they are scouting in teams."

"What might be the problem? I would think scrupulous attention to a treaty is to be lauded."

"Not if they think enemies will find out they are here."

"Enemies!"

"That is the word they used, though they did not name anyone." He sighed.

"The notion makes my neck cold, as if inimical eyes observe us."

Birdy chuckled. "If it helps, they find you and the princess intimidating."

"Me!"

"They call us peacocks. About you, they say you dance when you walk, like the princess, and they think we all sing our language, especially Anhar, when she reads to us at camp. And they are amazed that Colendi servants dress beautifully and smell like flowers." Birdy's voice changed a little, from teasing to reflective. "Though I notice Nifta no longer tucks flowers in those red braids of hers, and Belimas no longer arranges her hair in blossom-knots."

"They are unhappy. And who can blame them?" I spread my hands. "I move as stiffly as an old goat, my backside hurts so. My clothes are always damp and grimy, and my new scent is essence of horse."

The more I complained the more he laughed. I marveled over how that made me feel better as I walked back to my bedroll. Laughter was good—that was a common truism—but it was the quality of his laughter that warmed me, the shared companionship.

We had been proud of our ability to keep pace with the Marlovens until the day after my conversation with Birdy, when Ivandred gave the order for a hard ride, and our lancers relayed it to us.

"We've been on a hard ride." Belimas was too angry to keep her voice low.

"Too hard," Nifta mumbled. "I'm as skinny as . . ." She cast a look my way, then at Anhar, who was the thinnest of us all, and returned to her work without finishing her sentence. Nifta had been justifiably proud of her rounded shape, but it was true, we were all much more spare. It was not flattering to any of us. Our clothes would not fit when we reached civilization again.

"This has been an easy ride," Fnor said as she slung her bow over her shoulder and walked away.

"As if we haven't been shaken awake every day at Repose," Anhar whispered to me as we walked back to our tents. She took a quick look around, then twitched her hip one way, her chin over her shoulder, tossed her tumbled hair and fingered it, her nose lifted as if something smelled—it was Belimas to the life. I gasped, and from behind came a snort of laughter as Birdy walked by, his arms loaded with horse gear. Anhar and I both smiled back.

The Marlovens' idea of "on the road before dawn" meant waking just after the Hour of Reeds—three hours before Daybreak—so that everyone could be fed and the horses prepared, while the lancers went off in small groups to do whatever it was that they did each morning before we rode, and each evening after we halted. Hitherto, we'd taken horse around the Hour of the Bird, when the sun was at least a finger above the horizon. That, we discovered, was a rare luxury.

Lasva shared a horse with Fnor or one of her women, riding next to Ivandred. Each day's ride ended with silence, her face tight with tension. But she would not complain, or request an easier pace. One night, I was approaching our tent with dragging steps, after forcing myself to practice my spells on the pretext of fetching water, when I heard low, choked sobs from red-haired Nifta, then Marnda's angry whisper.

I already knew that Belimas longed to return to Colend, in spite of the disgrace that had sent her, Pelis, and Nifta on this journey. Now there were two of them. When they emerged to get their share of the never-changing rye panbreads with fried fish and cheese, one look at those lowered, reddened eyes, the compressed lips, and I knew they would have left if they'd dared. But even more terrible than this journey was the image of being alone without coin or even a common language. It was Adamas Dei, who had lived in this very same part of the world, who had written long ago, *Nobody wants a beggar to stay*. They had Colendi skills, but who in this horrible part of the world would want those?

That next morning, when Birdy brought a lantern to our tent to waken us, Nifta put out a hand to halt Anhar in the act of rolling her bedding in the tight form the Marlovens required. "Anhar. You actually were there for our war, last summer. We three were in herb-sleep because of the spy. What was the war like?"

Anhar flushed, obviously pleased to be the expert, yet she was too honest to parade a knowledge she did not have. "I saw nothing," she admitted. "Just the princess when she returned, all mud-covered, and her hand bleeding. No one actually saw the war."

"Lnand says it was not a war," Pelis said as she swiftly braided up her rope of brown hair—for those with longer hair had adopted the Marloven style, which was simpler to achieve and maintain than our more complicated loops and twists. "She said it was a brief skirmish."

"Skirmish?" Belimas said, tossing her head. "What is that?"

"A very small war, I believe," I said. And when all the faces turned my way, I added, "I saw the word in that record about Prince Ivandred's ancestor, Elgar the Fox. There were many assumptions in the record, things the Marloven writer thought everyone knew, so I can't define it further, except it seems that it takes many many skirmishes to make up a war."

"But two people were *killed!*" Belimas spread her hands, fingers stiff.

"War is when the entire kingdom is fighting another kingdom," Pelis said. "At least, I gather so. Yet Lnand also said that no kingdom has ever attacked their capital, which is ringed with great walls and has many guards. So we will be safe."

Belimas snapped her hand northward toward Thorn Gate. "What is to stop them from fighting each other within those walls? We've all seen the blood."

We looked at one another for answers that none could give, then Pelis shrugged. "Why frighten yourself with what-if? The point is, these very same Marlovens won our war, or skirmish, so they're sure to win whatever it is they think might be waiting."

"Ah-yedi!" Nifta flickered her fingers in the petals-in-the-wind gesture, meaning a flirt. "You just want to see that Lnand Dunrend riding about with a lance in her arms. So barbaric!" She pressed her fingers to her eyes. "How I hate this," she whispered.

"This what?" Pelis lifted her shoulders. "We're going to a barbaric kingdom. If we wish to find someone besides one another for rompery, then we must adjust our discrimination."

Pelis had been eyeing Lnand? Had Lnand returned her interest? Of course she had. Now I understood at least some of the motivation for our writing lessons. As Nifta and Belimas (who never ceased weeping, it seemed) gave each other, then Pelis, resentful looks, I walked to the stream wondering what else I'd missed—and saw Anhar had slipped away before I had. She was over by the horses, one hand fingering burrs out of a horse's mane as she talked to Birdy.

I'd assumed that the famous lances had been thrown away after the war—that is, the *skirmish*—with the Chwahir, for I hadn't seen any great sticks on the ride. I discovered the next day that the lances disassembled and then reassembled.

When Tesar and I climbed onto the horse (and I could get up by my-self now, though still without much grace) she seemed larger and harder. She was wearing chain mail beneath her black coat and carried a num-ber of weapons close at hand.

Fully armed also meant bows slung at their saddles. Bows! The forbid-den weapon! But the Marlovens had not agreed to the Compact.

"Are you going to . . . shoot arrows at persons?" I asked, my heartbeat thrumming.

"Not unless ordered," she replied soberly.

Once again, though we traveled so thoroughly together that our bod-ies touched on horseback, Marloven and Colendi were as if separated. I could see Lasva's fear in her wide gaze, in the tight grip of her hands. The Marlovens talked past us to one another, short, quick conversations.

When we camped, we found two riders waiting.

Once the fires were built and the tents set up, Ivandred drew Lasva as usual to the command tent. The rest of us could hear her sweet, polite voice and his deeper clipped one as we lined up for the excruciatingly predictable heavy bread, thick and stale, studded with nuts, the flavor a horrible mix of cloying honey, dates, and raisins, that mixed discordantly with the bitterness of their ubiquitous rye.

After we'd eaten, Lasva summoned us.

All her staff crowded into the main tent. Damp heat rose off us, per-vading the air with the pungent aroma of grimy human beings as we tried to fold inward and make ourselves inconspicuous, so strong was a lifetime's habit.

Then Lasva said, "Prince Ivandred has some troubling news. It appears that there might be . . ." She hesitated, hands clasping together.

I stared at her. How could I not have noticed how thin *she* had become? It was because of the shrouding of warm clothing we usually wore. But now she stood there in silk shirt and an overrobe the dressers had shortened and made into a tunic, and long riding trousers. These clothes had fit her when we commenced riding, but hung now from her straight-backed form.

"Trouble," Ivandred said, when the pause had lengthened into silence. "We believe trouble awaits. Treaty breakers. There might be fighting before we cross the border, which is a day or two ahead."

My heart rapped against my ribs. Nifta's breath hissed in. Belimas covered her face briefly with her hands.

"Belimas," Lasva murmured.

The dresser yanked her fingers down, her body trembling.

Lasva clasped Belimas's stiff fingers. "Prince Ivandred has two transfer tokens that can get two people safely to Darchelde, his family's castle. From there, his aunt can send you to their capital." She glanced over her shoulder at him, and on his slight nod, said, "It seems that further transfers are risky, as they could be warded. I do not know exactly what that means."

But I did. I understood those spells—though I would never have dared put them together. I also knew the difference between a general transfer, and the safer, specific transfers bound into the expensive tokens. They were difficult to make, for each must be unique. But they could get the user past wards placed to prevent transfer, or the far nastier ones that forced one to shift to another Destination.

Belimas shuddered, and Nifta said in a strange voice, subdued, but anger sharpened the sibilants, "Are we here for you to choose whom to take with you, your highness?"

"I am not transferring," Lasva said. "I hoped you would decide among you who will avail themselves of this opportunity."

As her gaze touched each of us, my instinctive reaction was to encourage her to look Anhar's way. This impulse caught me by surprise. Of all the staff, I liked Anhar and Pelis the most. But I was aware of an unworthy feeling of jealousy when Lasva asked Anhar to read, and the rare times I was able to speak to Birdy — however briefly — Anhar always seemed to be there.

Marnda stated in an angry, trembling voice, "At least *I* know my duty, if no one else does. I will stay by the Princess's side, whatever happens."

Belimas was startled by Lasva's statement. "But if there is danger—*you* must be kept safe, your highness."

Lasva smiled at her. "Thank you, Belimas. Thank you for your generous thought. But I believe my place is at Prince Ivandred's side. Though there is little I can do to help—in fact, nothing—*melende* requires me to stay and learn what must be learned.

"I've made my choice," Lasva said. "There would be no blame."

Belimas wept silently. Nifta's gaze flickered between us all, angrily, warily.

Lasva extended her hands, one to Belimas, the other to Nifta. "Once my things are sent to the capital. I will not need a hair dresser on this ride, nor someone to choose fabrics for my wardrobe. May I rely on you two to unpack and make my new chambers ready for our arrival?"

"Yes," Nifta whispered, fingering her ruddy braid with grimy fingernails—she who had always been so fastidious, even fussy.

Belimas bowed, still too overcome for speech. Lasva had given them escape and purpose. Marnda looked on, her head held high, bitterness crimping her mouth to a pucker.

Pelis, Anhar, and I helped the chosen two with a last sort-and-pack. They each clutched a transfer token tightly to their chests and vanished, along with another load of the princess's things; the magic transfer rippled through the air, blue-gold at the edges of vision, smelling faintly of burnt paper, feeling like the touch of metal before a thunderstorm.

Pelis made the Thorn Gate gesture after them, dropping her hand quickly to her side when she saw Lasva coming toward us.

"The prince wishes to explain our situation."

We crowded back into that stuffy tent where we were joined by Prince Ivandred.

He always seemed so cool, so distant, as if a film of ice existed between him and the rest of the world. But now the ice was gone, his manner hurried. He snapped open a map and knelt down to spread it on the low table, his pale braid silvery against his black coat in the lantern light.

"Here is Halia," he said. "Halia," to us, had always been the oddly shaped acorn on the map, stuck to the left side of the great southern continent that spread halfway around the world. "We used to be united under one peaceful government."

His gaze shifted from Lasva to me, his pupils so huge his eyes looked black, reflecting the lantern lights. "You saw it, in my ancestor's record.

It did not last." His callused fingers bisected the map with quick, slashing lines. "There were a couple of centuries of bad government under the Olavairs, who now claim their own kingdom up in the north. My great-grandfather reunited the heartland of Hesea with lands here in the south, the most important being Jayad Hesea. 'Jayad' means plains, you understand, so we usually say, 'the Jayad.' It is where the Jevairs hail from. Telyer Heyas was once a part of our kingdom but is currently an ally. There are some who would like to see either domain turn against us, and it is those ill-wishers we may have to face at the border, which is just beyond the Or Arei."

Or was river, we translated to ourselves.

"The only way into our territory is across a great bridge. If there is trouble, we will find it there," he said.

"I could swoon over that fine linen. Linen woven with cotton! Who would have thought? When it is wet, it does not squeak," Pelis said to me the next day, when we camped early. She wiped her hair back, hand streaked with mud. The days were long behind us when we would have been ashamed to be seen so.

We were grateful to stop in daylight, in a secluded little valley be-tween two great slant-layered stone cliffs forced apart by an ancient stream. Trees and grass had grown among the old tumble of stones, mak-ing a comfortable camp. The sun even shone, and the breeze carried the last lingering scents of grass and wild sage.

Anhar laughed as she snapped out her bedroll, then she bent back, hands flat against the back of her hips as she tried to stretch her spine. "Imagine thinking this a fine place. A year ago I would not have come here even for a picnic with my sister."

Pelis smiled, casting a self-conscious look over her shoulder in Lnand's direction. Usually Lnand looked back, but today the Marlovens were subdued. The intensity of their focus was on one another, not on us. They set up camp very swiftly, then moved off in groups as they usually did. We never questioned any of it. We were grateful that the order had come to light a fire and prepare a hot meal.

By the time I'd finished going through the princess's gold case (three letters, answered then burned) and washing out my riding stockings, I could see that something was amiss from the way the three Marlovens on cook duty talked in head-bent, earnest converse.

"Emras," Marnda scolded. "Here we find you, quite at your ease, yet everyone else has work and to spare. It appears that the only flour the outrider could obtain is wheat, and they are uncertain about the proportions required by wheat. You may teach them how to make our bread." This last she said in careful Marloven.

I turned to the three Marloven cooks, all young men who looked exactly alike to my eyes. I scarcely knew any of the men by sight or name, except for Haldren Marlovair, Ivandred's second in command, who was generally agreed among the women to be the handsomest of all the Marlovens. Prince Ivandred, while attractive, was too sharp of bone in his face, too square. Haldren had that perfect balance of bones and features so prized in Colend: the broad forehead and the tapering jaw that gave a hint of heart.

"We tried making this bread once before," the lead cook said with a sweep of his hand, palm outward as though pushing something away. "Very bad."

"I suspect you used the wrong starter. Your rye must use a sourdough starter." I did not say that starter breads were only made on Colend's borders where wheat did not grow easily. I followed him to their cook site, then knelt down and carefully uncapped little stoneware spice jars in order to sniff (very few of those) and looked into bags. From another lifetime ago came the voice of the court's second breadmaker: *unless you are the queen, you don't make what pleases you, you make what you believe will please them.*

Would that be a rule for any aspect of life? I wondered as I measured the crock of butter with my eye. Courtiers say what they think will please those who say what they please. . . .

The ingredients and the flat steel pans dictated quick-breads with plenty of butter beaten in. I was aware of Birdy watching intently as my fingers worked through the well-remembered tasks. Presently the comforting smell of baking bread rose.

It came out flaky and light. I served it and stood back to observe the result.

"Why this worm shape?" one of the Marlovens murmured softly.

"To hide the lack of flavor?"

"Silly peacocks." A chuckle.

Though the Marlovens were disappointed—and I was disappointed by their disappointment—we Colendi cherished every melting bite.

"Oh, the aromas of home," Birdy whispered to me in passing, his juggling silks arcing high up in long ovals.

He turned—and I turned just to see him. Our eyes met, and we laughed again, but though my gaze stayed on him, his moved past me, and his mouth curved in a different sort of humor. I glanced back, and there was Anhar, giving him the same smile.

Then he moved on, the silken bags in motion.

Ivandred had gone off twice to confer with Haldren and the newly re-turned scout, Retrend Senelac, who was the youngest of the lancers. He was slim in build as are most youths, but as a Marloven lancer, he was too disciplined to be weedy. Whenever there was laughter among them, one was certain to see Retrend's bright red head.

Ivandred came back from his conference, his step quick. "Lasva," he said. "Would you read some of that poetry?"

Lasva's chin lifted, betraying her surprise. "I would and gladly, but I must confess that Anhar or Emras are the better readers. Too often I stop to consider a phrase or word, and I cannot change my voice."

Ivandred assented and Anhar, nearest the book, took it up and began to read. Though he was still, I sensed that Ivandred's attention divided from the way his gaze would cut left or right in response to a quiet step, even the thunk of a horse shifting its stance by clopping down a hoof.

The truth is, my attention was also divided. Anhar seemed to share Birdy's friendship, which I had thought exclusively my own, because of our past—our shared knowledge—our shared humor. Now she was per-forming a duty I had thought exclusively mine.

The next poem was written in Sartoran, and Anhar handed the book to me, murmuring that her accent was not good enough for performance.

I took over the reading, and when I reached the end, the impulse was there to offer to translate it. At a sign of assent from Ivandred, I did so, though I was aware of discomfort. I knew the impulse came from the wish to show up Anhar's lack of knowledge. *I am no better than Tiflis when we were young,* I thought as Ivandred looked up, the firelight ruddy on his tense face. "The patient willow. Is that a symbol for a man who cannot raise the staff?"

"Raise . . ." Lasva repeated, but when Retrend muffled a snicker into his arm she gathered the meaning, and she too laughed softly, which seemed to set the Marlovens a little more at ease, judging from the shift-ings, the exchanged smiles. "Ah," she said. "To a Colendi, the willow symbolizes a grieving lover."

A couple of the Marlovens whispered, and Ivandred leaned forward. "Why would someone make a song about such a person?"

I laid the book on my knee as Lasva said, "Do you not have tragic songs?"

"Many. But they are about heroes falling in battle. Or a lover is killed, but the song finishes with vengeance or triumph." At our mute surprise, he said, "Some ballads about feuds are comical."

Haldren flashed a quick, surprisingly shy grin. "There must be twenty ballads about Marlovair against Senelac."

Retrend snickered again, the firelight glinting in his ruddy braids. "Fifty."

Ivandred laughed, a soft sound. "But we have no songs about someone who sits under a tree to mourn." He opened his hands, palms up. "Different ways, we have."

Lasva touched her fingertips in the gesture of Harmonious Assent. "Sometimes the lover is a symbol for an issue in court. Now it is my turn for a question." At Ivandred's open handed gesture, she continued. "In Colend, as you saw, when we travel we display our family symbols on plaques. You carry your symbols on flags. They are very fine," she added, gesturing in heart mode, "when the wind is true. But most of the time, wind is . . . wind. And that makes it difficult to see the flag symbols. So, why flags?"

Ivandred smiled as his people whispered briefly to one another. "Flags make the wind visible when we ride fast," he said. "When people see them, they think that the king or commander is lord of the riders, the animals, the ground, and the sky. Lord of the wind. It is . . . a symbol of power." He tapped his head.

His smile faded. "You will see them flying on the morrow."

SEVEN

OF BANNERS IN THE WIND

The next afternoon, under steel-colored skies, we topped the last ridge, and gained our first glimpse of the long river valley called the Jayad. A few twists and turns through rocky spires and outcroppings brought us low enough to spot the mighty bridge over the Or Arei, a cluster of slanted clay-tile rooftops around the near foot. The river was far too wide to cross by horse and too swift-moving for barges, after all the recent rains.

"See the bridge?" Lnand's voice lightened. "Beyond that lies our homeland."

We reined in shortly thereafter, screened by an ancient hedgerow growing wild alongside a rough trail that was once a road.

Ivandred trotted alone to where Retrend waited. The two dismounted and walked up the roadside to peer through the tangled, thorny branches at the moldering remains of a castle not too far from the mighty bridge.

Below the bridge rose a pall of dust.

Ivandred called for Tesar, who guided her horse out of position.

"They're wearing Jevair green," Ivandred said to her. "Are they Jevair?"

The horse shifted its weight as Ivandred passed a spy glass to her, and she peered just past my ear. Everyone waited, then she handed it back.

"It might be our spring-green, after several seasons in the sun." Tesar's tone was also uncertain.

Lasva gestured in Deference mode. "We know nothing of military matters, as I am certain you are aware, but my staff knows a great deal about matters of cloth dyes and fading. Might Pelis take a look?"

All the Marlovens turned her way, looking as surprised as if a rock had spoken—or a peacock had taken up a sword, as Ivandred turned his palm up.

Pelis took the spyglass and stared through it longer than the situation warranted, but we could guess from her stiff manner and her red face that she was making absolutely certain.

Lnand muttered something. Pelis made a Deference, then lowered the glass. "I wish we had Nifta with us, for she is the most knowledgeable about fabrics." She grasped the ends of her brown braids then said, "But I know something, too. At this distance, and with the light behind them, I am not going to state conviction, but I think that is fresh dye."

"Those battle tunics are a different shade," Haldren said. "Are you certain it's not sun-fading?"

"The difference in shade is due to a difference in fabric. From the hang, I would guess you are seeing three different weaves, which will take dye variously. But it is fresh. I would say the green was mixed with dye made from sun thistle petals, and recently at that."

"A ruse, then," Ivandred said. "Retrend? How close did you get?"

"Not close enough to hear."

"We will dismount. Rest the horses. Wait until night."

Fnor rode up. "I smell snow," she said, fist striking over her heart.

Ivandred lifted his head, studying the clear sky. "We will ride just as the sun sets."

He walked with Lasva up a goat trail to sit under a tree, but once she was comfortable, he went off with Fnor and a black-coated Marloven to confer.

Lasva beckoned to me. At the other end of our column, Birdy's voice rose briefly as he and those caring for the animals got busy watering, checking shoes, and swapping the baggage onto fresher horses.

Marnda halted when she found Pelis sitting on a rock, her sewing in her lap, needle poised, her tired face inward seeing, and began scolding in that fretful voice that had become habit.

I passed them to join Lasva on a mossy natural bench below a tangle of firs. She rested her back against an old stone with weatherworn carving on it, her wrist bone a pronounced knob.

"Sometimes," she whispered. "I think about walking through the ballroom just before dawn. The air smelled of snuffed beeswax candles, and the empty space carried that curious resonance after music has been played."

She paused, and I waited.

She didn't speak again.

The shadows were slanting halfway up the cliff behind us when Haldren and another Marloven passed down the line, handing out oily twists of rough hemp. Tesar put hers inside her coat. Lnand did the same.

We mounted swiftly and rode down the last of the trail into a tangle of twisted old firs, aspen, and a variety of oak that seemed thicker than those in Colend, as if they strove to grow against a constant wind.

When the road leveled at last, Ivandred motioned Haldren into his place next to Lasva, before the big banners. Lasva had her own mount. Fnor and her three bow women rode on the outside of the column.

The Marlovens put on their helms.

Ivandred said to Lasva, "Remember. Haldren is me. Ride by his side as you would ride by mine, and he will bring you to safety." His gaze shifted to Haldren, whose jaw tightened.

Then the prince and a chosen lancer trotted down a trail under cover of thick pine forest, and vanished from view. Retrend rode alone down the trail to rejoin his waiting partner and to scout ahead of us.

We rode on as shadows merged and began to deepen into darkness. After a time I asked, "Tesar? Is it permitted to ask why Prince Ivandred left us?"

"'Is it permitted to ask,'" she repeated. "Heh. The words are ours, but you put them in so odd an order. Is that what you say where you live? And do you reply, 'No you cannot ask' if such is true?"

"We might say, 'I shall inquire if it is permitted,' because then you are not denying your questioner. So no one present is at fault."

"Is there fault in just words? 'Melende' . . . I heard the princess explaining this word. She says it is not the same as our honor. Is that so?"

"I think honor in most languages has to do with obligations. And one's . . . oh, perception of the rules of society, or one's perception of oneself with respect to one's society."

Hoof beats approached from the road ahead. Haldren raised his hand for a halt, as Retrend galloped up the trail, then pulled up, face flushed behind his helm. "They're coming to meet you."

Haldren said, "Let's meet them. Use up some of this road."

"What's amiss?" I asked Tesar as we began to ride at a brisk trot toward a stand of trees.

"We expected them to wait before the bridge. It is a position of strength." She snorted. "Haldren is supposed to keep them talking until the prince is in place. We can do that on the road, but the rest of the plan requires us to be at the bridge."

Lnand spoke up from where she and Anhar rode next to us, "No plan survives intact." Her tone was akin to ours when we scribes remind one another of the First Rule.

"So, what will you do?" I whispered.

"Adapt—and get back to the plan as soon as—"

Haldren jerked his fist up, and the column fell silent.

The air had been still, the banners sagging bundles of black fabric, but as we rode toward the bridge cold drafts of fitful wind stung our faces and lifted the banners. On one side, a wingtip of the screaming eagle flickered, as if in flight. On the other, the flame-like ruff of the fox flared yellow-gold in the glow of our torches.

It was near full dark when we emerged from the trees to find large warriors blocking the road. They stood side by side with shields up, spears grounded, the only movement the flicker of ruddy torchlight. Their number was at least twice ours, probably more. I was sick with dread, unaware of pressing hard against Tesar in an unconscious wish to hide.

"Prince Ivandred of Marloven Hesea," called a man with a deep voice.

"Who wishes to speak to Ivandred of Marloven Hesea, and why?" Haldren put his hand to his sword hilt in its saddle sheath.

"We are an alliance for peace. Prince Ivandred is invited to confer to the mutual benefit of our alliance and Marloven."

"Prince Ivandred has not been ordered to speak in the king's name," Haldren shouted. "Your alliance is therefore requested to follow established forms. Send a delegation to the king of Marloven Hesea, who speaks for all Marlovens."

Tesar's breath hissed in.

"What is it?" I whispered.

"The way they're looking at each other. For a leader—"

Then a hoarse man shouted, "We demand the peaceful surrender of Prince Ivandred and his party. If you surrender in peace, we promise no harm will come to any."

"Prince Ivandred only surrenders to a prince. Who among you is his equal in rank? Come forth and state name and land," Haldren shouted

back, after another tense pause during which warriors shifted and whispered. "If your prince is there, we will ride in peace to yon party," he
added, nodding toward the countless Jayad warriors either standing in
clumps or walking slowly back and forth along the west bridge just
ahead.

"But . . . then we'll be surrounded," Pelis whispered.

"That's what we hope they'll think," Tesar breathed. "Sssh."

Lasva said to Haldren, "Where are the negotiators?"

"Who?" Haldren asked, his gaze on the enemy.

"The heralds from both sides, who negotiate distances and signals. If
you do not have them, what is to prevent . . . something horrible?"

Haldren's jaw sagged as he looked her way, his profile stark against the
clouding sky.

Tesar whispered, "Their leader isn't there. And heralds don't . . ."

The shiftings ceased. Hoarse Voice's tone lightened with satisfaction.
"Agreed."

Nothing made any sense—except that sense of danger.

I could feel Tesar's body shifting. Later, when I was able to see this
experience through others' minds—and I am coming to the how and the
why of that very soon—I chose Haldren's memory. He could feel the
others' focus as he led our party forward. Haldren did not question his
prince. It was right to meet the threat of dishonor by riding for glory,
whether the glory be in songs after their deaths, or enjoyed in life.

It may have seemed right to the head and heart, but the body does
not anticipate glory. It wants the sweetness of summer days, the warm
grip of love, the wind at one's back, good food eaten with those you
trust, and the shared drink of companionship. And so the body fights to
survive through shortened breath, acrid sweat despite the wintry air, and
the need to pee, though you whisper the Waste Spell again and again.

The body fights the will, but the will must prevail, *and pain is how the
will gains strength*—

"Halt there."

The command rang out from the wall of big shield men ahead.
Haldren's cousin Tdan, who bore the fox banner, smothered a curse.

Haldren reined in, readying his words. He felt the shared will of all his
band behind him in their tightened knees and focused gazes, the horses'
coiled rumps and ready necks. He peered to the left, southward along
the river bend, marshy land obscured by darkness and rain, then risked a
glance to the right, past Tdan's blade-tipped lance. The torchlight from
the big bridge gleamed along the edge of the blade, silver to gold.

Better to think about the sharpened blades and the animals' ears canted forward than to think about magic. It was rare he saw Prince Ivandred raise magic. It felt sinister, and instinct balked at the prince with only one other, riding alone at the head of an eerie army, as if formed of smoke and bad dreams.

"Prince Ivandred—" came the shout, choking off at a clamor of voices from the direction of the ruined castle.

Heads on both sides turned.

"It's a trap . . . a trap!" An enemy's voice rose to a howl. "They're attacking from the north!"

"They just spotted the prince's ghost army," Tesar breathed. "Ready yourself for a run."

Shouts rang out in relay, causing a confusion of the milling warriors. Captains summoned their own ridings or bands—twos and threes then nines galloped toward the distant lights, swords and spears brandished. The body of enemies seemed to shift about to face the many lights emerging from the other side of the ruin.

Except for one group, who galloped toward us in two efficient lines, their intention obviously to reinforce those now surrounding us.

Haldren shouted, "Now."

Tesar grunted as she pulled her oil-soaked hemp out of her coat, slapped it over the blade of her lance, jerked the point out as the torchbearer rode by, touched his torch to it, and moved on to the next. The hemp flamed up in orange and blue streamers. All this took about ten heartbeats. Ten more and the horses leaped into a gallop.

My memory is a confusion of lights, shouts, some screams, and noise. Fire whirled around me in dizzying circles as the Marlovens spun the lances in their hands, flames streaming. I could make no sense of anything, so I cowered down as small as I could, my fingers gripping the base of the horse's mane.

As I said, I found myself in a terrifying chaos. But I can tell you what happened.

Most of the enemy had ridden toward what they believed was a massive attack, only to discover darting lights too quick to be held by living hand and shadowy forms charging in a wedge though kicking up no mud. At the lead, screaming a high-pitched "Yi-yiyiyiyi!," rode two Marlovens. In their case, horses and swords and screams were real. The rest were phantoms.

The pair slashed straight through the center of the already wavering line, sending riders scattering. The lines serried and stopped, shocked faces turning as the living pair galloped toward the bridge, where the rest of us were headed.

The enemies reformed and chased, howling for blood. They could see cartwheels of flame riding down the meager line left to guard access to the bridge. Someone blew a signal on a trumpet, over and over.

Back to us. The horses skidded and neighed, steel clashed, flames whooshed—terrifyingly bright—and we were past the bridge guard. The enemy, impelled by that trumpet command, set fire to the buildings at either end of the bridge. The wind caught the flames and flung them outward. Fire spread at frightening speed.

Too fast. The distinctive smell of singed olives burned in our nostrils: someone had drenched parts of the bridge with barrels of cooking oil. We rode straight through rising walls of flame on either side. The gap between them narrowed fast as flame ate at the oil-soaked wood.

"One . . . two . . ." Tesar hunched down. Cursing steadily, she aimed us at a gap and we were through. She galloped on another fifty paces or so then pulled up and shoved me out of the saddle. "Rescue," she said and galloped back to the bridge, leaving me where I'd fallen.

I scrambled to my feet, staggering as the world slid and jerked, slid and jerked. The bridge fire roared skyward, spreading fast and bright. Silhouettes of locals emerged tentatively from their houses at either end, backtracking hastily as steel-swinging, shouting riders dashed past. In the strengthened light I counted our people. Haldren and the rest had easily defeated the small party at this end of the bridge. It was clear the alliance had never meant for us to get this far.

But we were not all present. Missing were the four bow women, Ivandred and his partner—and Birdy, leading the remounts.

Then I saw them silhouetted in the middle of the bridge, as flames shot upward at either end. Birdy ripped off his tunic and flung it over the eyes of the plunging, flat-eared lead horse. As the animal ceased panicking and stood splay-footed and shivering, Birdy's hands ran along its neck, soothing, as he looked back and forth, back and forth. Then he flung his arm over his face, gripped the horse by the halter, and with desperate courage plunged toward our end, the other animals pressing after. Five steps and they were obscured by smoke.

A roar went up from the far end. Ivandred and his companion reached the foot. The four bow-women broke formation and formed around them. They charged between the fires, straight at the party defending the foot of the bridge.

A horse screamed. Birdy and the animals would die unless the fire at my end was doused, and the only way to douse it was by magic. And Ivandred was too busy fighting at the far end.

I knew the spell. I knew what to do. But I'd only played around with candles. I dropped to my knees, trembling fingers shaping the first part of the spell meant to consume flame. My lips began the words but almost at once a sense of heat roared in my head, my nostrils filled with the scent of singed hair and silk—

Sip the cup. No, bigger than a cup. Huge! I imagined an enormous cistern of steel, rapidly gabbled the spell while *seeing* flame pour into my imaginary cistern, like a waterfall in reverse—the cistern grew wider and wider, but I could hold it, I *would* hold it.

Heat intensified, my eyes burned—with the last frantic gasp of control I snapped the last gesture and word, and collapsed into the grass, blinded and retching.

Gradually the waves of nausea diminished, leaving me aware that I was not blind. I lay in darkness, staring up at smoke-blurred stars. As I comprehended that, the last of the smoke blew past, and cold spots bloomed on my face like wintry kisses: snow. Clouds were moving in.

Galloping horses reached us. "Here she is," someone snapped in exasperation.

"Orders?"

Ivandred's low, urgent voice, "If they chase, we'll form up. But I don't think they will. Let's not tempt them. Someone pick up the princess's runner. From the smell, she was overcome by smoke."

My head throbbed, bringing the nausea back in a throat-stinging surge as someone hauled me to my feet. Not Tesar—the sweat-scent was male. I reached blindly to steady myself, my fingers closing on a hank of what I took to be horse hair, but softer, and loose, one end sticky, the smell an evil metallic tang. When Ivandred passed up the line, torch flaring, his horse's sides steaming and flecked with white, I discovered that the thing hooked to the saddle was a part of a human scalp with long hair hanging in a coil.

That time I did not manage the Waste Spell.

EIGHT

OF ISOLATED VISION

"... burned?"

Tesar's voice roused me, concerned, but defensive. "I don't understand. I set her down well upwind of the fires."

"The wind changed. It must have. It was fierce on the bridge. All directions. I think now I know what 'firestorm' means." Birdy was within arm's reach, judging by his voice.

Wearily I opened my eyes, as Birdy crouched in front of me, his face smeared with soot right to the absurd ears sticking out from his filthy hair that hung down in unkempt strings. "How badly are you burned, Em? We checked you over and didn't see any scorched flesh."

"She must have breathed smoke." Lnand was hoarse. "Haldren said there was smoke rising off her clothes when they first found her. She stank of it. If there's a burn, we have salve."

"Breathed it," I whispered. "No burns."

"Try to sleep."

I shut my eyes, aware of the sway and jolt of a wagon for about two breaths.

I woke to the sound of two men conversing softly in Sartoran.

". . . and that one breathed smoke. She'll cough it out in a day or two." That was Ivandred.

An unfamiliar voice responded pleasantly. "So these here are the pair you summoned me to see?"

"Yes. Four died. I will not lose these two."

Light flared, not the orange of flame, but the clear silver of a glow globe. I saw only bales of hay.

The newcomer still sounded amused. "This boy's shoulder is in shards. Even for me it presents a challenge."

Ivandred said flatly, "Insurmountable?"

"No. But it will take time. Such healings must be done in stages, so the body can do its own work—as much as it can." A pause and then, "You know the cost."

"Just teach me the magic. Or point me to where I can learn."

A quiet laugh. "The woman will be dead by morning if something is not done immediately. The boy will never raise that right arm above waist level, if you do not shift away the bone shards."

"Teach me."

"Ah, Ivandred! Your stubbornness is amusing but futile. No, I will not argue. We haven't time for one of our conversations on the verities." The man's voice altered to a brisk tone. "Now clear your people out so I can concentrate."

Ivandred's footsteps chuffed rapidly away through the hay.

A finger touched my forehead, and an odd pang flashed through my inward vision. I opened my eyes, only to find a vague face-shaped blur, half-obscured by tiny flickers of light, as if I stared at the night sky reflected in water.

"You and I," the man said, "will talk later."

I dropped into slumber.

I woke to the rise and fall of voices singing the Marloven memorial chant they called the *Hymn to the Fallen.*

We began moving again later that day.

The Marlovens' helm tails had thickened. That obscene detail was no dream.

From that point on I exerted myself to avoid ever touching those helms or permitting one to touch me, though I knew it was absurd. Hair could not hurt me. But symbols are strong. They shape the meanings in our lives.

I had nearly killed myself with only one spell. Now I knew with visceral conviction how very powerful magic was. We take it so for granted, with those little magics we use every day to make life comfortable. I needed to learn more. Sometimes I flexed my toes in my slippers, feeling as if that little ring burned me with the weight of its implied responsibility. How could I possibly know Norsundrian magic from any other kind of magic, if I could barely contain one spell?

Someone had commandeered a wagon in which Fnor and Retrend still lay gravely wounded, seldom awake or aware for very long.

For a few days, I lay with them as Anhar tended us. I gazed up at her face: the color of her eyes, which turned to amber when light shone from the side, and the little hollow in her upper lip. She gently washed the smoke from my face with a warm damp cloth that smelled of some herb. She pressed her hands over the hay before we lay down, to make certain there would be no bumps to vex our muscles. Without being asked, she did all these little things that — when you are so hurt all you can do is lie there — become more important than wars or even the wheeling of the stars.

Sometimes I opened my eyes and Birdy was there.

Once he smiled at me. "Drink up, and then you can sleep." He flicked the ends of my hair, a brief yet compassionate gesture. I wanted to weep, but it would hurt too much.

Within a few days, I could sit up, eat, and drink; within a day after that I could take care of my own dishes. I also became aware of Marnda's fretful voice summoning Anhar to other duties. So I took over the task of caring for the severely wounded, which enabled me to ride in the wagon beside them, my knees up under my chin. Anhar appeared with food, always making sure we got ours hot.

The best part of those long days was when Birdy came. He would sit on one side of me and Anhar on the other, and report on our progress.

One night Birdy appeared late. I had been lying there with my eyes shut. For a moment we just sat, three tired, grimy people far from the home we'd known and loved. Then he breathed, "Oh, I'm so glad you're here."

I opened my eyes and discovered that he was not talking to me. The campfire light beat over his features, touching his ears that stuck out so appealingly, as he smiled across at Anhar.

And she smiled back. Then he leaned forward—he was very tall—and their lips met directly over me. When they separated again, their breathing was ragged. They thought I slept, so I closed my eyes again.

I also considered a strange conversation I'd overheard, or thought I'd overheard, half convinced I'd dreamed it. That healer Ivandred had brought to us—I could not recall for certain the language in which he had said, "We will talk later." My forgetfulness suggested a dream.

We traveled more slowly, not just because of the wagon but because it snowed twice. The second time, the snow stayed.

When we reached the Faral River, Ivandred rode up a hill overlooking the cross-roads and peered intently toward the west.

"He thinks the enemy came from there," Lasva said to me, for she'd joined me on the wagon that day, to take a turn giving sips of water, or whatever was needed, to Fnor and Retrend. Fnor had wakened enough to discover that her sister was dead. Little was said, but Lasva sometimes just sat, head bowed, holding Fnor's hand.

"West of the Faral?" I asked. "Isn't that what used to be Choraed Elgaer—where Elgar the Fox came from?" There had been a map in the scroll I'd translated from Tharais's text, which I had copied out for Tiflis.

"It is now called Totha and wishes to be independent." Lasva lifted her head to glance at Ivandred, still on horseback atop the rise, reins loose in his hand. "There is a peace agreement with Marloven Hesea, but he said things are . . . complicated."

"'Totha,' is that . . ."

"From Tenthan, Elgar the Fox's home territory."

Prince Ivandred rode down the hillock and ordered us to cut up northward into a narrow valley rather than follow the Faral River to where it branched into the Marlovar.

And so we began the last leg of our long journey.

Marnda had been silent since the time we were invalids. She was like a stunned bird, eyes open but blank, eating by rote, only rousing to oversee Lasva's care and to scold Pelis and Anhar—who were busy sewing a suitable gown out of the last hoarded length of silk. But her voice was no longer shrill.

We had assumed that a kingdom whose prince could not afford to travel in the proper style would be penurious in the extreme. Our first introduction to Marloven Hesea was nothing like what we expected. There were inns, but to our eyes they were more like military posts, swarming with warriors. The stables were enormous. The rooms were plain, small, but warm, and the food, after the dreary travel fare, was hot and plentiful. No money changed hands—this was our first introduction to the complicated system of duties and barter that was more common than money in this kingdom.

Despite those inns, we camped as usual.

By the time we passed through low, rugged mountains, like those on the other side of the Telyer—sheer with naked rock of many warm colors, unlike the green, smooth hills of Colend—Fnor and Retrend were awake for longer periods. I had regained my strength, and practiced Marloven with them as I helped them to eat, drink, and to shift position.

Our cavalcade climbed steadily, then descended into a valley of shifting shades of silver, white, and pale blue crowned by an enormous castle with eight towers. It was my first sight of the Marloven honey-colored stone that could look like gold when the sun sank toward the western sea. I never thought I would admire a castle—a building made for defense rather than beauty—but Darchelde was beautiful in an austere way.

Marnda recovered her old spirit as soon as that castle was sighted. She pleaded with the prince to halt the entourage so that the princess could wash her face and hands, have her hair dressed, and wear the coronet that Marnda had secreted among her personal effects. Lasva tried to remonstrate, but Ivandred smiled. "You shall have it as you wish, Runner Marend. Ah. Marnda."

Very soon Lasva rode beside the prince, her hair arranged in shining coils once again. She wore the Lirendi colors in filmy layers of royal blue, darkest around the square neck and with each layer lightening to silver. It was a beautiful gown, but meant for a ballroom, not arduous travel. Marnda climbed into the wagon, anxious that the many layers would not snag on the splinters or become mired with grime. She waved me away from the wounded with a gesture worthy of Queen Hatahra, and took her place at their heads.

Ivandred gave the signal to ride, and the lancers ululated a shrill "Yip-yip-yip!"

People came out of sturdy houses with tiled or slated roofs to stare at us as we crossed the valley on well-tended roads. Their gazes lingered longest on Ivandred and Lasva. We'd begun the winding road upward to the castle when riders galloped down to meet us. Over their coats were tunics with either eagles or fox faces worked across the backs. They closed around, accompanying us as, from one of the eight castle towers, out-of-tune bells rang in a dissonant, monotonous clang.

"Alarm?" Lasva asked. She and Ivandred were directly in front of the wagon.

Ivandred's answer was too low for us to hear, but Birdy turned just enough to grin. "It's a welcome ring," he said. And in our own Kifelian added, "They don't seem to have carillons."

I hope their horrible bells do not ring the hours, I thought, but kept it to myself.

We rode through a huge open gate, under castle walls bristling with warriors—men and women—armed with swords, spears, and bows. When a trumpet sounded (thankfully not discordant) these guardians sent up a great shout and struck fists to chests.

The lancers rode in strict control until we'd entered an enormous courtyard. Ivandred released them by raising his fist and opening the fingers. The column broke into individuals all talking and laughing, as riders in fox tunics or eagle tunics, friends and family, reached to take charge of gear and extra mounts, pelting everyone with questions the while.

A woman approached, walking with a swinging stride, and everyone gave way. She smiled at Ivandred and laid her hand to her thin chest when she came abreast of Lasva, but all her attention was on the wagon. She vaulted lightly up and crouched down beside Fnor. Her hair was entirely silver, her bony face lined, emphasizing her resemblance to Ivandred. She had to be quite old, but she was vigorous. "I am Ingrid Montredaun-An, Ivandred's aunt, and sister to the king," she told me. "Give me a report on her state, please? On them both?"

I began to speak, but Marnda sent me an angry glance, then said, "I am Princess Lasthavais's Seneschal, your highness."

We soon learned that Ingrid was the jarlan of Darchelde, Ivandred's ancestral territory. Jarl and jarlan were titles somewhat like duke and duchess.

Ingrid-Jarlan issued a stream of fast-spoken orders, then turned to me. "My first runner will see you and these others comfortably established."

Our party was promptly surrounded by a genial, curious mob. Birdy was swept along with the horses in one direction, Lasva and Ivandred in another, leaving Marnda, Anhar, and Pelis with me. Marnda climbed down from the wagon, moving more quickly than I'd ever seen her as she scurried to take her place directly behind Lasva. They vanished inside.

Anhar whispered to Pelis and me, "I hope their floors aren't covered in horse manure."

"Or that the beds aren't bedrolls on the floor," Pelis whispered back, her lips compressed against a laugh as a tall older servant handed them off to a younger and beckoned to me to follow.

This older woman wore a long robe over trousers and a thick tunic, the colors contrasting gray shades edged with saffron. Everyone looked alike. I could see that none of our people could tell the Marlovens apart.

My first glimpse of the great hall inside the massive iron-reinforced doors at the front of Darchelde castle filled me with wonderment. The hall was so enormous that the vast fireplace I glimpsed at one end was as large as the queen's formal parlor at home.

From there, we climbed steep stone stairs, the stairwell narrow and bare. The woman in gray and saffron pointed me into a small room on the third floor with the bed on a platform and space for a trunk. She talked so fast that I hadn't a hope of following her words, once I winnowed out "bath" and "stairs." I didn't care about anything yet beyond getting a bath and changing my clothes.

The baths turned out to be in the basement, a long, long way down dank stairs.

"It's stone *everywhere* upstairs," Pelis whispered when we met at the baths a short time later. "Is this a prison, perhaps?"

"No torture instruments," Anhar said, bowing in Unalloyed Gratitude, causing Pelis to sniff a laugh. "And though we are consigned to dormitories like children, at least they are warm."

Dormitories? I did not tell them that I'd been given a room to myself; though it was small and mean by Colendi standards, it was private. And privacy was important to us.

"At least these Marlovens have discovered vents." Anhar turned to me.

"Who was that woman who escorted you? A scribe? I didn't know they had scribes!"

"I don't know that they do, yet," I said. "She was introduced as 'the jarlan's first runner,' whatever that implies."

Anhar said, "I thought they only had runners in the military."

"According to *An Examination of Greatness*, they were also a kind of seneschal, and scribe, and maid," I said as we stepped down into the steaming water.

"At least the baths are civilized," Pelis said, sighing as her long hair fanned out like fronds of walnut-shade in the water around her. "Dormitories!" She splashed her hands up in shadow-ward.

"We don't have time," I said. "There's the banquet to get ready for."

"Oh, we know." Pelis sniffed the air and made a face. "While you were off wherever you were, we had Marnda scolding us like a pair of kitchen pages."

Anhar ducked down, then came up, hair streaming over her round face. When she was wet, her wide eyes and round face pronounced her Chwahir heritage. "Here is my prediction," she said. "After all the time and care in making that royal-blue gown, we will be throwing everything away. You'll see. It's going to be gray linsey-woolsey, perhaps with a single spangle where it can't be seen, for variety. And she'll wear it for a week at a go."

I had been so busy resenting Marnda's usurpation of my time, I hadn't considered how the dressers would feel to be superseded in a land where everyone seemed to dress uniformly, and only once in the day.

The banquet hall was another vast chamber, mirror image to the great hall. The public chambers were plastered smooth and painted over with just the sort of enormous figures that Queen Hatahra had decreed should be torn down in Alsais's old palace. Only these were not lifelike, but highly stylized—great raptor shapes, horses at the gallop, manes and tales flying, some with riders on their backs shooting arrows from those same oddly shaped bows. The raptors all soared, talons extended, beaks open in screams.

I looked away from the walls to the people I must live among. The tables were low, guests seated on cushions. The prince and his party sat on a daïs well forward of the enormous fireplace, which was partly screened, and in the manner of that particular type of castle, very well vented in that these central fireplaces provided heat for the rooms directly above.

The people looked alike at first glance: mostly blond heads, everyone with braids, and the clothing shades of gray, black, and undyed, with contrasting edgings of yellow or dull gold; the only variations were fox faces or eagles embroidered in wool on the backs of many of the tunics.

Lasva still wore the blue gown—for she had no other formal robes. Her hair was bound up with a single strand of pearls, falling in ringlets down her back. In the time it took me to enter the room and walk along the wall toward the daïs, I observed how many of the Marlovens looked her way as they talked in low voices.

Lasva saw me, smiled, and lifted her hand. Marnda stood among the servants behind the main table, some holding pitchers, others ready to fetch and carry.

As I neared, Lasva and Ivandred finished a whispered conversation. He gripped her hand below the level of the table.

"This is my first runner, Emras," Lasva said to the jarlan.

Marnda stepped forward. "I have already learned where the kitchen is and how things are done here. I would be honored to serve." Her voice shook as she glared at me.

Lasva said, "Emras, I hoped you might consent to take charge of the wine."

Marnda had to step aside, her hands trembling. I took my place beside her, stunned at her rudeness in *public*. It made no sense!

I forced my attention on the service of the meal. The Marloven plates were wide and shallow, the only utensils spoons and very sharp knives with which they speared bites of the roasted turkey or fish or potato. The spoons were for eating something that smelled peppery and seemed to be made of lentils and garlic. They broke apart hot biscuits to mop up juices or gravy.

The runners stood behind their master or mistress, pouring wine, or fetching food when it was either pointed at or tapped with a reaching knife.

Conversation was loud enough to mask the noise of eating. Lasva borrowed Ivandred's knife to press her food into accommodating bites. Marnda hovered, anxiously watching that thin hand rise and fall.

The jarlan smiled my way when her runner handed me a pitcher of wine. Before she could speak, someone blew a trumpet in rising chords. The Marlovens stilled. The hubbub of voices flattened to whispers—*harvaldar*—then they, too, stilled.

Warriors entered with a quick clatter of iron-heeled footsteps, swords at the ready. Ivandred's head moved minutely as he tracked this efficient spread through the room. Their gazes shifted everywhere, and I belatedly noticed that everyone above the age of ten or so had their hands in sight.

Then two strong young men entered, supporting a thin, elderly figure between them.

Everyone in the room stood.

The runners around me picked up Ivandred's, the jarlan's, and Lasva's dishes. Others appeared, a little out of breath, holding fresh dishes at the ready.

This old man was Haldren-Harvaldar, the Marloven king—the man who at least half of the male lancers and jarls were named after. I will refer to him as *the king*.

His face was seamed with lines, his skin burned as brown as tree bark. Though he limped heavily, he shook off the young men impatiently as he neared the table. Ivandred led the salute: the stone walls threw back the sound of hundreds of fists thumping wool-covered chests, making me think of arrows striking into hearts.

The king touched his fingers to his chest and lifted his chin in question. Ivandred stepped aside, so that the king could choose his place.

He stepped between his son and Lasva, then motioned impatiently. Everyone sat down, including Ivandred and Lasva as the king eased himself, wincing and grunting, onto the pillow that Ivandred had vacated.

As the hovering servants moved forward to set fresh dishes and cups before the king, he turned Lasva's way. His nose made Birdy's hawk beak seem delicate. "Let me sit next to the princess who picked my son out of all those prancers and dancers of the east. Heh! How did you win her, Van? Have you a hidden talent at romping about to tootle-music? How did you look trussed up in ribbons?" His laugh sounded like a whinny. "Tell me how a Marloven courts a Colendi. Or did you steal her, Van?"

"Contrary." Lasva tipped her head, hands at Oblique. "I stole him." She smiled, the dimples flashing.

The king pounded the table with his fist, setting the dishes jumping. His whinny deepened to a guffaw before he began coughing. "Damn!" He coughed again, and gasped.

"He, in his turn, protected our kingdom," Lasva said.

"Yes, Van will protect the kingdom. He'll ride the border again, heh!" The king coughed more, waved off his hovering runners, then gasped, "Eat, eat. D'you like my sister's food? Is it as good as what you eat there in Ribbon-Land?"

"It is very fine," Lasva said, nibbling a fragment of rye bread.

The king speared bits of turkey, roast potato, and greens, watching Lasva the while.

She had grown up being the focus of a room full of people, and her manners were superlative because she never flaunted them. Neatly, deftly, gracefully, she used the knife and spoon in the Marloven manner, as if she had always done so.

The king seemed bemused by her calm. When he spoke again, his voice was less harsh. "Heh! I like that sister of yours."

Lasva made The Peace. "She was well pleased with the alliance."

"She can use us as a stick to shake at those Chwahir north of her." The king whinnied a laugh that snarled into another coughing fit. "That's what happens with us here, our allies use the threat of us coming over the border to control their neighbors. He laughed and coughed harder, spraying bits of bread over his plate and part of the table. "But who was to know those damned Olavairs would back down after they found out about Van and you? I thought you people didn't have an army."

"We do not have such a thing organized," Lasva said. "But the nobles must serve if called upon."

"Either they're formidable from a distance, or it's your treaty prowess they're afraid of." He creaked with laughter, gulping as he tried not to cough. "I had the heralds bring me some history—" His voice hoarsened. "—and it seems you never met anyone over a treaty without your going away the winner, eh?"

Lasva smiled, hands open in self-deprecation. "In truth, my ancestors have worked hard to avoid conflict."

"And yet you haven't been ground to dust. If we didn't brandish swords left and right you can be sure our enemies would grind us to dust—eh, son?"

Ivandred struck his fist to his chest.

The king turned back to Lasva. "So, I hear someone down south gave you a little fun to break the journey."

Lasva bowed, hands at Harmony, and smiled.

The king eyed her, grinned, and turned to Ivandred. "I want your report on what happened at the river."

Ivandred's concise words were shorn of emotion. He ended with the numbers of dead and wounded, and then the number of dead on the other side, which caused the old man to crack out another whinny as he dipped a broken rye biscuit in the turkey juice. All the fear, the effort, seemed as distant as those bland numbers.

The king grunted from time to time. At the end, he poked the knife point toward Ivandred. "Who were those in green? Jevair vows they weren't his."

"They weren't. Too sloppy."

"Totha?" the king asked, leaning toward him.

"Perhaps, though it was not Totha forest-green. Dyed to look Jevair."

The king scowled. "Damned soul-rotted presumption!" He coughed and sat back. "I want you to go down there and crush Totha. It's time to remind the jarls that we keep our promises." He threw down the last bit of bread and opened his hand toward the room. "Here they are, the Western Ride under two flights of Fourth Lancers. They are not here just to eat up my sister's food and make merry now that you are home."

"The First Lancers?" Ivandred said.

The king's jaw worked. "In the north. Where they belong, watching those treacherous Olavair snakes. If you are any kind of commander, you can use what I give you. Go on! I want you back by Convocation! Olavair needs to hear that, ribbons or not, you haven't forgotten you are Marloven."

Ivandred stilled.

"I'll take your princess to the city, where she can use those Colendi treaty skills New Year's Week."

Ivandred rose and saluted. The old man saluted back then lifted his wine cup in both hands, slopping the red liquid as Ivandred gathered his commanders with a glance. The king slurped wine as Ivandred and all the warriors in the room except the king's guard clattered out, leaving some two hundred half-eaten meals, Ivandred issuing orders as they went.

When the king had drained the cup, he set it down, wiped his face on his sleeve, and whispered to Lasva, "Come, Colendi princess! Send your woman for your gear. Andaun gave me transfer tokens."

"Can you not let her rest, Brother?" Ingrid-Jarlan said.

"Heh! If I can stand it, she can." The king wheezed a laugh.

"May I summon my staff?" Lasva said, rising.

"Staff! What more d'you need? You're not commanding an army. I've got two women of yours already tearing up the old queen's suite. I gave them a free hand. Yes, I promised your sister, and I keep my word, as she'll discover. But you don't need another pack of women."

"If I may, I would like to explain to my people that I will send for them. May I take one, at least?" Lasva gestured my way. "My . . . my first runner?"

Marnda looked shocked, then her face mottled with anger.

The king waved a hand. "Yes, yes, first runner, of course! The rest can catch up by wagon. We'll find a use for 'em later."

The jarlan made a subtle signal with her forefinger, and her first runner handed her jug to me with a glance eloquent with apology, then touched her hand to her heart and beckoned with the other to Lasva. "I will show you the way."

Marnda followed close on their heels with a fearful, almost furtive look back, but no one paid her the least heed. I hesitated, then stooped to set the jugs on the table, my heart pounding. The king also ignored me and began to talk to his sister. His hoarse voice faded behind me as I ran to catch up with the others.

This time I did not struggle to conquer my anger with Marnda, determined to take my place. Indignant questions piled against my tongue: how could I possibly obey Queen Hatahra's orders if I was left behind? How would I catch up, if no one gave me a transfer token? How long would be this wagon ride, especially in winter?

When I reached the doorway to Lasva's chamber, Marnda was already pulling things together. After weeks of living in tents, we were all very good at fast packing and unpacking. I could tell Marnda knew I was there, but she did not even look at me, as if she could erase my existence by ignoring me. Lasva sped across the stone floor, her tiny, gliding, court steps so odd in this huge chamber with its fresco of stylized dancing horses. "Emras," she murmured, and in Old Sartoran, which Marnda did not know, "she fears that I am in danger, and she was my heart-mother all my life . . ."

What about the queen's orders? I looked past Lasva to where Marnda worked, her movements quick and sharp. Marnda knew my orders. Yes, she *did* know my orders. In the time it would take for me to catch up with them by conventional means, surely she would be able to watch out for signs of Norsunder as well as I could. (I was still feeling uncertain about magic.) Marnda was the one I had to talk to, anyway, in order to write to the queen.

All that was reasonable, but there remained the duty imperative. And yet here was Lasva, waiting for me to decide, as Marnda worked on desperately, as if her hands packing things would make her wish into reality.

It was Lasva's permitting me to decide that caused me to relent. This was a temporary separation, I reminded myself. And there was a good chance I could learn things from the king's sister.

I bowed my acceptance.

Lasva touched my hand. "Thank you."

Having established her place as Lasva's guardian, Marnda said to me, "We will make things ready for your arrival."

They left, going back to the hall, where a drum roll was in progress.

There was no purpose in my following. No one seemed to need me. So I stayed upstairs, where Anhar and Pelis met me. "What happened? Where are they going?" and finally, "Are we safe?" Anhar asked.

Pelis was picking up things Marnda had flung aside in her haste. She straightened up. "We're safe. Enough."

Anhar sat on the bed Lasva never got to sleep in, her hands clasped tightly. "What do you mean? Is Princess Lasva in danger?"

Pelis sighed. "It's happened just as Lnand said it might. Only it happened sooner than anyone thought. Anyone except old Marnda. As if she could scold that king into proper behavior!"

"What do you mean?" Anhar looked skeptical. "Prince Ivandred has to go back to that place we passed. That I understand. But at least the princess doesn't have to be in the middle of the fighting. So why is she in danger?"

I saw it then. "Lasva is a . . . " I groped for the right word.

"A hostage," Pelis said.

Anhar's eyes widened. "A hostage? I don't understand."

"Because the king sees love as a weakness, and Ivandred is in love. So the king can use her to control his son," Pelis said, hands warding Thorn Gate.

NINE

Of Secrets within Secrets

Next morning, one of the jarlan's runners summoned us to a room where we were startled to discover the rosebud carpet hanging on the wall like a tapestry. I stopped as if I'd walked into a wall and held my breath so that I would let no mirth escape.

How could I laugh at the jarlan for not knowing what the rosebud mat was for, when I could not identify the purpose of the room we'd been brought to? There was no bed or bath, yet it did not look like any parlor I'd ever seen. There was only the plain, low wood table surrounded by cushions. On the table lay a slate, chalk, some ink, and a rough-looking straw-colored paper. Until I'd entered this castle, I'd never considered how uncomfortable it would be not to know a room's purpose. I did not know where to position myself.

"This tapestry is very beautiful," the jarlan said, entering from a side room. "I will look at those rose shades all through winter, and be reminded of summer. However, your mistress only had time to give it to me and not to instruct any of us in the care of such delicate weaving. It seems too fragile to hang long, so does it remain up for a season? And when I store it away, should it be laid in with attar of roses?" She turned expectantly from me to Anhar to Pelis.

Anhar looked down, hands tightly pressed in The Peace. Pelis said, "Anything you wish, my lady, ah, Ingrid-Jarlan."

The jarlan uttered a short laugh, then said, "Let us try another trail." She turned to me. "Someone said you are a scribe. In this kingdom, scribes make copies. Why would a princess bring a scribe across the continent, unless she thought she was coming to a land of illiterates? Or do scribes serve different purposes in Colend?"

My guise now gone, I outlined scribe duties. She listened with the same narrow-eyed detachment I'd seen in Ivandred when he looked at the maps, then said, "If I had to define what I am hearing, and what I am not hearing, it seems that you are in fact the princess's first runner."

Not certain how to answer, I made The Peace.

"And so, Seneschal Marend, or Marnd—"

"Marnda."

"Marnda usurped your place because her function changed?" The jarlan leaned forward. "Or because your queen did not retain her?"

I hesitated, reluctant to suggest that Marnda thought Ingrid-Jarlan's brother, the Marloven king, the primary danger to Lasva. And Marnda's action had been so odd, so desperate, as if she could defend anyone! She'd sounded like a madwoman, or one bespelled. How to put any of that into words, especially in a language I knew so ill?

The jarlan drummed her fingers on the table, then said, "When the seneschal sees how big Choreid Dhelerei is, she will probably not want to be a runner. I expect you will be summoned soon, and all duties and perquisites will be straightened out. Before that time, perhaps you might employ yourself learning more of our language and custom. The archive is directly above us." She pointed toward the ceiling. "I will have someone open the vents." This was a clear dismissal, so I bowed and left as she turned to the dressers. "Now, for you two. Until I receive orders, I can put you to work, which will define *your* duties and perquisites while you are among us, but first, what exactly is it that 'dressers' do. . . ?"

The archive had once been part of a private suite for Ivandred's ancestors, at the front of the castle overlooking the main court. The doors were beautifully carved, animals in flight: raptors and horses.

The first door opened into a scrupulously clean chamber with that atmosphere of emptiness that suggested it was seldom used. The air was still and frigid. An old-fashioned bed framed with more wood carvings of horses was the only piece of furniture. I understood that the bed, alone in that bare room, was significant, but not how. Beyond it was another set of tall carved doors, and here I found the archive in a long room with high windows, below which shelves were set. Between these were narrow spaces where shields hung. The floor was bare stone, with two low tables in the center, the legs oddly shaped, like raptor legs, with talon feet. Flat cushions lay all around the tables.

I was surprised to find this archive at least as large as any in Colend. Were these hand-bound books and scrolls all about nothing but horses and war? I felt the first breath of heat from hidden vents. Sliding my hands inside the sleeves of my woolen robe, I walked along the shelves, which were not labeled as ours were. Small sigils along the top of each bookshelf indicated types: a lily above Twelve Towers' copies of royal records; a scroll for plays—none newer than a couple of centuries; a poppy for records of the lands along Halia's north shore. The adjacent wall turned out to be made up entirely of very old records of the Venn.

I decided to start with what I knew, which was *An Examination of Greatness*, my reasoning being that I was so familiar with the Sartoran translation, having rendered it in Kifelian, that if I read the original, I might master their language the faster. So I stopped at the crown sigil, which turned out to be extremely old records from the Iascan days. Most of it was written by either the once-royal family Cassadas, or their scribes. These were all previous to Elgar the Fox and his contemporaries. I did not find anything on Adamas Dei of the Black Sword, though I recalled references to his having lived somewhere in this region, or one nearby.

The bells clanged discordantly: midday. The entire morning was gone, and nothing to show for it but dust on my cold fingers.

I ran downstairs and spotted a pair of runners vanishing at the other end of one of the long halls. The prospect of returning to my search got me through a boring meal of cabbage rolls and rye biscuits. I knew no one, though I looked for stable hands, hoping I'd at least see Birdy. But maybe they had their own dining area.

After the meal, when I turned the wrong way down a hall, I spotted his dark hair among a lot of blond heads. He said in Kifelian as I neared, "We stable hands are in dormitories, too."

I did not tell him that I had a private room. I put my hands together to gesture commiseration.

He went on quickly, "But I get Restday evening free, and our perquisites—it's much like pay—extends to the town pleasure house."

"They celebrate Restday here?"

"That's what I was told. Anhar and I want to know if you will meet with us at Barleywine House at Hour of the Lamp?"

I signed assent and turned away, almost stumbling into the jarlan, who looked at me in surprise. I said quickly, "I thought I would compare *An Examination of Greatness* against the original, to learn your language the better. But I could not find it in the archive room. Is there another archive?"

"*Examination* . . . ah." She passed her fingers over her lower face, her gaze blank. Then she said, "You will find it under the eagle sign, at the very end."

"But does not that section begin a full century after the time in question?"

Her brows lifted. "You are observant. I did not think anyone knew our history outside of our own people! You will find it there because it is regarded as a record of instruction," she said.

I waited, and when she did not offer to explain further, I made The Peace and ran upstairs. The archive was empty and perceptibly warmer. I looked for the eagle sigil. When I found nothing labeled *An Examination of Greatness*, I took down each book one after the other, until I reached one called *Indevan of Choreid Elgar's Reorganization of the Academy, as dictated to Savarend Montredaun-An, the Fox*. And below that, a drawing that was just recognizable as the Fox Banner that Ivandred and his lancers carried, only the fox face was flatter, rounder, the ruff not flame-like but more like thistledown. It still had the strange bird eyes.

I opened it and found a life of Inda Elgar at the beginning, only compressed into a skimpy summary of the main events. Most of the book was detailed instructions for teaching warriors, right down to how meals should be served, and what the boys (it said boys) should wear.

None of this had been in the book I translated.

I paged back again, looking for one of the many Elgar battles so vividly described in the record that I had translated. I found one—with no details offered, only a reference to a ballad that used Someone's story based on Someone Two's letters. There was also a dismissive reference to another ballad sung to a "stolen" melody and riddled with errors in service to the Olavairs, like Elgar's having been born in Lorgi Idego. Idego? I remembered a place along the north coast of Halia had been called Iday-ago, but the Marlovens had changed the name to something else. Obviously the change of names during Elgar the Fox's day hadn't stuck.

I put the book back. How strange that there were what seemed to be two versions of the same record. Perhaps there was yet another.

The room was warmer, and I had nothing else to do. So I walked back to the shelves with the oldest ancestral records, and one by one took them out. The earliest were the toughest to read, being written in either a phonetic Old Sartoran that was spelled according to local pronunciation, or in Venn, which I'd once tried to learn on a dare, then never used again. Gradually the books appeared in a writing more recognizable as the modern Marloven, with Sartoran vowel marks. In none of these did I find references to Inda the Fox, though I found many instances of the names Indevan, Algara, Algara-Vayir, Choraed, and Elgaer.

I stopped when the ancient inks became impossible to read. Dark was falling swiftly. I looked around. No waiting glowglobes. Obviously this room was too seldom used to warrant such an expensive luxury. However, lanterns sat in protected sconces high up on the walls, waiting to be lit, and there were also trimmed lamps on the two central tables. I raised my hands, delighted with this chance to practice my fire spell. Then I glanced at the windows above—and realized my light would be seen from without. How foolish would that be, to hide my secret all this way, just to have all those guards on the castle walls see light flare in the row of windows?

So I dropped my hands. It was then that I sensed the elusive presence of magic.

I want it understood that at this point I could have abandoned this quest to find the missing record. I had little interest in Inda Elgar, and none in their war academy, either historically or presently. But the anomalies were interesting, and so was the presence of magic that could not be accounted for in a room full of books and scrolls.

The bells rang the watch change, which was also the call for supper.

The next morning was Restday. I returned to the archive, which was full of weak, wintry morning light.

Restday. I still carried Lasva's golden case. The Restday letters had tapered off to one every week or so from Darva, always asking how Lasva was. It had been a week since the last. I would have to check when I returned to my room.

I walked the perimeter of the archive, the only sounds my breathing, and the hiss of my house slippers on the stone floor. Shelf after shelf, row upon row of books filled with hidden secrets, lives I'd never heard of, actions and decisions and customs unknown. But at that moment my goal was to explore that hidden magic, not to read and to learn.

I closed my eyes and groped along the shelves, brushing my fingers high and low in slow deliberate arcs. When I reached the space between two of the bookcases, there was a brush of invisible silk.

I opened my eyes. The shelves were stocked with rolled maps on one side, and on the other, guild records. I'd walked past both several times. The wall between the shelves had the most boring of all the shields, flat, and dull. But when I tried to focus on the details it was indistinct. Illusion!

I stretched out my fingers . . . and they passed through the shield to brush stone. The sense of magic flared. I moved closer, felt for the illusion again, and found a pattern of what I can only describe as blue-ice points. I stepped back, committed the wall and the plain shield to memory, then snapped away the illusion. Before I did anything else, I remade the illusion. I'd never made one that lasted any longer than a bubble, but I knew how to do it.

It worked.

Behind the illusion, a door had been fitted into a plastered wall so neatly the outline was just barely visible, one end covered with stiffened paper to hide the hinges.

I looked around for a handle, then remembered the icy points. I brushed my fingers slowly over the door until I found the pattern.

Someone had gone to considerable trouble to hide this door. I hesitated, then shrugged away the implicit warning. I was curious, a puzzle-seeker, not a political conspirator. I would remove nothing, destroy nothing, I just wanted to solve this magical problem, because solving it would aid in my quest to understand magic and thereby to follow the queen's orders, even if I couldn't be with Lasva.

There was a great deal I had figured out about the book I'd memorized, extrapolating from how the fire spells worked. If you could summon fire, you could employ similar patterns but substitute water for fire. More difficult were the spells for shifting wood, and even stone.

That which could be burned could be changed. I'd worked my way mentally through most of this magic during that long journey in the wagon as I tended Fnor and Retrend. My knowledge was purely theoretical, as I hadn't been alone long enough to test any of it.

Here was a door ward. In the book it was listed as an elementary spell, but to a beginner like me, it presented almost insolvable difficulties. I say "almost" because I did solve it, after working past midday, missing Restday wine and bread, suspecting no one would think twice about my absence.

The shadows through the north windows were long and thin on the opposite walls when the door finally opened onto a narrow hallway.

Cold, dry air blew around my face, smelling of stone and paper. I ran back to the table, fetched a lamp, and lit it by magic before venturing into that hidden alcove.

The hall progressed a short distance then turned, revealing steep stairs that had to be above the hall outside this room and perhaps above the one with the empty bed. The ceiling of the upper corridor was low— I had to bend over. The air blowing along it was warm. After a few shuffling steps I wondered if I was in a very old set of vents. My neck and back ached and my legs shivered when at last the corridor ended at another stairway, and I stepped into a windowless room that contained a table, a glow globe, and two chairs. On the table lay a stack of paper and books. The air was warm and dry.

In the wavering lamp light I saw a slanted handwriting, brown with age, in that old Iascan alphabet:

An Examination of Greatness
(A Title Inda Would Have Despised)
Written as a cautionary as well as an instructive tale
for whoever comes after me

And in long, swooping letters:

Fox Montredavan-An

This was the original, then. Why was it kept in this secret room?

I lifted the top leaf. I had just enough time to make out the words *I first met Inda when he was ten, on his way to the academy in the year four* when a flicker at the edge of my vision caused me to look up as the stone wall on the other side of the table dissolved like a thousand black moths fluttering and breaking into ash.

Cold air eddied into the secret chamber, bringing a complication of scents: cedar, bergamot mint, and a hint of smoke. Just writing those words prickles the hairs on the back of my neck. As long as I live, I will never forget that smell.

At the time, I was startled, and embarrassed to be caught where I had no business being: I could of course have no notion that I was about to meet the sixth of those important people I mentioned at the beginning of this testimony, whose lives, in crossing mine, brought me to my prison.

A man walked through the wall I'd believed to be solid and gave me an amused glance. He was about Ivandred's height and built much the same—on the slender side—moving with that economical control, the habit of readiness that I would discover characterized those who've had a lifetime of training in defense.

Other than that he was nothing extraordinary to look at—his skin was the brown of most folk, hair a few shades darker and tied back simply, his robe of light gray old-fashioned weave, done in the interlocking chain pattern that had been popular centuries before. Eyes hazel, a color common in that part of the world.

"I wondered if you might find your way here," he said. "Though I did not expect it to be within a day." He spoke as if we'd known one another all our lives.

"Are you Sigradir Andaun?"

His eyes crinkled briefly. "No. Ivandred calls me Herskalt. It will suffice."

At least, I thought gratefully, this is not the most dangerous man besides the king. "Herskalt? May I be permitted to ask if this is a title or a name?"

"Think of me as a tutor," the man said. "And so you may ask your questions."

"Thank you. Did you have some kind of ward on this record? I was seeking it just to find the original," I explained. "I intended to learn the Marloven language by comparing it to one I translated."

"Yes, I am aware of that particular version. If you are curious, the one you translated is Princess Tharais's attempt to shorten the one you see before you, leaving out the entire point of it, which was how to educate Marlovans." He pronounced the word the way that Prince Macael had, *Mar-LO-vahn*, and not *MAR-lo-venn*, as did everyone else. "So much of what Fox described has become family tradition, though that has changed in recent generations, as you will no doubt discover."

I said, "You know who I am."

"Of course," the Herskalt replied, hands opening in an ironic mimicry of Harmony. "I did tell you we would talk, did I not?"

Now I recognized that voice. "You are the healer! You spoke Sartoran."

The Herskalt snapped his fingers, and the shadowed entryway behind him was replaced by stone. "From our conversation so far, it is clear that you require practice in Marloven."

The air around me tingled as the Herskalt sat down in one of the winged chairs. "I want to know why you kept your heroic effort at the bridge a secret. That was truly impressive magic, young scribe."

"How do you know I had anything to do with that spell?"

"The residue of magic was still on you, and Ivandred did not perform those spells. There was no one else who could have. You used your skills effectively. Yet you permitted the prince to attribute your admirable effort to unknown mages."

I did not know what authority he had, though he obviously had magical knowledge. If he was connected to the Sartoran Council, surely he would give me some sign—mention Greveas—maybe refer to the ring on my toe, which no one had seen outside of the bath. Oh yes, did not Haldren-Harvaldar forbid the guilds from contact with their Marloven brethren?

"I am not a mage," I said finally. "I chanced to learn a few things. I've had no training."

"That," he said, "was evident. I am endeavoring to determine whether it would be worth my while to instruct you. Why do you want to learn magic?"

I was preparing some words about academic curiosity when he said, "Permit me to rephrase: why do you want to learn magic outside of the established process?"

"To understand it," I said.

"Not to use it?" He was skeptical. "Yet you used it at the border."

"That was an emergency."

"So you would put it to use in emergencies?"

"Yes," I said thankfully, for that accorded with the queen's orders and with my own conscience. "*Only* in emergencies."

"And yet you do not want to return to Alsais, or go to Sartor, and go through the established process."

I remembered Olnar's description of his studies—how long it had taken. I thought of being sent to the kitchen for six months, and though it had been valuable in many ways, when I'd returned, if it hadn't been for Birdy, I would have lost my sense of place. How much worse would that be now? "I would love to learn it on my own, if I may. I know how to study."

"Very well, then. I will match lesson to student. When you can figure out how to transfer to this room, I will commence teaching you. That sloppy door spell down in the archive will be replaced. Find your way here and read that record. We will then proceed."

I controlled the urge to exclaim that it had taken me an entire day to figure out how to get past that secret door—and that no one used the archive, so why go to the trouble of replacing a ward? I did not know the custom of this castle any more than I knew magic. So I made The Peace, and said what was topmost in my mind, "I would be grateful if you would honor me with your reasons for offering to teach me."

He smiled. "As I said, I am a tutor, and presently there are no household students to teach. And you will put your magic to use in emergencies. This kingdom is going to have need of such skills, as you will no doubt soon discover."

He made a gesture that seemed casual to me—fingers moving slightly in a pattern too quick to catch—and vanished, leaving the air to ruffle that secret room, disturbing the pages of the record.

I bent over it and began to read, at first with difficulty because of the old orthography and phrasing, but as always, persistence caused me to sink into it until I began to see and feel a different time and way of looking at the world. It was a way I did not relish, and the Inda in this record began to make me wonder who Birdy might have been if he were born in Inda's time and place.

Birdy! I was supposed to meet him and Anhar in the village! As soon as this thought floated to the top of my consciousness, I also became aware of tired eyes and a stiff neck. How long had I been reading? This room was located so deeply within the structure of the castle that I could not hear the bells. I replaced the ancient pages with meticulous care and, without much hope, moved to the wall that had seemingly dissolved. Yes, it was solid stone. Perhaps there was a room adjacent, one that might even have a door, but I wasn't going to find it today.

I made my way back through the vent, dusty and webby as it was, and thence to the door. At least it had a latch on the inside. I opened it to find the archive in darkness. How late was it?

I shut the door and fled to the bath.

As I emerged, the watch-change bells rang. I had missed the evening meal and whatever ritual the Marlovens shared for Restday. Dressed but still damp, pulling on my outerrobe as I ran, I made my way downstairs wondering how I could get to the bottom of the mountain. My frantic run eased when I heard laughing voices from the direction of the servants' area. I ran past the drying rooms and found a small stable yard where runners and kitchen people were climbing into a wagon hitched up to plough horses.

"Going to Darchelde Town?" someone addressed me.

"Yes," I said, thankful as someone pulled me up into the wagon and more people crowded in behind me.

In all the weeks we'd traveled with the prince and his lancers I had never heard as much laughter as I did on that journey down to the trade town. The talk was entirely ordinary—who was seeing whom, cranky chiefs, anecdotes about odd or annoying fellow workers. Then a girl pulled out a hand drum and rapped a complicated tattoo to which others began to sing a rousing ballad in a style completely unlike the subtle melodies I was used to. The rhythm counterpointed the drum beat, and the rise and fall of the melody echoed the trumpet chords we'd heard from time to time.

I discovered that this was the last wagon, that the castle people were expected to report for pickup to the town's bell tower before the dawn bells.

The town was crowded with locals and castle people. Drum beats and singing issued from doorways as they opened and closed. The town square was bounded by shops and stables. Except for the stable, Barleywine House was the largest building, people spilling out into the frigid night air, drinking, talking, and laughing. I dodged my way through the crowd, standing intermittently on tiptoe to search.

A few people glanced at me in surprise, and one woman said, "What's your game, Blue Robe?"

I dashed on past, frantic again—then a hand touched my shoulder. I looked up into Birdy's happy face. Even his ears seemed part of his grin. "You're here." At his shoulder was Anhar, her glossy black hair startling among so many light-colored heads.

I grinned back, ready for a pleasant evening of talk and good food and whatever music Marlovens had to offer.

Then Birdy said, "I arranged for a room."

"Privacy at last," Anhar said, hands opening in the flower gesture signifying joy.

Privacy. My pleasant anticipation turned into the heavy inward tightening of disappointment, even alarm. I tried to speak, but the crowd had thickened. Marlovens were oblivious to shadow custom, and if there were rules for deference, they were not apparent. With determined politeness Birdy used his height to navigate, repeating "Pardon my trespass," over and over, as Anhar and I trailed in his wake.

"Hah, foreigners!" A young man gave a laugh full of meaning.

"A threesome? Hail the peacocks!" his companion responded, and Birdy reddened as he made The Peace.

We passed the common room, which was a roar of noise and thick with the smells of food and ale.

Anhar was flushed and smiling. For her, this was the best moment of a long, dreadful trip, and she tingled from head to heels, though she looked my way from time to time. She was puzzled by my behavior. Until the fight at the bridge, I had kept my distance, though I was never condescending in word or action. When she'd tended me, she'd broken the invisible barrier against touch, and I had not rejected the most intimate attentions.

And so . . . what did that mean now? One more flight of stairs. "The workers have the rooms on the second floor," Birdy said in apology. "But we're almost there."

The place was scrupulously clean, yet there was an undertone to the scents, an unfamiliar, musky undertone, not quite like clothes too long worn on a summer's day, but close. I did not like it.

The door Birdy sought had three poppies painted on it. There was a bed on a platform and, behind an alcove, raised off the floor, a rudimentary bath—that is, it was small, made of wood with porcelain or ceramic tile inside. But the water was hot, and the edges of the tub glittered with the promise of the water being clean via the same magic spell used on baths, buckets, wells, and city canals the world over.

We crowded into the tiny chamber, laughing at the tub. I'd known Birdy since I was small; we had been private but never intimate. This was new territory. I felt crowded, uncomfortable, at the very same moment the other two were aflame with desire. All the world had shrunk to this moment and this space.

Birdy was waiting for us to move first. So we stood there, looking at the tub, and when the silence had grown, I looked up, and there was my own question in his face. In her face.

He grinned again. "Ah-ye."

He reached for me first and so quickly that this moment, although meant to be tender, was desperate and clumsy—our teeth bumped—I backed away, my hands up. Birdy regarded me in dismay, but then Anhar crossed in front of me, so all I saw was her long, glossy braid, clean-smelling, rinsed with expensive herbs she must have hoarded against just such a moment.

I ducked behind her, glad to relinquish proximity—someone trod on my toes. I fled to the door, then paused with one look back as Birdy hopped on one foot as he tried to kick off his trousers, then fell over, catching Anhar by the ankle. She whooped with laughter, and it was apparent what was going to happen—and that they were not even going to make it to the bed.

I flung myself out, then leaned against the door, my body clammy with revulsion.

I held my arms tightly against me.

Love had bloomed—of a kind. I was very sure that I was in love with Birdy. Thinking about our conversations made me feel air-light, drenched me with color, and I liked to linger over his image in every detail, from his old tunic to his hair escaping from his braid in tufts, and his big ears, his beak of a nose. He was Birdy, but when he was close to me, his breath hot and shaky, his hands reaching, I wanted peace and air.

For the first time, I comprehended that love, at least for me, had nothing to do with sex. I was *elor*—I didn't want him, or her, or anyone. Not in that way.

TEN

Of the Riding Moon

I took the first cart back to the castle, leaving them to follow as they would. The next time I saw Birdy, he addressed me as if nothing had happened. "Emras. How are things progressing?"

"I met the prince's tutor. I have new books to read."

"Excellent!" He began backing hastily away. "On duty now. But I wanted to see you . . ." His hands rose, but a crowd of runners walked between us, and I did not see the gesture. When they'd passed, he was gone.

So I retreated to my little bedroom to continue my experiments.

Fourthday, the first blizzard of winter struck. I scarcely noticed, for by then I had transferred enough bits of paper that I attempted to shift a cushion from platform to the bed. When the internal wrench died away, I knew I was going to try to shift myself next, in spite of my dry mouth and unsteady limbs.

If you judges are also mages, you understand the danger of which I was so blithely unaware. I did know, as everyone does, that transfer is risky, which is why we have Destinations. When one pulls something out of the world, there must be a specific place to reinsert it. Without specificity there is the threat of the object being lost outside of the world. Vexing if it's some*thing*, deadly if it's some*one*.

I had no idea that magic students are not permitted to transfer for at least three years, sometimes longer. Some are never deemed able to learn. And there I was, given transfer as a goal, untaught, as my first lesson.

"Fit the lesson to the student." I'd been challenged, that was all I knew.

As a scribe, I was taught to be methodical. I wanted badly to write everything out, but I resisted the impulse. One encounter with the king was enough to make plain that that danger had been foreseen. If his whim led to my personal effects being searched, there must be nothing to find but Lasva's scrollcase.

I used that scrollcase to experiment on, transferring bits of paper to the desk and back again. Then I tried larger objects. I knew exactly what to focus on: Fox's record. I could so clearly see that slashing handwriting, the aged-gold papers. Speaking rapidly, I performed the transfer—

—and magic punched me through stone and steel, or so it felt. I tumbled over the top of the table, onto the memoir. Pages delicate with age crackled warningly beneath me. Appalled, I struggled up, swallowing hastily as I recovered. When I could stop my hands from shaking, I carefully straightened the pages. There was enough linen content in that paper to spare it from my rough entry.

I sat down and resumed reading, skimming over battles. When I came to a conversation about magic, I bent close, puzzling out the old-fashioned hand and the outdated language. Venn—magic—and what was this? Mages who . . . ?

At first I could not believe that I had the right words. When I read a little farther, horror bloomed in tendrils of ice through my chest: I *had* read correctly. The Venn mages had used magic to kill people by transporting rocks into the center of their victims' chests.

I dropped the pages, sick with nausea. I was determined not to read any farther.

The air flickered, and there was the Herskalt. I stared at him, breathing hard as I tried to find a neutral way to express my repudiation of that record. He did not look at the pages. His attention was on me. "Perhaps we should begin with a review of what you *do* know," he said, as if we'd seen one another only moments before.

I took a moment to breathe in and out, to regain my equilibrium. The scribes' First Rule prevented me from offering an opinion of his record. It was an historical artifact. My opinion of it was not required.

Matching my manner to his, I began to recite my memorized book. A short way in, he held up his hand. "I see. You have committed to memory an instructor's private text, without comprehending the basic knowledge underlying it, or how to put this knowledge to use."

"I've figured out some of it," I said.

He seemed amused, though his expression did not change. "I gather you wish to achieve higher magical knowledge, without undergoing the tedium of what the Mage Council calls the Basics. These are what the young mage students term 'Bells and Spells,' because of the tricks of memorization and the simple spells designed to accustom mages to employing magic."

"I know how to memorize and to study."

"If you expect to understand anything about the higher level magics, you need to know what the lowest water-speller or wandmaker knows. So I will give you a set of spells without the bells."

His air was one of patience, his implication it would take a week—a month—to master what he gave me. I was back the next day, the only challenge being the transfer.

He walked through the wall. "You are trying to impress me with your diligence," he observed. "Will you remember anything next week or next month?"

"I know about quick memory and long memory," I said, and made The Peace so I would sound conscientious and not peremptory. "I will repeat the lessons until they settle in long memory. May I ask what manner of illusion you employ for dissolving that wall between this room and the one beyond?"

His smile deepened. "What convinces you there is a room beyond?"

"The vents in this castle have been partially rebuilt since the old days of wood fires, before fire sticks. Some of the vents seem to have been made into chambers. Like this one we sit in now. Also, there is the fact that you arrive without demonstrating the effects of transfer, which makes me think there is some step between illusion—where one sees a wall but feels nothing but air, as had been the case in the archive below—and actual transformation."

"Very observant indeed," he said. "I commend your teachers for their skill in training an effective mimic."

"Mimic?"

"You say you wish to help this kingdom in emergencies." He tapped the Fox memoir. "Yet you did not trouble yourself to thoroughly read this record that engages with your princess's new kingdom." So he was aware of my skimming? Once again I began rehearsing words that would appear neutral, yet still express my total disengagement with his record, but he went on. "That suggests that the magic you wish to learn is the easy trickery: gathering sunlight into glowglobes or purifying water. Perhaps creating air tunnels to the sky on hot days, to bring down the cooler breezes."

Now was the time to offer the first of my rehearsed reasons. "I do not see the utility in reading details about ancient wars, fought according to ancient custom. Such things are not just unpleasant but uncivilized."

"The Colendi being the pinnacle of 'civilized.'" He betrayed amusement in the crinkle of his eyes, though his demeanor remained serious.

I thought of diplomatic qualifiers to mask my conviction that we were at least more civilized than the Marlovens, but he raised a casual hand. "'Mine is superior to yours' is never a fruitful discussion, whether the subject is governments or ways of baking bread. I wonder if you were so busy skipping the details of battles (admittedly there are many) you also missed the discussions of statecraft and power. Is it more civilized to educate one's sister as a commodity to be sold, rather than as a war chieftain?"

Now he was talking about *my* history. And not just history, but people known to me. "Queen Hatahra did not educate her sister as a commodity to be sold," I retorted.

"Then you must tell me why she saw to it that Lasthavais's days were filled with lessons in art, dance, music, and deportment, with nothing said about statecraft; and why she was surrounded by maternal women whose positions depended on their anticipation of the princess's every want, so she would never have the time or the inclination to look past the surface of Hatahra's power?"

"That isn't true," I stated. "I was there, and the princess told me everything. I was in sight of the queen when she spoke with Princess Lasthavais nearly a year ago, at the New Year's ball, and the princess came straight from that conversation to me to repeat it. The queen had always intended to have an heir. She told the princess that if an heir was not born within a year, then lessons in statecraft would commence. Before then, she wanted Lasva to have a good life, the life she never had."

"How many of the queen's words have changed between leaving her lips and reaching my ears?"

"How much does anything remain free of the *hearer's* interpretation?" I countered, for we scribes had long lessons in this matter, from the very beginning. That was one of the reasons why we drilled so diligently in parroting—so that we would not alter the speech of others.

"Not at all," the Herskalt said. "Or effectively nothing. Which is why I always go to the source of important moments, if I can."

"If there was a way to do that, there would be no scribes. Or written records."

"There is a way. But it is rare, and even when one is in possession of the means, not all are able to endure the method."

"To gain the truth, I would endure much." Giddy with the possibilities, I made a full Peace deference. "Please teach me."

"Let us approach the question from a parallel path. You say that the princess told you everything."

"Everything of import, yes."

"We shall test that statement."

From a pocket inside his robe he brought forth a thin disc of what I took, at first, to be metal. It lay in the hollow of his palm like a pool of ice-filmed water, the light reflection too diffuse for metal, but more lucent than stone. The more I looked at it, the more my attention drew downward. I caught myself and rocked back. My body reacted as if I'd been falling nose downward, but I hadn't. Nausea curled inside of me, but I controlled it with my breathing, eyes closed.

Then I held my breath and looked again, my hands braced on the table to convince my body that I was not falling. It was not a pool, it was a disc, the hand did not move, *I* did not move—so my mind repeated until the whisper of other voices caught my attention, and the silver filled my vision, then closed around me like a circle of light.

. . . I heard Lasva's voice as if inside my own head: *Let me tell you about my beauty. I've never told anyone this, outside of—when I was, oh, about ten, and as full of self-importance as a child is who has discovered what rank means and what admiration means.*

It was Lasva's voice, but no words I had ever heard. Yet from the flickers of image, the sounds, even the smells, it was recent . . .

Have you ever slipped into a pair of someone else's shoes? You know immediately they are not yours, even if the size is. Now imagine your mind thrust inside someone else's skull, with all their experiences imbuing each thought with unfamiliar associations and emotional reactions that fit strangely. Even the smell of cinnamon is different for someone else.

I steadied myself firmly on the table as my mind worked to separate the images that had never belonged to me from images of my own. The former were now mine in memory, but encased by the *Lasva memories*: the painting gallery, Ivandred standing an arm's length away, looking at "me" with the ardency I'd only seen in him when he regarded Lasva. Smells, sounds, words, experienced differently from the way I would:

she was far more aware of scent than I, but not as sensitive to sound. Her words seemed to come from inside my head, but I had no control over them, and they shaped differently. My identity fractured as my mind struggled to separate *me* from *Lasva*, even while it accepted her memories as my own. Nausea clawed up the back of my throat. I whispered the Waste Spell as sweat broke out all over me in a painful tingle that turned cold.

I had self again. We were separate, Lasva and me. Her memories were *her memories*, even if I now shared them.

I opened my eyes, and met the watchful gaze of the Herskalt. "How is this possible?" I whispered.

"It is possible for those who have the discipline," he said. "And the training. Want the rest of that conversation?" His smile deepened. "Because we now both know that your princess did not, in fact, tell you everything."

Ambivalent, almost flinching, I still could not help but turn my expectant gaze back to the silvery pool in his palm, and this time the fall into the disc was swifter.

The images of the portrait of Lasthavais Dei the Wanderer echoed as if seen in facing mirrors: there were Lasva's memories of her ancestor's portrait, as the queen-consort of centuries ago danced a village jig while hiking up her exquisite brocaded skirts. Lasva had many memories of that portrait, for she'd visited it over and over from the time she was small, and those memories flickered past me, quick as flame. Then I was back, facing Ivandred.

Emotions chased through Lasva, as strong as taste, color, and smell: regret, rueful laughter, gentle mockery. And over it all a desperate hunger to will the attraction she felt for Ivandred into love.

"So I listened to this catalogue of my flaws: eyebrows too faint, nose too pointed, upper lip this, lower lip that, ears not quite another thing, until they had thoroughly assessed every single feature, then they moved on, leaving me feeling like . . . like a commodity handled in the marketplace."

She looked up at Ivandred, the hunger so acute and so painful I was flung out of the circle—then caught and flung back. I perceived the Herskalt shaping the perception, creating a bubble of awareness around me.

Then he let the bubble pop, and I gazed down into Lasva's face from a perspective I'd never had in life: from a taller person's view, one who noticed the length of her eyelashes, the shudder of her bosom beneath the flimsy gown. It was a distinctively male awareness. His senses organized differently from mine, with a strong erotic component that sent a thin thread of fire through my vitals, the urgency more painful than pleasant. Even more disturbing was the echo of his thought, a memory of the Herskalt's wry voice, *Most foreign kings and queens make speeches. They want to be remembered, and no one will tell them, or can tell them, how very boring they sound.*

Voice distorted into mushy loudness, and once again my identity shredded, now going three ways, tumbling between the "now" of the scene, the now of my body crouched in the hidden chamber, and the then of three people's memories. I was propelled out of the circle, into swimming black motes.

And I found myself lying on the stone floor. Excruciating pain lanced through my head at the tiniest move. For a time I could only listen to my own breathing, evaluating each one. This breath was a good one, the next bad. I tried to move. My stomach surged. Another good breath. A third, deeper.

Gradually my awareness included the wash-and-thump of my heart, which sent counterpoint pangs hammering in my skull. The nausea quieted, the pain eased enough for me to become anxious about lying there alone on the floor. Where was the Herskalt? Would he really leave me there to die?

No. Teachers did not do that.

It's a test.

I knew all about unexpected tests. I'd endured six months of one, and as a result became first choice for royal scribe.

I could overcome this pain. It took a long time to achieve a sitting position, though I had to grip the leg of the table for the world swung and hitched so mercilessly I knew I couldn't stand. *And I still have to transfer.*

No, I couldn't bear that. I opened my eyes a crack and caught sight of something lying on the table beside the Fox manuscript. It was a slim book. I slid my fingers over it, then tried to fully open my eyes.

No one knew where I was, and I had not eaten or drunk anything. The pain in my head nearly struck me unconscious again. I was just able to sweep the book off the table. I lay down again, the book clutched to me, and slid into sleep.

When I woke, I braced myself and underwent a transfer, straight to my bed, then slept again. I woke feeling feverish and clammy, my skin sensitive, my eyes confused by a gradual change in the room: dawn.

I made it to breakfast. After a few bites of bread and some water, I began to recover.

Nobody showed the least interest in my having missed meals. They went about their daily affairs as if I did not exist. I did not see Birdy walking the outer hall, which meant the weather had cleared enough for the animals to be exercised again. So I returned to my bedroom and opened the book. It was entirely written in Old Sartoran. Another test!

It was tedious and difficult. The language was archaic, and the magic concerned binding ships against water, mold, and other types of damage. This knowledge was nothing I would ever use, and for that first day, as the headache slowly diminished, I wrestled with impatience. But work steadied me, and when I became accustomed to the rhythms of the words and the antique turns of phrase, I began to gain a rudimentary awareness of how magic must balance against the natural inclinations of things to fall, or to be rent apart by forces such as wind, waves, and weather.

The days were marked by study and by the occasional glimpse of Birdy, who always seemed to be busy.

When I finished the book, I transferred to the secret chamber, where I found a new book, thinner than the Old Sartoran ship preservation text. It was written in more modern Sartoran: spells for securing a forge and for separating and returning to the ground the impurities caused by smelting. This topic was even more tedious than ship-binding, but again I found myself absorbed.

Birdy was an indistinct and bulky object in the drifting snow, yet I knew him at once. Only his eyes were visible between his muffler and knit hat, but the tiny lift to his brows sent warning through me. Something was wrong. He had been on the watch for me when I crossed the small court between the stable hands' wing and ours.

He bent toward me, murmuring in our language, "When the prince arrives, I'm to go with them to Choreid Dhelerei, the royal city."

My throat constricted. We stood so close together to avoid the howling wind, that I can still recall the pale blue light on his profile, nestled within the muffling of his scarf, coat, and hat, as well as the tiny gleam of reflected light in his pupil, the way his jaw moved, and the vibration of his voice in his chest, next to my ear.

I said, "I am sorry you are going."

"You are?" he asked, and the disbelief in his voice chilled my nerves.

"I am," I said. "Come inside. We have a sitting room for staff, just inside that door."

There were a few others in the room. We found a small table opposite the fire and sat down at either side. He stretched out a hand then pulled it back and flushed. "Anhar says . . ." He hesitated.

"That I am *elor*?" I asked.

"Is it true?"

"I think so. That is, I haven't really thought about it since I was fifteen or sixteen, and all of you went off to the pleasure houses without me. When I did finally go, all I wanted was the company. Nothing more. And gradually . . ." I shrugged.

"You don't feel anything?" He leaned forward, his forehead wrinkled. "I feel something for you. I can understand if I'm not attractive . . ."

"I love you," I said. "I think. I'm pretty sure. I just don't want physical love."

Birdy sat there, eyes averted, hands loose. Then he turned back. "I don't know what I feel," he admitted. "I think I grew up wanting you, before I even knew what want was. I don't know if I can love without . . ." He opened his hands. "Without all of it."

"What about Anhar?"

"What about her? She knows how I feel." He ran his fingers back and forth along the edge of a table, as if he must touch something. "I know how she feels. We started with homesickness. Though she was glad to leave." He looked away, as if reluctant to reveal things told him in intimate moments. Then he continued softly, "We both missed Colend in unexpected ways. Every time I ride out . . ." He was barely audible over the rise and fall of a ballad that someone in another room was singing, punctuated by laughter and the tap of drums. ". . . I see the same pale sun riding low in the north, and it throws me back to riding when I was a boy."

"Riding?" I asked.

"I first saw the moon ride the horizon when my mother put me on a horse. When I think back to my visits home I see bare hawthorn and smell the evergreen on the cold air. I hear the ice, like broken glass, no, like crystal wind chimes, running in the streams." His voice was slow, and dreamlike.

"Tell me about your mother," I said. "I know nothing about your family. You remember, how we were not to speak of such things at scribe school, so that those whose families were not traditionally scribes would not feel left out."

Surprise twitched through him. "And you obeyed? Ah-ye, most of us spoke as we pleased, we just knew better than to brag. My mother trained horses for the Baron Lassiter until a whole year went by and she still wasn't paid. That was when their household broke up. My mother chose to go to Sarendan with the baroness and her daughter. I visit when I have home leave. You would like Sarendan, I think. I hear that it's as beautiful as Sartor."

"Baron Lassiter!" I thought of Lasva's romance. "How well did you know any of the Lassiters?"

"Only saw them if they showed up wanting to ride. My sister and I spent most of our time in Alsais with my uncle, who started our scribe training early so we'd be selected at the testing."

"And you were chosen."

"Along with you."

"But when you went to your mother, you learned about horses."

"All New Year's Week we rode and rode, no matter how much it snowed."

The queen had known about Birdy's background, but I hadn't. I thought about that, and about how strange it is that one can read and read about the many kinds of love, but only experience teaches one to widen one's perceptions to include another.

ELEVEN

Of Mercy

"What is the news from home?" Pelis would ask from time to time, always in a whisper and with sideways glances.

It took no insight to comprehend that she was hungry for crumbs from Colend, so I gave her the gossip gleaned from Lasva's scrollcase, the only two items of import being that Ivandred's cousin Prince Macael had returned to Colend to visit court ("He wants someone like our princess," Pelis observed, and added, "but there isn't anyone like her.") At the end of the month came the news that Macael and Ananda were to return to Enaeran to wed.

"Lady Ananda," Pelis said, kissing the backs of her fingers in Willful Blindness. "Did you know her own servants call her Lady Demanda? How long before that pretty Enaeraneth prince regrets *that?*"

———

Birdy and Anhar vanished on Restdays, so I studied the magic lessons I found waiting for me each time I transferred to the chamber: how to purify water; the capture of sound; the formation of a cleaning frame.

The Herskalt himself came once, and I asked to learn about wards instead of all this basic stuff I would never use even in an emergency. He replied without any sign of emotion, "Review the definition of emergency." And his assignment? To make a fire stick by myself.

That meant finding a suitable piece of wood and then repeating the sunlight-gathering spell over and over during daylight hours, then focusing it down to a spark. At least a thousand times.

After that, my lesson was in the construction of a cleaning frame, which was enormously complicated magic.

On the morning after I reported to the Herskalt the success of my cleaning frame, I went in to breakfast. When I'd been sitting there a while, the dining room went silent.

I'd begun sitting alone. I knew it was absurd. I knew that Anhar and Birdy (when he was there) would include me if I sat with them, but there was this part of me that wanted them to seek me out—to value me as me, though I was not a sex partner for either of them.

I heard Anhar's light voice on the other side of the room and forced myself not to look, though there was that in her tone that convinced me she sat with Birdy. I closed myself mentally into lesson review so thoroughly that I was startled out of it by the rap of heels on the stone floor—a sound distinct in the sudden silence.

I turned on my cushion just as Ivandred reached me. Too many years of training forced me into a deep bow. Then I remembered that Marlovens do not bow and jerked upright. So powerful was Ivandred's presence that no one laughed as I accidentally knocked my cup to the floor.

Ivandred gave me a slight smile, then said, "The Haranviar has asked me to bring you to Choreid Dhelerei." "Haranviar" was their title for a crown princess. "We depart as soon as we change the horses and eat." He was mud-splattered to the waist, his hat spangled with melting snowflakes.

I fled, rejoicing. I would be traveling with Birdy, I would see Lasva again—she had asked for me! Oh, the joy of knowing there is a welcome, that one is wanted! I would—

I would no longer be learning magic.

I stopped. The disappointment was so sharp I just stood there, a hand braced against the smooth plaster of the wall. Then I thought, *I transfer to the chamber by magic.* So the Herskalt lived in Darchelde? Transfers could be done from anywhere in the world, though I understood that the longer the transfer, the harder it was physically. But people did it all the time. I had done it, when I went south from Alsais to Ranflar each New Year's Week to visit my parents, though I'd used a transfer token. I did not think that the relative distances were all that different, and the spell was second nature by now.

These thoughts took no more than a pair of heartbeats, then he said, "Tell the rest of your people." And he walked away.

So I would not lose my magic lessons, I thought happily as I ran up-stairs to tell Anhar and Pelis and to pack up my few belongings.

As soon as I reached the courtyard, Lnand and Tesar emerged from the gloom, bulky in their snow-stippled winter gear, their noses red and faces scarf-hidden. "How is Retrend?" one asked, and the other, "How is Fnor?"

I gave them a quick report on the two, who were recovering steadily, then:

"Mount up," Haldren called.

As the noon bells clanged we clattered out of Darchelde's great court, the walls lined with people in spite of wet, sloppy snow. Ivandred sa-luted the towers and the gate, and then we were off.

We each had horses to ourselves. Birdy rode directly behind us. Knowing he was there made me a little less afraid. I hadn't spared a single thought for Tesar since we'd first arrived at the castle, but I missed her steadying presence as I rode.

How soon we forget unpleasant things! The unending cold, the dis-comfort of fast riding, the horrible travel food, had faded out of mind. Each came back with an unpleasant jolt.

We rode hard that day. The prince had sent scouts ahead so that fresh horses were waiting, which meant a great deal of galloping.

It was difficult to see anyone inside the bulky woolen hats, mufflers, gloves, coats, and the like. As the sun set, and we slowed not to camp but to change horses again, I overheard someone cursing and the tail end of someone else saying, ". . . dead long before New Year's."

I remembered what the king had ordered: *I want you back by Convocation!* Ivandred was expected to execute his orders and cross half the kingdom by New Year's Firstday. But that was only three days off. I'd seen the big map on the wall down in the dining room enough times to gauge distances. Even if we galloped all the time, we could not possibly reach Choreid Dhelerei in three days.

We rode through the night, torches streaming.

The first dawn was bleak and blue. I shivered with cold, hands and feet numb. Ivandred called a halt at last when we reached a frozen river. A check made it clear that we could get across, we did not have to seek a bridge.

As the warriors dismounted to lead the animals across the ice, I became aware of squeaking snow near me, and hoped to find Birdy. Instead, Ivandred gazed down at me through bloodshot eyes as he clutched a carefully wrapped roll of cloth against his chest.

"Come," he said hoarsely.

Too cold and tired for anything beyond the briefest spurt of astonishment, I bent into the wind and followed him some paces away, until we lost sight of the others. The howl of the wind guaranteed we would not be overheard.

"We can talk here." I could only see his blue eyes, which seemed so expressionless to me as he went on, his breath clouding, "The Herskalt says that he is teaching you."

"Yes." I made The Peace. "Our queen ordered me to watch over her sister, and learn about magic if I could."

His head turned. I saw how exhaustion-marked his eyes were. I could see the effort it took for him to speak.

"Yes," he said finally. "I learned magic for the same reason. To protect the kingdom. My father . . . does not know."

So that's why the Herskalt lived at Darchelde, I thought.

Ivandred looked around. "He said you read Fox's record."

"I read some of it," I said, hoping he was not about to examine me on its details.

He shrugged, his arm holding the rolled cloth protectively against him. "There is the Marlovar Bridge," he said.

Snow obscured all but an arched line over the river.

"I used to come here often," he continued, "whenever I rode either way. By transfer, once I learned how. Somewhere nearby was where Inda hid. He was not quite twelve. Saw the shape of the attack. Within four years he was famed over the world. At sixteen, I . . ." He gazed into the whirling white of the departing blizzard. "It's a merciless measure of success," he said finally, his voice rough.

Then he gestured with the rolled thing. "Here is his wedding shirt, worn by my ancestors for several generations. We have not had a gunvaer—that is our word for queen— for a century, but everyone knows of this shirt. In their eyes, I will not be married to Lasva until I wear it and we say the vows before Convocation."

Another pause.

"My father forced Andaun-Sigradir to ward the castle so that it is impossible for me to transfer. I can only use transfer tokens made by Andaun. They alert the Sigradir to my presence, and he tells my father." He looked my way. "Or I can be sent, which will not alert Andaun. I will give you the Destination pattern for the royal castle. You must transfer me."

"I can do that," I said.

I'd transferred myself enough times by now to know how to do it. Transferring another was essentially the same—except for the knowledge that another's life depends upon your skill. He described a Destination that he'd made outside the city gates and beyond the perimeter of the wards. "Got that?" he asked.

"Please repeat it once more?"

He did. I took off my gloves so I could see my hands, as I couldn't feel my fingers performing the right gestures. Wind flayed them with tiny needles of ice, but I was fast, and he vanished.

I struggled back into my gloves, stumbled downwind and discovered the rest of them had crossed the river. I found them awaiting me on the riverbank, and shortly after that we encamped on a farm, in a barn, the exhausted warriors busily caring for the animals.

On New Year's Firstday, I felt Lasva's scrollcase fill with notes. When we camped, Haldren brought out some hoarded distilled drink and passed it from hand to hand. The Marlovens began to sing the *Hymn to the Beginnings*:

Marloven of ancient day, riding Hesea Plain
Wide as the wind's home, free as the falcon.
Led by three war lords wielding the wreath:
Montrehauc of the mountains, first of the lords.
Montrevair of the plains, makers of kingdoms,
Montredaun-An war leaders, Marloven kings.
Allies united 'neath gold-eagle banner . . .

At the same time, two weeks away in Choreid Dhelerei, Ivandred stood beside Lasva, who shivered in a gown of royal blue silk. Ivandred gripped her hand tightly. He wore the four hundred-year-old shirt, which was far too wide for his slim body, and too short. It came down to the tops of his legs instead of mid-thigh. Lasva had been afraid that the sight would cause smirks and averted eyes, but the moment they walked out to stand below the king on the royal daïs, the entire room went silent with awe at the appearance of that age-yellowed cloth. They all knew what it was, covered over with crooked embroidery of birds and horses, ships and suns, and animals that Lasva couldn't identify.

Lasva could hear Ivandred's breathing and feel the tension he tried to lock inside as he took the sword the king handed him, and gravely held it out so that she could close her hand over part of its hilt, the second time she had ever touched a weapon. His fingers in the icy air were cold, and so were hers, but together they made a little warmth as they spoke the words of marriage-union, which bound them in the eyes of the Marlovens.

She had learned the words but they meant little to her. Meaning had shrunk to the steady pair of ice-blue eyes meeting hers, and the quiet desperation she saw there, that he tried so hard to hide. So she spoke the words, pitching her voice to be heard, as she'd been trained, and shuttered away the ironic knowledge that for all those listening her marriage in Colend, brilliant as it had been, had no significance.

When they finished, she felt Ivandred's fingers tighten, and his hand guided hers as together they lifted the sword skyward, signifying prince and princess, future harvaldar and future gunvaer.

Then the king's raspy squawk rang out as he led the *Hymn to the Beginnings*:

Riding the ranges, valiant and venturous,
Marlovan war kings shielded the holdings
Jarls sworn and loyal, round the high throne.

In the king's hall, and in castles all over the kingdom, as well as around our low fire in a barn, people sang words similar to those I'd read in the record, up there in Darchelde tower—but then, the language had changed. As yet I had no interest in why.

War-drums and danger, all days and weather
Broken like spear-shafts, bones of the enemy!
Flame-flensed and flindered all traitors' shields!
Such was the conquest by Montredaun kings.

As soon as the song finished, someone started another, and then another, as a fiery beverage was followed by jugs of cider. Though we had so little in common with these Marlovens, for this brief time, we were united in our humanity, our shared exhaustion and wish for comfort, and our hope in the year's turning.

The hot cider and the distilled liquor warmed us. It was followed by the local beer, which I'd never tasted before my arrival in this country. It was delicious, made from barley and oats. It warmed the insides as effectively as the cider, and it tasted better than that sticky-sweet, rye-based travel bread, which I nonetheless choked down until the edge of hunger was gone. I joined Pelis and Anhar, where bedrolls had been spread out against one wall of the barn. Pelis soon fell asleep. Anhar gnawed determinedly at travel bread gripped in both hands, wisps of her black hair—usually so tidy—draggled around her blotched countenance.

I stretched out between the two dressers. Anhar's shadow slipped over me, but I was comforted by her presence, remembering how she'd cared for me after that terrible fire. She seemed unaware; yes, her eyes were closed as she worked determinedly at the bread.

Rhythmic movement caught my attention, the whirl of color in time to a galloping rhythm. On the other side of the barn Birdy sat, juggling his silks in small circles, the rhythm steady, the circles perfectly described, braiding the air in a neverending pattern. Watching it was oddly soothing. He smiled at me, but then his gaze shifted to Anhar, and the quality of his smile changed. I can hardly say how. Something in the muscles beside his eyes, the upper lip, conveyed tenderness. Special meaning. I lay down to sleep, a last drifting thought, *He knows how to juggle. When did that happen?*

PART FIVE
THE FOX BANNER

ONE

Of Hymns and Beginnings

Halfway through New Year's Week, we halted in a snowy field with nothing in sight. The Marlovens all got out their best battle tunics and affixed banners to their lances, which were snapped together and carried once again. Even the horses were curried, though some of the snowdrifts were chest deep.

Lnand leaned over. "We're nigh the city."

Anhar muttered, "They have to furbish up for that?"

"I suspect it's like arrival at Lily Gate," I said.

"Ah-ye. I didn't think they had any manners at all," Anhar said cheerfully.

We mounted up, riding in strict column over a hill, and there, on the horizon, was Choreid Dhelerei, the biggest walled city I've ever seen. It appeared, through the light snow, to be built on three hills, with too many towers to count. When we neared enough to see the figures on the gate, Haldren raised his fist, and the horses moved from trot to canter and thence to gallop.

Horns blew from the walls, echoing from tower to tower. As we approached the gates people scattered. We galloped through the gate without a check, the banners streaming, clattered up a street that was lined with people, most of whom either cheered or touched fingers to chests.

The walls here had poles from which banners flew. The highest tower flew the great stylized gold eagle against the black of Marloven Hesea.

We approached another gate, only somewhat narrower than the city gate, and stopped in an enormous courtyard, the animals blowing and steaming. Stable hands ran out to the halters as we dismounted.

Among the many runners in subtly different versions of the typical austere Marloven coat or robe were women in dark blue belted over-robes with fine bleached linen robes beneath. They picked Anhar, Pelis, and me out and led us up a crowded spiral staircase made out of stone. Bare stone. The only thing that made many parts of this castle seem less than a prison was the stone's warm sandy color.

Ah-ye! How dismal I found that castle! It was cold, the air was stuffy from inadequate venting and far too many people walking the halls, and the halls were unconscionably long and determinedly bare of any attempt at civilization. Servants in various dull colors moved to and fro. The hallways were no more than long stone tunnels.

Anhar's eyes were wide. Pelis walked head down, her brow contracted. We stopped before a wooden door carved over with Venn knots of barley-beards and little four-petal flowers. Women carrying steel weapons stood guard at these doors, but after exchanged glances and some signal I did not catch, they let us pass.

Inside lay a colorful Bermundi rug, predominantly crimson, worked in geometric patterns and giving an otherwise sparsely furnished room some warmth. There was a single low table with plain cushions on either side, and a door on each side wall.

One of these doors opened, and a gaunt old woman entered. I recognized Marnda only after she'd taken a few steps toward us. She too wore the dark blue overrobe with an inner robe of undyed linen. Her gray hair was braided.

Her expression when she saw me was unmistakable relief. "You are here at last, Scribe Emras. Dressers, you two go that way." She gestured to the door on the other side of the room. "Ask for Gislan. She will tell you what is expected."

Pelis sent back a somber glance as they went. As soon as the door shut, Marnda said, "Follow me."

She opened the door behind her, and we passed into a room with a leaping fire; two enormous chairs with great winged backs sat on either side of the fireplace. I'd glimpsed similar chairs at Darchelde. The chair legs were like those of birds, complete to talons.

Marnda said in a dry voice with the faintest trace of a quaver, "Those chairs are built to keep the sitter safe from assassins creeping up behind."

"Ah-yedi!" I made the shadow-ward.

Marnda gripped her hands. "This castle is Thorn Gate come again. And that king is the worst of them all. Emras, I crave your pardon for usurping your rightful place, and I earnestly beg you will assume the position of first runner."

Since this was what I had come all this way to do, I bowed a full Peace, acknowledging the difficulty she must be feeling to make such an admission. I said, "This way I can truly determine if Norsundrian magic aids this king, as our queen ordered me to do."

"Norsunder!" she repeated, shadow-warding. I wondered how many times she'd had occasion to make that gesture since her arrival. "I could not think Norsunder any worse than what we find here, yet this king reviles against Norsunder as much as anyone. More." She drew a deep breath. "He summons our princess at irregular hours. He talks to her like, ah-ye, like a pet, only do people threaten pets? Not that I have heard him speak any threat directly. He doesn't need to. I have had to stand behind him for hours. They call it 'watches,' and you must stand until your bones want to break."

"I will take that duty," I said.

"You are truly loyal. I will remember that, when our queen . . ." She looked away.

When our queen calls us home, were the words she wanted to say. But when would that be?

Her voice regained a little of the old briskness. "Let me show you everything before they return. The prince and princess are attending on the king at this moment, in the Great Hall, with the jarls. If they do not run into the meal time, Lasva might bring back those women again, and we will have these rooms filled with them and their runners. This is Lasva's private interview chamber. Through here is her public room, which, as you see, has a door to the hall, which would be one door down from where you entered . . ."

She flung opened doors to a suite fully as large as the princess's suite in Alsais, though the pages' chambers at home were finer. ". . . but it was empty—and oh, the webs! It had been at least a hundred years since a queen had possessed these rooms, you see. There was some furniture in the back rooms that they despised as Olavair. They seem to revile against these Olavairs, though they once ruled. It is all of a piece."

She touched her lips in the moth kiss then opened yet another door. "This is the princess's bedroom. He comes in through the other side— those are his rooms beyond. Across the hall from his rooms are the king's. Your room is here, where you can hear her if she opens her bedroom or summons you from the personal chambers."

She pointed to a door, as yet unopened.

"At least our staff has private rooms, though they are ugly little closets, like this." She glanced at the door to my room, still shut. "Their equivalent of a seneschal is not unlike my position in Alsais: Gislan will be glad to leave it all to me. I took care to let her know how our princess likes things to be *nice*." A little of Marnda's old pride showed. "You will have four runners attendant on you, two for night and two for day. The guards are commanded by someone else, but you can request of them anything that pertains to safety. The runners fetch things or take them away."

Marnda finally opened the door to my room. It was oddly shaped, long and narrow. The window was a slit, looking down into a tiny court formed by this and another wing of the castle. Directly above was the sentry walk: a warrior's shadow moved along the building adjacent, cast by the faint, low sun. The bedroom was bare stone, swept clean, furnished only with a bed and a tiny desk with a stool. Closet indeed.

"At the far end of the hall is the tower where that mage lives." Marnda raised her hand against Thorn Gate. "Will you know Norsundrian magic if you hear it?"

I was about to reassure her with the knowledge that I'd met Prince Ivandred's tutor at Darchelde, then remembered that the king did not know that Ivandred was a mage.

"I will," I said, aware that I was not as sure as I sounded.

But that was what Marnda wanted to hear. She breathed out in relief once again and left the subject. "Do you have the princess's scrollcase?"

"Ah-ye," I exclaimed. "I do. It is full of letters, but I dared not stop to deal with them."

"If you will entrust it to me, I will take care of it."

I pulled the scrollcase from my gear, feeling one burden fall from my shoulders as I dropped the rich gold into Marnda's hand. Before either of us could speak, a door opened somewhere, and women's voices reached us.

Ahead of the newcomers came Lasva, seeming to float ahead of the free-striding, pale-haired women. They were all dressed in brightly colored overrobes of a simple line, made of fine linen. I soon learned that they wore family colors. These were their formal robes. The edges were embroidered in complicated Venn geometries. Each woman wore a kind of embroidered sash-belt low around the hips, the clasps worked in gold or silver, usually in the form of claws or talons, the sash ends swinging in front with each stride. Only Lasva's was still; she was startling dressed so, in black and gold, with a cream-linen under dress. Her hair was braided in the Marloven loop, which framed her face.

Marnda hid the scrollcase in her robe, bowed, and vanished.

Lasva did not seem to see her. She flung her arms wide in the Bird on the Wing, as she had the first day I met her, but her fingers flexed into stiffness for a heartbeat, expressing or releasing tension; the old, artless rush of words was stemmed.

"My first runner is here," she said to the women behind her, and to me, "Emras, you must be exhausted! You shall begin duty tomorrow. Today you may rest. We have everything in hand."

She led me back toward the little room that would be mine. In Kifelian she murmured, "I am very glad you are here. You must help me turn this place into less of a prison." She waved at the long windows set deep into the thick stone walls. "Here and there I've seen evidence of once-lovely windows, of fine rooms made to let in light, but then they were all bricked up by Ivandred's ancestors, to protect the castle."

She sighed, without waiting for me to answer. "Oh, Emras, I so need your observation. They seem to take me as a birdwit. Even my name is gone, though I must say," her voice deepened with irony, "their attempts to say 'Lasthavais' correctly make me glad to keep Lasva. At least they can say *that*." She flicked her fingers in Rue. "The king seems to find my ignorance not just entertaining but reassuring." Her eyes narrowed. "He goes on at great lengths, teaching me the rudiments of warfare, though he will not tell me anything about how he manages his state. Not that anyone can't see it's by force. Yet he's not ordering deaths every day— they wouldn't stand for that. If you read any of their history, you will find that their kings are not any safer than anyone else, it just takes more people to successfully attack them."

She sighed the way Marnda did, a long breath in an attempt to ease strain.

Then she warded it all, a quick gesture very like Ivandred's flat-handed motion. "We haven't time. Later I will tell you everything. But first, what did you do for all these weeks? Did the jarlan keep you occupied?"

This would be my moment to tell her that I was learning magic in order to protect her. Except that the queen had seen fit to separate Birdy and me out when she gave those orders. And here was Lasva, under the king's eyes all the time. Many thoughts streamed through my mind in the time it took for my heart to beat twice, but these two in particular:

the horrible things I heard about this king, and Queen Hatahra's orders. My instinct was very strong: I must keep my magic studies to myself.

And so I lied. "I studied history," I said.

"In Alsais," Lasva said to me the next morning, "my sister's presence was more felt than seen, except at the Rising. Everyone knew she was there, but the mood of the court seldom reflected her mood."

She paused, and I made the Peace in agreement.

"Here, these frightening warriors and their guards and their servants are all aware of the king's mood. Even when they do not see him."

"I felt it the moment I walked in." I would never commit the vulgarity of saying that I had smelled it in that faint tang of sweat, though it was true.

"Today, when you take your place behind me, please observe. I have been longing to talk to you about . . . everything. But I will not tell you what to see. I want to see again through your eyes."

As I walked behind Lasva into the Great Hall, wearing my new robe of dark blue over beautifully soft, finely woven undyed linen, my mind entered a fugue composed of memory and unfamiliarity. For a giddy moment I was fifteen again, taking up my station as observer in Alsais's beautiful octagonal fountain chamber, aware of being in public yet expected to remain unobtrusive.

"Since the civil judgments did not last past yesterday and there are no military judgments to be witnessed, today is what they all look forward to," Lasva said. "The exhibitions and, tonight, promotions. Then tomorrow the jarls and jarlans can start for home."

"They do not stay all New Year's Week?" I asked, surprised.

"Ivandred says the king doesn't like them around any longer than they like being here. If there is nothing to keep them, they leave."

Lasva laid her hand against her heart, head inclined slightly. We fell silent as a guard opened the door for us. We entered an enormous throne room and approached the king on his daïs of black marble. Ivandred was already there, seated on a cushion below his father's throne. It, too, was carved of black marble.

I joined Ivandred's first runner, out of the king's vision, but within sight of the vigilant guards behind the king, who stood with spears grounded, other hand resting on sword hilts.

I took up my observer stance, unused for half a year.

"What did you see?"

"Color, first of all. Brilliant color in those overrobes and in the sashes. It surprised me, because so far in this kingdom all wear browns, grays, undyed linens. Except for the three all in black."

"Those three are First Lancers," Lasva said. "There are many wings of King's Lancers, but the perceived elite is the First Lancers, followed by the Second, Third, and Fourth, with somewhat less prestige. Only those four units can wear the black robes at formal affairs."

"Is there significance in the colors? Crimson, green, cyan, violet, yellow, royal blue—which was the most unsettling. Am I to understand that royal blue is not reserved for the king, here?"

"That is correct. These others are representative colors for jarlates."

"Where are the owls and the marmots and the sigils of the Inda history?"

"They have gone out of fashion, just as our dyeing our hair silver. Except for the eagle on the king's banner and the fox for the heir, both in the black and gold of the royal family. The rest of them can use any colors except black, silver and gold, but they only wear them to Convocation and a few other rare and special events."

"But one wore gold trim to his white robe," I said.

"That is Ivandred's cousin from the Telyer, whose family were the kings previous to the Marlovens. Mar*lov*ans," she corrected herself. "There was a language shift under their King Senrid, who brought Ivandred's family back to the throne. It seems important to them to remember the distinctions."

"And that very old man who wore a gold sash, with a robe the color of Colend's royal blue?"

"That is the Jarl of Olavair." Her voice dropped. "That family ruled until the beginning of the last century, and in the north they still call themselves kings. Though not in the hearing of southern Marlovens."

What did she want? What did I miss? I thought again about the milling men, their voices sharp and quick. "At first I thought all those wearing baldrics were men, but that is not true."

"The baldrics mean they have been trained at the Academy." Her gesture opened westward, toward the high walls we'd glimpsed on the ride into the castle.

"Are they all trained there, the jarlate offspring?"

"Not much is said about that place. Ivandred told me that, of those who *do* attend, many are sent home at the three year mark and more at the six year mark. Only those who stay for nine years can become lancer captains. Jarls who stay that long are very highly regarded by all. In war, they can command their own people—under the king—instead of handing their people off in levies."

I was already so bored my jaw ached. Levies, war, command . . . what a horrible place!

"What did you think of the exhibition?"

"I liked the dancing after dinner better than the horse riding before, however skillful it was. The danger frightened me. Though there was danger in some of the dances—when the fellows did that heel drumming and waved swords around."

"The women used to, too, but they were forbidden to wave their knives around after a dance some centuries ago, when the dancers then turned on a king and his adherents and assassinated them. Actually, I believe women assassinated a king twice. So women will often do the drumming for the sword dances."

"Ah-yedi!" I made the Peace. "Like the songs we heard when traveling, these songs have strong melodies, and I liked how so many of them sang when dancing."

"So you perceived only the danger of the Academy youths' exhibition?"

I thought back to the sudden quiet, the expectation after a distant bugle peal.

Servants threw open the opposite doors and in raced nine young riders all in black—dressed like the lancers. The horses' hooves struck sparks on the stone floor as the animals raced in nose to tail. The riders sat with their hands on their thighs, weapons hooked to the saddles but untouched as the horses galloped in patterns, leaping, wheeling, and once rising to strike with their front hooves.

In Colend courtiers often rode horses in similar fast and dangerous patterns, so I heard. But they didn't fight in patterns, sword to sword, or shoot arrows at targets as they galloped by, much less leap down and exchange blows in a fast flurry of whirling hands, glinting steel, and black fabric.

Then, quick as they came, they were gone. By then the air had warmed considerably from all the human and animal exertions. Stable hands came in to wand the droppings, after which a line of servants brought in food. My astonishment that food would be served where animals had been cavorting was mirrored in Lasva's stiff back. My throat closed, and

I had to swallow a couple of times, reminding myself fiercely that the droppings were gone—that customs differed—but my stomach settled only when I reminded myself I was here to serve and to observe. Not to eat.

"I perceived great skill in the exhibition," I said at last.

"What else did you see?"

"That the king sat between the two of you."

"He always does."

"Does he always breathe like that? I know they have healers here. There was a good one who tended our wounded."

"I'm told that the king's healer died of old age twenty years ago, and the king doesn't trust anyone younger not to try to assassinate him." She clasped her hands. We were seated in her private chamber, an almost bare room save for a rug worked with Venn knots, a carved chest, a table and cushions. "What did you notice about individuals?"

I concentrated. "There was that one very tall man with the hair more pale than Ivandred's, and the yellow robe that seemed to be edged with silver. He fondled the hand of the pregnant woman to his right, who was quite beautiful. But he kept watching Ivandred."

Lasva's hands clasped together tightly, then dropped to her sides. Another important person? "Yes. That is Danrid Yvanavar, a new jarl. The woman is his wife, sister to Haldren. Her name is Tdiran."

"It struck me as odd that she would not look Ivandred's way, nor he hers, unless this Danrid-Jarl forced their attention by speaking to both."

"Yes," Lasva whispered. "What else?"

"Oh, it is difficult to explain, as their mannerisms are so different. What can they mean?"

"Look past that to human characteristics."

"But those are puzzling as well. I saw Haldren's eyes a-sheen when he gained his promotion, at the very end. Was that joy or sorrow? I thought our lancers all expected to be promoted to the First Lancers."

"The king chose to separate them to different companies."

"So the king was not pleased with them?"

"Ah-ye! It . . . it's . . ." Lasva stopped, and spread her hands. "All I truly understand is, the king is making certain that the First Lancers and Ivandred are kept completely separate in all ways. He even keeps us separate, at times, though at other times he has ordered us to produce an heir. Ivandred and I have decided that I will take the birth herb."

"So . . . the scowl the king gave Ivandred at the end of the dancing. That was not from pain or from regret that he could not dance?"

"Did you not see, how they all danced around him?"

I thought of Ivandred moving so freely, with such casual strength and grace. How for the first time I had seen his face lifted in joy, even grinning. And how they all grinned back, *the garden arch*. Would not the king rejoice to see how much they love Ivandred? Another thought, more astonishing. "Does he not trust his own son?"

"No." That word from a Colendi was shocking; she wanted to underscore the truth.

The next morning early, I'd just finished dressing when there was a peremptory rap on my door. I knew it would be a Marloven because we Colendi scratch, but I was startled to find Ivandred standing there in his fighting blacks, hair braided and looped for travel. "Scribe Emras. I have a request."

My surprise turned to astonishment as I stepped back so that he could enter. The light from my tiny slit window harshened the juts of his cheekbones and eye sockets. Tension and exhaustion tautened his skin. He had looked better on our headlong gallop above Telyer.

He thrust the door shut. "First, I am trying to understand your position. Lasva does not know about your magic studies? Last night I asked when your scribes began their magic lessons, and she was surprised. Said that they are not taught magic."

Swiftly I told him what I'd told the Herskalt, and to my immense relief he accepted that with a brief nod. "That was shrewd on the part of your queen. As a result, Andaun-Sigradir is not aware of your being a mage, so you are not warded."

Gratitude flooded me with relief.

"I'm here with a request," he said. "I need you to make me transfer tokens."

My gratitude made me wish to serve. But there was also doubt, caused by that pervasive sense of danger. "That much magic performed, will the Sigradir not sense it?"

"Yes. Perform your spells outside the castle. You are Lasva's first runner, which grants you Restday free."

I made the Peace, then said, "I have never performed this task. I do not know how long it will take."

"It's lengthy," he said grimly, touched two fingers to his heart then opened the door, and was gone with quick step.

I found Lasva in one of her chambers. This one was barren except for a little side table and embroidery tambours placed at either end of the room, each with cloth set in. She wore riding clothes of soft cotton-wool—trousers, overtunic, and an open robe over that. They were all undyed, and the neutral shade of cloth emphasized her russet coloring, the gold-glinting dark hair wound up in braids, and her blue eyes.

She was pouring out steeped leaf, which filled the air with a summery scent. "Ivandred has been sent by his father to follow Olavair all the way north," she said, handing a cup to me.

"Why?" I asked, because we were alone.

"The king says it is necessary. Oh, Emras, it is all so complicated." She finished her cup and picked up her fans. She'd had new ones made, I saw. They were black on one side and gold on the other.

"Strategy," Lasva said as we progressed down the room in Altan fan form. "When I was young I never thought about such things, but listening to the king has taught me the concepts of strategy. He talks of war, but I?" She whirled, fan snapping out in a perfect flat arc, and glanced over her shoulder, smiling. "I translate what he says into terms of people. Ah-ye! My strategy is twofold: to keep the king happy, if I can. And two, to try to gain the allegiance of the women of this kingdom. They appear to think I have no wit, because I have no experience to match theirs," Lasva went on. "Ivandred asked me to understand his people. He is a man of very few words. One might say that words cost him."

"Cost?" I asked.

"Your observations about Tdiran Marlovair, or rather Tdiran Yvanavar: she wore the Yvanavar colors, though Ivandred calls her Marlovair. I think it is habit, and I think they have a history. I asked him last night, but all he said was, *There is no use in talking about Tdiran Marlovair.*" Her voice dropped low, unexpectedly hard. Then she tipped her head. "You perceive?"

"It is not the words, it is the tone," I said.

"Ah-ye. He has difficulty putting words to what happens in his head and heart. It could be he has so long guarded his speech that words do not come easily. I sense there is more. As for Tdiran, I tried to speak with her, but she was reticent. They all were. They talked freely enough among themselves, but with me, it was like a girl's first day at court. Everyone smiles at her but otherwise take no notice, for she can have no influence."

When she reached the wall, Lasva began speeding up the pace. I was soon damp. It had been so long since I had practiced.

She increased the pace until our arms were swinging. At the end of the form she leaped, whirled, and struck her fan across one of the tambours. Its fabric ripped cleanly, straight across. She snapped her fan shut and laughed soundlessly at me. "You seem surprised! Yet it was you who first demonstrated the cut."

She bent to the tambour and frowned. "Not as clean as I'd like. The strike wasn't strong enough at the start, so I put more effort into the middle, causing this sawing effect. I will work on that."

I saw then that her fan had real steel at the tips instead of the wooden cat-ears. Seeing the direction of my glance, she held the fans out. "Ivandred had them waiting for me," she said.

"How much fabric do you spoil, or do you not do this every day?"

"Oh, I end with the grand slash each morning. It feels so satisfying, though I do not know why. And when I am summoned to attend on the king, I mend it again. It gives me something to do with my hands, and he sees it as frivolous and harmless. Satin-stitch, chain-stitch, interlock, feather." Her forefinger tapped at the cloth, and I saw the tiny, even stitches. "He has seen me sewing nearly every day, but has yet to ask what it is. So much of the world is hidden to him. He seems to value only that which has to do with force."

We set the fans aside as she said, "I will order you a set."

I made the Peace then left, anxious to get going before anyone could stop me with demands. I'd decided that Restday would be my time to visit the Herskalt.

Then I thought, why should I be limited to daytime? There was no doubt a lesson awaiting me in that chamber, which had lain there for weeks. If the Herskalt was asleep, or busy with his teaching, or elsewhere, I could leave a note asking for lessons in making transfer tokens, and in the meantime I could experiment.

But I hoped he rose early, as I'd decided to transfer well before dawn. I was ready for another attempt at the *real* magic.

TWO

OF THE SNAP OF A FAN

"Here you are in blue again," the Herskalt said, looking amused.
"The runners wear blue." My face heated. "Of course you
know that."

His amusement deepened briefly, but he didn't say anything.

"Perhaps you know why they chose blue? It being the color mages wore
in Sartor for centuries. Also scribes. We were taught that scribes and mages
were once conjoined, though each says its practitioners were first. Is there
a connection, according to what you mages have been taught?"

The Herskalt motioned with his hand. "You have to look much further
back."

"To?"

"To the beginnings. Colors symbolized power. Blue was the power of
the mind, contrasting with crimson, the power of the sword. From there
developed the usual overlapping, often conflicting infinitude typical of
human endeavor, translated out into a rainbow of symbolic colors."

"You make it sound like everything in life is about power," I said.

"Many would agree," he replied. "Judging from her actions so far, your
Lasva appears to comprehend, if only by instinct, that the birth of lasting
power arises not in one's own mind, but in the minds of others. I refer to
the way she endeavors to beguile the king."

How did he know that? Ivandred must communicate with his old tutor, or maybe they had friends in common.

I said, "I don't understand. Will you explain?"

"If you were to go to Colend right now, mark off a territory, and declare yourself queen, what would happen?"

"People would laugh at me. And perhaps Queen Hatahra would summon me to explain myself."

"Yet it was no different when Martande Lirendi dealt with the Chwahir threat, then looked around and decided that since he was doing the work of a king anyway, why should it all go to Sartor's glory? Why not to his own? Most of his friends lauded the idea and dedicated themselves to making it happen. It is said that the smartest and most ambitious persons in Sartor's court followed him and became dukes and barons."

I pressed my hands together, not certain how to answer. My instinct rebelled at this airy dismissal of our great, visionary king, then I thought, *This is a test.*

The Herskalt touched the book I had brought back, and it vanished with a glint of light and a brief stirring of air.

"It's the same with anything," he went on in his reasonable tone. "A poet declares his work will be lauded universally. If others like it, they laud it. If they don't, they despise him for his temerity, they defame his poem, and he's forgotten as soon as the laughter dies away."

"How do you know people's motivations?" I said. "Do you use that magical object? I should like to master that," I said, referring to the disc that had allowed me to inhabit others' perspectives.

His chin lifted as though he was mildly pleased. "You need far more discipline before you can use the dyr to look at the past through others' eyes."

"Dye-r-r-r, dy-re," I repeated, trying to get the "eye" sound matched to the "r" at the back of the throat in a single syllable, the way he articulated it. I wanted to split the "eye" into two syllables, *die-ur.* "That is what the thing is called?"

"It's the traditional term. So: have you a subject you wish to study, or shall I assign you one?"

"Ivandred wishes me to make him transfer tokens."

The Herskalt's brows lifted. "Ah, excellent plan. He never seems to have time to practice much less complete exacting projects such as transfer tokens. So. How would you begin?"

I told him what I'd been thinking, and he taught me a way that was far better than the laborious method I'd put together. I learned more about the connections between spells in the doing, and then I used one of my own tokens to transfer, as I was not certain of my strength after all that work.

I'd set the Destination for the narrow hallway outside my room, which was rarely used by anyone but me. As soon as the transfer reaction faded I was aware that something was wrong. I turned around in a circle, then noticed that all the doors were open, including my own. I went into my room and hid the two transfer tokens I had made under my bedding. Then I went out. I heard Lasva's voice through the open door to her outer chamber.

". . . can't find her? Where could she possibly be?"

I stopped in the doorway and made a full bow. "You sought me, your highness?" I said in our home language, though she preferred us to speak in Marloven.

Lasva whirled around, her hands out in that tense Bird on the Wing. "There you are! Where did you go?"

My body flashed with heat as I offered her a lie. "I went out to learn my way around, as I am always lost. But I lost myself yet again."

Lasva clasped her hands together. "They have no street signs here. To confuse an invader, I am told."

"I crave your pardon, your highness."

"Ah-ye! You are here, and today is Restday, and I did say you had it free. It's just that the king desires us all to join him at noon for the ceremony. I wanted to make sure we all knew that."

She turned around again, her blue gaze going from Marnda to me and back. "I also have another question: Where is my scrollcase? I could not find it in view upon your desk, Emras."

I glanced Marnda's way. The seneschal clasped her hands in the Peace. "I requested she give it to me upon her arrival, your highness, so that I might deal myself with the correspondence."

"So there has been correspondence?" Lasva asked. "But why have *you* dealt with it, Marnda?"

"It was on the orders of her majesty, your royal sister," Marnda said, making a full bow over her crossed arms. She spoke from that position. "Your royal sister instructed me to do what I could to turn your eyes west as soon as might be."

"So there were letters? I ask because Darva did promise to write. Whatever the others might have said, I relied upon her, at least." Lasva lifted her head. Her eyes were wide, so wide I could see light reflected in her pupils though I stood some distance away. Her color was high, her mouth tight—a new expression, difficult to define, it was so different from the Lasva I knew. "Though I never asked, did I, Emras? I gave you my scrollcase, and then I never asked."

Another turn, and she clasped her hands. "I should have liked to have made that decision for myself. Were the letters answered or just disposed of?"

I said, "I answered them, until my arrival here."

"I answered the New Year's letters," Marnda said.

"Did you save them?" Lasva's gaze switched between us.

This direct question forced the probability of a blunt negative. I could see it disturbed Marnda as much as it did me.

Even so, neither of us could bring ourselves to say "no" to our princess. "I believed it was according to the queen's will to burn them, lest they fall into . . ." Marnda halted there. *Into the wrong hands* was an absurdity she could not speak. What would be the wrong hands for Lasva's letters from people in faraway Colend, about the trivialities of court?

"I would like to hear what you remember of them." Lasva turned my way. "You, I know, can be trusted to recall those that passed under your eyes, as well as the words you wrote in response over my name."

Marnda and I both made the full court obeisance, though she'd asked us to use Marloven custom. The event demanded no less.

"We shall begin with Emras, then, as she had the scrollcase the longest. Until the king's summons." She paused. "Emras, I understand that you were under my sister's orders. But why did you not tell me? I would have agreed. You must know I would have agreed."

The intensity of her unwavering gaze unnerved me, and I bowed my head. "You sailed the river below Willow Gate. I could not bear to hurt you the more."

"From that am I to understand Kaidas was frequently mentioned in those letters? Especially if Ananda troubled herself to write. I admit that I lived at Willow Gate for much of the autumn, so . . . yes, I think I can understand your dilemma, Emras. I think I can here." She touched her forehead. "But not here." She touched her heart. "I told you when we first met. I want there to be truth between us. So tell me now. Are there any other secrets that you keep from me for my own good?"

If I told her the queen's orders, then I must tell her the rest—that I studied magic. This knowledge would have to be hidden from the king who so distrusted his own son that Ivandred was, in his turn, made to hide his own knowledge.

The desire to protect her was as strong as my hunger to gain more knowledge. And so, yet again, I lied. "You have them all," I said. After the rude words left my lips, I recognized how much time had passed between her question and my response. I had taken too long to consider my answer, and she knew it.

Lasva said, "Then please begin. We can practice the while."

Memorization being long habit, I recited all the letters. I even tried to match a little of the voice of the individual correspondents, if I knew them. I strove to please her, to entertain, to demonstrate that my loyalties were true, even if my word had not been.

She listened without speaking as we performed the Altan fan form side by side, her profile giving no clue to her thoughts. I'd reached the letters received during our ship journey when the summons came, and we had to put away our fans.

Though it was Restday, and though she'd said she would try to spare me the tedium of those long attendances on the king by relying on her Marloven runners who were used to him, she did not lift her hand to dismiss me. Nor did she summon anyone else as we walked out of her chambers and down the long hall to where the king sat on his cushion, hemming and huffing against whatever disturbed his breathing passages.

She gracefully laid hand to heart.

"Well, here you are," the king said, coughing. "Now. The jarls are gone, and many were the fair words about your hosting. What are you going to do with your time, eh? Eh?"

She addressed the king by his full title, using Colend's court accent to make a caress of his name. "Should you like a tapestry to be made? I note many places where one might grace your walls."

"Tapestry? Hah! What d'you think my people would make of a big cloth full of ribbon dancers and flowers, or whatever it is you put in your art?"

Lasva made the gesture of Harmony. "I thought I might make one celebrating your ancestor, the one who first united your kingdom."

"Hah!" He coughed horribly. "Old Savarend! You won't show him being stabbed in the back, I dare swear." He cackled, then coughed.

"I would surround him with representatives of all the jarl families."

"I like that. I like that. Put my old friends, my most loyal friends, up close in front."

Lasva hesitated a heartbeat, then assented gracefully.

"So. How far did you get with your map, eh, girl? Start at the top."

"Olavair is the farthest north, bounded by Fath, Tiv Evair, and Khanivar."

"When was Fath created?"

"At the Treaty of the Rivers."

"Year?"

"4094."

"And south of it?"

"Tiv Evair."

"Why do they hold out with two names?"

"An internal treaty, between the jarl family, whose name Tya became Tiv under King Senrid in the year 4285, and the federation of free cities . . ."

On and on it went—names and dates without the reasons why one should remember them, until the king summoned his subordinates for the Restday sharing of wine and bread.

Perhaps Lasva wanted me to learn them, too. She would know that I only had to hear it to remember it all, but if so, she could have said so. I was being punished, and I accepted the rebuke with sorrow. She might guess that whatever I withheld was on orders, was intended for her benefit—but she knew I was lying.

———

He sent Lasva away with scarcely more respect than he'd dismiss a runner, and we were free.

All the way back to her chambers I formulated possible responses. I even considered kneeling down to offer full confession. I wanted her forgiveness, the flow of converse which I had lost once, on the way to Sartor. It had taken this long to recover it, only to lose it again? No!

But when we reached Lasva's chambers, she said briskly, "I believe he expects the tapestry to be set in the contemporary mode, and here I was ready to order you to discover the oldest families and their traditional clothes. Well! I must ponder. Who would have thought that my idea, meant to keep my day filled with unexceptionable activity, would already be so fraught. The rest of the day is yours, Emras."

In sorrow I made The Peace. I had been dismissed.

Confession would have to wait.

I had to go outside the castle to make transfer tokens. I found a secluded path between the boundary of the kitchen garden and the yards where flax was turned into linen. One yard abutted the end of the garrison where the women guards lived.

To secure an excuse to be over there, I'd taken on the task of running messages back and forth from the guardswomen's captain to Lasva, an extra task the runners were happy to relinquish to me. I had to choose a time when no one would notice how long it took me, so I went directly after bathing, before the time when Lasva liked doing the Altan fans but after her breakfast with Ivandred—when he was there.

After I delivered messages, I would retreat to my hideaway and pull from my pocket a selection of carved wood shank buttons. The Herskalt had said that the material did not matter, and I could not requisition the usual metal discs without raising questions.

I worked my spells. By the time I reached the last button I was bent over, my teeth clenched. The spell kept dissipating on me, like trying to catch and hold water.

When at last it was done, I sat down with my back to the fence to recover. It was getting easier each time.

THREE

Of Regret and Remembered Bells

One morning, when I emerged from the women's side of the baths in the sub-basement, I chanced on Birdy and Anhar, who were coming from the area where genders mixed, a wide room furnished with nothing but stone benches. As a place to congregate it offered nothing but the dank smell of wet stone, yet people strolled about in the warm, humid air, talking, flirting, exchanging news.

They saw me at the same time. Birdy grinned. "Em!" He looked younger, with his hair wet and slicked back off his clean, shining face, his long body clad in a shapeless robe. He approached within a step of me, then halted abruptly, an awkward halt that described an invisible boundary around me. "I have seen so little of you. What has the princess got you doing?"

"Lasva is planning a tapestry," I said, though surely Anhar had told him.

We said little more than that, but the next day, there they were again, and I sensed that they were waiting. Once again we talked about the details of daily life, so unimportant a subject I was surprised when Birdy suggested we take advantage of one of the benches. But I agreed, for it was good to see him again, hear his voice. But all the while I was anxious not only about my magic work for the day but also about questions that might lead in that direction.

Later that evening, when I went to Anhar to get my nails trimmed, and as always, she smoothed the tension from my fingers, palms, and feet, she said, "You do not object to my touch."

I had shut my eyes as I reviewed my latest lesson. This question seemed to come from nowhere. I asked, "Have I been rude?"

"Not to me."

Then I understood, and discomfort made me twitch my fingers from her grasp.

She let go. "Will you explain? I am trying to understand. Is it Birdy who doesn't attract you, or everyone?"

"Everyone."

"Ah-ye, *elor*. You are the first I have known, so may I ask just to learn: Are the rest of us repulsive?"

"No. Yes, if I feel crowded. I like people. I just don't want them . . ." I shrugged, hugged myself with one arm, my half-finished nails brushing over me as if insects crawled up my sleeves. "I don't seem to have whatever it is that you feel when you let someone that close."

"So my touch, when I rub your hands or your neck, it's not unendurable." She took my hand back to begin the next nail.

"Far from it. But the effect is to make me sleepy, not ardent." I said, gesturing pardon for intimacy with my free hand. "You and Birdy share ardency, for that I am glad. For him."

"And yet our natures differ, too. He is inclined toward exclusivity, and I am not. But he is my favorite." She gave me a considering glance as she began the last nail.

"And so?" I asked, sensing that she had something further to say. "The direction of your query?"

"My mother held a conversation with my sister and me," she said, "before my sister chose to hire to a pleasure house with her skills. You know, my mother taught us both not just the arts of the nails but also of massage."

I remembered her telling me long ago that she'd wanted to be an actor, a player. But this did not seem the time to ask about that. "We learned how the body reacts to muscle work. It is like the making of lace," she said. "Boundaries interweave, cross and recross. Those who like sex cannot imagine anyone not wanting it. Those who like power assume everyone does. So much depends on what patterns of behavior we expect—are taught to expect—grow to expect." She leaned toward me and said quickly, "Birdy likes to talk to you in the mornings. I think he misses your conversations."

"I miss his," I said. "I do love Birdy, but we have all been so busy." I think my sorrow showed, too, for I did regret avoiding him.

"And so he devised this plan to catch you when we are all clean, so that you will not find him objectionable. Emras, do not take away those morning talks from him."

"Now I feel terrible," I said.

She smiled. "Do not. Please talk to him instead, like always."

And so I shifted my magic-making to the free watch at night, when the rest of the staff went off for social pursuits. It meant being outside in the dark, bundled up against the cold, but that was incentive to work faster. And it gave me extra time for talking to Birdy each morning in the communal bath alcove. At first we spoke in our own language, but gradually we became more accustomed to Marloven, and we were back to our old debates, just like our student days—what we'd learned of Marloven history, customs, and culture—funny stories about servants or horses. Anhar often met us. She listened in silence at first, and gradually joined the talk.

We on Lasva's staff spoke Kifelian whenever we were alone. We talked endlessly about minutiae that at home never would have been worth comment: foods, scents, the exact shade of the canals on winter mornings, who first put out window boxes, the cries of the canal boaters. The feel of silk on our skin. The sweet songs of Colendi bells, scarcely noticed before now but well remembered. Sometimes, when we were all together, just us, we sang—or, at least, three of us sang. Belimas always sat silently, her face so long set in sullenness and resentment that the soft folds of her skin in candlelight were beginning to resemble grooves.

"Hour of the Leaf," Nifta would say, and I would take the high bell, "Dinga-dinga ding-ding-ding!"

Pelis, on a lower note in the same chord: "Ring-rung-ring, ring-rung-ring!"

Anhar: "Dong-dong . . . dong-dong . . . dong-de-dong."

Nifta, in a low moo: "Bon-n-ng!"

Lasva ordered Marloven foods, so the rest of us arranged, with tortuous complications worthy of state diplomacy, to find bakers willing to make our breads—an indulgence that used up most of our pay.

Ananda sent a herald with not only a letter but a gift, a gaudy brooch. *This wedding gift was from the Duchess of Alarcansa. I assume it's a com-*

mentary on my presumption in surpassing her in rank when I married Macael and came to Enaeran. Having laughed over it, I pass it on to you, to remind you of our foolish youth.

We did not hear anything about what Lasva thought of the letter. We often saw her wear that brooch when she attended the king. It was so heavy it pulled at the fabric of her gowns. None of us dared ask why she wore it.

Side by side every morning after breakfast, Lasva and I worked through the Altan fan form. We often talked, but gone was intimacy, which made the thought of confession more difficult. I was afraid not only of the risk, should that terrible king hear, but what if the result was a greater divide between us?

She chose subjects for conversation that interested us both—history, reading. She was never petty; she simply erased her inner life from our discussions. It was exactly like the days of her simulacrum, only that had been unconscious and borne of grief. Now she closed herself in consciously.

Gradually she sped up the fan form until some days we whirled through it so fast, our fans snapped in and out. I usually stopped before the final cuts, but now she had four stands, one at each wall. She liked to whirl from one to another, building speed until she ripped the cloth across with one stroke, left hand, right, left, right. The first time she succeeded in cutting all four cleanly on each stroke she laughed aloud like she had when I first met her, her arms hugged against herself. But it was not the free, joyous laugh of those days. It was one of triumph.

As I got faster at making tokens and, thus, had more time to myself, I would take walks around the city. I tested myself by finding and identifying the signs of magic. If you are not a mage, think of these as seeing sigils etched in the pale glow of moonlight, or luminescent moss. The colors had to do with intensity, from old spells fading into a dull blue to the bright yellow of newly restored spells. Complicated chains of spells—necessary for just about anything to do with water, for example—were like Venn roses, circles of interlocking links. Sometimes, if the wind was not too bitter, I'd pause and count them, observing where they connected and how: sometimes interlocked, at other times layered.

I had to learn every step of the sorts of magic we took for granted. I put water-purifying spells on cups, buckets, streams.

I had to take apart the Waste Spell while reading its history. I learned how the spell first shifted waste to a specific location, until that became a noisome sump; how the spell was altered and altered again until it shifted waste to soil that met certain specifications; how that had to be altered to prevent cities from being ringed with evil swamps; how it was altered to remove the waste directly from the body; how it was broken into components when shifted to the soil, that it might become useful material again, the more swiftly.

With these lessons came an appreciation of the *power* of magic.

Ivandred came and went without any of the staff seeing much of him. He used the tokens I made him to visit Lasva of nights, then he would be gone again before sunrise.

We only heard about his triumphs—the settling of the southern border, the routing of a foray by the principality of Stalgoreth against the jarlate of Tlennen—which sent the king from triumph into dark moods whose cause no one understood, which seemed to increase the universal tension.

The king sometimes prowled the halls during the night. Lasva heard from Fnor that he was looking for traitors meeting in conspiracy. I could tell when the king had been by due to the scent of stale sweat and elderberry-ginger steep that he drank in great quantity. Those halls were frigid in winter, the air so still that aromas lingered for a day or so.

I'd begun exploring the castle to identify where wards were anchored. Whenever I smelled sweat and elderberry-ginger, I retreated rapidly.

The king transferred away twice and was gone for a week each time, which freed Lasva's day. She spent her free time studying and working on the tapestry under the watchful eyes of the king's closest servants.

FOUR

OF TURNED CUFFS AND MOUSTACHES

Everything changed that spring.
On a Restday evening as the snows were beginning to melt, I found the Herskalt awaiting me when I transferred to Darchelde.

He took the book I held out, and I settled in my chair, awaiting a test of my knowledge.

He said, "It's time to use what you have learned. Your assignment is to pick apart Choreid Dhelerei's wards. Eventually you will rebuild them again, but for now, you must only note the transfer traps and the personal wards—some of which are centuries old. You must accomplish this without breaking Andaun-Sigradir's own alarm spells. Then you will do the same for the castle itself."

I said in surprise, "Does he know I am to do this?"

The Herskalt smiled. "Of course he does not. He would be obliged to alert the king."

"But . . . that's . . ."

"Dangerous? If you plan to assist in protecting the kingdom, will you refuse any challenge that includes risk? That would limit your usefulness in any emergency."

"Will the Sigradir not know immediately that the wards are not his?"

"He will not test them if you give him no reason to do so. Begin simply, with caution."

The next day, the king summoned Lasva. Over the course of three weeks, she'd finished the design of a tapestry depicting the unification of the kingdom under Ivandred's ancestor who became first king.

When the message came, Lasva said, "Attend me, Emras."

I resisted the persistent urge to make The Peace and instead laid my hand over my heart in the proper sign of respect, then followed behind as she made her way to the king's formal antechamber. There was still a daïs, but a table and cushions replaced the imposing black marble throne, and the room was smaller. Also warmer.

I took up my stance and prepared to review lessons when the king took me by surprise. "You've summoned the guardswomen's healer, girl."

"I have, Haldren-Harvaldar."

"Does that mean you are with child?"

"I am."

The old man cackled, leaning back and forth, slapping his knees. I stared at the back of Lasva's glossy head, hurt that I had not known, but aware of the thrill of newness. Of possibility.

The king said, "We'll make sure he learns kingship."

Lasva agreed, and from that I understood that she had tried to beget a boy, probably at Ivandred's wish. Fresh sorrow at our lack of communication hurt me. As the king went on at tedious length about the right way to educate a prince, and Lasva agreed to every word, I consoled myself by reviewing my lessons on wards; not until the end of the session did I see that the king was watching Lasva suspiciously. Her very compliance seemed to disturb him, and he dismissed her abruptly.

On the way back, she said in Marloven (for she'd forbidden us to converse in our own tongue where others could hear), "I've written to Ingrid-Jarlan about those robes, Emras. I forgot to mention that she answered last night, sending me sketches. How vexing! She located, probably at great trouble, a single surviving scrap from those very old days, a sketch someone had done of the first Savarend to become king, surrounded by his friends."

"What is amiss?" I asked.

"Moustaches! The men wore these long moustaches in those days. It looks like worms crawled onto their faces and died there. Their hair was loose, too, and from the look of the sketch, seldom cleaned or brushed, though perhaps the sketch was made on their arrival from a long ride. Their clothing looks like what the stable hands wear when they ride. The point is, they are not suitable models for a tapestry."

"I thought we were going to put them in modern dress."

"I just wanted to see if the old-fashioned dress looked better, because modern dress seems absurd when we're depicting an event of centuries ago."

"But we do not know anything about the actual event."

"Correct," Lasva said, as we passed the women guards. I felt their gazes. "So all must be symbolic." And when we were inside, the door closed, "Some of the king's jarls were not in any of the old lists, either, which creates another sort of difficulty. Modern dress it is. But we'll surround them with artifacts of history. That ought to lend the whole sufficient . . . glory."

Her tone changed on the last word.

That night, I began a new castle exploration. I was not about to begin replacing wards until I understood the entire structure of their magic. It was easy enough to see that most had been laid around the mage's tower, going outward like the spokes of a wheel. There were so many that surely I could use a tiny spell just to illuminate the system.

Until then, I'd been careful to avoid the area everyone called "the old tower." This massive round structure was jammed awkwardly between the main building and the garrison, where I'd never set foot. The tower was at least four centuries old. In the old record, it was termed the Harskialdna Suite. My first foray was just to walk its extreme perimeter, sensing the wards.

Here is where I must begin discussing magic. Those mages about to sit in judgment over me will see the attached set of spells in specific; the scribes who read this testimony will not know what I'm talking about.

I am going to resort to metaphor, color and chain. I discovered the most amazing series of interlocking links protecting the Sigradir's chambers, surpassed only by those protecting the king's. These chains, or rings of chains, were also layered so deeply that I detected seven different hands. Maybe more beneath. Older spells were colder colors, the blue of the ocean, shading to the pale silver of ice. Newer spells glowed red like the heart of a fire. I would not accomplish my task soon. It would take at least a year, probably more.

So, where to begin? With the most recent spells. Only when those were adjusted could I dare to go deeper. And I would begin as far away from the castle as possible, in hopes that adjusting the city wards would not alarm the Sigradir.

However, after an entire day spent walking around the city and following the newest chain of spells, I discovered that the most recent ward entwined the city and the castle . . . and the lock for the entire interlace of spells was strongest at the tower.

It took a week to comprehend the structure, and then to duplicate the lock in memory before I dared to unlock and replace it.

The rest of that day, and the day after, I used all my skills to remain unnoticed, dreading a magical (or military) summons. When there was no outcry I ventured more bravely, working rapidly to dissolve the entire ring and replace it with a stronger, neater structure. The work was exhausting, and that ring was only one out of thousands forming hundreds of interlocking chains that were further connected by interlocked Vennknots of protective spells.

But I had succeeded in completing one. I had done the work of a real mage. What did that make me? A scribe attempting to be a mage, I thought as I walked the upper corridor on the third night. It was late. Marlovens retired early and rose before dawn. At this late hour, the king's hall was guarded only by a pair of roving sentries.

I was so certain that I was alone that I nearly ran straight into the king and his mage as I passed the rooms that were to be the nursery.

I heard voices inside. An unknown voice said, ". . . that the book exists, but if it does, it's far away in the land of the Venn. And it will be hidden well, as they are forbidden by treaty against the performance of any kind of magic. It is the only source of that set of spells, I promise you, Haldren-Harvaldar."

The king's raspy, gaspy voice was immediately recognizable, "Get it, Andaun! Get it! You must find out who has been tampering with your magic any way you can. It has to be a conspiracy, and I will flay whoever is behind it."

I backed away and fled, sick with terror. My work had been detected!

The next day, I decided to avoid the castle altogether and study the city wards. I would dare nothing until I understood the entire structure—and how, if possible, to work without detection. I planned to begin at the castle's outer perimeter, at the other end of the great parade court between the castle and the high wall of the academy, and work outward from there.

I sloshed across the rainy courts behind the castle, ignored my old token-making site, and ventured into new territory. At the perimeter of the garrison I was stopped by unfamiliar guards.

"I'm the Haranviar's first runner," I said.

They didn't stir. Their swords prevented me from moving forward. My heart hammered against my ribs, and my mouth dried: I'd been caught, not by magical wards, but by stumbling into one of the king's guard perimeters under specific orders.

A guard was sent off and, not long after, the king himself appeared, gasping for breath. "What's this?" He peered at me, and his face changed from suspicion and anger to wariness. "This is one of the peacocks," he said to the guards. And to me, "What are *you* doing here?"

"The tunics," I said. "For the tapestry. The princess—the Haranviar— asked me to observe the guards' formal tunics, so we can draw them." This was entirely true, but it had happened two days before. It was the least suspicious excuse I could think of.

The king waved me aside impatiently. "Go on, go on. Tell the watch captain to summon a pair in formal gear." And to me, "No one is permitted here but my guard. If you are sent on an errand here, you must ask a runner to accompany you."

The swords lifted. I passed one way, and the king the other, coughing and muttering.

My skin crawled. I abandoned my real task and, under the eyes of the watchful guards, toiled out into the rain to the command side of the garrison, where I wasted my own morning and that of two young guards who posed for me in the heavy, long, quilted black-and-tan tunics that they wore for their formal Convocation. When I'd made the sketches, I returned to Lasva's chambers.

She looked at me in surprise. "I already have these," she said. "Pelis did them night before last. Did you not see?"

Blushing mightily, I said that I hadn't. As I added my sketches to the pile on the great table, Pelis whispered, "You did not think my sketches good enough?"

"I forgot you made them," I returned, full knowing how stupid that sounded as she had given them to me on her return.

For the remainder of that week I confined myself to study and review. There was far more danger than I had thought, but why? I did nothing immoral, illegal, or threatening to the welfare of the castle inhabitants. The danger was entirely in the king's imagination.

I had detected seven hands involved in the creation of the interlocking chains of magic around Choreid Dhelerei (and my walk hinted that there were more, here and there, like knots in a grain of wood). Was it possible the king's fear was based on some hidden truth? In other words, was one of the seven hands a Norsundrian?

I wanted to know, but I also wanted to do. The potential elegance of the structure of chains, so hidden from everyday eyes, appealed to me as strongly as once had the most perfectly written manuscript, embellished with gold leaf flourishes.

Was it distance from the city that would keep me undetected, or speed? During the next week, I practiced on the least important set of spells, the water-cleaning spell at the stable. I could not imagine the elderly Sigradir prowling the stable to test his water-cleaning wards. I practiced until I was so fast that there was scarcely any time between the breaking of the spell and the establishing of a newer, stronger chain. Now I held the magic more firmly and rarely got that sense of dangerous heat.

The day before Restday, I was in the staff dining hall eating the midday meal when we heard the thunder of horse hooves.

Everyone moved to the open windows to look into the enormous stable yard below, where a double-column of riders galloped into the yard at top speed, reining in almost nose to tail. It was an impressive sight: the perfect control, the lances on the foremost riders never wavering, so the yellow and silver banner lifted freely in the breeze.

On one side of me, a runner snorted. "Look at the mud on those yellows."

An off-duty guard said, "Typical Yvanavar strut." She turned away, muttering low-voiced to another woman, ". . . must be a hot ride in the saddle. Why else would she choose him?"

"Tdiran was always . . ."

Their voices were subsumed under a louder male conversation on my other side, about the forebears of the horses. I remained long enough to observe that the host wore their formal battle tunics rather than their regular riding clothes. As the handsome Danrid Yvanavar dismounted and stalked toward the tower that led up to the governmental chambers, leading a train of warriors and personal runners, I understood that this was some kind of political mission, perhaps the equivalent of arriving at Lily Gate at the Hour of the Crown, with musicians in attendance, strumming historical airs.

Judging from the resulting sense of tension, the significance was more dire.

The next morning after breakfast, I found Lasva on her knees in the room that had been set aside for the tapestry. The loom had been built, and the warp was ready. At last Lasva was happy with the drawing and had begun stippling it onto the undyed warp yarn with ink. As customary in Colend, she'd begun with the border.

When I entered, she said, "Let me just finish this row, then we can take up our fans. I'm eager to begin the weft work." She indicated the table full of yarns waiting behind us, some of the colors having traveled across the entire continent before Nifta, who was our expert in threads and fabrics, was satisfied.

Pelis was in the process of setting the yarn balls in baskets according to hue.

"This fox face is so strange," I said, putting my finger to the central figure in the border pattern, which was made up of various symbols used by Marlovens over the years. "It looks a little like an eagle from one way, and a fox from another."

"I thought it was a lion at first," Pelis said, her head tipping to one side, then the other.

"Here's what astonished me," Lasva said as she measured out a very complicated Venn knot. "My discovery that Ivandred's great-grandfather, who reunited the kingdom, was everywhere hailed as the true king."

"So romantic!" Pelis exclaimed sardonically, eyebrows aslant, and in Kifelian, "It's amazing any of them get born."

"How much of it really happened and how much was rewritten by the victors?" I asked, catching myself after I'd spoken in Kifelian.

Lasva gestured Harmony—not quite a rebuke—and she continued in Marloven. "They tend to burn a great deal of their forebears' records. It has been quite an expedition, to piece out the missing years. Yet the archive is full of records detailing the lineage of their horses, and the patrols made, and exact countings of people, horses, and animals found there."

"I thought the idea of 'true kings' was confined to the Sartorans," I said, "—the belief that there must be a Landis on the throne of Sartor. We Colendi certainly never made any such claim."

"Lirendis are traditional monarchs." Lasva fluttered her fingers in mockery, then put hands on hips. "I've tried to combine all the symbols that evoke kingship. There are so many! Like Khanivar's marmot, emblematic of the Khani family, who came from—"

The door banged open, and guards clattered in, swords drawn, but held point up. Behind them came the king, his face waxen as he looked around, then the hard, almost mad suspicion corrugating his face eased slightly when he saw the tapestry loom.

We all stood, hands over our hearts.

"Where is my son?" the king demanded.

Lasva spread her hands, eyes wide in surprise. "I do not know, Haldren-Harvaldar. Is he not riding somewhere in the north?"

The king went out again, followed by his guards.

Lasva set aside her drawing tools and signed for me to follow to her inner room, where we took up our fans.

Once across the room, then back again, in silence. Then she whispered in Kifelian, "Ivandred warned me that if I beget a child, his father might seek an excuse to kill Ivandred in one of his fits of anger."

"Why?"

"Because an infant would be easier to control." She flicked the fan toward Thorn Gate and said in our language, "Perhaps you did not know, but Ivandred's sister told me that their father killed his own father the day he came of age." She sped up the pace.

Whirl, slash, whirl, slash. To the wall and back we stepped, fans snapping and cutting the air. "How do you educate a future king?" she said finally. "I never thought about any of these things before. I want this child to be civilized, to understand the necessity for peace. To understand love. Yet if it's a boy, he must survive in this . . ." Her voice trailed off.

Snap, snap, slash! Four times she whirled and struck, ripping the cloth in a perfect cut. Then we took the cloths down, she handed me two, and we went to sit in the next room to stitch them up again. When she spoke again, it was in Marloven. About plays.

FIVE

OF LIGHTNING RUTILANT

*Z*athumbre is the Colendi term for the breathless, charged air when the sky is tumbling with lurid clouds and you know that lightning is about to strike but you do not know where. Our words, as usual, come from the Sartoran (*zathre*) but as usual there is an added meaning: the charged atmosphere of high, uneven, violent emotion, signified in the intensifier *umb*.

In Colend, violent emotion might be expressed in a fan of contrasting colors snapped open to shock the eyes, or in *the arrow*, that is, a deliberate straight line walked through a gathering, paying no attention to the proper deference. Both, implying transgression, will cause the susurrus of whispers like the rain after thunder. We even have a term for the wake of whispers after a moment of *zathumbre*.

With the arrival of Danrid Yvanavar, we lived in a state of *zathumbre*. The attack on the bridge, the Jevair imposters, had formed the context for Marloven life: anticipation of not just emotional but physical violence.

But life must be lived, and we began the tapestry. We all behaved with strict attention to detail, with soft voices and deferential politeness, but the storm broke, as storms will.

Storms are experienced differently, depending on where you are when the clouds roll overhead. For some, this storm had begun years ago. Perhaps even generations. For us Colendi, it began with the king's summoning Lasva.

She set aside her ink and stippling pen, then cast me a look, her lips tight, her pupils huge. "Attend me, first runner?"

I set aside my yarns (for I was embroidering in the tiny details that cannot be woven) and followed her to the throne room.

Ah-ye! How I remember the sharp smell of male sweat on that heavy, cold air, the shifting eyes of the guards as we followed the king up onto the marble daïs. Before we could take our places, once again the cobblestone streets rumbled with hundreds of hooves.

The king paused, one step on the daïs. He swayed, then jerked his hand at the guards. "Alert," he rasped, the single word sending him into a fit of coughing.

As some guards unsheathed weapons, moving closer to the throne, others ran to the doors to shut and bar them, staking position at either side with their spear-banners held at the ready. The king dropped heavily onto his cushioned throne, snorting in his breath.

Lasva sank with swift grace onto her cushion, head bowed, palms on her thighs. I took my place behind her, distracted by how purple the king's huge ears looked, contrasting with the paleness of his hair. Why would I notice such things when I felt danger all around me? Perhaps my fleeing wits caught on any little thing they could comprehend, rather than be swept away entirely by my helplessness before the terrifying sense of imminent danger.

The king drank from the beaten gold wine cup waiting beside him and straightened up, then he beckoned Danrid forward. But before he could speak, a loud rapping on the door echoed through the vast stone chamber.

"Who hails?" one of the door guards called, with a quick glance toward the throne.

"Ivandred," came the prince's voice, clear in spite of the thick iron-reinforced wood.

"Let him in. But only—" the king began, then pawed at the air in the direction of the door as he began coughing again.

The doors were opened, Ivandred walked in, mud-splashed to the waist. He paused at a minor scuffle behind him as the guards labored to bar his men from following. Ivandred flicked his hand out behind him in the "halt" command, and the doors shut on his attendants.

"Father," Ivandred said. He reached the throne in a few swift steps, then saluted, hand flat over his heart. "I rode myself to examine the terrain. Danrid's charge is false. Olavair remained on their side of the river."

"I protest this slur on my honor as Jarl of Yvanavar," the tall man protested, coming forward. "I was well within my rights as defender of my—"

"Tuh . . ." the king tried to speak, but choked on the words, gagging and hurring.

Ivandred cut through. "It was entirely specious, a ruse intended for one purpose: to ruin Haldren Marlovair—"

"Tuh . . ." the king tried to shout, but only hacked wheezingly.

"Marlovair disobeyed an order!" Danrid shouted.

Neither Lasva nor I understood the politics, but one thing was clear: the conflict between Ivandred and Danrid had gone from covert to overt.

"Take him!" The king's voice was so guttural he was almost incomprehensible.

Both Ivandred and Danrid stilled as the king pressed both fists to his chest. The noises he made were so horrible I found myself struggling to breathe for him. He lurched toward Lasva, pawed at her arm as he said, "Guard . . ." the next word was unintelligible, then he groaned and fell backward, his hands loose.

The guards looked at one another, hands gripping their weapons. Danrid's eyes narrowed, but he had no weapon. Neither did Ivandred, as weapons were forbidden in the king's presence. They looked at one another, then Ivandred lunged forward, kneeling down in spite of his mud, to lift his father's head from the cold black marble of the throne arm.

The king's mouth had gone slack, his breathing labored. The guards' gazes shifted between the two men and Lasva, most frequently back to her. The guards' own lives depended on what they did next. The king had said "take *him*," but no one knew which "him" was meant.

So Lasva said, "We should get the king into his bed and summon the healer."

The guards obeyed with such alacrity their relief was plain. The king had said nothing about "her" and the princess had given an order. Thus, at a moment most dire, there was a clear chain of command.

"Unlock the doors," Lasva said briskly, and the door guards leapt to do that.

The ones around the throne worked together to make a kind of carry-all with their arms. They did so in an efficient manner that I would come to recognize as part of their field training. Moving together, they lifted the king and bore him off.

Lasva said, "I will attend the king until the healer arrives. First runner, attend me, please." This last to me, her tone urgent.

"I will go with you," Danrid declared, with a glare Ivandred's way. "To make certain nothing happens to the king. And that his orders are . . ."

Danrid's personal guards had stepped up to either side of him.

"Heard." Ivandred finished, as his glance flicked past Danrid to Lasva. I could not see her, but I sensed that some kind of signal went between them, quicker than a heartbeat, and then Ivandred shifted his attention to the angry jarl. "Do that. Do that, Danrid."

The jarl's cheeks reddened, and he made the barest flick of his fingers over his chest, a belated gesture that reminded me he ought to have saluted.

And so I slipped into the most disparate group of people I had ever experienced, as the guards followed Lasva down the corridor. She seemed to float, gliding swiftly ahead of the guards bobbing behind, their heavy boots clattering. Runners accumulated behind us. Counterpoint to them was Danrid, following me. His breathing stirred my hair, he was so close to my heels. At a corner I glanced back. Ivandred was nowhere in sight.

So there had definitely been a signal between Lasva and Ivandred.

The king's rooms smelled musty and sour. "Open the windows," Lasva ordered the servants.

"The king has not permitted the windows to open for ten years at least," whispered the oldest servant, his hand at his breast.

The other said in a low voice, "He has forbidden the garrison healer to come near him. He . . . he feared poison." The man looked away.

Lasva turned her palm up. "If he will not permit the healer here, then we must do our best for him ourselves. Fresh air might do him good, wouldn't you agree? He is fighting so hard for breath. And steeped leaf. Perhaps we can talk him into sipping it."

No one argued with that. One runner went to struggle with the nearest window, and another left, as the guards gently laid the king on the bed. The old servants fussed about, tugging the king's tunic straight over his bony knees and his sleeves straight over the gnarled wrists, and then, hesitantly, began to tug the royal boots off. His knobby feet in their stockings looked abject to my eyes before they covered him with quilts.

The jarl gestured for his men to wait outside the chamber, then he took up a station at the window closest to the bed, where he could see everyone.

Lasva beckoned, and I joined her by the far window. The jarl looked our way, then back at the king as the old servants brought elderberry-ginger steep, more blankets, water, and a change of clothing.

A servant entered with something on a tray. The king groaned.

Lasva crossed the room quickly. Before she could speak, the oldest of the servants leaned over the bed, his low voice a rumble as he coaxed the king to waken and take a sip of the brew he held ready.

"You drink it first," Danrid commanded Lasva, startling us all.

The old servant's amazement altered to mottled anger.

Lasva said calmly, "I believe we are confusing the king's runner's perception of chain of command."

The jarl glared from one to another of the servants, then pointed at me. "She can drink it. In case someone saw fit to send up poisoned steep."

Lasva addressed me. "Scribe Emras, you may regard what you just heard as a request."

The jarl stared at Lasva, and she gazed back. Now I understood why Danrid was with us. I'd thought he was going to attack the king, and Ivandred had signaled Lasva to be present to avoid that. He was waiting for the king to rouse himself, and complete an order for the guards to seize Ivandred. Danrid meant to witness the order, and see that it was carried out, and until then, protect the king from *us*.

There was so much tension in that room that I said to Lasva, "I do not mind heeding the jarl's request, Lasva-Haranviar. I cannot believe the kitchens would send up poison."

I took the cup from the hands of the old servant, turned the brim the way we do when we share Restday cup with family, and drank down the hot liquid, which was fresh and aromatic.

There was a besorcelled handkerchief on a side table. I wiped the rim and handed the cup back to the servant. In silence he poured another cup, then stood there with the cup in his hands as he stared down at the still figure on the bed.

The king had fallen asleep.

After a time, Lasva said to Danrid, "Shall I send for refreshment? Or you could send your own people, if you fear we conspire against you."

Her smile was sweet, her voice warm. The man flushed and made that negating motion. "Send anyone you like. I think no one in this room is conspiring." His high tone had dropped closer to normal.

The king's second personal runner said, "I will order a meal." He added with faint affront, not quite in Danrid's direction, "And personally supervise its preparation."

He went out, leaving another silence suspended in time.

When he returned with a row of tray-bearing servants, Lasva extended a hand to Danrid in invitation. He sat down stiffly across from her at the low table at the other end of the room, and Lasva drew Danrid by gradual degrees into speech. Too trivial to record here, it was an exercise in the Colendi arts of filling time with pleasant chat, and gradually Danrid's short, abrupt responses lengthened into sentences. Encouraged by her, he described his land, and the horses raised on the northern studs, whose ancestors all came from the Nelkereth plains to the east.

Finally Danrid laughed, a short, husky bark. When he smiled, the fellow was handsome. Lasva met my eyes, and then flicked her gaze to the window. The king's rooms were built along one of the outer walls, which were so thick that benches had been carved into either side of the window alcoves.

She wants me to witness, I thought, as I slipped into the alcove and sat down gratefully on the stone bench.

Time passed, marked only by the gradual shifting of the shadows along the stone. Though I knew I was to be a witness, there was nothing to mark in the talk, which had shifted to riding, lessons in riding, carriages, and differing customs. Their voices blended pleasantly, Danrid's acrimony having dissipated like morning mist. I shut out the difficult, rattling breathing of the king as I began reviewing my magic lessons.

The ochre rays of the sun had nearly reached the toes of my slippers when the old servant startled everyone by exclaiming in a low, pain-rent growl, "O my king . . ."

I leaped up. There were no swords, no threats. No one had moved from their places. The jarl and Lasva came together to the bedside. I stopped behind Lasva's shoulder as we looked down at the still figure of the king. The slow, rattling breathing had stopped.

Lasva turned to me. "You must summon the prince," she said.

The jarl stared from the king to her and then to me, his demeanor hardening to the tension I'd seen on our arrival. He yanked open the door, snapped his fingers at the two men who waited there with the king's silent guards, and the three of them moved away so swiftly that they were gone when I reached the top of the stairs.

From the doorway behind me, Lasva said softly in Kifelian, "Before he does, if you can."

I halted then went back to the silent guards at the door, who were staying at their post until ordered differently.

"Where is the prince?" I asked, half expecting them to ignore me.

"Guardhouse," one said.

Because I am determined to tell the truth as I understand it, here I must admit that after that, I dashed along the halls, full of my own importance at bearing this epoch-changing news, my emotions untarnished by the slightest vestige of regret. But after I'd encountered four sets of guards who crossed their spears at my appearance before allowing me to pass, I noticed there were more guards than usual. Thereafter, I found a pair at every intersection—male and female—with young runners here and there, ready to sprint. Everyone's eyes tracked me as I passed.

I approached the prison, deep within the garrison part of the castle. I had no wish to see the spectacle of a dungeon in reality, yet here I was, approaching the thick, iron-reinforced doors to its gates. Anticipatory horror tightened my nerves as I walked up to the guards. One pulled the huge door open.

"The prince is in the lower level," the guard's tone with the last two words conveyed meaning that I had not yet the experience to catch.

I stepped inside, instinctively fearing that I would never again emerge. There were no instruments of torture hung about in readiness for use. The stone walls were exactly like those elsewhere in the castle, save for the varied shapes of rusting iron bars outside the ancient, warped glass in the few window slits.

A tall boy emerged from a side room. "Are you the princess's runner?" On my assent, "They just came up from below." He opened his palm toward the first door along the hall.

From habit my steps were soundless as I walked through the empty outer chamber and approached the inner one. The only light was from a lantern hung on a hook high on the wall to my right. Ivandred and Haldren Marlovair sat together on a bench below the window in an otherwise bare, clean-swept cell.

I must describe this still-vivid image: the prince still mud-spattered from his long ride, the hilt of a knife visible at the top of one of his boots, his body leaning as the two sat forehead to forehead. The prince's right hand braced the back of Haldren Marlovair's head, the tendons in his fingers standing out. Haldren, too, was disheveled, but the grime in his skin and clothing and the smell of sweat were so stale they had to be days old. His profile was drawn, his eyes closed as Ivandred said in a low, husky voice rendered sharp and clear by the bare stone walls surrounding us, "You know he's a liar, and I know he's a liar, but I can't accuse him before the Convocation without proof. That will be his excuse for civil war. It's the law, Haldren. Everything according to law."

Haldren whispered, "I am not a coward."

"Everyone knows that. Danrid looks like a coward to accuse you."

"Then . . . do what you will. Shoot me. But not a coward's punishment."

I had frozen in place outside the cell, so I saw every detail and heard every word. I knew I shouldn't disturb them, and yet I had news that was too important not to impart.

"It was the king's will, Hal. We both know Danrid hears what he wants to hear, but Len was on door duty, and he assures me that it was clear enough spoken that everyone in the throne room heard it. You know the importance of heeding the king's last command, sorry as it is, until he can rescind it. And I will get him to rescind it as soon as he wakens, I promise you that."

Haldren whispered something too low for me to hear, after which Ivandred said, "If we both survive this day, you will ride at the head of the First Lancers as commander, whatever happens. You have my oath, brother in shared blood."

In shared blood was in Marloven a compound word that I had not heard before, and I did not understand its import then. I knew only that I was not meant to witness this conversation.

Haldren lifted his voice. "My honor is in your hands."

I had begun step by step to back away. But my movement must have stirred the air, or maybe it was their eternal wariness, for both heads turned.

For a heartbeat two pairs of shock-rounded eyes stared at me from faces taut with strain. Then Ivandred's eyes narrowed in a twitch of anger at my trespass. He straightened up, his jaw hardening.

Haldren's eyes closed as the prince let him go, and he sank back against the wall.

"The princess sent me to tell you that the king is dead," I said, falling into old habit: I gave him the words in Lasva's intonations and accent.

His eyelids flashed up in brief surprise. "Where is she now?"

"She stayed with your father," I said.

"Danrid Yvanavar?" he asked.

"He left ahead of me," I said. "But I do not know what was his destination."

"It matters little." Ivandred's mouth creased in a brief, bleak smile as he gazed down at Haldren. "He will have discovered by now that I have the castle secure." He did not wait for Marlovair to respond. "Come, Scribe," he said to me. "There is much to be done." And in a low voice, "Bide. Remember my oath."

He walked out, me scurrying at his heels. I heard the runner shut those iron-reinforced doors behind us, one, two, and three—leaving Haldren still in prison.

"Can you remember orders?" he asked over his shoulder as he sped through the garrison, everyone in sight standing still, fists to hearts, eyes tracking us.

"I can," I said.

He issued a stream of orders that are immaterial to list here. They were mostly summons, or curt sets of words to be spoken to this or that person. We parted at the foot of the stairway to the king's rooms, and then I began to make up for my long day of standing by running all over the castle.

Every person I spoke to listened to me with exquisite intensity, indicating that although I was in the center of great events I barely comprehended how great.

The watch change in the middle of the night was the first time I sat down. Marnda had left a meal waiting in our staff sitting room, along with a candle. The precious summer steep had gone cold, its surface oily. I ate the bread and butter, then pillowed my head on my arms. I'd meant to rest only my eyes, but I woke when my legs had gone numb.

I heard singing. The room was dark. The candle had gone out.

The rise and fall of voices was faint but gradually swelled in volume as more voices joined, and then slowly passed as I rubbed at the painful needle-pricks in my legs. I couldn't yet stand.

The singing faded away again as Pelis came in, bearing a tray with food and a candle on it. In the wavering light she set it down and swiftly set out the fresh bread, some oat slurry, and more of our precious steep, from the refreshing smell. My eyes prickled at the scent of home.

"The singing is them bearing the king away." Pelis's brown hair blended with the shadows. Her eyes were wide, the pupils dark as she whispered, "Lnand told me all the guards are on readiness alert."

A rustle behind her, and Lasva joined us. "There you are, Emras," she said. "I looked in your room. Thank you, Pelis."

Pelis gave a faint sigh as she made The Peace and withdrew.

Lasva moved into the light, her eyes marked with exhaustion. She sipped from a cup she carried. "What did you see in the king's chamber, Emras? Ah-ye, I misspeak." She raised two fingers. "There was so very much to see. What was your impression when Danrid gave you that order to taste the cup?"

I said, "He was about to insist? Perhaps, might have used force? There was the tensing here and here." I touched my shoulder and my jaw.

Lasva laced her fingers together around her cup. "Yes. I think . . . there is only a pretense of regarding me as Ivandred's equal in their chain of command."

The word "barbarians" shaped my lips, but she forestalled me with a forefinger. "As we treated King Jurac of the Chwahir. A semblance of respect, but if Jurac had given orders as the queen does, no one would have obeyed, at least, not without her corroboration."

"The Colendi are loyal to Queen Hatahra," I said. "No one feels loyalty to the Chwahir king."

"I have been pondering the ephemera of hierarchy," she said, setting the cup down, "and of my own place, if I am truly to be an aid to Ivandred and not just a decoration. Either I request Ivandred to order these people to obey me, or I find a way to inspire loyalty on my own."

Loyalty.

Here, *at last*, was my opportunity.

I stood up, so that I could make the full Peace, and then I dropped to my knees before her. "O Princess Lasthavais," I said, my words tumbling out. "Now that the king is dead, I must unburden my heart and confess the secret I was ordered by the queen your sister to withhold from you: I have begun to learn magic."

My heart was so full of remorse and sorrow that I misstated the queen's orders, which as you have seen, were not about learning magic but about discerning whether Norsundrian magic was at work in Marloven Hesea—something the Sartoran Mage Council, through Greveas, also wanted to know. But what I told Lasva was what I now believed, and so I explained about the book I'd arranged to get from my cousin, and my secret studies. I told her about the spell I did at the bridge, and how I discovered Ivandred's teacher, the Herskalt.

But did I tell her everything?

No.

When do you keep secrets from those you love most? When the knowledge of them would cause nothing but hurt. So I reasoned as I approached the Herskalt's disc, the dyr, and its lessons. As I neared the subject and saw how taken aback she was when I told her about my being able to send Ivandred to her on New Year's, I thought for the first time, would she have granted me permission to experience her secret thoughts had I asked? Though I had not chosen to do so, I had participated as a learning exercise. Yet my learning exercise had been through her memories, never willingly shared. And so I did not mention the dyr.

The blue light of dawn painted us with shadow, turning the candle light to dirty smudges, when I finished.

Lasva said, "I asked you once for personal loyalty, but now I wonder if I asked too much." As I moved to protest—to implore, to explain—I even considered, for a reckless moment, the relief of confiding everything, including the dyr, but then she raised her hand. "Ah-yedi! I hear your good intentions in every breath. Yet is true fidelity possible? My sister issuing orders to my own staff that I was not to know about. Not just you and Marnda, but this Herald Martande, whom I do not even know."

Is she doubting my loyalty? I thought in despair when the prince's step approached. "There you are," he said to me. "Have you explained? Yes, I can see. Good. I am in desperate need of more transfer tokens, and Andaun is gone."

Lasva said, "I take it you would like Emras to continue her duties with magery?"

Ivandred said, "She could be of immeasurable value. The Herskalt—my tutor, I told you about him. He has cautioned me for years to spend more time at my studies, but I can seldom get the time. This scribe could take up where I left off."

"So shall it be," Lasva said. "Emras, so shall it be."

I bowed, forgetting my Marloven salute in my overwhelming relief. Ivandred then dismissed me to rest before I began the hard work of making those tokens. As I retreated at last to my room, I wondered two things: where Sigradir Andaun was, and if he knew about the dyr.

SIX

OF SECRETS AND SYNCRETICS

W hen I woke, my head ached, but there was a pervasive sense of relief that I identified as soon as I sat up. The king was dead!

Did anyone mourn? Though I would never find that castle beautiful, it seemed less oppressive as I walked into the familiar rooms, knowing I would never again hear that disgusting rheumy cough or fear the threat of royal whim.

A tray of biscuits sat on our table. I meant to eat one and then transfer to the Herskalt, but scarcely had I taken a bite when Lasva entered, her manner so like that of her younger days, my heart lifted. "There you are! Come, Emras. Let us continue our good habits. We shall begin as we mean to go on," she exclaimed as we entered the practice chamber. "So long ago seem the days when we supped surrounded by flowers, midway through a ball!"

She shut the door so that we were alone, and lowered her voice. "While you and I endured that long deathbed wait—and Danrid Yvanavar no doubt considered whether or not to kill us—Ivandred made certain that everyone else in the castle understood there would be a lawful change of government. They know their history. The first to die after a violent change of kings have usually been the servants of the old king."

I gasped as my nerves chilled all the way to my back teeth. "I never considered that."

"We wouldn't," she whispered. "In Colend, the monarch dies, and there is an orderly progression, with dignity and grace. Sometimes with true grief and sometimes with affectation of grief over anticipation of change. But here?" She snapped a fan open. "Our weapons! You know how the patterns come in pairs, and we have practiced them side by side?"

I nodded in wonderment.

"We have never tried them face to face. Let us experiment."

"How can a dance teach us to fight?"

"We shall try this one thing. Slowly, Emras. We will begin with the simplest movements. On my count, now."

I fell automatically into place, my hands and arms beginning the familiar movement, but with Lasva facing me—her fan moving opposite mine—I faltered, distracted by the fact that her arm was in the way, she was too close. I fell back, confused. It felt much like learning to sing in part for the first time.

"Ah-ye," Lasva whispered. "It's true. Look. Do the three first steps again. Forget about me. Just do them, very slowly, as slow as the drip of honey."

I raised my fan, stepped, swept, and there was Lasva's arm, blocking the fan, and forcing it downward. My other hand came up in a block, and there was her fan in its pretty horizontal sweep at the level of my neck.

The next step was the twirl, which avoided her block, then the shift from one foot to the other and the side-sweep—and there she was, stepping past me—this time I blocked a sweep from her.

Amazed, I faltered again. We stared at each other. "It *is*," she whispered, her eyes wide. "It's a lesson not in dance, but in fighting. Come, let's go through the entire pattern. Slow, now, on my beat."

After so many strange events, it was another strange experience to find Lasva attacking me, and myself warding her blows. We performed the entire pattern through three times, Lasva's forehead puckered with concentration and then puzzlement.

When we finished, she said, "Do you see it?"

"I think I do, yet in true fighting you would not know exactly what your opponent is going to do next, would you?"

"Perhaps you would, if you are experienced enough? Ivandred said something to me about how one first has to learn patterns, so that one does not have to think. Like, if I tell you to ready your pen, you know exactly what to do."

I made The Peace, then asked, "Are we then going to commence striking one another with our fans?" I tried to keep doubt from my voice, but she laughed softly, one forearm pressed against her middle. "Right now your time is better spent with the magic lessons."

How my heart filled with joy! "May I begin, then?"

Lasva smiled. "Go, Emras. When you return, I might ask to see you perform magic, if does not discommode you."

I found the Herskalt waiting for me.

"The king is dead," I said. "But you knew?"

The Herskalt gave me that wry smile. "Ivandred was here last night."

I opened my hands. "Then why are we here? Why do we not meet in the castle?"

"There remains the matter of the wards that you have yet to penetrate. Your assignment now begins in earnest, for in those protections are built lethal wards. All on the king's orders, I hasten to add. Do not blame poor old Andaun. But those wards must be dismantled all the way to the fundamental spells, which are a snarl and patchwork that wastes magic. You are to establish a clean structure that will be all the stronger and remove all those personal wards against people who have been dead for centuries, as well as those against us living."

"Us? Where are these other mages?"

The Herskalt laughed silently. "The Guild Chief of Sartor, for one. The king had poor Andaun discover who the strongest mages in the world were and ward every one of them."

"Yet my question still stands. I cannot be the only mage student. Would it not be much faster if someone with more experience attends to the task? Where are Sig—ah, Andaun-Sigradir's own students?"

"There are none."

"How can that be?"

"A combination of reasons, beginning with the deep distrust Marlovens have for mages, or anyone they cannot vanquish with a sword. There's the king's distrust. Andaun lost the two he'd begun training; one was killed, the other disappeared. Then he became too old, and too bound up with the king's frantic demands for safety, to begin training a new one. So when you appeared along with Ivandred, with your fast ability to learn. . . ." He laughed again, no sound—a quick flash of teeth, the crinkle of eyes. "The royal runners can do some very limited, very basic spells, but there is only ever a single royal mage in this kingdom."

"Why are you not appointed?"

"I first came to serve as Ivandred's teacher. His studies, as I am sure you are aware, have been intermittent at best, and so I promised myself elsewhere. I come when I can, because I conceived a liking for Ivandred and sympathy for his position. Now there is you to keep me returning, for you are that rarity, a natural."

I gestured my thanks, warm with pleasure.

"Ivandred was specific. He wants me to train you to replace Andaun. As tutor to the new royal mage, I am assigning you this crucially important task, which only you can perform, as I cannot enter Choreid Dhelerei. And it must be done from inside."

So I was not just to be a mage, but the royal mage! As I made a gesture of protest, he said, "You object? Or am I seeing trained scribal hypocrisy?"

"Hypocrisy!" I repeated, far more disturbed by the accusation than about the putative position of royal mage.

"I suspect you were about to tell me you could not possibly be a royal mage—that you scribes keep the purity of the First Rule, non-interference?"

"We don't interfere in governments," I began, "and we certainly don't participate in wars."

"Have you ever paused to reflect on how animals do not recognize kingdom boundaries?" The Herskalt made The Peace, gently mocking. "Political boundaries are conditional. The Scribe Guild is supposed to ignore them, for example, but what Sartor is trying to foster is a kingdom in secret, its power the control of information."

"We don't control information," I began.

"Scribes can be as dangerous as the most war-mongering, wild duke. More so, because he is outright in his intentions. You move secretly, you dress simply, you influence from behind the carefully cultivated façade of virtue. The scribes, together with the heralds, who were once scribes, have an international legal structure. They control information that kings desire. Within kingdoms, they handle the records of lives. Do you know what they do with that information? Do you really think that no one looks at numbers of marriages, births, and deaths; that policy is not formed on the details of lives—details culled by scribes and heralds?"

"Information that betters lives."

"Information about defense. About offense. Your King Martande the Scribe got ahead because the smart and creative people who felt stultified in Sartor fled to him. He also saw that princes and dukes become interested in legal structure to support and sustain them as soon as the question of inheritance comes up. His kingdom was born not as a result of that fight with the Chwahir. That would have remained a battle, with a statue at the famous site and a few ballads and tapestries. The kingdom was born in recognition of his claim, and in making laws to legitimize that claim, he insured against a series of warrior dukes fighting one another to be king after his death. Everyone in power wanted Colend to survive." The Herskalt leaned forward. "Emras, what I am trying to tell you is that influence is not all bad. You do, however, need to be aware of what you are doing."

"But I have never . . ."

He opened his hand toward my foot. "Your toe ring. You seem to have forgotten it. Assuming that your Sartoran friends could transfer in a flood of magical spies—which the border transfer wards specifically prevent—how would that not be interference?"

"I did not see it this way."

"Of course not. Emras, do not distress yourself. Ivandred does not want a political royal mage. Far from it. You are very well suited to the position because you consciously maintain a political distance. I only ask that you understand that with power, ignorance is not an acceptable excuse. You must learn as much as you can, but you must be very careful. Think through your actions."

"I agree with that." I took a deep breath. "As I am called to serve, and I have the ability, I will do what I am asked. There remains my original orders, to seek signs of Norsunder, and it seems logical to begin my search in Andaun-Sigradir's tower."

The Herskalt gave a voiceless laugh. "Andaun is no more Norsundrian than you are. He was constrained to do what he did by his master's obsessive fears. The Sartoran Mage Council has been pointing accusatory fingers at the Marlovens for generations, accusing them of magical alliance with Norsunder and castigating Marloven culture as a recruiting ground, because the Marloven kings wanted the Council safely warded beyond the border where they couldn't interfere."

"That is a comfort to hear. Do you know where he is so that I may interview him? Ask if I may copy his books, and learn what he's done, to enable me to be more effective?"

"He's not just gone from the castle, he's gone from the kingdom." The

Herskalt gestured, hands turned upward. "Ivandred told me that the poor old man was gone before the next watch bell, once he heard about the king's death. I do not know the particulars of his late interactions with the king, but no doubt they were sufficiently dire. So." The Herskalt touched one of the magic books on the table. "There is no danger from the king or his former mage, but there is still danger from hidden traps. You cannot be complacent. Remember, because I am warded from entering Choreid Dhelerei by any means—even walking in—I cannot be there to help you."

"I will proceed with caution," I said.

"Return to your duties, Scribe Emras. Both of us have much to do."

For the first time, I transferred back to the royal castle in Choreid Dhelerei with a sense of anticipation without equal dread, to find someone utterly unexpected standing in the middle of the staff chamber.

"Birdy!" I exclaimed. I was about to proudly proclaim my astonishing new status—as if by speaking it aloud I could make it more real—but halted, disconcerted by his wary stance, his unsmiling mouth.

"I asked permission of the princess—the queen." He was speaking in Kifelian. "To say my farewells."

"Farewells?" I repeated witlessly.

He looked aside, at the closed door, then back at me, his mouth thin. "Lasva is sending me away. I am returning to Colend with Belimas, who asked to be sent back. I am not being given a choice, it seems: the Marlovens have enough stable hands, and Lasva says that she can write to her sister herself."

He took a step backward toward the door. I followed, instinctively desiring to close the distance between us. "What happened?" I asked, my wits entirely flown. "I don't understand."

He passed a hand over his face. "This isn't working," he mumbled into his palm. "Lasva is angry because of the queen's secret orders." Birdy met my gaze, his sober, the tenderness that I thought an inescapable part of him utterly absent. "But that is not what upsets me most. I did not know what to think or to say when Ivandred said he would send us by magic— using tokens *you* made for him. Emras, why didn't you tell me?"

His voice was raw with grief and betrayal, and I felt the impact as strongly as any physical blow. "The magic was a secret," I said, utterly inadequately.

Birdy made an impatient gesture, as though to strike the words out of the air. "I was there when you received your orders," he said. "And I can understand what made you keep the secret while we were traveling. But you could have whispered to me on the ride. Or when we talked every day, Emras. *Every day*, we met down at the baths, and talked about everything. I thought we talked about everything, for you picked the topics, I made sure of that. How could you possibly think I would be incapable of protecting this secret? If you didn't trust Anhar, why didn't you ask to take me aside? She would have understood. She has always understood. Always deferred. She knows quite well that all the Colendi think her a lesser being because one of her parents was a Chwahir." His voice cracked.

"Ah-yedi, that is not at all—" I exclaimed, my hands out in shadow-warding. "It was *never* that. Never! I kept my secret to protect us *all*. You, too. Even Anhar! *Think* what would have happened if the king had heard a single word!"

He looked aside. "I did not consider that," he said as quickly as I had—as if he, too, willed the gap closed between us. "Yes. That makes sense. Yet you could have asked me." He made that impatient gesture again and flicked his hand up in Thorn Gate. "Enough argument, even with myself. Let it be past." He drew an unsteady breath.

I could not forebear speaking, though I was horribly aware of that day when he left for Chwahirsland. "Will you write to me, Birdy?" My eyes stung with tears.

"Yes," he breathed, his expression softening when he saw my tears. "Yes. I already told Anhar I would write to her. Every day. But . . ." He looked away. Then back. "I was going to buy her a scrollcase, which would cost half a year's pay. But you can make them. Will you make one for Anhar?"

"Of course I will," I promised, and his face eased.

It was then that Anhar burst in, too distraught for politeness. They hurled themselves into one another's arms and kissed fervently, roughly. I looked on, my breathing as ragged as theirs, but my emotions were grief and loss—and a little disgust at those moist, sticky noises.

He broke off, and when Anhar, always so quiet, could not suppress a sob, he left. She sank onto a cushion, her hands over her face. "Why did you do it?" she keened. "Why did you lie to him?"

"I didn't. I couldn't tell him. It might have gotten us all killed. He knows that." I knelt beside her. "Do you want to go back with him? I could speak to Lasva."

"And do what?" Her mouth was bitter. "Back to the world of people humming under their breath, and making plans *between two* in my hearing?" She dropped her hands. "I hate this place. But I know when I'm better off."

She ran out.

Ivandred stroked Lasva's eyebrow with a gentle thumb, then the line of her jaw. "I would do anything to see you happy," he whispered.

"Your wish makes me happy," she returned.

"You say that, yet I see here and here you are angry." He touched the taut flesh on her temple and the tight muscle along the pure line of her jaw. "Give it to me," he said.

They had fallen into a pattern. A lifetime of careful training required this ritual. She was conscious of the necessity as she said, "I am not angry with you."

"I know what to do with anger," he said. "Give it to me."

She raised her hands and put them against his chest. She watched the flick of his eyelids at her touch, the twitch of his lips, and she pushed. And had to step back, because she could not shift him.

Why should his strength be so alluring? She did not question. It just was. She pushed harder, and once more stepped back. So she pushed again, harder, a shove.

"Give it to me," he said and took hold of her wrists.

She used the Altan fan twirl and twisted them from his grasp, then struck at his hands, in play and not quite play. Once again he took her by the wrists, a firmer grip, and she freed herself more violently, and this time she dealt him a ringing slap. His head turned sharply, the red marks of her fingers imprinting the line of his cheekbone. Her fingers stung, and he smiled. "Better. But not good enough."

She used the fan strike with her hand, whirled out of his grasp, and took a step. This time the force came up through her planted foot, centered in her hips, and her body torqued as she swung.

Then he caught her fist, and they grappled. Freed of all constraint she swung at him with all her might, and he fought back. Grunting with effort, her eyes stinging—why were tears always so close? She was angry! Angry . . . and the heat flared.

"Obliterate me," she whispered, and sank her teeth into the palm of his hand.

Afterward she felt as if she'd tumbled into the air and sunlight. There was ache, but it was good, for her nerves were unsheathed, the more sensitive to the fading throb of climax. She floated free, empty of emotion.

Ivandred still lay beside her when she woke. She was not aware of moving, but she had discovered that even the sound of her breath changing would bring Ivandred instantly awake and aware, his body still, his fingers closed around the knife hilt never far from his reach.

She met his watchful gaze on the next pillow and smiled. "I dreamed of wings," she whispered, habit making her sorrowful at the purpling scratch on his neck and on his shoulders. He always insisted he never noticed such things. It seemed to be true. He could not remember how he'd taken some of the scars she had examined with her fingers.

"Wings?" he whispered back. "How is that?"

She had not had one of these dreams since . . .

Her mind slid away from Kaidas and reached for the dream, whose images were already dissipating. But familiar patterns lingered: she always woke a little dizzy from seeing the land below, the wandering ribbon of streams, trees seen from overhead resembling round green sponges, the spires of the palace like spindles just below her fingertips. Dizzy but triumphant from the memory of happiness coursing through her veins as she drifted high on the air, the sun warm on her wings.

That memory of happiness always betrayed her, for there under the memory was the ember of anger. Where did it come from? She was not an angry person. Her earliest memories were Marnda's kindly, firm tone whispering over her head as she sat on her ponder chair, *Princesses are never angry. It makes them ugly, and princesses are always beautiful.* She could not get up from the ponder chair until her anger was conquered— and the last time she'd had to sit on that chair, she was no older than eight.

"What can I do to help you?" she asked, willing away the memories.

"What can I do for you?" He searched her eyes, as if trying to find the thoughts behind them. For in his way he was sensitive to muscle movement, and he sensed the complexities of her mood, though he could not understand them. He wanted her to be happy. He would do anything to make her so. "You have already done much, from the moment you gave up your home to come here. I would have stayed in Colend for a year. I think you know that. But you gave that up for me, and so." He opened his hand toward the bedchamber. "And so we wake up here, instead of arriving straight to a dungeon, with Danrid as king. I wake up every day grateful to you."

"I want to be busy. I want work that matters. You must tell me what a queen does."

His expression altered as he considered, his twitch of shoulder, upward glance a little helpless. "We don't have any custom for a gunvaer, not anymore."

"New custom is not welcome?"

"Right now, they must see a continuation of agreed-on custom, all according to law. Do you see? If I obey the law, that forces the others to do so."

"Will continuation of Marloven custom end the troubles, then?"

"Continuation of custom might circumvent the most obvious problems," he said. "There are two things that we must do immediately. One, the city needs to see a proper memorial for my father. And we need to make ready for the jarls to arrive for renewing their vows as I take the throne."

"And after?"

"Olavair is going to make a move, I am certain of it. And in the south, I had no time to settle Totha. My father knew I did not have time. I hit two castles from which I suspect raiders have originated. Left one of those false Jevair-green tunics on a lance to let them know that I had seen through the ruse. I want that to suffice, but it probably won't."

The watch bell rang then, and it was time for him to rise and get on with his tasks.

Lasva went straightaway to her own chamber, and there, wrapped in silk and imprisoned inside a beautiful darkwood box with herons inlaid in cedar, lay the lover's cup.

She craved the peace of emptiness. She lifted her hand to fling the lover's cup into the fireplace, but the light caught in the fine porcelain, glowing like something alive—the wing of a butterfly, the fragile curve of the ear of a young girl, as heedless of her own beauty as she was of the beauty of summer sunshine. Living hands had ground the ingredients to make this cup, had shaped it and fired it; wishes and dreams had been set into its constituents, and every touch of brush had been laid on with . . .

Love does not last.

Why should art suffer, even if the humans who made the art were as transient as those butterflies? And so she dashed through to the private chamber where we did our fan form and thrust the box into my hands. "Hide it away," she said, with tears along her lower lashes, her mouth tight. "Do not tell me where it is." She whisked herself out.

I opened the box, lifted the heavy silk wrapper, and stared down in astonishment, recognizing at last one of the infamous lover's cups Tiflis had chirped about. I took the thing to my own room and looked around desperately. I had three pieces of furniture: a bed, a desk, a trunk. How could I hide anything?

Magic, of course. I set the box on the desk, cast an illusion over it, and returned, where I found Lasva stretching, her voice brisk, her gaze bright. We worked through our fan forms in the old way, and then faced one another, striking and blocking in the dueling dance, as she talked about how our lives would change.

Lasva then faced me, and I knew that here was the conversation that I had been dreading.

But she had seen that. "We will not talk about my sister's orders," she said. "I understand the dilemma you were placed in. All of you, but you especially with this astonishing command to learn magic. It was to my protection. Ivandred was expressive in your praise. He was far too graphic in his description of what would have happened to you had the king discovered what you were doing, and he insisted that only my ignorance would have protected me from sharing the same sentence. So I comprehend your silence."

I bowed low, wretched with my falsity, for I hadn't known about *that* threat. However, I also knew that to speak was to worsen things.

She continued, "I will only say this: your duty is no longer to my sister. It is to me, and to Ivandred. Regard our wills as united."

I made another full bow.

"He has spoken with you about magic," she said, still with that intent gaze. "What about?"

"Only the tasks at hand. Except once. Before New Year's. He was very tired. Rode with us as long as he could. But when we stopped, he took me aside and showed me Marlovar Bridge. He talked about Inda, who was Elgar the Fox." And at her gesture, I repeated the entire conversation.

"He never said anything like that to me," she observed, and I bowed again, sick with apprehension that yet again I'd done wrong. But she said quickly, "Oh, Emras. I think it's entirely due to the way you scribes are trained. You are easy to talk to. Safe. You stand there so quietly, and we are raised knowing that you cannot interfere, that you must keep our secrets. Merely, I am surprised that he should find it so, having not been raised the same way."

She took a step, hands under her elbows, and I was astonished and disturbed to see a fresh bruise where I thought the edge of her robe had cast a shadow at her collarbone. There was another on her wrist. Who could have bruised her but Ivandred? I had regarded him with the same wariness I regarded all the Marlovens, but also with the respect due his rank. Otherwise I spared him as little thought as ants think about the eagle drifting overhead. The sight of that bruise, however, evoked repugnance, even loathing.

But Lasva's severity eased—she did not have the demeanor I would expect from someone abused. "Though we talk—much—about the kingdom, he seldom speaks of his inner life, and I am trying to understand him. It will come. " She let out her breath. "You and I find ourselves in new ranks of life. You must make the transfer tokens he asked for, as they ease his tasks. But for me, you must search the archives for something on queens—gunvaers. The good ones. What do they consider good, here? Did they ride as warriors at the head of lancers? Even with the best of intentions, I do not see myself performing such a role well."

"If I may suggest without attempting to interfere?" I hoped this contravention of the rules would please her.

She made an impatient gesture, dashing away Colendi custom.

I said, "You might write to Ivandred's sister. Or to his aunt."

"His sister was mostly raised by his aunt, and she spent summers in Enaeran," Lasva said. "But Ingrid-Jarlan? That is a very good idea, Emras. If anyone knows what a gunvaer traditionally did, it would be she."

The jarlan came almost at once, and it was apparent to both Lasva and me that she was cognizant of everything that had happened. It became clear that she'd had steady communication with the captain of the female guards.

Ingrid-Jarlan looked around with open curiosity, indicated her approval with quick open-palmed gestures, and then Lasva invited her to sit, gesturing me to the scribe's post.

The jarlan dropped down cross-legged at the table, sipped the Sartoran steep and blinked, her head a little tipped. "That has an odd flavor," she said. "The taste reminds me of the smell of summer grass after rain. Now. To your purpose. I have been thinking about it. You have to know that I am at a disadvantage. My father, who had grown up hearing about how the women assassinated one of the last of the Olavair kings, refused to send me to the Academy. No one will accept a ruler who hasn't been trained," she said.

"So there are no customs of queens?"

"The last truly great gunvaer was Hadand Deheldegarthe. In Colend, did all compare your sister to your famous great-grandmother?"

Lasva made The Peace as she considered her answer.

But the jarlan did not expect one. She leaned forward. "Hadand's daughter-by-marriage, who grew up under her tutelage, when our female academy was as great as the men's, was the worst gunvaer in history. Among her many culpabilities, she disbanded *our* academy."

"What was its purpose?" Lasva asked.

"The girls spent two years here, the first to ensure that the quality of their training was universal, but the second was really for them to know one another, so that they might band together to communicate and defend the kingdom. When Fabern-Gunvaer disbanded their training so that she would have more free time to pursue her lovers, that communication was lost within a generation. And so was our influence. We have never regained it except in short periods, when a king's mother or sister was very strong. But if you wish to understand what makes a great gunvaer, then you must read Hadand Deheldegarthe's letters."

Lasva said, "I have not found any such in the library here."

"Tchah!" Ingrid lifted the back of her hand, a gesture of rudeness. "The Olavairs destroyed everything they could of my family's greatness. But Hadand's daughter and niece saw that coming, and they made it their own work to collect all her letters before they died. I have them in the Darchelde archive. I can send them over." Her lip curled. "There are very many. And difficult, for the language has changed somewhat. But if you read them, I promise you will understand what a gunvaer does."

The jarlan retired to rest before the midnight bonfire. Lasva summoned me to her own chamber, and said, "You saw the day the king died that the guards listened to me, but that was not because I had authority, it was because I spoke in an absence of authority, what they call a clear chain of command. Does that match your perception?" She had switched to Marloven.

I made The Peace.

She twisted her hands together, then flung them apart. "I made an oath. I mean to keep it. And *melende* requires me to establish my own authority, instead of relying on that which Ivandred gives me. I can achieve nothing here if he must endorse every command I might give."

I bowed over my pressed palms, completely out of my depth, for all my training had been toward my absenting myself from influence—the Scribes' First Rule.

Lasva gazed at the wide, flat Marloven plates on the table, then to the glimpse of barely-begun tapestry in the far room. "What *can* I achieve? I do not want authority just so that I can walk first through a door. I had a lifetime of that. Yet I am not and never will be, a war leader. Perhaps I can fill a need that they do not see. The Colendi have avoided war for centuries by refining the art of discourse, which becomes negotiation when the subject is a treaty."

I bowed again.

Lasva got to her feet. "Go and rest. I have no idea how long this memorial bonfire might go, but judging from their usual habits, long or short, we will rise before the sun as always."

SEVEN

OF THE ADUMBRATIONS OF POWER

E mras:

I am writing in Old Sartoran partly as practice (I am a herald again, as you shall discover) and partly because I have no idea how safe your circumstances are. There is a third "partly": I vowed not to write until I was settled.

As soon as the residual stresses of the transfer magic cleared, we breathed the sweet air of Alsais again. Rejoicing at the sound of the carillons ringing the quarter after the Hour of Spice, Belimas began to weep, repeating "Home, home, I never thought I would see it again," which matched the emotions in my heart.

Imagine the irony when we discovered that Alsais would only be home in memory. In truth, I do not think Belimas was there a full day before the queen gave her a year's pay and sent her off. I heard this from my sister as I awaited my interview with the queen (something Belimas was not granted). I got much the same, though with thanks for my service. All honorable, polite, and definite: there was no place for me either in the palace or in Alsais.

I went straight to the heralds. What had I done wrong? Nothing. I went to Halimas, who had championed me during the days when you and I were students. What did I do wrong? Nothing.

So I took a boat into Alsais, made my way to the scribe shop, and used some of my new wealth to get myself a magical scrollcase, and then awarded myself a night in the finest inn that had space. Do you remember the Viridian Fane? From my room overlooking the Crown Skya Canal, I sent a note to my mother.

Within a day I had an answer: though I was welcome, she could only offer the customary week of family visitation time but no place. My sister who had never trained as a scribe? Gone as a caravan farrier for merchants. My mother suggested that I go to the Baron Lassiter, as our family had served them for generations.

So my third night was spent in my old bed at Lassiter House. I did not fit the bed any more than I fit the place, which was overrun with the staff of the Baron's new lover, a Lady Yirlath. He interviewed me the next morning. Said he, "I can always find you something to do, for I owe your family that much, but you are too smart to serve as a postilion, and besides, you're not handsome enough."

"Handsome!" said I.

He laughed. "Yirlath's daughter is trying to make a splash in Khanerenth's court, and the fashion now is for matched sets of pretty horses and postilions. I suggest you go see my son, the Duke of Alarcansa. I think he's still there—it's early for court. He's richer than most kings. If that poison-piece he's married to boots you back down the stairs, come back to me, and I can put you out with the yearlings, at least, because I know you won't break their gaits."

Thus my fourth morning found me in Alarcansa, and though I braced myself to face the grown version of the Icicle Duchess (at the Hour of Stone, in a room so formal I would be intimidated just to breathe its air), I found myself waved in by the Duke, whose impatient stride was a younger version of his father's. "Your timing is excellent. I must return to my duties at court in two days," he said to me, and then beckoned for me to walk by his side. "If you were a scribe, I'd send you back. I know it is unjust to judge them by the perfidy of a single member of the guild who betrayed my father, but I can't look on those smooth scribal faces without wondering what machinations are going on behind them. They affect virtue, but do they practice it?"

He raised the three fingers in Insinuation, which caught me by surprise, after months of Marlovens and their largely meaningless gestures.

Did your mind insist on ascribing meanings to them, too? "Heralds, though, I like. You either proclaim the news or you archive it. You don't make it. My career as a queen-appointed commander is attached to the palace heralds . . ."

Oh, I could hear Birdy's voice reading the words, which caused my throat to hurt. I could not prevent myself from wondering what he wrote to Anhar and if he wrote as much. Or maybe he wrote less, but revealed his inner self more?

. . . and then he indicated my stable-worn hands and said, "Your mission was obviously quite fraught. We can amend that, at least."

I found myself in the bath alcove, sitting side by side with him as our nails were tended, and I don't mean the quick trim and buff expected of us servants. We had the entire course, beginning with hot water with citrus blossoms, oils, and oh how good it felt to have the knots smoothed from my hands and feet, as we conversed.

He asked for my experience, and I told him, including the inexplicable ending to my career as a royal herald.

"No more inexplicable than my glorious career," he said.

Have you ever heard the man speak? He's a master of cordial irony.

"How," I began, "if I may be permitted to ask—"

"Ask as you will," he said, signing shadow-pardon for the interruption. "The queen apparently liked my style in my total failure to rescue the princess last summer, but not enough to keep me in Alsais over winter. She was here not quite three weeks on her progress. Heh! She was not best pleased with a supper of a single olive served on a five-hundred year old plate, surrounded by a wreath of lettuce, and poetry for dessert. The duchess and I extolled the art of austerity, wearing the same unadorned clothing for two weeks running. On her way out, the queen left orders for me to present myself again on Flower Day. So, what color is it to be?"

By then, you will infer, we were nearly finished, and there was only the nail polish to consider.

I signed deference, saying, "I know not how I leave this room, whether as free man, postilion, or herald."

He laughed again. "I like you—you don't mince and whisper like a damned spying scribe. Herald it shall be, though we never had any at Lassiter, so far as I am aware. If there is a family archive, I never saw it. The Definians have a full staff, but they will fit you in if I will it."

And so my nails were painted with a gloss suitable for heralds while his were tipped with gold for court. We put our slippers on (you can imagine how good it feels to wear slippers again, after half a year confined in blackweave boots), and he walked with me to the Alarcansa heralds' chambers.

I have yet to meet the principle members of the household. The duchess is indisposed (Kaidas's man told me on Day Five that she's not sick, merely recovering from the recent birth of a child, but she seems to believe the world would not recover from the spectacle of a Definian whose waist is not spanned by a man's two hands together) and the other Definian, the one everyone used to call Tittermouse, was sent last fall to Alsais as lady-in-waiting to the royal princess.

So far, life is pleasant. The duke remembered my name when he saw me next—always a good sign—and said he wishes to hear more about my experiences. Whether he does or not, I appreciate him saying it. Last of all, I will describe how they celebrate Flower Day in Alarcansa, which was merry. I haven't danced so much in my life.

Flower Day, the great spring celebration. Marlovens, needless to say, didn't bother with such frivol. We'd made our own celebration, Nifta finding flowers somewhere (for Marlovens did not have flower gardens). I had begged the kitchen to let me bake some lily breads. The assistant baker seemed intrigued, following me closely as I worked.

Then we sang songs until we were so homesick that I don't think anyone enjoyed it, though we pretended for one another's sake.

I say "we," but Lasva was not there.

The memory hurt as I skimmed Birdy's description, then my eye caught on Anhar's name. He asked about her, hoping things were better for her with Belimas gone. He finished:

Right now my labors are largely make-work—gathering the weekly reports from provincial guilds from the scribe on the transfer desk, sorting and recording the information. It's a job a prentice could do, but there is no prentice at present, and I do not mind the labor. I will learn more about Alarcansa, if this is to be my home.

When Ivandred departed on his journeys, Lasva and I sat through long, quiet evenings, as she struggled with Hadand-Gunvaer's letters, and I studied. Some experiments I could do in the castle, but because of the wards, sometimes I had to make my way outside the gates of the city.

The structure was a messy tangle. I would have to find a way to address the illogical, patchwork layers of the recent years—desperate measures ordered by a king who feared shadows—before I could delve to the mysteries beneath.

At the Marloven Convocation, New Year's Week, the jarls repeat their oaths as given on their appointment. That is strictly according to law. Then, on the fourth day, the jarls can bring judgments against one another, on behalf of their people or themselves. The people can also bring judgments against their nobles, though apparently very few take advantage of this.

At the Marloven coronation, there is a reversal. Each jarl brings grievances and demands to the new king, from which they work out the new oath that will be repeated at every New Year's Convocation of this king's rule. Once their new oaths are sworn, there is much feasting and singing and martial demonstration, then all go home.

And, just as in Colend, any noble can be replaced.

As the jarls began appearing with their cavalcades (they were permitted two ridings, eighteen armed attendants, plus servants) the castle took on an atmosphere of tension at least as great as the worst day under the dead king. The staff did their best to relieve tension with wry comments about the guests. One cook told me, when I carried the breakfast dishes down, that everyone was flying about seeing to far too many tasks. Then she added, "At least one thing, it's not at midnight anymore."

One of the female guards cracked a laugh. "My grandma told me they used to talk of scraping resin off the stone for months after, so many torches. What a stink it must have raised!"

Midnight for a coronation? I thought as I fled. *I will never get used to this place.*

The jarls who had little to dispute were the earliest arrivals. Also early were those allied with more powerful jarls. Once a jarl had settled his, or her oaths, they gathered each day to witness the interviews of the newcomers, and to see justice or judgments carried out. There were three jarlans besides Ingrid-Jarlan of Darchelde: a short, tough old woman from Sindan-An and two around my mother's age, from Zheirban and Torac.

The first time I'd ever seen Lasva's impassive female guards express emotion was when Fnor returned. The smiles, even chatter, surprised me. Yet again I saw that celebrative mood when Ingrid-Jarlan arrived. Not only that, but the quick exchanges of personal talk made it clear that there had been frequent communication.

The jarlan walked everywhere with Lasva, who seemed to float along the stone corridors next to the free-striding jarlan, both dressed in black robes over linen under robes dyed goldenrod. Lasva wore one of those worked chain belts on her hips, but she refused to attach a knife, even when the jarlan suggested it. "It is important to us," she said. "Ivandred has given us our dignity back, in permitting us once again to wear our knives."

"Until I can use them the way you do, I would rather wear my fan," Lasva said. At her belt hung a fine black and gold Altan fan.

The day that Danrid-Jarl arrived with his enormous cavalcade of servants behind his eighteen riders, we watched their approach from the upper windows. "Can he really need so many servants?" Lasva asked Ingrid-Jarlan.

I was astonished, thinking that even the Duke of Gaszin had not traveled with so many attendants.

"They are most certainly warriors garbed as household runners and servants. I think I see three in cooks' aprons," the jarlan stated, and she uttered a crack of laughter. "Three! He does have a sense of humor, arrogant young soul-eater."

Lasva touched her fingers together in The Peace. "Does that mean we are to expect an attack?"

"Not here!" The jarlan gave another laugh. "If they were mad enough to break the truce that everyone understands is in force at Convocation or a coronation, they'd be dead before they reached the first stairwell, and well they know it. It is as close to a challenge as he dares to come. Don't the Colendi know of challenges?"

Her amusement irked me, but Lasva said only, "We do. There is the shadow trespass, and in court, there are many, such as the moth kiss. I am thinking that perhaps this gesture here is the Marloven equivalent of a moth kiss, if this Danrid does not intend a battle, yet brings them anyway."

"Shadow trespass, as in walking in someone's shadow?" the jarlan asked, brows crimped. "Terrifying."

"It is an affront," Lasva said. "A challenge."

The jarlan's chin lifted in a small jerk, reminding me of Ivandred. A family trait? "I see," she said slowly. "Very . . . hm. You must see your place in a room differently, and how you stand in relation to others. Is everyone watching for where light is placed?"

"Customarily we light all four corners of a room. But that can change."

The jarlan was thoughtful. "I wonder if this is akin to standing to someone's left when you are not shield brethren. It is presumptuous. Or standing within sword reach of the right hand, in challenge." The jarlan gave a deep chuckle. "As for these below, if I know my nephew, they will shortly discover themselves housed with the sweepers and scrubbers at the back of the castle and offered work there, until their jarl leaves. I hope they may enjoy it."

She inclined her head. The yard filled with fully armed guards, everyone orderly, as that mass of "servants" was deftly cut out and marched toward the east side of the castle. The surprise was how many of the guards and supposed guards suppressed laughter, as if all conspired in some obscure jest.

But though Danrid Yvanavar arrived making an expensive, elaborate challenge in jest, his late arrival was also understood as a different gesture: by arriving last, he was assured that everyone of import in the kingdom was there to see justice carried out.

Lasva had found me a place in the gallery to witness Danrid's interview, for the throne room was packed, the silence so tense it almost rung. I fully expecting to be elbowed to the back by burly Marloven retainers, but one of the heralds appeared and drew me into their own gallery. This was the first time they acknowledged my existence. As I was introduced around so swiftly that faces and names were a blur of similarities, I thought, *And so their loyalty to the old king shifts to the new.* Whatever they privately thought of the old king or the new, they were patently welcoming me as scribe to the new queen.

The heralds' gallery ran below the clerestory windows all around the walls except above the throne. (Later I learned that the gallery doubled as a defensive platform for shooting arrows through the tall narrow windows.) Two gray-haired herald-scribes were on duty at the rail, with an unimpeded view of the throne daïs below, pens busy as one recorded the king's words and the other the petitioners'. I wedged in between the stone rail and a pillar. Danrid would be next. For now, Ivandred stood still as a statue below the few, shallow steps of the daïs, head bent, concentrated on the jarl standing before him.

But for the rest of us, Ivandred was the center of attention, tall in his black and gold, the thin circlet wrought of black steel making his hair look gold in contrast. When he moved, glints along it highlighted the edges of interlocked leaves in a stylized wreath.

Danrid waited a few paces behind. He also stood out, so tall, his sun-yellow silken tunic so bright against the black of those on the black marble daïs. Venn knots in white silk glinted with subtle threads, to hint at princely silver.

The young jarl from Tlen along with Khanivar's heir—the oldest son and older brother to the Lan who had died at the bridge—stood at Danrid's left, in the position of shield brethren. Ingrid-Jarlan, as governor of Darchelde, stood a scarce step from his right, the old jarlan from Sindan-An firmly at her side.

The vows finished, and Ivandred lifted his head.

Danrid stepped forward with confident stride. Instead of barking angrily, as he had when the old king first collapsed, Danrid was almost friendly and addressed Ivandred jovially, except his laughter carried a note that caused my shoulder blades to tighten, my heart to thump in wariness. All I heard were the words "fathers" and "oath" as a young herald—he looked no older than I had been when I was first assigned to Lasva—whispered to me, "The king did not invite Tdiran Marlovair."

"Why should she be invited or not?" I breathed.

"If he had invited her, everyone would know she was to replace Danrid as Jarlan of Yvanavar."

"But she was not born there," I whispered, as below, Danrid was saying in ringing tones, ". . . salute the valiant . . . defend the nation, from holding to stronghold . . ."

My companionable young herald gripped his lower lip between his teeth, then whispered hastily, "Danrid insisted on full adoption. She is legally Yvanavar. So our king could do it." And, almost inaudibly, "I wish he had."

". . . crown of black steel, symbol of justice . . . our vows under law." Danrid's speech ended with emphasis on the last four words.

Ivandred said clearly, "Justice shall be carried out according to law."

Danrid saluted, mock-solemn, his voice rising. "Then I have nothing more to ask."

And so we all ended up in the great square between the castle and one side of the high academy walls, breath clouding, as, with deliberate ritual, Haldren Marlovair was chained to a post and flogged.

I shut my eyes, but the sound made me ill, and I could feel Lasva shiver as her side was pressed against mine. At that moment, if anyone had offered me a transfer token home, I would have gone.

When it finally ended, a murmuring and a rustle went through the gathering, and Ivandred walked down to take a stance beside the blood-soaked figure hanging by the wrists, knees buckled. Ivandred lifted his voice.

"Haldren Marlovair disobeyed orders, and justice has been served. That was my first order as king."

I glanced Danrid's way. His mocking grin made me hate him.

Then Ivandred said, "My second order is to raise Haldren Marlovair to Commander of the First Lancers. He and the First Lancers will accompany me on a ride to the northern border."

A gasp, and then a huge shout echoed off the castle walls and back again. Danrid's smile had frozen into a rictus of fury. In the tumult that followed, everyone talking to his or her neighbor, Lasva flicked her fingers to me, and we threaded our way through the crowds.

We entered the castle, and as soon as we reached the relative quiet of a hallway, Lasva said, "Ivandred told me last night. We will be leaving as soon as the last one of the jarls is out the gates. Yes, I am going, and so are you—Ivandred specifically asked for you, in your capacity as mage."

"Why should we go anywhere? Do kings here have Progresses, like at home?"

She gave me a tight smile at the slip about home but lifted a hand toward Thorn Gate. "Their version of a Progress. Did you not notice the Jarl of Olavair's absence at the coronation? Everyone else did, and they all know it means nothing short of a declaration of war."

EIGHT

OF THE FOX BANNER UNFURLING

The staff stood before Lasva, and she studied us with that intent look. Marnda, of course, was exempt from travel due to seniority, unless she wished to go. She didn't. Nifta had recently been assigned to oversee the import of Colendi silks, which promised to be a lucrative trade. She would stay behind as well. I had never seen her happier.

Marloven female runners would accompany us but, of the Colendi, aside from Lasva and myself, there was only Pelis and Anhar. One would join us to care for whatever niceties would be possible. I was riding as a mage.

Pelis clasped her hands pleadingly, for we were to travel with the First Lancers, and she had not seen Lnand for weeks. Anhar waited quietly, head bowed. I was in the self-effacing scribe pose, but I felt Lasva's questioning gaze as I stared at Anhar, strong in my ambivalence.

Lasva must have seen something in my demeanor, for she said, "Anhar, you will go with us this time." And when Pelis could not hide her dismay, Lasva added kindly, "Next journey, Pelis will accompany me."

Anhar bowed, her expression closed, and we were dismissed to pack. We left early the next day.

I was so pleased with my ability to stay on a horse that for a short time I mistook the Marlovens' occasional smiles in my direction for friendliness or encouragement. Finally I saw the mirth.

When we camped that night, Anhar sent a speculative glance at the distant camp, only visible as tent silhouettes outlined by a ruddy glow.

"Why aren't the lancers riding with us?" I asked as we began clearing the ground of little stones and tufts of grass that could be felt under the bedroll.

"Pelis told me before we left that Lnand told her that they will keep their distance until Haldren can sit a horse."

"I do not understand their notions of honor," I muttered.

Anhar shrugged, and began to shake out the fine-woven sheets that had recently arrived from Colend. She fluttered her fingers toward Ivandred's tent, visible through the open flap. "Think he'll come in here or she'll go in with him?"

"Won't they sleep apart?" I said. "I don't think she likes tents now any more than she did last winter."

"They never sleep apart," Anhar stated and then flashed a grin. "You're in that nice room away at the other end, where you lie at your ease of a morning—"

Lie at my ease! Then I recognized her tone. She was making game of Marnda. "Ah-yedi! So tell me this, you who knows what the Marlovens say and think. Why are they smiling at me?"

Anhar made the formal Peace, in the mode of one who divorces herself from an unpalatable truth and said, "It's not you, it's the way you ride. I overheard one of them when they set up the tent. He said . . ." She repeated a Marloven phrase that means, *the hop of a bean on a frying pan.*

So! From dancing peacock to bouncing bean. I had to admit to myself that though we Colendi move much more gracefully on foot, Marloven riding was grace in action.

Anhar and I shared a tent. That night, she wrote a quick note by candle light. I felt her glance before she closed her scrollcase.

Also that night, Lasva invited Ivandred to her tent.

Like Colendi royal progresses, Marloven ones require hospitality from the governor of any land the ruler crosses. We stayed at Marlovair for two days. Everyone understood it was to permit Haldren to recover, though absolutely nothing was said. Instead, the king was fêted, we were fêted, there was an atmosphere of vitality and purpose that I saw in every single face, right down to the dogs running about. It was extraordinary, how deeply felt was Haldren's honor as the new Commander of the First

Lancers, yet how nothing whatsoever was said about what he had suffered. If, that is, you overlook the spitting whenever "Yvanavar" was named.

"What has Yvanavar to do with Olavair attacking?" I asked Anhar when we left Marlovair at last. I'd had to attend Lasva, which meant all I heard was genial talk about unfamiliar people.

Anhar, however, had been able to mingle with the staff and so heard all the gossip. "Everyone knows Yvanavar's looking the other way while Olavair invades Khanivar, which Olavair claims is *his,*" she said with the light tone of one who enjoys having the information. "I still don't really understand, but it goes something like this: everyone except Olavair, who is by all accounts a pompous rooster, knows that Olavair cannot possibly win against Ivandred."

"That much I have already gathered."

"But there are two things that Ivandred can do which might weaken his new kingship. The first, he can wait and call up the warriors each jarl owes. It's called a levy."

"They all swore that, did they not? Why should it weaken him?"

"They say that the kingdom should not be raised unless there is real invasion."

"This is not real?"

She opened her hands. "How do I know what kind of invasion is real or not real? I heard that it would take half the summer to get the messages out, and to assemble everyone at the extreme northern border. And there are political consequences when this is done, having to do with trade and what we at home call taxes, but they call royal dues. Or, he can order the First Lancers to ride against Olavair, even though they are not a large force, and they will be led by poor Haldren, who is . . .yedi!" She signed Thorn Gate. "You know what happened to him. Everyone chirps that Yvanavar is seeking a way to claim the throne."

"Why doesn't he call all the rest of the King's Lancers? The Second and Third and Fourth?"

"He could, but then we all wait around for weeks—months—until they can get here. They are at the borders of the kingdom." She waved a hand in a circle, then went on in a low whisper. "I heard one of the woman guards in the bath saying that if Ivandred chases Olavair all the way back to his capital to force peace, then he is effectively cut off from the rest of the kingdom—because he will have to return through Khanivar and Yvanavar, which adjoin."

"And so these two jarls, who just spoke oaths that we all witnessed, will betray him?"

"The runners say that they wouldn't dare revolt outright. Until they gain more support, they will pretend to be loyal, but if they can keep him cut off from the rest of the King's Lancers, they could perhaps pressure him into granting their demands, and weaken him as a king."

"So Ivandred will be a hostage in his own kingdom?" My thought was, *we* would be the hostages. "But aren't we heading for Yvanavar?"

"Yes. It's deliberate, a challenge, everyone says. And they predict that the Jarl of Yvanavar would not dare do anything now, fresh from the coronation. He will wait until after Ivandred has this battle with Olavair. And when we reach Yvanavar, they will obey the laws of hospitality strictly but not offer an oat or a blade of grass more."

She was right.

Our stay at Yvanavar weeks later was rigidly correct, from Danrid to his wife Tdiran, whose attitude toward Lasva was distant but polite. Though I was there when the baby was brought out, and Lasva's exclamation of delight over the beauty of their son (who looked exactly like any other infant) caused a faint smile in the mother, so quickly smoothed I knew it was inadvertent.

I also saw her gaze rest on Lasva, who did nothing to hide the thickening of her waist when her open robe gapped.

We stayed over one night, then rode west instead of north, a direction whose significance was utterly lost on me, though not on the First Lancers. To me it seemed as if the tension underlying Yvanavar's strict attention to protocol traveled with us, for gone were the songs and the hilarity. The morning practices were longer, and the columns tighter. Everyone who had weapons wore them in easy reach.

The second day, when we camped, the drums came out again: it was Midsummer's Night. Lasva rode mostly by Ivandred's side, so I had seen relatively little of her, and our only conversations had been about travel things.

This night I caught her walking around the perimeter of the campfire, her silhouetted profile somber in the firelight, as Marlovens drummed and heel-danced and leaped around the flames in spite of the night's warmth.

Then it came back to me, what had happened last year at this time. Or, rather, what had not happened—the elopement of Lasva and Kaidas. But she was not going to share what she felt.

Marlovens on the road did not celebrate long into the night, because they rose so early. As the celebration wound down I retreated to the tent I shared with Anhar, and I caught her finishing her nightly note. I did not try to read it but could see that it was only two or three lines. Endearments? A report? Did he write back each night?

I, too, had corresponded with him, long letters each way, too long for every day. One week often stretched to two. Both of us were busy and had little free time.

Again, I'd assumed that the trip meant I could not continue my studies until I remembered that I could transfer to Darchelde. But I thought it better to obtain leave, so one night, I walked out in hopes that I might find Lasva or Ivandred. I asked one of the runners and he pointed. There was the crunch of boots in soil, and here he was, limned by ochre glow of the dying fire. That wreath coronet was gone—the Marlovens seldom wore ornaments, except when riding into war.

"Emras-Sigradir," he said.

I still could not quite believe the title, but I performed the proper deference, hand to heart.

He said, "This is excellent, for I had thought to speak to you on the morrow, and here you are. I have a task for you."

"More transfer tokens, Ivandred-Harvaldar?" I asked in surprise.

"I have yet eight." He grunted. "Twice in a week is about as much as I can bear for any distance longer than half a day's ride. Twice in a day gives me a headache for two days afterward." He looked at me with interest. "But you find it easier?"

"Not at all," I said. "However, I hold hopes of learning to mitigate the effect, for I've seen little reaction in the Herskalt. At first I thought he was transferring from one room to another."

"Above the library at Darchelde?" he asked. "No, there is no other room."

He was so formidable, I was a little afraid of him and certainly wary. But there was also the knowledge that we had the Herskalt in common, so I dared a question: "May I ask his background?"

Ivandred lifted a shoulder as he glanced around the orderly camp. In the distance someone tapped a hand drum, and voices rose and fell in a ballad with the characteristic galloping beat. "We know little about him. He arrived when my aunt sought a tutor for Thar and me. This was when we were young. My father sent us to Darchelde for summers—I was sent as a warning that I could be replaced as heir. He had no idea how much I liked to be there. Anyway, the Herskalt did not come from Sartor, which was important to my father. He said his homeland was somewhere west. Across the water. Hin, or Han, it began with."

I once had to memorize the world map. For the first time, the litany of names did not come easily to my tongue, which disturbing realization I would cope with later. I concentrated and brought to mind the drawing I had made and colored with my own hand. "Hanivah, on the continent Goerael?"

"Could be." Ivandred's disinterest was plain. "Here is my question. I need magic to aid me in warfare."

"Warfare," I repeated, shocked. "Is that not—" Diplomacy caused me to hesitate, but the ring on my toe, the voices of many teachers, forced the words out. "Is that not the purview of Norsunder?"

Ivandred made that impatient gesture, as if swatting something aside. "Norsundrian mages—if we're to believe they still exist—rip souls from your living body. Maybe smite hundreds to death. I want something that will aid my front line." He must have seen something in my expression, though I tried to mask it, because he said, "You know little of war, I see. If it's going to happen—and it will—I want a fast, hard attack that will be so fast, and so hard, that the other side loses their taste for battle."

"But to kill . . . with magic . . . even if I knew anything even remotely like that . . ."

"People," he said, "are going to die. That's what happens in battle. I want as few of my people lying on the ground as possible. There is no magic for killing, at least, not available to us. Just as well. To kill with a word, a gesture . . ." He shook his head. "It would be too easy. What I seek is something that aids our people. A spell that, oh, makes the other side's horses slip in the mud, say. Fouls their weapons. Or clouds their vision."

I discovered that my toes were clenched in my shoes, the ring cutting into my flesh. "Have you discussed this with the Herskalt?"

"Of course. Early on, when I commenced learning. He wanted to teach me such spells, but insisted I practice basics first, as such magic is dangerous. I understand that. Like learning how to fight before riding to battle. You don't carry a sword into battle and expect to achieve anything without training, no matter how sharp that sword is, or how tempered the steel. I have never had the time to master both. So I come to you."

I said cautiously, "I will have to study. I know of nothing now."

"I don't expect anything now. It's a defensive preparation only. Against the future."

"I was going to ask your permission to visit the Herskalt while we ride. I could leave a token for myself to transfer back to. And if Lasva-Gunvaer had need of me, you would know where I am for summons."

His forehead cleared. "Excellent. Do that."

He turned away, and the two runners standing out of earshot approached him. I walked away, thinking, "defensive preparation?" Then came the obvious: *Danrid Yvanavar*.

I should not have been surprised that the Herskalt was not there.

I had not finished any of my current assignments. I knew he did not live in that small space. Yet I had so many questions my disappointment was sharp enough that I did what I never had before: used the waiting pen and ink, which I had assumed were for translation purposes, and wrote him a note, stating my questions in proper order, using my best scribal hand, for he seemed to warrant no less.

Then I transferred back.

"There you are," Ivandred said, striding through his people a week afterward.

I stood next to Lasva, who was silent and tense. All around us the Marlovens moved about purposefully, but the signs of nerves were there, the sharp smell of sweat. Later the Herskalt would explain these as the distinctive scent of fight or flee, the extremity of human survival emotions.

Through the milling crowd stepped the Herskalt, his plain robe of gray swinging. It was the first time I had ever seen him outside of Darchelde and among others. He was no taller than Ivandred, built much the same, and he moved with the same martial stride. But the Herskalt exhibited an inner stillness—that is, he made no unnecessary move, and when he did move, it was not abrupt, restless, or even calculated.

"I am here," he said, smiling. "As you both requested." To me, "I apologize, young scribe, for my lateness in responding to your request for enlightenment. I was away, on my appointed tasks."

Ivandred waited for him to finish with scarcely concealed impatience. "We are going to ride soon."

"I will bide here with your gunvaer," the Herskalt said with a smile at Lasva. Ivandred gave him a salute expressive of relief then vanished quickly beyond the tents.

The Herskalt touched us each on the elbow. "Come. We shall view the attack from a better vantage."

Once again, he performed transfer magic that was so easy it was like stepping from one room to the next. In this case, from one room to a hilltop. Lasva looked around, and I said, "Will you teach me that?"

"You have much to learn before you can manage the shift," he said. And before I could demand a definition of "shift" he said, "But right now you must witness the consequences as grandiosity clashes with royal will."

We stood on a rocky promontory, overlooking a broad river valley. Olavair's force was enormous—so large that we could not see the ends of it within the placement of the hills. In comparison, Ivandred's force seemed small, and the Herskalt commented on it.

"Ivandred did not call for the oath-stipulated levies," he said.

Lasva gave a short nod, her arms tightening across her front, as a fitful summer breeze toyed with a loose strand from her braid. Ivandred had obviously explained his reasoning to her. What dreadful pillow talk, I thought.

The Herskalt smiled in my direction, as if he could hear my thought. But of course he could not. He held no dyr, and I felt no "presence." For the first time I wondered if it was possible to listen to minds as events occurred, instead of from the distance of memory.

"Does that not place him at a disadvantage?" I ventured a question.

Lasva was silent, her profile severe.

"It's problematic," the Herskalt agreed, as if the forming lines of horse warriors below were painted figures, like in Martande's great mural, and not living, breathing people and animals. "But if his skill can prevail, it will serve not only as a blow to Olavair's attempt here to move into Khanivar but also as an even more devastating political blow to Ivandred's ambitious jarls."

Lasva spoke at last. "He said he trusted our speed would disconcert Olavair. But they await the First Lancers. There will be no surprise."

"There is seldom surprise when armies find one another," the Herskalt answered in an amused tone. "Unless one army has been asleep. However, Olavair has not completed his preparations. He was counting on Ivandred calling the levy, which would have given him at least two months more. And in his haste, he has chosen ground ill-advisedly."

Olavair's colors were a bright summer blue glinting with gold—the royal gold. The Marlovens lifted the eagle banner, but that was not where everyone's attention went as the First Lancers rode up and into formation, lances upright.

"Ah," the Herskalt said. "Ivandred is going to be a great king."

And I heard the Senior Scribe Halimas's voice echo in memory, *I require each of you to tell me what greatness is.*

"How do you come to this conclusion now?" Lasva asked, too strained to phrase the question in court form.

There was no evidence in the Herskalt's demeanor that he expected court form as he said, "Marlovens are bonded by their constant drill. But a great leader binds them to ideals. Watch: the First Lancers' banner is now unfurling for the first time in this new reign. And—it is not the eagle of the Montredaun-Ans. Nor is Ivandred unfurling it himself. See him alone, there?"

Below, Ivandred sat his horse as if born to ride and pulled on his helm—not a plain one but the helm of a king. He would stand out to his people.

He would be a target.

He turned his head, obviously a signal to Haldren Marlovair, who rode up beside him, lance raised. It was heavier than the lances I'd seen before, black and bulky.

"Ivandred could unfurl the banner as king. But he has given that honor to his commander."

A wind seemed to move through the riders below as Haldren Marlovair snapped his lance in a movement that took both skill and strength, and the Fox banner unfurled.

"Ivandred has bestowed on the First Lancers their own identity, through his personal symbol, which used to belong to the Montredaun-An heir. Now the Fox banner belongs to the First Lancers. See? It heightens their bond through their loyalty to one another. And to him. Just as they are about to sustain the most brutal part of battle, the first charge."

Lords of the wind, Ivandred had said.

"So . . . if Ivandred's skills prevail, it could be over at once?" Lasva asked.

Below on both sides, trumpets called, and all the banners streamed and snapped as warriors on both sides braced up or moved into line.

The Herskalt uttered a chuckle. "At once? No. Only surrender can happen at once, and even that does not transpire in a moment. This conflict will probably be fought in steps; it depends not only on how good Olavair's defense is, but also how far Ivandred is going to push, assuming he wins this encounter."

The First Lancers' charge began slow. This was a charge? The horses walked sedately, riders' lances held upright, pennants flapping.

The inchoate noise changed in volume.

I raised my hand to ward the wink and gleam of sun on helm and steel weapon, and what I had taken to be rain (impossible, for there were no clouds) resolved into a hissing, humming stream of arrows arcing over the heads of the chargers into the solid phalanx of Olavair defenders, standing shield to shield between two hills. The center of that phalanx was packed with warriors fifty deep, maybe more, many with shields held over their heads, throwing the sun's rays mercilessly back at us as the arrows rained down like hailstones.

Most arrows bounced off harmlessly, but not all. The ranks serried a little and, along the tops of the two hills, warriors for Olavair appeared, heads low, as they drew bow and began to shoot at the slowly approaching First Lancers.

A barely audible trumpet blast, and up came the Lancers' shields, helms just topping them. The arrows clattered into the shields and slid off the horses' caparisons, as the animals began to trot, Ivandred at the center.

"The king could command from the second or third line, but you see he leads at Haldren Marlovair's side. That binds them all the tighter."

Lasva's fingers gripped white on her elbows as the trot quickened to a canter, and the gap began to narrow. The warriors bent low behind their shields, the pennants on the upright lances snapping, the horses' tails streaming. It was a stirring sight.

Then on some signal that I did not perceive, the First Lancers changed direction as if they shared one mind and lengthened their gait into a gallop. They did not run straight into the middle of the shields, but obliquely, toward the left flank, as Haldren lifted something to his lips and a hoarse moan rolled from hill to hill, like the death cry of spectres. The Olavairans wavered.

"Ah," the Herskalt said. "Good."

"Good?" Lasva asked, her voice sharp, for the first time ever. "Do you see the way to end this?"

"Ivandred gave them leave to wind the Venn horn. As you hear, it is a dismaying sound. And there is the charge."

My appreciation of the glory and power of the sight below ended as suddenly as did many lives, with the first smash. Lasva turned her head away as if she'd been struck, but I stared, appalled as the lances lowered at the last moment, the riders' postures altering to a brace before they plowed into the defenders, driving them into a mass of writhing, shouting, bleeding flesh plus metal and flying hooves and clotted mud.

". . . the danger is that the center will come around and swallow them, but see, the skirmishers are attacking the front lines, who now are useless as there is no cavalry attacking them. They are packed too deeply to do much but resist the arrows, and their skirmishers can't get through to engage with Ivandred's," the Herskalt said.

"People are dying," Lasva said.

"Yes," the Herskalt agreed. "This is what happens in war."

"You will pardon my dismay," Lasva said, her voice trembling as she struggled for courtly modulation. "At this affect of indifference."

The Herskalt said, "My emotions, whatever they may be, do nothing to alter the suffering below." He glanced my way. "Until there is no more war, my intent is to find ways to limit the suffering."

Beyond his shoulder, Lasva's chin lifted, and her expression became one of intent as she forced herself to look again. So did I, in a vain effort to spot Ivandred. But when the mass shifted, revealing mangled bodies trampled into the churned, blackened mud, my stomach heaved, and I shut my eyes as the terrible noise went on. Close by, the Herskalt's light, dispassionate voice went on. ". . . I am certain that Ivandred explained that the Olavairs are not permitted to stay past their third year at the academy. If they go at all. This man refused to send his son, for he wanted to keep him loyal to Olavair, and the academy has a distressing tendency to knit its product into a common bond. He had to send his grandson, but pulled him at age thirteen." And after another of those horrible surges, revealing more dead: "Marloven strategy has for centuries centered on warfare from horseback. But styles change as the theatre of war changes."

"Theatre?" Lasva repeated, her voice husky.

"A place of significant events or action. Oh, Khanivar is down. A shame! He was the best of the old generation. That is going to make things more difficult for Ivandred."

"How can you see?"

"The signal is Khanivar's crimson-and-white banner: *Jarl down*. He was eighty-two, did you know that? Marloven men are notorious for not admitting to their ages if they can help it. Even a man above eighty wants to be perceived strong enough to lead."

Lasva's fingers shook before she clasped them over her upper arms. His dispassionate tone, that of the lecturer, was something new to her, as the Herskalt added: "Ivandred requested I enlighten you. I endeavor to comply." When she inclined her head, he went on, "In the Academy, they are taught the rudiments of war from horseback. That is what Olavair took away fifty years ago. He had learned the basics of fighting, but he never learned to command. He flattered himself, and his followers have been careful ever since to agree in every point of his self-praise. Like the late king, he is known for his temper."

"This is insupportable," Lasva whispered in Kifelian.

An eternity later, the Herskalt spoke again. (It was still daylight, but I could not tell you how many hours we stood there.) "Ah! He's lost control of the rally. There they go, straight for the river. If their retreat is as messy as I suspect it will be, Ivandred will dispatch his skirmishers to make life interesting for them."

Trumpet signals traveled through the strengthening breeze. The fighting did not end at once. There were surges in the mass, shouts and clashes, but more spaces opened up, revealing the terrible cost.

As the battle sounds below diminished, and I could hear Lasva's breathing. Her gaze was unwavering, even after Ivandred emerged, riding along his forming lines on a new horse, apparently unhurt, though that black coat could very well hide wounds. His helm, encircled by a wreath of black steel, glittered in the light.

"It is time to descend," the Herskalt said. "Ivandred desired me to educate you both as much as I was able, and I trust I have done so. You now have a better understanding of what is at stake."

Lasva said, "Yes. I thank you." She looked away then back. "Do we walk, or will you bring us via magic?"

The Herskalt did not answer, but shifted us again, without painful effect or apparent effort.

Lasva and I found ourselves alone in the middle of our camp, where all around us purposeful activity was carried out: wounded to certain tents, from which groans and cries of pain issued; the dead were laid out in the center of camp, their coats neat, their weapons and helms at hand; horse pickets in a long line, busy with people tending them, everywhere laboring to bring order after the horrible destruction.

Lasva made straight for Ivandred, who was mud and blood spattered from boots to eyebrows, his hair clotted. He sent a bloodshot look our way, then said, "I must see to the worst hurt."

Lasva joined him. They walked together from cot to cot, or from bedroll to bedroll. No one had prepared me for the stenches attendant on mortally wounded flesh. The king stopped by each wounded warrior who was well enough to perceive him. Lasva reached down to smooth pain-furrowed brows, to touch straining fingers. When steaming cups of green kinthus were brought around, the fumes heady, she helped to steady heads and hands so that the elixir might mask pain, even though it did not restore rent flesh or shattered bone.

Ivandred stopped the healer, who protested hoarsely that he "dare not talk," then explained rapidly that one of his colleagues was dead and the other lay in the tent behind us with a cracked skull. Half his prentices were away with the skirmishers, and half of those left also were wounded.

Without saying anything to anyone I disengaged from Ivandred and Lasva and followed the man to his next cot. At first I carried freshly steeped cups of green kinthus to the wounded, who—when the pain elixir relaxed them—were then tended. I listened as the healer performed his spells. Though the more complicated spells were beyond me, I quickly grasped how to keep loosened teeth in the head and how to secure a bone once the fracture had been set, so that it may be safely bandaged. This spell I performed over and over, as Ivandred went out to preside over the Disappearing of the Dead. As I worked, I heard the mournful rise and fall of the *Hymn to the Fallen*. Was it echoing faintly from the hills, or did the sound carry from the Olavairans? The idea that they sang the same song struck me as hard as that first brutal smash.

It was very late when, at last, the worst were seen to and the wounded lay in the pain-free haze of kinthus. I slipped away to seek Anhar, who would know where our tent was, but just as I was crossing the square between the lazaretto and cook tents, Anhar herself appeared. She scudded across the square, blue-black braids swinging like bell ropes, her Colendi gait out of place in a war camp. "I have been seeking you! Come, Emras."

Ivandred's tent was larger than anyone else's. From its sparse, collapsible furnishings, it was clear that this was where he held his war councils. I stepped inside, then almost rocked back at the strong smell of the Marloven warriors. No courtier would have stepped in personal proximity to another in such a state, but Lasva sat on the pillow behind the low table with the huge unrolled map, as composed as if she sat in the queen's formal parlor with aromatic breezes wafting through.

As always, the light came from one source, throwing shadows onto the tent walls, and as always the runners were oblivious as they moved about efficiently. Ivandred was issuing orders, and the runners vanished one by one, as Lasva listened in silence.

". . . might try to rally at the riverside in the next day or two. At least that is probably what the old fool is planning, but keep the skirmishers at the ready. Strike whenever you see an advantage," he said to the last runner, who struck his fist to his chest and ducked out of the tent.

Leaving the three of us alone. Lasva said, "Ivandred."

Exhausted as he was, his dry, cracked lips twitched in a brief smile at her pronunciation of his name. He opened his palm toward her.

"Please give me a week before you commence your war again."

"What?"

Lasva repeated herself with clear enunciation, "Please give me a week before you recommence this war. I intend to negotiate a treaty of peace, if I can."

Ivandred stared at her as if she had begun speaking in a language he had never heard. I know I stared, my emotions a flood of relief, of anxiety. *Oh send her, send her*, I thought.

His lips parted, and he blinked rapidly, then drew his grimy sleeve across his face with one hand as he reached for the cup his runner had set down earlier. "I do not understand."

Lasva open her hands. "Do you want this war?"

"Of course I do not want it," he said impatiently, then he drew breath. When he spoke again, his tone was even, but with an undertone of question.

I clasped my hands tight, for all my training had imbued me with the importance of the First Rule. My mind bloomed with questions as Lasva said, "I know nothing of war, as you are well aware. But one thing we Colendi are trained in is negotiation. Let me go talk to this jarl, or king, and offer whatever terms you think best, and let me see if I can bring an end to this death and destruction."

Ivandred shook his head. "There is no negotiating with the old snake. I tried. My father tried. He will agree to anything to your face, and slither off to do exactly what he wants as soon as you are safely away."

"You insist on killing him?" she asked, her eyes narrowing.

His palm turned up. "I only insist when someone comes at me intending to kill me. But I find it strange, your reasoning. I think it your customs that I do not understand. For Marlovens, it's a mercy to die if you lose. To be spared leaves you with a life of dishonor. In Colend, you said the duels are fought with wit. But if you lose, do you not see scorn in all eyes for your weakness?"

Lasva's fan made a complicated swoop and swirl, one he could not interpret. What he saw was her shiver. "Our cruelty is not with steel, yes, but we too can be cruel. It took me a lifetime to comprehend it. But we also learn the art of compromise, which means leaving both sides with honor. I think . . . I think I know enough to try to achieve it. I want to try. What about the man's son?"

"He's long dead. Mestan, his grandson, was sent against me today. When I left him, he was alive but barely." His brow furrowed. "There is his sister." His tone had changed, as if a new idea had occurred. "Nanjir, who will be in command of Olavair while her grandfather is in the field. I've only met her twice, but I found her to be straightforward."

"Then let me go under a white flag and talk to her. Please do not object with observations that I might be captured or killed. I know. That is why I suggest taking Emras with me. If I cannot talk myself out of a fraught situation, then she can take us away by magic. But at least let me try. In this, perhaps, I can attempt to be a gunvaer, instead of playing the role of one."

I could see that Ivandred hated the idea of her riding into danger. He looked from her to me and back again, frowned at the map, then tapped his forefinger on the stylized castle labeled Yvanavar. Then he lifted his head. "If you'll take a couple of my people as runners."

Lasva clasped her hands under her chin and bowed over them. "I would be glad of their company and of their guidance. When would it be best to leave?"

He blinked rapidly again, then said, "What would be best, and what would suit you might be different. Leaving under cover of darkness would be the safest, but I would not have you go without rest."

"I have rested enough. I was once used to dancing all night until dawn. I have not exerted myself today, except in spirit. I do not think I could sleep."

He moved suddenly, taking her in his arms with such force and desperation that I withdrew from the tent. Tired as I was, relief made me giddy. If Lasva could make peace, then this horrible fighting would end, and perhaps with it the question of my making magic for war.

NINE

OF LASVA-GUNVAER'S RIDE

L nand and a tough older lancer called Keth were our escorts. We traveled the first few legs by night, and the constant vigilance of our guides, the quiet urgency behind their getting us to eat a little faster, travel a little farther, sleep a little less, made us both so anxious we were silent almost the entire time.

And I could not rest when at last we stopped, because I felt obliged to make transfer tokens for Lasva, Lnand, and Keth, as I was as yet unable to transfer more than one person at a time.

Lasva spent time bent over the thick book of Hadand-Gunvaer's girlhood letters, as we shared a lamp. She pored over the girlish scrawl, fighting yawn after yawn. Once, I glanced over her shoulder and a surge of pity arose in me when I saw a long page of boring details about horses, dogs, cats, marmots, and the different flight patterns of falcons. On the facing page there appeared to be interminable descriptions of war games. But Lasva stuck grimly to her task.

Lnand and Keth traded guarding and scouting. It seemed they never slept; one was always awake when at last I shut my eyes and already up and doing when I woke after scant sleep.

I was grateful for summer. The moon's light was a great aid—that and the lancers' skills. Though we'd left the battle zone within a day or so, we were not out of danger, for we traveled ever deeper into enemy territory.

Our first encounter with Olavairans was on the fifth day, subsequent to a discussion between the Marlovens and Lasva, who insisted we not take Nanjir Olavair by surprise. "In a negotiation, you want to preserve . . ." She turned my way. "How would we translate *melende*? Call it honor. We try to preserve our own honor, of course, but not at the expense of another. We must not travel by stealth, at this point. Give her time to anticipate our arrival."

Lnand and Keth did not hide their doubt, but they didn't argue, either. They had all their weapons at hand, which made them look very fierce indeed. My worry about war had shifted entirely to worry about what was going to happen when we encountered the Olavairans—if we'd be able to transfer before they shot arrows at us.

The encounter came at last one morning, when we rounded a hill full of roaming sheep and came face to face with a party of guards who wore sky blue tunics over their battle clothing. They were young and, until they saw us, were laughing and joking. The sight of Lnand and Keth stiffened them into wariness in a heartbeat. I watched all those gazes travel up the lances to the white pennants tied onto each, and suppressed the weird flutter of laughter behind my ribs, even as I clutched my token in my damp fingers.

Lasva said in her soft, melodious accent, "I am Lasthavais-Gunvaer of Marloven Hesea. I request an interview with Nanjir Olavair." And she held up a ribbon tied scroll.

They gazed in astonishment, and from one of them came the hissed word, "Assassin."

Lnand gave a laugh and squashed it into a peculiar hiccup.

The patrol leader eyed us, chewing his lip, then spoke a curt word, and the patrol surrounded us. Lnand and Keth stiffened, reins looped loosely around a clip, hands to weapons.

"Disarm yourselves," the patrol leader commanded.

"We never lay down our weapons except by order or in truce." Keth's deep voice was flat with warning.

"We are here to propose peace," Lasva said encouragingly. "Would you honor me by showing me the way to Nanjir Olavair?"

The patrol leader looked between Lasva and our escort. I have recorded my conversation with Lasva about authority. Here was a situation that illustrated the dilemma. Whether or not they recognized her name, it was clear that she had little authority here. Their attention was all on Lnand and Keth. Authority lay in the Lancers' reputation as well as their powerful presence.

Lasva said, "We will not attack you." She brandished her scroll again. "I am here to discuss a treaty with Nanjir Olavair."

They reacted on the word "treaty," some surprised, others exchanging glances. One repeated the word softly.

"We will take you," said the patrol leader, in the dubious tone of one who would just as soon dump the problem into someone else's lap. "Follow."

None of them approached Lnand or Keth, nor did they speak to them. I could not tell if we were prisoners or envoys; I believe we started out the first in all but name. I also believe that the patrol did not attempt to disarm Lnand or Keth only because they wanted reinforcements first.

Lasva modified her horse's gait so that she rode next to the patrol leader. She asked his name and then began to comment admiringly about the flowering trees we passed, which had been planted as some kind of border marker. She commented favorably on the distant mountains to the north, purple and hazy on the horizon. The color of the sky, the scents on the wind, even the fine road were all given their due. I could see little signs of impatience in some of the patrol, and one made a comment in which I heard the word *witless*. Lasva certainly did chatter, in her pleasing accent, sometimes making courtly gestures with the scroll so that the ribbons fluttered.

Gradually, as the road wound up a set of hills, her comments became questions. First one, then two, all easy to answer. Nothing personal. She asked the name of the region, and who owned the fine castle just appearing on a promontory to the south, and did the captain know its history.

By the time this history had been related, a couple of the others had joined in to add their knowledge. Lasva turned to each, smiling, thanking them for their addition, asking names. And so it went. By the time we glimpsed the gated city between two forested hills, they were all talking and laughing, bragging about Olavair's history, and telling her the best places to see. Lnand and Keth watched in all directions, alert as ever, as if any moment they would be expected to spring into battle. I just observed.

As soon as we sighted that city, the captain—in a much more friendly voice—sent one of his riders on ahead to notify the princess of our arrival. When he spoke the word, "princess," he cast a quick glance Lasva's way, but she showed no reaction to this evidence of the Olavair family's royal claim.

The good relations continued as we entered a wide brick courtyard. Then the captain became more formal as an elderly herald in resplendent sky blue requested Lasva to follow. The captain fell in behind me, and an honor guard—or some kind of guard—made up of at least twenty armed warriors formed up behind Lnand and Keth, at a distance of about two paces.

In this manner we were escorted to a sizable room with tables and chairs that looked tall and uncomfortable to us who were used to cushions and Marloven mats. Again, I was not certain if we were prisoners or guests. A servant offered food and drink, which Lasva accepted with gratitude. Then the far door opened and a tall, gaunt young woman about Lasva's age strode in, her chain belt ending in long tassels that swung at each step.

She took us in as we surveyed her. She had a broad, thoughtful brow and bright red hair drawn up in a complicated style. She glanced from Lasva to me, took in my rumpled blue robe, and shifted her attention away, making clear she knew I was a scribe.

She said to Lasva, "I see you bear no weapons. Perhaps we might converse better alone?" She pointed at Keth and Lnand.

Lasva turned to them. "I will be safe enough," she said, her finger and thumb touching to remind them of her token.

Lnand and Keth betrayed their first uncertainty. I suspect they'd been ordered to stick to her side, but here was an implied order to withdraw. "My scribe must attend me of course," Lasva said to Nanjir, but her tone addressed the lancers, who both glanced my way. Then they withdrew, and the entire clanking entourage went with them, shutting the door behind the last.

"Well," Nanjir said. "This is a new situation. Marlovens—and I count half my ancestors among them—usually dictate terms on the field of battle or after they occupy one's home."

"I am here to try something different," Lasva said. "In the style of Colend."

Nanjir then said, "I trust you will not be insulted if I summon my own scribe."

Lasva made The Peace, a gesture that caused Nanjir to stare, lips parted. "You really are from Colend," she exclaimed, and Lasva laughed as she extended the scroll.

Nanjir took it but kept it between her fingers as she walked to the door, spoke to someone right outside it, then returned. "I take it you are an envoy from Ivandred?"

Lasva said, "You may regard me as such, if it smooths the path of our discourse."

Nanjir sighed. "I don't know my path," she said plainly. "A few days ago, your Ivandred did his best to kill Mestan, my brother. Of course, Mestan was trying to kill him," she admitted.

Lasva's fingers fluttered in shadow-warding, ending at Thorn Gate— none of which Nanjir understood.

The door opened then, and a scribe appeared, in another shade of blue, but recognizable immediately. How absurd, that my heart would leap so gladly! I hoped it meant that our peace mission would be successful—that the war would end.

"What hear you of events?" Lasva asked.

"What hear you?" Nanjir countered.

Lasva made a pretty gesture, not quite Life's Ironies, and when she observed Nanjir's mystified gaze, she clasped her hands. "Nothing directly," she said. "My escort has received very cryptic notes with some sort of military meaning. From that I am to understand that there has been little progress one way or another." She leaned forward, her voice dropping to softness. "I am here because I hope never again to witness what I did the other day."

Nanjir said, "Yet after Ivandred gave us a battering, he's been harrying our flanks. My grandfather is trying to hold his position . . ." She broke off.

"In hopes of the arrival of Marloven allies?" Lasva asked gently.

Nanjir looked away then changed the subject. "I remember that Ivandred would not write letters. We thought this was on orders from his father."

"My understanding is, he has misgivings about the magical scrollcases. I admit, I do not yet understand his reasoning, but we are new-married, and there is much yet to discover about one another, as well as about my new home."

Nanjir looked away again, then slid the ribbon off the scroll and unrolled it. She laid it down on the inlay table between herself and Lasva. "It is a map," Nanjir commented. "A good one, too." She leaned forward. "I see a line drawn at the River Tar."

"Your traditional border, I am told," Lasva said.

"My grandfather is determined to acquire traditional land down to the Khan."

"What tradition?" Lasva asked. "I beg your pardon for my ignorance. I thought that the area in question at present constitutes the jarlate called Khanivar."

"It does," Nanjir said. "It used to be Khani-Vayir." She pronounced "Khanivar" as two words. "And before that, it belonged to us, the Olalia. Khani-Vayir was created in a treaty marriage." There was a brief silence as Lasva waited, and Nanjir finally added, "Six and a half centuries ago."

When the Olalia swore fealty to the Marlovens and renamed themselves Ola-Vayir. It remained unspoken, but I am certain they were thinking it as I was.

Lasva raised her hand and said, "Please educate me. I am trying to comprehend your customs here, and so any trespass is inadvertent. But are your people loyal to this land between the rivers? That is, do *you* regard it as part of your kingdom?"

"Kingdom," Nanjir repeated, leaning her elbows on her knees. "I thought the next thing you would say would be the reminder of my grandfather's being forced to swear an oath to old Haldren, the former king."

"My comprehension of the question is not royal status, which Ivandred acknowledges as firmly as he does the familial connection, but the status of the trade treaty between our two kingdoms."

Nanjir's eyelids flashed up. "I . . . see." Her tone said, *It is too easy.*

And so it went, as a meal was served and half-ignored. Lasva begged enlightenment, went over the map, asked general questions about history, about families, and Nanjir's own experiences. All the little questions one asks at court to set a visitor at ease, but Lasva guided the questions around in wide circles, over uncontroversial areas, slowly bringing the circle in. When Nanjir's tone changed, or her gaze, or her hands, outward would go the questions again, back to what was safe.

A day and a half passed like this, with our hostess vanishing every now and then. We would retire, Lasva to read and I to study, or we'd walk in the garden—with Lnand and Keth in sight, and those two, in turn, watched by an impressive host of guards.

Judging from the increased tension in our hosts, it became apparent to us that this war, or skirmish, or battle, was not going well for Olavair—contrary to their expectations.

Finally Lasva's circles narrowed to three facts: Nanjir did not want the war; the brother, badly wounded, no longer wanted the war and was apparently writing a furious series of letters to his sister; the grandfather was angered enough by his wavering progeny to launch an attack.

The First Lancers were waiting.

Lnand and Keth were extraordinarily silent all through that next day.

Late that night Nanjir came to the guest suite to say, "My grandfather is dead. Ivandred has halted at the River Tar. My brother says the Marlovens are ranged along the bank." She pinched her brow with trembling fingers. "Mestan and I will be sharing the crown, and he has agreed to your treaty. I will sign now—we will keep the trade treaty. But you say that Ivandred promises protection if we are attacked from the north, or from . . ." She looked away, and her chin jutted as she looked back. "If Danrid Yvanavar attacks us. Haldren-Harvaldar was a vicious man, but so was my grandfather. Right now your danger is not from us. It is from Danrid, for there is no greater peril than moral righteousness."

"Yvanavar is where I intend to go next," Lasva said.

Nanjir leaned toward her. "Talk to Tdiran."

Lasva bowed over her hands. "I shall do my best."

No more war, I thought, rejoicing. *No more war!*

Though I had not had any training in state matters, I'd sat through the lectures on herald scribes and their duties. I was expected to serve in this capacity, which in this instance was easy enough. The Olavairan scribe and I both wrote down the wording as dictated, and with celebratory enthusiasm I offered to make the Sartoran translation to be sent to the Heralds' Archive there—though I suspected that the Marlovens had not sent any treaty to them for centuries. I hoped that the world seeing this treaty would cement it into reality. No more war for the Marlovens!

"There is no necessity," the Olavairan scribe said in the stiff voice of personal affront. "We have a long tradition in place which I trust is sufficient."

Although I apologized sincerely for my ignorance and assured him that their protocol was more than sufficient, my mood of release—of hilarity, of joy—did not diminish. No more war! I stood by as witness as each new queen signed, and I took charge of the precious scroll for the heralds in Choreid Dhelerei.

When we were alone, Lasva asked me for paper and drew on it a single letter, then folded it and sent it to Ivandred in her scrollcase. "It is so strange," she said. "That Ivandred does not trust these things. Is the magic so easy to violate?"

"I was told as a student that it was nearly impossible," I said. "But I will find out."

Four days later (we traveled much faster by day, and on the road) we reached the river, where a good portion of the Olavairan army still remained.

I had envisioned a crowd of people whose relief would match mine. No more war! Everyone could go home again, and take up their lives! I could work on magic without having to waste time inventing war spells!

We were met by a delegation that took us to Mestan, newly a king. He was badly wounded; though the healers had done what they could, he was obviously in great pain. Lasva and I were conducted to him by silent Olavairans. He could only speak a word at a time, but Lasva offered a stream of questions, which he answered by sign.

I showed him the treaty, Lasva wished him a swift recovery, and we left his pavilion, and traveled between two rows of Olavairans. My shoulder blades tightened as I gazed about me in amazement, then concern, then resignation. Many of those faces were angry, some tight with extreme reserve. A few were curious, but it became clear that whatever quarrel lay behind this uncivilized behavior had not been resolved.

At best, it had been postponed.

My mood plunged into gloom, worsened by Ivandred's request for a magical aid in battle—which I now would have to heed, or leave. Where did my moral duty lie?

With Lasva, I kept telling myself. I had sworn to serve her, and she made it plain that she served the cause of peace.

Lasva bore herself as she always had and neatly stepped onto the waiting ferryboat. As soon as Keth and Lnand were in with us, each holding their horses by the bridle, we set out.

Ivandred was there on the other side, still and watchful until Lasva reached him. I think he meant to greet her with kingly formality, for everyone was watching (including, no doubt, the Olavairans with field glasses, from the other side of the river) but the moment their hands touched as he helped her from the boat he drew her into his embrace and kissed her, then he let go and stepped back.

Lasva gestured to me, and I handed him the treaty, which he did not look at. Clearly Lnand and Keth had been in communication with him.

"We are to return to Choreid Dhelerei now?" Lasva asked.

"You can," Ivandred asked, his voice so low I scarcely heard him. "If you need. I was going to ask you to ride to Yvanavar. The treaty has to be announced. It would be an honor if you took it to them, while I ride to Khanivar Castle to hear the new jarl's oath." His voice dropped even more. "It also forces them to stay in their castles separately in order to receive us."

Lasva's chin lifted, and I stared, astonished yet again. If I understood him correctly, he did not want fighting breaking out. "Ah-ye," she said. "I will be happy to do that, the more if it will prevent any more lives being destroyed."

"Then you can take half of the worst wounded. Tdiran will look out for them."

"Talk to me about Tdiran," Lasva said the next day, when our cavalcade—slow because of the wagons of wounded—set out for Yvanavar. "What did you observe when we visited Yvanavar before the battle with Olavair?"

"What little I saw, Tdiran was civil," I said.

"Put it in our terms."

It was strange. Though my thinking was still in Kifelian, applying courtly language to this situation felt a lot like putting on a pair of shoes that I'd worn too long, and then cast off.

"Lily Gate," I said.

"Yes, yes. That matches my impression. The determined formality, yet when she spoke it was always to the others, and to me, only politesse. Did you see her when Ivandred was present?"

"She did not look at him, except to speak to."

"Except once. Before our departure. The Garden Arch, when he left the room. Oh, Emras." But she did not follow that with an observation.

So we fell silent. She reached down a hand, stroking absently the square, thick book she was halfway through reading, until she said, "I think I know what to do."

By the time we reached Yvanavar, I had worked it out in my head. My duty lay with Lasva, who was adamantly against war. She had also made oaths to Ivandred and his kingdom. So. Perhaps I could please everyone if I invented something that would fit his requirements yet make death-dealing more difficult.

I had two ideas. Both had to do with shifting water, something I'd learned a bit about while working the purification spells. If, for example, I could raise minute bits of water to seep into arrow wood, then they could not be used. And what if I could raise water from the ground into vapors to hide armies from one another?

I would bring these up with the Herskalt on our next tutoring session.

The Yvanavar castle was built alongside a curve in a river, surrounded by a ring of hills with a beautiful road topping them. Silhouetted horse riders appeared and vanished down into valleys as we rode, passed on by dipped flags and hand signals.

The castle itself was built out of stone the color of honey in sunlight, rare in the east, and almost ubiquitous at this end. As with most Marloven castles, you could not just ride up to the front door. There were angled sweeps of stairs to either side, making frontal assault difficult. The doors were massive, iron-reinforced. The one at Darchelde was beautiful with carvings. This one was plain.

The jarl and jarlan both came to the door, as was proper for welcoming someone of superior rank.

The tensed lower eyelids and the tightened jaw betrayed anger in Danrid Yvanavar's handsome, smiling face. I watched Lasva's quick gaze assess him as she returned the greetings, and how her attention turned solely to the man's wife, the jarlan Tdiran, a tall woman, at least as beautiful as her husband. They made a mythic pair, like songs and stories, standing side by side, but the subtleties of muscle, angle of head, the flicker of an eye provided a stream of impressions, not quite clues.

Two things I was sure of: that the woman had far better self-control than the man did. She was impossible to read. The other thing I saw was that he watched his wife as closely as he watched Lasva.

It was clearly understood by the formal words of greeting that they acknowledged the honor of the gunvaer's having personally brought the treaty, but no tone or demeanor betrayed the gratitude you would expect of someone so honored.

I was motioned forward (my role now being scribe and herald rather than mage) as Keeper of the Treaty. I unrolled the thing to display it and watched Danrid's light blue eyes brush indifferently over it. He then turned to his wife. Tdiran's gaze moved from side to side—she read at least half of it, then began uttering the conventional offer of hospitality.

We staff were bustled off to be entertained and effectively shut up for safekeeping. The wounded were escorted to the barracks lazaretto, and Lasva was conducted inside, the jarl at her right, the jarlan at her left.

The first break in the fog of formality was the next morning. As first runner, I had the freedom of Lasva's suite. Thus I was able to signal when the jarlan came to greet her. On Lasva's orders, we arranged for Tdiran to find her in the middle of the Altan fan form.

As Lasva had surmised, Tdiran had too much respect for drill—even a type of drill completely foreign—to interrupt, thus she witnessed the spectacle of the fan she had seen dangling apparently uselessly at Lasva's waist circling with its pair, faster and faster, until they slashed the fabric that I had fastened in the collapsible easel that we had carried along with us. Lasva was so good by now that the slash was a loud, effective rip.

Then I stepped aside to watch the jarlan's reaction as Lasva set down her fan and assumed her overrobe. Thus I saw Tdiran's gaze go from the slashed cloth to the fans, then down Lasva's form to rest on her bare toes. Then her lips parted, and her teeth bit into her soft lower lip, her expression impossible for me to define.

So I transferred my gaze to Lasva's feet, to find nothing out of the ordinary. Her feet, like the rest of her, were beautiful, and beautifully tended. Was it the silver polish, or the neatness of her trimmed nails, the absence of callus or rough cuticle? Or was it the delicate gold ring on her middle toe, carved with minute blossoms?

Marlovens did not color their nails. From their raggedness, especially toenails as seen in the baths, I had wondered if they cut them with knives. Then Tdiran came forward, her tone betraying a cautious interest as she greeted Lasva.

Later, Lasva said, "What did you see?"

I explained, and Lasva's brows went up. "I observe surprise," she said.

"I am very surprised. I do not see the connection."

Lasva chuckled under her breath, and kicked out her neatly booted foot. Then she looked at me askance. "Emras, I forget your age, except that you are younger, but surely you are far past the age of interest. Do you have a lover?"

"I do not," and then felt obliged to say, "So far I am *elor*."

"Ah." She signed Understanding then said, "Then I will confine myself to observing that it is not my feet that draw her attention, it is the thought of my feet in proximity to Ivandred's. The fans show that the peacock has teeth, if you will permit a very awkward metaphor. The feet . . . there is a question about what a Colendi can do for a Marloven within the intimacy of the bedchamber. I am trying to understand how it all fits together."

The watch bell rang and we parted, she to join the jarl and jarlan for a meal.

The night after we left Yvanavar, Lasva bade me walk with her out into the twilit field that smelled heavily of wet grass and moist soil. When we had paced side by side a distance from camp, halfway between the silhouettes against the fire's glow and the barely perceived silhouettes of the perimeter riders, she put out a hand to stop me.

"Tdiran talked. A great deal. So did I, though I revealed very little. She revealed three things," she said, holding up her fingers. "First, since the days of Hadand-Gunvaer, Marloven history has been hard on the women, who can't always match men in physical strength but can in wit. The laws have varied wildly, it seems, and I mean to read up on them. One of the absurdities Tdiran spoke of is called the Time of Daughters, when families could only have one son. As a result, many boys were dressed and raised as girls, as the girls also trained in war."

"Yedi!" I exclaimed. "Did they identify as both, then?"

"I asked her that, and she said that such a question is impossible to answer, except that ballads from that time will switch gender pronouns in what will seem a careless way, but isn't. She also talked about old politics and how the Olavairs would bribe their supporters by promising lands belonging to those they did not favor." Lasva signed Thorn Gate. "Oh Emras. I cannot tell you how my heart chilled when she said, 'We are cruel to our enemies, many say, but we are crueler to ourselves.'"

I made The Peace.

Lasva signed with the second finger. "Next. She cannot explain what happens to them in the Academy. Part is an oath that they don't break, but some is an experience that is impossible to explain unless you've shared it. She offered me an example. She said that when he was growing up, Danrid was always first. But in the academy, he was supplanted by Ivandred, who had once looked up to him. Emulated him. Loved him with the passion of youth."

Her voice dropped, low and rough. "The day that Haldren was flogged. I looked away, at the others, so that I could avoid making a memory I could not rid myself of. And I saw Danrid tight against the seam."

Cold shock through every nerve and muscle made me shiver, then came the inward revulsion of disgust.

"Yes." Lasva's face lifted. I stood with my back to the distant campfire, so its light fell full on her face, where I saw a cold anger tightening her features. For a moment we stood thus, she so still she might have been a statue of her Dei ancestors. "That, I will never forget."

"This is the man Tdiran Marlovair chose over Ivandred," I observed, too amazed to remain circumspect.

That was fine with Lasva. She did not want circumspect. She wanted her own emotions mirrored, shared, reinforced. "That is the third thing," Lasva said. "She did *not* choose him. He wanted her—she says it has much to do with the fact that Ivandred wanted her. So I said that I had seen subtle signs—the trick of gaze, the draw of breath—that in Colend would mean shared intimacy."

"Danrid and Ivandred?" I exclaimed in disbelief. "I thought they hated one another."

"Ivandred was the first to fall in love and the first to grow out of it. She thinks Danrid never did. Such a passion, if unrequited, can turn to anger. Even hate, which in no way lessens the desire."

She fell silent, gazing past me to the campfire, her eyes so wide I could see tiny leaping flames reflected in her pupils. Her breathing changed as she remembered *Obliterate me*, a memory echo that Tdiran intuited and acknowledged softly with, *You understand*. And Lasva had returned, *I understand*.

She roused herself. "She was ordered to marry Danrid by none other than the king. She broke off the relationship with Ivandred, claiming it was personal, entirely to protect him, because she was afraid of what might happen if he found out. But she has now given me leave to tell him the truth."

She paused, looked away, and I wondered if she was thinking of the Duke and Duchess of Alarcansa. Then she faced me again, her voice brisk. "So far, there is one lesson I can take from Hadand-Gunvaer. It is the nature of this net of communication with the kingdom's women. I am going to attempt to recreate that, if I can. Emras, I want you to make a scrollcase for every jarlan in this kingdom—" She paused, studying me. "Or is there a difficulty of which I am unaware?"

I gestured apology as I said, "It would take time to lay the necessary spells. There are a thousand repetitions or even more. And that's after I find someone who can get the gold necessary to make the case."

"Ah-ye! And I understand gold is rarer in this kingdom, as it must be brought from far away. Very well. I know what to do, then. My sister tendered me a substantial sum as a wedding gift, in case I should have need of such. I will use some of it to order cases, if you give me exact specifications. I want them finished before the women show up for New Year's Week."

TEN

OF RENASCENCE

I vandred had the entire city up on the walls with trumpets, drums, and cheers to honor Lasva's arrival. He embraced her right in front of everyone, there in the enormous stable yard, and twined his fingers with hers as they walked inside.

After a meal, I transferred to Darchelde and the secret room.

Within moments the Herskalt appeared. When I told him what Ivandred wanted—and my reasoning behind supplying it—he said, "Excellent thinking, Emras. However, I see that your magical knowledge, while improving steadily, is still lacking. You cannot add water to wood by magic, not without great difficulty. Think of the difficulty of waterlogging an arrow by spooning water over it. How long would it take you? It is far easier to construct a spell that squeezes water out of the wood, for here, the specificity of the arrow works for you. I will give you the appropriate book, and you may add that to your studies, along with your work on the Choreid Dhelerei castle wards."

"These wards," I said. "I believe I see the entire structure more clearly now. The layers of spells are impossibly deep. Far deeper than I thought."

He smiled. "Yes. They go back to the years the Cassadas family ruled in that city, which they built. After the Marlovens took it, they reinforced the castle both architecturally and, later, magically."

"It's thousands upon thousands of spells. It might take me ten years to accomplish."

He said, "Then that will be ten years of good work."

I suppressed my desire to sigh. "I have had another thought." I hesitated, thought about what I had already experienced, and plunged on. "I confess, I'm not sure whether my reluctance is because of being trained not to interfere, or because there is a . . . a moral trespass here, but . . ."

He waited, neither encouraging nor scorning me.

I tried again. "You have said that Ivandred will be a great king, and most Marlovens agree, except this Danrid Yvanavar. I believe that Ivandred wants to avoid war. But from all I've seen, Danrid Yvanavar is quite willing to cause fighting if he can gain whatever it is that he wants. I understand that the dyr can only be used to look at past memories, but could we not use it to determine his true motivations as well as his plans?"

The Herskalt did not exhibit any consternation, repugnance, or surprise. "He is warded. But if he were not, which moment would you choose from his life from which to gain this knowledge?"

"I don't know. But we could begin looking on the day of the coronation, perhaps. His enmity is obvious. His thinking at such times has to be germane."

"That would be an excellent place to begin," the Herskalt conceded. "Were he not warded, as I said."

"Can the dyr's magic be warded, then?"

"It can. A very old spell," he said, flashing a quick smile. "Or, human nature being what it is, the dyr would be in use every day in political circles, would it not?"

"This is the first time I have ever considered the political consequences of this kind of magic," I said.

"Yes. And I see your ambivalence. Your thinking has been carefully hobbled by years of the Scribes' First Rule. Promulgated by the Sartoran Mage Council, whose strategy centers on the airy belief that it exists above politics, in order to do good."

Though his hazel gaze was exactly the same as ever, his voice deepened with irony on the last few words, then resumed an instructive tone. "The Sartoran Mage Council has not changed its method of teaching for centuries. Any system is, understandably, dedicated in part to perpetuating itself. They teach not only magic. As you discovered in your brief conversation with your brother, they successfully alter their students' views of the world to fit their own. Thus, you have learned more in not quite a year then your brother did in four. But then their first year is entirely spent on shaping the student's views and on memorization training. So if you were to discuss your training with your brother—telling him how much you have learned in so little time—it would be human nature for him to feel affront, and to scold you and deem it his duty to report you to the Council."

I bowed my acquiescence, aware of sharp regret. So there would be no writing to Olnar about magic, at least for a while—at least until I better understood my new place in the world. I'd thought to surprise him with the news of two mages in the family when I wrote on his next Name Day. My gratification would have to wait.

The Herskalt lifted his hand. "Dyr aside, what makes you believe that Danrid Yvanavar harbors perfidious intent?"

I exclaimed, "Was he not behind the war with Olavair? Does he not hate Ivandred and wish to take over his throne?"

"Do you really believe human motivation so simple?" the Herskalt retorted with a humorous glance. Then he said, "Perhaps you need some context. Within living memory of Yvanavar's older generation—whose bitterness has influenced the succeeding generations—Yvanavar lost its traditional lands to the Faths. What they have now is a small corner of less desirable land."

"I have gathered that much."

"Perhaps you do not understand what that means to the man himself. Danrid Yvanavar is two years older than Ivandred. He was, until Ivandred joined the academy, an emerging leader. The Yvanavars have long felt that they had a claim to the throne."

"Yes, I know that. His family talks of a legitimate claim."

The Herskalt smiled. "Your irony when you say the word 'legitimate' tells me you do not understand how important a justified transfer of power is."

"Justified because of the accident of inheritance?" I countered. "Yes, we have studied how stability is established through accepted accession, but—"

"But you are about to tell me that Colend's transfers of power are all peaceful. That shows me you do not understand the importance of Marloven Hesea to Danrid Yvanavar. Imagine yourself raised in his house, believing yourself, as heir, a great leader, because you are quick and strong and on all sides all you get is encouragement and flattery. You are raised to think that accident of birth put Ivandred Montredaun-An in the heirship, but if Ivandred is not strong or smart enough to handle the challenges of kingship, why should not a better leader, one with equally legitimate claim, lead the Marlovens?"

The Herskalt opened his hands in mimicry of the Colendi gesture for Query. I glimpsed hard calluses across his palms before he put his hands on his knees. "What you do not know—could not know—is that in his striving to better the training of his people, Danrid has of late hired a sword master to train them all—including himself. He recognizes the need for improvement, for the good of the kingdom."

"This is new to me. Is Ivandred aware?"

"Yes. But he does not know the sword master and probably will not. Danrid will go to great lengths to keep the king from poaching him, is my guess. The point being, this sword master has convinced Danrid, especially after that foolhardy ruse with the Olavairs, that Ivandred is just what Marloven Hesea needs to regain its ancient glory. And so Danrid's attitude is undergoing considerable alteration, because his loyalty goes first to his people but second to the kingdom."

Emras:

I've not only survived my first meeting with the duchess, whose reputation here is more formidable than Queen Hatahra's, but I seem to have fit into the rhythm of days. The work is interesting enough, and there are those occasional visits from the duke. It surprised and flattered me that on these brief visits home he never fails to speak to me. Not just that. He always comes to me, rather than summoning me. He asks about my experiences in Marloven Hesea and never seems to find any detail trivial, though I was taught that travel anecdotes are as much a trespass on another's patience as boasting about one's family . . .

"So that fog spell will raise an impenetrable layer of vapor between the two forces," I said to Ivandred some weeks later. "It doesn't last very long, and like I say, you have to pace out the place you want to raise it, and say the spell each time, but it should suffice if a party of warriors seems about to attack you. Maybe it will halt them long enough to send a peace party," I said, and when Ivandred signed that he understood, I said, "And here is my spell for drawing the moisture out of an arrow."

I demonstrated the spell on an arrow, then broke it between my fingers. "As you can see, it becomes so brittle that it would be useless for shooting." My secret hope was that this spell would be lead the Marlovens to join the Compact forbidding any weapon that is not wielded in hand—and help take them toward the same place in civilization as the rest of the continent. "The arrow spell has to be used one at a time, and, as you see, you need some proximity, but it could be of use."

"This is good work, Sigradir," he said.

"I hope that they will contribute to peace," was my response.

He gave me that open-palmed gesture that meant assent. "Come spring, you will fulfill my oaths to the kingdom by renewing protection spells."

I was surprised, for in spite of his "sigradir," I still thought of myself as a scribe who happened to be studying magic. "What about the Herskalt? Surely he can do these tasks much better than I."

"Asked him. After my father died. Said he's an instructor, and his time is already promised. Comes to us because he thinks that you will make a great mage." He tapped two fingers to his heart in salute to me. "And after a year or so of making reinforcements, you should be expert at it." He turned away, then back. "Also. Lasva tells me you are still holed up in that servant's chamber. Why have you not moved into the tower? I gave orders for it to be cleaned out for you, all except the library. That you'll have to sort out yourself."

I gazed at him, my first reaction dismay. It wasn't the moving—I had so few belongings that I could probably carry them all in a single trip. It was . . . the residue of bad memories of the king? Reluctance to move farther away from Lasva? The sense of permanence that moving implied?

"When you wish," he said and walked away.

I tried to make time to experiment with healing spells. I knew that there must be training for anything major—I would never risk people's lives with my experiments. I could help with binding a broken bone, however, if the healer was not in reach, and someone was injured in the stable or in the practice yard at the garrison. I rather liked being summoned to their aid. It made me feel important, and Haldren Marlovair, who had moved into the tower at the north end of the castle (when he was not in the field) always went out of his way to thank me for these extra attentions to his people, the rare times our paths crossed.

This brought us to late autumn and the cold winds that promised winter. The yellow leaves were clattering across the stones when Pelis crept into my room and shook me awake.

My head pounded. I had been up late working at converting the snarl of ward spells to a clear, tight pattern of interlocked wards, which had apparently plunged me into turbulent dreams. It took me a few moments to recover place and time.

"The babe is coming," Pelis whispered.

I rose and dressed, in case Lasva might need me, though I could not imagine what for.

We had discovered that Marloven custom for birth was different from ours. In Colend—at least, at court—women preferred to experience the effort and physical awkwardness with only personal staff at hand, or a sister if she had one, sometimes with music played from beyond a stout screen, some say to bolster the mother's spirits and others say to help mask the messy aspects of bringing another life into the world.

The Marlovens, we were told, used to require the family to be there by law, a consequence of the Time of Daughters and subsequent sneaky practices with switching babies. Within the last century that law had been rescinded, so that an entire family might be there only if the parents wished.

But I found it strange to discover Ivandred with Lasva in the birthing room, muddy to the thighs, his hair wind-tousled. Since the last we'd heard he was somewhere in the south, he had obviously transferred straight to us.

He was holding Lasva's hands, whispering to her as she gazed at the far wall, her face rigid with concentration and, finally, extreme suffering—she, who had experienced so little physical duress. But pain lasted a very short time, and there was the new prince, a red, wriggling mite with a newborn's misshapen head, his eyes so squinted it was a while before we saw their murky blue.

"Name," she murmured, barely audible. "It is a boy. What shall be his name?"

"Do you have a preference?" Ivandred's voice was low and tender.

This surprised me, for in Colend such things are discussed well in advance.

"There have been no men in my family for several generations," she said. "And as for the famous names—Martande, Lael, Mathias—too many people now wear those names who I don't particularly wish to remember. What about your family?"

He spoke so promptly it was clear he'd thought about it. "Kendred.

Family name, but far enough back that there are no expectations. Obligations."

"Kendred. I like the sound of that." She shifted. "Go, and permit us to be tidied," Lasva whispered.

Ivandred looked down at himself and smiled. "Not just you."

Soon a fire stick was warming the clean, orderly room. The babe lay on a soft towel, and Lasva looked tired but content, her hair brushed and braided.

At her request, one of the runners brought in a shallow bowl filled with Sartoran steeped leaf, which gave off a refreshing scent. In Lasva's hands was a small dish of green kinthus, which the healer had advised her to drink before attempting rest.

Lasva asked me to stay, once she'd been restored to order, the babe in her arms. Everyone else had been sent out.

When Ivandred returned, he wore fresh clothes, and his hands were red from scrubbing. I faded back as he approached the now-neat bedside, but in truth I doubt he would have noticed me if I'd stood on my head and barked like a dog. He knelt down, and reached toward one of those jerking, waving arms. He touched a small hand, the fingers outspread like the petals of starliss, and his eyes gleamed with tears.

"We should talk about Kendred's Name Day party," she said.

He glanced up, lips parted.

"We Colendi always celebrate the birth of a baby and acknowledge our Name Days with little gifts until coming of age, and notes thereafter, to remind our beloveds, *I am glad you are here*. I miss that custom and intend to institute it for Kendred."

"I agree," he said. "The Herskalt once told me that some of our strife might stem from how little family feel there is, when too many put off having heirs until they are old. My father . . . you know what happened. Let us have that tradition again."

The babe let out a wail. Ivandred stilled.

The door opened and in came the Marloven nursemaid, a stout middle-aged woman with smooth fair hair. Marnda was on her heels.

"I will take him to the cry room, so you will not have to hear him," the nursemaid said cheerily as she saluted Lasva and Ivandred. Then she reached to take the infant from Lasva's arms, but Marnda darted around her, hands agitated. "We may begin as we are accustomed," she said.

Lasva looked from one to the other in distress.

The nursemaid said as if to a small child, "We all begin with crying and wailing. It does no harm. The sooner we learn that life is lived to a schedule, the better."

"In Colend," Marnda stated, "infants are surrounded by love. How else do they learn trust? Schedules can wait upon walking and the Waste Spell."

Ivandred said, "We all were left to cry until the bell. How else to learn discipline?"

Lasva's eyes were enormous. "No," she whispered.

The word shocked Marnda and me; the Marlovens scarcely noticed. Lasva closed her arms protectively around the baby. "We will avoid putting him in a room alone to cry. He is half Colendi! We can teach him a schedule—discipline—our way."

Ivandred gazed at her, then at the infant. There was no sign of the extreme ambivalence that later I discovered he felt. At last he said, "He has ten years until he has to begin training for kingship. For now, do as you see fit."

Marnda shot a triumphant look at the nursemaid, who saluted again and left. Ivandred retreated after her, and Marnda took over to instruct Lasva in how an infant must be fed.

The babe was soon settled and asleep, securely bundled in warm clothing, nestled against his mother. Marnda insisted that Lasva drink down the green kinthus. I could see by the way Lasva winced and moved her legs that the attendant soreness had set in.

"I do not want him unhappy," Lasva said.

"He will not be," Marnda responded firmly. "I know how to raise an infant. Cry room." She signed Thorn Gate with emphatic movement. "He will have a civilized upbringing." She marched out, head held high.

Lasva's eyelids drifted. But she was not yet sleepy. "Emras. Come. Listen to his breathing. Is it not charming?"

I said what anyone would. I doubt that she heard me, for she gazed down at the babe and said slowly, "So strange, the power of love. I never particularly thought of children except as a duty, but he is here and so is love. A well of it, that I did not have to create. What did my foremother, Lasva Sky Child, say to her king? 'So powerful is love, freely given, for it cannot be taken, even by an emperor.' The Marlovens say that no one can command love, it's as wild as the wind."

I sensed that she did not want my comment, for she stared down into the baby's face, the firelight reflecting in her eyes. She bent to kiss him, and he stirred at her warm breath on his face, his mouth making little motions. Then she looked up at me, her pupils huge from the effect of kinthus. "I did not expect the strength of this love, " she murmured, as she wormed her forefinger into the infant's grip. "I'm beginning to think that *rafalle* is an illusion, part of the ephemera of youth. There is a reason that someone named that emotion after something ephemeral and intangible. But *this* love . . . like this moment. No pain of the past. No worries about the future. It is perfectly in balance." Her whisper slowed. "Ivandred doesn't write. He doesn't *talk*. He loves me with hands and lips and body, but our minds are separate, for he is chary of words. Is it that words have betrayed him? Or perhaps it is that harsh training that drives a wedge between the inner life and the outer. *Cry room!* It explains much, do you not think? They learn not to express any emotions beyond the field of what they call defense. I do not want this child growing up like that. He will have love and gentleness." Her eyelids fluttered, she slid her arm protectively around the baby and closed her eyes.

When I walked out of that room, I found Ivandred waiting. "Does she sleep?" he asked.

"Yes."

"Is she happy?"

His question took me by surprise. "Yes," I said, because it was easiest, it was polite, and happiness formed part of the truth.

He looked away, but his manner did not release me, and I knew he was considering what to say. So I waited and in my own mind tried to think of ways to define the intense, complex emotions I had witnessed in Lasva. But when he spoke, once again he took me by surprise. "There must be a way to clear snow off of a road by magic."

"There is always the transfer spell, but you know its limitations. You must be specific about the amount, and the more you send, the more difficult the spell. Several strong people would probably be faster."

His lips curved into almost-smile. "Not if the road is between here and the border."

I closed my eyes. "I know there is some kind of spell . . . I read about it somewhere. But it requires a great deal of labor. For one must lay it down along the road first, section by section. And then that spell is tied to some object which, when certain words are spoken, will complete the transfer, and shift snow to the side, at least for a time. But it is very expensive. I know that Sartor's nobles and royalty possess such objects, which their highly paid mages keep in good order."

"Find out how to make it for us," he said. "You can lay down the road spell when you go around the kingdom renewing the protection spells. I will order your escort to keep you to the military roads. For the other part, all you need to do is teach one of my lancers how to layer the transfer spell onto an object. They will see it done."

I bowed my assent, and left, pitying whatever young rider was going to be stuck with this tedious chore.

You now know how I was able to see events through the eyes of participants, though I was not present. What you do not yet know is why. That will come.

On the last few days of the year, the jarl cavalcades arrived one after another, sometimes two and three together. The entire castle was on alert when Yvanavar arrived.

Lasva made it her business to greet them all Colendi style—not just friendly chatter, but inviting them to refresh themselves, rather than dismissing them to their suites after the formal salute.

She had me with her, my runners at hand to be dispatched in case anyone needed anything. So I was there when Danrid and Tdiran rode in, surrounded by their cavalcade, looking so spruce that they had to have stopped somewhere beyond one of the hills to change into their formal wear. As the two dismounted, the walls were lined not only with the regular sentries but the curious. The jarl was wary, his smile humorless; the jarlan looked about with darting glances, as if seeking someone who was not there.

Lasva did not make the mistake of ordering Colendi scrollcases. In Colend, notes carried by messengers were always folded into shapes, as I have said. But intimate notes, given directly from one person to another without being touched by an intermediary, were always tied in little scrolls with thin ribbon, the colors symbolic. So Colendi scrollcases were flat on the bottom but rounded on the top, and always as artistically made as one could desire or afford.

Here, the scrollcases were rectangular and flat, the easier to slide into a coat pocket for travel. Lasva designed the scrollcases herself. Each had at its center the family device, framed by Venn knots and stylized running horses and soaring birds.

At the New Year's dinner, we watched the jarlans touch and examine the scrollcases. You could tell instantly who already had already learned to use magical scrollcases and who had never seen one before, by the way they handled them.

Lasva said, "As you know, I come from the other side of the continent. So I am regretfully ignorant of your history. I am doing my best to repair that. Therefore, I am hoping that you will recommend the best histories for me to read. That includes memoirs and letters written by your own ancestors. I would like to correspond with you about history," Lasva said. "These scrollcases will enable me to write to you, and if you wish, for you to write back. All you have to do to write to me is to tap twice in the center of your family device after you close the note inside. Otherwise you may use the scrollcase any way you wish, for I know many of you have personal magic signs."

I do not think that I was meant to overhear, but Lasva was so used to my presence coming and going that she was probably unaware that I paced behind her as she walked with Tdiran out of the dining hall that first night.

When they reached the hall, Lasva said to Tdiran, "Go talk to him."

Tdiran glanced her way, her brow furrowed warily.

Lasva touched Tdiran's wrist. "I know he still thinks of you."

"What does it mean in Colend, to invite one to talk to one's spouse?" Tdiran asked. "Gossip says that you change partners like you change clothes."

In Colend's court, what is promised and kept or broken is far less important than the style with which such matters are conducted. Here? Did the knives come out? Did they duel over broken promises? I could see Lasva regarding Tdiran warily, then she said gently, "Ivandred and I have made no vows of exclusivity. As for Colend's way of life, friendship is cherished. Talk to him."

Tdiran saluted and walked away.

In spite of the tension gripping us all, from the wall sentries to the kitchen runners, Fourthday's judgment gathering in the throne room was far less contentious than anyone had expected. I was surprised less than most, after the Herskalt's words, for Danrid made no trouble. Far from it. As the Herskalt had promised, the Jarl of Yvanavar spoke passionately about the glory of Marloven Hesea, quoting lines from old ballads, judging from the galloping rhythms and the percussives of alliteration. His manner was fervent as he looked forward to regaining the prestige of the old days, under Ivandred's leadership. His mood seemed to infect most of the jarls, infusing the events with a celebratory atmosphere. As that was the last day of business, I think it is fair to say that the festive mood heightened to one of hilarity.

While everyone withdrew to their suites to put on their silken battle tunics and robes for the last meal in the Great Hall, Tdiran found Ivandred between the garrison command building and the residence wing.

When he saw her, so tall and strong, her long hair hanging down like a cloak over her shoulders, its color of corn silk in the summer sun, all his old feelings were there, powerful, sweet, and painful. Every step she took toward him increased the pain and rekindled the anger of two summers before.

She held out her hand. "Lasva promised me she would explain to you what I kept to myself for your protection." She studied his eyes. "You are angry. Perhaps she did not understand? I know our language is new to her."

"She explained," he said. "It was my father's interference that came between us." He shook his head. "You let me think you didn't want me. I understand your reasons, and I honor your attempt to spare me pain. Maybe even death. But I can't . . ." He looked down, feeling the old struggle against the danger of words.

She stepped forward and laid her strong hand over his heart. He closed his eyes, for he could feel her pulse counter-beat to his, he could smell the wild bayberry and myrtle she used to rinse her hair, and desire reawakened. But then came the image of her standing thus, heart to heart, with Danrid, and a memory overlaid that image with his own beating pulse, the mingled scents of horse and sweat and mud after a banner game, and Danrid's soft voice, his hot breath stirring Ivandred's hair . . . and the strength of memory drove him back a step.

"Talk to me, Van," Tdiran whispered.

He took another step back. They'd never had to "talk." They'd always understood one another with a look, a tug. A slap.

Again, his mind supplied the vision of Danrid flushed and sweaty, ardent and angry. Smiling with cruel anticipation as he used his strength to lure, to subdue. Pain and desire in equal measure. Danrid's hands on her . . .

Ivandred's gut churned. "We can't go back."

He sidestepped and walked away from memory, away from *her*. He could never touch her again. Then came another image, more powerful even than memory, because instinct said it was possible—probable: Danrid's elusive smile aimed at Lasva, the low purring voice as he bent to whisper in her ear, the easy power that enticed and then chastised, knowing instinctively and intimately, the blurred border between the two. That would be far worse than losing Tdiran. It was an unbearable image.

He knew that Danrid would be unable to resist trying.

The dinner was torture. He forced himself to patience, to give time to each jarl and jarlan. But the relief was physical when at last it was over, and Marlovair had reported, and at last, at last, he was alone with Lasva as she nursed the child in her chamber.

And though he'd begun their relationship determined to acknowledge the Colendi freedoms, he could not prevent himself from whispering, "Make the ring vow with me, Lasva."

She was taken completely by surprise.

"In the vow," he continued, "it says, 'I will cleave to you until I am taken beyond life in this world.' I will never want another woman."

She said, "But what about Tdiran?"

His hand flicked out, repelling. "Old friend."

That moment is as indelible in my mind as this ink on my defense. For I was there. I'd slipped to the other side of the room, not directly behind him—he did not like people behind him—but on the periphery of his vision. She could see me, but I was part of the furniture. Her attention was on him, as their fingers met. His profile so intent, hers so still.

Then she said "I will," as softly as he, so as not to disturb the babe, who was now making small noises.

He let out a breath of relief.

. She whispered, "What is your custom? Must we do it on a festival day, or Midsummer? That is when royalty in Colend has customarily made vows of fidelity, which they then renew each year."

"No. I will send the herald in charge of the Montredaun-An vault. There will be rings to fit us among those my ancestors left. Ring vows can be private. Have nothing to do with kingdom matters."

The ring exchange was held the next day. The only witnesses were Haldren Marlovair, several of Ivandred's personal guard, and Pelis, Anhar, and I for Lasva. It was a quick ceremony, in fact so quick you could scarcely call it a ceremony in the sense that Colendi understand the word.

As they stood there before a roaring fire, he in his warrior gear, weapons glinting, and she in plain robes of cotton wool in his colors, the ruddy light on their faces made their emotions clear enough: he so ardent and so intense as he gazed down into her eyes and spoke barely above a whisper, only for her to hear. She, looking up, her profile the smooth courtly mask that first appeared the summer after Kaidas left to marry Carola.

Her voice was soft, and distinct, and I, who had spent so long listening to every word she spoke and trying to descry the emotions behind it, heard not ardency but determination. Each word was an act of will.

ELEVEN

OF SARTOR'S SHADOW

"Now that the kingdom is quiet," I said to the Herskalt the week after New Year's, "and the pressing magical repairs are done, I am ordered to embark on a kingdom-wide tour to reinforce all magic as the snows melt in spring. I am told it will take most of a year."

The Herskalt gave me a nod of acknowledgment.

"Before I depart, Lasva has given Anhar and me permission to visit home for a week. I can make the transfer tokens, so we are spared the usual prohibitive cost."

"True," the Herskalt said. "But is it wise to leave the kingdom?"

I gazed at him in surprise. "Is there something amiss that I do not see?"

"Remember our discussion about the Sartorans and your unorthodox training? This has been a problem for Marloven mages for generations."

"Ah-ye!" I exclaimed. "I did not consider that. But in Colend I am known as a scribe."

"But you will be visiting friends and family, yes? Do you trust them not to speak about your new calling? If they do, and word gets around as it does, Queen Hatahra could summon your hosts."

I'd told the Herskalt that I wished to visit my parents, but I meant to spend most of my time with Birdy. I longed to tell him everything—to regain the free exchange whose preciousness and importance I only understood when it was withdrawn. So the Herskalt's words startled me.

"Why should my queen summon him?"

The pronoun slipped out, but he did not remark on it. "Because the Sartoran Council will probably send an emissary to your queen if any word gets out about your studies. You do know how scribes share news and talk."

I thought uneasily of Greveas and the ring on my toe, though I had done nothing wrong.

"Look at it this way," he said. "Would you put your friend in the position of having to harbor your secret from his queen, and from the Sartorans?"

"I think he would gladly protect me, once I explain the reasons," I protested. "Birdy and I trust one another."

"He trusts you not to speak or do harm. Try to comprehend the difference between that and keeping secrets that transgress against guild rules."

"I intend no harm, and we trust one another to be open."

"You will tell him about the dyr, then?"

"The dyr! Should I not?"

"Don't scribes have trade secrets?" He smiled. "Knowledge is important, on that we are agreed. Finding out the truth gives you greater understanding. You need that, as a mage."

"I understand that, but—"

"Perhaps, at this juncture in your studies, you need the truth of experience, compared to your own perceptions." He gestured, and there was the dyr again. "Think about your friend, this time."

I stared at the gleaming object in his hand, and my desire to see through Birdy's eyes—to see myself—was abrupt and irresistible.

"Shut your eyes and select a memory shared by you and your friend. Perhaps a crucial moment, one wherein you had doubts about someone else's motivation. It need not be negative. In fact, I think it would be better if you chose a situation that did not make you angry or defensive."

My mind reverted to that encounter when Birdy left for Chwahirsland. "The moment I want to see is one when I was a teen. It had no political importance, and there was no anger or threat to me."

"I think such a memory an astute choice: thus you will learn to compare your own perceptions of an event with others' real perceptions—not what they want you to hear about said events. Or what you want to believe."

Guided by his whispered words, I watched myself through Birdy's eyes on that day just before he left for Chwahirsland.

I did not record this memory of his when it happened because I think it is better placed here. Seldom is it pleasant to see oneself through others' eyes, but in this one instance it was so poignantly sweet to be looking on my young self—my round face so unmarked by time and experience that it looked to me like unbaked dough. But to him it was dear. I had to laugh as he tried to find a hint of curve in my plain white linen robe, but my moment of humor was rueful, almost painful, as he struggled not to reveal his hopes, and his ardency.

He used his juggling to distract himself, to hide his sweaty hands (though he had come straight from the baths, his hair still wet). What a disaster! There I was, pompous as only the young can be as I scolded him for juggling at the table.

The diving of bold birds is an apt comparison to the swooping of your silken bags, I said, oh, so self-righteous, my voice much higher when heard through someone else's ears. *But if I have to point out the analogy then it is clumsy.*

I'm the clumsy one. It's just that . . . we leave tomorrow for Chwahirsland, he said in an agony of hope and fear.

And there I sat, my lack of concern killing him inside as I said, *I thought you wished to go.*

But . . . Chwahirsland, he said hopelessly, and there were all the dreams he had of me missing him, of me opening my arms to a first kiss. Nothing. All I offered was a platitude, my disinterest plain, and his sorrow and humiliation hurt me so much that I fell out of the memory, my head aching as if I'd someone had taken a hammer to my skull.

"Drink this." Something cool and bitter was pressed to my lips. I swallowed, choked, forced another swallow.

Very quickly the pain receded, replaced by a cool fog that kept my thoughts at a distance.

"You have not only experienced the truth, you have also discovered the danger of personal exploration with the dyr," the Herskalt said. "We all have done the same. Mages have to learn to disengage emotionally. Do you see that now?"

"Yes." I had difficulty finding my voice. "What did I drink?"

"Kinthus."

"You had it ready?"

He smiled. "Mage students at the higher levels often face this dilemma. It is expected."

The conflicting emotions were still there, behind that fog. I couldn't feel them, as I couldn't feel the headache, but I knew they were there as I knew the headache was still present by the pulse of heartbeat behind my eyes. "I don't think I can do that again. Not to him."

The Herskalt inclined his head. "The knowledge we gain from such sessions becomes difficult to hide from those we are close to."

I forced my lips to move. It took an effort. "We are told that the Old Sartorans talked mind to mind. How did they prevent that sense of trespass?"

"By using mental shields," he said. "It is very much like learning to ward scrying, except you are not using a glass as a focus. It is inside your head, reinforced by magic." He smiled. "Some are warded from the outside, as I have already explained about Danrid Yvanavar. If you follow the typical pattern to the next step, you will be tempted to look at my experiences, if you did not already know that I was shielded long ago."

For the first time, it occurred to me that he might have used the dyr to delve into *my* memories. I was afraid to ask if it was true. Instead I asked, "Will you teach me that mental shield?"

His smile deepened as if he knew my thought. I reassured myself that what I felt was probably what everyone did. His voice was noncommittal as he said, "You will learn it when your studies reach that point. So let us address your progress with the castle wards."

———

I did not go to Colend.

I was in the staff room when Anhar returned from her visit. On her arm was a basket full of delicious Colendi pastries. I was startled to see her hair dyed that light ashy brown again.

Pelis raised her brows. "Anhar, why that terrible color? Or is it all the rage?"

"It was what my sister wanted," Anhar said, flushing.

Pelis paid no attention. She was trying to see into the basket. "You brought us lily breads! And lemon-cream cakes? I can smell the vanilla bean!"

Anhar pulled the basket from Pelis's eager fingers. "These are for Emras. Birdy and I packed them together."

Pelis turned to me, and of course I had to say, "We shall share them."

Anhar went on to describe, in detail, the newest plays in Alsais.

The next day, her hair was back to its natural hue.

———

Scarcely a week after Anhar's return, came two surprising letters.

First, one from my parents. I'd corresponded with them ever since making myself a scrollcase, but I never mentioned magic. Our letters were entirely about the family doings, irrelevant to this record until now. On my Name Day they sent me congratulatory notes and a gold piece, and Tiflis also remembered, writing a long screed about how busy and successful she was, but I did not hear from my brother at all.

I did not know what to make of Olnar's silence after I'd written on his Name Day. I had hesitated about writing to him on mine, for I did not want to tell him what I was doing (I knew what he would say) and yet I did not want to lie. So what had we to talk about?

Here is the letter I received from my parents.

Emras,

We received a call from a Mage Council representative. She is a very friendly young person who claims to be known to you. Olnar vouches for her: Greveas. What she had to say surprised us exceedingly: that you have begun magical studies with a mage outside of the Council? You can imagine our concern. Olnar says further that he attempted to transfer to you but found he was warded, whatever that means. Please explain? You have not mentioned any such things in your letters—we have just finished rereading them all.

Deeply disturbed, I sat right down and wrote a fast response, telling them about the queen's orders and my subsequent decision to learn magic directly instead of learn about it (thus protecting Tiflis, who got me that book). I explained that my lack of information about my new studies after the death of the king was nothing more sinister than habit, and that I was a beginner, my job to renew the protection spells.

As for Olnar being warded, that was because Marloven Hesea's border had transfer wards that were fairly old and fairly strong, specifically against mages from the Sartoran Mage Guild. I said that maybe the new king would order those removed, but someone with more skill than I would have to see to the removal.

Wondering if I'd hear from Olnar next, and if he would still scold me for my unorthodox method of learning, I folded my note, opened the case, and discovered another letter.

It was not from Olnar, but from Birdy:

Emras:

*I hardly know what to write! Somehow someone chirped after
Anhar's visit. Not that I thought that your lives in Marloven Hesea
should be kept secret, but old scribe habits keep me from talking about
my personal life. Anhar insists she did not talk to anyone about you, so
someone must have been listening to us.*

   *The Chief Herald summoned me at the Hour of Stone to an au-
dience with no less a personage than a mage from the Sartoran
Mage Council. What did they want to talk about? You! Who was
teaching you, what you are learning, and what you had done. I told
them what I knew, which in retrospect, I realize is very little. They
would not tell me why they were so concerned, but they made me
promise to contact them if you ever come to visit and to share any
letters in which you detail your magical studies. I am writing to you
to let you know, so that you may contact them yourself. I do not
understand why this high personage should be making me into a
go-between.*

This hit me such a blow I walked out of my room as if physical distance would lessen the pain.

As one does instinctively when emotions are overpowering, I turned
toward the light and nearly ran into Lasva, who was walking the hall
with the baby clasped in her arms. I had forgotten how she often prowled
around, walking back and forth with a fretful baby, so that Marnda could
sleep. In those first few months, the young prince was colicky, and Lasva
was adamant that he not be left to cry it out.

"Emras," she exclaimed. "You look like Thorn Gate come again. What
is amiss?"

I told her. She followed me to my room, and when I was finished, she
said, "Who is this Birdy? Do I know him?"

"You knew him as Herald Martande. Sent back to Colend."

Lasva gazed at me as she hefted the heavy, slumbering infant up
tighter in her arms. "Herald Martande? A lover? You are not *elor?*"

"Not my lover," I said quickly, for well-drilled in me was the old rule
about how royal scribes were never to marry. Even mates were frowned
upon, for one's loyalties must not be divided. But such things no longer
mattered. "He's my friend."

"I can see he is important to you. I could have kept him here. Why did you not tell me?"

I stared at her, my lips moving. So deep was my training, I could scarcely get out the words *First Rule*.

But she understood. "Emras, I am sorry, most particularly because it seems my sister is right after all. I know how much she resents Sartor and interference, though they use other terms. Even in my earliest visits to Sartor for the music festival, I noticed that ineffable superiority the Sartorans feel for all the rest of the world whose kingdoms are not four thousand years old."

She hefted the baby again, glanced into his face, and gently laid him on a cushion. He was too deeply asleep to notice. "Ah! Then I can let poor Anhar sleep. She has been up reading to him every night while he cuts these wretched teeth."

She pressed her fingertips to her forehead and dropped her hands. "If Herald Martande ever wishes to return to us, we will find him a place. I will give orders to that effect." She looked around again. "While you are on your journey, I will have your things transferred to the mage tower." She peered into my face and said quickly, "Nothing needs to change, except your experiments probably require more space. And my staff complains of a burning smell, as if cloth were singed, when you have been very busy. I would be honored if you would continue the fan practice with me, just as usual, on your return, and you may always eat with us."

She left me feeling ambivalent about the prospective change. My resentment of Sartor's officiousness annoyed me so much that I decided I owed them no explanations. I had never made any oaths to them. The only promise I made was to alert Greveas via the toe ring if I ever discovered any Norsundrian influence. That promise I would keep—though I didn't know how much good it would do, if Sartor's mages couldn't transfer into the kingdom.

TWELVE

OF THE LINEAMENTS OF LACE

L *asva:*

We have passed through Eveneth and Zheirban, and are heading southward toward Marthdaun. Though I promised I would write frequently, I have so far reneged as I would not trespass against your kindness and concern by demonstrating my lack of skill at making interesting a journey divided between riding and performing basic but necessary spells.

You asked for my impressions, but all I have to offer are journey details—the mud, the emerging haze of green which close up looks like a fine stubble, the many unfamiliar birds crying overhead as they search for seed or prey, the distant horizon. The cold. If you will, do me the honor to reflect upon your own journeys.

I lifted my pen, scribe training prompting an objection to my tone. Duty did not require an opinion.

You will remember red-haired Retrend. Haldren Marlovair put him in charge of my riding of Lancers. He says he has yet to regain his full strength and confessed one night at campfire that he will probably

*never have the honor of leading a first charge, but he is proud to have
attained the captaincy of skirmishers, whose practice I see if I rise early
enough. They gallop around in circles on the plains, shooting their arrows accurately backward as well as forward. When the first-years
have picked up all those arrows again, I know it is time to end my own
practice and prepare to resume the journey.*

Would Lasva really want to read the details? I was grateful to her for
having assigned Anhar to see to my needs. Lasva had told the Marloven
runners that only a Colendi understands the little habits and rituals that
make life comfortable for another Colendi. But even the most skilled
poet would struggle to make the grubby details of travel interesting.

Nor would I write about the tedium of repeating the road spell for
throwing off snow, as Ivandred had requested. So I ended that letter
with an apology for its brevity, reminding her that I was keeping exact
records of each spell for the Chief Herald. I could copy it for her if she
wished.

The following night I was surprised to discover a letter from her in
my scrollcase when we halted for the night.

Emras:
I honor you for your exemplary concerns on my behalf—

Ah-ye, was she still thinking of my having hidden my mage studies?
But she was never petty.

*—and I cherish your forbearance, for I do recall the details of my
own travels. What I desire to see through your eyes are the people
you meet, and what transpires. I told you before you left that reading
Hadand-Gunvaer's letters was wearisome because of the language
difficulties and because so very many of the details of their daily lives
are uninteresting or obscure. But now that my darling Kendred needs
me less as he gains the strength and curiosity to explore his world, I
am reading more. And corresponding more. (I will return to this anon.)*

*The young Hadand, in going from girl to young woman—from
anomalous princess to queen—gains in interest. Especially when I discovered that a great many of those interminable references to pets,
birds, and animals were actually codes.*

*As Ivandred would say, what is my strategy? Through Hadand's
letters I am beginning to perceive two kingdoms, interlocked, for neither*

exists without the other: what I think of as the kingdom of trade and the kingdom of guards. This is profoundly new territory to me, and as yet I cannot seem to express my ideas to Ivandred, who repeats that there is only one kingdom, and that he is sworn to keep it whole, and further, during the time of Hadand-Gunvaer's letters, men and women both guarded, the first from without, the second from within.

But I perceive a difference, and it is not so simple as "men fought and women traded," which would not be true. Hadand became queen after she herself dueled the leader of a conspiracy. It is odd that the man she defeated was an ancestor of Danrid Yvanavar, and that the two times I mentioned this ancestor, everyone hastened to assure me that his son was a hero, and that the family was quite loyal thereafter. As for Hadand's letters, my runners (who follow my progress with interest as they define terms for me, and identify names and places) keep warning me about "Andahi." I located Andahi on a very old map, for there is no such place now. It might not even be the right place, for it lies far, far north, entirely outside of Marloven Hesea. Apparently some battle occurred there, but that is for later reading.

She wanted more details, but how could I give her what I did not have? By describing exactly how the Marlovens did their best to shut me out and otherwise limit me?

The Jarlan of Marthdaun sent an honor guard—everyone dressed in their formal colors—to meet us at the city gate. The jarlan herself met us at the castle gate, a tall, weather-beaten woman of some forty years. She walked at my horse's bridle to their enormous stable, where the jarl waited to greet me. He seemed tall, though when I dismounted he was not much above my own height, but so massive was he through the chest and arms that he seemed like a mountain on legs.

"The young king speaks well of you, Sigradir," he said. His voice was low and rough as gravel.

Then this imposing couple closed in on either side of me to conduct me up the stone steps into a typical castle, opening into a great hall, which led off to smaller chambers.

There, with rather intimidating ceremony, they offered food and drink. As we partook, they enumerated the things that needed magical reinforcement.

When we rose, there was no conversation, or even an offer of a bathe or a rest. They clearly expected me to get right to it. So I did.

Most of what needed doing I had already done on an earlier visit for emergency repairs. As before, I added extra layers, repeating the spells until my head buzzed and specks swam across my vision. My intention was to ensure that no matter how much use these various things saw, there would be no need for a mage for at least ten years. I did not want to make this arduous journey again anytime soon.

When I could do no more, there was another meal waiting. I stared down at those wide, shallow dishes full of steaming rice, sweet-pepper fish, cabbage rolls, and rye biscuits, and swallowed convulsively, unable to speak.

"She needs to bathe and lie down," came Anhar's voice.

The jarlan, who had been with me every step of the way, returned a noncommittal answer, and soon I floated in the bath, my eyes closed, as Anhar's fingers smoothed the knotted wires around my head, my jaw and neck, and my cramped hands. Oh, the relief! I wondered idly if her clever hands, so sensitive to the hidden pain in muscles and nerves, made sex into an art, and I thought, of course they do. The vivid image of her lying with Birdy imprinted against my eyelids, but absent was that small ball of disgust at the notion. All I felt was gratitude that he found that elsewhere, and the sense of our abiding bond, like being aware of the sun lying below the rim of the world before Daybreak. Love—from the devouring intimacy of sex to the undemanding touch of tenderness—is as mysterious as magic.

"What was that?" Anhar said.

"Did I speak aloud?" I discovered I had the strength to respond. "What you do . . . is magic."

She laughed, a soft sound. "It's training. Like your own."

"It feels like magic to me," I said idly as I climbed out of the bath.

I did not think anything more of it as I employed what little strength I'd regained to record each spell I'd performed. The strict accounting, which I was to turn over to the Chief Herald, was a part of the king's fulfillment of his vows.

Thinking about how I, at my extreme distance, thus functioned as an extension of the king's will, I crawled at last into the bed and fell into profound sleep.

I woke to Anhar singing the carillon pattern of the Hour of Leaf. As well that only two tasks remained, for it was clear from the way that the jarl and jarlan gravely thanked me after I finished that there would be no relaxing, no sharing of entertainment, no extra night of rest. I was expected to move on.

Once again the formal farewell, a reverse of our arrival: the jarl and jarlan walked me to the stable; the jarlan, as commander of castle life, paced beside my horse to the castle gate, and an honor guard accompanied my own guard to the city gates, the lancers exchanging last conversations with their friends among the Marthdaun guards. As we galloped away, I had the distinct sense that we couldn't be gone fast enough.

Once we were out of sight of the city and had slowed to a more comfortable walk, I was so irritable about the prospect of an aching night on the ground when I could just as well have slept in a bed, and so mindful of the total lack of conversational detail to report to Lasva, that I observed to Anhar, who was riding next to me, "They might have invited us to stay the night."

Her brows shot up. Then she said something that I did not expect: "You did not see that they are afraid of you?"

"Ah-ye! My understanding was, they call us 'peacocks.'"

"So they do."

"And I myself was once likened to a bean on a hot pan."

"Very true."

"And the jarl, so very grim. The jarlan, imposing. The both seeming as soft and welcoming as an avalanche."

She tapped her fingertips together on each point.

"And yet, you say they are afraid of me? Might I beg you to explicate?"

She said, "You are a mage."

"Why? They know I come to mend and to secure. I attended to their own list. I did nothing that was not requested."

With an air of gentle mockery, she made The Peace on each point. "I think . . ." She gazed upward, then said slowly, "My thought is that they fear what you *might* do."

I laughed, but as the sun sank toward the flat horizon, my circumstances began to connect in my mind. "So . . . Retrend and the lancers, are they there to protect me, or to protect the Marlovens from me?"

"Both, I suspect," she said.

"Yet their king studied magic."

"He is their king."

"And I am a foreign peacock who rides like a bean popping on a hot pan."

Anhar let her mirth show at last.

"I am delighted to serve as amusement," I said with so high a manner that the mirth erupted in a soft laugh.

"From what they all say, Totha is going to be far worse," she said, with another laugh. "And here I am a coward." She sobered. "Cowards know how quickly circumstances can become fearful. From girlhood I worked to stay unnoticed, except when I wished to be a player. In life? I tried to be furniture, which calls for the skills of a player, but in another way. No one threatens the furniture," she finished with cheery irony.

A few days later, Retrend announced that we were near the border of Totha, and to my surprise called a halt not far from the bank of a river, though it seemed to me we had at least another hour's riding time left.

Anhar and I retired, and I discovered a letter from Lasva waiting. I could tell from Anhar's quick, intimate smile that she'd heard from Birdy.

I had been staring, and she glanced up. "Do you want to see it?" She held out the strip of paper, her gaze steady. "You can read it, if you like."

"I thank you for the offer," I began, preparatory to refusing.

She shrugged. "He seldom says anything that could not be cried out at city center at the Hour of the Bird. I assumed that the private thoughts, the complete thoughts, were reserved for his letters with you. I know that his letters to you are long," she added, still with that steady gaze. "I saw him writing to you, one night when I was Colend, when he thought I was asleep and safe from being bored." She stared out at the campfire, the silhouettes of the Marlovens as they stomped and twirled to the tap of drum and the cadenced ballad. "He wrote a long time," she went on, her tone slow and reflective. "Sometimes he looked up, and then he would lean over the paper the same way he leaned toward you when the two of you got into one of your arguments about history. I think those aren't letters. They're conversations. Probably in your scribe form."

"It is true," I said. "We were drilled in those forms. It's comfortable."

"You value these conversations by letter."

"Yes. I look forward to them."

"But you don't want to be closer to him?"

I let out my breath in a long sigh. "It is not him. It's everyone."

She studied me as she ran the strip of paper through her fingers again and again, not quite an absent motion, for the pull of paper was slow, as if she felt the curve and stroke of each letter that he had inscribed. "It was always you first," she said slowly, still studying me. "I knew that. We even talked about it the month before he left. I accepted that, and in his turn, he accepted that I would not go back to Colend except to visit."

How strong was the urge to say that I wished I could go back! In spite of the ambivalences, the hurt I saw in him that we did not feel the same sensations. But I dared not explain about the mages and Sartor, not after those accusatory letters. The less she knew the better for her.

In any case, she did not have magic on her mind. "Just now you looked down, and you recognized his hand. And then there was that in your face." To illustrate, Anhar touched the middle of her forehead, which puckered with a mock frown. "My little letters each night are like the soft words before bedtime. They are never profound. They are not words to be archived, or even remembered, not that kind of conversation—the elegant form, the expressions with a lot of Sartoran worked in as decorative language that he shares with you."

There were so many things I could say, but what came out was, "You do not wish to return to Colend, and live with him?"

She gestured irony. "You would not ask that if you met the Duchess of Alarcansa."

"I saw her once or twice, when I was still a student," I said. "They called her the Icicle Duchess then, even though she was merely acknowledged as heir. Does Birdy find duty with her so onerous? He has said nothing in his letters." As I spoke the words, a quick sense of regret, almost constraint seized me: though I did not talk about *everything*—meaning magic—to him, I had assumed that he told me everything. I hated the necessity of holding secrets from him and wondered why he should hold any from me. There were no Sartoran mages looming in shadow over him.

"His duties are at a remove from the family," Anhar replied. "And he has been befriended by the duke."

"The Duke of Alarcansa?" I asked, surprised.

"Yes. He joined us twice while I was there. I'm given to understand that he and the duchess are opposites in that way. He was certainly very informal, and he seemed to like hearing about our lives in Marloven Hesea."

"Our lives?"

"We Colendi," Anhar explained. "Lasva in particular. He encouraged me to join the conversation and share any experiences I wished to." Anhar gestured irony. "Except for Birdy, he was alone in encouraging me to speak."

Here was another secret I would not tell: that the Duke of Alarcansa had painted Lasva a lover's cup. "Is the duke interested in the Marlovens, then?" I asked.

"Yes." Anhar closed the flap and slipped out of her robe so that she could prepare for sleep. "One night," she said, as she hung up her robe on its peg to air, "the second or third that I was there, the duke came to us for the first time. I was so surprised, first to see him and then to see how informal he was with Birdy. I forget how it came about, but the Duke asked what would happen if someone leaped into the middle of Marlovens at a meal, waving a sword threateningly. Birdy said that they would all attack. The Duke said that if such a thing happened to Colendi, they would run away."

"As would I," I said, as she crawled into her bedroll and turned her head away from my candle flame. She chuckled, and composed herself for sleep.

I turned to the letter from Lasva.

Emras:

My forming idea is this. The Marloven women, in guarding and guiding the cities, fostered trade. The jarls and their men, in riding around looking for trouble, kept away would-be invaders. It seemed to work, from the brief historical references, except when either of these two "kingdoms" attempt to assume the other's role, there is disaster. The kingdom of trade, accustomed to being defended, cannot defend itself, for tools are not weapons. And when the kingdom of guards tries to trade, everyone else sees them as making war.

Hadand and her people are so interesting. On your return, you must read from the letters of the old Jarlan of the Marlovairs, whose blunt style and trenchant view of the world makes me laugh.

But there is my other task, my attempt at building this net that Hadand inherited and propagated with such wit and brilliance. I fear that such wit as I possess is too characteristically Colendi (which is, to most of my correspondents, the equivalent of incomprehensible.) As for brilliance, you know what they call us: peacocks. So beautiful to look at but regarded as silly. No Marlovens put peacocks on their banners.

The rapid crunch of footsteps broke my reverie. Anhar also sat up, her black hair a waterfall against the dull tent wall. "Something's wrong?"

It felt late. The Marlovens had not sung or played drums at campfire like they usually did if there was no rain or snow. The quiet, interrupted by unprecedented noise, caused me to open the tent, gasping in the wash of bitter cold. No lights whatsoever.

The quick footfalls, the jingle and rattle of gear, the muffled thud of hoofbeats reached my ears. I strained to see but couldn't. My heartbeat pulsed in my throat as I pulled on my coat and plunged outside the tent, where I found Retrend standing guard, sword drawn. There was no moon, it had already sunk, leaving us only weak starlight to see by.

"What is it?" I asked.

"Scouts heard at least half a wing out there."

"Could they be travelers, or on training?"

"No one rides in this darkness without purpose," was the brief reply, as his head turned in one direction.

I made an effort to contain the questions he obviously could not answer. My pulse was still quick. I could transfer out, of course. I had four transfer tokens with me. If the impossible was possible—if for some mad reason someone intended us harm—I could save three lancers and Anhar.

Or I could . . . do something.

My first thought was of my magical fog. I pulled on my shoes, then stood in the door of the tent, listening. The muted thunder of many riders seemed to come from everywhere to my untrained ears, but Retrend's entire countenance acted as a beacon.

The riders, whoever they were, proceeded slowly along the river's edge. That made my task much easier. I took a moment to gather my strength, to concentrate. To remember the water's edge, where we'd gone for a drink before eating. Magic must be exact.

From the water I drew vapor. Again and again, building the mist. What direction was the air moving? I pulled off my glove, licked my finger, and held it up. Good. The mist could be left to drift on its own, so I kept making the spell over and over until my head buzzed with my effort.

I opened my eyes and staggered; my sight was blurred, and I had to sit down, but even so, I smiled in triumph. The entire camp was thickly enshrouded in swirling, drifting mist.

No one was going to be finding us, whoever they were, whatever their purpose. They would have difficulty finding their own feet.

I crawled back into my bedroll and dropped into sleep.

The next day, we crossed the border into Totha, our lancers alert and wary.

Nothing stirred. The first village we came to seemed empty, until we reached the center, where we found armed people awaiting us.

We drew rein, and Retrend turned my way.

"I am here to renew the protection spells," I said.

"We will accompany you," was the reply, from a bleak-faced old woman. She gripped a knotted stick that looked very much like a weapon.

So it went, in that village, and in the two castellated towns we visited that day.

That night, Lasva wrote again:

Emras:

Ivandred spent the morning issuing orders that I believe concern you in the South. I cannot believe that the friendly, appealing young jarl and jarlan from Totha would be secretly planning some sort of vile attack. When I asked Ivandred, he said something about their desire to withdraw from the kingdom and set themselves up as king and queen on their own. I do not believe it. I cannot believe it. I am well aware that my sentiments are going to appear trite. I know that I am not the first mother to stare at my precious child patting his hand in rain puddles and think of him lying broken and bleeding in some faraway land. Every single one of these young warriors came from loving hands. Surely no one would deliberately cause a war over borders and titles, which are no more substantial than air.

She used words with such emphasis that her request carried the gravity of an order. She wanted me to find the evidence that someone somewhere else was behind these indefinable threats, but not the "appealing young jarl and jarlan."

The next morning, I carried Lasva's questions to Retrend and put them as my own, lest it seem like I was interfering with his orders by invoking Lasva's name. He was distracted as they mounted up, with their weapons out, alert for trouble. He said, "We are sure to find out before we leave Totha."

One or two of the others in earshot seemed to find his words funny, for they uttered short laughs as they went about securing and tightening things.

Anhar mounted her horse silently, so pale that her Chwahir ancestry was pronounced.

As the day stretched into a week of tension, I gained the sense of a people whose entire life was a preparation for battle. My honor guard was paced by another, larger, honor guard that stayed between us and the locals.

Mindful of Lasva's request, I wrote to her:

> *Everywhere I went, all week long, I was watched from a distance, sometimes by crowds. But those Tothan warriors on horseback, riding restlessly back and forth, kept me from speaking to anyone. And no one came near enough to speak to me once I'd been told what was needed. Though I travel to keep the king's vow—to complete necessary tasks that make life easier—I always feel relief when we leave. And we resume our travels on roads without plinths or signposts.*
>
> *So far, no sign of the jarl and jarlan.*

In spite of the rigid politeness with which I was addressed, you would think a mage was little better than a thief. Anhar, however, was regarded as no threat. In the course of seeing to all the little details of life—laundry, food, and fodder—she was able to cross outside of those armed circles. She asked small questions or exchanged easy comments, and learned about how people lived. Though no one discussed politics.

Glad to have something to report to Lasva, I wrote:

> *As we were told, the word "Elgar" is never heard around this region. Yet according to Anhar, a nearby mossy structure is called Indasbridge, and down the Valley, the village is known as Indascamp. We stayed in a very old house that was made of golden stone. It had weather-softened contours and wide windows and doors that opened onto little gardens, making it clear that it had been built a century or two before the castles. Anhar was told proudly that Inda Harskialdna had been caught by a storm and stayed there with some of his relatives. And this morning, when she went for bread, someone pointed out a plateau on which nothing at all was built. This was apparently where Inda had died.*
>
> *The Marlovens do not build statues or commemorative buildings here, either. Their memorial art here is like elsewhere in the north, on display inside their halls: those mounted weapons, shields, and banners once carried by heroic ancestors.*

If the lancers thought war was imminent, they didn't talk about it, in spite of their wariness, the way they carried weapons in hand, and their constant patrols. Human concerns like anyone else's aired around campfires at night, or as we walked the horses through valleys still streaked with snow, over roads laid to accommodate speed and terrain. These roads never described pleasing curves, so that one might enjoy a vista from varying angles.

There was little art as *we* understood it. The closest they came were the galloping ballads which invariably described heroism, battles, chases, and so forth. As we crossed those flat plains, so unlike the gracefully undulating hills of Colend, cloud castles flourished in the unimpeded sky, and toward nightfall the extravagant colors of Marloven banners were steadily drenched. Twilight, at last, reduced the storm to the charge of a single head-lowered horse, ridden by a muffled rider. I was beginning to see the world in their metaphor and resented it.

And then came the attack.

———

"Tomorrow we reach the border and head north," Retrend said. There was no mistaking his relief.

I should have taken that relief as a warning, but I, too, was relieved. The next day, as our horses struggled along the road under a heavy downpour, the scouts splashed back, calling out military terms that I did not understand, but this I did: "Forming up beyond the ridge."

I had been riding with my head bent so that rain would not run into my mouth as I muttered the road spell. I broke off as Retrend wheeled his horse back in my direction.

"The king thought they wouldn't come until after we crossed the border. Where the First Lancers are waiting."

"Why would anyone attack us? We've done nothing wrong!"

"Their intent is either to capture or kill you."

I wanted to cry out, *Why?* "Who is attacking?" I asked, arms pressed against my churning middle.

He opened his hands. "We may as well say Totha. It will make no difference soon. They risk reprisals by attacking us within their border. They must be claiming a new border, based on some ancient treaty, to try sidestepping the laws of peaceful passage." He looked around as if there was some sort of sign in the gray, rain-curtained landscape.

I saw Anhar's painful expression at my side, and remembered what she had said about no one being threatened by the furniture.

There were too few of us for anyone to be overlooked if our pursuers were intent on slaughter. "It makes no sense," I muttered.

From my arrival on the subcontinent of Halia I had experienced all the varieties of fear, from wariness to thick, choking terror. The terror was back and as sudden as those flames on the bridge, but this time, shadowing its heels was anger, as I watched Anhar's terrified eyes flicking back and forth between us.

Retrend and the lancers betrayed no such surprise or disbelief. In their faces I saw grim desperation, the revealing tic of a thundering heartbeat in the veins at neck and temple. They had expected an attack—but it was coming too soon.

"I can transfer to the king," I said. "Or one of you can, because you'll know how to report."

"But he can do nothing. He's a day's ride away," Retrend said bleakly.

Fear feeds rage, I discovered. I was trembling with it, angrier at each breath. "What do you suggest we do?"

"Find a defensive position. And defend to the last," Retrend said.

There were mutters from the lancers. I heard a few words—"honor," "retribution"—but I stopped listening. The prospect of fighting to the last had meaning to them. It didn't to me.

I had done nothing wrong. I would do nothing wrong. This magery I was learning was good work—*peaceful* work. I cared nothing whatsoever about the "honor" of dying in a brutal, messy way.

It could be that I am the only person whose mind, especially at moments of tension, will insist on bringing up memories that I would rather stay buried: in this instance, a painfully vivid image of what I had read in Fox's record about those Venn mages.

I would never do something as evil as transport a rock inside another living being. However, as my heart drummed behind my eyeballs, I thought, Why should I not defend myself against someone coming to kill me for no worthwhile reason?

This and all my other concerns jumbled rapidly through my mind, as Retrend motioned to the lancers. They began to move about purposefully, one drawing Anhar away toward the remounts. "You won't want to be in the front line," the woman said with the sort of humor typical of Marlovens.

With one backward, pleading glance my way, Anhar obeyed, as if obedience would restore order.

I said to Retrend, "How long until they come?"

Retrend glanced at the scout, who couldn't be any older than seventeen. "A watch. Maybe," this fellow said in his adolescent honk.

Watches were six hours.

"If we were to survive, could you make it seem that it was by some military ruse. At least, to Anhar?" I asked Retrend, whose brows shot up, and I felt obliged to explain, "Mages have politics as well as everyone else. I can't do anything about the attackers, and of course the king must know whatever transpires, but if I can spare Anhar, I would."

Retrend clapped his fist against his chest, the sound a fervent expression of his hope in spite of all that talk of dying for honor, I thought.

I said, "What will they do?"

He replied with a grim smile, "With so few of us, it will be elementary: they will ride up in column, surround us, and see to it that none of us survive the circle."

"Ah-ye." My throat was so tight it was difficult to speak. "Where will they break?"

This time he looked around. "We will take up our position on that hill, using those trees as cover. So, they will break outside of bow shot, approximately there, just behind that stump."

"Good. Then have your people collect as many small pebbles, this size—" I made a circle on my palm. "As many as possible and bring them to me. I'll tell you where to place them. . . ."

I would never transport rocks inside of other humans, but I had no compunction about transporting rocks inside of other rocks. Two things, I had learned, cannot possess the same space at the same time. One is impelled away from the other; the larger it is, the more violently it is flung away. Often in pieces.

As the Marlovens brought my pebbles, I placed a destination transport spell on each, which I told the lancers to scatter along the route the attackers would come. I asked Retrend to position his people so that the break in the column would occur abreast of the tree stump on the one side, and mossy remain of a stone wall several paces away. I spelled until my head swam and I was staggering, but I kept at it until I'd completed my plan.

We could hear the rumble of horse hooves, when I said, "It is ready."

Retrend signaled with a gesture, and his lancers took up their places behind the rough trunks of the cluster of droopy wild pepper trees, and strung their bows. I stood behind the first tree, with Retrend, struggling to calm myself with Altan breathing, with little success. My veins sang with fear-excitement. I had to trust it to get me through more spell-casting.

Amid a splattering of mud and rain the attackers came, exactly as Retrend had predicted. Bows creaked around me—soft curses at the way the weather interfered with snapvine and bow tension—then the first twenty or thirty pairs reached my first avenue of pebbles, and I performed the spells to transfer each pebble's mate inside. I'd bound these together in twos so that the transfers would be simultaneous. Even though the pebbles were small, and side by side, I felt the build of heat very swiftly, and I thought I caught the singe of cloth and hair as I rapidly closed the spell.

The transfer was nearly invisible to us, as pebbles shifted inside pebbles, causing violent breakage, the bits hurling outward. The result was a sudden surge of angry, panicky horses as the line broke. Horses neighed and reared. Warriors fought and regained control. Their leaders shouted, and the line pressed on, though slower, their shields raised.

When the leaders reached my boulder and stump, where Retrend guessed their column would break, I activated my second transfer. The resulting fragments of stone caught their horses full on the sides, and the riders at an angle just inside their shields, which were aimed forward.

One shouted, two horses crashed together, and the person carrying the banner lost it and tried to reach for it. His horse spun on its back legs, and he fell with a crash in the mud.

Still, the leader shouted, rallying them.

That was all I had! My spells were done! Desperate, I stepped out, and for a single heartbeat I stared into that blanched, grim face, his eyes wide with fear, jaw jutted with determination.

I spread my hands, whispered the easy spells of illusion, and lightning danced on both my palms. I could do nothing with a mere image, but as I hoped, the warriors were too ignorant of magic to recognize stage artifice.

They broke and retreated in chaotic haste.

Slowly, slowly, the Marlovens eased, first the tension of arrows nocked to bows, then their bodies. They remained in position until Retrend raised his hand. He motioned the scouts to follow the attackers. Within the space of five breaths, I heard galloping.

They were gone. They were gone, and I had driven them away. The relief was intensified by a flush of triumphant sweetness. Oh, the exaltation! *This* was the power of magic.

I dropped my head and clasped my hands inside my robe in an effort to hide the heady joy that made me so nearly dizzy. I used Altan breathing as I followed Retrend through the leaf-strewn duff and down the hill to where Anhar waited, holding the remounts' line in a death grip.

"You did it?" she asked. "You fought them off?"

Retrend glanced my way; I did not trust my voice not to tremble. He said, "Couldn't see in the rain." It was clear he hated lying. He raised his head and said more sharply, addressing everyone, "They might be back. I suggest we run for the border, cross country. You and you on point. . . ."

And that is what happened.

We used my glowglobe for night travel. At least the rain had lifted by then. The tired horses and riders plodded on, everyone's lower limbs caked with mud, until at last someone gave a shout of relief. The outer perimeter riders spotted us just as another band of rain overtook us.

Soon we were inside the First Lancers' camp. The voices around me were high with hilarity as the warriors joked back and forth. Anhar and the remounts were led off to the horse picket, where I knew someone would help her set up our tent. I sat on my horse unable to move. My head throbbed, and I was shivering with cold and reaction, joy and trepidation, exhaustion and nervous energy by turns.

Ivandred emerged from his tent. As always, I was a little startled by his appearance, though he had never said anything remotely threatening to me. It was more that I could not disassociate him from bloody scalps, red-streaked swords . . . and that bruise on Lasva. The lingering joy subsided completely.

He seemed not to notice the rain that dotted his coat in dark gray splotches and beaded in his pale hair. "Report," he said.

I began to search for the best words, but Retrend, long experienced, uttered a military summation of the situation, wonderfully succinct.

Ivandred glanced briefly at me and back as he said, "You say they carried a banner. Whose?"

I could not recall the color, much less the device. My memory was of a sodden mass of fabric blotched with unremarkable color.

"Old Algara," Retrend said unerringly. "Brown and silver owl on white."

"Where are they now?"

"Evrec is shadowing them."

Ivandred flicked up his hand in acknowledgment then said, "Proceed as ordered. Same road. Leave them to us."

Retrend thumped his fist against his chest and walked away, talking low-voiced to a couple of his lancers. Ivandred turned to me. "How did you accomplish this spell with the rocks? I thought it was impossible to transport something into something else, but Retrend makes it sound like you did."

"Using the transport spell we are taught, it's impossible. But the Herskalt made me take it apart and reconstruct it, so now I understand how to modify it," I said, and explained. Ivandred listened closely. I wondered if he was thinking of trying to spray pebbles at enemies—if he did, I thought, it would be far less terrible than using swords and lances. I coached him until he understood, then I said, "I was hoping that as little about my part would be said as possible. I cannot help what the Totha attackers will say, of course, but our folk."

"Do not worry about the Tothans." Ivandred's voice and his face were devoid of emotion, but again I sustained that thrill of dread. "As for your request. I understand what you want. And I concur." He lifted his chin toward the busy camp. "We train all our lives to defend ourselves, but the idea that some mage, even a little thing like you, could wiggle a hand, mutter something, and cause one of us to drop dead, it is disheartening."

It is exhilarating, I thought, but enough dread remained to enable me to hide the reaction. "Yet we know only Norsunder does that kind of magic."

He made a negating motion. "We know that is not true."

I thought again of those terrible Venn mages. I had refused to read any more of Fox's memoir, so I did not know the specifics, but I knew that these Venn had fought Retrend's and Ivandred's ancestors, and in some ballad there was probably a bloody description of what had come to pass by magic.

He let me go then, and I retired to our tent, but I was not permitted to rest.

"There is something they are not telling me," Anhar said, arms pressed tightly·across her front. "Did they cut scalps away from those people?"

I flung up my hands to ward Thorn Gate. "Nothing like that," I exclaimed without thinking.

She exclaimed in surprise, "Then what is so terrible?"

I thought about her words, and Ivandred's words, and found a sliver of truth, while still protecting her. "I used stage magic. It frightened them away."

"Oh-h-h-h," Anhar nodded, then winced. "And they are ashamed that they do not have bloody scalps?"

It would have been easy to agree, but I had already been dishonest enough. "It is more like such a ruse will never work again. Surely some-

one somewhere will explain to the Tothans that it was merely stage illusion."

"Then next time, they will attack," she murmured, grim again.

But next time, surely, I will have a plan, I thought, as I curled up to
sleep.

PART SIX
GLORY

ONE

OF THE VAGARIES OF FAME

Three or four days later, when we camped, out came the hoarded distilled liquor. Anhar and I were considerably surprised. The lancers used swords in wild and exciting dances, with much whirling, martial posturing, and heel drumming in counterpoint to the hand drums.

When I asked Retrend if there was a festival day we were unaware of, he grinned, offered me a drink from his flask, and said, "The king and the First Lancers found the attackers."

"Found?"

"They won't be talking to anybody."

He turned back to the celebration as I comprehended what it meant: they were all dead.

My emotions were a turmoil, but foremost was my awareness of no desire to celebrate. I retreated to our tent, where Anhar asked the expected question. "Good," she said fiercely. "I am glad. They were going to kill us, people who did them no harm. Who they had never met! Aren't you glad?"

"I was glad the moment he said it," I answered. And I had been—a pulse of angry vindication, but it lasted only as long as the walk to the tents. More lingering was the memory of the leader's face, his nose with a bump in it, jug ears a lot like Birdy's. His horror, then the tightening of determination. I would swear he hadn't wanted to kill us, but that determination made it plain he would carry out his . . . orders? Duty? Honor?

We traveled on. The long, alternately dusty or muddy road was broken by the occasional pleasure of Birdy's letters. The Marlovens acknowledged Restday by passing around a wine flask, but otherwise we traveled like always, and if they had other festival days, those went past unnoticed by us. Maybe the ballads or dances changed? I was never certain. I did transfer to Choreid Dhelerei on Flower Day, to visit the baker who made rolls something like Colendi lily breads. I brought those back to Anhar, who wept as we ate them in silence, the homesickness sharp and poignant in the lack of music and flowers and pretty silken clothes.

Birdy cheerfully described the plays and banquets celebrated that day in Alarcansa, not knowing how eagerly I read, nor how much it hurt to read. He had been promoted from trade statistics to vital statistics—recording and sometimes amending birth records. He was not only required to witness at births, he must now attend hearings if parents parted, or if a parent wished to adopt another parent into a family.

Sometimes I thought about what the Herskalt had said about scribes and power and controlling information. Not that Birdy gave any sign of such intent. He delighted in people, no matter what degree, in all their variety. I relished these small, vivid glimpses into the lives of Colendi I would never meet, appreciating their very ordinariness. As for me, I wrote about what I saw, the language, historical artifacts. I talked about everything but magic.

We passed northward again. By subtle signs (and lengthened drills) the lancers revealed the anticipatory tension that I associated with Yvanavar. We camped one night short of the border. The Marlovens performed a vigorous dance in commemoration of some important battle long ago, then a flask of distilled liquor passed from hand to hand.

I heard the tail end of Retrend's conversation as he offered the flask, ". . . and I will see and talk to this mysterious sword master—see if I don't."

"Stake?" came the laughing challenge.

In answer Retrend pulled from his boot a favorite knife, and cast it down to stand in the soil, hilt upright. Those who were wagering against him offered weapons in their turn, amid whoops and crowing laughter.

I walked away to where Anhar was setting up our tent. "I wonder if anyone keeps the same set of weapons all their lives? Or if they get traded all around in these wagers of theirs, I asked.

"Who cares?" Anhar said.

There was no sword master, mysterious or otherwise, while we were there.

We were scarcely out of sight of Yvanavar's gate when Retrend looked around, the low sun barely striking a glint in his red hair, as he made certain the Yvanavar escort was not lurking about.

Then he exclaimed, "Well, that was disgusting."

One of the older lancers said, "I thought it was too early for the jarl to be heading south for Convocation. Even at a walk, he'll get there a month ahead of time."

"The jarlan told me that he is making stops at Torac and other places," I said.

"Tlen," Retrend said with meaning.

"Tiv Evair," someone else said with the same heavy emphasis.

I mentally shrugged away politics I couldn't even pretend to understand.

Retrend turned my way. "Did the jarlan mention the sword master?"

"Not a thing," I replied. I did not tell them that the only conversation I had with the jarlan was about myself. *I am told that you are a Colendi scribe.*

So I was trained.

In Colend, are all scribes taught magic?

Either explain or say nothing, I could almost hear the Herskalt's advice, and so I said, *Scribes are taught in Colend as they are taught everywhere. I learned magic after I left.*

And Tdiran looked at me just the way the courtiers at home had looked at Jurac Sonscarna.

". . . sword master was on a field run with the young ones, that's what I was told," someone said.

"Banner games," Retrend replied. "A little late in the season for that."

"I'll take my knife now," said one of the others, and amid laughter, the weaponry began to change hands as the payoff of the earlier wager, momentarily halting when Anhar spoke up.

"I know his name."

Everyone turned her way. She reddened. "The upstairs maid talks a lot. I listened. The man's name is Hannik, and she said he comes from some small place beyond the Jayad."

"Hannik!" Tesar repeated, and half the lancers laughed.

"What is droll about this name?" I asked.

"Only that every third man is named Hannik down that way," Retrend said, with a salute in Tesar's direction. She grinned and lifted a shoulder.

"Why?" I asked.

They all found that funny.

"Haven't you heard that ballad, 'The Rat and the Lion'?" Retrend asked, grinning.

"Yes. Several times. It's about all these animals, each verse a separate one. A rat outsmarts them all and then chooses the lion as its companion after outsmarting it, too."

"Nobody explained? It's about Princess Rat, when she married Hannik Dei," Retrend said.

Tesar added, "This was way back when it was all Iascans here. Before *we* came." She struck her fist to her chest. "The 'rat' is Princess Siar Cassadas. In all the stories, she looked like a rat. Hannik Dei was a tall, blond fellow, son of the famous Adamas Dei of the Black Sword."

Anhar said, "The Hannik the Yvanavars hired as sword master is blond, too."

"A blond named Hannik," Retrend repeated. "That narrows it down to a few thousand fellows."

Everyone found that hilarious, then they began discussing patterns of drill, both old and new, with the easy knowledge of a lifetime of experience.

Anhar rode at my side, looking distracted.

I made certain attention was elsewhere, then asked in our own language, "Is aught amiss, then?"

"Rat." She made a shadow-warding. "In Colend, we grow up with the fine statues of people famed for talents or actions that benefited others. And we use the gardens or the buildings that royalty and nobility build when they haven't fame for anything else. They want to be remembered. What did this princess build, or do, to be remembered? Yet for all these centuries, she is known as Rat for her buck teeth."

We had two weeks of the year left when at last we rode into the courtyard of the royal castle.

It seemed both strange and curiously familiar—as if I'd been gone a lifetime, or only a few hours. Nothing had changed. That impression altered the moment I rounded the stair to the Residence part of the castle, for instead of the ubiquitous smell of dusty stone and old meals, my nose encountered a dank smell that startled me: the long stone hallway had been smoothed over with plaster of a soft gray, so pale it reminded me of moonlight. Midway along, several young men and women were busy—artists, creating huge stylized frescoes of running animals, swooping raptors, all in shades of gray and silver overlapping.

The doors to the queen's chamber opened, and runners emerged. Gislan, the tall, somber woman who oversaw the communications between Lasva, her staff, and the female guards, appeared. She touched her fingers to her chest, then said, "I will show you your new chambers."

One cannot say that Marlovens do anything in great state, but her pace seemed deliberate as she walked me the rest of the way down the long hall to the double doors leading to Andaun-Sigradir's tower.

There was no lingering scent of old man sweat. The plain stone had been scrubbed clean, the oddly shaped main salon with its many doors rendered as comfortable as possible by an astonishing sight: candlesticks of blue crystal, shaped like birds; tables and bed covered in garlanded damask of pale blue; everything straight from Colend. I wondered if these were the furnishings that Lasva would not let herself possess.

I had glimpsed the bed in a bedchamber, a single slit window deep set in the massive walls letting in a modicum of natural light. Two more chambers lay off the main one in the other direction, one a workroom, the other full of the books Andaun had left behind.

I ran my fingers along spines and scrolls: most of them old, careful records of castle and kingdom renewal spells, twin to what I had made on my journey. A few books of magic . . . but those on the upper levels appeared to be long-unused elementary spells, books, or experiments. Nothing important. Of course he would have taken those with him. I did not look at the bottom shelves, tightly packed and perfunctorily dusted.

"Thank you," I said to Gislan, though I knew whose orders lay behind the labors. "Will you show me the way to the Chief Herald?"

I knew where the heralds' wing was—beyond the Great Hall—but I had never stepped inside. It was a bewildering maze of narrow corridors and rooms. Gislan left me outside a chamber with a stream of runners coming and going. The old Chief Herald was talking to a circle of heralds. When he saw me, he stopped talking, and took the scroll that I had labored over during my long year of travel. By now it was sadly rumpled and smudged in a way that would have gained me deportment marks from the Senior Scribes—who would never have imagined a scribe, much less a mage, traveling and living as I had.

He made no comment on the state of it, but read rapidly, his brow furrowed.

Then he gave me an approving eyebrow lift. "This is exactly as I would have done it myself. Thank you, Sigradir."

"Of course," I said and departed, wondering if the peacock had grown a feather or two.

I headed to the queen's chambers, to find Lasva approaching from the opposite hall. Though she dressed in the Marloven robe, she still moved with the gliding step of a Colendi; her curling dark hair was braided, but she'd twisted it up in a flattering knot, instead of wearing it fastened in loops behind the ears.

"Emras. It is good to see you back." I noticed she did not say "home," and wondered if she was aware of the distinction.

I made a full bow and spoke my thanks for the tower room.

"Are you pleased?" she asked.

I praised everything, from the fine Colendi bedding to the furnishings, as she smiled with delight, then I said, "Will the king be expecting me to report?"

"He walked down to the garrison to meet your escort, and they are probably deep in *I did this with my sword* and *that with my arrows*," Lasva said, leading the way into her suite. "Do you like what I'm doing in the hall? I got the idea from Darchelde. I finally figured out why the Marlovens are so resistant to art, especially when it is combined with comfort. Why they end every discussion with, *what suited my ancestors suits me.* Do you remember the mural in the old palace, how King Martande was depicted so much larger than life?"

"Scribe Halimas told us that it was a symbol of power, and of greatness."

"I suspect the Marlovens think their ancestors *were* larger than life. All those songs about truly frightful deeds, couched in terms of glory. If they lived in bare stone rooms, it made them stronger. Emras, I think they lived in bare stone rooms because they were learning how to live in castles. It is so clear from Hadand's letters that they still thought of themselves as traveling people. Their travel furniture was probably sparse when brought from tents inside halls, and maybe stone seemed comforting if you are used to being awoken in the middle of the night with a sword at your neck. But I seem to be the only one who thinks that our Marlovens now equate comfort with complacency. So I must use all of their symbols of strength and power to create art. And maybe, someday, I can sneak in some comfort."

She laughed as her hands swooped in great swirls, following the line of an arch-necked horse, and out and up toward a high-flying hawk. "I went through so many designs, and as always Ivandred said, 'Do whatever you like.' But I read in Hadand's records what they thought of the queen's suite, which sounded lovely and civilized."

"Queen?"

"Wisthia. Foster-mother to Hadand. You need to read these records, Emras. You will be fascinated, I promise. Anyway, I watched faces as I showed my design around. Lips spoke the Marloven equivalent of soft words, but faces . . ." She touched her upper lip as she sneered. "They have plenty of honor, but no *melende*. So then I took Kendred to visit Ingrid-Jarlan in spring, as I think I wrote to you, but I didn't tell you I was making sketches. And here is the result in the hall. I had Pelis watch from a vantage after the first set was done. No one said much, but she told me that people slowed, and looked, and mostly their gazes were approving. As long as the symbols suggest powerful creatures, ah-ye! Then art is permissible." Her lips curled with mirth.

We were interrupted by an unprecedented noise that at first I could not identify, being unused to children. The prince entered with the peculiar stumping, tippy-toe gait of baby turning toddler. He waved his arms, exclaiming nonsense as drool threaded down his dimple of a chin. He was a sturdy child, his eyes wide and blue as the sky. His feathery curls of hair were as light as ducks' down, though underneath his hair was just beginning to grow in thicker, promising a darker color.

The sound of that babble caused Lasva to whirl around and clasp her hands. Her attention arrowed to the child as if nothing else existed. To my amazement, she began to babble back in a high voice, causing the child to laugh a joyous, slightly husky sound that reminded me of Lasva's laugh when I first met her.

Marnda appeared, cooing and clucking like an old hen. As the boy lurched from object to object, grasping things in both hands and attempting to gnaw on them, Marnda gently disengaged each candlestick, pen, book, and tasseled table cover, then she tried to guide him to some of the toys she carried in a large pocket of her robe. But the boy looked at those with disinterest.

He tugged at Lasva's robe. She sat down and pulled him into her lap as she said over his head to me, "One thing that I have learned from Hadand's letters is the importance of letting the child meet other children in play. I never had that. From as far back as I can remember, court children were introduced into my presence in their best clothes, and we all behaved impeccably, or we would be whisked out to sit on the ponder chair."

In spite of her caressing fingers, the child seemed to be aware of her attention on something else besides him and began to fret loudly. Lasva bent her head, kissed him soundly, and murmured to him in a cooing voice.

Kendred put up his fat arms and stood in her lap, reaching for her braids. He yanked hard on one as he tried to climb her. Tears sprang in her eyes, but she gently disengaged his fingers, then Marnda swooped down and snatched him up, saying, "You must treat mama with respect. You hurt mama. Time for the ponder chair."

As soon as Marnda said the words *ponder chair*, the little prince began to howl as loudly as any of us Colendi had, a sound that diminished rapidly as he was carried off to the nursery.

Lasva tucked up the loosened strands of hair with one finger as she said, "Ivandred would have us strike Kendred's hands when he does that. He says that that is the Marloven way. He says that the boy will get rough handling in the Academy, and that Kendred must get used to it as soon as he can. Ivandred says, How will the boy survive the first day? But then all he would tell me is that they have to pass the gate." She looked worried. "What does that mean? Hadand's letters only described what she saw of her brother at what they called 'callover,' when they line up of a morning."

I told her what I had read early on in the Fox record: that the boys had run down a row of other boys who slapped and kicked lightly at them, after which they all have their hair cut so that they looked the same.

Her brow cleared. "Well if that is all there is!" She took a turn about the room. "There is so much that I cannot control here. So much that they say we peacocks cannot understand." She touched her lips in the moth kiss. "But I will never accept violence as a way of life. I am struggling to understand how it is necessary for defense, if others come at you with violent intent. And it has happened in this very castle. So I understand when Ivandred tells me I cannot knock out windows to let in more light. I must work with awkward spaces as I can, using a mirror here or there to reflect what light comes in." She pointed inside a small, narrow chamber with a wall mirror that reflected the two slit windows. "And living things." She pointed at potted plants. "I had a lot more of them in summer, which brightened things considerably and made the air much fresher. But there was not enough light, except at the very height of summer. These are the only ones left. I will try with different varieties come spring. Say the word, and I will have some put in your tower."

I spoke my thanks, and she said with a facility that made me think her words rehearsed, "It is good to have you back. Emras, I know that when you first came to me I regarded you somewhat as a living doll, an extension of myself, who would share all my interests, talk to me when I want to talk. Though I would never want to emulate Hadand's life—you cannot conceive the barbarity—I concede her wisdom. People have lives outside of one's own. She knew that from the start. Perhaps she got that from her mother, who was a great woman. If she had lived in Colend, I am convinced there would be statues to her in every town and plays written about her wisdom. Well." She opened her hands gracefully. "I just want to say how very glad I am that you have become a mage. You have a life outside of mine, but I hope I can still talk to you. I need people to talk to who will not say *yes, gunvaer*, but who will talk back."

Training formed words about the First Rule. But I kept those back and gave her the assurance that she wanted.

Then she let me go.

I returned to finish acquainting myself with my tower and to arrange my few things in an effort to make the place mine.

Last, I broke the illusory spell in my old window embrasure, and brought to my tower the Lover's Cup that Lasva had asked me to keep. After a moment's consideration of hiding places, I put it in my trunk. There seemed to be no danger anymore. Who would know what it was, even if they found it?

———

I was impatient to get to Darchelde. Three times during my year of travel I'd transferred there to find an empty chamber and a further book of study awaiting me. This new one I copied out—a habit I continued, now that I had my own library.

On this trip to Darchelde the Herskalt was there. The burst of joy nearly matched my happiness on the day Birdy returned from Chwahirsland. To the Herskalt I could confess my triumphant ruse with the stones. I could report on my studies and share the puzzling aspects of my work with the wards. Most of all, I needed him to comb out the tangle of my thoughts, as our counselors had done for us scribes.

He listened to it all, then said, "I was very pleased with your quick and innovative thinking."

My gratification lasted only a pulse, accompanied as it was by the memory of what had happened to those people. "The First Lancers killed them, I fear. I did not want to ask."

"Why not? Do you think that asking alters the events?"

"Because I feel responsible in part. And yet I know that those warriors could not have harbored any civil intentions toward us."

"Correct. Once you finished the spells for Totha, you were not only expendable but a danger. If they'd captured you earlier, they probably would have tried to hostage you against Ivandred for treaty purposes, but permitted you to continue doing your magic as the price for your life." His tone was matter-of-fact.

"Herskalt, I do not understand how people turn evil. And then Retrend and the lancers celebrated a massacre. I feel like these people here in the west . . ."

The Herskalt regarded me with a skeptical gaze. "It appears to me that time and distance from your Colendi have eroded your usually acute observation."

"The Colendi do not harbor evil intent," I retorted. "We don't go conquering back and forth. Well, I know we've had war, mostly with the Chwahir, but that was defense against invasion. And I know that our single emperor did conquer a vast empire, but he did it without evil intent. Or slaughter."

The Herskalt laughed.

I exclaimed, "I want knowledge, I want the *truth*. Why do I gain this sense that you regard truth as mutable, that the intentions of kings cannot be civilized?"

"Perhaps we should begin with the reminder that kingdoms—countries—governments are made up of human beings, each concerned with personal survival and comfort. The most widely read and popular histories reweave the truth to bind their audience together with high sentiment. You still believe Colend is the pinnacle of civilization, of moral achievement. I am trying to get you to examine your childhood convictions."

"So you imply there are no great kings, or that there are no great human beings? That everything is motivated by self-interest? Should we not have kings, then, is that our problem? Is the fact of kingship holding back the advance of civilization?"

"One of the few things one can safely accept about human behavior is that there will always be kings," he retorted. "Whatever they are called. One reason is that any kind of government in which people must choose their leaders requires the people to think of the common good if it's to function. Therefore, such governments are as inclined toward corruption as quickly, if not more so, than courts and kings. Kings control corruption by fear or force, by patronage, by what you Colendi call *melende*. Can you agree to that?"

"We were taught as much."

"Very well. Then let us proceed to the second reason: since we don't know what tomorrow will bring, most humans will follow anyone who promises a safe tomorrow, and more than that, an enjoyable tomorrow. So we are inclined to follow leaders who can both protect and inspire us."

I sensed an importance to the discussion, though it appeared to be an academic exchange, teacher and student. "What do you believe was Mathias the Magnificent's motivation for creating his empire?" I asked. "Everything we read in the archives pointed to the wish to spread peace by joining every kingdom under one benevolent set of laws. You will say that Colendi scribes and heralds will foster the Colendi viewpoint, and I can accept that, but—"

As I spoke, I remembered Greveas and the scribes entertaining themselves with discussions of which ancient records lied and why. Then the Herskalt twirled a finger in the Colendi fan gesture for Great Wind Over Little Matter.

I sighed and moderated my tone. "Assuming you disagree, how would I know your source is any more trustworthy?"

"By listening to the principles, of course," he said, and there was the flash of silver—the dyr.

Though we'd listened to people I knew—including a prince and princess—I had never considered the possibility of delving into famous crowned heads of the past. Remembering the long debates we'd had about Mathias's decision to cease empire-building, after we'd spent weeks combing through the existing records (as had the scribes of every generation since, I was certain) I said, "Can we see *that* moment? When he and the Enaeraneth king went off in private, then came back with the news that Mathias had reached the end of his empire building, and would return east?" I remembered some of the more creative surmises—made when the Senior Scribes were not in hearing—and hid a spurt of laughter. "The only thing anyone could agree on was that there was a mystery witness to that meeting, but there is no written evidence."

The Herskalt's smile deepened briefly. Obviously his years of study had featured similar discussions. "Both kings, sadly, were warded, so we cannot look inside their memories. But that is not true of others present. I trust you will find this one interesting."

I knew what to expect now and did my Altan fan-breathing as I braced myself.

I knew at once that I was in the thoughts of a female. There were a thousand subtle signals. That was the clearest impression. Thoughts, words, were distorted; meanings and pronunciations different. But emotions, those were clear.

This is Firel, sister to Alored Elsarion, who would soon become the Enaeraneth king. She was exactly your age. The thought came from the sky, in the Herskalt's voice.

Firel stood at the top of a curve of marble steps as a fantastic carriage pulled up, all gold and scrollwork, beautifully hinged—perhaps even aided by magic, so it never so much as rocked, much less jolted. The matched team of white horses pranced to a stop, and Firel admired the braided tails and manes, the well-bred heads tossing, then shifted her attention to the door of the coach as attendants opened it.

Out stepped Mathias as everyone bowed. Mathias's face was familiar from statues and pictures. Like Martande I, he really was as handsome as the art that represented him, for at that time he was in his mid-thirties, three years into his long and remarkable reign.

Firel's slow, appreciative gaze afforded me a clear view of his splendid form in the close-fitting clothes of the period.

He paused halfway up the steps, one foot higher than the other (Firel's gaze lingering along the line of his thigh), then looked up and laughed. I will not reproduce the archaic language, which probably would not be exact, but what he said to Alored was: "No one told me you were one of *us.*"

Firel turned, and with a wash of pride mixed with irony, observed her brother, who was about thirty. If possible, he was even more beautiful than Mathias, at least in profile: his hair was long and golden and, judging from the variety of shades, from lemon to amber, it was not hairdresser's art. His skin was russet shading to gold, his eyes under long lashes so light a brown as to also look like gold. His direct descendant, the lazy, careless Prince Macael, bore him no resemblance except for the light hair common to this end of the continent. *Alored is a Golden Dei—* one of the famous Dei descendants whose coloring was so distinct.

"You really did not know about the infamous duchess, my great-mother?" Alored said as he led the emperor past courtiers who formed a colorful wall on both sides of the marble hall.

Firel followed at her brother's shoulder, her gaze sweeping past the courtiers so fast they were a blur of faces, accompanied by a flutter of reactions. Then she paused, and again I nearly fell out of the vision: intense with a different sort of attraction, she gazed at a short, still man who stood alone, framed by a doorway. He had to be near fifty, long gray-streaked yellow hair pulled into a topknot on his head. I recognized the distinctive Marloven gray coat, tight-fitting to the belt, and flaring into skirts below; in his high boots, the subtle wink of polished knife handles. How could Mathias have looked past *him?*

The emperor assumed he was a guardsman, came the Herskalt's amused voice. *That is the Senrid-Harvaldar who reunited Marloven Hesea. Alored's Uncle Senrid. Came over the mountain with dragoons and skirmishers.*

"We're either famous or infamous, I find," Mathias said, in response to Alored's query about his great-mother, the "infamous duchess." He went on: "In Sartor I am known as Mathias Dei, son of Lasva Dei the Wanderer." He paused to greet Firel, whose reaction to him was so intense I felt unclothed. It was a relief to me, in spite of her disappointment, when Mathias turned back to Alored and said, "So. To our business. I trust you received my equerry, duly sent on ahead with my offer?"

"Among the bits of wisdom my infamous great-mother passed down," Alored said in his singer's voice, "was an exhortation to resist investing in ephemera."

"Of course empires never last," Mathias responded, as Alored gestured and a footman closed Mathias, Alored, and Firel into a white and gold room filled with arabesques and embellishments designed around moons, stars, and suns. "But it will be glorious while it does. And the day will come when it is no longer glorious. Then your descendants will sit down with mine over a spectacular dinner and negotiate a withdrawal from the empire, leaving in place an excellent trade treaty."

"By which you will benefit." Alored sat in a fine chair, and Matthias in another.

Unnoticed, Firel avoided the adjacent chair in favor of standing at her brother's elbow so that she could see Mathias's face.

"Of course!" Mathias said with an airy gesture. "You know we Colendi haven't defensible borders, so we must achieve with inventiveness what others achieve with valor."

Firel's attention strayed to Uncle Senrid out there in the hall somewhere, thence to the prospective evening ahead, and to a hatred of whatever ancestor had bequeathed her her plain looks. By then my head was pounding so hard it was difficult to discern voices, and the Herskalt ended the vision.

He gave me a cup of kinthus. When the pain had receded, I asked, "So was Mathias's withdrawal caused by this King Senrid, or not?"

"The war game occurred the next day. It really was a game to the Marlovens. Not so much to the Colendi in their splendid clothes, who limped off the field after an efficient thrashing. There was trouble between the Faleth and the Marlovens, the former taking exception to the thrashings. A handful of them died before the trumpets were blown."

"Yet there is almost nothing said about that in our records."

"To be fair to your heralds, all they saw was dust, all they heard was shouting, until the living combatants staggered off the field. The Faleth, ashamed of their losses, hid them. But the kings acted as if nothing happened, until the famous meeting later that night, the two of them alone . . . or not alone." The Herskalt smiled. "Mathias took his leave the next morning, with many expensive parting gifts going both ways, and rode eastward again, out of their lives. Senrid then helped Alored ride to the capital to claim his kingship . . . but that is Enaeraneth history."

I had no interest in Enaeraneth history. What caught my attention was how easily the Herskalt used their names—Mathias, Senrid, Alored—as if he had known them all.

That must come of seeing history through dyr magic, I thought.

"To your Colendi. Events came to pass as Mathias foresaw. How would you characterize his motivation, Emras? You may think about that. And this: since those days, many of your Colendi heralds took advantage of Mathias' precedent of skillfully fostering squabbling among neighboring kingdoms, which your Colendi diplomats could solve by inviting everyone to sumptuous balls and parties, and gently but firmly negotiating treaties favorable to Colend, all in the name of peace."

As I recovered from the effects of the dyr-vision, I stared at the centuries old pile of papers—the Fox memoir—still sitting there on the table. It seemed to mock my ignorance. "That should suffice for now," the Herskalt said and sent me back, whereupon I tumbled into bed.

I was awakened by Anhar, who came to my tower and burst into my bedchamber, her travel gear clasped to her. She was dressed in her old Colendi travel gown.

"You have been given leave," I said.

"She paid me well and gave me three weeks. I can spend one with my sister, and then go east to Alarcansa. On my return, I will be promoted: she has asked me, *me!* to be Kendred's tutor in Kifelian. She desires him to read and write gracefully in our language, and to be familiar with our best plays and poems." She smiled with her entire being. "I will spend my time in Colend collecting the very best works, and I will ask Birdy for polish in reading."

I said all the right words, though there was the old surge of envy of her freedom to return to Colend.

Her gaze was searching. "Emras?" she said on a note of inquiry.

I made a little fuss, rubbing my eyes and brushing my hair out of my face (it needed cutting again, I thought in annoyance) as I reached for an excuse to cover whatever she saw in my face. "I remember something you said, and forgive me if I trespass personally, but did you not wish to alter the color of your hair again before you return?"

"No. Not anymore." Anhar drew in a deep breath, and words cascaded. "I told you that I hate history. I never wanted to read it. I always liked plays, because they are not real. History lessons were full of thorns and nettles about the Chwahir. Platter faces. Hummers. Chalk skinned. Ugly, stupid, barbaric, evil and venal. Always *they. Them.* I don't feel like one. I do not speak a word of the language. I have never been north of the border. My father left when he was a boy, because he wanted a better life than the army. And he had it. Though he, too, had to endure the thorns and nettles. But people made us out to be *them.* So when I turned sixteen my mother told me to get my hair colored and style it to make my face longer. Go in the sun as often as I could to turn my skin darker. But now? After what happened at Totha? I don't care. They can look at my black hair and say what they want, but I *don't care.*" She held out her hand. "May I request a transfer token?"

"Here you go." I took one from the little carved chest where I kept my inks. "Give my greetings to Birdy."

"I will," she promised, and then vanished, the cold air in my room stirring in reaction.

I rose, my emotions in turmoil. I longed to see Birdy again, but I couldn't for the very reason I wished to: to talk out the confusions in my head. I had to protect him as well as myself from Sartor's well-meant but misguided investigations. Someday I would have to deal with that, but not now. Now I could at least write to Birdy:

When we were children, we asked questions. At scribe school we were praised for asking questions, and we wanted to know the answers. We delighted in finding them. I suspect that we stop learning when we leave behind that childhood habit, and so, in the nature of inquiry, I have questions about what heralds are taught about the writing of history.

We grew up with the conviction that Colendi are civilized, that they are peacemakers where others resort to war. It is startling to discover how others view us: For example, someone recently said that during the years the empire waned our heralds caused trouble so that they could make peace to our advantage. Birdy, were you trained to this end when you were sent to the heralds?

Someone had been hired from one of the pleasure houses to attend to our nails and to provide muscle relief when we needed. She was older, calm, efficient, but did not have Anhar's touch.

Days passed with the entire castle busy getting ready for the arrival of the jarls and their parties for New Year's Week. I continued my work, but my thoughts strayed eastward to Anhar and Birdy there in Alarcansa, and then southward to Darchelde.

From my limited experience with the dyr, I knew that some minds and memories were more accessible than others. Ivandred had been the most difficult, Lasva the easiest, probably because I knew her well and because we were both female and close in age.

I kept imagining the possibilities. Think of the understanding one could get, seeing famous moments from inside the participants! But how many of them had been warded against dyr magic? I was going to ask. I had to know, had to see more. Had to learn, I kept telling myself. The Herskalt wanted me to gain knowledge. Ah-ye, this was better than sifting through old and dusty records.

On the last day of the year, I took a walk around the city walls as I performed the spells I'd been working on. A year before, that much magic would have tired me to dizziness, but exhilaration kept me strong as I felt the old mess of wards disintegrate and reform in a structure as strong as the golden stone that formed the walls.

When I returned to the royal castle just before sunset, I heard the rare sound of many female voices emanating from the queen's outer chambers. Lasva had asked me to listen, for she relied on my perceptions of New Year's Week. "When I am in the midst of the jarlans," she said, "and all eyes are on me, I am so busy thinking about what I must say next, and how I must curtail my habitual gestures, my walk, so as to lessen the mannerisms of the peacock. I certainly don't see what they are doing when they think my gaze is elsewhere."

The air beyond the door did not carry the astringent aroma of crisp white wine, offered in Colend when New Year's Week begins. Here in Marloven Hesea it was the heady scent of the last of the festival barley-wine. It is these little sensory starts and jolts that keep a place from ever becoming home.

I shut my eyes and listened to the voices, so different on the surface from a court gathering in Colend. But there was a similarity after all, I thought. Though Colend's courtiers speak so softly in the trained cadences that rise and fall so smoothly, there still was that sense of self-awareness, and I heard it here, too: the sound of people pretending to civility, rather than the ease of relaxation or friendliness.

I told Lasva, who nodded in corroboration. "They still see a peacock."

The Great Hall was quiet as the Jarl of Totha—the others called him Bluejay—came forward to make his vows. I watched from above as he spoke in a wooden voice. He was a lanky, loose-limbed fellow, too well trained to shamble, but he reminded me a little of King Jurac of Chwahirsland, who had moved as if he never became accustomed to the length of his own limbs.

When Bluejay finished, Ivandred stepped forward and said his vows in the same voice he used for everyone. Not a word more or a word less. No mention at all of those Totha attackers, dead somewhere around the border, but every single person in that Hall had to be thinking about them. There was too much tension for it to be a secret.

The surprising thing was the number of looks furtively cast my way. Irritated and unsettled, I reminded myself of what Anhar had said: the looks were not aimed at me but at "the mage," who might be able to smite them with a whispered spell.

Smiting was what Marlovens thought about when they considered power.

The unwanted notice caused me to employ all my old skills at staying on the periphery.

There is only one other thing to report from that week.

The Jarlan of Totha was exactly my age. She was even small with a round face. But where I am spare, with thin hair of dull brown, she was as curvy as Nifta, with a great quantity of curly blond hair pulled back into looped braids behind a face that was the true heart shape so prized in Colend.

But she was not at all like a courtier. Her behavior all week was stiff and silent, her hands hidden in the sleeves of her robe, which was the dark forest green and silver of Totha.

Following supper on the Fourthday eve after the jarls and jarlans presented their requests for judgment, Lasva whispered to me in passing, "She asked to speak to me alone. Will you listen beyond the door?"

I felt like a spy, standing beside the door to Lasva's bedchamber, which smelled of the dried rose hips, starliss, and verbena that she had transferred from Colend. Lasva's tone was soothing as she offered her guest the best cushion, some freshly steeped Sartoran leaf, a cream cake.

The jarlan refused them all in a tight voice. Lasva said invitingly, "What is happening in Totha, Gdan? Please tell me. I promise you, I want peace. I would do anything I can to bring it about. Are there people trying to stir up trouble in your land? Do you need help?"

"Yes . . . No. That is, there are those who want . . . sovereignty. The way Olavair now has. And some want things to stay as they have been. Then there are those who want life to go back to the way it was in the old days. Except you really cannot go back, can you? No one in Totha speaks the old Iascan. We are Marlovens in all the important ways. We celebrate Rest Day like Marlovens." Gdan-Jarlan's voice lowered to a whisper. "But there is so much talk of war in the north. Everyone knows it is going to happen. And we also know that when the king calls the levy, it is our people who will be forced to go north to fight. No one wants to go north to fight Yvanavar or Olavair. We have enough problems of our own in the south, and many are afraid that if the king is dealing with the northerners, he will never get to us in time."

"Have you and Bluejay spoken with Ivandred about this? Surely you trust him. I know that the most important thing in his life is this kingdom and keeping it safe."

"There are different kinds of safe," Gdan began, almost too low to hear. Then came the swish of fabric and a quick step. "I am afraid I have said too much. Thank you for . . . being kind, Lasva-Gunvaer."

Lasva joined me. "She sounded sincere, did she not? I don't need you to corroborate that she doesn't trust me. It's not that she thinks that I am a liar so much as she thinks the peacock can wave her pretty tail and strut all around this castle, but she cannot fly with the Marloven eagle."

TWO

OF MEMORY'S ENCHANTMENT

I followed Lasva out to the balcony a day later, when she joined Ivandred in watching the last of the jarls ride out of the courtyard, as snow drifted lazily down from a gray blanket sky. He gave me an absent nod as he stretched out his hand to Lasva. It was an habitual gesture, not the peremptory palm down but one of appeal, palm up.

Lasva grasped his hand. He bent to kiss her fingers, then straightened up. It was all quick, with the unconsciousness of habit, as they turned their attention downward. I glanced at the two attractive profiles, wondering what was going on inside each silent head. Oh, to have a dyr of my own!

The impulse to see, to *know*, had been growing stronger by the day, becoming a hunger. When the last jarl was gone, Ivandred took Lasva off somewhere, and so I wandered back toward my tower. I was too restless to resume my work, so I turned my steps to the queen's chambers, to which I always had entrance. Except for the guards, no one was about. The runners had been permitted liberty days in relay. Pelis was busy putting the finishing stitches on the tapestry. Nifta had been sent somewhere on a trade mission. Marnda and Kendred were either asleep or outside.

I looked around, then transferred myself to Darchelde. The Herskalt appeared moments later. Was there a faint scent of wood smoke? It was gone too soon for me to be sure. I took my chair, saying, "I suppose that kings and others in power are protected against the dyr magic, but I cannot stop thinking about it. There are so many possibilities to find out the truth of important events."

The Herskalt said, "Very true. However, there is much to be learned from ordinary people. Discovering hidden motivations and reasoning will enable you to make more acute evaluations in your own life. As you gain magical knowledge, you are going to be called upon to make judgments that will affect many lives."

"So what do you suggest?"

"Begin to study people familiar to you."

"Not my parents," I said quickly, but what I was really thinking was, *Not Birdy.*

He said, "People with whom you have some connection, but minimal emotional involvement." He opened his hand, and there was the dyr. "I anticipated your question, and did some exploration of my own. I believe that this will be a very good place to begin, on what appeared to be a peaceful day's picnic, not long ago."

He whispered the words, and guided me into a vision of a warm day. Colend sometimes had such bursts of very late summer warmth, weeks after harvest. A group of people sat upon a silk quilt that covered a mossy bank. Behind them a few white-barked birch trees retained enough bright orange leaves to catch the low, slanting light of impending winter.

My heart yearned at the layered silk robes the two women wore, one in shades of soft blue, embroidered with long-tailed parrots and orchid blossoms in silver and peach, the other in shades of lemon and straw, embroidered with pale green cattails and butterflies. The man wore summer blue edged with amber. His embroidery was thistles in a geometric pattern. His head was bent as he played with a little boy of two or three. His short, curly dark hair hid his face. Was that jawline familiar? I wondered as he plucked up dandelions and blew on them, sending tufts into the air that the child tried to catch in his grasping fingers.

The man laughed and looked up. Yes. I knew that face. He was the Duke of Alarcansa. I shifted my gaze to the two women, and recognized the seated one in blue with the perfect profile and elaborately dressed golden hair. She was known as "the duchess" at seventeen: Carola Definian, now a real duchess. The one in yellow was tall and thin. Tatia.

Her ruddy hair was also dressed elaborately, though with knots of ribbon as embellishment, instead of gems.

We'd looked through the eyes of a servant, who was waved off by an impatient gesture from Tatia.

Then the vision smeared, causing my insides to lurch, and now I looked down at the top of the duchess's head. Beyond her the man and boy played, the colors distorted in a way difficult to describe, until the first thoughts whispered into my head: anger. We looked through Tatia's eyes.

Go on, one slide of those slippers on a rock, brat, she thought. But no, the Hummer would catch him, then Carola and the Hummer would fuss sickeningly over the brat, Vasande, as if he *had* fallen and cracked his stupid skull.

Memory flashes. Pain nearly slew me as jolting, rage-burning images provided context: distracting a nursemaid by sending her for something to drink, then luring the small boy to play near one of the indoor pools. The toddler laughed . . . climbed up . . . fell in . . . Tatia scurried away, her laughter screaming through my skull; then she looked back, and the rage surged through me as scalding as vomit when she saw the baby swimming to the side. How angry Tatia was that the Hummer (for such was her name for Kaidas) had taught "the little maggot" to swim!

I nearly withdrew, but the Herskalt kept the vision steady as again the memory provided a horrifying image, this time high on a wall, but again the frustrated rage when Carola appeared and intervened, dismissing the two maidservants and the footman whom Tatia had carefully distracted. Carola's anger doused Tatia's, causing fear which was scarcely less terrible to endure than the rage, scolding as Tatia herself was sent on degrading errands until the servants could be replaced.

She was the heir. *She* should rule Alarcansa, not this disgusting worm of a brat. Why should Carola birth an heir thirty years before anyone of her age thought of such things?

I could not bear this woman's thoughts another heartbeat. I tried to end the vision, but it smeared . . . and I found myself caught in a wash of sensory impressions that cleared away, establishing a caressing perspective on the child and man.

"It is a refreshment to the spirit to see them together like that, is it not?" Carola asked her cousin, richly enjoying the way that Tatia snorted like a lapdog in frustration. "Would it not be charming for him to have a sister or brother to romp with? Perhaps several of them."

Carola laughed to herself at the forced pleasantry with which Tatia replied. She entertained herself with imagining another child. A beautiful daughter, who would enter court exquisitely trained. Carola toyed with the notion of her daughter courting the Royal Princess, who was almost certainly going to look like a toad in silk.

I would be ruling court now if I had had the wit to court that fool Lasva, she thought. If only she'd had the long vision to see it at seventeen. Lasva's self-centered acceptance of everyone's admiration, her sentimental assurance that everyone loved her . . . it would have been easy to swallow disgust and flatter her. But that was the past. She had longer vision now, which could benefit a daughter.

As Kaidas chased Vasande around in a circle, and the boy laughed, she suppressed the image of the beautiful daughter. What if he monopolized her as much as he did Vasande? Whenever Kaidas was in Alarcansa, every free moment was given to Vasande. Carola gritted her teeth against bitter resentment. Kaidas never came to her freely. She always had to summon him. She would not lose what time she had to another child, not until her interest in him died. Some days, she hoped it would die soon.

On this bitter thought, the Herskalt shifted us to Kaidas, whose emotions buffeted me like a wind storm, so fierce was his love for Vasande, and so strong was his longing for freedom.

That was as much as I could discern before the headache threatened to overcome my wits. Already I was dizzy and sour-mouthed with nausea.

Once again he had a cup of kinthus waiting for me. When the pain and nausea had lessened, I said hoarsely, "They are evil people, the Definians."

"They are angry people."

"Bitter as iron gall. Why is that? They are wealthy, they have everything they want."

"They do not have everything they want. They have everything others want. Experiences shape us, but so do the choices we make in reaction to those experiences. Tatia craves her cousin's title. The other cousin, Falisse Ranalassi, ran away and learned to sing. In your terms, the latter chose the path of civility—art—and the former pretends to civility."

The hunger was there again, this time to dive into this other cousin's mind, to know through experience what shaped Falisse Ranalassi. Uneasy at the intensity of my own passion I asked, "Is it not a trespass, to delve into people's secret thoughts like this, unasked?"

"Almost everything we do in life is a trespass by someone's standards.

You Colendi object if someone steps on your shadow inside a house, but in other kingdoms, no one notices shadows. Ask yourself this instead: will you do harm or good with the knowledge that you have gained? And ask yourself if you ever have enough knowledge, when you are making decisions that will affect other lives?"

I made The Peace. My thoughts tumbled in painful confusion. Knowledge, the gaining of knowledge, that steadied me. Knowledge led to wisdom.

"I believe the time has come to let you explore on your own." The Herskalt laid the dyr in a shallow dish of thin porcelain, chased round the rim with tiny red-centered golden blossoms and blue laurel leaves—it was not Marloven, whose styles were variations on interlocking figures. I had this sense that it was *old*. "I am going to be busy for a time. I have a very difficult set of wards to set up. I believe you are aware of the dangers of using this magical artifact, so you will follow my instructions exactly."

I was so amazed I couldn't speak. But I did not need to. I am certain my longing was plain in my face.

"No more than one memory a day—if I am not here, and you lose consciousness while under the influence of the magic . . ."

The idea was so terrible that I made a gesture of repudiation that I could not control. He left the sentence unfinished and said, "You must always come here. If you take the dyr anywhere, there are powerful wards that will alert interested mages to its presence. You may find yourself in a difficult situation, and again, I would be unable to rescue you."

I assented, reflecting on all those castle wards still awaiting replacement. The sooner I freed the city of ancient bindings and granted the Herskalt access, the better for us all.

He issued a long list of magical instructions specific to the circumstances, so useless to duplicate in this defense.

Two days later, Anhar returned. She burst into the tower and thrust open the door to my study, bringing the scents of Colend with her, and a basket of fresh pastries and late-season berries, plus a letter from Birdy. Her eyes were wide as she said, "You certainly stirred him up the night after I arrived. That next day he went off to the archive, and every time I turned around he and the duke were talking about this record or that, or Birdy was scribbling this letter." She laughed as she handed me a fat scroll tied with the green of sincerity—far too lengthy to be stuffed into a scrollcase without being put in three separate sendings. I sat down and opened it, with her looking on; my worry about magic was foremost in my mind.

Who have you been talking to, Em? Is Lasva turning on her land of birth?

That is not to deny that some heralds didn't interfere in foreign affairs. We were told about them and shown how short-sighted such a policy was. Did Lasva really say that "all heralds were educated to cause trouble in other kingdoms" or is that the careless hyperbole of discussion?

The Duke of Alarcansa and I both agree that Colend has never set out to make trouble for other kingdoms. Many name Mathias the Magnificent, our single emperor, as the height of ambition, but if you read all his records, he firmly believed that the creation of his empire was an exercise in civilizing people. There was a Lassiter as equerry on that famous journey, and I finished reading his account last night. According to the words he heard spoken by the emperor, Mathias's definition of civilization was food, shelter, and meaningful work for everyone. His military strategy (if you can call it that, when there was little or no actual fighting) was to push his indefensible borders out to defensive ones.

When he approached a new border, and invited the rulers of the kingdom to talk to him, he explained at length—you can read the records written AT THE TIME by herald scribes from both sides, as one of our exercises was to compare them word for word, translating them back and forth from Sartoran to Kifelian—that he was constantly formulating experiments to better all three of those for the good of all and that he invited client kings to actively contribute.

His laws were set to protect all people and their property. Show me any empire that has done the same. Including that Marloven one. I've been reading its history, as much as I can. There is scarcely anything available, unless you want to send me copies.

I glanced rapidly down the rest and found that he'd listed every source he had to hand, with salient quotations copied out in a handwriting that got more hasty and scribbled toward the end.

I looked up, to discover Anhar waiting, her expression curious and intent. She was going to report back, of course. Relieved that the question of magic had not come up at all, I said, "We studied this question when we were young, but it's interesting to delve into it now—except that I don't have access to Colendi records anymore." I pointed to the pastries. "Nifta is back, and Pelis is restless, as it's been snowing since New Year's Lastday. Shall we go to the queen's rooms and share these out while they are fresh?"

I still walked to the queen's suite each morning at the daybreak bells to spend an hour with Lasva doing the Altan fan form. Twice she asked me if I had begun reading Hadand's letters, and both times I told her that, so far, my tasks had precluded this reading, but if she desired me to do so, I would lay aside another task.

I was aware as I repeated those words a second time that she would take the reiteration as an oblique question: is this an order? If she ordered me to read those letters, I would. I believe she knew that. What I did not see at the time was the hurt I caused in putting her in that position; I just wanted to be free of the obligation. I knew that she was seeking something from them, but I had no time for toiling through four-centuries' old letters in search of the long dead queen's inner mind, not when I had the means to visit people's thoughts directly. I consoled myself with the thought that gunvaer affairs could be safely left to the current-day gunvaer. I had my own tasks.

I was tempted to venture into Hadand's mind with the dyr. All I required was one letter to use as a focus. But the Herskalt had warned me about people with whom I had no contact, and I feared that the distortion of old-fashioned Marlovan would be difficult to endure.

And anyway, how would I explain my sudden expertise to Lasva? Telling her about the dyr was impossible, not without admitting what I had seen. Because I suspected that her first question—it was only human nature—would be, *Did you use it on me without my being aware?*

It was a relief one morning when she said, "If you are busy with your own tasks, Emras, you are free from practicing the Altan fan. I am teaching some of the guardswomen—I find that nothing reinforces good form like being required to explain it. But I fear it would be unforgivably dull for you to revert to the very basic steps." She smiled. "But you are welcome to continue eating with the staff, as always."

I bowed and withdrew.

By then I'd been back to the dyr three times. I'd begun with Tatia, Falisse Ranalassi, and Carola, separately at first, and the day before the above, the three together the day of the fight in the salon.

I was so deeply involved that I actually forgot about my letters to Birdy, until I woke up after falling into bed, and discovered his last letter on the floor; though servants did come through to clean my rooms, I had told them not to touch any papers or books. They obeyed assiduously, apparently unwilling to have any interaction with anything that might be magical, and therefore dangerous.

So I picked up the letter from the floor and read it through. After a day of work at the wards, I sat down to answer:

Birdy:

If I read your words correctly it appears to you as if Lasva has turned on her homeland, and because of that, I've done the same. Oh Birdy, the truth is very different. I have resisted reading Marloven history because I am so busy dealing with Marlovens in the present, but from what I hear in ballads and stories the Marlovens tell on themselves, they imposed their empire by military force onto people who had no loyalty or interest in being Marloven. They demanded loyalty through fear and punitive laws instead of inviting it. Worse, they claimed pre-eminence of a cultural entity, the Marlovens, which by our definition is evil. Colend does not claim pre-eminence of any cultural entity.

We do make it plain by misdirection, however, that we consider the Chwahir a sub-eminent cultural entity. But the Chwahir do the same to us, according to what we were taught. The Chwahir as well as the Marlovens exalt themselves by praising the violence by which they prevail, and they constantly seek to advance in the skills of war.

I am merely attempting to look at how and why kingdoms form. As a child, I understood that they just were, with King Martande bettering everyone else. I am looking at all my unquestioned assumptions as there is little else to do in the grip of winter. How I envy you in Colend's temperate weather!

———

I was so busy with my secret pursuit (meted out to myself as a reward for work) that Birdy's letters sat for longer and longer periods before I'd remember to answer them. I had closed myself completely into the world of magic and other people's lives.

> . . . but according to what we heralds are taught (and I will search out the sources in just a moment), each development of war, from stone to fire, steel to arrows, has cost the civilization that made them.
>
> Next day. Last night the duke came to visit. I brought up this topic. He corroborated my point, quoting what the queen said to him the first year he was appointed Commander: War material has to be made, like everything else, but unlike everything else isn't used in trade, in sustenance, or to make life better. It is spent to cause death.
>
> You remember our class in the history of kingdoms. First tenet, humans like hierarchies. Second tenet, shifts from small kingdoms to large was in part due to the need to raise, train, and supply royal armies. King Martande did away with royal armies, requiring his nobles to supply said warriors on need. Then he set about creating policies that would preclude that need.
>
> Do we claim moral superiority? Sometimes. But what does it really mean? That Colend's determined policy of avoiding war is simple practicality? We can look at the world in terms of survival and necessity, denying such ideals as honor and loyalty, compassion and mercy, and so on, but in that case you may as well deny the existence of knowledge and wisdom, because such an argument also denies the validity of human reasoning—and renders meaningless such concepts as virtue, because it denies free choice. And virtue depends on free choice. . . .

I ran my gaze down the rest of the letter, and saw Lasva's name. Again, Birdy intuited that my quotations from the Herskalt were not my thoughts, but he seemed to be attributing them to Lasva. And again, here was Kaidas involved. Might this protracted discussion be an indirect way for Kaidas to communicate with Lasva?

I should straighten out the misunderstanding, I thought as I laid the letter down. But later. Writing such long letters, engaging every point, was more fatiguing than interesting when I already had so much to do: there were still kingdom emergencies and castle spells of various sorts to repair, from new water-purifying spells on buckets to wands to make for the stables. The stewards brought their lists to Gislan, who gave them to me once a week. I found that I was much faster if I dispatched these tasks in the middle of the night, when there were fewer people around to distract me with their questions and curiosity or to offer me unwanted advice.

The second layer of castle ward spells had been easier to dismantle and replace than the first, but then overconfidence nearly caused me to fall into a very nasty magical trap. I might have but, as a way to perceive wards, I took the time to refashion my spells into colors. In the middle of a very tangled chain there was a single wink of blood red. I almost overlooked it. The "red" spell was a transfer worked into the structure around it. This transfer would have sent me between time and place, with no destination.

That frightened me into slowing down to beginner's deliberate pace again.

When I discovered Birdy's letter and forced myself to take a night to answer it—with an introductory paragraph about how Lasva had been too busy to talk these things over with me—Birdy responded within two days.

> . . . *In our first class as heralds, they taught us the four characteristics of monarchy: the stability resultant to dynastic succession; protection, which your Marlovens seem to put first, but we define through awareness of our neighbors and constant negotiation; independence of other nations' problems and demands, and law and custom.*
>
> *In Colend, each branch of service emphasizes the public good over the monarch's personal interests, and we are assured by the queen that royal education teaches the same. Loyalty is to Colend, not to the body sitting on Colend's throne; even though she serves as its symbol, she still serves, as do we.*
>
> *The duke wishes me to remind you that common law is the law of custom. That can be as strong as a king, and the heralds give that legitimacy, as opposed to so-called natural law, or the law of strength. This is not to say that natural law precludes moral precepts, but it requires far more prudence because while there is the chance that political decisions may be wrong, who can prevail against someone who uses strength instead of communication to "convince" those who do not agree?*

Was that last bit a moth-kiss aimed by Kaidas at the Marlovens?

I pulled paper forward to reply, beginning with a fair statement about Marlovens (who, I had witnessed personally at the border of Totha, were ready to sacrifice themselves for what they believed was the good of the kingdom, whereas I couldn't name any Colendi who would) when I thought, *But Anhar told Birdy about that incident.* Which ended with mass slaughter because of my magic.

Birdy might be trying to delve deeper into my life, this being an indirect prompt to get me to talk about magic. I tossed the letter aside to deal with tomorrow.

Two months of tomorrows later, I forced myself to answer it, quoting from Scribe Halimas's lectures about kingdoms, service, and the Scribes' First and Second Rules, which were still the guiding principles of my life.

Unnoticed by me, half a year passed.

With the removal and reestablishment of the Choreid Dhelerei's top, or most recent, set of wards, Ivandred now had complete access to the city. I knew that he wanted more spells. I wanted to give him as many as I could that would make warfare impossible, or at least difficult. The spells I'd already given him I'd named Fog, Water, and Rock, and the specifics are in my magic books, which you already have.

But the Herskalt still did not have access—the wards against him had somehow been placed deeper. And so I continued the ward project.

As spring ripened into summer, Fire's idea came to me when I reached the bath, to find it full of kitchen staff. They were commiserating with a young kitchen worker who had become impatient while making cabbage rolls, and had dropped water onto the hot flatsheet smeared with pressed olives. The result was horrible splatters that flew up and burned her hands and her cheek.

What if I could send little globs of water-encased oil into torches, causing them to splatter? It would sting, like my rocks, but no one would be hurt. The sting might be enough to cause horses to break order. Torches would waver and even be flung down as untrustworthy. No one could be busy killing other humans if their horses and torches were fractious.

I took torches and oil into my experiment room. By now I was not only at home in my tower, but I also could not imagine how I'd existed without four rooms and Andaun's library, scant as it was, all to myself. I worked until the acrid stink nearly choked me, but the result was worth it when I showed Ivandred. He listened with his customary lack of expression, then had me take him through the magic a step at a time. At the end, he said, "I can take this with me to practice with the First Lancers on Midsummer games. Excellent work, Sigradir."

That praise I used as an excuse to visit the dyr, though I'd been the day before.

By now I had finished with Falisse Ranalassi, known as Larksong, whose life I am not detailing here. But I had reveled in her audition. In fact I had twice revisited that particular event. Oh, the joy, the *power* of looking out at a room full of people and knowing that you have the ability to bind them in awe and wonder! It was more intoxicating than using magic to burst little stones and drive off warriors set to kill you. We all want to be admired, emulated, remembered.

If I was to be a great mage, then I needed greater understanding. And so I left the pleasure of Larksong's happy life and turned my eyes to her most vivid memories of Carola . . . from inside Carola's mind.

Why am I cold? I thought impatiently. Summer shouldn't be cold.

But when I glanced through the tall, narrow windows set deeply in the thick stone walls of my work chamber and thrust my fingers into my armpits, I was astounded to discover the sun setting. I had not eaten all day.

I walked out and down the hall to Lasva's staff chamber, where I found the others finishing a meal. They greeted me with muted surprise, and I realized I had stayed in my rooms for . . . how many weeks?

Pelis said, "She's alive!" And sang the carillon for the Welcome at Lily Gate, causing Anhar to laugh. The Marloven runners ignored this sally with the absence of long habit. Then Pelis said, "Did you really throw lightning and thunder at warriors from Totha, the spring before last?"

"It was stage illusion," I said.

"Told you," Anhar put in, as she reached for the clay pot full of freshly steeped leaf. (I had recently visited her past. Never any memories with Birdy, but I'd looked at her audition with the players and discovered that she was very good indeed, especially at comedy. But it was clear in the faces of her judges, who responded to every quip with a twitch of affront, that they were seeing a Chwahir mocking the Colendi.)

"The lancers all insist Emras's lightning was a real attack," Pelis replied.

"I didn't tell them that it was illusion," I said.

The others laughed, then Pelis said, "That was probably smart. Much more frightening for those terrible people and their arrows to think you could shoot back lightning at them. "I wish you knew spells for mending clothing! Marnda insists these Marlovens don't know a proper silk-stitch."

"We don't," said a new runner, a teenage girl with freckles and braids the color of cream. The other Marlovens regarded the peacocks with tolerant scorn, as the Colendi regarded the barbarians with tolerant scorn.

The conversation shifted to Kendred. Anhar led by relating little details of the prince's life—adorable mistakes he made in his reading and writing. I was amazed that everyone seemed to find them as entertaining as Anhar did. But I did not know the child, and so, my mind turned back to a particularly involved knot of wards. By now I could discern the different creators of the wards and how they thought. I was five layers down, but this next was horrific, and I did not have to look up the history of that period to know that whoever reigned had been afraid of his or her own shadow.

". . . Emras?"

I looked up at the sound of my name, to discover that everyone had left except Anhar.

"I asked," she said patiently, "if you would like me to bring you anything from Colend. I'm going to Alarcansa next week."

"Next week?"

"It's nearly New Year's," she said and then regarded me intently. "What is it you are working on now, to make you so absent?"

Irritation flashed through me, and I banished it. The question was perfectly normal. I busied myself with a bite of honey-smeared biscuit until I knew my face and voice were under control. "Wards," I said.

"Which are?"

"Elementary magic, but very, very tedious. Like stonemasons' workers, you don't want them laying stones awry." I patted the bare wall behind me. "I have to clean up all the old wards and lay new ones. Thousands and thousands of spells. Like laying walls, it might be tedious, but it has to be done."

It was all true, except for the elementary magic part, but who would know the difference?

Then she unsettled me by saying, "It's just that we never *see* you. I thought you might have been sent on some exciting tours for the king. And glad I am not to be sent along!" She warded Thorn Gate.

"I am as busy with tasks for the king as you are in training the prince," I said, knowing it was inadequate.

She seemed to accept my words, then indicated my hand, in which I held my biscuit. "Do you want me to do your nails? You don't like Starand?"

"She's adequate. But not as good as you were, so it's easier to do them myself. I have a clipper," I said. "And I thank you for the offer, but are you not free of that duty?"

"I still do it for some. Like Birdy—he likes my touch, though they have the best of everything at Alarcansa. Which they will remind you, if they think you might have forgotten." And when I bowed my thanks, "Ah-yedi! If you ever change your mind, you can always find me when I'm off duty. As for my visit, if you can think of anything you'd like me to bring back besides cream-cakes and nut-rolls, let me know." She fluttered her fingers, then whisked herself out of the room, and I was alone.

I helped myself to another biscuit and turned back to my problem—if I could see a way to the center of the knot, I promised myself, I'd look at Carola's last day at court when she was seventeen.

THREE

OF CINNAMON AND ZATHUMBRE

Another year passed, the only event to report being Ingrid-Jarlan's death. She was sitting with her women in the morning, as always, and interrupted a series of orders to ask for some listerblossom steep for a headache. The runners were debating whether or not to summon a healer, as the jarlan had never mentioned any kind of physical weakness before, but by the time they got back with the requested leaf, she had leaned her head on her hands and died.

You could see the generational divide among the guardswomen by the sincere mourning in the older faces. Lasva and Ivandred went to Darchelde for the memorial bonfire. On her return, she summoned the entire staff, saying briskly, "Since there are no cousins to inherit, the king has decided that Darchelde will be set aside for his son as a retreat. Anyone who would like to be transferred there as caretakers, speak to me."

It was an opportunity for the older staff to obtain an easy post. None of the Colendi volunteered, and life returned to normal.

I reached the seventh layer of wards—and with it, discovered that some mages had the skills to bury nasty transfer traps or personal wards—that is, warnings that an individual had crossed a particular boundary—into lower layers. I had been all ready to report to the

Herskalt (saving the news until I saw him face to face) that the seventh layer had been put down roughly two centuries before, so he should be perfectly safe entering the city.

But now I understood why he told me I must replace them all: while I did not believe that Andaun-Sigradir could have inserted personal wards so low in the entire structure, someone else might have had the skills to do so.

With the dyr, I discovered that all Carola's waking thoughts seemed to be bound up in conjecture about the smallest details of Kaidas's life, and a horrible, distorted semblance of Lasva. The motivations that Carola attributed to Lasva reflected her own.

I went back to that day in the salon, which I'd already seen from Falisse's and Carola's eyes. This time I looked at it through Tatia's eyes. Tatia, who had tried to contrive the death of a baby.

Tatia inspired the same horrified fascination that I think causes others to travel to witness executions, or to walk over the sites where some terrible event occurred.

Since the Herskalt was gone, I got into the habit of writing him long letters, discussing my reactions and surmises, letters I would find exactly where I had left them on my return. But I did not cease to write them, for I discovered when I read them through that they functioned to give me distance from my own mind.

There was also Ivandred's standing order.

I saw him rarely, but he always asked about my progress, accepted my words with a gesture, and I would be left to retreat to my tower, freshly motivated to have something better to report at our next encounter. Each time I saw him was a reminder of how terrible war was, and how I must find ways to circumvent it.

Bringing me to *zathumbre*, this time not metaphorical: the stormy spring that year provoked me to experiment with weather. I knew the magic for bringing cold air from the clouds into hot rooms, something that better-trained herald mages did for palaces. It was tedious magic, for the mage had to maintain the spell in person by creating a sort of air tunnel, or funnel, so that hot air and cold did not mix. My reasoning was that if I experimented with that spell, it would harm no one—we all lived with a variety of weathers—but might it not be an effective way to summarily put a stop to battle?

But I could not experiment close by. I understood enough about violent weather to know what it would do to growing crops. Where could I go? I asked that question of the Herskalt in one of my letters, then set the matter aside.

You will be aware that I was actually mastering magic at a prodigious speed, but you must remember there was no school, no set of peers with whom to work. My measure of progress was the castle and city ward project, and so I was only aware of my limitations, and how much work had yet to be done.

It was the day after Midsummer when I left that letter about weather magic for the Herskalt.

I walked out of my tower to the gunvaer's suite to join the others for a meal—made incommodious by Kendred's high shriek as he ran around playing games with two of the guards' children. Pelis told me that Lasva insisted their play be unfettered, which seemed to mean door-banging, shouting, and throwing things about in some kind of wild game that only almost-three year olds could invent.

So I finished my meal in haste and walked out to get exercise. I happened to be near the garrison when riders appeared, making way for a train of wagons bringing in wounded warriors. I didn't ask what happened. I just added myself to the squad of healers and healers' aides, and once again I performed those spells I'd first learned at the Olavair battle. Now they seemed simple. My mind turned eagerly to a new task—one whose good effect I could see immediately and whose mastery could be measured with satisfying rapidity.

I had found a new challenge—I would study healing!

I delved into the library of magic books that Andaun had left behind and, sure enough, found an old record of healer magic done for the garrison. I was a month into my new studies when I shifted to Darchelde and discovered a note in an unknown hand where my pile of letters had been. It said only, *Excellent progress—here is a Destination to use for weather work. You will be in the Ghildraith mountains, where there are constant storms. It is therefore a considerable transfer, so take tokens to use for your return.* The note finished with a facsimile of the Destination tiles on which I must form my focus. That meant I had to make myself tokens—but that was relatively easy by now. I began making up a few each night before I went to sleep. The rote magic functioned to calm my mind.

The Herskalt had not commanded me to drop the study of healing, but this was a hint that I'd strayed from the king's work. After all, there were healers aplenty, but only one Sigradir—me.

And so I transferred to the new Destination. It took me the space of three breaths to discover my error. It was frigid, and though the sun was in the same place in the sky, it was different, the light intense, the shadows extraordinarily sharp. I drew in a deep breath, almost giddy. I braced myself and transferred back. The rest of the day I spent on ward work, but the next day, early, I dressed in winter clothing, brought paper and pen for taking notes, and transferred again.

As that year wore on, I noticed with each successive visit that the sun's position that far north was increasingly higher than it was in the south. The air was correspondingly colder, though I was closer to the belt of the world. I had to be very high up indeed.

And here I took the greatest joy, regardless of my toes often going numb despite thick socks and sturdy boots, and despite my body trembling in the knife-cut of the high winds. I tested myself to the limit, reveling in the speed with which I controlled the internal heat-build of powerful magic and the snap of release as my mass of hot air, pulled from below, thrust up into the cold and sparked towering monuments of clouds that billowed and colored through darkening hues from startling green to deepest violet. And then the lightning danced and shivered from cloud to cloud, releasing thunder that shook the world below my feet.

By New Year's the weather was too vile for me to visit that Destination, but I could call up powerful lightning storms. What I could not do was control where the lightning would strike.

A few days before New Year's Week, the entire castle staff went into the usual frenzy of cleaning, airing, and preparing, which stirred me out of my cocoon. In the midst of these interruptions, Ivandred came to my chambers. "You have something new for me?"

After I explained (apologizing for the fact that I still could not control lightning's strike) he said, "It's excellent. Surpasses my expectations. I don't know how much more magic I can manage in the field and still command. Teach me this spell, and that should suffice."

I worked him through the spell several times until he had it. Then he said, "Put your time into the wards. I need the Herskalt's experience. Surely you have felt the need as well."

"Oh, yes. Is it possible we could hire him from whoever he works for now?"

"That's my plan. But he has to have access to Choreid Dhelerei."

I asked, "Could he not teach you, or guide you, from a place outside of the city? He can't be refusing to help you until I finish the wards!" I

could not believe the Herskalt would be petty, though it was a little reassuring to think of him having human failings like the rest of us.

"Not at all. That is, he visits me if I ask him to, and advises me. I don't
understand why he cannot stay," Ivandred said. "Probably has something
to do with the work he does elsewhere."

"I will redouble my efforts," I said.

And did to the exclusion of everything, and everyone, else.

It was the smell of cinnamon that broke the wall of my isolation.

Winter had been extraordinarily difficult, with a very late spring.
Each time we thought the snows were over at last, and we'd see the
ground with little green tufts, yet another heavy storm would boil up on
the northeastern horizon.

I'd gone to get a meal and found no one in the queen's suite, except
the duty guards, who looked glum, almost grim. Was something terribly
amiss? It could not be. Surely someone would warn me. . . . I walked out
in search of those I knew. When I got farther down the smoothly plastered hall with its stylish, running and soaring figures, my nose encountered a faint, familiar scene. I turned toward it, walking until I identified
the heady aroma of cinnamon and spice mulled into hot wine.

This was unprecedented! I followed it downstairs to discover the
Great Hall filled with castle folk, the younger people trading off drumming and singing as everyone else talked, laughed, and danced in big
circles.

Lasva was in the center of a group of women, looking like a teen again
as she stepped and twirled, her robes whirling. She knew every step and
every gesture, but nothing could make her look Marloven: grace had
been drilled into her from early childhood, and smooth were her movements out to the fingertips.

Surrounding her was a circle of teen-age girls and young women,
kicking up their heels so that the silk-stitched interlocked patterns along
sleeves and hems gleamed in the torchlight. I watched how girls cast
glances over their shoulders at the young men drumming, gave hips an
extra roll, backs arched a little more.

When the song ended, the young men put the drums down and raced
onto the floor, as older folk and some of the women took up the drums.

Now the boys began to show off, some crossing the circle with flips
and twirls, others glancing back at the girls as they stomped their heels

and leaped higher. I didn't know a step of any of these dances, though I'd once loved to dance.

When the men finished (roaring in counterpoint to the drums, which the girls thundered in antiphon) the air filled again with the heavy, sweet scent of mulled wine as wide, shallow cups were passed hand to hand.

It's Flower Day, I thought. *Today is Flower Day, the spring festival at home. No, not home anymore.*

Someone nudged me, and I jumped. Turned. A guard I recognized held out a cup, and I took it, caught by the sight of my hands. They looked like a stranger's hands. I'd been working so hard for so long, but I had only seen the papers, the results of my work, or others' memories . . . I had made none of my own.

That was it, I thought as I gulped the warm spiced wine. I had not eaten in so long that the wine's effect mounted to my head in the space of three heartbeats, leaving me blinking rapidly against stinging eyes as someone took the cup from my unresisting fingers, sipped and passed it on. I had made no memories with anyone, not for a long time.

Again a cup went around and again I drank as the drumbeat thrummed through my bones and sinews and blood.

In the center of the room Lasva moved, hands held high, palm to palm with other women. Their feet brushed and stamped in a complicated rhythm that set their robes swaying as their hands stayed steady, or almost steady. When someone faltered and broke her touch on one of her partners' palms, the watchers crowed and laughed, and she had to sit down. As the circle got smaller, the beat quickened until Lasva was left with Tesar and one of the weavers. Round and round they went, their steps a blur until Lasva whirled away, laughing, and declared all three of them winners.

Alone, and no one noticed. Who could blame them? The unconscious became conscious, as I counted up the months since Birdy's last letter and discovered how long it had been.

In the center of the room, it was the men's turn. Out came the swords. It was not the strange, almost somber dance with two swords laid on the ground that I had seen before the battle in the north, and never since. This dance was performed with laughter and mock challenge, the swords thrown back and forth, wielded in arcs and circles, then passed on.

Compared to Colend, these dances might seem crude. They were certainly not graceful, nor full of the oblique innuendo that Colendi courtiers enjoyed. The way that people watched one another was open, desire made plain, challenge overt. And there was Lasva in the middle of them, having created a Flower Day all of her own, though she had no flowers. But the Marlovens did not miss what they did not have, and it was clear that the real meaning of the day—the celebration of spring, and youth, and growth—was a success.

And I had not known about it. I had not even remembered the date. High shrieks caught my attention as Prince Kendred led a stream of other five-year-olds in and out among the adults. From their gait it seemed the children were pretending to be horses.

Kendred was small and light, his curly hair darkening to chestnut. In the middle of one of the dances he dashed into the center of the circle, though the other children faltered, not quite daring. He ran up to Lasva and caught her robe. She whirled around, exclaimed in surprise, caught him up and kissed him soundly, as a roar of approval and laughter went up around us. Then she set him down and would have taken his hands to dance with him, but he declared in his high voice, "It's a women's dance! I'm not a women!"

"No you're *not*," came a shrill voice from a little girl. "You have to get out of the circle, Kendred-Laef!"

Kendred dashed away as another laugh sounded, and I caught Marnda talking in our home language, querulous with old age, "Look at this—did not touch a bite, and I fetched all his favorite foods. I really think Prince Kendred lives on air, because he does not eat enough to sustain a bird."

Anhar said with a voice of authority, "This I know from my cousins. When he starts to grow, he will eat." And from there, "Did you hear what he said the other day, when we were reading *The Tales of Peddler Antivad*?"

"What did he say this time?"

I moved away, bored and a little grieved. It was not that I disliked the prince. I didn't know him well enough to like or dislike him. I did dislike his noise—so unlike anything I'd ever experienced. We never made such noise, I thought as I distanced myself. From my earliest memories I gained praise for quietness and neatness. My last session on a ponder chair was after Tiflis and I had argued about some paints when I was no older than six. *I do not care who began it,* my mother had said kindly. *We use our words to find agreement, not to foster disagreement. Sit for a time and reflect on how you might have arranged to share, then join us for supper.*

The remarkable thing, I soon discovered, was that Lasva had known even less freedom than I had. Her earliest memories were of kindly but firm hands disengaging her fingers from something forbidden, and admonishments if she tried to run, or leap, or shout, always beginning with the phrase *A princess must . . .*

"Emras!" Lasva herself was there, her entire countenance expressing pleasure. "Emras! I am so glad to see you here. Come! Here is food. And places to sit. Or would you like to dance?"

I declined, without telling her I did not know the dances. She stayed with me until I had a plate and a cup of my own, but I could not eat: the fast I was breaking was the hunger of the heart. I watched with the dizzy languor of emotional starvation as she tripped lightly off to dance again, leaving me surrounded by people having a good time, while I remained effectively invisible. I forced myself to take a bite. Another. But my eyes blurred as I watched them all: Pelis, fingers entwined with a blonde potter; Nifta head to head with a tall, somber herald; Marnda gesticulating as she talked to a couple of silver-haired women on the far side of the room.

Anhar kissed the assistant baker with the attitude of a lover, and I thought, When did that happen? She left him to join the dance, every bit as graceful as Lasva, but part of the circle instead of in the center. She danced on her toes, her fingertips up in Bird-on-the-Wing, while around her hands flapped or gripped into fists of concentration or dangled, as dancers concentrated on their steps. Did she still write to Birdy? Did she dance when she went to Colend? I had never asked. I had never cared, though she had been thoughtful enough to bring me back little gifts: pastry, and letters.

I put the wine cup down. It was making me maudlin. Yet I could not blame the wine for the sorrow aching in my chest. No one noticed me because I had cut all the connections we make to others by asking such small questions, *Did you dance in Colend?* and *Who is your new friend?* And then listening to the answer.

I slipped out, my emotions in a turmoil of self-pity worsened by the unaccustomed wine, and returned to my tower to discover a letter waiting in my scrollcase, which I had bespelled to form an illusory candle flame when a letter transferred in.

It was from the Herskalt: *We need to consult.*

Grateful—desperate to get away—I transferred immediately. He was there waiting. When I met that acute gaze, the urge to defend myself, to explain the smell of wine that surely accompanied me made me flustered, but all he said was, "Ivandred is in the field, as I'm sure you know."

"I did not, actually," I said. "I probably have been remiss, if I am to be of use to the king and queen. I have been unaware of events outside my tower."

"Recollect that Marloven kings prefer their mages to be unaware of events, until their services are needed," the Herskalt replied. "You've done nothing amiss. Your progress is excellent."

Somewhat steadied, I said, "Am I going to be needed, then?"

"Not at this moment. I suspect the trouble will come within the next few months, and it's probable it will be in the south," the Herskalt said.

"I thought Totha was settled after . . . after what happened." I knew it was weak to avoid stating the truth, but I could not get my lips to form the word *massacre*.

The Herskalt's lips twitched. "Suffice it to say that Totha is only part of the problem. Jarl Bluejay has been flattered by his cousin in Perideth into thinking that he deserves an independent kingdom. What Perideth wants is the Jayad. And Totha as a buffer."

"Does Ivandred know all this? What am I to do?"

"You will continue doing exactly what you have been: working on those wards."

"I have been working so hard."

"I read your notes here. I presume they were for me," he said, touching my papers, now neatly stacked. "I hasten to give you credit for hard work. But I think you have lost sight of magic's potential by miring yourself in details, then coming back here to lose yourself in the lives of individuals who will never make a difference in the world, in spite of their intriguing minds."

"What should I be doing?"

"Let us combine two lessons in one," he said as he made a curious gesture with his first two fingers and picked up the dyr.

The adjacent wall that I had wondered so much about vanished. Beyond it lay an impossibility in the middle of a castle late at night: a garden in daylight. He led the way, and I followed, distracted for a moment by the long tail of brown hair he wore neatly tied back. My own hair was just as long—unnoticed until now, as I had not bothered to get it cut.

He stepped onto grass as I put my foot through the divide between the hidden chamber and the garden. I tried to study the transition but my eyes slid away. I forced my gaze back, but black dots dappled my vision as I tried to bring the doorway into focus. At that moment, my foot stepped through, encountering sudden cold. It was a shock, like the touch of ice that burns then goes numb.

But just as my lungs contracted on a gasp, I was through, and the cold was gone. I looked around, though there was nothing to see that would explain the imperceptible disorientation: the garden was surrounded by a hedge of thick flowering trumpet lilies. The grass was thick and green, the flowers growing in scattered profusion summer bright. Some I recognized, and some I did not.

"Sit down," the Herskalt invited, indicating a marble bench. He sat down beside me and put his hands on his knees. "Today's lesson is about ordinary people who choose to influence those in power and whose choices therefore affect nations."

I was about to protest but halted. I was no longer a scribe, and further, I had exerted myself to influence Ivandred with the spells I had given him to avoid battles.

The Herskalt gave me an approving look. "You are finally learning that influence is not the equivalent of evil. Nor is it always good." His hand flickered in a complicated sign, and I jumped when without any warning, a semblance of a familiar place formed around me: the staff dining room in Alsais's palace.

I say a semblance, though at first it seemed we were there. But there was no smell, no sense of air moving; further, I was still seated and nobody could see me. I could also see the Herskalt next to me as he indicated a smiling man of about thirty, his face round, his curly hair a rusty red whose color reminded me of Birdy's when we were young.

"This is Kivic, a Chwahir spy hired as a bridle man," the Herskalt said. "From this garden we can move back in time in a limited way. I believe it will be instructive for you to see the world through his eyes."

He did not give me time to recover from my amazement— I found myself in Kivic's head as he watched Torsu, the dresser he eventually killed.

The Herskalt's gestures—the impossibilities made manifest—the ease with which all of this occurred, struck me anew with the power of magic. Once again I felt like the most clumsy beginner. I *had* to learn how to do these things!

At first Kivic's murder of Torsu did not affect me, because it meant so little to him. I did not believe she was really dead until I looked down at her, feeling her lifelessness through "my" hands. That is when I recoiled, closing my eyes and clapping my hands over my ears, which was stupid because my mind was trapped inside his.

But then I was alone with my own thoughts, and the Herskalt rose from the bench. Once again he gestured with two fingers toward the hedge, which vanished, and we stepped through into the hidden chamber.

Giddy with amazement, I sat down abruptly as he replaced the dyr in its porcelain bowl. "Where is he now?" I asked. "I remember the queen saying something about demanding restitution."

"You may find out on your own. I have given you the means to understand him, and also Lasva, so that you may better serve her. But you seem to prefer your reticence."

"I do not want to look at myself through her eyes," I said. "The dyr feels like trespass enough."

"You do not have to look at yourself through her eyes," he replied. "If you do—and many of us could not resist—you will merely discover what we did, that few people are as interested in us as we are ourselves. They regularly misconstrue our motives. They judge us according to their own personal standards and believe them universal. You will learn nothing about yourself. However, you could learn a great deal about the people most important in your life through their experiences—specifically the ones that brought you all here."

Why should I *not* look at Lasva's life through her own eyes, and just avoid the circumstances in which I was in her thoughts? That very evening I had been mourning my lack of connection. I knew that I would never use what I learned against her, she who had been so good to me. If anything, by bettering my understanding, I could better my service.

"I will," I said.

FOUR

OF A NOTCHED TRUNK

I discovered that I could not write to Birdy. It was too awkward—I could not tell him about my dyr studies.

So I immersed myself in Lasva's life and Queen Hatahra's memories—though at first I was as frightened as if she could catch me at it and have me exiled. I found her just as daunting from the inside. Davaud was unexpectedly sympathetic, though we had thought him so dour from our distant perspective. Thence into Kaidas's memories.

As summer waxed and waned, I put more effort into the wards—and extra effort was required, for I discovered that the Marlovens' additions were simple, almost simplistic, compared to what I found below.

The characteristics of the tenth level mage captivated me. I was almost certain that a female mind lay behind the structure. Her protection-spell skills far surpassed mine, so much so that I had to stop and comb through those old dusty books belonging to Andaun-Sigradir in search not only of magic spells but also of the history of the castle through a mage's eyes. I found lessons on protections, akin to the all-but-forgotten elementary magic text that I had memorized while crossing the continent. These spells seemed clumsy, fussy, and were definitely slow. The constant stresses about carefulness and preservation reminded me of Greveas, all but forgotten. Was this unknown mage Sartoran? If so, why the structure that appeared to be based on Venn knots?

Once again I had to slow down, but my reward was new insight into how magic was layered into keyed enchantments.

I brought that knowledge to the dyr. Without actually touching it—I was far too cautious for that—I attempted to tease apart the layers of enchantment that I could perceive around this object whose material was still unidentifiable. Not quite metal and not quite stone.

And so I came to the end of that year. I made sure to attend Kendred's sixth Name Day celebration. My reward for an evening of anecdotes about children, the prince, and elementary lessons was Lasva's happy smile when I entered her chamber. Ivandred was not there, which should have served as warning for me. But I, in my ignorance, looked out at the sentries walking the wall, their breath clouding as they slogged through a heavy early snow, and thought, at least the season of war is ended for another half-year.

How wrong I was became apparent when gossip arrowed through the castle that the Jarl of Totha had not come to renew his vows. "Snowed in—what a fool excuse!" Such words passed from lip to ear. They seem to want trouble, I thought at the time, and withdrew to my tower, shaking my head over the unaccountability of Marlovens.

It was not quite two weeks into the new year when an unprecedented event occurred. I sat at my desk, my sketches of that tenth level before me. What was missing?

Lasva threw open the door to my work room, fans swinging, eyes wide and blue. She was too distressed to speak in their language. "Emras, what have you done?"

I turned so quickly I almost fell off my stool. "Your highness," I said—I, too, fell into old habit as I responded in Kifelian and scrambled up to bow in the full peace. "I? Done?" I began to point at my sketches, wondering how to put into words what I was working on.

"Magic. The Jarlan of Totha says that Ivandred slaughtered hundreds of them using magic. *Hundreds*, Emras. That can only have come from you."

"Impossible," I declared. "All I've taught Ivandred is how to prevent battles."

In answer Lasva held out a much-folded piece of paper, obviously sent via scrollcase.

Lasva-Gunvaer:

You promised to be our advocate. I call upon you to heed that promise before there is nothing left of our land but ghosts. Has Norsunder truly allied with the king? How else could he loose fire and lightning against us, destroying our weapons and killing our warriors by the wing at one strike? It will take us days to Disappear the dead whose lives were destroyed in an afternoon. I do not know yet if Bluejay lives. I fear by tomorrow my children and I will be dead, in which case you will have no one to answer to.

Gdan of Totha

I looked up, confused by a half-familiar name. "Bluejay?"

"The jarl," Lasva said. "One of the many Haldrens. Emras, can you take me to Gdan, and then to Ivandred? I have to try to make peace."

"Take you to her by magic?" I asked. "Lasva, they might . . . not make a truce."

Lasva said bleakly, "Then they don't. I must find out about this Norsunder accusation. Oh, Emras, please see the necessity of haste! You must know their Destinations—don't you have that written down somewhere?"

"Destinations might be in one of the records I have yet to peruse," I said. "But I can do better, though it will hurt, I fear. These transfers are harsher because there is no time to lay down the relative protections around each Destination—" I stopped explaining when I saw her anxiety. "I can transfer to her scrollcase, if you can give me her scrollcase sign. If she has it with her, we will transfer directly to her."

"Please take us. Or send me, if you must."

The instinct to self-preservation caused me to hesitate. The danger was obvious, and I had already experienced a threat to my life from those people.

But I'd been spending weeks looking at moments in Lasva's life. And though the Herskalt appeared to speak truth when he said that no one has the interest in us that we have in ourselves, his general remarks did not otherwise apply to her. She really did love us all. The rare glimpses of me (that is, when she was aware of me) in the memories I chose came with emotional surges of fondness, sometimes humor. She thought of me as such a steadfast, earnest little thing, sometimes puzzling. Even that terrible day when she so abruptly went silent, I was right about the cause, but she did not resent my ill-concealed weariness. *Emras cannot fix my pain and it pains her*, that was what Lasva had thought.

I said, "Let me get my cloak."

When the transfer reaction wore off, Lasva swallowed several times, then whispered, "Now I know why everyone says they smell singed cloth near your tower."

There was no time for my surprise. We found ourselves surrounded by a startled group of people whose oddly round faces hardened from surprise to intent. Most of them had shorn their hair, so it clustered around the tops of their heads.

Lasva walked straight to Gdan of Totha, who stood surrounded by young warriors. Gdan threw up a hand. "Halt!" she said to her followers, some of whom started to converge, hands on weapons. "She is here by my desire." And to Lasva, "Come within. Tell me you can halt the king before he destroys us all."

We were in a low building made of stone and timber. Windows on two sides made it clear we were not in a castle. Farmhouse? Gdan opened a slat door to a tiny room crowded with people seated on woven mats around a low table.

Lasva's gaze rested on a young man whose nearly white hair was so short and fine that it reminded me of duck's down. Gdan, seeing the direction of her gaze, lifted her chin. "Our defenders all cut their hair. They do not want their scalps worn by their murderers."

"I loathe that practice," Lasva stated plainly.

Gdan looked surprised, then made a gesture. "Of course. You are Colendi."

"I am Colendi, which means I would much rather talk out problems than fight. You asked me to intervene. I will do that, but I must first understand your side of the conflict—what it is you want and where you are willing to compromise."

"Compromise," Gdan repeated, frowning.

Lasva opened her hands. I think she meant to emulate the Marloven gesture for truth-sharing, but it turned into the Colendi Opening of a Flower, the invitation to intimacy. "In Colend, this negotiation would last for weeks, amidst pleasant talk about plays and poems, between balls and dinners and journeys along the canal for idle flirtation. But if there is imminent conflict, well, must we not be as plain as we can? That means telling me what you wish, what you can accept. What . . ." She hesitated, then said firmly, "What you will refuse."

Gdan leaned forward. "But all we were doing was securing our northern border."

"I beg your forbearance, but do you not share a border with other jarlates of Marloven Hesea? Why should it require securing?"

"Because we had word that Tlen was going to send wings against our northern lands on the excuse of securing *their* border. When we heard that Marthdaun had allied with them . . ."

"A moment," Lasva said. "A little background for the lamentably slow Colendi, may I beg? You and the jarl did not come to Convocation to renew your vows."

"We sent a message to the king—we were snowed in."

Slowly, patiently, Lasva worked through questions, her gaze steady as she looked for the signals of guile. I did not see any, but I was not court trained. Lasva herself was still, her hands loose in her lap. Finally she said, "As for the lightning . . ."

And every face turned my way, then averted, as if I would strike them dead with a look.

". . . did anyone see it?" Lasva asked.

In answer, Gdan motioned toward one of the warriors. They were all muddy, almost indistinguishable. The one she indicated was not just muddy. There was a darker stain on his coat: blood. He leaned back against the wall, his shorn hair hanging in his eyes. Lasva looked away quickly then braced herself to look back.

"My riding mate died so I could run to report," he said, his voice cracking. "But I was there. I saw our arrows turn to ash in the sky. And I saw lightning hit the middle of the front lines . . ." He dropped his head forward onto his breast, clamping his jaw shut.

Again I felt the weight of accusation against me—I saw the signs in quick, covert glances, and the tightening of hands on weapons—but it was not nearly as profound as my own sense of shock and betrayal. Words piled up, but I couldn't speak them. No one would understand, and no one would believe me if I said that this magic was meant to frighten, perhaps to drench warriors, horses, and ground. Not to kill. The truth seemed to lie with the fellow barely out of his teens who struggled against grief.

Lasva rose to her feet. "I believe I have enough," she said softly. "Where are we? In relation to the battle, to . . . to the king and the others?"

"They are probably camped on the other side of the ridge," an older man said in a low voice. "We could send someone with a white flag, if you want to ride out and find them."

Lasva looked my way. I signed assent, and she said, "We will find him."

I had never transferred to Ivandred. Truth to say, I was not even sure I could. If I had not been so angry, I might've been afraid to try. The distance was short—the transfer was a sharp jolt, which, coming so soon after the previous one, left me with a bitter taste in my mouth and a headache behind my eyes. Lasva gulped for breath, one hand pressed to her chest. Then she drew in a shaky breath and looked around. I did as well.

We found ourselves directly outside of Ivandred's tent—probably within arm's reach of his scrollcase, but on the other side of the canvas. Startled guards had closed around us, weapons ready, but when they recognized Lasva they took a step back and saluted. They did not look at her, but at me, hands hovering near hilts and bows.

Lasva pushed aside the tent flap and walked in. So great was her perturbation that she did not even glance to see where the shadows lay, for as always there was only one glowglobe.

Ivandred, Haldren, and two or three others were gathered around a camp table with an unrolled map. They, too, were muddy. I did not look closely to see how much of that was blood. My attention went straight to Ivandred, who gazed at Lasva with eyes red-rimmed from exhaustion.

Ivandred said, "Out." The word had the same effect as a Colendi pointing down in the shadow challenge.

All his leaders but Haldren moved past us; Haldren stayed.

A puff of cold air replaced the stuffy, sweaty atmosphere as Ivandred and Lasva faced one another. A shadow shifted behind them, and I sustained a second shock when the Herskalt stepped forward. "Emras," he greeted me.

"I have just come from Gdan," Lasva said to Ivandred. She held out the jarlan's note. "She said that they were reinforcing their border because they thought that people from Tlen and Marthdaun were attacking *them*."

"Look here, Lasva," Ivandred said pointing to his map. He glanced my way. "You too, Sigradir."

His gloved finger traced the hilly border between Totha and Marthdaun, then eastward along the border of Tlen, toward Ivandred's oldest ancestral land. This hilly border ran alongside a river. On the north side were many little villages and market towns. I recognized a few names. Next to a great many of them were little markers. Ivandred touched one. "These are the targets for teams of Perideth's best. They were riding in support of Bluejay's defensive wing. Bluejay had no idea that Perideth was using him as an excuse to make trouble up here in order to deflect me from a land grab in the south."

"How do you know that?" Lasva asked.

"Fnor was the scout who discovered the ruse. Do you want to talk to her?"

"Fnor," Lasva repeated and drew another deep breath, her hands pressed tightly together. "I accept what you say. I remember you told me that the King of Perideth entertained malign intentions in the southern reaches. And I remember that attack at the bridge. I also believe Gdan. She is afraid that you are about to massacre her people."

"I plan to ride through, straight to Perideth. It will be a salutary ride," Ivandred said.

"What does that mean?" Lasva asked. "Does that mean killing everyone in sight with bolts of lightning? Or putting them all to the sword?"

"They broke their oath. I intend to keep mine. My real target is Perideth. Totha is in the way for both of us. Bluejay should have thought of that when he allied with his cousin against me."

"But I am not convinced that he did ally against you," Lasva said. "I believe Gdan. Her skills at dissembling must be great indeed, if she is lying."

Ivandred let out a breath of tiredness. "She is no liar. She and Bluejay are simple. He has always believed anyone he likes. Anyone who flatters him. And his cousin has made much of Bluejay's great ancestors, telling him that he inherited Inda's strategic sense. From all the signs, Bluejay has shifted loyalties."

"What I understand from Gdan is that she is loyal to Totha, first and foremost," Lasva said. "She seems to think that Bluejay feels exactly the same. Ivandred, I'm here to try to save lives. I beg you to find a way to spare Totha."

While they talked, the Herskalt drew me aside. "I trust I am not about to hear that everyone dies anyway," I said. "That is no justification for that spell being altered to kill people. There *is* no justification for that—for war."

"Warriors ride into battle knowing that they may have to kill someone. Knowing that their own lives are at risk. War is a different moral paradigm."

"There is nothing moral about it."

"Emras, look again at the map. Listen to what you were told. Perideth intends to make war against Marloven Hesea. Ivandred is sworn to protect his people, and the only means he has to do so is to meet violence with violence."

My throat had closed. The Herskalt touched my arm and shifted us by transfer. Once again it was painless, as effortless as stepping from one room to another. I looked around the Darchelde chamber, blinking tears from my eyes—tears that stung the worse because of the dust on my face from my day of labor on the wards.

I clasped my hands, determined to get control. "I find it so difficult to believe. Is this King of Perideth so different from other humans that he will not negotiate, he cannot understand that people in other countries have the right to live in peace? Is he no respecter of laws? How do they function in Perideth with no laws?"

"He is using war to gain an end. War is a form of human endeavor. The protection of law cannot exist until Ivandred controls the threat of violence."

"True."

"Further, you have to admit that war creates no new situation. It simply worsens the strife that is already there. One of the ugly truths about the human condition is how close we are to strife at any given moment."

I wiped my eyes, my voice unsteady. "It does not help when strife is consistently seen as glory and honor."

The Herskalt said gently, "It's bearable—just—if they know that their families will mount their weapons on walls for future generations to venerate, that there will be songs with all their names. Emras, Ivandred knew that you could not bring yourself to give him spells that would supplement fighting tactics. He took the responsibility for altering those spells himself."

I was about to point out, with all the bitterness in my soul, that I would be responsible, that I would be condemned for that magic, but I did not. My reputation was not the important matter here, and I had to accept my part of the blame—if anyone would blame me besides Lasva. The Marlovens were far more likely to heap praise on my head, while avoiding contact with my person.

The Herskalt said, "Ivandred reached them in two weeks. It was an astonishing ride, the more because, tired as they were, they ran straight into battle, Ivandred every step of the way with them."

I made the shadow ward. Someone else could admire this martial expertise, but I could not.

The Herskalt said, "The First Lancers took the advance force utterly by surprise. This was in part due to your road spells, which struck snow out of the way, and in part due to their constant drill. Would you condemn yourself for the road clearing spell?"

"I condemn war," I said.

"This attack appears to be bringing about a peace negotiation far earlier than Ivandred had hoped," the Herskalt said. "He had foreseen a long, grim winter of chasing down the disparate Perideth attack teams one by one. Have you ever seen this kind of search? What happened today—yesterday—was on the field of battle, between people who had, at least in some part, chosen to be there. Emras, you will have to come to terms with the darkness in our natures. Surely you have been seeing that in your dyr studies."

I had no answer to that. I would have argued, but he said, "I am afraid I have to return to my own duties. I owed Ivandred that much time, but I can spare no more at present." He faded through the wall again, leaving me alone.

I stared at the Fox memoir on the table, unable to form a coherent thought. Possibly because I was so overwhelmed, my mind reached past the recent horror to the problem I'd been struggling with before Lasva's appearance: the vexing structure of the tenth level. As I stared at that manuscript, it gradually dawned on me that this Fox had written the memoir around the time that tenth layer had been put over the castle.

The Marlovens had been ignorant about magic, that much I'd gathered. I knew that many monarchs hired mages for important spells, on the understanding that they would perform their spells and then promptly leave.

But this tenth hand was so different from those who had formed the previous nine layers, what if I might find a name, or even a hint, in the Fox record?

I think it was no more than desperation to escape the inescapable that I reached for the top page of the pile that I'd been ignoring for several years. Once again I commenced reading. But this time, I forced my way determinedly past the detailed account of Inda the Elgar's early life in search of any words about magic.

I did not transfer back to the royal castle until my head was sodden with exhaustion, my body aching from the base of my spine to my skull. It was the only way I could hope to get some sleep; I was afraid to lie in bed with my mind lurching and spinning around my errors, the consequences of my magical studies, and how could I not have foreseen what Ivandred would do with my spells?

As soon as I lit a glow-globe in the always gloomy main chamber, there was a sound from without the double doors. A tall guardswoman opened the door. "I was instructed to inform the gunvaer as soon as you returned," she said, pointing to the light.

"Which watch are we in?"

The woman glanced at me in muted surprise. "Sunset watch change half a glass ago."

I'd read all night and most of the day, then. No wonder I felt as if I'd fallen from a roof. Or had transferred four times since the last time I'd slept.

She stepped aside in a manner that made it clear I was to go, just as I was. So I forced myself to follow her to the queen's suite, which seemed an intolerable distance. Glances and whispers relayed ahead of us, and Lasva came scudding out of her chambers to meet us in the staff room. "Emras, you are back at last! Where did you go? Never mind. About your magical affairs, I am certain. Come. Let me show you."

She led me to her own room and pointed at a battered carved trunk. The usual Marloven symbols decorated it, unevenly made. But when I saw a row of notches along the top, chills rung through my nerves.

"Gdan sent it to me," Lasva said. "In thanks. Did you know that Ivandred agreed to a treaty? That is, the people from Perideth are to withdraw beyond Totha's border. The First Lancers will ride through and see them gone, but there is to be no fighting if the retreat is orderly. Oh, my dear, apparently there were more of them than anyone thought. Far more. Before I transferred back here—Ivandred gave me one of his tokens—Gdan gave me this. You haven't read Hadand's letters, so you won't understand who Tdor Marth-Davan was, but—"

"I do know," I said, staring down. "She was Inda Elgar's jarlan." Some of Fox's record was written from Tdor's own view.

"This trunk is four hundred years old," Lasva said. "Sent back to the Algaravairs from Enaeran. It is regarded by the Tothans as a treasure."

I scarcely heard her, because I was staring at that chest while thinking. *How could I not have seen? Those memories written so vividly from inside the minds and hearts of people Fox had never met: someone—either Fox or someone he interviewed—had a dyr.*

FIVE

OF SWORDS AND THE ABSENCE OF CATS

As winter passed, Lasva wrote ceaselessly to the jarlans in her effort to weave her net of peace among the women. I made a conscious effort to involve myself more in others' lives, though the cost was a reminder of why I'd gradually withdrawn. I did not know half the names in local gossip; I was not amused by the interminable anecdotes about what little Prince Kendred said and did. Everyone smiled on his noisy antics, and Lasva—if she was present—praised him and kissed him before he ran out again, to my great relief.

Pelis had finished the tapestry, which was duly borne off and hung in the antechamber outside the throne room. She then got the idea to begin another one as a surprise for Lasva, so she talked about it only when Lasva was busy elsewhere. Pelis, still homesick, was inspired to make it a Colendi tapestry—completely forgetting, or ignoring, all Lasva's reasoning for making the Marloven-styled one. After all that I had seen with the dyr, I knew why reminders of home pained her. But how could I explain, and not open myself to questions that might lead to Kaidas?

I tried. "Have you noticed that Lasva does not have any cats?"

"Cats?" Nifta repeated—for she was there, a rarity these days. She traveled a great deal, seeing to the burgeoning silk trade.

"Cats?" Pelis said, hands up. "She hasn't cats because she has a child now."

"I would love to see a tapestry with the rose garden, seen from the Grand Skya Canal," Anhar said, to which Pelis and Nifta at first agreed, but soon began to amend to include other symbols of Colend, and I gave up.

Before a month had passed, I found reasons to make my visits to the gunvaer's suite shorter and shorter . . . until I began skipping days. I divided myself between the wards, the Fox memoir, and the dyr.

All three had become inextricably entwined. In the Fox memoir I found the mage—a Venn named Signi Sofar. Her magic was layered so evenly that the "draw" from magic's pool of potential was minimal. Her skill was such that it took me a long time to perceive just how very complex her structure was.

It also gave me clues to the magework beneath, which was different yet again. Far older: the layers beneath were not separated by a generation or two, as the previous had been, but a century apart, maybe more. And this work, in turn, led me to experiment with the dyr. I proceeded very carefully, for the spells binding it were so powerful I could feel the brush of them against my bones if I stretched my hand just above the object—I did not dare to touch it. I wrote down those spells, one by one.

I don't think I would have dared to try what I did next, had I not still carried a residue of anger against Ivandred, underscored by anxiety that he would use magic in war again. I'd been trying with little success to see Ivandred through the dyr. I knew he was not warded against transfer, and the Herskalt had helped me to see from Ivandred's eyes the first time we used the dyr. But for some reason it was extraordinarily difficult to glimpse much from his perspective for very long, and most of that was about Lasva or his journey across the continent—and there, Macael Elsarion's perspective was far easier.

Then there was shifting in time. One stormy day I dared the two-fingered gesture that I'd seen the Herskalt perform. I was amazed when the wall vanished, and there was the garden. Why not experiment?

I picked up the porcelain bowl, careful not to touch the dyr, stepped into the garden, and reproduced the Herskalt's gestures. I finished with Kivic's memories until his death, then moved back in time to Torsu. Knowing what would happen to her—and its swiftness, catching her by surprise—was rendered easier to bear by her contempt for me and for the rest of Lasva's staff.

Because those memories were so easy to call up and see, without the usual physical cost, I experimented further. Where in the world was this garden? I tried several spells, all of which were warded in such a way that I got this disturbing sense of the unseen walls and ceiling silently closing in on me. The fact that the timeless garden, with its lack of direct sun (and its absence of shadows) showed no change was even more disturbing. I became aware that I was breathing through my mouth, my skin was clammy, and my shoulder blades itched unbearably; in haste I made the access gesture, stepped into the Darchelde chamber, set the bowl down, and stood there trembling.

"How can this be?" Marnda's voice was shrill with distress.

I had avoided the staff room for several days. In spite of the fact that the next day would be Kendred's Name Day (which would of course provide the content of the day's conversation) I was determined to keep my promise to myself. I walked over there at Daybreak to discover the Colendi gathered in a knot. None of the Marlovens were present.

"How can he do that?" Marnda exclaimed.

Lasva entered through her door a moment after my entrance. The Colendi all whirled around, and eight years of exile among Marlovens could not prevent any of us from making the profound court bow to Lasva.

Lasva did not pretend she had not heard us. "The king has decided to start Kendred at the academy earlier than is customary," she said, her hands pressed tightly together. "He has explained his reasoning: there is so much for a future king to learn. Kendred must begin early on the purely physical training, so that he is accepted as a leader by his future captains. And when they are refining their training, he will be learning statecraft."

She used the future-must-be mode in Kifelian, which prompted another full court bow. Now there could be no more public discussion, though of course the staff would continue to opine and wonder in private.

Lasva sat down to join us and, into the silence, requested Anhar to read us some poetry.

After the meal, everyone went about their duties in a suitably chastened mood. Lasva put out her hand to stop me. "I get the sense that there is something missing. You know they will not talk about what happens. But Ivandred . . . ah-ye, I can feel his . . . ambivalence. When I asked, he said that Kendred must begin early, because one of the things he would have to study would be magic. With you."

Back came all my feelings of resentment and betrayal. There was no use in declaring to Lasva that I would not teach the boy war magic. As I'd read in the Fox memoir, once evil magic was used, it was difficult to suppress short of killing everyone who knew it.

And that was another problem. As I walked back to my tower, I reflected again on those deceptively easy labels, light magic and dark magic. The definitions were too facile to mean much. Dark magic spent magic, yes. But the most benign spell, sloppily performed, could spend magic. So did that change it from light to dark? Or was darkness a question of evil intent? Transferring stones into the hearts of enemies, as those Venn mages did in the Fox memoir—definitely dark magic. But my Rock spell, so small, meant to sting and not to kill, I would have characterized that as light magic. Yet Ivandred had magnified that same spell. At what point did it change to dark magic? And did that make him a Norsundrian?

I knew he was not a Norsundrian. I had seen enough of his memories to grasp that his entire life was dedicated to his kingdom. Lasva was second in importance, and his son came close after. This was not an evil man, but he had done an evil thing. Yet he did not believe it to be evil. He was convinced he had done right, according to military strategy, and to his oaths.

So I transferred to Darchelde, picked up the porcelain bowl, made the transfer to the garden. I would not attempt any ward magic. I meant to focus the dyr on the current moment, though hitherto it had always been memories. I would proceed with caution—and choose a first host who was unlikely to notice anything amiss, if the magic somehow obtruded itself into notice. Someone I knew but with whom I had no affinity. Who better than a child? I chose Kendred for my first experiment.

Again, it was extraordinarily easy. I looked up through Kendred's eyes at Ivandred, full of love, a little awe, and a little impatient. "I *know*, Da. They been telling me all week, tonight we will have my Name Day, and tomorrow, when it's my real Name Day, I get to go through the gate."

Ivandred looked away, then back at his son. "You don't know what it means, to go through the gate."

"But I get to find out tomorrow." Kendred hopped from toe to toe.

"Cam and me, we're going up to the shooting range after my riding lesson, 'cause the captain said he'd let me pull his bow, if . . ."

Ivandred looked around again, then knelt and put his hands on Kendred's shoulders. His strong grip held "me" steady. Kendred's impatience turned to question. "Da?"

"Remember what I tell you, son. We all went through it. And we survived. Will you remember that?"

Kendred spoke in a scoffing voice, but his fear knotted in my middle. "The big boys said they beat you up and throw you in the dungeon. But that's just stupid. They can't do that to me. I'm going to be king."

"The big boys who have never been through the gate are stupid to talk about something they don't know," Ivandred said. "Your mother wanted you to learn her ways. They are good ways in her country. But you are Marloven. Yes, you are going to be a king, and that means you don't defend just yourself, you defend the kingdom."

Kendred recovered a little of his bravado and said stoutly, "I know. I have to be the best. Everyone tells me that. And I will try, I promise, Da."

Ivandred bent down, kissed the boy on his forehead then walked away. Kendred did not spare his father a thought. The impatience was back, impelling him to run his fastest to the stable as he thought about bows, arrows, and some other children whose images flickered through his mind and whose names I did not try to catch.

That night, I attended Kendred's party in the queen's rooms. All his friends were there; sturdy castle children whose parents were guards or artisans. From their talk, they were all war-mad. One solid little girl was deferred to because she could already pull a bow and hit the center of the target at fifty paces. The children teased Kendred with the freedom that no court child would have had in Colend, and several expressed envy because they knew they would never get chosen to go through the gate.

Since my experiment had been successful (leaving me wondering if I had managed to learn something that the Herskalt did not know) I was curious enough to return the next morning. I had taken my place in the garden, the dyr bowl on my lap, as Kendred walked down to the castle and through the mossy stone archway between the great hall and the throne room, to the tall gate beyond which lay the mysterious Academy. He shivered with excitement, a little fear, and some impatience as he tried to tug his fingers free from Marnda's tight grip. But she held on. At his right, his mother walked, her hand warm and gentle on his fingers, her thumb caressing the top of his hand.

When they reached the gate at which a tall boy stood straight and still, Lasva bent to kiss his hand then let go and stepped away. Kendred smiled up at his mother, warm with love, which vanished when he realized that Marnda still held his left hand.

"Marnda," Lasva said.

"I will walk him through," Marnda said. I could hear the fear and suspicion making her words quiver. Kendred only heard her strong Colendi accent, and a flush of embarrassment made him feel hot as he tried to free his hand. "I can go alone."

"Gently, Kendred," Lasva whispered.

Kendred covertly tugged against Marnda's grip as he stood still, his gaze on the tall boy in the gray coat. Kendred longed to be that boy. He did not even look up when Marnda finally let go, though he heard her muffled sob.

When he stood alone, the tall boy spoke at last. There was no smile, no sign of friendship as he said formally, "Who presents himself at the gate?"

Kendred said proudly, "Kendred-Laef Montredaun-An of Marloven Hesea. I'm seven, but I am coming here anyway, because I have to learn to be a king."

The gate opened wide enough to permit one small boy through. Wildly curious and excited, Kendred peered through the gap. All he saw was a sliver of dusty ground as the boy said, "Enter."

Kendred walked proudly into a wide square of hard-packed dirt. That much he'd expected, after trying to stare over the walls from the upper rooms of the castle. At one end were archery targets, and along the side, a rail for horses. It was swept clean otherwise. In the distance he could make out children's voices in cadence, and somewhere else, the deeper tones of oldsters like that gate boy. Kendred gave a little hop as he crossed the wide square to where a couple of men waited, one young and one old, before another gate between two buildings that had no windows on the square. He was really here and younger than anyone!

The older man said, "Montredaun-An?"

Just like in the military! Kendred grinned. "That's me!"

In silence the younger man opened this new gate. Kendred marched through, and caught his first glimpse of others—walking in pairs, each on the same step, or carrying weapons. His grin widened—then blinding pain.

I recoiled, almost falling off my bench as Kendred hit the ground hard. "My" face throbbed and stung.

"Defend yourself," the younger man said.

Kendred gasped, then scrambled up, though his arms and legs felt strange, like someone had put water inside him. He turned to the older man instinctively for protection, to see a hand come down and hit the side of his face. Again he fell. "Who are you going to call for help?" the older man asked.

"See? There is no help," the young one said and kicked Kendred in the side.

"Defend yourself," the old one said and reached down to slap Kendred again.

Kendred curled up, but when the slaps continued, he kicked out, hard, fiercely glad when his foot encountered something. The old man stepped back, and Kendred rolled to his hands and knees. His eyes, blurred with tears, made out another line of boys and girls, but they didn't pause in their march, didn't so much as look his way.

No one was going to help him.

I survived. Kendred remembered what his father had said. That meant this was supposed to happen. Kendred got to his feet, dizzy, desolate, angry, and swung out as hard as he could at the nearest tormentor. His fist encountered air, and again someone hit him. Down he went.

"Who is going to defend you?" they asked. And again, "Who?"

Not Da. He wasn't there. Ma couldn't come in. No one!

"Are nice words going to save you?"

A kick against his back as he lay sobbing.

"Dancing and singing? Or telling everybody you're a king's son, is that going to save you?"

"*Who* is going to defend you?" came the inexorable voice.

You don't just defend yourself, you defend the kingdom, his Da said in memory, and after another hard slap, and the question, Kendred yelled, "Me! I'm gonna!"

The slaps and kicks stopped. A hand closed around his arm. He recoiled, crying hard, and no longer caring as snot pinked with blood dripped down onto his shirt. The hand lifted him up and set him on his feet.

"When you leave here," the old man said, "no one can ever get you down again."

"When you leave here," the young one said, "you will win every fight. Against one or a thousand."

Kendred gulped, trying to get control of his sobbing.

"You got in one kick," the old man said. "That's more than some manage, and they're ten when they come."

"But air-swings only hurt the passing fly," the young one said.

Kendred eyed them, shoulders hunched. He was dizzy, and one eye was swelling. They were big and strong. Nobody could defeat *them*. That boy at the gate, he looked strong enough to fight anybody. "I wanna learn," Kendred said. His voice was squeaky, but they didn't laugh at him for it.

"Then follow me," the young one said. "To your first lesson."

I stayed with him a little longer, but his aches and pains, the stream of new terms and rules, and my own creeping fatigue, forced me out. I blinked around the timeless garden, my entire body throbbing with reflected pain from Kendred. The air was suffocating. I returned to Darchelde to recover.

When I returned to the royal palace, I avoided the queen's rooms, and I worked at my wards. I resolved not to tell Lasva what I'd seen. I did not know what would disturb her more, the rough treatment of her child, or the way that Kendred said *I wanna learn*. All his careful teaching about civility, using words instead of fists, it all went away before violence.

And that led to my resolution: I had to hear about incipient violence first. So I would use this new skill to listen to the jarlans, and maybe the jarls (if they weren't warded) and find a way to let the information get to those who could circumvent war. If I heard intimations of trouble before the trouble could begin, would that not be a deterrent?

It took less than one month to discover how foolish were my expectations.

I still could not find my way to strangers. It was like transfers. One needs a specific, either a face, or an event that gives one access to the participants. Once I learned how to work my way from one familiar person to someone they interacted with, I discovered that most people while away their days with inconsequential matters—sleeping or eating, or riding, dressing, or chatting. All the little vexations of daily life: annoyance, concealed (sometimes not well concealed) dislike of someone close, pique, greed, distrust, yearning, boredom, and always defense, war, strength, skill. It was a relief to hear laughter, even if I did not understand the joke, or to find them asleep. Occasionally I caught them in intimate moments, and my physical sense of violation expelled me. Not once did I arrive to find someone plotting or holding a politically crucial conversation.

I could almost hear the Herskalt, *It's human nature.*

One morning, in reaction to this inner mockery, I left Marloven Hesea entirely and returned to Colend for relief. And why not start at the summit? With a practiced ease that would have astounded me in years before, I reached for Queen Hatahra—to recoil at the blast of fury.

"Duels? *Duels?*" she exclaimed, glaring at Kaidas, who stood before her, resplendent to my eye after so many years of the Marlovens' gray and black (except at New Year's Convocation).

Faintly in the background I heard the carillon for Hour of the Harp as Kaidas bowed, rigid. "I beg your majesty to honor me with permission to repeat myself: I did not know. And the only defense that can be made against the two was that they agreed there would be no fighting to the death."

"They should not be *fighting* at all," the queen retorted. "Send these two hum-bumblers to me. I do not have the slightest interest in the cause, so spare your breath. They are both going to discover the delights of working on their home estates for the next ten years. Maybe twenty!"

Kaidas bowed again.

"My lord duke. I acquit you of blame in this matter. You are here in your martial capacity by my express desire, because we believed we had need at the time, but the *possible* has somehow become *probable*—and not from the Chwahir!"

Kaidas bowed again.

"In fact there has been no sign of trouble with that hummer Jurac for years, and there won't be consequent to the new water treaty, so I believe it is time to retire our Defense with due honors. I am going to award you with a medal tomorrow at the Rising, and send you back to Alarcansa. You may remain for a peaceful New Year's Week at home, and when you return in spring, it shall be as the duke, without sword. The practice hall will be restored, probably to a private theater, since performance is popular again among the courtiers."

Kaidas bowed.

I shut my eyes, disengaging from the queen. From the garden, everything was so much easier, but I had to be careful, for if I stayed too long, that sense of suffocation gradually closed me in. Accelerated if I attempted to experiment with the ward magic.

I drew in a cautious breath and then reached for Kaidas. I found him striding away. The sight of the marble halls and soft carpets of the royal palace struck my heart with such ache that I almost lost him. I had to suppress my own emotions as he paused twice to bow to curious courtiers, their beautiful clothes and graceful poses also sorely familiar. The styles had altered little, except for the fashion for short hair, garlanded with fresh flowers.

All wanted to know what was said in the queen's chamber, that much was clear. But Kaidas was not talking. When he reached the beautiful Alarcansa suite, he let loose a laugh of relief.

Then came the memory, no more than a flicker, but I recovered enough to recognize young Darian of Ranflar, now about twenty, and a Gaszin cousin energetically plying their rapiers as they stood self-consciously, free hand poised in the correct position, faces flushed and startled when Kaidas appeared.

So much for the Defenders, Kaidas thought. *If I'm fast, I can be home in time to see Vasande for New Year's Firstday.*

I completed Signi Sofar's wards. The eleventh layer was simplistic by comparison—it was the first set of wards laid by the Marlovans after they had conquered the royal city. The personal wards were all against specific individuals, mostly Ivandred's ancestors. I even saw the magical print of a ward against all that family, but it had been long since disassembled, though not removed, probably by the unknown hand who had laid the seventh layer.

The eleventh layer took me two days, but then I came to the most difficult of all: the wards laid by the Cassadas mages of Iasca Leror.

From here I began to count anew—that is, in descending order, because I was able to determine how many layers I had to go before I reached the fundament. These layers were all bound to one another. The evidence was clear that these mages had known a great deal more about magic than the Marlovans had. And, like Signi's spells, they were carefully constructed, drawing magic so minimally that the wards were still quite strong all these hundreds of years later. To set a spell so that it would complement a later spell, that was elegant, used very little extra magic, and I was determined to learn how.

But added onto these wards, a much later mage had deftly intertwined personal wards. Think of it (you who do not practice magic) as a persistent ivy plant reaching its roots down into stone. Even if the plant is pulled away at the top, those roots are still alive down there.

I was so busy that at first I was only peripherally aware of the castle beginning preparation for New Year's Convocation.

I did notice that Lasva was absent, her expression pensive, and I attributed this mood to the absence of her son. The queen's rooms were certainly more quiet and orderly—no toys scattered about, no footprints to be swept away. Marnda's querulous voice was absent, a relief that I did not question.

Lasva's emotions were so intense, the pain and sadness and anger and hunger were so raw, that I looked at her less often. I tried Kendred one time, in hopes of finding him content, which I could then convey in some indirect way to Lasva. The result was excruciating physical shock: the boy lay in his bunk weeping, his body a snarl of pains and aches. Why didn't Da save him, he was a king, and Ma couldn't save him because she was too gentle. *No one* could save him! The echo of his wretchedness both physical and mental debilitated me so much that I was unable to transfer until my nerves and muscles—reacting to a beating I had never received—recovered the fact that they were undamaged.

I withdrew into my tower to bury myself in the wards, to be interrupted a few days later by Anhar, who came to request a token for her yearly return to Colend.

After she left, I prowled around my tower, unsettled. The atmosphere of the castle seemed unbalanced. I attributed the sharper voices, the sense of heightened alert to the preparation for New Year's, and consciously avoided everyone.

So I decided to see Kaidas's return home. I wanted to see Birdy again but safely, through Kaidas's eyes. I could not bear the thought of listening to Birdy himself. My guilt oppressed me, for I knew that he would think I had rejected him. And in a sense I had, but only to protect him.

Mindful of the seven or so hours that Colend lay ahead in the progress of the sun, I chose a morning hour and discovered Kaidas in the middle of a party. He breathed in the scents of mulled wine and dried flowers as softly modulated voices conversed. We really did sound like we chanted or sang, I found, after these eight years of consonant-sharp Marloven. Kaidas's interest in the guests was mild. He wanted to go upstairs to the schoolroom: memory, suffused with annoyance, Carola saying, *Vasande may stay among company for a turn of the glass. He requires practice being social. But his manners disallow his remaining.* And Kaidas's annoyance increased to sharpness when she added in her calm lisp, *By the time I was eight, I could be trusted an entire day downstairs,* thereby indicting Vasande's Lassiter half for their son's shortcomings.

Kaidas remained on the other side of the room from Carola, but I got the sense that it was from long habit, because he scarcely looked her way. I was intrigued by the fact that they did not speak to one another. Something had changed with her, and as Kaidas suppressed his impatience to escape to the schoolroom and talked on about a horse race with people I did not know and had no interest in, I considered shifting to Carola to find out what had happened. Especially as this party did not include scribes or others in service.

But then, on Kaidas's periphery, Tatia walked by, her glance so ugly that I shifted to her, to be knocked out of the connection by her wrath. The boy! I braced myself and returned.

Tatia had crossed the room by then. She was fawning on some distant cousin whom she secretly despised. I shut out her voice (and as much of her poisonous emotion as I could) and reached for memory. There was the cause, a recent conversation that Tatia kept recalling, ever more angry: Carola saying *I want a daughter who is mine. I don't care how long it takes, or what means are necessary. With or without Kaidas, I will have a child who is mine, and she will be a daughter.*

And when Tatia tried to offer remonstrance, Carola turned her shoulder. *Tatia, my mind is made up. Now that Kaidas is home for good, he and I will address this matter. It is none of your concern.*

It's time to get rid of that brat, Tatia repeated to herself. But how?

There is no use in prolonging this appalling episode. Over the next two days, as Tatia pondered the way to avoid blame but hurt Kaidas and Carola the most (with mounting self-justification) I pondered what to do with the knowledge if she did make the transition from what-if to action. Because this much I'd learned: people entertained what-ifs in their minds, usually without expecting them to happen, no matter whether the accompanying emotion was vindication, idle longing, or simply entertainment.

I checked in once on Kaidas, at the Hour of Rose, when most work was done for the day. And this time I caught him visiting the place where Birdy lived—a cottage shared with three other scribes. Birdy had a little sitting room of his own where the three sat, spiced wine and elegant bread-bites at hand. Oh, the leap of happiness when I saw Birdy's face—a little older, but otherwise the same, and so very dear.

". . . sorry your correspondent has neglected to respond," Kaidas was saying.

"I think I bored her into abandoning it," Birdy said ruefully. "Neglect was never her weakness."

In the background, Anhar spoke, "Emras is always busy. We seldom see her, sometimes for weeks on end."

"I trust we will not abandon our discussions, especially now that I am returned for good," Kaidas said. "I hoped we could pick up from where we left off, our comparison of our empire built on trade, and the Chwahirs' built on tyranny."

"I don't think it's fair to say it's built on tyranny," Birdy said. "When I was there, they were fond enough of Jurac."

"They don't have to hate a tyrant," Kaidas said. "You should have heard the Chwahir ambassador in the past couple of years, ever since Jurac's Folly. Everything is for the good of the Chwahir."

Birdy said, "There was a lot of that when I was there. Old signs, old rules. Always for the good of the people."

"Which is more overbearing than the tyrant everyone hates. I wonder if Jurac really believes that everything he does is for the people's good? If trying to capture Lasva was to improve the Chwahir culture? He would not be troubled by conscience—he could perpetrate far worse rules than the evil king of ballads, and still think himself just."

Birdy laughed. "From what I could tell during my time there, the Chwahir are loyal. When they aren't, they have a habit of rather summary execution of their monarchs. So the king has to talk up the Good of the People . . ."

Oh, how it hurt me, to hear them talking back and forth with such ease and interest! Nearly overwhelming was the sense that I had lost something precious. It was better not to listen to Birdy at all, even through Kaidas. Those old feelings were better left unstirred.

I returned to Tatia and discovered her carefully unpicking the hidden support seams on Vasande's saddle, as she rehearsed the next step constantly in her mind: bring baked oat-and-molasses treats to the stall of Vasande's favorite horse, and while the animal was feeding, insert a small stone under a back shoe. It was no longer possible, as the queen had said: it was probable.

I still hadn't found a way to reveal her plot without revealing myself. But I felt I had to act. I could not prevent a kingdom from going to war, but I had the information to save one child. I needed only the means.

So many things can go wrong with anonymous notes, beginning with the person never finding it, but I did not know what else to do. After tearing up too many attempts at an explanation without revealing the source, I finally settled on a scrollcase note to Kaidas: *If you wish to save your son's life, observe your son's riding lesson tomorrow. Do not reveal yourself.*

If Carola was still spying on him and got to it first, I did not know what might happen—except that Tatia would probably try another way. But he opened it and stood there puzzled, asking himself useless questions as I writhed with impatience.

I spent that night between Darchelde and the garden, constantly checking. Kaidas slept, but his dreams were a distasteful mix of memory and erotic components. I left quickly and returned to work another hour or two on the wards.

At the Hour of Daybreak, I found Kaidas in the Alarcansa barn hayloft, looking down at the stalls from above. I stayed there, gratified at his shock when Tatia stole into the barn, moving like a shadow. Kaidas watched her talking to the horse in a cooing voice. All he could see from above was that she was doing something at the animal's hindquarter.

Before she scurried away she looked back once, her mouth twisted in a smirk of relief and triumph. He climbed down the ladder. None of the stable hands were about. He let himself into the horse's stall, and ran his hands expertly over the horse's back, legs, and finally, finally he checked the shoes. I waited in agony lest he miss the stone, but he was too expert for that. He pried it loose, soothing the horse, which had shifted uneasily, ears twitching back.

He stood there looking down at the stone on his palm, and then moved to the gear. Again he ran his hands expertly over everything, turning buckles and straps over, until he inserted his finger beneath the saddle—and jerked it out again. Then he called, "Benisar!"

A shout came from the far end of the barn, where there was a faint glow as the stable hands began their day. "My lord duke?" came a call.

"Bring a lantern."

Kaidas waited where he was until the swinging yellow light appeared in the hands of a surprised stable hand.

"Did you see Lady Tatia in here earlier?" Kaidas asked.

"No one's been here, that is, no one came through the palace door," the man answered, staring at the saddle, where Kaidas wiggled his finger through the hole. The man flushed. "I'll turn off Solin this day—the Young Heir's equipment is his responsibility—"

"This is not Solin's fault," Kaidas said. "Thank you." He hefted the saddle and started toward the palace, ordering the words he was going to speak to Carola and anticipating her questions and her refusal to believe anything he said about her cousin.

My concentration was beginning to blur. I released the contact, and my head swam. Swiftly I transferred to Darchelde and fell onto my seat, gulping air.

When I dared to return, I found Kaidas in the middle of ordering servants about. They seemed to be packing. I was going to delve into his memory, when I decided to see it from Carola's perspective.

I shifted—and found her closeted with Tatia, who wept, her thin hands covering her face. ". . . but he's lying," Tatia sobbed. "Someone is. Who wouldn't even come forward—how could you believe an anonymous note?"

"Tatia, the fact that one of my servants was driven to be anonymous deeply disturbs me. Have they been corrupted? I am going to interview every servant, and if you have ever threatened any of them, or done anything like this before, you are going to make restitution."

"I didn't *do* anything. That Lassiter hummer lied about me! He's always hated me!"

Carola paused, seized by memory: Kaidas, saying in the even voice of decision, *I beg to make it clear that I do not hold you responsible for Tatia's action. However, I do hold you responsible for the poisonous atmosphere of this place, which I am ever more aware of on each return. I am going to remove my son not just from Tatia's murderous intentions but from your anger. You are an angry woman, Carola, and anger begets anger.*

"Kaidas has never lied to me," Carola said to Tatia. "Whatever else you want to say about him I will not defend, except for this: he has always told me the truth."

"*I* have always told you the truth."

"I no longer believe that."

"How could you accuse me, your most loyal companion, friend, cousin. You have called me sister!"

Carola turned away from her cousin and stared out into the courtyard. *Kaidas is right. I am so angry*, she thought. *I am so angry that I never knew I was angry.* The anger had dulled down into pain and shock.

She turned around, and the anger flared. "You lied *for* me, Tatia. You lied *for* me to the entire court, when you slandered Lasthavais Lirendi. The moment Kaidas left my chamber I sent the Chief Herald to petition the queen to have you written out of the line of succession. You can kill us all, but you will *never* have Alarcansa."

SIX

OF SWORDS
AND THE PRESENCE OF CATS

As I transferred back to the royal castle, I resolved never to look at Colend again. The matter with Tatia was finished, and the cost was too high. Besides the chance of discovery, there was Carola's assumption that her own servants had written the note and her determination to interrogate them. This was a consequence I'd not foreseen. I did not know what collateral damage my action would do to innocent people.

Then there was the hurt I felt at seeing Birdy, even through someone else's eyes. I did not need all those old feelings stirred up.

"What is your progress, Scribe?"

"I can see the remaining layers of wards," I said to Ivandred. "There are eight."

He gave me a nod of approval, and walked away. As always, I felt relief, and an exhortation to work harder.

Once again I buried myself in work, but my reward was always another visit to the dyr.

As I ran to the queen's suite, I overheard the guards talking in the high voices of celebration. The only person inside was the duty runner, a young Marloven girl. "Where is the gunvaer?" I asked.

"Not here," was the reply.

"Do you know why the bells are clanging like that?"

She grinned, her eyes wide that the Sigradir was ignorant. "Victory ring," she said. "Perideth fell. Jayad is safe, and Perideth—Fera—is ours again."

A day later, the entire castle went wild again. The triumphant king had transferred back, to make military arrangements. Word winged all over that he would stay long enough to preside over a midnight victory bonfire, then he'd be off again. I did not expect to see him and so was surprised when everyone snapped into rigidity while I was at the garrison, busily putting purifying spells on a load of new buckets that would be heading south on a supply wagon.

I finished my work and found Ivandred waiting. "Walk with me," he said and, when we were out of earshot of the others, "You've done well, Sigradir. How is your progress?"

"I believe I have seven layers left."

"Here is some incentive to get the wards finished. When you do, the Herskalt says he can return to us for good. I am giving him Darchelde in the interim."

I said, "Do you need me to go to Perideth, that is, Fera, to establish protective wards?" and then came the question, "Who is going to govern there?"

Ivandred smiled. "You really are the ideal royal mage," he observed with an open-handed, friendly gesture as we started up the stairs. "The Herskalt was right. You have no political aspirations—you don't scheme, you don't even think about such things."

"I think about peace," I said.

The amusement went out of his face, leaving him looking tired, even tense. "Yes. I know. I want it, too. But everything I do to bring peace . . . turns to mirage. Recedes." The guards at the door opened it. When we'd passed through, he said, "The Herskalt promised to see to the Fera wards. He says that these castle ones are the most important of all, and only you can do that. As for governing, I offered Captain Tesar the jarlate. They all know that she's the best of the skirmish captains. She's got relations all over the area. They look up to her there. But she turned it down. Rather stay a captain with the First Lancers than leave them to be a jarlan."

He started toward his chambers, where already there was a crowd waiting for him, many gathered out in the hall. At the sight of us, they all fell silent.

He turned his back on them, blinking rapidly. We had stopped directly under a glow globe; at Lasva's request I'd replaced the torches inside the castle, though outside on the walls they stuck with tradition. Ivandred's eyes were dark underneath, and I wondered how much sleep he got. "I need the Herskalt," he said in an undervoice, in his accented Sartoran. "His grasp of strategy is so . . . I don't see as far as he does. I need him for the kingdom. I need him for the Academy, and the changes he foresees there." Ivandred was soon swallowed up in the crowd waiting to speak to him.

I remembered Fera-Vayir from the Fox memoir, a huge area of land at the southern end of Halia.

I started toward my tower, sick with reaction. All victory meant to me was more war. I did not get far before I was intercepted by Anhar, who had been waiting quietly behind us, properly out of hearing. "She wants you."

I could feel her gaze. I slowed my steps. "Is there something I should know?"

Anhar whispered in our language, "Are you happy?"

I was taken aback. "Happy? What prompts this?" I thought immediately of the horrible Totha magic and wondered if rumor had somehow placed me at this latest battle.

Anhar looked down. My mood shifted when I thought, *she feels sorry for me!*

She said, "I only wondered," as we passed the suite guards. Then she sped away as, behind me, I heard one say tolerantly to the other, "There they go again, talking peacock. You think they celebrate victory with cream cakes?"

"Either that or bonging like bells," the other said, to mutual chuckles.

I found Lasva in her study. I could see my own emotions in her face.

"There will be a midnight bonfire tonight. Singing and drums. That sword dance. If you call it dancing," she said, her fingers opening toward the hall beyond. "They expect it, but you do not have to go. Emras, shut the door, please. I know that you are under orders yourself, but I need you as I never have before."

"Should I know more about what is going on? I only know what Ivandred told me."

"Which is?"

I fell into old scribe habit and repeated his words as exactly as I could.

Lasva was walking back and forth again, from wall to wall, as she listened. "That matches what I know. I wish Tesar had taken this promotion. Hadand talked about the loyalty that comes of surviving terrible events together. Like war. Saving one another's lives, so I guess I can comprehend her preference to stay with the First Lancers. But because she did not accept the promotion, Ivandred has to either choose another southerner who has a lesser claim in others' eyes—which will annoy the northerners, who are all land-hungry—or else give it to a northerner and offend those in the south." She drew a breath. "Especially Danrid Yvanavar."

"Is he plotting against Ivandred again?"

"Oh, no. All the letters say that he is full of praise— 'greatness' and 'glory. ' I find that I do not trust that, it is such a change."

"The Herskalt once told me that he is the most loyal of Marlovens, whatever else we think of him."

"One can be loyal, yet have ambitions that will harm . . ." She shook her head. "Where is it going to end?"

"I don't understand," I said. "Ivandred wants peace, Yvanavar wants peace."

"Yvanavar wants glory." Lasva walked slowly around the perimeter of the room. "As for what happened. The king of Perideth was putting together an alliance to invade the Jayad and Totha, on two fronts. Ten years ago, if you asked me what a front was, I would have talked about artistic embellishments." She snapped her hands down in the shadow-ward, her fingers stiff. "In secret, this king had his people breaking the Compact and practicing with arrows. Which is the reason one of his putative allies slipped the information about the invasion to Ivandred."

"What do they call that, defense or offense?" I asked.

"I call it war." Lasva's voice was low and rough. "I call it a moral trespass, for war is nothing less than the organized murder of other people's children." Her walking so close to the wall, her step so quiet and deliberate, it was more like prowling. As if the room were a cage. "I can't talk to anyone about this. I had to send Marnda home. She's now part of my royal niece's staff. Marnda never recovered from the fact that Kendred did not look back. At either of us."

She lifted her chin, her mouth a thin line as she struggled to contain tears. Then she said, "Ivandred wants another child, Emras. I told him I wouldn't until there is peace. He said, 'I am doing my best to bring you peace.' That's what he said. And now this war." She walked again, as beyond my slit windows across the quad, a ruddy light intensified: they were lighting torches all along the walls. "He wants a child who will learn magic."

"I thought I was to tutor Kendred," I said.

"Oh, he changed his mind. Said there is too much work, magic and command, for one person. He says that an eight year gap is good, for a second son, or a daughter, who would always look up to Kendred . . ." She whirled. "Is it always thus, that we are born to someone's purpose? I was born because of a quarrel between my mother and my sister. Nobody knows that."

I suppressed the words, *I know.*

"A quarrel." She looked skyward, tears gathering in her eyes. "Yet all my life I believed I was born out of love and to a greater purpose. Or are we all chance creatures? Why did the Birth Spell work for an old woman in her seventies, having a quarrel with her daughter, yet it did not come to my sister for years and years? Tell me, Emras."

"I would if I could. My mother would say that however you were born, you are now loved." My voice caught—I had not exchanged a meaningful word with my parents for going on five years, and that only in Name Day letters, but now I wished my mother were here.

Except that I couldn't tell her anything important.

"Love," Lasva repeated, clearly anything but comforted. "I used to know what that means, but I am not so certain of anything anymore." She lifted her chin again. "I do know *melende*. I will keep that promise I made to Ivandred: I will bring no second child into a kingdom of war."

She started toward the door, then turned. "Did you know that this room was where Tdor Marth-Davan once lived? But you haven't read Hadand's letters, have you? Those women were smart, and passionate, and worked for peace. How could they admire that Inda they called Elgar? It is true that he cleared the strait for which he is named, for free trade, but what does that truly mean? It means war, people killing others' children."

That I could fairly answer. "Inda made war because he had to. It's in the full version of the Fox record, not the truncated one that is copied now, all about war and glory. There's a passage that Savarend Montredaun-An wrote, when Inda visited him at Darchelde." I went into recitation mode. *"Inda kicked his heels on the battlement for a long time, then said, 'There's only one way for us to stop looking for war even if we won't stop training for it.'*

'Take the sword from their hands? That will not happen.'

'Not while we are recognizably Marlovan. But if we shift the honor from the kill to the art, might that be a step toward peace?'"

Lasva gazed at me, lips parted. "Taking the sword from whose hands? Marlovens?"

"I think they were talking about the Academy."

"He's talking about their war games. Who would *want* to play war games?" Lasva cried out, then resumed prowling. "I am being hypocritical, Emras." The words were low, as if wrung out of her. Gone was the pleasing Colendi cadence. "Is Norsunder just a metaphor for our own evil? It's in us. It's in *me*. Emras, why is it that strong effort can produce mutual pride—if everyone bands together to rebuild a fallen house, or to shore up a bridge on the verge of crumbling, thus saving lives. Then it's forgotten. But if the same amount of effort is put into a cavalry charge against Olavair, or Perideth, pride keeps the warlike bits of people like Inda living on in hearts and minds through ballads for generations."

There had been something in the Fox memoir. Hadn't he called his own banner—that banner with the strange fox face, that was carried so proudly by the First Lancers now—*the banner of the damned*? I had to go back and look at it again.

Lasva spoke on. "Why do sex and pain go together? I see it in myself, Emras. I am ashamed of this want that I never discovered in myself until I came here. I can't blame the Marlovens, for no one has ever used violence against me."

"It is not just here," I said. "At my Fifteen test, Scribe Halimas talked to us about how Martande Lirendi used his personal beauty as a kind of armor when he rode to war."

Lasva flung apart her hands in Bird on the Wing, her fingers stiff and angry. "I am beginning to wonder if war isn't caused by Perideth or Olavair, but by sex."

"Sex? I thought sex was good."

"It's good for you, we're taught. I do believe that. But, like everything else, there is angry sex, prideful, dominating sex. There is sex where pain heightens the pleasure." She glanced my way and flicked her hand in Rue. "There are also hatred and greed, but when war is propagated by kings and their political boundaries, I can see the sexual drive. The best sex that Ivandred and I have ever had was after one of his wars. I can see the release of having come through alive, but there was the pride of triumph."

"So you feel that men are to blame?" I asked, as a roar went up somewhere outside, and then drumming rumbled in syncopated tattoos. Above that, the rise and fall of many voices in song.

"Women take their share. Watch their eyes, how they follow the man who looks like he might attack anyone in the room if he desired. They respect a woman who can shoot an arrow into a target at a hundred paces—Tdiran did not listen to me until I slashed a cloth with my fan. These Marlovens are angry, because they were raised with violence by those who should keep them safe. Yet they say, *It's better this way, so you can fight the world.* What a way to insure that the world fights!"

I thought of poor Kendred but said nothing.

"So they like angry sex." She whirled around. "Yet I like angry sex. Oh, I am ashamed to admit it, but it is the truth, and no one ever laid an unkind hand on me. Maybe we humans are Norsunder, yet I do not *feel* evil." She drew in a breath. "And we are capable of art and compassion. Ingrid-Tdiran valued the rose carpet as art. And she had the compassion to send Tharais to Enaeran . . . I guess my answer is to go on and use all my wit and strength to, ah-ye, to fight that side of my nature. There I am, using the word fight. Control. Inspire."

She walked to the door. "I have to go downstairs and be seen, Emras." She turned. "At least the question of magic and teaching will not arise until Kendred is permitted to visit us when he turns eight. I got that much of a concession, since he's already broken tradition by going there so young—"

There was a scratch at the door. "Enter," Lasva called.

Anhar walked in, her face solemn as she carefully bore something in her hands.

Lasva looked puzzled. "What is this?"

"A gift. For you, your majesty," Anhar said in Colendi—and in Lasva's lap, she put a lanky orange kitten with a white ear and hind paw.

"Where did this cat come from?" Lasva asked in a high voice.

"I am to say that this is Anise, third generation from Pepper."

Lasva's eyes widened. "Pepper was one of my cats. I do not under-stand."

Anhar gave me a quick glance, her countenance peculiar, smiling and yet uncertain. Then she addressed the floor between Lasva and me. "You once said that if Birdy—if Herald Martande—wanted to return, he could always find work in the stable. And it seems they need help, with so many gone to the south or about to go north. So, ah-yedi! He is here—and he brought another with him, who is now working with the curriers. We know him as the Duke of Alarcansa."

SEVEN

OF A TAPESTRY SKETCH

Lasva stilled, her expression closed. "Please convey my thanks for the gift." She pressed her fingertips to her mouth to hide the tremble of her lower lip, lifted the kitten, and said to me, "I had better see this little creature settled, then prepare for the bonfire."

I followed Anhar out. As soon as the door was shut, Anhar closed her eyes and bowed her head. "Maybe it was a mistake," she said in a low voice. Then straightened up. "Or maybe not. It might take time. They brought that kitten all the way across the continent."

"You knew they were coming," I said.

"It was my idea," Anhar admitted. "She's so unhappy, and, ah-ye! On my last visit, the duke parted with the duchess, and he wanted to go far away. Farther than Lassiter, where his father and his father's new wife are. He did not want any of the duchess's money, and Birdy did not want me to pester you for transfer tokens. So I returned here and arranged for them to be hired. It wasn't difficult. They remembered Birdy, and trained people are needed. They worked their way across the continent."

"They?"

"The duke—he says we should call him Kaidas. That is how he's known in the stable. Anyway, he brought his little boy, Vasande. Come with me tonight, after the watch change. We often eat together. Birdy so wishes to see you."

She whisked herself away. I'd thought Kaidas and Lasva's relationship was a secret I'd shared with Lasva. She had been so careful, bringing him in and out of her suite by the back way—sending me out in her clothes to parade along the Isqua's Assent at the Hour of the Lily—but Anhar, I had learned, was both observant and quiet.

Who was she, really? In her own way, she had influence. How do we measure influence, I wondered as I walked back to my tower, my emotions in turmoil. What did Anhar do now that Kendred was in the Academy, other than water potted plants?

As always, my instinct was to shift to Darchelde, use the dyr, and delve into . . . whose mind? I could not bear to look into Birdy's. The duke would be little better, if his constant companion was Birdy.

I fretted around my work room uselessly until I noticed something in my sketches—had to adjust it—tested the spell, and the next thing I knew the watch bells were ringing beyond my windows, and Anhar appeared in a fresh robe, her hair fixed in a Colendi style.

I brushed drawing chalk off my sleeve. "What are your duties now?" I asked as we walked out.

She laughed. "I'm the Seneschal. You didn't know? Your tower seems to be more guarded than the city."

"I cry pardon," I said. "I have been so busy with my assigned tasks—"

"Oh, everyone knows how hard you work, Emras. And I have seen you. I cry *your* pardon, but I cannot help finding it funny, how powerful you are said to be, yet how . . . ah-ye . . . oblivious."

She chuckled as we ran down the stairs. The stable had living quarters over it, noisy dorms at one end, where younger folk lived, and at the other end sets of four small rooms built around a central gathering chamber. Each had a table and mats all around it. Into one of these shared salons Anhar walked, me on her heels.

The sound of Birdy's voice after so long made me prickle all over, and I ducked behind Anhar as she spoke her greetings. Sitting cross-legged on a large mat in a corner was a cluster of children, plates on their laps, laughing as they ate; a fair-haired boy ate neatly, his fingers passing small bites behind his lips in Colendi style. His eyes were black.

". . . and here is Emras."

Anhar stepped aside, and there was Birdy. He stooped over me, held out his arms, then dropped them quickly to his sides. "Em," he said. "I forgot what a little thing you are." He ducked his head to peer into my face. "You are thin as a leaf. And you look tired. What do they have you do, bespelling horse stall wands all day and night?"

"Something like that," I said. "But I like it."

"You were always a good worker," Birdy said and gestured. "Meet Kaidas."

The duke made The Peace and spoke a formal greeting, as if we were first meeting. I responded in kind as we sat, me at the empty place at the end of the table, Anhar at Birdy's side, their thighs touching. The three stable hands adjacent to me exchanged uneasy looks and left, taking their plates with them, the last one calling to a girl in the corner, "Marend!"

The girl heaved a sigh and got up to follow.

Kaidas put his brows up, and Birdy said, "It can't be us, so it has to be you, Em. Are the rumors true that you slew half an army with thunder and lightning?"

"I used stage magic to frighten a . . . a what did they call it? A wing. However many that is."

"Eighty-one warriors," Birdy said. "How did it get from that to a slaughtered army?"

"The king used some of my spells in another instance," I said. "I wasn't there."

The atmosphere of hilarity sobered, then Birdy shook his head and made an effort to lighten the atmosphere again. "Do they really think you're going to sit down to supper and then smite them with lightning?"

Kaidas said, "I think it's more like they are afraid if they say something amiss she'll mutter something mysterious and their pricks will fall off."

The children in the corner howled with laughter at the word "prick" as Anhar observed with hands at Neutral, "One was a woman."

"Her nose?" Kaidas offered.

One of the children said, "Breasts!"

"You don't have any," a boy said scornfully. "And two things can't fall off for one spell."

"I don't have any *yet*," the girl replied just as scornfully. "So one falls off."

"Maybe your butt falls off," another boy said, causing another howl of laughter.

"That's two things," Vasande observed, two fingers up.

The children went on suggesting body parts as the adults looked my way, then back, and raised their voices tolerantly over the children's. I comprehended two things: that this was normal talk, and that I had missed a cue, perhaps to wave my hands mysteriously and intone something while gazing at someone's body. But I had never done that sort of thing, even as a child. For the first time I wondered if Tiflis had dropped me when I went to the kitchens not because I'd been shamed, or even because I wasn't showing her how to do our work, but because I was boring.

". . . can actually move my elbows," Kaidas observed.

Birdy grinned my way, breaking the unhappy thoughts. "You ought to sup here every day, Em. It's nice to have the room to ourselves for once."

After that it was all chatter. Twice before the end of the shared meal Kaidas asked about Lasva indirectly and listened closely to Anhar's answers. When he finished his meal, he rose, saying, "Vasande. Time for lessons."

The boy executed a perfunctory bow to us, then reluctantly followed his father out.

Birdy turned toward me, and I rose when I saw the curiosity in his face. "I had best get back to work."

Birdy's lips parted. Anhar dug her elbow in his side. He blinked, then said, "I hope you will join us again, Em. Soon."

"When I can," I said.

Kaidas caught up with me before I'd gone fifty paces.

"I'm here to see Lasva," he said, dark gaze searching my face. "Anhar is a romantic. What do you think? Is Lasva happy? Do you think she will talk to me?"

Though all our lives had changed, old habits persist. My hands came up in the scribe's neutral pose, and I expect my face smoothed into scribe mask, for his own expression altered.

"Forgive me," he said. "This should not tax your scruples: if she asks, tell her I seek only an interview. If she asks."

"I will," I promised.

"What did he say?" Lasva was waiting in my rooms when I returned, dressed in her black and gold robes that I usually saw only at Convocation.

"He seeks an interview."

"Why did he come?"

I said cautiously, "Anhar was there in Alarcansa when the duke decided to leave. Did she not tell you?"

"I have never asked about her visits home. I thought my questions might be an intrusion," Lasva said. She passed her hands over her face. "It is better as things are. I must join Ivandred."

———

On his way out of Colend, the kitten cradled in one arm, Kaidas and Vasande had stopped in Lassiter to say goodbye. *You were wrong, Father. Love does not die.*

So you are chasing across the entire continent after a woman who hasn't written a word to you in ten years?

That I am.

The baron had laughed. *Ah, son! I will say this. Even when you act the fool, you do it with style.*

Lasva and Kaidas saw each other the next morning when she went down to the women's side of the garrison to talk about the New Year's roster with the guard captain. Kaidas was in the training yard. He saw the flurry of women guards, and in their center Lasva walked, outwardly like the Marlovens, yet she seemed to float between the long-striding guardswomen.

She knew he was somewhere in the castle and looked around as she hadn't for years. And there he was, taller than she remembered, broader through the chest. His hair was short like laborers wore it, thinning at the temples. The same and not the same.

Their eyes met. Both waited for the other to turn away, then unheeding guardswomen walked between them, and they were lost from one another's view. She turned her steps away, aware of her dry mouth and shaky limbs. It had to be old habit, but even if it wasn't, they were not the same people they had been . . . and love never lasts, everyone said.

She caught sight of her tightly clasped hands and the ring glinting there.

Lasva summoned me later that day. "I think it is time for me to make a journey and talk to the northerners face to face. I will start at Sindan-An, which is almost as pretty as Colend, if you look past the ugly stone castle. I am going to circumvent this war if I possibly can."

She left that day, and I buried myself in wards, inspired by the relief I would feel once I'd relinquished the kingdom's magical guardianship to the Herskalt. No matter how hard I worked, how much I studied, I was never going to understand things like the Herskalt could.

I did not intend to return to the stable, but when Anhar invited me to join them downstairs for Altan fan practice, I could not resist trying just once. It had been so long since I'd done my fan routines I was afraid I'd forgotten, but I swiftly discovered that the body remembers.

Anhar had begun to learn it—and so had Kaidas, apparently as a warm-up during his Defense days. So the five of us (Vasande alongside his father) worked slowly through the forms, and Birdy and I fell right back into our old discussions.

It was self-conscious at first; I had the sense that he'd thought out his questions beforehand. The universality of literature, the effect of interpretation. But from there we launched headlong into all the old byways: food, and its effect on culture, Kaidas admiring local pale ales and rich stouts, and Birdy observing that barley grows well everywhere, even in Marloven Hesea, which is noticeably colder than Colend; the differences between honor and *melende*, especially in court, where what mattered was the style with which affairs were conducted, sometimes more than soft words exchanged during the Hour of Reeds; the Chwahir, Sartor, and political casuistry.

Birdy never asked me about my work.

Two months later, at the height of spring, I received a letter from Lasva:

Emras:

I now understand why I like Sindan-An so much. The first time I was here, I knew so little of Marloven history. This area was reclaimed by the Iascans not long after Hadand was gunvaer, in the first of many treaties of relinquishments by the Olavairan monarchs. It has only been a jarlate (and the smallest) for almost three generations, so though everyone speaks Marloven for important affairs, I notice that ordinary folk converse in their dialect of Iascan (which has Sartoran roots) for day to day affairs. It is so good to hear Sartoran, even if it's not easy to follow. And there are gardens here—flowers have not entirely fallen out of custom.

That is the good thing. The thing I do not understand is this prejudice against trade outside the kingdom. That is, the Marlovens scorn outside goods, but I notice that ordinary folk express a cautious interest.

Everyone is deferential to my face, but where do they get the idea that Colendi are dedicated to decadence and debilitating luxury? I never heard any of this before, but recently someone has been maligning me and warning that my influence will destroy Marloven Hesea because luxury leads straight to the ruin of kingdoms. I have attempted to explain that the ruin of any polity is not the result of luxury itself but more a result of those who expect luxury as a right of birth and not a reward. They agree, but give me that look like, Here speaks the peacock, what can she possibly know?

Time passed. Summer's heat settled over the city. So great was my wish to drop the Sigradir post into the Herskalt's hands that I worked exclusively on the wards, either studying and sketching the structure, or sifting through the former sigradir's messy library, bit by bit, paper by paper, looking for anything about wards. I resented the Sartoran Mage Guild's arrogant exclusivity—I should be able to order the books I needed.

If that library was organized, it was on a system that made sense only to the old sigradir. Either that, or he had built atop older material that he'd inherited. My library excavations paralleled my magical excavations, as I recovered forgotten strata of magic spells, notes, experiments, scrawled in old-fashioned handwritings.

My reward was on the bottom shelf, clearly neglected for centuries: a small scroll squashed flat between a record of household magical spells that dated back seven hundred years, and a Brennic book of stage illusions that had probably been brought by Taumad Dei, who built a theater near the castle during Inda's lifetime.

The scroll was written in Old Sartoran, which I hadn't perused for ten years. Here I found, clearly laid out, some of what I had been struggling to formulate on my own. The most important thing, though, was the comparison between dark magic wards, which are mostly traps, and mirror wards used to reflect magic—think of a mirror set behind a candle sconce—so that less magic was required to sustain a spell.

The first type of spell required strong magic, bound to a protection (with lethal effect). The second was a series of small spells, interlocked in now-familiar chains.

My immediate reaction was, *Now I've got the basics for the bottom layer of wards.*

My second reaction was, *Most of the magic I have been making is the first type.*

I was going to write a letter to the Herskalt when I blinked at the paper, my head feeling odd, as if it might float away from my body. Again, I'd forgotten to eat, and I couldn't remember when I'd slept last. Yet I could not possibly sleep. On impulse I decided to shift to Darchelde and walk through the castle in hopes of finding the Herskalt at a meal, or in one of the other chambers.

I was aware of noise coming from the direction of the stable, but no one was about inside. I passed along quiet corridors, appreciating the decorative touches that had been too austere for my Colendi notice when we first arrived, such as the Venn knots worked into doors and high on walls, the patterned tiles, the carved doors. As I gazed up at them, I sensed magic worked into the painted or carved patterns.

I breathed in, my senses heightened. I felt magic everywhere—the Herskalt's signature. As was to be expected, if he was renewing the protective spells, though my work should certainly have been good enough for another eight to ten years. Also, the spells felt stronger than protective magic, but that might be the peculiarity of walking in an enormous castle without anyone in sight.

I transferred back to my tower when a series of yawns made my eyes sting. The sooner the Herskalt took over, the better, I thought, and went to bed.

One morning, when I walked up to the staff room after an early session with the fans, I discovered that Lasva had returned. I was shocked when I saw her with the strong morning light full on her face. For the first time, I noticed subtle signs of aging in fine lines at the corners of her eyes and across her brow. She was still beautiful, but in the way of a statue, cool as marble.

"Emras," she said. "I hoped to find you out of your lair." She gestured to her private room, and I walked inside, breathing the subtle floral scents that always brought Alsais to mind.

"Was your journey successful?" I asked.

"I did my best, but someone was ahead of me. Everywhere I went, I had to answer, ah-ye, misapprehensions about me. About Colend. It's as if someone did their best to undercut anything I would say. In Tiv Evair, they had the idea that I'd made a secret treaty with Totha at the northern jarlates' expense, culminating in my being given Tdor's trunk, which had not left Totha for three centuries."

"What secret treaty?"

"I don't know." Lasva opened a travel bag and pulled out a ribbon-tied roll of heavy paper. "Then there was Tlennen, who had heard that I wanted to turn Marloven Hesea into a nation of traders. The warriors would become caravan guards." She fluttered the roll of paper in Mock Horror.

"Better that than warriors," I said.

Lasva smiled. "I think so, too, and how could I summarily take their weapons away from them? Then I reached Tdiran Yvanavar." Lasva untied the ribbon and began to lay out the papers on her desk. "She told me the truth, that the north has decided the peace treaty I made with Olavair was a peace without honor."

"How?"

"Because of the granted right of sovereignty." She tapped her head. "Such things—kingship and borders—it's all up here. I understand why people want to be kings, but the people they rule? Why should anyone care if your leader calls himself king or jarl, so long as they are left in peace? But somehow, the ordinary folk in Yvanavar and Khanivar and Tiv Evair have decided that Olavair's being a sovereign nation dishonors the rest of Marloven Hesea. They have always hated the Olavairans. Emras, my mission was a failure. I returned to consider something else, something to try at New Year's Convocation, perhaps." She frowned down at the papers, which I could see were sketches.

"May I ask what those are?"

"Certainly. Tdiran insisted that I honor her with my advice—it seems that she's been taken by the notion of reviving the art of tapestry-making. They have looms, of course, but she has no idea how to lay the whole out. I don't know how serious she is, but I promised I'd try to make some sense of these sketches." Her lip curled. "Not that a battle has to make artistic sense."

"They want a battle scene?"

"The Battle of Andahi, to be precise, where the Yvanavar ancestor, named Hawkeye, achieved a great triumph just before he died on the battlefield." She shook her head. "I suspect they want him at the moment of triumph, judging from these sketches of Danrid, who of course is the model for Hawkeye. This runner is a fine artist, isn't he? It's a remarkable likeness of Danrid, to the toothy smile. And Inda Elgar is to be posed in suitably martial triumph next to him."

"According to the Fox memoir, Inda Elgar was on the cliffs above," I said, glancing down at the sketch she laid next to that of Danrid.

What I saw made me bend down to look closer, for whoever had made these sketches had caught the Herskalt, or someone who looked remarkably like him.

"The Fox writer might have gotten it wrong," Lasva said, looking through the rest of the drawings. "Unless he was there."

"He wasn't, but . . ." *He had someone's memories—he had a dyr,* I thought, and tapped the drawing. "Who is this?"

"Some guard captain, I think. I don't know—he has a familiar face, doesn't he? Hemma, Hanas. One of these odd names."

"Hannik?" I asked. "He's the Yvanavar sword master." Lasva had seen the Herskalt twice, as far as I was aware, once at the Olavair battle and right after the Totha one. Both times she was distracted by other matters, and it was clear from her expression of mild query that he had not stayed in her memory.

But I knew that face well.

"One of their riders made the drawings during training," Lasva said, as she laid the rest of the drawings out on her desk and frowned at them, shifting them this way and that, then standing back to observe the whole.

"May I borrow this drawing?" I asked.

"Certainly. I have him from three angles, as I do Danrid and his favorite cousin. But these two are the best for the purpose of the tapestry." She tapped the two in the center, turned her ring around on her finger, then fluttered her fingers in Rue. "Is Kaidas still here?"

"Yes."

"Then I suppose I must interview him. I perceive my cowardice in avoiding him. In Colend, there are a thousand ways to say *our old love is dead* without ever making a trespass against *melende*. I suppose I owe him that much, though I really do not know why he came."

The problem with the dyr, I thought as I walked out, is that at once you can know too much about a person—that is, facts you might not have wanted to know, and that you certainly cannot share—and yet not understand the person at all. So it was now. I could not understand Lasva's reaction to Kaidas's continued presence.

However, at that moment there was a more pressing puzzle: Hannik.

I transferred to Darchelde, where I half expected to find the Herskalt. He was not there. If Hannik was his brother (he did not look old enough to have a grown son) or even a cousin, it seemed odd that he wouldn't have mentioned it when we talked about Danrid Yvanavar. So I would explore the question on my own.

I settled into my chair, laid the drawing on the table, concentrated and found Tdiran. She was in the nursery with her son, and the daughter who was four. The boy was turning cartwheels as Tdiran admired his looks—annoyance at the thunderstorm keeping her in—Dannor was definitely left-handed. Then the boy knocked over the castle the girl was building with small wooden blocks, which set her screaming. As Tdiran dealt with them, I searched her memory for Hannik . . . and there.

Admiration suffused the memory of a straight-backed figure astride a horse. From the distance he did look like the Herskalt, except his hair was bright, catching the light and drawing the eye. I had to make an effort to look past that long streaming tail of sun-glinting hair . . . illusion?

I searched farther back in her memories for him. Only once did she watch him, but it was from a distance—drilling the men. Tdiran's erotic response to the man's speed and expertise forced me out of that memory. I could find no conversations. Tdiran never seemed to see—ah, echo of conversation, *Why don't you bring him inside?* And there was Danrid in Tdiran's memory, shrugging. *I have tried.*

Can you order him?

No. That was our agreement.

You can't give your sword master an order?

Danrid flushed angrily, looking out a window. *That was the agreement we made. Tdiran, he had me pinned down. He could have killed me, and no one would have known. I've never seen anyone fight like that, he knew every strike before I made it. If he doesn't want to talk to us, he doesn't want to talk to us. I want our people to fight like that. If we do reclaim the north, no one is going to stop us.*

I tried to access Danrid, but as the Herskalt had said, he was warded. All I could "hear" were distorted emotions, and the sound of his voice, but no sense.

So I returned to Tdiran's memory of watching Hannik in training. I tried to access him from there. It was like bumping into a shield of polished steel. Vertigo seized me, forcing me out.

On impulse, I tried to reach the Herskalt and got the same thing, the shield of steel.

So I shifted back to my tower, and for the first time, wrote a note to Ivandred: *I must consult you.*

I sent it and turned to my ward sketches. I was in the middle of an experiment using the slow but subtle magic as set out in my scroll, when I received an answer from Ivandred: *We are camped beside the bridge at Or Arei.*

Where I had first performed magic. I would never forget that place.

When the transfer reaction wore off, I found myself standing in the middle of a camp clearing a few paces from the royal tent, which was exactly like the others only larger, with the Fox Banner suspended from a lance stuck in the ground at one side. At the other, the black and gold Marloven screaming eagle in flight. Above it curved the magnificent bridge. The air was cold.

Around the camp the lancers moved about purposefully. A few stood near the campfire, from which emanated the smell of pan bread baking, a combination of rye and olive oil that threw me back to those days when we first arrived.

As I crossed the muddy ground to the royal tent, I caught sight of Tesar, who lifted a camp cup to me in greeting. Then she went back to her conversation; I saw her laugh, her breath clouding on the air.

I raised my hand in salute, amazed that she could turn down a high rank and a castle of her own just to stand around a muddy camp, weighted down with weapons, eating dry pan bread cooked over a fire instead of properly baked in an oven. Is this love? I wondered. Not the tender passion, as we Colendi would say—though maybe she was in love with someone here—but the kind of love that binds a group into one? Loyalty is one of the great loves, Martande I had written.

Ivandred appeared at the door to his tent, and Haldren Marlovair passed me by, raising a gauntlet in salute, chain mail jingling.

"You have a report?" Ivandred asked. "Wards are finished?"

"I discovered a text by accident that might speed me along. It's a kind of magic that, ah-ye, you may not wish to hear the details." His silence I took as tacit agreement, so I unrolled the drawing, and laid it on the camp table beside the ever-present map.

He glanced down. "It's the Herskalt. Looks like he's demonstrating an upward block against attack from someone on horseback. So?"

"This is Hannik, the sword master in Yvanavar."

Ivandred's brow lifted. "He must have a brother." The brow furrowed. "I can't question Danrid directly, because I cannot interfere with who the jarls hire to train their own people, or how. He might take questions as interference."

"If Hannik is the Herskalt's brother, it seems he would have told you."

"The Herskalt's never said anything about Hannik, other than a report on the fact that the man is a loyal Marloven. The Herskalt talks that way about everyone, as if he knows them. So far, what he's said has proven to be true."

I knew why, but I dared not tell Ivandred about the dyr, if he didn't already know. And he couldn't know. As sure as I could be about any-thing, I was certain that Ivandred, who spent most of every year riding around inspecting his kingdom defenses and preparing for attack, would order me to produce the dyr by any means necessary, so that potential enemies' thoughts could be listened to.

Ivandred said, "I'll ask him. He should be here soon to see our innova-tions in shifting from line to column—" He seemed to see my confusion, and gave me a half smile. "He's been advising me in methods of consoli-dating tactical command through inside lines without dividing my force. Our frontal assault is our best weapon, and . . . heh. I see you are lost. We both have our expertise, Sigradir. Would you like supper?"

He walked out, opening his hand toward the campfire, where Haldren and the other captains sat together on a log, camp plates on their laps, their faces ruddy in the reflected firelight.

I discovered that I was hungry, but stronger than the prospect of camp food was the desire to think about what I'd just heard and to do so at the ground where I'd lain after nearly burning myself to death calling fire from the bridge. The inner perimeter guards saluted me as I left the camp and walked toward the bridge.

My initial thought was that the Herskalt hadn't used the dyr to help Ivandred on his battles, or I would have seen it at Olavair, and I am sure I would have heard about it subsequently. So Ivandred definitely did not know about its existence.

I could see why people hated mages, if they found out mages kept such vital secrets. Secrets are another form of power. What had the Herskalt said about the control of information?

The village had long since been rebuilt, the roofs replaced with tile. Stone had been fitted into the cracks where the old timber had been. It was habit by now to assess magic spells, and here were the expected protections binding the bridge supports, laid by myself during my long journey. How isolated I had felt, how afraid! But not nearly as afraid as the day of that attack, was it really ten years ago?

The residue of magic broke my thoughts. I stepped onto the bridge, sifting the layers, and caught a familiar signature below mine. The Herskalt's. He'd been there.

I remembered the first time I heard his voice. We could not have been far away when he'd healed Retrend and Fnor. I walked closer, extending my hand. Sometimes touching a thing will bring the residue into focus, but only traces remained.

So I transferred back and got to work.

EIGHT

OF EVIL MAGES

Lasva mulled the problem of Kaidas. He'd brought the granddaughter of one of her cats. She felt she owed him an interview for that, but nothing she did was unobserved. For the first time, this mattered. She did not want speculation or rumor starting about someone she intended to see as little of as possible, as all it would bring would be pain. So she must interview him in circumstances too ordinary to be remarked upon.

She walked through her rooms, looking for suitably ordinary circumstances, noticed that her oldest pair of fans was missing, and went in search of Anhar. She found her consulting with the linen-draper. When Anhar interrupted herself, Lasva said, "My old fans. I hope that means you've begun to learn the Altan form?"

Anhar bowed. "You said once that if I wished to learn, I could borrow them. Birdy, that is, Herald Martande, holds a morning practice in the stable rec room."

Lasva had been very proud of the three Marloven runners who'd taken up the fan form, with whom she now practiced each day. But she said, "Ah! I have long wished to practice with other Colendi, and Emras has been too busy these past few years."

Anhar said, "She has been practicing with us most days."

Lasva smiled. "Is there room for one more?"

When you are a queen, Lasva thought, there is only one answer to that, and she saw the effect the next morning when she walked in behind Anhar.

I was as surprised as the others to see Lasva enter. She greeted everyone with grave courtesy, giving Kaidas no more or less attention than she did the others. She took up her stance next to me in our old way and waited while everyone adjusted around her. Kaidas stayed on the other side of the room with his son, who had attracted a gaggle of small children.

It was this son who Lasva looked at, as she did not want to be observed staring at Kaidas. The boy was fair, black-eyed, with a heartrendingly familiar grin. But he did not have his father's easy style. There was wariness in his tight shoulders, in his quick glances. He laughed at himself readily when he stumbled with fan or with the Marloven language: the other children seemed to be delighted by his accent.

In short, Vasande had already made himself popular.

As you might expect, after the time I'd spent listening to Kaidas and Lasva, I was intensely interested in their meeting now. And so, over the next couple of weeks, as I tried to master my scroll's magic forms, I visited their thoughts with the dyr.

There wasn't much to descry. His intense reaction to her appearance that morning was to be expected—so intense he made my head throb with his mixture of hard-reined erotic response and the sharp disappointment when she didn't speak to him except in polite greeting. But she was there. That was all the hope he consciously permitted himself.

She kept putting off the interview. She was busy, the time was not right, too many people around. Yet she returned to fan practice each day.

As the rest of that month veered between hot days and the first intimations of autumn, Anise gained two companions, then three—for once someone adopts a cat, more of them seem to appear.

I was not surprised to be asked to make little houses for their waste like the ones Lasva had had in Alsais. I used Adamas Dei's magic to make them, for by then I'd discovered who'd written my scroll.

Political casuistry . . . the universality of literature . . . translations . . . history and whose truth to trust.

Truth.

What was the truth? Again I had this sense that I was seeing pieces of a puzzle. It struck me when I reached the last section of Adamas's text, where he talked about building a mental shield against the magic of mind-listening. The startling thing was Adamas's wording: *It is good prac-*

tice to prevent the invasion of one's intellect by idle eyes in the Garden of the Twelve.

Idle eyes in the Garden of the Twelve. I had seen the phrase before. It was not until the next morning, when I was moving through Altan fan practice (with Lasva there, the conversations had ceased) that I recovered it: the Fox memoir, specifically the interview Inda Elgar had at Ghost Island with the strange, scar-faced Norsundrian named Ramis, who had calmly predicted his own death. Had he used a dyr? That was a disturbing idea, that Norsundrians might have access to the dyr, too.

———

Three weeks after Lasva joined us in Altan fan practice, the Marlovens found the gunvaer's new area of practice sufficiently uninteresting enough to overlook. Of course the peacocks would flock together—everyone thought that a very good joke.

One rainy day, when practice was over and I'd left for my tower, Kaidas was aware of Lasva listening as he explained to Vasande and his friends how the Altan fan form was actually not Colendi at all, but far, far back in history it had come from Chwahirsland. The old stories were that Chwahirsland was great, back in the days of dragons, but that the great leaders and makers left when the dragons did.

As soon as he finished his historical lecture, the children ran off (undoubtedly shedding most of his words unheard) and he found Lasva walking next to him. She said, "Before I left Colend I gave my dear tabby Pepper to Darva. How did you come by Anise?"

"On my way out of the country I stayed with Darva, and here was the new litter. Darva asked if I might take one west."

"What made you decide to come?"

Here was his moment at last, the one he had rehearsed all across the continent. Even dreamed about. But the Lasva in those dreams had been the young princess, tender and ardent, always on the verge of laughter, and not this woman more beautiful than marble, and about as warm.

However, he did not see the indifference his father had predicted so easily, from the comfortable summit of experience. There was that in the tightness of Lasva's upper lip, the tilt of her chin, that hinted at emotions immured behind a wall of stone as thick as these around him. *Anguish.*

So he swallowed his words of love, and did not mention how court still talked with regret about *back in the princess's day*, because her leaving had somehow taken all the sunlight and music out of Alsais, leaving only false glare and civilized noise.

When you cannot say what is in your heart, what is left? "I gather Anhar did not tell you what happened New Year's Week?"

"I never question my staff about their personal time."

Kaidas took in her guarded expression, her hands gripping the fans, and knew he had it: talk of Colend hurt her. *Begin easy.* So he tried for a light tone. "It's sordid enough that I felt it best to take my son on an extended tour. Very extended. Birdy made this kingdom sound interesting."

"Interesting enough to labor in a stable?" Lasva asked.

"I may as well do it here as anywhere else," he replied. "You'll remember the state of Lassiter affairs. It has not changed, my father having run through both my marriage settlement and his current wife's, and he convinced me years ago that I could never earn a living as a painter." Kaidas hesitated, then took the greatest gamble of his life. "At some point we'll take ship and cross over to Toar. Then onward."

And waited with sick certainty for her to invite him to continue his trip, or ask when he was going to leave, because anguish can turn to anger, and anger to bitterness.

But she turned away—saying nothing—and he slowly drew breath. No conjectures. One hope: tomorrow he might see her again.

She had thought that proximity would be the worst, and she could endure it. But no, talking—hearing his voice—seeing the subtle changes of his expression from delight to the quick lift of brows as he mused some inner thought, then the change in the curve of his lips from rueful humor to a flash of sorrow, quickly hidden again—oh, *how* it hurt! She tightened her grip on her hands until the ring cut into her finger, following Birdy and Anhar out as she talked to Anhar about some castle business, without hearing anything said.

Ivandred and his First Lancer captains arrived at the gallop, horns blaring from tower to tower across the city. He showed up in my lair within a short time after his arrival, and, as always, asked me about the status of the wards.

"I have four levels left," I said. "They are so interlocked. This type of magic is new to me. But I discovered that it was taught by Adamas Dei."

Ivandred whistled softly.

"I'm having to learn it on my own, because I haven't heard from the Herskalt at all."

"I have," Ivandred said as he looked around my tower, and I wondered if he was imagining the Herskalt there instead of me—a far more powerful mage, and someone who could advise on everything, from strategy to training. All I could advise on was styles in scribal writing.

But then he turned back to me. "You won't hear from him until you finish your task, and we can all meet here in Choreid Dhelerei to plan the future."

"Is Hannik the Herskalt's brother, then?"

"No. He's the Herskalt himself, using a family name, he says." Ivandred flashed a brief smile at my astonishment. "He kept his identity a surprise. Said he knew I'd be pleased at the discovery, and his purpose was to bring my training to the north. Foster unity of purpose among the Marlovens. The rivalry with the south could be put to use on the training field. We are only as worthy as our opponents. I know that from my own training days." He indicated my tower. "So your orders are clear: finish those wards. Leave the military training and commanders, to me." He left.

Was he angry with me? I had to know—and so I turned to the dyr. By the time I got to Darchelde and my listening post, he'd gone to Lasva. I found him just as he crushed her in his arms, whispering, "I had to be back for Kendred's Name Day visit." When he began kissing her, I left them.

Later on, I revisited to find them lying side by side, Ivandred running his fingers up and down her ribs to her hip, a gentle but absent gesture. She was instantly minded of Kaidas's clever fingers that gave pleasure as well as took it, but such thinking only cut deeper into her heart. *I have to send him away . . . tomorrow. The weather is too bad now. It would be terrible for his son. I can be strong.*

Ivandred said, "I'm going to take all four divisions of the King's Lancers north to meet the Herskalt—Hannik—and the northerners, soon as spring clears the plains. I wish you would come with me."

"If it's a peace mission, I would most happily accompany you. But if your purpose is another of your interminable war games, I fear I would make myself a nuisance."

"Lasva, I will tell you again, I mean to keep the peace, but—heh! Was that a cat just now, running into your wardrobe?"

"Her name is Anise."

"Colendi?"

"From Colend, yes. I do not know 'anise' in Marloven."

"Someone sent you an orange cat all the way from Colend? We do have cats in Marloven Hesea." He smiled.

"I know. And perhaps you will see two Marloven tabbies when you go in to breakfast, as Patter is fond of egg. The runners named them Patter and Tuft. But yes, Anise was brought from Colend."

"Brought? By whom?"

"Kaidas Lassiter. Who now works in the stable, along with Herald Martande. Back with us again."

"Why would a stable hand bring a cat across the continent? Who sent it?"

"It was his own idea."

Ivandred rose on his elbow, frowning in perplexity. "A Colendi comes all the way here to work in our stable and brings you a cat." His brow lifted. "He brought it for *you*." His tone changed. "A former suitor, or lover?"

Lasva had hoped that this conversation would never take place. But hope always betrayed one. "He was never a suitor," she said. "Being at the time an indigent baron."

"I don't remember meeting any Lassiter. But then I've forgotten most of their names."

"You were not introduced."

Ivandred said slowly, "There is one I remember. The day we scuffled with that northern king. The man who met us on the way back to your palace."

"That is he."

"A former lover, then. Here to see you."

"I believe so," she said steadily.

He sat up. There was a new scar on one shoulder, angry red, slanting below his collar bone. She had not even known that he had been wounded. Again. His hair fell over it. She brushed the lock aside and traced her finger gently over the length of the scar, murmuring, "I think our souls scar as our bodies do."

Ivandred stared at her, wary, perplexed. "Your soul is free of . . . of scars and tarnish. I need that, Lasva. I need you."

"My soul is scarred, too," she whispered. "But I am here."

Ivandred let his breath out. "Do you see him? Lassiter?"

"See?" she repeated, thinking of the many varieties of the word in our language, and the dearth in Marloven. So she defined it. "Yes. Every morning, when we Colendi practice the Altan fan form. Then each of us goes about our daily tasks."

Ivandred gazed intently at her, then passed a hand over his face. "I do not want to become my father," he said and reached for her. "If it pleases you to practice your fans with Colendi stable hands, including a former lover, then so be it." She sat unresisting as he gripped her shoulders. "Lasva. Give me another child."

"I will and gladly," she said steadily. "As soon as I know that that child will be born into a kingdom at peace. I do not feel it now."

"Nor do I," he admitted. "That's why I'm going north in spring. I want to see Danrid and the rest of them face to face. In the field. Every day. Not in a crowd for New Year's Week. Find out what's galling them under their saddles, and form them into unity of purpose, as Hannik says. He will be there to help. Strange, to think of the Herskalt as having a name. If it is his name. When I asked, he said that the name Hannik would suffice. A strange man, he is. Not ten years older than I am, yet he's so knowledgeable. So good with command. Stronger than a tree, too. Sometimes I wonder why he isn't a king."

Lasva had no interest whatsoever in Hannik. She took Ivandred's hands from her shoulders and pressed them between hers. "Bring me peace, Ivandred. And I will do my best to keep it and to raise your children to propagate it."

Two days later, crowds lined the stone walkways around the palace. I hadn't realized how highly people regarded the little prince. Rather than squeeze into the crowd, I took myself to Darchelde, and thence the garden, to watch with the dyr.

I oriented myself through Lasva's gaze, as she stood beside Ivandred to watch the Academy gate open. But her thoughts were turbulent, a dizzying mix of erotic memory, sorrowful awareness of Kaidas somewhere in the castle, and anxiousness to see her son after a year.

Kendred walked out, thin, even weedy, his upper lip lengthened as he tried to suppress a self-conscious smile; I shifted to his thoughts. They were turbulent, too. He was pleased, but shy of all those staring eyes, after a year with only the Academy. His heart pulsed with baffled love when he spotted his parents. His mother with tears in her eyes. His father tall and strong. But neither had saved him from Them. (Image of towering instructor brandishing a withy cane.)

Then he caught sight of Vasande—a boy his age, one he didn't know—among some of his own castle friends, and his interest sharpened before his mother's arms closed around him, and she smothered him with kisses.

I disengaged, stepped out of that airless garden, and set down the dyr. As had become habit, Adamas Dei's words about the idle eyes in the Garden of the Twelve prompted me to practice the mental shield. I already had the habit of shutting out the world, so the conscious building of a mental wall from within had come easy. Then I turned my attention to the magic over the dyr, but I assessed it using Adamas Dei's magical approach.

This time I could see the layers clearly. I could even have removed them, with no more difficulty than snapping a series of spider webs. If the Herskalt were to set that as a lesson, I would prove my prowess as a mage!

After these experiments, I checked back with Kendred. He was not with his parents at all—his vantage made me dizzy as he lay on his stomach in a tower crenellation, his elbow jammed up against someone else as he stared down at the neat alignment of rooftops. ". . . and there. That last one? That's where the scrubs sleep. Everybody is ten except me, but we're supposed to have seven-year-olds in spring." Kendred flushed with morose triumph. "I'll still be a scrub, but they'll be lower." He envisioned himself thrashing a younger boy—faceless, weeping loudly.

"We don't have any academy. Not like that." It was Vasande—and they were speaking in Kifelian.

"Truth?" Kendred's foremost emotion was scorn but under that was envy.

"We have lessons at home."

"You must lose all your wars."

"We win them."

"All? Mother wouldn't talk about wars, except that King Martande the First won against the Chwahir."

"All," Vasande repeated, and though Kendred was not looking at him, so I couldn't see his face, perhaps Vasande saw some of Kendred's resentful anger, because he added, "My Aunt Tatia tried to kill me. That's why I am here."

"She did? I only had one aunt, and she was *old*. How did she do it? Sword? Knife? How did you fight her off?"

"I wasn't there."

"Oh." Kendred's disappointment verged on disgust.

"So show me how tough you are," Vasande said. "Cam says you're supposed to come out of there tougher than anyone. Let's scrap."

"Behind the bake-house is where we always go."

I disengaged. The prince had obviously rejected the day of activities that Lasva had planned, and with the unthinking selfishness of children, had run off on his own pursuits. No matter how much it hurt her, she would never constrain him. I did not want to hear her emotional pain, so I listened to Kaidas, who was on duty. He and the stable hands were busy with the newly arrived horses, the latter bragging about the exploits of the First Lancers.

Kaidas's thoughts veered. He remembered the single glimpse of Ivandred he'd had so far, when Lasva rode on his horse after the rescue from the king of the Chwahir. Now a king of a huge kingdom that was about to become bigger, if the gossip was right. *If I can see them together, I'll know what hope I have*, that was the gist of Kaidas's thoughts, over and over. The rest was a confusion of what he'd say in this instance or that. . . . I left him, as by then my head was panging.

But the yearning to see more had not abated. So I worked through the layered wards on the dyr again, a soothing task, until the headache abated enough for me to look again.

To be hit with Lasva's heightened distress as she stared down at Kendred, who said proudly, "He's nine, he's bigger'n me, but I thrashed him good." He turned his head, and she reacted with pain at the blossoming bruise on his cheek. "Da, what They teach us, it works, it *works*."

"Did this boy challenge you?" Ivandred asked. "You did not attack him?"

"Yes," Kendred said. "He said, let's scrap. He said he didn't think the Academy was any good."

Lasva left them. She ran down to the stable, where she found Vasande being cleaned up by his father. Kaidas gazed at her over Vasande's head, but she did not address him.

She knelt down beside Vasande. "I beg your pardon on my son's behalf," she said, working hard not to let him see the sorrow that filled her heart. "You are a guest. Fighting is uncivilized behavior."

Vasande had been holding a cloth to his bleeding nose. "I said we should scrap," he mumbled. "I didn't think he would hit so hard, he's so puny."

Lasva looked at Kaidas and Carola's child, helpless, grieved.

It was this grief that Kaidas saw.

Lasva sensed his scrutiny. She turned her attention to the boy's wide black eyes framed by long lashes, fair hair, bones already showing the planes of his father's, the same cleft in his chin. "Are you happy here?" she asked, though she hadn't meant to.

The parallel to Kaidas's thoughts unsettled him, and he walked out in search of healer's steep.

Vasande jerked up a shoulder. "I hate my mother," he told Lasva calmly.

Her throat ached. How unbearable it would be if her own dear son said such a thing! Guilt for sending her own son to that horrific Academy, combined with memory, prompted her to say, "Please don't hate her. I know she loves you, though maybe you do not yet see it."

The boy regarded her steadily, his face unchanged—*melende*. "She hates everybody," he said. "She hates *you*."

"I think she did," Lasva responded and then spoke a secret thought, and not about Carola, whom she had never known. "Sometimes . . . ah-ye, how to say it. Sometimes hate is misplaced love."

But she just confused the boy. "Did she lose love? For you?"

"Not for me, though I did try to become her friend. But I wonder how much love she learned from her father. Though she inherited great wealth, as you know. Perhaps it makes more sense to say it this way, that I think her inheritance of love was very small. You probably know that when people have little of a thing, it's soon spent. And they cannot find any new."

"We don't have any money," Vasande stated, in the same matter-of-fact tone he'd said *Let's scrap*. "Not anymore. We did in Alarcansa. My father says that maybe I can go back and be a duke, but he can't go back."

"Do you want to go back?"

"My Aunt Tatia tried to kill me." Now he was bragging, though his tone was morose. "Ow." He winced when he daubed his nose. "I'm supposed to have healer steep."

"Your father went to get some. Shall we find him?"

As they walked out together, I left them, as by then black spots swam before my eyes. I stumbled out of the garden and put my head down on the table. It took a long time to recover enough to transfer. I'd listened far, far too long with the dyr.

The next morning, I felt as if I'd fallen down stairs, but I forced myself to the fan practice so that no one would remark on my absence.

The result?

"What did you do to your eyes?" Anhar gasped. "They are red as cherries."

"Translating an interesting text," I said. "Very late."

At her shoulder, Birdy stared in horror and disbelief.

I hated myself for yet another lie and took up my stance. At the end of an excruciating practice, and since Birdy didn't believe me anyway (I thought irritably) I decided I might as well stay in my tower until my eyes cleared.

I set myself the task of finishing the translation of Adamas Dei's text, which I knew would help me replace the wards that much more easily. There were few pages left, but this translation—this magic—was more difficult, complex, challenging, than anything I'd done yet. He talked about mirror wards that stepped not only outside of place but outside of time.

The latter, he said, was the basis for Norsunder.

When I reached that, I could not halt my experiments, I *had* to know, to understand. Once again I sensed pieces of a vast puzzle assembling around me, just out of sight. This vague misgiving grew to anxiety as Adamas carefully set out what he'd learned from his tutor—a mysterious figure he never named—about Norsunder's magic.

This text was a lesson in how to fight Norsunder's magic at its fundament.

While I labored at that text, Kendred vanished back into the Academy. New Year's approached, arrived, and oaths and judgments went on below as I kept studying.

With the first clearing of the new year, Ivandred came to see me. I told him that I knew what to do with the those remaining four layers of protective wards. I had assessed the structure clear down to the first, establishing layer. I promised him that after a couple weeks of work it would be finished.

He gave me his characteristic short nod of approval and walked out. Shortly thereafter he rode out side by side with Haldren Marlovair, the Fox Banner streaming, the deep, mourning bawl of the Venn horn louder than the brassy trumpets pealing chords from the towers.

I had five pages left to translate. Ivandred was gone, so there was no hurry to complete the ward project. For my own satisfaction, I decided that I would finish the Adamas Dei translation first, and then, to celebrate, I'd attend to the wards. Then I could send the text to the Herskalt along with the news that the wards were finished at long last.

The morning I finished translating the text, I walked out of my tower in a daze, my feet taking me by habit toward the queen's suite. When I turned the first corner I was nearly knocked down by Anhar, who righted me and greeted me with a smile. "You're with us again! What did you find this time?"

I was so tired that someone else seemed to use my voice. "An old scroll. In my tower library. Been there for centuries."

"Of course you had to drop everything and translate it," Anhar said, laughing. "What scribe, even if she's become a mage, could resist? But—if you will forgive a trespass—you look as if you could use some exercise."

We had arrived at our practice room. Lasva was already there. As I took up my fans I stared down at my feet, blinking. My memory supplied the day of my Fifteen, and my own feet looking like half-furled fans. I swayed with vertigo, as if I was looking in the dyr at my own memories. I had to shut my eyes and breathe.

Once I began the first move, my body took over, and oh, it felt good to breathe and step and swing. Gradually the world reassembled itself around me. They were talking.

The word "Chwahir" had caught my attention.

". . . there was never any chance that the Chwahir were going to come over the mountain again, after the Great Flood," Kaidas was saying, as we stooped, slashed, and snapped our fans.

"The Great Flood?" Lasva asked.

They're talking, I thought. *Like the old days, even though Lasva is here. When did that happen?* I had not listened with the dyr for days, and the urge to go right then was nearly overwhelming.

"Spring of 4412," Kaidas said. "You were not hit by it here?"

"We had a very, very late winter, and then we went almost straight into summer," Lasva said. "I threw a Flower Day celebration in the castle because it was still snowing once a week or so. We did hear about some flooding up north. I gather this was widespread?"

"Down the northern end of the entire continent," Kaidas said. "That is, the spring storms curled in an enormous spiral over the western mountains, instead of spreading out over the continent. So from Lorgi Idego to the Brennish peninsula there were swollen rivers and floods. When the winds changed that summer, the sky dried up. Chwahirsland went almost overnight from frigid to heat. No rain at all that year. Almost as bad the next, so we ended up renegotiating the treaty. We gained more of their ore, in trade for releasing some of our dams on our side of the mountains and redirecting the flow."

"Tell her the rumor," Birdy said.

"Which one?" Kaidas laughed as his fan clacked shut then spread, and he twirled around on the balls of his feet. "Queen Hatahra was fluently skeptical about the Sartoran Mage Guild's insistence that some evil sorcerer had taken up residence in some mysteriously hidden prominence in Ghildraith just to perform evil weather magic."

Shock sent my nerves running cold, and I counted back. It couldn't possibly . . . no. Relief flooded through me. It was true that my experiments had taken place in those mountains, but they were a vast and mighty range. More than one mage could have been there, and anyway, I'd stopped when winter froze the air around me, late in 4411. The year previous to the one in question.

"Weather magic?" Lasva asked. "I thought that was forbidden, save in drought conditions, when the mages, at great cost, would do something to cause clouds already present to drop their rain."

"It *is* forbidden," Kaidas said. "From what we heard at court, the mages don't like to interfere with a local storm because of the consequences farther on. If we end a drought, say, over Eth Endra, then that can worsen conditions as far away as Sarendan for the next season, or even two."

"How is that possible?" Anhar asked. "Emras?"

I said stiffly, "I have not studied weather magic." *Ignorance is no excuse for the powerful, isn't that what the Herskalt said?*

"Don't ask me, either," Kaidas said. "Hatahra flat refused to believe it. She said that the mages were making up alarmist rumors to explain bad weather in order to hike the fees they charged against governments. All this was before the royal princess produced some book or other from her own magic studies that authenticated the rumor, after which we didn't hear another word about weather." He chuckled. "All I can say for certain is the result: that and a pair of fools going after one another with swords is one of the reasons why I am here training fine young colts, and not swanking about court in Alsais, trying not to sit on my sword."

Was I the cause of that disaster? I concentrated on my breathing as my body went clammy. *Finish the form*, I told myself.

"What I do not comprehend," Lasva said, "is why anyone would do such a thing? I do not mean the pair of fools, I mean the evil mage. Though I can imagine that my sister inquired closely into the intent of that pair of fools."

"Evil has its own purpose," Kaidas said. "So we're told. Tip a rock for the fun of seeing an avalanche. No thought to anyone below."

"It wouldn't have to be evil intent," Birdy said.

"Surely you do not claim a benign intent?" Lasva responded, her fan flicking upward in mock horror.

Birdy said in that musing tone that was so familiar, hiding a question beneath. It had been this way when we were young, and he'd gotten a mark for undue influence. "What if there was no intent at all ? What if someone merely thought to experiment? Someone who has, perhaps, slowly shifted from doing what is right for the common good to justifying doing what feels good?"

He knows. He knows that I was the one.

Then he said, "Emras, are you all right? You look pale."

"You have been sitting too long," Anhar said. "Would you like me to fetch you some healer's steep?"

I opened my eyes to discover the others still working but all looking my way.

"I am fine," I said. Again, my voice sounded like someone else's. I wanted to offer an excuse, as I always had, but the words dried up.

Somehow the practice ended, somehow I got away. I stood in the middle of my workroom, shivering as I stared at my desk. My recollection was as clear as always: I had asked the Herskalt about damage to the Marloven crops, and he'd responded that it was an excellent idea, that he'd made me a Destination square in the Ghildraith mountains, where there were always storms. Nothing about further damage.

Was it possible he did not know? But how could I find out if what Kaidas said was true? I had no books about weather magic. Maybe that was my answer. Because it was forbidden?

Adamas's text, the form of magic that I had mastered, the words I'd heard . . . idle eyes in the Garden of the Twelve.

Overmastered by need, I shifted to Darchelde, took up the dyr, and faced the wall. Where exactly was this garden? *Garden of the Twelve.* I shuddered. Now I was just scaring myself. Any garden could be marked off by strong wards.

Like mirror wards that displaced location. And time?

I looked around me. The secret room, I already knew, was accessible only by magic. The ward, so complicated-seeming on my first visits, was easily descried now. I could use the Herskalt's own ward and mirror it from the inside to create my own secret chamber, hidden within his.

Then I created a magical barrier blocking off that transfer wall between his chamber and the garden. No one was going to come here from that garden, whether it was in Norsunder or not.

Inside my new secret chamber, I employed the interlocking chain of mirror wards that Adamas Dei had taught me, link by link, layer by layer, until I had made a facsimile of the garden, displaced from the physical world. This was an exhaustive method, but it avoided the burning power of what Adamas Dei called dark magic. The kind I was used to.

That timeless sense coalesced around me.

When it was finished, I took the dyr into my lap. I concentrated on Fox, whose voice had become so familiar through his writing. I reached for the day he faced the same Ramis who had told Inda that he was watched by idle eyes in the Garden of the Twelve.

Even with the mirror wards, the reach so far back in time wrenched my skull from the inside, distorting color and sound, but I didn't need to hear the words. I'd already read them. All I needed to see was the man with Fox, whose face was marred down one side. Illusory magic. But illusory scarring did not keep me from recognizing the plain brown hair, the still body, the amused hazel gaze of the Herskalt.

NINE

OF THE MUTABILITY OF TIME

M y first thought was that it was impossible. Fox had lived more than four hundred years ago. Except that there was no record that he had ever died. Just that he'd sailed away. Beyond time, some insisted.

A few of the rumors even placed him in Norsunder.

And that brought me back to the Herskalt, who had not told me the consequences of weather magic. I could not believe he didn't know the possible effects. So if he knew, then . . . My thoughts ran to the Garden, and from there to the Garden of the Twelve, which Ramis had implied was in Norsunder.

I had my sign of Norsunder at last: the person training me.

Disbelief was my strongest reaction, followed by question. Why?

The next reaction was anger. My first impulse was to wrench off the toe ring I'd worn for ten years, toss it, and hand off the problem to Greveas or her superiors. However, I could not do that. First, Sartoran mages had been warded from transfer at the border. It would take weeks, maybe months, for Greveas to arrive the usual way.

And what would happen to me when she got here? Would I be clapped up somewhere, unable to act, because of my evil deed, however unintentional?

My neck ached, my eyes burned. I was thirsty. But I had to think this matter through.

I tried examining my evidence from the perspective of time: my first magic spell, there at that bridge. Anyone could have soaked the wood with oil, but the weather had been so bad that only magic could have spread that fire. And I'd found traces of the Herskalt's magic there. That was not proof that he'd accelerated that fire, but if he had, why?

Another of his tests, to see who was strong enough to extinguish those flames by magic? Then came Darchelde and the archive, and again I was tested, and survived. Was the weather magic a test? If so, what was his purpose? A Norsundrian lord, capable of powerful magic, spends all this time helping Ivandred with his political unrest and army training, and trains a scribe to become a mage?

Something was missing. And maybe I was not capable of seeing it. What had Birdy said? *Someone who has, perhaps, slowly shifted from doing what is right for the common good to justifying doing what feels good.* Someone who has gently but firmly been guided from moral certainty to casuistry.

The urge, the *need* to break the shroud of secrecy and lies was so overwhelming that I raised my hands to transfer right then. But when I tried to stand I staggered, giddy to an astonishing degree. My hand clutched the table as I steadied myself, causing the porcelain bowl to rattle, and I remembered the dyr.

If the Herskalt was truly a Norsundrian, whatever his purpose, he would need the dyr to listen to us all.

Second certain thing: he had not been here since my arrival, so he could not have listened to me, which meant he could not know that I had seen him in Fox's memory.

I have to take it, I thought, gazing at the dyr. But I remembered what he'd said about transporting it. Whoever he might be, so far he had not lied outright.

I had not yet replaced those last four layers of wards over Choreid Dhelerei, but I knew the traps and personal wards. Though I did not recognize any of the names, one thing was for certain: no ward against the dyr. Therefore, the ward against transporting it had to be buried somewhere in the Darchelde protections. There were a lot of these. But I could bypass them by placing one of those false walls—a transfer access—similar to the one that opened to that garden. Only the access way would open directly to my tower in Choreid Dhelerei.

Tired as I was, having a goal restored me enough to perform the necessary spells. Then I finished by removing the spells around the dyr. My mood was dark enough for me to think, *If something happens to me, it's no more than I deserve.*

Nevertheless, my heart pounded unpleasantly as I picked the dyr up and then turned it over in my hand. It felt like it looked, a heavy object not quite stone and not quite metal.

I dropped it into my robe's inner pocket, where scribes usually kept their tools, then stepped through my access way into my tower.

Nothing happened.

I looked around again, startled to find the room so warm, especially as the fireplace was bare. The air was not only warm, but fresh. I wandered to my bedchamber, but my jug of fresh water was empty. I could summon a runner . . . I could get water on my own . . . But it felt good to sit down on my bed and then to stretch out my aching body.

I woke when someone gave a gasp.

I opened my eyes to discover a runner staring at me. An image of myself, starkly staring—pale, even gray-faced, struck me behind the eyeballs, and I closed my eyes. "Water," I whispered, my hands over my face.

Surprise, dismay, the urge to run goaded me before the door shut.

Oh. The dyr in my pocket was bringing me the runner's emotions. In spite of the throbbing headache, I rebuilt my mental shield. The reward was blessed quiet. I was alone in my own skull.

The door opened, and the runner was back with water. I drank down two glasses, gasping for air, then wiped my eyes on my sleeve as I became aware of the rustle of cloth, the manifold breathings of several people.

"Emras?" That was Anhar, speaking quietly. Cautiously. "You're back."

She and Pelis and two more runners gazed curiously at me.

"Where have you been?" Pelis asked.

"Been?" I repeated witlessly. "I was on an errand," I said in Kifelian, "I was just here yesterday. Wasn't I?"

Anhar and Pelis exchanged looks, then Anhar said, "If you were, no one saw you. No one has seen you for eight, almost nine months."

I gave a cry of dismay; I wanted to disbelieve them. "The Fox vision," I said. "That single glimpse must have thrown me out of time for nine months. I did not know that time would be so unreliable—" I stopped myself before I loosed incomprehensible babble about magic. "I'm glad I didn't listen to an entire conversation, I might have vanished for a hundred years."

I became aware of painful silence and looked up. Four sets of eyes stared back at me.

The time for secrets to end is now, but don't be stupid about it. I rubbed my eyes, gathered my wits, and switched to Marloven. *Normal. Sound normal.*

"I need a bath," I said, and watched the runners' faces clear at that. Pelis as well.

As they all turned away, I caught Anhar's robe. "Get Birdy," I whispered wordlessly.

Her brows shot up. She gave a slight nod, ducked around the others, and fled.

Nine months? Reaction wrung through me, my limbs watery.

Birdy and Anhar arrived together, both breathless. "I had to say you sent for him," Anhar said. "He was on duty."

"Please tell me what I've missed," I said, no longer trying to hide my urgency.

Birdy came up to me, his gaze searching mine. "Will you tell us what *we* have missed?"

My heart beat hard. "I will," I promised. "Where is the king?"

"He's been in the north since spring. Lasva went to join him early in summer."

"She was in Olavair," Anhar put in. "Talking to the Northern Alliance. She says they want Ivandred to agree to the Compact against arrows. They all have their hair cut short."

"Prince Macael's brother hired mages to cause an avalanche in both passes," Birdy said. "High and low. There's no crossing over to Enaeran."

"Has Ivandred declared war?"

"It has not been declared. But he's been riding around up there, exercising the army. You know how the king can call up levies if the kingdom is in danger? Well, levies have been raising on their own, volunteering all across the north—"

"Yvanavar, Tiv Evair, Khanivar," I said.

"Not just them," Birdy said. "Sindan-An, Tlen, and Fath as well. They seem to have united in one purpose, to regain their hereditary lands. Their cry is 'river to river.' I guess that means the glorious Marlovan empire of old, which was bordered between the rivers all up and down Halia. But Ivandred has held out against declaring war against the northern kingdoms. He says that no one has broken any treaties."

"A moment," I said. I shut my eyes, released the shield and concentrated on Lasva, partly to test my reach with the dyr—and there she was,

desperate to keep her voice even, to hide her anger as she said, *Danrid,
permit me to disagree. Heroism is not overlooking wounds, tiredness, fear, in
order to kill others, but in overlooking wounds, tiredness, fear, to save others.*

I snapped the shield close again.

"Em?" Birdy had knelt down directly in front of me.

I took a deep breath. "I believe I am in trouble," I said. "And if I am
right, so is Ivandred. And Lasva. And the kingdom." I reached for the
water. "This will take some time."

Anhar said, "Then you had better eat something. You look dreadful,
Emras. No trouble, I've found, is the easier to solve while hungry."

"You are right," I said. "I'd be grateful for some bread and cheese."

Anhar whisked herself out. Birdy stomped purposelessly to my desk,
glared at it, then came back, decision in his face. "Emras, the truth is, I
came back because of you. Not so much because you didn't write—
people do get tired of other people and move on, I understand that, I've
done it myself—but there was something in your last letters, an evasive-
ness that was so unlike you. Unlike who I thought you were. Ah-ye!
That is not what I meant to say. I thought, ah, how to say it? That you
were turning into a Marloven. And it was all right," he added hastily.
"Lasva had married one, she meant to be one. But Anhar said you were
in trouble."

"Anhar? Trouble?"

"She couldn't tell me what it was. Only that you worked harder than
anyone else, but you didn't talk to anyone, and you seemed to be living
under the shadow of Thorn Gate. And we began to wonder what they
were making you do."

"She never said anything to me about that."

"Oh, she did. She tried. You fended her off." He gave the old gesture
for south-gating, and when I stirred to protest, he went on quickly, "She
told me early that Lasva and Kaidas had been lovers right before they
both married, which made sense of all his questions about Lasva. Because
each year, he always came to me for news of her. So last year, when the
duke wanted to leave Colend, Anhar and I thought of Marloven
Hesea—so Kaidas could speak to Lasva, and I, you." He gave a short sigh.
"But you didn't want to talk to me. Ah-ye*di!* This was much easier in my
head, when I thought it out a thousand times, crossing the continent. I'd
say how much I cared, and you would fall into my arms." He hugged
himself, making smooching noises, then grinned crookedly.

"Birdy, I can't do that."

"I know. I know. It is not your nature. I am joking, see? Only it's not a joke if no one laughs, is it? The other thing I thought you might say would be, *Birdy, I was so lonely.*"

And I said unsteadily, "Birdy, I was so lonely."

He dropped down beside the bed, all the humor gone. "Talk to me, Em. Just talk. Tell me why you pushed us away, even after we found out you were a mage."

"Yes," I said. "That is what I intend to do." Now that the time had come, I did not know where to begin. With my first lie to Birdy? Or should I begin at the end and work backward? "Kaidas and his son. Are they still here?"

"Yes." Birdy frowned down at his hands, then said, "Fan practice had become the best part of our day. I am willing to guess it was Lasva's, too. All we did was talk. But there was one day, late in spring. Kaidas was telling a story about one of his colts. It was funny—he'd been kicked several times, and then this colt nipped him, and he fell . . . yedi! The point is, we were all laughing. Anhar could not remember hearing Lasva laugh since she was first hired, back in Alsais. Kaidas and Lasva looked at each other, and she turned away, and wiped her eyes, and next thing we knew, she and some of the guard women were riding for the north."

"I can find out what happened," I said, figuring that this was as good an entry as any.

"You can?"

"Right here. Right now. At least, I think I can hear a memory from here." I closed my eyes and concentrated, but the moment I lowered the shield and reached for this memory of Birdy's, there were his thoughts: worried, tender, fearful, uneasy. I forced the shield up again, before my mind could delve into his.

"Emras?" he said, on a new note.

"I think I'd better begin back in Alsais," I said. "When Tif sent me a magic book, because I asked."

I was still talking when Anhar returned. The sight of food woke my appetite, and though I kept talking as I ate, which is vulgar behavior in Colendi, the other two gave no sign that they noticed. They were concentrating too hard on my words.

When I reached the recent events at last, Birdy said, "Have you listened to me?"

"Only that once."

"Can you hear me now?"

"I have the shield up." I tapped the top of my head.

"Try," he said, watching me intently.

"Are you sure?"

"I just want . . ."

"Proof?" I asked, knowing that I deserved his disbelief.

"Ah-ye, I believe you, it's just that I want to know what that thing can do. May I see it? I won't touch it."

I took the dyr out of my pocket and laid it on my hand.

"How can a thing make others hear thoughts? Might I try it?" he asked.

Fighting my intense misgiving, I laid it on his hand. He looked at me, then quickly to Anhar, as if to avoid hearing my thoughts, then stiffened. He was within arm's reach of me, which was the distance I'd always maintained from the dyr, so I heard the clamor of his emotions, Anhar's, and mine echoing back at me through the distortion of Birdy's perception.

He gasped and snapped a strained look my way. "It's like you poked me from inside my skull." He threw the dyr in my lap. "That's enough of *that*. It's . . ."

I heard *evil*. I put up the mental shield again.

"Dizzying," he said. "So this is what mages learn to use?"

"Yes. That is," I corrected myself, wondering how much of what the Herskalt had said was true. "So I was given to understand."

He grimaced. "I think you'd better start by questioning everything that man told you." He shook his head. "I can't even think, my head hurts too much. Anhar, what think you?"

"I'm not a planner." She gestured Rue.

"You are deft at seeing what is there."

Anhar said slowly, "That kind of trespass, it is almost as evil as days before written history, when there was sex without consent."

I made a warding, too distressed for words.

She gave me a glance of sympathy, but went on. "You could say no, not the same—the person doesn't feel it—but this is even more intimate, and the scars here and here." She touched her head and heart. "Would be terrible if you revealed these things to others. And what if you can use it to force ideas into someone's head? Like the enemy commander that you mentioned, could you bend this commander's thoughts by your will to force him to lose a war?"

Birdy turned my way. "Can you?"

"I do not know. I never tried any such thing. I only listened."

"Without consent," Anhar repeated, and I winced. *This is a direct consequence of my actions.* "So far, from what you say, the only evidence we have of any mage using this dyr is Ramis, who you think is your Herskalt."

"From Norsunder," Birdy said. "So we can assume evil intent."

"Can we?" I said. "Oh, make no mistake. I will never again step into that garden. I see it was set up to lure me, and the trap could snap around me any time. I even know the magic for it. But why would someone from Norsunder spend all this time to help Ivandred train his army? Is that evil? Lasva thinks any war is evil, but the Marlovens all seem to want their kingdom reunited. They aren't evil people."

Birdy said, "I don't think we can define Norsunder and its goals while sitting here."

"We have to figure out this man's goals if we are to convince the king," I said. "And the key is Darchelde. That much I am certain of." The euphoria from the meal had worn off, leaving my body feeling leaden. My throat hurt, which I attributed to the amount of talking I'd done—more than I had in years. "I beg your pardon, the both of you. Though I know how inadequate it is."

Anhar said, "You have mine. Easily given, as your trespass against *me* was so small." Birdy nodded as she said, "The hardest pardon lies ahead of you."

Lasva.

"I know. But first, perhaps, I ought to contact the king about the greater matter."

Anhar put her palms out in *Do not cross my shadow.* "Carefully, yes? Because the single advantage you have is that this Norsunder mage might not know yet that you know."

Birdy said soberly, "If this Hannik-Herskalt finds out you have that dyr thing, he's going to come after you."

My bath did not refresh me. Instead, I emerged shivering in spite of the warmth, and my skin hurt. By the next day, I was so ill with fever that I could not get out of bed, much less do magic. But I wrote to Ivandred, saying, *I am here and have news for you.*

He wrote back almost immediately, telling me to transfer and use his scrollcase as a Destination.

I was sitting stupidly in bed, the scrollcase and note on my lap, when Anhar came in with a tray of food.

I showed her the note, then croaked, "I don't know what to do. I need more information—Ivandred is going to want proof, he's going to ask questions I cannot answer."

"Emras, tell them you cannot transfer. You are clearly ill. Birdy also told me to tell you that he knows where to begin some research, that is, with whom. Eat this. I'm going to take away this cider and brew you some listerblossom."

Oh, the relief just to be able to share! My already raw throat tightened with tears as I wrote to Ivandred.

The answer was almost immediate, and it was from Lasva.

Emras! You vanished! Hannik feared that your experiments had done something dire to you, for he says that he has not had any contact from you, either. Emras, we are riding for home. All around me everyone talks unity, loyalty, the bond of the ancient Marloven. They sing the Hymn to the Beginnings with fervor on Restday. But the word peace seems to recede farther into the future.

For three days I tossed on my bed, my mind crowded with nightmarish images. Even after I remembered the dyr long enough to crawl out of bed and close it in with Lasva's lover's cup, the fever raised every fear I'd endured, going back to childhood. I was in the kitchen again, but it was not the kitchen at Alsais where I'd spent six months. It was Darchelde's kitchen, only seen once, a distorted room filled with bread dough to knead, but my hands were tied. Sheris, who I had not thought about for over ten years, followed me up to the secret chamber, reaching with her fingers and saying, *Your family hates you, Emras, everyone hates you.* She metamorphosed into Carola, who offered me a cup full of poison, the cup beaten from gold, with the raptor-eyed fox etched round its rim. *Drink it, before the Sartorans catch up with you.*

I ran away, into the jarlan's old room, where the walls had been replaced with mirrors that reflected one another into infinity, as I ran and ran and ran, ever more lost in darkness.

But the worst of all was Lasva, presiding sorrowfully as she whispered over and over, *Why did you betray me? Bring me the dyr, so we can have peace at last.*

I'd wake up gasping, to find myself drenched with sweat. Anhar was often there, and once, Birdy, holding out a cup. Frightened, they brought me green kinthus as well as willow bark, and that enabled me to sleep dreamlessly. When I woke at last, I found Anhar sitting beside my bed, teasing a small kitten with a feather tied to a string.

"What is happening?" I whispered, my voice quite gone.

"The king and queen are riding back," Anhar said, flicking the feather up. The little cat arched its tail, wiggled its behind, and pounced. "They're going to celebrate harvest up in Sindan-An. Something bad happened there, that's the rumor, anyway."

I hoped whatever it was had not happened to the jarlan, who was one of Lasva's staunchest supporters. She'd already lost her middle-aged son and her older granddaughter at Olavair's battle. But I could not waste my strength on politics, about which I could do nothing. With recovery came the weight of anxiety and the sense of impending trouble.

"If you are awake, I'm going to get you some food."

"I am ravenous," I discovered.

"Excellent! The healer said an appetite means recovery." She smiled and scooped up the kitten. "Come along, Rosie."

I had to know the dyr was safe, and I could use it to assess what was going on. I got out of bed, clutched at the wall as I swayed, light-headed, then I trod to the box, and banished the illusion. The dyr was safe, exactly where I'd laid it. I picked it up, ready to project myself—and back came Anhar's words about intimate trespass.

I knew that. I'd known all along that there was something wrong with what I did, but the urge to listen, to know, was so strong. And the danger was now so great. Given how many times I'd used it, what was wrong with one more?

I reached, and there was Lasva, her lower back aching as she rode, her lips gritty with dust as Ivandred and Haldren talked. I could hear a few words, all of them military. I delved into Lasva's memories for her last sight of Kaidas, and there it was, so powerful I reeled back and fell into my chair.

. . . and there I was, mud to the eyebrows, and that colt dancing around with his tail up and his ears saying, "How smart are you now, two-leg? Put a halter on me, will you?"

Lasva laughed. And the laughter released an overwhelming flood of anguish, sweet and yearning and sorrowful, and so intense my throat constricted as she thought, *Oh Hatahra, how very wrong you were. Love does not always die, but how can death's pain be worse?*

"Emras? Are you here?"

I jumped, glanced around my room as my head panged—and somewhere on the road days and days north, I felt Lasva looking back down the long column of riders. "Emras?" she said again.

She'd heard me! I flung the dyr to the stone floor, where it rang and spun. Some of those spells I'd removed must have been a protective ward of some kind that prevented victims—objects—targets—*people*—from hearing my thoughts when I listened.

I forced myself to my feet, retrieved the dyr, my mental shield firmly in place, and I threw it in the box.

Then the long journey to my bed, where I dropped flat. I had time to take two steadying breaths when Anhar was back. "You're flushed. Is the fever back?"

"I walked to my desk," I said—and hated the lie. "To test the dyr," I forced myself to say.

She grimaced. "Don't. Eat this instead."

I was halfway through a thick savory soup, accompanied by a hot rye bun slathered with honey and a hunk of cheese when someone scratched at the door.

"Birdy," Anhar said. "Enter!"

Birdy walked in, greeted us, then gave me another of those puzzled, slightly wary glances.

"What's wrong?" Anhar said.

"Remember tall Nashande, who was a year ahead of me when we were scribe students?" Birdy asked. "He's a royal archivist now, and I trust his discretion. So I asked him to do some excavation into the records about this dyr. Apparently just looking at those records sends some kind of spell alert, because this just arrived, after three days of silence."

He held out a tiny scroll. "It's addressed to you, Em," he added. "It's from your brother."

"Olnar? But I haven't heard from him since . . ."

"Read it," Birdy said gently.

Birdy, will you share this with Emras after you read it? Exhort her to respond!

Emras: I am going to assume that your friend Birdy, who is known to be in Marloven Hesea, is inquiring after an object made of a substance called "disirad" that vanished from the world during the Fall of Old Sartor four thousand years ago. This much you would have learned had you been properly taught. We do not know the purpose of dyra because so many records were destroyed in the Fall, but we do know that there is at least one in existence. It is in the possession of a Norsundrian commander, and it has been used to throw kingdom-wide enchantments. There are other rumors of uses, some too harrowing to describe, but this much I can tell you: All of these uses are evil. If you have even seen a dyr, we have to know! I do not know why you never answered any of my letters, but Emras, what are you doing and why? Who have you become?

I looked down at my half-eaten meal, sickened. I set aside the tray and covered my face with my hands.

"Emras?" Anhar asked.

"I can't eat any more. I am sorry. The food is good, but . . ." I tossed the letter down, my mind working rapidly.

Anhar picked up the tray, sending a worried look at Birdy, then left us alone.

"Birdy," I said. "You've read this."

"Yes."

"First, I never received any communication from my brother. When we came to this kingdom I sent a Name Day greeting, describing our journey, and received no answer. Then the Herskalt convinced me that Olnar would only scold me for learning magic on my own, and that once he found out, he'd be jealous at how much faster I'd learned. I believed that, because Olnar hadn't answered me."

"You were always competitive," Birdy observed.

"We *all* were. We worked harder because of it." He assented, and I said, "Do you have any desire to use the dyr?"

His hands flicked out in the shadow-ward, his upper lip curling with repugnance.

"The Herskalt," I said as I felt my way through the tangle of thoughts, "never quite lied. But he didn't tell me all of the truth. It's like the mirror wards in that garden, distorted reflections of what's real. Though the Sartoran Mage Guild is probably not as controlling, as venal, as he led me to believe, I think there is a little truth there. I do remember some of the things Queen Hatahra said."

"She had definite opinions," Birdy said with a quick, somewhat humorless grin. "But I don't know that I'd go to her first on the subject of mages and magic."

"But she had some convincing observations about mages in history who tasted power and liked it. Birdy, everything I've been told for the last ten years is suspect. My own morals are suspect. But I know three things. First, the Herskalt is going to be desperate to get the dyr back. Second, I have to confess to Ivandred and Lasva, and though I suspect she will feel the way you do, he will see it as an aid to kingdom protection. Third, I can't seem to stay away from using it. There's a craving in me, which probably means I've turned into an evil mage."

"An evil mage would justify its use."

"Don't you see? I *do* justify it. Birdy, I used it not an hour ago. I know how much it's going to hurt Lasva, how betrayed she is going to feel . . ." I caught myself. "That is my personal burden. The dyr is a world burden, and the only thing I can think of is to ask the greatest favor I ever have from you: to take it and dispose of it."

"What? Me?"

"Yes."

"Em, may I remind you that I know nothing about magic?"

"That is exactly why I am asking you. The Herskalt cannot trace it if you carry it in that box. If it moves by normal means—walking, riding, aboard a ship—then magic won't find it. All its tracer wards are gone. I saw to that before I left Darchelde."

"Should I throw it in the ocean?"

"Yes. Perhaps not. What if the mer folk find it? What will it do to them? I think the only safe thing is to bind it to some future date, when maybe mages will be wiser. Will know what to do. Yes. The Sartoran Mage Guild might be angry, but on reflection, they might decide they are well rid of it. As for Norsunder, ah-ye! I hope by the time you reach wherever you are going that I will have solved that problem."

He gave a short nod, his jaw working.

"The box will be carefully warded. The rest you will have to do, but it won't be difficult, just laborious. I will write it all out and set up the enchantment, which is a series of interlocked spells. All you have to do to finish it is to choose as key the family name of someone who seems to be established and sensible. You'll complete the spell by naming one of their descendants many generations away. Very specific. That will make the enchantment pretty much impossible to break, if someone finds it. Don't tell anyone what it is, or where. Including me."

Birdy looked around the room, then said, "Where do I go?"

"As far as you can get." I crossed to my desk, where I kept the few coins left over from my days in Alsais. I took them out and stared down at them. For some reason hot tears blurred the gold on my palm and tickled my cheeks. "This is what I'm worth? Olnar asked who am I, and I don't know, Birdy. An evil mage—ah-ye, I can see you are going to protest, and I know I'm overstating it just for the comfort of hearing it denied. But maybe I shouldn't hear it denied. I am morally suspect, a mage who can destroy weather patterns for half a continent and place dangerous wards. I am even an evil scribe, for I've broken the First Rule so many times I can't even count them, and I helped others break the Second."

"You are Emras," he said, "and I love you."

I met his eyes at last, startled, apprehensive—but I did not see in his gaze the grasping desperation of *zalend*, or the poetic passion of *rafalle*. It was the warm and steadfast love of human for human, necessary and infinite as light and air.

"I love you, too," I said.

TEN

OF A WITNESSED GLANCE

B irdy was gone when I woke the next morning. When Anhar brought me breakfast, she told me he'd left at first light. I was still too weak to walk downstairs any appreciable distance—and in that castle, everything was an appreciable distance.

The time was coming—soon—when I was going to have to act, but just then, it passed with the cold trickle of snowmelt as I tried to recover.

Anhar finished her daily tasks and offered to read to me from Hadand's letters, which I had avoided all this time. I could read them myself, of course, but I found her voice soothing and even entertaining, as she employed her talent at altering her speech to match the tone of the writer. I found it interesting and oddly cheering to hear the female perspective on the lives presented in the Fox memoir.

And so that day passed, and another, and the days turned into a week. Restday came and went, the castle filling with the rich aroma of harvest barley wine, and here and there, mulled wine spiced with cinnamon, a Colendi scent. Some peacock things had been accepted, like many of our pastries, now made by bakers all over the city.

Gradually I recovered my strength as the week stretched to the thirty-six days of a month, and another week after that. As my strength returned, so did the impulse to reach for the dyr. It was a hunger, its absence like losing sight and hearing. The only way to endure it was to keep busy, because somehow, I had to put the puzzle pieces together.

My first project was to test my scrollcase. At first I detected nothing amiss, until I went over it carefully, then found a tiny mirror ward, so cleverly built that it was easy to overlook. Think of a sliver of lead hidden in filigree. I left it alone, and made myself a new scrollcase.

Then I set myself the task of solving the mystery of Darchelde. That meant shifting to my secret chamber, but Anhar made me promise to work only eight turns of the hourglass before my return. So I stepped through my transfer access way each day armed with an hourglass. From inside my secret chamber, I began systematically assessing every spell in that vast castle, from the highest of the eight towers down to the cellars.

Choreid Dhelerei began the preparation for New Year's Week, as rumors flew about war, defense, threats. Each morning before I left for Darchelde, I joined the fan practice with Anhar, Kaidas, and Vasande. Gone was the wit and range of discussion, until one day, after the children had run out, and it was just the three of us adults, Kaidas closed the door and said, "You hear everything in stables, and there is war in the air." He flicked his fan in Imminence.

Anhar said, "How can you tell? They always talk this way."

Kaidas snapped the fan shut. "I can't quite describe it. But it feels like it did before our fight with the Chwahir up at the border. Only that, I have learned since being here, was barely a skirmish." He lowered his hand, his gaze serious. "I think my son and I ought to depart. I am weak enough to permit myself a last indulgence: I will take my leave of Lasva face to face. There's nothing else I can do for her."

I was not done with my assay.

Desperate to finish, I began staying longer at night, though Anhar wouldn't sleep until she'd seen me safely in my bed.

Then one morning we heard the distant horns announcing the coming of the king, soon followed by the thundering arrival of Ivandred, Lasva, and a swarm of warriors through the gates. Sick with trepidation, I waited for the inevitable summons, as word flew through the castle that the First Lancers were not among the arrivals. Deep in my own set of worries, I paid little heed to the news.

The summons came immediately.

We arrived at the same time in Ivandred's outer chamber, so rarely seen by me. He dropped tiredly into one of his great wing-backed chairs, his boots and the skirt of his coat mud-splashed, his hair damp from a fresh fall of snow. Lasva had somehow contrived to neaten herself between dismounting and coming upstairs to his room. She sat in the chair next to his, feet together, hands pressed together.

"Hannik couldn't ride in with us," Ivandred said. "When we talked last, you had a few weeks of work ahead to replace the wards, and that was nearly a year ago. What happened, Sigradir?"

"Instead of removing and rebuilding the last four layers of wards, I have strengthened them," I said. "If you order it, I must release the personal wards, which will permit Hannik—the Herskalt—to enter this city. But you should know that I believe he is a Norsundrian. "

"What?" Ivandred half-started out of his chair, then sat back, scowling at me.

Lasva blanched.

I clasped my hands tightly. "This is what I have learned and how I learned it."

Though the danger was from Ivandred—and I knew he was going to be angry—it was Lasva I watched as I confessed. Not everything. That is, I told them what I had done, but not everything I saw; I kept from them only the names of others whose lives I had penetrated.

Like Kaidas.

Lasva's eyes closed at I described the first betrayal of her memories. After that every flutter of her lashes, subtle tightening of her lips—every wince that she tried to hide, but couldn't—stabbed me deeper with the knife of guilt.

At the end, I waited for them to pronounce judgment.

Ivandred said, "This object. You say it is not here?"

"I thought it better to get rid of it. If the Herskalt gets it again, he will use it against us both. As well as against anyone he wishes."

Ivandred stared down into the fire, a vein beating at his temple. When he looked up, he said, "You say you only listened to me in private? With my wife?" Disgust lifted his upper lip. "Anyone knows how I feel about my wife."

"Yes." I did not mitigate it by telling him how few of those scenes I'd watched. I should not have seen anything at all.

Lasva said softly, "Emras, I would have told you anything you wanted." My throat hurt so much I could barely speak. "I know," I said.

Ivandred looked my way, his expression altering to consideration. "He was keeping you busy."

"I see that now," I said. "At the time, he told me that I needed to understand people in power, how they thought. In order to help Lasva. And you."

Ivandred lifted his chin. "He said the same thing to me. Only he told me what they said. Told me what they thought. Private conversations, concerning the kingdom. He let me think it was intelligence-gathering. Even my own runners couldn't get that much information." He traced a curious sign in the air—then opened his hand. "I wonder if they've been compromised?"

"They?"

Ivandred pressed his fingertips to his eyes, then dropped his hand. "My runners, the king's runners. They learn a little magic. Nothing like what you know. During the bad years, before we regained the throne, they were the only organized force, you could say. My family had a sign." He slashed his finger in the air, making that same curious sign. "You recognize the letters of the alphabet? If you draw them that way, they look like an eagle in flight. It was a signal . . . ah, it's no matter." He struck the air with his hand. "I always feared that if he could tamper with scrollcases, then anyone might. In this, I trusted my father's suspicion. But I had no idea about this dyr." His brows lifted. "The fact that he never told me is the most damning evidence against him. He would know how I'd use it."

"Instead, he would use it to command you."

"Or to aid me in my plans?" Ivandred gazed into the fire, so tense he did not seem to breathe. "He has worked hard for Marloven Hesea. All spring and summer I heard nothing but talk about Marloven glory."

Lasva looked from one of us to the other. "I believe, if you will permit my intrusion, that he told you both what you wished to hear most."

"Again, why?" Ivandred said.

"I have been worried all along that this man has trained you Marlovens not to use weapons so much as to be a weapon," Lasva said.

Ivandred gave her a quick look at the words "you Marlovens."

"The warriors," she corrected herself, and then fell silent, so all we heard was the beating of the flames and the echo of a clarification she should not have had to make.

Ivandred stirred, one fist tightening, then he said, "Hannik rode down to Darchelde with the First Lancers."

Darchelde again!

Ivandred went on, "I will go there later on this winter—just me, and not the rest of the lancers, as we'd originally planned. As soon as New Year's Week is over, I'll send the Second Lancers to patrol the middle plains, Third to the northern border, and Fourth to the east."

"There is a lot of magic over Darchelde," I said uneasily, knowing how inadequate were my words, how unconvincing. "Far more wards than necessary for protection."

Lasva said, "Maybe you should send orders to the First Lancers, giving them home liberty for the winter."

Ivandred's smile was bleak. "I don't trust any means of sending orders. We know scrollcases are compromised, and runners can be ambushed. The First Lancers are accustomed to the garrison at Darchelde—nothing will happen to them there. It's been our winter camp whenever we could use it. Herskalt and I often met and conversed there. I do feel that I owe him a chance to explain himself."

"What did you learn from my memories that you could not have learned by asking me?" Lasva asked.

We were alone in her inner chamber, which was determinedly Marloven in look, but smelling like a Colendi herb garden.

How can one honestly answer such a question?

"That is misspoken." Lasva caught herself up. "Ah-ye, Emras, you look like poor Haldren did, before his own friends put him up there to be flogged. I do not want to make you suffer. Let me ask this. Did your trespass cause anyone harm? Do not answer 'yes' without thinking. I know you know it was wrong. But did you do harm."

"I don't believe I did," I said cautiously. "I can't say for certain."

"Very well. Did you do anyone any good?"

"Only once."

"Tell me."

I had made an oath that I would answer every question with the truth. So I told her about Tatia and Vasande. At the end, she said, "Yet it was not by your mental whisper, say, or by your wish that Kaidas came here?"

"I did not know they were coming," I said emphatically.

Lasva prowled her room, then paused, her fingertips resting on the carved box in which she kept her letters. "Sometimes I miss court in

Alsais, and sometimes I think about how I can never go back. Court is where love is mixed with business, and business with love. People hide their emotions as we hide our bodies behind layers and layers of silk. Our intent was to gain ascendance by being agreeable, to serve or to disserve, and intrigue and pleasure took up our time." She looked my way. "Court is a kind of dance, tumult without disorder. Is that a kind of war? Is war in whatever form all we are capable of?"

"Adamas Dei said that we are capable of infinite mercy and infinite beauty," I said, my throat hurting. "As well as infinite cruelty."

She prowled around the room again, then stopped before me. "I find that it is necessary to redefine relationships at various junctures in our lives. Perhaps it is too early to do so, but I want you to know this, Emras. I recognize your love, and you have always had what I could give. You abrogated my trust, but you regained some of it in telling the truth about what you did that had magical and political consequences —and in being merciful about not going into all the intimate details." The name *Kaidas* remained unspoken, but I think she heard it as clearly as I did. She took a deep breath. "Shall we begin again from there?"

I could not answer, so I gave her the deep sovereign bow.

New Year's Week arrived, the atmosphere as tense as my first New Year's in Marloven Hesea. Danric Yvanavar's speech was especially fine, spoken in the rolling alliteratives and galloping cadences of their ancestors. He, or someone, had worked a long time on that call for restoring the glory of the Marlovens. He wrote for posterity, using every emotion-hitching word save the crucial one: war.

So I refuse to record his speech.

The gist of it was repeated by the Jarls of Tlen, Tiv Evair, Khanivar, Fath, and the new Jarl of Sindan-An, who (it was rumored) had drowned his great-aunt, she being too tough to kill via a riding accident or a fall down stairs. I did not understand the significance of these six jarls' similar speeches until the last day, which I will come to very shortly.

Each morning, Kaidas asked Anhar, "When should I see her today?"

And each day she answered, "Not today. It's oath day, then the banquet," or "Today she is hosting a memorial for the Jarlan of Sindan-An for all her friends," or "Today is the riding and shooting exhibition—then they go straight to the great hall for singing and dancing."

Near the end of the week, after he'd gestured Assent and walked off, she whispered to me, "I hope he will change his mind. If he leaves, it's going to break her heart."

"Having him here is breaking her heart," I said, and Anhar gave me a quick glance. "She told you that? She's not so much as mentioned his name to me since they came back."

"Nor to me. But here is the last thing I saw with the dyr." And I described it.

Anhar listened then wiped her eyes on her sleeve. "I don't see any happiness for either of them."

"Maybe she will find a measure of it if we win peace," I said. "And he will find it somewhere else. But he's going to have to leave first."

Anhar flung out her hands, then dropped them. "I'm going to have to ask if she'll see him. But I'll wait until Lastday."

Why did the structure of Darchelde's wards distort when I sketched the layers?

I'd done everything right, but my sketches were impossible. I had to find out why.

But I didn't dare walk around Darchelde to make a physical assessment. The Herskalt had tracers all over the castle. If I dissolved one, he'd be on me in a heartbeat, and in a contest of physical strength, I was going to lose. So I had to build another transfer 'wall.' Almost weeping with despair, I stayed up all night constructing this magical access way, then connecting it to one of the towers where the Herskalt's magic distorted.

I finished it in the Hour of Repose—the last before Daybreak—and tiredly raised my hand to gesture the last spell, revealing what was beyond.

Shock gripped me by the vitals with such ferocity I stumbled back and fell over my wooden chair. I watched that incalculable darkness, terrified it would swallow me as I gabbled the spell to thoroughly eradicate the access way I'd spent all night constructing.

Then I sat there on the floor, my arms and head on the chair seat as my heart thumped frantically and my mind struggled to comprehend the enormity of what I had discovered.

I had it now. I had been given a mountain to climb, with a path laid out before me. As I toiled upward, here was the spreading tree representing prospective knowledge, and there was a towering cliff of glittering rock represented by the dyr, all of which filled my vision and guided my steps up the path. So I never thought to turn around.

But now I'd turned around at last, and there was the world—the puzzle—the *plan*, laid out below me.

The Herskalt had created numberless access ways like the one connecting to the Garden of the Twelve, in order to turn the castle into a massive Destination Chamber. *Once the transfer was made, the entire castle could exist in Norsunder or in the physical world.*

That meant not only could the Herskalt take anyone in the castle to Norsunder, but Norsunder's army—however many warriors they had accumulated over the centuries—could be brought from there to here, something hitherto considered impossible.

I walked into my tower as dawn broke on New Year's Lastday. The snow had cleared at last, leaving a sky as brilliant as gemstones and far colder.

I found Anhar rushing around supervising the removal of jarlate belongings. They were all riding out.

"Where is the king?" I asked. "I have to talk to him."

"With Lasva on the balcony, seeing them off," she said. "They're all leaving at once!" She threw out her hands in Bird on the Wing, then fled.

What had I missed? Usually the jarls departed one by one. In Hadand's letters we'd discovered that they didn't like their trumpet salutes to be merged with anyone else's, and fights could start over one expecting the other's entourage to give way.

Tired, shivering with both cold and reaction, I scurried down to the second floor balcony that looked out over the royal stable yard. Snow creaked under the horses' hooves. Lasva was there beside Ivandred, but as soon as she saw me, she beckoned to me, her breath frosting as she said, "This is the last of them. I promised an interview. Will you accompany me, Emras?"

I glanced past her at Ivandred. "I need to talk to the king."

Lasva's gaze was wretched as her hand came up in the spywell sign, which I had not seen her use in years. Yet she did not move away from Ivandred, which I understood as conflict between honor and desire. "Can it wait? I think you had better be there."

"Interview." Anhar had kept her promise to Kaidas, then. There was going to be no happy outcome to this interview, but if they needed the safety of me present as a third, I owed Lasva that much. Surely the king was not going anywhere for this moment, I thought dully as I followed Lasva downstairs to one of the warren of rooms adjacent to the stable.

Here Kaidas stood, his gear set against the inside wall. Vasande was visible down the hall, talking in a cluster of other children.

As soon as Lasva walked in, Kaidas said, "I have to go, Lasva. There is war in the air, which is no place for my son." And when she bowed her head in assent, he said quickly, his voice pleading, "Come with me."

She recoiled as if struck.

"Ah-ye! I beg your pardon," he said, taking a step toward her, then halting as if he'd hit a glass wall. "Your ring." He indicated her gloved hand and retreated into full courtly mode. "I honor your vows. I will not put you in that position." He should have gone then, but he stayed, the words unsteady and quick. "If you will in turn honor me with one last conversation, do you think you can bring peace when no one seems to want it?"

"I think they do want peace," Lasva said—and she, too, should have gone, but she turned away and looked back, as if she could not deny herself this one last sight of him, the sound of his voice, the exchange of words, ideas. Connection. She walked randomly, her gaze lowered, her hands holding her elbows against her. "Though I don't know if we understand the word 'peace' in the same way. A Colendi thinks, How can there be peace when . . . ? When Ivandred was crowned, his first act was to have his best friend—more than a friend, his trusted . . . if he had had a brother, he would have been Haldren Marlovair. And yet he had him flogged."

"How is this possible?" Kaidas exclaimed, appalled.

"Understand this. It made Ivandred very angry. He was forced into it by a political maneuver. But he stood there just the same, because it was the law. And afterward? As they all went away, did they exclaim *We must change our laws!* Or: *How can we do this to one another and say we live in peace?* No. They admired Marlovair's bravery. Some had even counted the strokes, commenting about how long he'd held out before his legs buckled, before he passed out the first time."

"Did Ivandred explain the reasoning?"

"Yes. He said that orders must be obeyed, or life would be far worse. And I've seen enough Marloven violence to believe that. All night long Ivandred watched over Haldren, offering him steeped leaf that he made up fresh himself, though we had to ride the next morning. Yet he said nothing about changing laws." She looked Kaidas's way. "Don't you see it? When everyone agrees on accepting such violence as normal, talking about efficient killing of enemies in lance strikes, admiring a brother's style when being flogged. . . . Yet they share the same emotions as us, it . . . is a consensus that defines what is real, what is possible, differently than we do. But I believe that could change, because there is also music in these people. Do you know how many ancient songs I hear traces of in their ballads, extolling the same emotions we value? Our souls share much. And I don't believe a one of them wants to see any child of theirs die on the battlefield, or at a flogging post, in spite of all the fine words about glory."

She turned again. "As for those they fight, there is no innocence and peace. The former king of Perideth ran away and hid when he saw he was going to lose, and has been fostering unrest ever since. He, too, is willing to spend lives other than his own to regain his crown."

"Lasva. I know this much." Kaidas's face lifted. "If I share your work, then we are united in thought as well as memory. Let me help in this way: I was going to take Vasande south, and maybe west to Toar. But how about this? Stable hands always find work and always hear gossip. If I overhear something you might need to know when I travel through Perideth, shall I write to you?"

I could see Lasva's inward struggle, then she said, low-voiced, "Yes. Do that. Write to me."

She was permitting herself this one small connection with him. It was so clear to me, and it clearly was to him as well. Impulsively he took a step toward her, and another, and she didn't move. He held out his hands in mute appeal, and slowly, slowly, hers lifted away from her elbows and opened. And their hands met, palm to palm, as Lasva and Kaidas stood there, gazes locked.

For them the world had shrunk to one another. But pressing on me was the wider world's need. I was edging backward toward the door, when I caught a shift of air, a quick step beyond my shoulder.

When I turned my head, the open doorway was empty, but I heard the rapid diminishment of footfalls, and I knew who had been there with such dreadful certainty that I began to run.

I was short of breath far too soon; I did not catch up with Ivandred until I reached the courtyard, to discover him in the middle of swarming horses and warriors, checking gear, strapping weapons to saddles, tugging on coats and hats.

I ran to Ivandred, heedless of my lack of coat or hat. "It's not what it looked like," I said to him. "Please listen."

He paused beside his horse.

I stood there shivering, my lips rapidly numbing. "It's not what it looked like. He was saying good-bye—Lasva would never—"

His head bent, but I could see in the curve of his cheek the sharp pain of unhappiness, even grief. "I know," he said as he flexed his ring hand, then dropped it. "I know. Everything honorable. The both of them. But she never looked at me like that." He turned to grip the reins.

"Ivandred-Harvaldar, you cannot leave," I said desperately, hopping up and down on my toes. "I just found out what the Herskalt has done. Darchelde is a transfer chamber. That is, he—the Herskalt—Hannik— *whoever* he is, he can complete the spells, and all of Norsunder can be brought into Marloven Hesea through your ancestral castle."

His chin jerked up, his hand tightened on the bridle. I could see that he was too grieved to comprehend, or too angry to care that Norsunder was on his ancestral doorstep, so I said, "I think it's the Fox plan again."

His head snapped my way. "The what?"

"That is, Fox never had any such plan, but he wrote in his memoir about how Norsunder used that evil Venn mage who manipulated his king to come here in order to conquer. Remember what they intended? They were going to loose you Marlovens against all the rest of the Sartoran continent. I really believe that the Herskalt wants to do the same to you. "

He said slowly, "That has to be what *It's just beginning* means."

Now it was my turn to stare.

Ivandred's expression hardened. "This is why I'm riding out now, instead of next month. Why I went inside to take my leave of Lasva." He paused, then went on in a flat tone, "Just before the watch bells rang, one of my people overheard Khanivar's fool of a first runner complaining. I just finished choking it out of the idiot. Danrid and five others made a secret pact with Hannik. They mean to force me to ride north in spring to conquer the rest of Halia, in the name of Marloven glory. And Hannik promised them that's just the beginning." His teeth showed briefly. "Danrid won't know I'm right on their heels. I'll stop them cold."

"You won't stop them if all Norsunder is coming through that gate. The Jarls and the First Lancers will find themselves under the Herskalt's command."

"All the more reason for me to ride out," he said. "The First Lancers won't take orders from anyone but me, on pain of death." He stopped, gazing skyward, and I suspect he was thinking the same thing that I was: what does pain of death mean when you are dealing with a place beyond time?

He laid his hand to his horse's bridle. "I have to go. I will try to stop him. But I can't do anything about the magic."

"I can," I said, though inwardly I was not sure at all. "And I will," I vowed.

His lips curled in what was almost a smile as he touched his hand flat to his heart in salute. "Good job, Sigradir. " His chin lifted. "Tell Lasva."

"I will," I said inadequately.

He vaulted into the saddle. Then—without any fanfare—they rode out and away.

I stumped back inside, my feet completely numb as I sought Lasva. "Where did you go?" she asked.

I looked around—and there was Kaidas, with Vasande at his side, each clasping an armload of gear.

"You'd better not venture south," I stuttered, my teeth chattering. "Whatever is going to happen, I think it's going to start there." And then, switching to Sartoran, I told them what had happened. Everything— Lasva and Kaidas each cut a fast glance at the other when I got to *She never looked at me like that*, but said nothing.

At the end, Lasva said to Kaidas, "You know that nothing has changed. Except . . . we might need help. Will you stay?"

The man had mucked stables across the continent on hope. "Love," he said, "is stronger than armies, because when they are all dust, it lives. I will do anything. You have only to ask."

ELEVEN

OF THE BANNER AND DAMNATION

I t had taken the Herskalt twenty years to make those spells at Darchelde, and I had two to three weeks before the six jarls and Ivandred arrived there, after which it would probably be too late to act.

But I also had Adamas Dei's text. I still did not comprehend it completely. Even when I toiled word by word through a sentence, my head felt giddy, as if too many ideas tried to crowd into my skull. But I could build spells word by word, and I knew the structure of the dark magic that the Herskalt had taught me. These would have to be my advantages, because surprise had gone with the dyr.

I opened the text, dipped the waiting pen in the inkwell, turned over the hourglass, and got to work.

You have in the accompanying magical text my hour-by-hour notes on what I did, though perhaps those have been consigned to the fire by my judges. Think of it this way: my strategy was to use the Herskalt's own structure against him, by building a chain of mirrors that reflected his chain of mirrors. I worked feverishly, each emptying of the hourglass recorded with intensifying dread.

But time on this side of the divide is as remorseless as any Norsundrian lord.

At noon midway into Firstmonth, under a light drift of snow, the six jarls clattered into the Darchelde stable yard. I stepped through my transfer wall, tousled and shrouded in my sturdiest winter gear, to report for the last time to Lasva. "They are gathering in the great hall. Ivandred cannot be far behind."

"Emras, I must be there. I need to see what transpires," she responded, reaching for her coat. "Can you make that happen?"

"I can, but I don't know how safe we are," I said. "I haven't detected any sign of the Herskalt. That fills me with misgivings. It would be far better if I knew where he was."

"When Ivandred arrives, I must be there," she repeated.

And so I took her hand, made the sign, and we stepped through my wall into Darchelde. There, I picked up my two paper lilies, which after far too much time spent worrying and arguing with myself, were the physical vessels for the only two "cage" wards I'd been able to make: if I could get one to close around the Herskalt, it would force him back to Norsunder. I knew better than to assume success with one try. I wished, as I shifted us directly to the gallery above the great hall, that I'd had time to make a dozen.

At least I had a transfer token, bound with a complicated interlocking of wards meant to get me past anything. I'd made it so strong that if I held onto Lasva, I was fairly certain it would transfer us both.

We looked down at enormous fireplaces at either end of the vast chamber that hearkened back to another age. The walls were plastered, decorated with gigantic stylized horses and eagles and wind-blown riders, surrounded by interlocking knotwork patterns. These latter glowed ruby-red with magic potential.

A mighty table built of timbers from century-old trees, each leg ending in raptor claws, had been arranged before one of the fireplaces. From the looks of the gathered jarls and their attendants, as they stamped and rubbed their hands, the heat from the roaring flames did not reach very far.

The servants had just brought hot food and drink when Ivandred arrived at last. Everyone stilled as he walked down the center of the hall of his ancestors, Haldren at his left in shield arm position, their heels ringing on the icy floor.

"Van," Danrid said. His friendly tone, magnified in that vaulted hall, sounded false to my ears, his laughter a bark of anger. "This is a surprise."

Ivandred said, "Let's understand one another. Here's an order, plain to all. King to sworn jarls: disperse. Go home."

"But we have made a pact," Danrid replied, standing away from the table. He reached to his shoulder and pulled his sword.

"A pact for the good of the kingdom supersedes a bad order, even from a king," the Jarl of Khanivar said pompously, looking at the others for support.

His cousin from Tlen spoke up. "Your own ancestor, King Senrid, made that claim when he reunited us."

"Van, you've let a woman tie you by the prick," Danrid stated with cordial contempt. "Do you really want to turn us into a nation of shop-keepers and caravan guards?"

Ivandred ignored Danrid and said to the others, "I do not want Marlovens riding under the banner of Norsunder. Our souls are our own."

Danrid's brow twitched at that. Some of the others stirred and whis-pered.

Ivandred looked upward, then around the chamber, and raised his voice. "I know you are listening, Hannik. Or whatever you call your-self—I refuse to malign 'Herskalt' any further, a once-respected title."

Between one moment and the next, the Norsundrian we'd called Herskalt appeared before the fireplace, facing Ivandred, who stood di-rectly below me.

I gripped my first lily as the Herskalt glanced sideways at the jarls. Desperation gnawed at me—I had to catch him facing away. He must not see the magic coming, not at this distance, or he'd have time to ward it. "Each one of you swore to ride to war and glory," he said to the jarls, and to Ivandred, "What matter whose glory?"

"My glory," said Ivandred, "is in keeping faith with my wife."

Next to me Lasva stilled, unbreathing.

"With her, I keep faith with my family. With my family, I keep faith with your families, Yvanavar, Tlen, Tiv Evair, Sindan-An, Khanivar, Fath. With our families, we keep faith with our kingdom. My mistakes are my own, but I can fix them. Because my soul is my own."

"Too late for that," Hannik said.

Then everything went awry. Ivandred raised his hand in a familiar sign—the Fire spell! Frantic with dismay I drew breath to halt him, for I'd been certain there would be sword play, and in the moment the Herskalt was busy with steel, I'd planned to make my move.

Lightning flared; Hannik vanished a heartbeat before it could reach him. Lasva flinched as Ivandred's lightning, which had been sent toward Hannik before the fireplace, rebounded as no natural lightning had ever done, and shot—aimed deliberately by a will expert in cruelty—straight at the six jarls, as Ivandred watched in astonishment.

Lightning flared terribly around hair and clothing, amid high screams of pain and amazement, then hurled their souls to infinity as their bodies drifted to the floor in puffs of ash.

"I need you intact," the Herskalt said to Ivandred, emerging once again from nothingness. "I have great plans for you. Glorious." The word rang with mockery.

Even if he was an image—a projected illusion—my cage of mirror wards could propagate up the link to him. As he passed underneath, I opened my lily, the magic streamed downward, twilight blue, and closed around him with a faint cobalt glitter as the Herskalt's image looked sharply up. Then froze.

Ivandred looked up, too. And saw us. "Lasva?" he whispered, face drawn with pain.

"I don't think that's going to hold Hannik," I said. "You'd better get out—"

Ivandred didn't hear me. "Lasva, why are you here?"

"I had to see you," she began.

The cobalt figure pulsed with a ring of light, then began to coalesce into a different form: taller, more slender. Long hair, whiter than snow. Whoever it was had the skill to draw the magic from my cage ward and use it to build power. Layer by layer.

"Get out," I pleaded.

"Lasva, I did everything for you," Ivandred said. "I could have conquered all Halia. I held them all off, because you wanted peace." He wasn't bitter, or even angry—he spoke with the pain and bewilderment of a man trying to understand.

"I know." Lasva leaned dangerously over the carved rail. "And I loved you for that."

"But you loved him more. Is that it? You always did?"

She opened her hands, an expression eloquent and disconsolate. "I tried—"

Those words, simple as they were, impacted him with the force of steel.

"*Look.*" I pointed at the figure not ten paces away, rippling with white-hot coruscation. Streamers of magic bled from the wards all through the room, purple and green and red, drawing power inward.

Ivandred turned to Haldren at his side. "Get them out of here."

"No," Haldren replied. "Where you lead I follow. Even into death. So I swore."

"Haldren, I am damned, but you can save yourself."

"Then the damned will ride together," Haldren said, and from behind came shouts: somewhere underneath us, out of sight, the First Lancers had gathered to protect their king.

"Show us the soul-eaters!"

"We will fight!"

"You can't fight that magic," I said urgently to Ivandred.

"We can't run from it either." He looked around as if blinded.

"*You* can." I made my decision, clutching the transfer token in one hand, as I tossed my second cage ward down. "Ivandred, take this. It's the only way to save your people. Get as far away from the castle as you can. The Herskalt might have a cage ward waiting somewhere on the road, just like this one. If he tries to close it around you, open this."

His hand came up automatically to catch the paper. The words "Save your people" forced him to act. He stepped back from the incandescent figure, glanced upward at us, as I called, "She will be safe!" and with that he began to marshal his followers as they clattered rapidly out of sight and away.

I gripped Lasva. "Get the servants outside. What I am going to do might bring the castle down."

"What about you, Emras?"

"I'll be fine," I lied. "See? Transfer token. But I can't take servants, so go!" And as she started away, "Your lover's cup—it's in my trunk."

Lasva glanced back once, but decision cleared her brow. She'd seen the transfer token, which meant I could escape. But the castle servants had no such aid. She vanished down the stairs to lead them out to safety.

I turned my attention back to the impossible glowing figure, evidence of magic far beyond my skills. But I had Adamas Dei's chain of mirrors . . .

A halo of magic formed around the figure, shrinking slowly toward the upraised hand, as I whispered over my transfer token, weaving a new chain over the layers already there. The magic halo thickened to a ring, forming into a ball of violet effulgence. Right before it touched that outstretched hand, I dropped the token directly into the center of it.

The result could not have been more dramatic: my mirror ward smashed the coalescing power outward. Air hissed on a high note, like a shrieking wind, as the lightning exploded. Plaster blackened, tapestries whooshed into blue flame, then drifted in ash; the building rocked under the onslaught.

I staggered, then gripped the balcony. Now it was time to release my wards bound to the Herskalt's access ways: one up high, a second off the kitchen, the third in the tower over the garrison, the fourth in the basement. Everywhere I'd found spells ready to force a connection between Norsunder and the world I reflected the magic back onto itself, again and again, and in a random lack of pattern that it would be impossible for him to keep up with, wherever he was.

Crack! Resounded from the biggest tower, where four hundred years ago Fox had sat on the battlements with Inda, talking about how beating did not bring out the best in the academy youth, but having a common goal did. The rampart exploded in a mighty clap, raining stone chips beyond the outer walls as below, terrified servants and stable hands fled.

My balcony swayed. I nearly fell over the edge, so flung myself backward. A carved pediment with owls and vines and eagles crashed down at my feet. I transferred to the tower directly above the secret room, which overlooked the road leading down into the town of Darchelde.

I rejoiced for about a heartbeat when I made out Lasva, her hair a tangle, leading a straggling band of servants—many clutching whatever they could grab up—as they exited the big gate in the wake of the First Lancers, who had leaped on their horses, weapons to hand, lances snapped into place, with drilled speed. Ivandred was leading his force away from the castle, obedient to my directive, because he had no defense against magic, only a driving need to save his people.

I couldn't breathe as every muscle and nerve in my body urged them faster. *There's going to be a cost*, the Herskalt whispered in memory from the first time I heard his voice, as Ivandred and the First Lancers galloped in perfect formation down the road toward freedom—

Toward a faint, forming shimmer. And there it was, the expected ward.

Only larger than I had believed possible.

Beyond the hill curving above the town the air glittered as if a gigantic hammer had smashed diamonds into a million shards. They winked and shimmered as they blended and then merged in a writhing rope of darkness that vibrated through the air, shattering rock, shivering winterbare trees, and making my teeth rattle. It stretched between ground and sky, thickening into roiling darkness.

In the road, Lasva's group staggered, some falling to their knees in the snow churned up by the lancers, hands clapped over ears.

The rope of darkness began to open into a chasm. Ivandred made one last gesture of defiance, flinging his hand high as he snapped open the little paper—which merely drew the focus of that vast access way to Norsunder.

The entire column of lancers was swallowed by the chasm. Then it slammed shut and vanished in a tumultuous reverberation of thunder and a whirling gout of lightning that blasted those shaken trees, and set roofs aflame all through the town.

I had won: Norsunder could not enter Marloven Hesea, and thence the world.

But the Herskalt had won: Norsunder had captured Ivandred, and the best trained of all his warriors.

TWELVE

OF MY SURRENDER

My vision flared, darkened, then returned in blurs and shadows as in the town below the mountain, people boiled out of the buildings, running crazily. How could it be so silent?

My ears itched. Furious with the futility of my efforts, anguished at my failure to save Ivandred from the Herskalt's trap, I wiped impatiently at my ears. And looked down at fingers smeared with blood.

Then the frigid air stirred, and the Herskalt appeared next to me, his arms full of cloth—a fold contained a crookedly stitched ship. I'd seen that in Lasva's memories . . . Inda's wedding shirt?

The Herskalt said—and though I'd been deafened, I heard the words inside my head—"Well done, Emras, for a beginner. But as you see, not sufficient. Come along."

I raised my hand in repudiation, and he laughed. "Do you really think that you would fare any better with Sartor when they catch up with you?"

"Watch me," I said—that is, my throat worked, but I heard nothing as I threw at his face the toe ring that I had been clutching in my hand.

He disappeared before the ring bounced off the honey-colored stone, then it, too, vanished. I held my breath, expecting anything but more silence.

Of course. First, the Sartoran mages had to discover that the border ward against transfer had been lifted. That, I'd set in motion the previous week, using Adamas Dei's spell so that it would quietly propagate itself.

Then they would have to dare the castle, which was still creaking. I walked inside and down the cracked stairway to the upper level of the residence wing, silt dropping from overhead. Here and there fires smoldered. The place was a ruin, the air purple with snarls of dark magic. Wearily, sore at heart, I forced myself to assess each of my access ways. Every one of the Herskalt's transfer wards had been thoroughly obliterated. I was not going to be able to rescue Ivandred, but at least the Herskalt could not get back here without a very great effort.

I kept walking, increasingly dizzy, through the empty castle. Lasva and the servants were somewhere on that slushy road between the ruined castle and the burning town. At least they were alive.

I picked my way down the remains of the grand staircase, avoiding the great hall and the ash where those six men had died. I wiped at my cheek, where a bit of flying stone had scored, and daubed with my sleeve gently at my right ear, which bled sluggishly.

My head was still ringing from the explosion, echoing on a high singing note as I slipped between the iron-studded front doors. One had cracked, flinging splinters clear out into the muddy courtyard below the two sweeping stairs. I lowered myself onto the first step, shivering. Presently the air stirred, and two figures appeared.

Was that Olnar? Looking solid as our father—and a little apprehensive. Next to him was Greveas, also older than I remembered, hands up and ready for desperate measures.

Greveas said something. I shook my head and pointed to my ears.

Olnar's expression of extreme reserve broke into wide-eyed dismay, and he said something, reaching out to me like a brother rather than a judge.

"It's done," I whispered.

And so, my judges, am I.

THE END

OF THE SCRIBES' THIRD RULE

This last part, no one has yet seen.

I was taken by Greveas and Olnar to Sartor as a prisoner. In my warded rooms deep in the Mage Guild, a healer was sent to me. She was able to restore the hearing in my right ear—one painful pop, and a rush of slightly flattened sound filled the silence—but my left was damaged so severely that it would take years to repair, I was warned. The implication was, who would pay for it, given my anomalous position? I said that it could wait.

Half a year after my arrival, they brought me a letter from Lasva:

Emras,

I hope this will get to you. Your friend Birdy promised to send it to a herald in Alsais who knows your brother. Such a torturous route begins to sound like the diplomatic circles I grew up with.

The truth is that I write to you for reassurance. I do not trust my memory, though I see those terrible final moments over and over in nightmares still. The disappearance of the First Lancers, that I heard about from too many witnesses to disbelieve, and I did see the skyward gateway to darkness, high above the trees.

What I cannot believe is that Ivandred killed those six men, foresworn or not, and I am fairly sure I never heard him claim the Fox Banner as the "banner of the damned." Rumor rippled out ahead of me, as it does, and by the time I had dealt with the people of Darchelde, establishing them with others in the farther reaches of Montredaun-An, I returned to Choreid Dhelerei to discover that Ivandred had become the evil king who slew his staunchest supporters then rode into Norsunder to escape retribution.

Every jarl had sent a relative seeking justice, or pre-eminence; they were prudent enough (perhaps scared enough, after hearing what happened) to stay home themselves, to guard their own territories.

Tdiran Yvanavar was there for both her adopted territory and for her brother's, as Haldren and his cousin were with Ivandred. I told Tdiran that Ivandred sent the lightning at Hannik, then it leaped sideways to strike the six.

She said, whether Ivandred killed them or not, would it do anyone any good to believe the dead foresworn, much less allies of Norsunder? I understand that, but my heart grieves to hear people justifying themselves by tarnishing Ivandred's good name—the same people who praised him on every side during their foolish war game last year.

But I understand the kingdom-wide sense of dishonor. Marloven Hesea has had enough trouble, and there is more promised. Gdan and Bluejay have stayed staunch, riding back and forth along their border with the Second Lancers (now called the Southern Wing), in case the King of Perideth carries out his threat to take revenge by carrying a war of destruction to my doorstep. I am going down there over Midsummer to win a treaty if I can.

The Olavairs have allied themselves with the northern kingdoms by signing the Compact. I am told they made great ceremony of burning all their arrows and breaking their bows, though the Jarlan of Marthdaun muttered that every basement is probably stuffed with extras that can come out at a moment's notice.

Nanjir Olavair used her influence to get the allies to agree not to cross our border, as long as the Marlovens do not carry bows and arrows outside of our border. In spite of the heated words, I suspect none of them really want to test their prowess against the Third Lancers, who though not Ivandred's chosen best, are deemed formidable enough.

I closed the Academy just before spring. I do not think I could have done it had not the kingdom still been unsettled by the events of winter, and I believe somewhat reluctant to send their children here. Kendred is angry with me one day and glad the next. He brags about how tough they were, but oh Emras, when he flinches if someone raises a hand at the edge of his vision, or wakens crying in the night, my heart aches. He is also angry with his father in a way I cannot understand or explain, though to other children he brags about him.

He talks of all the things he will do when he turns twenty and becomes king.

Kaidas stayed true to his offer, so I sent him in his capacity as Duke of Alarcansa to Sindan-An when it looked like fighting was going to break out between Fath and Tlennen over that area. Kaidas has managed to make himself popular—the Iascan language retains enough Sartoran roots for him to have learned it fast. The remnants of old Iasca seem to value his being a Colendi, and they are united in not wanting to be subsumed under any of the neighboring jarlates.

At New Year's Convocation I am thinking of giving out medals and awards to ease the sense of dishonor. If people are going to re-envision history, let them get a sense of glory for protecting the border and working for the common good.

Your brother Olnar sorted all your papers and sent them away. He said that he will make the ten year rounds of the protections, but that we will have to find another mage after that—and he trusts that we will go through accepted channels. I agreed, but I told Anhar that I quite understand my sister's opinion of mage tact.

Before Olnar left, I tried to make him promise to send for me to testify on your behalf. His reply was diplomatic, which is to say, polite but noncommittal. So I am writing in hopes that you will see this and be able to answer. As for the cup, it is back on my mantelpiece, but in spirit only, for now. I think you will understand what I mean.

I thought I understood. She would defer to Kendred, so bewildered by these violent changes, and she would defer her own happiness because everyone in Marloven Hesea had to be expecting (or dreading) another mysterious opening between sky and ground through which the First Lancers might come thundering back at the head of a howling army of darkness. But she had given her word to Ivandred. Only the conviction that he was truly beyond life could release her.

The mages let me write to Lasva, so I explained that I believed that Hannik deflected Ivandred's magic to strike the six jarls, but I suspect no one will listen to her. I'm sure my reputation had also suffered. What Marloven would believe the peacock mage?

Soon after that came a letter from Tiflis:

Em:

I never thought that you, of all people, would find herself at the center of all kinds of rumors. Did you really blow up an entire city with magic? Did you send the evil Marlovens into Norsunder, or did you escape when they tried to take you there? They won't tell me anything, just sent me a formal notice that I have to travel to Sartor—at my own expense, though Mother said I can stay with the diplomats—to testify about that magic book I had managed to forget all about. And I will have to pay a thumping fine on top of it, Cousin Olnar says, for breaking the rules about magic books. I was peeved with you until Kaura pointed out how much notice we will gain from the whole affair, and that cheered me, you can imagine. If you write up what happened, remember your loving cousin—

Tiflis

Then came the one I had been waiting for. It was short:

Your commission executed.
Wherever we go, you will always have a home with us.

Martande Keperi—your Birdy

It was after I received that one that the wall inside me broke, and I cried.

———

Greveas made certain that my prison was comfortable, two rooms deep in the Mage Guild's building, with a window that overlooked fountains and a park. If I craned my neck, I could see spires of the royal castle.

I never tested the wards they put around my rooms. I suspect they knew that I could break anything they put up—as I knew that the smallest spell testing those wards would instantly bring them upon me. One cannot unlearn things, however one might wish. I had become a liability—an embarrassment— a mage ignorant of most forms of magic outside of basic protections, but extremely powerful with wards, the most difficult magic of all. Too powerful, judging from the way they pounced on the Adamas Dei text. Apparently it had been missing for centuries, and the likes of me should not have even seen it, much less translated it.

From time to time, as I wrote my defense, I was visited by this or that mage, and requested to go over exactly what I found in Darchelde and what I did. I had written out all my magic notes, but they wanted to comb over every detail so much that gradually I became aware that some of my skips—my shorthand—constituted important steps for them. Only then did I begin to comprehend that mirror wards were both rare and dangerous.

They were not happy about my summary disposition of the dyr, but as I had foreseen, they accepted that it would become the future's problem. Whatever Birdy chose to tell them was sealed up in their archives.

He continued to write to me. It gave me solace to write back, explaining exactly what was going on. His letters were full of news that could be read by any number of censors. He and Anhar went to Sindan-An to run Kaidas's household, once the house he had built was finished. Anhar's lover, the pastry-cook, soon followed to join them, and took over the kitchen. Birdy wrote cheery letters about cats, all their children, and the colts that Kaidas had begun raising, straight off the Nelkereth plains south of Sindan-An.

Lasva wrote as well, reporting on her ongoing work to hold Marloven Hesea until Kendred turned twenty—and her determination to educate a prince who would foster peace.

Two years after I commenced writing it, I handed my defense to Greveas. She took it away, and another year passed before they sent for me.

I was not permitted farther than one floor up, and down to an archive where a young scribe sat, poised to record every word spoken.

To my surprise, the first interview was with no less a personage than Scribe Halimas, white-haired and irascible. He grumbled a great deal about politics, then finally said, "They spent half a hear arguing about who would judge you. Queen Hatahra maintained that Sartor had no political rights to judge you, only her sister Lasthavais did. And Hatahra claimed secondary rights, as the one who had sent you to Marloven Hesea."

I had to laugh at that.

"They then asked if she wanted you back in Colend, and . . . ah-ye, it's that business about Norsunder, and no one quite knows what happened at the end. There are witnesses who insist that it was you who slaughtered those nobles by lightning, not the king."

"Neither of us did that."

"But they believe what they saw."

"What they thought they saw."

Scribe Halimas, said ironically, "And you saw to it that this mysterious disc, a means by which they could look back in time in order to corroborate what you did and didn't do, is safely removed from anyone's access."

"It's a Norsundrian artifact," I said.

"It's an artifact of Old Sartor," he corrected. "This much I've learned from colleagues at the northern end of the world, where more records survived the Fall. Probably had all kinds of safeguards in the olden days." He leaned forward. "The mages are in a hum because it's beyond reach, but I'm glad you did what you did. And so are many others. We have no defense against that thing, and a powerful mage corrupted by it . . . Ah-ye! Let the future worry about it."

"What's going to happen to me, Scribe Halimas?" I asked.

He looked down at his hands. "I don't know, Emras. Nobody does."

After him came heralds and royal representatives from various places. The most difficult interviews were with people from along the coast of the strait, where the Great Flood effects had been the worst. I told my story over and over again, to a range of reaction from sneering disbelief to knowing skepticism to a wary, conditional acceptance that I might really be as stupid as I sounded.

The only visitor they permitted other than official ones was my aunt, Tiflis's mother, who was too high in diplomatic circles to shut out. She caught me up on family news, and when she left, she said, "If they let you out, hold your head up, as a smiter of Norsunder ought. Remember the family *melende!*"

Nobody brought Marlovens to Sartor to speak in my behalf. The only witnesses spoken to were survivors of the magical duel at Darchelde—which, Olnar reported to me, was so blasted that it was going to take centuries for the dark magic to leach away. The mages traveled to Marloven Hesea to interview the former residents of Darchelde.

"But you eradicated the Norsundrian rift better than any rift has been blocked for centuries," Olnar finished.

"Rift?"

He looked skyward. "Ugh, Em. Your ignorance is almost as frightening as your skills." He grinned. "You can imagine the shockwaves going through the Guild at their methods of education, and how they communicate with the other guilds. 'How can we prevent another Emras from happening?' is on lips right and left."

He leaned forward and touched my hand. "But others say this: how can we test for greatness? You know that the definition of 'greatness' varies from land to land, from generation to generation. One kingdom's Someone the Great is another kingdom's Someone the Bloody-handed. We call this playwright great because he successfully flattered a prince, whereas the words of another are still remembered two hundred years after the great one is forgotten. But Emras, many mages are calling you great, because though you were carefully cultivated by a Norsundrian, you turned his intention back on him. A Norsundrian from Old Sartor."

"It's the nature of mirror wards," I said. "You have the means there in the Adamas Dei text and my notes."

"Which vanished like smoke the night we brought you here," Olnar retorted. "In spite of being very carefully locked up." He twiddled his fingers, indicating magical locks.

I shivered. "It can only have been the Herskalt. Or whatever he calls himself now."

"The same man who created the last rift, four hundred years ago, not very far south of where you were. He closed that rift after he took those ships—you know that story?" As I signed assent, he said, "And it took decades for the mages to eradicate the traces of that rift. Decades, Em." He waited, and when I just shook my head, he sighed. "So. As you are a scribe, you should be able to reproduce your translation of Adamas Dei's text."

"I can . . ." I began confidently, then remembered the difficulties of those last pages, all the material about Norsunder. It had often taken a full hour to translate a single sentence, and even then, I'd have to constantly reread because the sense of it would not stay solid in my head. "Ah. Most of it."

He sighed again. "Probably the parts we already have. Do try. And as a reward for your effort, I am allowed to ask: have you have any requests from us?"

"I do. May I take magic lessons?"

His brows shot up. "I will inquire."

I reproduced about three-quarters of Adamas Dei's text, then had to give up. I could not be absolutely certain of the last part, the most difficult of all. They accepted that in resignation, though I suspect that they wished they could use a dyr, evil or not, to claw the rest of it from the inside of my head.

They then fitted me with an armband so loaded with magical protections that the subtle buzz against my skin felt like velvet. I spent a little time assessing the layers, in deep appreciation of their thoroughness.

I am certain that a degree of irony prompted the assignment of my first class, which was with children no older than ten. But I took my place, pretended not to hear whispers about the "dangerous lady" and though the elementary lessons—Bells and Spells—were as boring as I'd feared, over time the rote recitations in cadenced Sartoran poetry, spoken by magic students for two thousand years, became deeply soothing to my spirit.

Instead of a first test after six months, I was taken to an interview with Greveas, who said, "We are fairly certain who your Herskalt was."

"He called himself Ramis, four hundred years ago," I said.

"Oh, he's older than that. *Much* older. The modern form of his personal name is Detlef, as we say in Sartor, but the Venn called him Detlev nearly two thousand years ago, when he appeared to smite their most powerful king, and there is evidence that he's even older than that, like from before the Fall of Sartor, four thousand years ago. There are mysterious references to a Dei-to Laif, or some such. Most don't survive dealing with him. You did."

"Because he let me. He's one of the Host of Lords? The authors of Norsunder?"

"No," she said pleasantly. "That would be your white-haired man in the column of light, the soul-eater himself. Detlef is their servant. But terrifying enough."

"And he got away," I said, harrowed by the extent of my failure. "He could come back any time."

"No he can't. Not easily," Greveas said. "Emras, he was born more than four thousand years ago. But in spite of his great power he's human. That means time is his enemy, and it's more powerful than any of us. He might not have let you go, so much as had to. You cost him dearly, is our guess. He spent a lot of time in the real world, especially at the end, to pull his plan together, which you smashed along with that castle. He won't be back for a while, is what they think now."

"He took the Inda wedding shirt," I said, cold inside.

"Then he's not done with the Marlovens," Greveas said, her shoulders lifting in a faint shrug. "That's their lookout, some day. Right now, the general trend of the ongoing discussion is to permit you to finish training in Basics, and let the experts gauge you. The question is restitution in the north."

After that, there was only the lightest of boundaries—the entire city of Eidervaen—and my only guard was that armband of beaten gold, worked with lilies and laurel leaves. I went to plays and attended the music festival. I even heard Larksong sing again, and I reflected on her past.

After my first year of magic lessons, they no longer kept me among the children reciting the basics. The lessons were everything the Herskalt had said—and yet he'd managed to distort the intent. We didn't just recite tables of historical facts, we deliberated the consequences of actions. We examined the records of mages and monarchs, discussing the latter with a freedom that would have been highly resented in court circles.

By the end of my second year of studies, I'd been promoted steadily and rapidly until I was working alongside people on the verge of adulthood—among whom I made friends.

And so, when at last I was summoned before the Chief Mage, an old woman whose reserve did not quite mask her amusement, she said, "We have come to our judgment, Mage Emras."

"Mage?"

"You have attained the first level, qualified to purify waterways, renew cleaning frames, and strengthen walls, roofs, and bridge supports," she said with gentle satire. "The conditions of your release are these: you will spend the next ten years making restitution by renewing protections through the kingdoms that suffered the worst damage from your actions." She must have seen something in my face because she said hurriedly, "We are not inhumane. No one but the local mage guild will know who you are, and they will have no objections to your presence as you will be doing their work while they collect their fee as usual." Her expression resumed its formality. "You will wear the armband for the remainder of your life, and once a year, you report to either Mage Olnar or myself. And," she added. "When ten years are completed, you are free to go."

"What about my written defense?"

"It served its purpose," she said. "It is now locked up in the Mage Guild's Archive."

I'd expected no different. I packed my two robes into my satchel, loaded up my trunk of books, and among them placed the invisible warded cube in which rested my original copy of this record.

Emras:

Kendred is now king.

His first order was to restart the Academy. I fought against it, but Tdiran warned me last year that I was swimming against a centuries-old tide. At least Kendred invited her to be one of the overseers. And she and I have talked a great deal about what we think is the emotional price for that kind of training. She says that they all agree that nothing will be conducted in secrecy—they will go back to Inda's rules again. I hope this means that some kind of compromise has been made between the Marloven eagle and the Colendi peacock!

I don't think I told you that Vasande Definian returned to Alarcansa. The duchess had remarried, taking Young Gaszin—now Old Gaszin—as her consort. Her daughter wants to go to Sartor to marry a prince. Vasande writes to his father that she will probably succeed.

Mother and son made peace, but on the condition that Vasande could adopt his father's name. His half-sister could be Definian or Gaszin or whatever she liked, but he would share nothing with Aunt Tatia Tittermouse—though she'd vanished years ago. I hope she found peace wherever she is.

After Convocation in six months' time, I will move to Sindan-An, which is now going to be a principality. As the new prince, Kaidas suggested we rename it Vasande, adding Leror for the Iascans, who, it seems, vastly approve. (But the name of the forested area in the north will remain "Sindan-An" as "An" in Iascan means "woodland.")

Kaidas has been painting scrollwork and vines and flowers and animals all around the doors and windows of the new house, which the various children can't seem to stay away from. We will soon have children of our own to smudge it.

The year I finished my restitution, I went to visit my parents, and then, at last, I crossed the continent for what I believe will be the final time. Oh, what joy to walk up the rose garden to the house (a house, not a castle, not even remotely defensible) near Crestel in the newly-named Vasande Leror, to be welcomed by Birdy and Anhar, Lasva and Kaidas— and to find waiting for me a room of my own! I am now Vasande Leror's mage, as well as a scribe.

So it is time to finish this record. Because Lasva was right: the Marlovens and the world have begun rewriting history.

Though I broke the scribes' first two Rules, I have kept the Third, which was to record the truth as I saw it. For that very reason I cannot send it to Tiflis: no one else is going to read our inner thoughts until we are long gone.

Though I found justice, and made my restitution, there is a greater injustice. Somewhere in Norsunder Ivandred abides with his First Lancers, who loyally rode behind him straight into darkness.

And that is why I kept this copy of my record. I will transfer to Darchelde's secret room, where I will lay this down with Fox's memoir, then seal the chamber. One day Ivandred is going to ride forth again, and I hope by then that the world will understand what happened, and that justice will vindicate the banner of the damned.